IN THE BELLY OF THE
ANACONDA

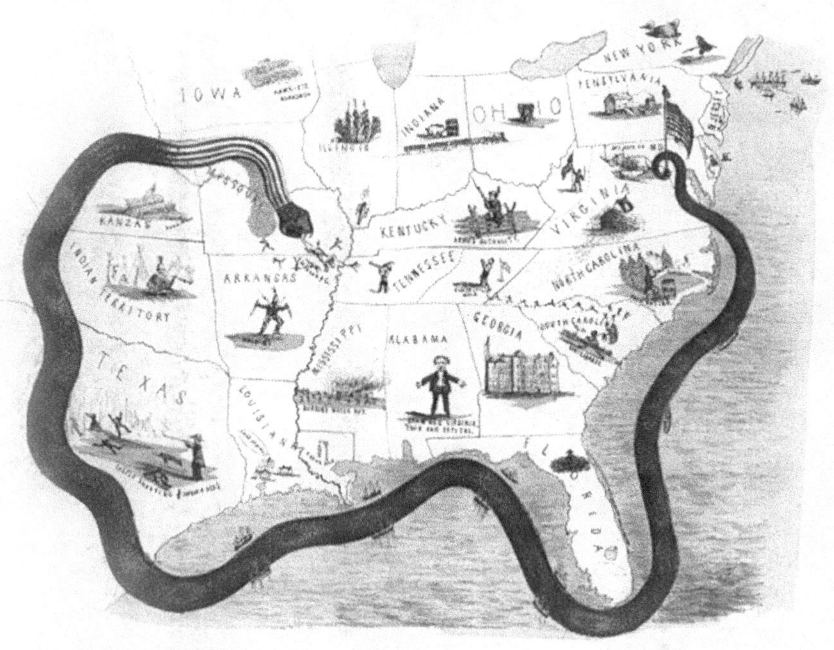

C. ARTHUR ELLIS, JR., PhD

IN THE BELLY OF THE ANACONDA

C. ARTHUR ELLIS, JR., PH.D.

Gadfly Publishing, LLC
Dalton, Georgia

Copyright © 2025 by C. Arthur Ellis, Jr., Ph.D.

All Rights Reserved. No part of this work may be reproduced, stored in a retrieval system, or transmitted in any form or by any means—electronic, mechanical, photocopying, recording, or otherwise—without the prior written permission of the copyright holder.

Publisher's Cataloging-in-Publication Data

Names: Ellis, C. Arthur Jr., author. | Aakif, Mirshad, illustrator. | Yumerov, Alper, illustrator. | Henriott-Jauw, K., illustrator.

Title: In the belly of the anaconda / by C. Arthur Ellis, Jr., Ph.D.; illustrated by C. Arthur Ellis, Jr., Ph.D., Mirshad Aakif, Alper Yumerov, and K. Henriott-Jauw.

Description: Dalton, GA: Gadfly Publishing, LLC, 2025.

Identifiers:

Library of Congress Control Number: 2025943540

ISBN	979-8-9997631-3-6	(Hardback, black and white Library Edition)
ISBN	979-8-9997631-0-5	(Hardback, color Collector's Edition)
ISBN	979-8-9997631-1-2	(Paperback, black and white)
ISBN	979-8-9997631-2-9	(e-Pub)

Subjects: LCSH Espionage--Fiction. | New Orleans (La.)--History--Capture, 1862--Fiction. | Louisiana--History--Civil War, 1861-1865--Fiction. | United States--History--Civil War, 1861-1865--Women--Fiction. | United States--History--Civil War, 1861-1865--Fiction.| Historical fiction. | BISAC FICTION / Historical / 19th Century / American Civil War Era | FICTION / Women

Classification: LCC PS3605 .L55 I68 2025 | DDC 813.6--dc23

"Life can only be understood backwards; but it must be lived forwards."
—Søren Kierkegaard

CONTENTS

1862
THE FALL AND THE OCCUPATION

1863
ROMANCE, RIVERS, AND ESPIONAGE

1864
THE RISE OF RECONSTRUCTION

1865
A MAN FOR ALL AGES

1920
EPILOGUE

PREFACE

Most historical accounts of the U.S. Civil War focus on battles and military strategy, often praising the generals who led them. Some works of historical fiction—such as *Gone with the Wind*—romanticize the planter class, offering an idealized view of Southern nobility while overlooking the brutal realities of slavery.

In contrast, *In the Belly of the Anaconda* follows the lives of the overlooked men and women who bore the war's daily burdens far from the victorious headlines or the gilded parlors of the Southern elite.

The title references the early days of the war when Union General Winfield Scott proposed a strategy of attrition known as the Anaconda Plan. Instead of aggressive land battles with massive casualties, Scott envisioned a slow, suffocating method: a naval blockade of Confederate ports and control of the Mississippi River, cutting off the South's trade and supplies, both foreign and domestic, until its rebellion was subdued. To Southerners, the plan felt like a giant serpent tightening its grip with each month.

This was most painfully felt in New Orleans, the Confederacy's largest city and commercial hub. Once the blockade intensified and Union forces seized the Mississippi's mouth, New Orleans lay trapped in the belly of the Anaconda.

The novel's central figure is Rachel, an educated and fiercely determined Southern woman navigating the shifting tides of war while facing personal loss, divided loyalties, and a conscience no longer at peace with her world. As her perilous journey unfolds, Rachel vows to dedicate her life to bringing about meaningful change.

Richly illustrated and based on thorough historical research, *In the Belly of the Anaconda* is also an ensemble narrative: a complex tapestry of voices from both the North and the South. Though divided by politics and war, its characters are connected through shared bonds of blood, soil, and commerce. Through their flawed, deeply human struggles, they reflect the nation's hope to become "one nation under God, indivisible, with liberty and justice for all."

PROLOGUE

CHANDELIERS AND SILK GOWNS
IN THE SHADOW OF WAR

On the evening of Wednesday, February 5, 1862, the East Room of the Executive Mansion glittered with opulence, as though the war beyond its walls had been momentarily banished by candlelight and Champagne.

Thomas Manget, a striking figure of a young man, stood in formal attire at the threshold, surveying the grand procession of Washington's elite as they gathered beneath the blaze of newly restored chandeliers and furnishings. Jewels sparkled at the throats and wrists of ladies cloaked in silk, while the polished shoes of generals and congressmen gleamed in the shifting light. The murmur of admiration rose like a tide: "Oh's" and "ah's" buoyed by the rustle of gowns, the clinking of glasses, and the lighthearted laughter of those for whom the war remained the distant sound of rolling thunder.

Thomas had watched war mount like a storm in his native South. Yet here, in the very heart of the Republic, the capital's high society swept it aside like a trifling concern, as if silk drapes and Champagne could hold back the rising flood.

He kept his glass of fruit punch steady in his hand, declining the Champagne offered freely on silver trays. As a Pinkerton detective, he could not afford to have impaired judgment. His dark eyes flicked over the assembly with the careful vigilance of a man who understood too well that danger came in many disguises.

A plantation near Baton Rouge was recently passed down to him, but he sold it without hesitation. His loyalty now lay with the Union. Still, the weight of that decision pressed heavily on him as he stood among the revelers, who treated the war lightly and toasted to victory as if it were already theirs to claim.

Across the expanse, President Lincoln and Mrs. Lincoln stood beneath the carved lintel of the doorway, greeting each guest with practiced civility as they entered from the Cross Hall. But Thomas saw the truth beneath their public faces: the pallor of worry in Mr. Lincoln's cheeks, the tightened lines around the First Lady's eyes. Their young son,

Willie, lay gravely ill upstairs, and despite the brilliance of the evening, sorrow weighed them down.

Mrs. Lincoln, intent on maintaining her vision of a European-style reception while paradoxically discouraging any festive spirit, had stationed the Marine Band in the hall to deter dancing. The musicians stood like silent sentinels, their brass instruments gleaming beneath the chandeliers. Yet despite her expressed wishes, the crowd's spirit grew restless, eager to participate in the festivities.

Thomas's gaze lingered on the gilded walls and French silk drapes, the gold-framed mirrors, and the vast Brussels carpet that muffled the sound of polished shoes and boots. None of this was accidental. He understood its strategy: the desperate bid of an emerging nation in turmoil for legitimacy in the eyes of foreign powers, with a rail-splitter turned President and the quiet woman who bore her title's weight with a mix of pride and unease.

The band's conductor, Francis Scala, raised his baton. "Ladies and gentlemen," he called, and the room quieted at once. "It is my distinct pleasure to conduct 'The Mary Lincoln Polka,' composed by my hand to honor our First Lady's remarkable accomplishments."

A flicker of discomfort crossed Mrs. Lincoln's face. Thomas noted it at once, but the applause swallowed her protest before it could find a voice. With reluctant grace, she stepped forward to offer an embarrassed curtsy. Thomas observed the sidelong glances from other ladies, some of whom appeared jealous that she was wearing the most elaborate gown in the room.

The band struck up the rhythm of the polka, and though the guests respected the First Lady's injunction against dancing, their feet betrayed them, tapping eagerly beneath layers of silk and taffeta.

Thomas marked the Comte de Paris and the Duc de Chartres, their military uniforms lending them an air of gravitas beyond their years. Beside them stood General McClellan, appearing uncomfortable, while his wife drew wary glances in her defiant gown of secessionist colors, a white dress slashed with scarlet velvet, crowned with red and white plumes. Thomas thought it was a bold statement, dancing dangerously close to treason in such a gathering.

When the steward finally unlocked the dining room doors at ten o'clock in the evening, a cheer rose, and the crowd surged toward the feast. Thomas hung back, letting others press forward to admire the spun sugar steamer, the sugar cannons, the candy flag waving bravely above its fragile mast at Fort Sumter, and trays of delicacies brought in by rail from New York. He could not help but see in it a hollow triumph. Sugar steamers could not hold a line against musket fire. Nor could gilded china and crystal deflect the iron will of a divided nation.

His ears caught the voice of a French dowager as she sipped her third glass of California wine, the lines around her aging lips revealing her distaste for the déclassé vintage. *"C'est apropos. Je me souviens, maintenant,"* she murmured, then, seeing her listeners did not understand French, added, "It reminds me of the ball before Waterloo. So many goodbyes, never to meet again."

Madame Mercier, the dowager's friend and wife of the French ambassador, raised her glass with a knowing smile, amused by the wine's effect in loosening the dowager's tongue. *"Dans le vin, la vérité."*

Thomas felt the irony in the exchange. *How many men here,* he wondered, *would be lost before the year's end? How many would fall beneath flags of spun sugar and bravado?*

Not far off, Thomas overheard Nicolay and Hay, the President's personal secretaries, conversing.

Nicolay leaned toward Hay and asked, "When will you inform the President about Senator Wade's note?"

"Not before tomorrow," Hay replied. "I dread Mrs. Lincoln's fury if she reads it tonight."

"I can fancy her reading it now," Nicolay said with a smirk, mimicking the First Lady's tone. "Are the President and Mrs. Lincoln aware that there is a civil war? If not, Mr. and Mrs. Wade are, and therefore decline to participate in feasting and dancing."

Hay suppressed a chuckle. "The Wades could not have made it clearer that they disapproved of tonight's celebration in the shadow of war."

Thomas was caught off guard when their conversation shifted to him.

"Who is that distinguished young gentleman?" Nicolay asked.

"That's Thomas Manget," Hay answered. "One of Pinkerton's newer agents. Hails from Baton Rouge, I believe. A lawyer before he took up this work."

Thomas kept his expression neutral, as though the conversation did not concern him, though he heard every word.

"Dashing fellow," Nicolay mused, "in that fine wool Brooks Brothers suit and burgundy silk cravat. He looks more like a fashion plate from *Godey's* than a spy."

Hay chuckled. "He can afford it. He's a planter's son."

"This war is tearing families apart," Hay added, his voice softer now, betraying his sadness. "Besides you and me, there isn't any citizen in this room, including the First Lady, who doesn't have relatives in the Confederacy."

As the secretaries drifted away, Thomas remained silent amid the opulence, relieved to hear that at least a few guests saw the night not as a celebration but as a gilded mask stretched over the face of war, a charade that could not endure. The river of blood would rise, and no confectioner's masterpiece or chandelier's glow would hold it back.

The grim truth was that the war had already swept through lives in the South like a scythe through ripe cane. While politicians and foreign dignitaries celebrated in splendor in the nation's capital, he knew that his friends in Louisiana would soon be burying their dead in the waterlogged earth, so sodden and swollen with grief that it would resist its grim duty, as if even the soil could not bear to swallow so many sons of the South.

1862

THE FALL AND THE OCCUPATION

1

WHERE IS APOLLO NOW?

Far from the glittering ballrooms of the Union capital, beneath a New Orleans sky heavy with clouds that seemed to mourn with her, Rachel Durand's carriage driver pulled his horse to a stop in front of Pierre Casanave's stables and mortuary at 122 Custom House Street in French Town. The driver then stepped down from his seat and offered a gloved hand as she exited the carriage, trying to avoid staring at the young lady despite her captivating beauty and striking red hair.

"Wish I had all that man's horses," the elderly driver said, gesturing toward the stables beside the mortuary. "Man with that many fine horses don't need to work no mo'. He go hire somebody else to work for him."

Rachel glanced toward the stables, noting the many well-bred horses and beautiful carriages. She particularly admired the American Saddlebred, which reminded her of her father's horse, Tempest, the one he had taught her to ride when she turned twelve. In her opinion, such fine horses were a testament to the proprietor's hard work and dedication to his craft. The man's words recalled the age-old warning from her mother against envy: "If wishes were horses, beggars would ride."

"Thank you, driver," she said, dismissing him with a streetcar shinplaster to save her dwindling hard money for larger purchases.

"Thank you, ma'am," the driver returned with a smile, admiringly tipping his hat and climbing back into his seat.

Casanave's funeral home was not the mortuary she would have chosen, despite its excellent reputation, because it was owned by a Creole proprietor born to parents of mixed

French and African descent who had little experience with Jewish funerary customs. Nevertheless, she had no say in the matter. When the Army notified her of her husband's death at Shiloh, they informed her that his remains had been sent to Casanave's funeral home. They explained that Casanave was one of the few morticians who was not overwhelmed by the daily influx of bodies arriving by rail from the battlefield.

The mortuary was a modest, red-brick building. Yet, Rachel understood that her carriage driver was correct about the value of all the horses. Funeral homes generated a sizable portion of their income by hiring horses and hearses for various events, including weddings, when floral garlands transformed them into celebratory carriages. She reflected on the irony of her husband hiring a hearse for their wedding a year ago, and now she was arranging one for his funeral.

Approaching the entrance, she twisted the knob on the weathered door and pushed it open to enter the receiving area. Closing the door behind her, the heavy scent of lilies and aged wood greeted her in a room adorned with dark mahogany paneling and lined with high-backed oak pews reminiscent of her synagogue. About to take a seat, she witnessed a well-groomed young Negro man dressed in a neatly tailored black suit stepping through a doorway at one end of the room.

"Good morning, Madame," he said. "My name is André. How may I be of assistance?"

"Good morning, André. My name is Mrs. Rachel Durand. I am here to plan my husband's funeral."

"Is Monsieur Casanave expecting you, Madame?" he asked.

"Yes," Rachel said. "Sergeant Burns set my appointment."

The attendant gestured to a bench. "Please have a seat, Madame. I will inform Monsieur Casanave of your arrival."

Rachel settled onto a bench facing the entry door and retrieved a lace handkerchief from her handbag. Wiping her tears, she looked at a vase filled with lilies on a plant stand in the room's far corner. She began to think about where to find floral arrangements for the funeral. Since the florists' shops were closed, finding fresh flowers had become almost impossible, especially with street vendors no longer selling from their carts. Neighbors with gardens were now coming together to share what they had. She would have to ask her friend Eugenia, who lived across town in a district known for its lush gardens and greenery, if she could provide some flowers.

"Madame Durand?" a voice called from a door that swung open unexpectedly.

Rachel swiftly returned her handkerchief to her handbag and stood to greet Casanave, a short, bronze-skinned man in his middle years with wavy hair impeccably styled in place with pomade. She admired the tailoring of his black suit and the flowered silk vest, both accentuated by a coordinated cravat and a large pearl stickpin.

"Parlez-vous Français, Madame?" he asked in a Haitian accent.

"Un tout petit peu, Monsieur. Je préfère l'anglais, s'il vous plaît."

"Certainly, Madame," he returned in passable English. He stepped aside from the door and motioned to her. "If you please. My office is this way."

Rachel stood to follow the proprietor down a short corridor, detecting the fragrance of lavender water in his wake. In a small room to her left, she noticed open coffins on display, ranging from wooden models polished like fine furniture to less expensive, woven-wicker versions. She stopped when the undertaker opened another door at the end of the hallway and motioned for her to enter.

Casanave's office was bare, except for a central oak meeting table for family consultations. He courteously pulled a chair for Rachel and sat across from her.

"I offer my deepest condolences for the loss of your husband," he said, his voice reminding her of the compassionate tone of Rabbi Gutheim when he had comforted her upon hearing the news of her husband's passing.

"Thank you," she said.

"I know this is a most difficult time," he continued with measured grace, "but we must attend to matters regarding the funeral. I would understand completely if Madame would prefer someone to act on her behalf."

"No," she said, choking back a tear. "I am his closest relative."

"Do you have a family vault?"

"No. We have a family plot in the Tememe Derech Cemetery." Rachel noticed that Casanave shifted uncomfortably in his chair when she mentioned the cemetery's name, which confirmed her suspicion that he was unfamiliar with Jewish funerary practices. She had heard troubling stories about Gentile undertakers who resorted to drilling holes in coffins and having their gravediggers stand on top to sink them into the waterlogged soil.

Deciding to address his apparent reticence, she said, "I sense, Mr. Casanave, that the mention of Tememe Derech Cemetery makes you uneasy."

"No, Madame," he assured her. "I am more than willing to meet your needs in your time of sorrow." Pausing, he shifted his weight. "However, it might be necessary to construct an aboveground retaining wall to maintain dry soil."

Rachel found his professional demeanor comforting. Perhaps her initial misgivings about his ability to accommodate her religious needs were unwarranted. "Very well. Do what you must."

"Do you have an inscription for the headstone?" he asked.

"Yes," she replied, opening her handbag to hand him a note. "And I will need to purchase a headstone as well. Do you have any pink granite?"

"Oui, Madame," he said, taking the note. Casanave read the wording for the inscription

and determined that it was brief enough to fit on his standard tombstone. He then penned "*granit rose*" on the bottom of the note.

"Good," she said, relieved that she would no longer have to worry about these details.

Casanave lapsed into a momentary silence, his expression turning pensive. "We will need to select a casket. Unfortunately, my supply is quite limited due to the blockade." He paused, then added, "I recommend a closed casket service, so there is no need to select an interior design."

Rachel stiffened, caught off guard. "And why is that? Why not a viewing?"

"I think, under the circumstances…"

"I want a straightforward explanation!" she demanded, tiring of his perceived evasion.

"Your husband perished at Shiloh," he ventured cautiously. "The extent of the casualties was so great, and of course, priority had to go to the wounded. It took quite a while before space could be made on the trains for the deceased. And then, only the ones who could be identified were sent home."

Rachel felt her heart pounding, and her hands began to tremble.

"Considering the heat and humidity this time of year…" He paused, expecting her to ask him to stop, but she did not. "Additionally, there were packs of starving dogs…"

"Stop!" Rachel shouted in horror, leaping to her feet. "I can bear no more!" Feeling the room spin dizzily around her, she fell back into the chair. She sat speechless for a moment, her heart pounding as she struggled to maintain consciousness. Then, she forced herself to summon the strength to choose a casket for the only man she had ever loved. "Mahogany," she whispered, still fighting to remain conscious as she once again attempted to stand to take her leave.

Making her way uncertainly down the hallway to the foyer, she glanced again into the room of open coffins on display. At the door to the waiting room, she steadied herself to turn back to Casanave. "Levi loved mahogany."

"Yes, Madame," the flustered mortician said, catching up with her at the doorway. "Fortunately, I have one mahogany coffin left."

"Please send the bill to my residence," she said, fumbling with her handbag to hand him her *carte de visite.*

"Yes, Madame. I am here if you need me."

Still feeling somewhat disoriented, Rachel sat down on a bench in the foyer, her mind haunted by her husband's tragic fate. She remembered her father, a classics professor, reading her the tale of the Trojan War when she was a child. She specifically recalled how Achilles, after killing Hector, dishonored his body by dragging it around Troy's walls, allowing feral dogs to tear it apart. She knew that the god Apollo had intervened then to protect the fallen hero from further desecration. Now, she wondered to herself, "Where is Apollo now?"

Grief-stricken by the profound sorrow of Levi's absence, Rachel dreaded the day when her younger sister, Sarah, would inevitably receive news about her husband, Jacob. The future was shrouded in dreadful uncertainty, adding to her grief. Would Jacob be listed among the wounded, the deceased, or those lingering on the brink of death? The dreaded possibility of being left alone cast a shadow over their ability to fend for themselves.

Rachel's fingers closed around Levi's gold pocket watch, returned to her by the Army, now hanging on a black silk ribbon that rested against her chest. Its soft ticking served as a fragile lifeline, bridging the chaos of the present with the peace of their past. Their engraved names gleamed faintly, a whisper of their shared dreams now shattered. She would never see his face again or hear his laugh, but the watch had come back to her. Its survival, like her own, was a quiet act of defiance against the destruction surrounding them. As she traced the engraving, a spark of resolve grew within her. If this small piece of their love could endure the horrors of Shiloh, she, too, could find the strength to move forward, not just for herself but for Sarah.

Turning her eyes toward heaven, she pleaded, "Why can't it be as it was? Why am I being tormented so?"

After a brief, tearful prayer, she remembered the words from Ecclesiastes that speak of a time and a purpose for everything under the heavens. She reassured herself, "I must be strong for Sarah now. She is so fragile. It's what Levi would have wanted."

With a newfound resolve, she stood and declared, "It's time for me to go home."

2

THE END OF DAYS

At half past nine, the ominous tolling of dueling bells from St. Louis Cathedral in French Town, overlooking the Mississippi Riverfront, and Christ Church, located at the corner of Canal and Dauphine, shattered the tranquility of a Monday morning.

Bong Bong…Bong Bong…Bong Bong…
Bong Bong…Bong Bong…Bong Bong…
Bong Bong…Bong Bong…Bong Bong…
Bong Bong…Bong Bong…Bong Bong.

The disturbing cacophony ended with the twelfth echo of the tolling bells.

Leaving Sarah in bed crying and curled up like a baby in the womb, Rachel crossed through the library and swung open the double French doors. She stepped onto her balcony, determined to discover what was happening. Everyone knew that the alarm was to ring only if the port of New Orleans was being invaded, yet she could not, indeed *would* not, believe that the enemy was approaching.

After all, she had read an article in the *Picayune* on the fifth of the month assuring the citizens of New Orleans of the ominous firepower of its two forts miles below the city, stating that "no flotilla on earth" could pass them in less than two hours. During that time, the invaders would be "fired upon by 170 guns of the heaviest caliber."

The article argued that, along with the fortifications, sections of the over seventy-mile winding passage up the muddy Mississippi from the Gulf of Mexico were so shallow that the deep-draft ships of the invading fleet, designed for maritime warfare, could never navigate past the numerous sandbars. Yet she knew that recent heavy rains had swollen the river, and the waters now ran high at the levee. Could the unthinkable have happened? Could the record-high waters of the Mississippi have granted the Union ships safe passage beyond Forts Jackson and St. Philip? Was the fleet approaching the city just as the tolling bells seemed to warn?

In the distance, trumpets echoed, summoning General Lovell's troops to assemble. Yet she couldn't help but wonder how rifles would fare against the thunderous cannon fire of an advancing armada.

Looking down her street, she watched as men left their homes, gripping shotguns and pistols with no time for lingering farewells. Terrified children clung to their mothers, who screamed or fainted as they bid their husbands wrenching farewells.

One man, dressed in his soldier's uniform, knelt on the street with his haversack before him, carving something on it with a penknife. "What is he doing?" she murmured, then realized he was carving his initials into the leather flap as a final mark to ensure he would be recognized among the casualties. Her heart twisted as she thought of her husband, who had at least left behind a watch engraved with both of their names, a testament to their love.

"It's not fair," she cried, clutching the wrought-iron railing. "Levi gave his life to keep us safe!"

A block away, toward the levee, she spotted molasses streaming down the refuse-filled gutters, flowing like rainwater after a heavy storm. Starving beggars crouched by the road-side, desperately rummaging for anything they could use to scoop up the precious food.

Terrified by what she saw, she left the balcony and hurried back through her library to their bedroom, where she found her sister sitting on the edge of the bed, holding herself and rocking, overwhelmed with fear. She fought to regain her composure and approached Sarah to offer comfort.

"We are doomed," Sarah cried. "They are going to burn down our houses with us still inside."

"No, they won't," Rachel assured her while stepping back into the library to assess whether they were in immediate danger. Her mind wandered to the news of General Lovell's troops loading supplies onto trains heading north. Who would be left to defend New Orleans now?

Rachel braced herself and grabbed her spyglass as she stepped onto the balcony. The skies had taken on an unnatural glow, casting an eerie light over the city. She leaned over the railing, lifting her spyglass to focus on the levee. Men were setting countless bales of cotton ablaze, torching hundreds of barrels of sugar and molasses, and reducing entire warehouses of goods to ash. Whole wharves filled with steamer ships and fine sailing vessels were engulfed in flames to keep them from falling into enemy hands. With wide, disbelieving eyes, she witnessed the grim *auto-da-fé.*

Rachel watched as sailors poured whale oil overboard, setting the water ablaze to create towering flames that sent thick, black smoke swirling into the sky. The inferno twisted upward, casting an otherworldly glow illuminating the city with a false dawn. She watched as Confederate ships fired their cannons at cargo vessels to command Earth, Air, Fire, and Water to invoke a dark Fifth Element: the very essence of destruction.

Below her balcony, Protestant women clutched their Bibles, and Catholic women held rosaries close. They drew their crying babies near and gathered their young children by the hand to lead them to church, seeking sanctuary and offering prayers for their families as Easter Sunday approached. Pastors, priests, and nuns struggled to calm the growing panic, assuring the crowd of God's promise to protect His faithful.

It was the first day of Passover, and Jewish mothers gathered their children to head toward the synagogues, where rabbis would read the Torah's age-old story of bondage and deliverance. Rachel knew that on this holy day of freedom, their prayers would turn toward deliverance from their invaders, seeking liberation from the forces threatening their city.

The improbable sound of a shofar cut through the chaos, drawing her gaze down to a street evangelist with wild, gray hair and fevered eyes, brandishing a massive ram's horn as he blocked the path of a speeding carriage. The carriage skidded to a halt in front of him, and a bejeweled madame leaned out the window, shrieking, "Out of the way, you crazy old lecher! Religion only struck you after that sad little prick of yours gave up the ghost." Turning to her driver, she called, "*Conducteur! Baton Rouge, s'il vous plaît! Rapidement!*"

As the carriage sped away, bearing the madame and her workers, the self-proclaimed prophet stepped back, raising the shofar to his lips to blow three long, piercing blasts that echoed down the street, pursuing the departing vehicle. He lifted his fist to the heavens and roared, "You whores of Babylon have brought God's wrath upon us all!" Dramatically raising the ram's horn, he proclaimed, "Behold! He commands the river to rise, delivering us into the hands of our enemies. Repent or be damned to the everlasting fires of hell!"

Feeling faint at the nightmare unfolding before her, Rachel withdrew to the safety of her library, latching the French doors behind her. Breathing heavily, she pressed her back against the doors to steady herself. Then she glanced toward the bedroom where her distraught sister remained in bed and whispered, "Dear God. What will become of us?"

3

RACHEL'S NIGHTMARE

Startled from her nightmare by a clap of thunder, Rachel bolted out of bed and raced barefoot across the soft library rug to unlatch the double French doors leading to her balcony. Stepping gingerly onto the damp flagstone, she gripped the cool wrought iron railing, its sturdy presence grounding her amidst the storm. She leaned forward, savoring the gentle night breeze brushing against her skin and the fresh scent of rain-kissed cobblestones rising from the streets below.

Chartres Street shimmered like a living Manet painting, with flickering gaslights casting dreamy reflections that danced on the wet pavement. Enchanted by the ephemeral tableau, she fancied that the eternal clash between nature and civilization had, for a breathless moment, reached a harmonious accord.

Stepping back into the library, she looked through the door at her sister in the bedroom, now tucked comfortably beneath her soft, billowing white down quilt. The sight was a picture of tranquility, an image of innocence that brought back memories from childhood.

Rachel recalled their mother paying them each a penny to hide under the bed during summer thunderstorms. "Hush now, girls," she would whisper at the sound of approaching thunder, "so you don't attract the lightning."

Rachel and her sister always doubted that hiding from the lightning kept it from striking. Still, they never questioned their mother, knowing they could take their pennies and run down the street to buy a piece of hard candy from Miss Fannie's confectionery once the skies had cleared.

Returning to the balcony, she stood mesmerized by the dazzling streaks of lightning that forked through the night sky, illuminating the landscape in brief, haunting flashes. Each strike conjured vivid memories of the surreal events that took place two weeks ago. In her mind's eye, she could still see the old man wandering the chaotic streets, blowing his shofar and proclaiming the End of Days.

She wondered how she and Sarah had endured so much that dreadful day: the soot so thick from burning cotton that they choked when they breathed, the constant fear that the fires would spread to their house and burn them alive, the terrifying thought of marauders breaking into their home and violating them, the humiliation of having their Stars and Bars torn down from government buildings and replaced by the dreaded Stars and Stripes. The list was endless.

Nonetheless, after a few days, sustaining a constant state of vigilance and anxiety became impossible. Gradually, both her body and spirit reached their breaking points, leaving behind a numb tranquility. Now, nothing seemed to bring her joy, and her determination to survive and protect what remained of her family was all that sustained her during the occupation.

She looked toward the river to see Farragut's ships still anchored in the harbor, looming above the charred remains of Confederate vessels scattered around them, high above the levee overlooking the city. But unlike her nightmare, there was no cannon fire now. Instead, an unsettling silence and a palpable sense of impending doom filled the streets. People were walking mindlessly toward the levee, as if spellbound, drawn by a morbid compulsion to gaze upon their fate.

After retreating once more to the safety of her library and securing the French doors behind her, she caught a glimpse of a traveling artist's drawing hanging on the wall beside the bedroom door. Just a few weeks ago, she had asked him to depict her in the garment she envisioned wearing for Passover this year, and she had been delighted with how realistic it turned out.

But in the light of the lightning flashes illuminating the glass panes of the French doors, she could not see the rich shades of orchid in her hat and dress, her vibrant red hair, or her sparkling green eyes. Now, all that remained was a somber palette of gray, like her life was now: drained of color and devoid of delight, forced into mourning for two years, dressed in widow's black.

She touched the portrait, reflecting that her dressmaking had been interrupted by fear of an impending invasion, and that she and her sister had not attended Passover services on the day the city burned. "Maybe next year," she whispered.

Without warning, the distant cry of a train's steam whistle broke the tense quiet. The rhythmic clatter of iron wheels carried her back to her childhood, when she would fall asleep to that familiar lullaby. Maybe she could find solace and drift off to sleep again.

Glancing into the bedroom, Rachel smiled warmly at the serene expression on Sarah's face. Would to heaven she could find the same peace.

She carefully closed the bedroom door and stepped into the adjoining library, where a side table bore a kerosene lamp. After removing the frosted glass globe, she touched a match to the wick and paused to watch the flame catch and steady. Satisfied with the gentle glow, she replaced the shade and settled into her father's leather armchair beside it, reminiscing about bygone evenings from her childhood.

She envisioned herself sitting on the plush rug, lost in her world of dolls, in front of the comforting crackle of logs in the fireplace. Seated nearby, her father indulged in the rich aroma of his Meerschaum pipe, a treasured memento from Turkey, as he transported himself to the realms of ancient Greece and Rome through the pages of his beloved classics, which lined the bookshelves along the wall.

As she gazed at the panes of the French doors, her reflection bore a striking resemblance to a daguerreotype likeness. Struggling to keep her heavy eyelids open, she watched as the lamplight gradually transformed the still image. A smile spread across her face as she beheld the enchanting scene: herself as a young girl in a flannel nightgown, nestled on her father's lap, listening to her favorite childhood story about Persephone's eternal return to usher in spring and new life each year.

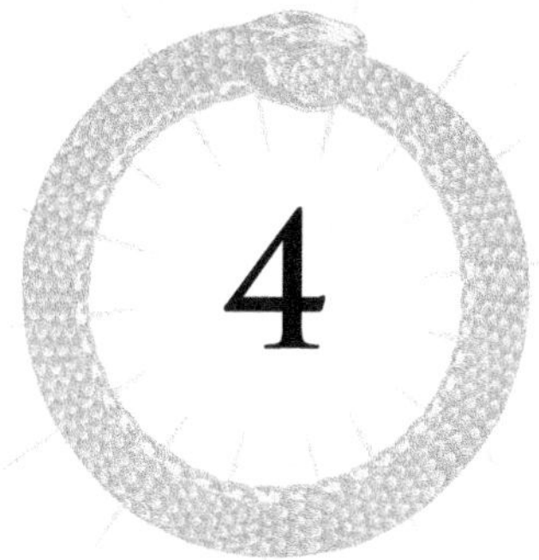

4

MUMFORD AND THE FLAG

The next morning, Sarah and Rachel, still in their nightgowns, sat on the library settee darning socks for Confederate soldiers.

After a time, Rachel set her darning aside, stood to stretch, and stepped outside onto the warm, sunlit balcony, where a flock of birds drifted in effortless formation across the clear blue sky. Their graceful flight stirred a fleeting warmth within her. For the first time since the devastation of her husband's death and the nightmare of the Union invasion, a smile broke through the heavy cloud that had hung over her spirit.

Suddenly, a flurry of wings startled her as pigeons soared away from the street, clearing a path for a buggy racing toward the French Market.

Leaning over the wrought-iron railing, she narrowed her eyes against the sun's glare, watching as the buggy slowed several blocks away, drawing near a jubilant crowd. She lifted a pale hand to sweep aside a cascade of thick red hair and shield her vision, but the light was too strong.

"Quickly, Sarah! Bring the spyglass," she called inside.

Responding to the urgency in her sister's voice, Sarah laid down her knitting, sprang from the rosewood settee, retrieved the brass spyglass from the parlor table, and hastened across the library toward the open balcony doors.

Rachel took the glass and trained it toward the gathering crowd between the French Market and the U.S. Mint, which stood sentinel at the corner of Decatur and Esplanade. "Can it be?" she murmured to herself.

"Let me see!" Sarah said, breathless, her eyes bright with excitement.

The two sisters, often mistaken for twins, took turns peering through the glass.

It had only been yesterday that Farragut's marines raised the Stars and Stripes above the Mint, shielding it from a hostile crowd with a line of soldiers bearing fixed bayonets, while the mayor was still negotiating terms of surrender. The marines had warned the onlookers that Union warships lay ready in the harbor to shell the city should the flag be disturbed.

And now, a day later, Rachel and Sarah witnessed three men clambering atop the Mint to tear down the Union banner.

Cheers rose as hundreds of onlookers tossed their hats into the air like kernels bursting from a hot corn pan. Neighbors poured out of their homes, voices swelling with cries of "God save the South!" until the anthem itself rang through the streets.

God save the South, God save the South,
Her altars and firesides, God save the South!
Now that the war is nigh, now that we arm to die,
Chanting our battle cry, "Freedom or death!"
Chanting our battle cry, "Freedom or death!"

Gooseflesh prickled across Sarah's arms. She joined in softly, her voice gaining strength as she sang with the crowd.

Rachel stood beside her, listening. An unexpected rush of joy blossomed in her bosom. She now understood that Sarah's recent hours at the piano, practicing that very song from the sheet music purchased at Blackmar's store on Canal Street, had been her quiet way of coping with their grim reality.

A sudden boom shattered the moment. Cannon fire from a Union vessel thundered across the water. Rachel quickly turned the spyglass toward the Mint and saw people screaming, scattering in all directions. Dust and fragments flew from a brick building struck by the blast.

Setting aside her fear, Rachel embraced her trembling sister and whispered words of comfort, as she had in childhood. She had to be strong, just as she had been every day since Levi's death.

"It's all right, Sarah. We're safe in our home. That was no more than a warning shot. It was meant to frighten, not to harm. Remember, Farragut still has kinfolk in this city."

Sarah, steadying her nerves, accepted the spyglass once more. "Rachel, look! Do you see that man being helped into a buggy? Is he wounded?"

Rachel took the glass. "I believe he is. But the crowd is gathering again. Look! They're tearing the flag into pieces and tucking the strips into their pockets. Keepsakes!"

"I can scarcely believe it," Sarah breathed, wringing her hands. "Those Yankee invaders mean to rob us of all we hold dear. Our men have gone off to war, and we women are left alone to tend to our homes and families as best we can."

Rachel restrained her anger. It was her duty to carry herself with composure and dignity, as expected of a widow.

"We must make their stay in New Orleans as miserable as possible," Sarah declared, setting her jaw and adjusting the whalebone comb in her carefully pinned hair. "We owe them none of our Southern grace."

"Look!" Rachel cried, handing the spyglass back to her. "They're lifting one of the brave souls who pulled down the flag onto their shoulders. Now they're marching toward the levee. Do you think they're bound for City Hall, where Mayor Monroe is said to remain defiant?"

Sarah squinted through the glass. "Perhaps. But with every block they travel, more and more people are tearing off pieces of that flag. By the time they reach Canal Street, there may be little left to give him."

A chant rose from the crowd like a rising tide.

"Listen," Rachel said, holding her breath. "They're shouting a name. Mumford… Mumford… Mumford… That must be their leader."

She stood tall, her heart full of admiration for the man who had dared defy the occupiers. "Shall we hurry down and join the throng?"

Sarah's eyes widened as she rested a protective hand over the swell of her belly. "The baby just kicked."

Rachel gasped, reaching to feel her stomach. "I feel it, too! So strong!"

But Sarah hesitated. "Prudence tells me we should stay here. I fear the press of the crowd. And Union patrols may fire again, now that no Southern troops remain to guard us."

Rachel remembered how her sister had chosen the name Prudence after an old Haitian woman, a healer of sorts, had rubbed her belly and declared, "You carry a girl child."

"Well," Rachel said, "if we cannot go to them, there must be something we can do to show our support."

Sarah narrowed her eyes toward the distant levee. "I detest those Northern women. Yes, their men are also far from home, but their cities are safe, and their children sleep in peace. They cannot fathom how violated we feel and how powerless our men must feel on the battlefield, receiving the dreadful news that New Orleans has fallen and knowing they are too far away to defend us."

Rachel nodded in agreement, relieved to hear the passion in her sister's voice. She had been worried by Sarah's silence of late.

A sudden shriek from the street broke their reverie.

They turned to see their elderly neighbor cackling on her balcony, upending a chamber pot. "There's more where that came from, boys!" she hollered, disappearing inside.

Below, a young marine let out a shout. "That hag emptied her privy pot straight on my head!"

Ladies in hoops and ribbons strolled past the drenched soldiers, hiding their amusement behind fans fluttering like a flock of colorful butterflies.

"Damnation, William," his companion grumbled, eyeing the spreading stain on his comrade's coat. "We've been made fools of by that old crone." He pointed upward. "Look at those two Southern Belles s mirking like we're some kind of sideshow."

Rachel and Sarah exchanged amused glances and stepped back behind the French doors, locking them with a satisfying click.

5

A Spy Among Us

Eugenia Phillips sat beside Rachel on the parlor sofa, her striking brown eyes shimmering with intelligence. Her neatly curled auburn hair, modest gray dress, and black lace-trimmed Beauregard cape were enhanced by matching black jet earrings and a pendant necklace.

Sarah blushed as she served their distinguished guest hot tea and a warm beignet on the inexpensive Blue Willow china and silverplate she had bought from a street vendor to replace her confiscated Wedgewood and sterling silver service.

Eugenia leaned over to the tea table to reach the serving spoon in the sugar dish, then unabashedly retrieved her lorgnette to examine the marking on the back of the handle. Sipping her tea through lips curled in a sardonic smile, she locked eyes with Sarah. "I see that 'Spoons Butler' has honored you by sending his minions to greet you, my dear."

Sarah blushed. "He has been aptly named."

"Don't be embarrassed, my dear. His soldiers visited me as well, rifling through all my possessions. Those of us who refused to sign the Oath of Allegiance are all mourning the loss of our valuables. They even stole my finest silk gowns."

Sarah gasped. "No! How horrible."

"Yes. And can you believe that when I asked the soldiers why they took my gowns, they informed me that it was to keep them from the Confederacy? It seems that some genius on our side figured out how to fashion observation balloons out of them."

"I've heard of those balloons," Rachel said. "General Beauregard recently sent out a call for silk dresses. I understand that he considers those balloons useful for gathering intelligence."

"Would I have responded to his call sooner," Eugenia lamented.

Rachel noted Eugenia's bare ring finger, devoid of her magnificent fire opal and diamond engagement ring, but chose not to mention it. "Where he manages to hoard all our valuables confounds me," she said, gazing down at the floor. "Fortunately, the gold coins my parents gifted me for our wedding last year are still concealed under the floorboards beneath our feet." She paused, her face growing sad. "Unlike my pearl necklace, which one of his soldiers pocketed from my *abre à bijoux.*"

"No doubt to impress some factory worker sweetheart back home," Eugenia suggested. "I doubt that his gift will be appreciated. I'm certain that the poor wretch is incapable of distinguishing fine pearls from worthless carnival beads."

Eugenia's *schadenfreude* brought Rachel some comfort, yet it couldn't ease the loss of her pearls or the indignity of the federal occupation.

Settling into their father's armchair, Sarah returned to the topic of Rachel's gold coins. "Father told us that those Liberty Head Double Eagle gold coins he gave you were minted right here in New Orleans."

"Yes, they were," Rachel said.

Eugenia reached for the serving tongs to help herself to another beignet. She grinned. "My husband refers to these as *pets de nonne.*"

"How clever," Rachel said, trying to divert attention from her sister's disapproving look at the vulgar expression, since *pets de nonne,* or 'nun's farts,' was a corruption of the original *paix de nonne,* or 'nun's peace.'"

Sarah sipped her tea with a displeased smile and quickly changed the subject. "I strongly suspect the Beast is hiding his spoils in a massive bank vault somewhere up North to retire in luxury."

"No doubt," Rachel said, pouring another cup of tea. Noticing that the teapot was nearly empty, she was anxious that she might run out of her cherished Twining. And with the blockade cutting off supplies, there was no way to replenish her tea caddy once it was gone.

"Worst of all," Sarah continued, "he stole our servants, Ginny and Rebecca, to cook and do laundry for his soldiers. Now, we must wear gloves in public to hide our chafed hands. Even worse, we are left without a mammy to help with the baby when she comes."

"Shameful," Eugenia said.

"No one in the family has ever had to change baby linens or boil the laundry with lye soap in that old cast iron pot in the courtyard," Sarah said. "We've always had servants."

"Yes. And the stench from our cast-off water closets out back is unbearable in the summer months," Rachel added. "With most of the men off to battle, I fear I won't be able to find anyone to remove them this year."

"I can't imagine living without a cesspool," Eugenia remarked, considering that when her family recently relocated to New Orleans, her husband chose a home across Canal Street. This allowed them to distance themselves from the Frenchtown Creoles and freedmen, providing a suitable environment to host their fellow lawyers, bankers, and wealthy merchants in refined settings complete with expansive lawns and gardens — and, naturally, the convenience of a proper commode draining into a cesspool.

"It's the price we pay for living in such crowded conditions in French Town," Rachel lamented.

"Speaking of stealing our servants," Eugenia said, "have you, my dear friends, been informed that as soon as the well-coiffed Mrs. Butler stepped ashore from the U.S.S. *Mississippi* and settled into the most elegant suite at the St. Charles Hotel, she appropriated Mrs. General Lovell's abandoned hairdresser?"

"Her hairdresser? She and her husband make a perfect pair," Sarah said. "She steals the beauty, and he makes off with the booty."

Eugenia chuckled at Sarah's cleverness. "Well said, my dear."

"I almost forgot!" Rachel exclaimed, retrieving a rolled-up broadside from her handbag.

Eugenia reached for the paper and unfolded it, her eyes narrowing as they fixed on the bold heading: "General Order No. 28." She looked up sharply. "Where did you find this, Rachel?"

"After I heard the milkman's dog bark to announce our delivery early this morning, I rushed downstairs…"

"Fancy that! A milkman with a dog trained to announce his deliveries. You must share this delightful fellow's name, Rachel."

"Certainly. I have his *carte de visite* in my secretary."

"Thank you, my dear. I do hope he delivers to my side of town."

"Now, as I was saying," Rachel continued, "when I bent over to pick up the milk jug from our stoop, I saw this broadside attached to the lamp post. Did you not see any of them along St. Charles Avenue on your ride to our house today?"

"No. I was perusing the *Picayune* the whole time. May I look at it?"

"Please do," Rachel said.

"Let me see," she said, carefully adjusting her lorgnette to read the smaller print beneath the heading:

> As the officers and soldiers of the United States have been subject to repeated insults from the women (calling themselves ladies) of New Orleans, in return for the most scrupulous non-interference and courtesy on our part, it is ordered that hereafter when any female shall, by word,

gesture or movement, insult or show contempt for any officer or soldier of
the United States, she shall be regarded and held liable to be treated as a
woman of the town plying her avocation.

Frowning at Butler's order, Eugenia rolled up the announcement and shoved it back to
Rachel. "I suppose he had to establish a limit of how many chamber pots could be doused
upon the heads of his soldiers before coming down upon our fair sex with an iron fist."

Rachel found Eugenia's contemptuous comment amusing. "He apparently intends to
brand every one of us 'women of the town.'"

"He's left many widows with few other means to earn a living," Sarah said. "From
what I hear from my friends in my sewing circle, the brothels in town are overflowing
with Yankee gold."

Rachel, still attired in mourning black for Levi, cringed.

Eugenia continued, "Mr. P. tells me that some *femmes de joie* have purchased tents to
establish their business just outside the Union encampments around the city. They only
accept gold coins, you understand. No paper money. She smiled. "Mr. P. was taken aback
when I asked him how he came by this information."

"Your husband would never…" Sarah interjected.

Eugenia chuckled. "I know, dear. I was just bantering with him. He's so much fun
to tease."

"I wish I had bought one of those souvenir chamber pots with a picture of that balding,
fat old buzzard on the bottom," Rachel said. "Yesterday, I saw a street vendor—an elderly
Creole man, as I recall—hawking them around the French Market yelling '*Mira, Mira*,'
at everyone he encountered until Butler's men shooed him away with their bayonets and
threatened to arrest him if he returned with his wares."

Eugenia laughed. "Yes, I saw that very same peddler and his cart. Such a delightful little
man. I had just opened my *porte-monnaie* to buy some for my friends when…"

Rachel interrupted, "I do hope you saved one for me!"

Eugenia's expression soured. "Alas, no, my dear. My husband thwarted the transaction
before I could act upon my wicked impulse."

"What a pity."

"None's the pity, my dear, since neither I nor my friends would stoop so low as to use
one for such a deed. It simply would have made a quaint souvenir to remind us of this
horrid occupation once our beloved General Beauregard returns."

"Philip is quite the gentleman, Eugenia," Sarah said, choosing her words carefully. "I
mean no disrespect, but I find it challenging to comprehend how you manage a harmonious
marriage with a Union sympathizer."

"Sarah, I don't remember telling you this, but Mr. P. was a United States Representative in '53 and later argued cases before the Supreme Court prior to our war for Southern independence. That's why we moved from our home in Montgomery to Washington. Now, he is an accomplished businessman and a successful attorney in New Orleans. He explained to me ad nauseam that the future of this city and our well-being depend on how well we can adapt to Union rule and tolerate their corruption and system of bribes. God forbid, but I strongly suspect that following the raid on our house, he signed Butler's Oath of Allegiance and traded with his brother's agents."

"Many merchants and bankers seem to share his views," Rachel observed, noting that Eugenia had prepared a meticulously crafted speech to defend her husband's reputation within her social circle, as Union sympathizers were not well-received among the old guard of New Orleans.

Sarah wrung her hands. "I maintain that he neglects our traditions and values that we have sworn to defend with our very lives."

"Sarah, my dear, I ignore Mr. P.'s errant political philosophy because of my feelings for him, and for the sake of our children and our livelihood. Besides, he has tolerated my efforts to support the Confederacy even to his peril."

Eugenia's defense of her husband only heightened Sarah's agitation. "Has Mr. P. considered what will happen if all these African beasts are set free in polite society with no oversight to enforce civility?" she asked. "I shudder to think of what horrible things they might do to my Prudence. We would have to establish a special police force to keep the brutes in their place."

"Mr. P. has told me that Lincoln is considering relocating many of them to Africa or South America," Eugenia said. "Even he has the good sense to know that the races can never mix in a civilized society."

"I just realized that your husband insisted you remain in your residence unless you were accompanied, Eugenia," Rachel said, seeing that her sister was increasingly upset by the conversation. "Does he know that you are out visiting?"

Eugenia raised her hand with a nonchalant wave. "Indeed, he does, my dear. He stood directly in front of me and instructed my driver to ignore any entreaty I might make to stop along the way to your residence, all the while shooting me a defiant look. He is, after all, fiercely protective of me and the children. My driver is still downstairs, awaiting my return."

"Speaking of which, how are your children?" Sarah asked.

"They are faring well, thank you. You know my dear servant, Phebe. She is taking care of them while I am visiting. She's been in quite a state since the mayor had to call off Mardi Gras this year."

"Oh, yes, Phebe," Sarah said, "that lovely rotund Irish Catholic lady. Everyone missed Mardi Gras this year. It's always such a grand pageant. Even though Christie's Minstrels is performing at the Camp Street Theatre, it's not the same."

Rachel maintained the decorum demanded of widows, choosing not to share that her ongoing grief from losing her husband and her parents in such short succession had left her drained of joy and unable to celebrate anything.

Eugenia poured herself the last of the tea. "I agree. I know my children were terribly disappointed to miss the festivities and the toys and treats the krewes threw out into the crowd from the floats. As for Phebe, no one could be more loyal. She saved me from languishing in jail when I was accused of spying last year. She has also continued to offer my daughters solace following the distress of our house arrest."

Rachel gasped. "Did you say…I mean, were you an actual spy when you lived in Washington?"

"My friend, Rosie Greenhow, trained me well. Did you know she passed intelligence to the Confederacy, contributing to our victory at Manassas?"

"No! You must tell us about that. But first, you must share everything about your ordeal."

Eugenia, a former child actress in England whose mother was a renowned star, beamed, apparently pleased to have an eager audience.

"Well," she began, "I was held under house arrest only two months ago. It seems like it was just yesterday."

"Oh my!" Sarah gasped. "You simply must share your story."

"Miss Eugenia, come quickly!" Phebe shouted, barging into the kitchen where her mistress was enjoying tea with her elderly widowed neighbor. "Soldiers are rifling through the parlor, turning everything upside down."

"Oh my!" her neighbor cried.

"Did they present a search warrant, Phebe?" Eugenia asked calmly.

"No, ma'am. But I didn't ask for one." Phebe nervously pressed her apron with her hands. "I'm sorry, Miss Eugenia. I didn't know what to do; I never…"

"No matter, Phebe," Eugenia said, brushing aside her concern. "I will handle this." Turning to her friend, now trembling and pale as a sheet, Eugenia touched her hand and said, "Excuse me, Delores dear. Don't worry. I will go to the parlor for a moment and resolve the matter. Please finish your tea and help yourself to another of Phebe's wonderful scones while they're still warm out of the oven."

Taken aback by the sudden intrusion in her home, Eugenia left her bewildered neighbor and stepped into the parlor. There, she found Union soldiers aggressively rummaging through drawers, scattering papers and books in utter chaos.

Maintaining her composure, she calmly addressed the ranking officer, "May I ask your name, sir?"

"I am Lieutenant Brown, Madame."

"If there is something you are searching for, I might be of assistance."

In response, the lieutenant extracted a piece of paper from his pocket and handed it to her.

"A warrant," she said, but quickly determined that it was a military order, not a warrant. "It indicates that you are authorized to search my residence for documents related to alleged espionage activities. Might I inquire about what led to the issuance of this order?"

"No, ma'am," he replied courteously. "But you may speak with your lawyer if you choose to do so."

Eugenia wrestled with the temptation to mention that her husband was an accomplished attorney with many political connections but decided to withhold that information, at least for now. Instead, she directed her attention to her visibly distressed servant. "Phebe, my dear, please step into the hall where we can have a word."

Phebe followed her into the hallway, where Eugenia discreetly gestured toward her writing desk, a piece she had acquired from Mrs. Jefferson Davis when the Davises left Washington for Richmond. "Phebe," she whispered, "I need you to go to my desk over there and remove any papers you find in the drawers. Find a secure place to hide them, somewhere these men will never discover."

"Yes, ma'am."

Just then, one of the officers approached the women, and Phebe said, "Officer, I am terribly thirsty from scrubbing floors this morning. May I please go to the kitchen to fetch myself a drink of water?"

"Yes, ma'am," he returned politely with the tip of his hat.

"Would you like a glass of water, young man?"

"Thank you kindly, ma'am. I'm fine," he said, returning to the parlor to join his comrades.

Eugenia stood her ground in the hallway while Phebe discreetly slipped into the kitchen. Shortly after, she reemerged, taking a detour to Eugenia's writing desk nestled in an alcove along the hallway where her mistress could see her. There, she methodically emptied the drawers of papers, crumpling them up and tucking them into her bosom.

Amused by the sight of Phebe's ample bust, Eugenia held back a laugh while remaining vigilant of the soldiers' whereabouts. As Phebe rejoined her, another soldier approached, eyeing Phebe's bosom, but passed by on his way upstairs without questioning her.

When Eugenia returned to the parlor, she discovered one of the soldiers rummaging through her handbag. She saw that he had taken her memorandum book and put it on the sofa table alongside several twenty-dollar gold coins.

Stepping to the back of the sofa to look over his shoulder as he leafed through her book, she taunted, "Four yards of tape—treason! Five pieces of ribbon—important dispatch! Bill at Harper's—the government will pay!' Turn the page, sir," she urged, "and you will find something more awful still."

Disregarding her mockery, the soldier turned the page to find a clipping from the *London Times'* account of the battle of Manassas.

Eugenia's smile lingered as he held the newspaper clipping. It was a keepsake sent by Rosie Greenhow to mark the Confederate victory. To the soldier, it seemed to be nothing more than an innocuous clipping from a British newspaper reporting events in the United States. Yet, to Eugenia, it symbolized her friend's secret celebration of the significant contribution her espionage efforts had made to the Cause.

Within minutes, Brown and his soldiers gathered in the foyer, conversing in subdued tones. Lieutenant Brown then approached Eugenia. "Mrs. Phillips, inform all household members that they will come with us."

"I beg your pardon. Upon whose authority?"

"Mrs. Phillips, you are being detained for questioning until the matter is settled. Refuse, and I will bind your wrists."

"And may I inquire as to the reason for my detention?"

"You are accused of spying for the Confederacy, Madame."

Eugenia laughed. "Spying? On what evidence? Have you found something in my house that has made you suspect me of being a spy?"

"Madame, I do not have to answer your questions. However, you must come with me, along with the others in the household, or I will be forced to shackle you and drag you into the carriage waiting outside."

"But my neighbor and my servant have nothing to do with anything you accuse me of. My youngest daughter is playing with her dolls upstairs, and her older sister is reading. Do you truly suspect a child of nine and her eighteen-year-old sister capable of espionage?"

"Madame, please. Don't make this difficult."

"My husband is currently at his law firm. If I provide you with his address, will you kindly inform him that you are detaining his wife, our servant, our neighbor, and our daughters?"

"You may do so, and I will convey the message," the officer replied. "I will also apprise him of the location where you will be held. I presume you are familiar with it."

"Oh?"

"Yes. It is the residence of your friend, Rosie Greenhow."

Eugenia was forced to treat the matter seriously for the first time in this improbable episode. How could they have possibly connected her with her friend, Rosie? They had always met discreetly in the park near Rosie's house, sitting on their favorite bench like two strangers feeding the pigeons while surreptitiously passing notes between them. Who could have possibly reported them? It certainly wasn't the pigeons.

One of the soldiers led Eugenia's two daughters and her neighbor into the parlor to join her and Phebe.

"Where are they taking us, Mama?" Emma asked tearfully, holding her doll.

"We're going to visit a friend, Emma," Eugenia said, bending down to hug her.

"Where's father?" Salvadora asked, still holding her copy of *Great Expectations*.

"He's at work, darling. He will join us shortly."

Lieutenant Brown said, "Men, take these ladies to the carriage, and I will be with you shortly."

One of the soldiers saluted. "Yes, sir," he said, opening the door for the detainees to exit.

Outside, a black military carriage awaited. Eugenia knew that Rosie's house was only a few minutes from hers and decided to use the brief transit time to consider her options.

Could Philip file a petition with the Army to obtain their release? Could he demand the particulars of the order? Would he be told the extent of the evidence officials had on her?

Once inside the carriage, Eugenia's two daughters sat by her side. Emma sobbed softly, snuggled beside her mother. "I love you," she said to them, feeling a tinge of guilt for what her spying missions had done to her family.

Within minutes, the carriage pulled to a stop, and one of the soldiers opened the door for the passengers to exit.

"Come along," Lieutenant Brown said.

Eugenia was surprised to see how Rosie's front yard was overgrown, as her friend was always so proud of how neatly her gardener kept it. She had not had the chance to speak with her in several weeks and now wondered if she had been jailed.

"This way," the lieutenant said, conducting the women and children through the front door. "Up the stairs, please," he directed, gesturing to the broad staircase.

Two flights up, Lieutenant Brown led the entourage to a narrower staircase to the attic. Eugenia ascended the stairs first, followed by her daughters. Phebe assisted the elderly neighbor up the stairs to the small landing at the top.

"Oh!" exclaimed Eugenia, entering the doorway and stepping into the attic. Much to her surprise, it had been rummaged through in the same manner as her house, and there was a foul odor saturating the air. Several soiled mattresses with no bed linens littered the floor.

"This is where your friend kept her house slaves," the officer said. He smirked. "I trust that you will find the accommodations suitable, Madame."

"What crimes have we committed that we are thus treated?" Eugenia asked, disgusted at the stench of several half-filled chamber pots scattered about the room. "What charges were made against us? Who made them? And on what facts were they founded?"

Lieutenant Brown made an abrupt about-face to leave without answering her barrage of questions.

Eugenia's heart sank at the click of the door locking behind him, sealing her party within their makeshift prison.

"So, how did you manage to get out of this dilemma?" Rachel asked, finding herself engrossed in Eugenia's story.

"Mr. P. persuaded several individuals in high positions to advocate for us. You can imagine our astonishment when, about three weeks into our confinement, Colonel Thomas Key, General McClellan's Judge Advocate, and Mr. Stanton, Lincoln's Secretary of War and a family friend before the war, visited us."

"So, what did they say?" Rachel asked, impressed by Mr. P.'s political connections.

"The interview was brief, and our story was soon told. I was surprised by Judge Key's statement that he had heretofore been ignorant of our position, but they both left us with the promise that we would have 'fair play.' What that meant, we were left in our miserable attic to ponder."

"You were released shortly after?"

"Yes, after several excruciating days of confinement in that wretched environment, Mr. P. was informed that we were banished from Washington. He was then told that we had to dispose of our personal property and house quickly, but we were not allowed to leave our residence to make the necessary arrangements. Mr. P. managed to dispatch Phebe to call for an auctioneer, and everything was sold for pennies on the dollar. It mattered not since no price can be placed upon freedom."

"So, how did you get to New Orleans?" Sarah asked, enthralled by Eugenia's exploits.

"First, Union guards shipped us like livestock to Fort Monroe, where our belongings and our persons were thoroughly searched. Fortunately, they did not discover the gold coins I had sewn into the lining of my dress. From there, we were conveyed south into Confederate territory, where we were kindlier treated and taken to Richmond. Mrs. Davis and the President invited us to the Confederate White House for an evening of dining and entertainment fit for royalty. Although I found the fond attentions of numerous guests exhausting after our tedious journey, I cannot express the elation I felt at enjoying a warm bath with a bar of lavender soap and being reunited with civilized society in elegant surroundings."

"Providence was certainly looking out for you and your family," Sarah said.

"After Richmond, we remained in Savannah with relatives and then eventually traveled to New Orleans, where Mr. P. felt we would be far beyond the enemy's reach."

"As everyone had assumed," Rachel said, considering the bitter irony that the fall of the Confederacy's most prominent and affluent seaport was the Union's first major victory.

"We are so very grateful that you and your family are with us in New Orleans," Sarah shared, reaching over to clasp her friend's hands, "even though now is certainly not the best of times."

Rachel said, "Eugenia, I know that it must be difficult for you to be confined to your house now, especially after your terrible imprisonment in Washington. But I think Philip has wisely counseled you to stay where you and your children are safe while he endeavors to support the family."

"Thank you, my dear friends," Eugenia said, her voice softening. "We will meet at schul this Shabbos to pray with all of our friends for President Davis that he may deliver us from this scourge."

"Thankfully, we will be safe to pray in our synagogue as we wish, unlike in the churches, since none of Butler's soldiers understand Hebrew," Rachel said with a hint of a smile.

"Yes, thankfully," Eugenia agreed. "I can understand why Butler would forbid public prayer for Union soldiers to perish from yellow fever, but Phebe often complains that her priest is even forbidden to pray for fallen Confederates."

"And let us not forget our friends in Baton Rouge," Sarah said. "From what little we heard on the telegraph lines before the Yankees cut them, they are faring worse than we are. The last message reported that the city was shelled by Farragut's ships in retaliation for onshore resistance."

"Then there is your Jacob," Eugenia added, "and your unborn child. Let us pray for them as well."

Sarah reached for Rachel and Eugenia's hands and recited a prayer for deliverance that she remembered from the Psalms of David. *"Adoá-i Elohá, Bekháh khasiti; hoshiéini micól rodfa-i-ve-hatziléni:* My Lord God, in You I have taken refuge; save me from all who pursue me and deliver me."

The words settled upon the friends like a blessing as they murmured their Amens with bowed heads.

REPORT

OF THE

SANITARY COMMISSION

OF

NEW ORLEANS

ON THE

EPIDEMIC YELLOW FEVER,

OF

1853;

PUBLISHED BY AUTHORITY

OF THE

CITY COUNCIL OF NEW ORLEANS

— Quod sol aique imbres dederant, quod terra crearat sponte sus.

Lucret, tib. v

NEW ORLEANS:

PRINTED AT THE FICAYUNE OFFICE, 06 CAMP STREET

1854

6

First Do No Harm

While the city buzzed with Butler's oppressive orders, Dr. Smith, a silver-haired octogenarian comfortably attired for the evening in his silk smoking jacket, took a contemplative sip of bourbon. With a hand unsteady from palsy, he reached for the 1854 New Orleans Sanitary Commission report on the yellow fever epidemic of the prior year, nestled among the timeworn volumes crowding his library shelves.

Settling into the comfort of his leather armchair, he set his whiskey glass on the side table and laid the heavy tome across his lap. Propping his slippered feet on the richly dyed leather of a Turkish ottoman, he packed fresh tobacco into his well-worn briar pipe, tamping it down with his father's ivory lady's leg tamper. He opened a tin of matches, selected one, and struck it. The tobacco crackled to life beneath the flame. Satisfied with the steady glow, he extinguished the match just before it singed his fingers. Leaning back, he took a slow, luxurious pull, savoring the rich burst of flavor and the sweet, mellow aroma of Virginia's finest tobacco.

Leafing to the title page of the Commission's report, he read, "*Quod sol atque imbres dederant, quod terra creárat sponte sua.*" A gentle smile crossed his face. "What the sun and the rains had given, what the earth had created of its own accord."

Contemplating the advances in medicine illustrated by the volumes on his bookshelf— Lucretius, Hippocrates, and Descartes — he reflected on their teachings. From Lucretius's *De Rerum Natura*, he recalled lines that accurately described epidemics as natural phenomena, consistent with Hippocrates's observations in *Airs, Waters, and Places*. Turning to Descartes's *Traité de L'Homme*, the groundbreaking treatise that rejected the Church's idea of the soul as the force that animates the human body, he admired the insights of the philosopher-turned-physiologist.

He particularly admired the logical rigor and scientific method of Descartes's treatise since it represented a significant departure from the theological explanations that had dominated thought from antiquity into the 17th century. However, it was not published until after Descartes's death, as fears of religious persecution loomed large following Galileo's lifetime house arrest for proclaiming his heretical heliocentric theory of planetary motion.

Regrettably, even in the modern era, scientists were unable to grasp the true origins of yellow fever. In this void of knowledge, religion often intervened to provide explanations. Although the medical community had progressed beyond purely supernatural interpretations and recognized the disease's link to tropical ports, their understanding of the cause of yellow fever remained rudimentary. The outbreak's timing, during the peak of shipping season in the hot, rainy summer months, was attributed to a mysterious "miasma," thought to emanate from the filthy conditions of a city desperately lacking sanitation workers and proper drainage and sewer systems.

Without a known cause, there was no cure for yellow fever. Survival depended solely on luck, and for the fortunate, the acquired immunity that came with enduring the fever's ravages.

The Commission's report was an epic undertaking, coordinating with health officials across the Caribbean and South America to gather insights from their experiences combating a disease that thrived in tropical climates. The exhaustive document spanned nearly six hundred pages, from maps pinpointing high-outbreak areas, or "nests," of the disease in New Orleans to tables cataloging barometric pressure, temperature, rainfall, and other conditions present during the summer contagion. It also offered recommendations for health officials and city leaders on quarantine and sanitation measures to prevent future epidemics.

A curious note on page thirty-one mentioned a vast number of mosquitoes and houseflies during the 1853 outbreak. Since no one could confirm a connection between the insects and the disease, the observation was ultimately dismissed as coincidental.

He vividly remembered that summer when nearly a quarter of New Orleans' 30,000 residents were struck down with high fever and black vomiting. The horrific images of contorted faces—especially those of infants and young children— haunted his nightmares.

Despite the Commission's detailed recommendations, including the call for a quarantine, merchants and politicians downplayed the report to the public, fearing it would cripple the city's economy. As a result, another deadly epidemic swept through just four years later, in 1857.

"The Devil and Tom Walker," he muttered, recalling Washington Irving's cautionary tale of greed. "Like Tom Walker, who sold his soul to the Devil in the swamp for treasure, these merchants and politicians traded their souls for gold while thousands died."

He had sworn to his colleagues that he would never reveal the Commission's report to General Butler, despite knowing all this. Doing so would make him a pariah among his peers, all of whom had declared their ignorance about the cause of the disease.

A part of him couldn't fault his colleagues for despising Butler, especially after the general had meddled in their medical practice by attempting to seize the city's entire supply of quinine to send to Union forces battling malaria.

Not long ago, Dr. Moore, his elderly pharmacist friend, made a grave mistake by giving a few ounces of quinine to someone with a pass who later smuggled the medicine across the line into the Confederacy. For his attempt to ease suffering across enemy lines, he was branded a traitor and sentenced to hard labor, shackled with a ball and chain at Fort Jackson, further down the Mississippi.

Were it not for the brave and resourceful women of the city, who cleverly hid bottles of quinine in their infants' underclothes and delivered them to tradesmen skilled in crafting secret compartments in horse collars, New Orleans would have been helpless to alleviate the malaria afflicting their beloved soldiers.

Then there was what happened to his close friend, Dr. Mercer, when he sought an audience with Butler to plead for Mumford's life after he had hauled down the Union flag over the U.S. Mint. Mercer desperately implored, "A scratch of your pen will save him." Butler coldly replied, "True, Doctor. And a scratch of that same pen would put you in his place."

Even if he could overlook Butler's cruelty, would the general comprehend the Commission's study if it were shared with him? And if he did, could he raise the labor force needed to clean the gutters and sanitize a city without a sewage system? And even if Butler managed to assemble such resources, would he finish before the yellow fever season struck?

Yet, despite these doubts, there was the troubling knowledge that the Confederates were planning a silent war of disease. The occupying Union army, unlike the locals, lacked immunity to yellow fever. Confederate whispers spoke of General Lovell marching back into a decimated city, liberating it over the bodies of dead Union soldiers littering the streets.

The plan was not far-fetched. Confederate generals, many of them trained at West Point, were aware of the devastating effects of yellow fever in Saint Domingue, where Napoleon Bonaparte lost up to ninety percent of his troops. That catastrophe and European financial pressures forced the emperor to abandon his New World ambitions and sell the Louisiana Territory to the United States at a bargain price.

Were his fellow physicians, like the bankers and merchants of New Orleans, making a deal with the Devil? By withholding the Commission's report from Butler, were they indirectly complicit in the hope that disease would rid them of the occupying force?

As a Christian, the decision weighed heavily on his conscience. Should he betray his compatriots and give the report to Butler, or remain loyal and conceal it? And what of Butler's threat to set fire to the city if yellow fever broke out?

Recalling the ancient Hippocratic oath, "First, do no harm," he shut the Commission's report and set down his pipe. "Dear God, when does my silence transition from mere omission to complicity in mass slaughter?"

Gathering his strength, he pushed himself upright, only to send his cane clattering across the floor. Startled by the noise, he exclaimed, "Eureka!" and steadied himself long enough to step to the bookcase and slide the Commission's report back onto the shelf. Beside it, his eye fell upon a much slimmer volume, his friend Dr. Riddell's *On the Nature of Miasm and Contagion*.

Published in 1836, the treatise boldly questioned the accepted miasma theory of yellow fever, daring instead to suggest that unseen microscopic organisms—"animalcules," as Riddell called them—were the true culprits. The theory was still dismissed by many as fanciful, yet within its pages lay a vision of disease spread not by foul air but by living agents, a vision that hinted at the promise of prevention through simple acts of sanitation.

He thumbed quickly through the familiar chapters, a wave of relief passing over him when he confirmed that the book predated the controversial study he had vowed never to place in Butler's hands. Closing the slim volume with a gentle snap, he smiled. "Thank you, my friend," he whispered. "You've no idea what your work will accomplish, now that it will not fall on deaf ears."

With that, he eased himself back into his chair, Riddell's treatise resting against his chest. He savored a slow sip of whiskey, then reached for his pipe, the smoke curling upward as his conscience, at last, grew quiet.

7

THE HANGING OF WILLIAM B. MUMFORD

At ten in the morning, Philip Phillips tugged the reins of his black stallion to guide his phaeton toward the edge of the boisterous crowd gathered in front of the U.S. Mint in New Orleans, situated near the levee at the corner of Esplanade Avenue and Decatur Street.

In his mid-fifties, Philip was a strikingly handsome man with a Roman nose, bronzed skin, and deep-set, keen brown eyes that bestowed upon him the dignified air befitting his esteemed character as an accomplished attorney. He wore impeccably trimmed, elongated Burnside whiskers styled after those of General Burnside, whom he had met in Washington.

With his wife, Eugenia, and her friend, Rachel, beside him, Philip's eyes swept the restless crowd with growing unease. The charged atmosphere, thick with shouts and shifting bodies, heightened his concern for the women's safety. He was particularly wary of a group of clearly intoxicated men gathered near William Mumford's gallows, as the area was heavily guarded by a line of Union soldiers with fixed bayonets.

Mumford's gallows were built to obstruct the Mint's front steps, yet the crowd's more agile members managed to scale the sides of the columned portico behind the execution scaffolding to get a closer view of the hanging.

Butler had caused the scaffolding to be erected only weeks after he had presided as both judge and jury in Mumford's hasty, closed-door trial. He deliberately selected the site for Mumford's execution following the Spanish tradition of executing criminals at the scene of their crimes, fully aware that many in the crowd would understand that this was his way of branding Mumford a felon.

Mumford, a man of average height in his forties, stood at attention on the scaffolding, his hands shackled behind his back. He wore a dark suit, a white collared shirt, and a black felt hat. His prominent forehead, striking brown eyes, and aquiline nose were the only visible features of his face, as his thick brown hair and full, neatly trimmed beard obscured his lips and ears.

"Let him go!" one woman yelled, while several men raised their liquor bottles and jeered. "Old Butler's just pullin' a fast one. He ain't fixin' to hang nobody!"

Eugenia shifted uncomfortably in her seat, glancing at the handles of illicit pistols sticking out of the pockets of some rowdier men in the crowd. She turned to Philip. "No one believed that this day would ever dawn. Banishment to Ship Island, or perhaps Fort Jackson. Everyone agreed that such would be the punishment for his drunken defiance."

"His act was committed before the city's surrender, so it was not even subject to military law when he and his friends pulled the flag down," Philip said.

Hearing this exoneration from her attorney husband, a flicker of pride crossed her face. "I knew that the Beast could be petty, but I never believed that a simple act of drunken rashness would come to this."

Rachel gestured toward Butler. "Behold! The Beast sits astride his horse: short, rotund, neckless, cross-eyed, bald."

"Look!" Eugenia exclaimed. "I think that's Mrs. Mumford approaching the Beast.

Rachel, wearing her mourning attire, expressed a sense of shared grief. "Such a pitiful sight in her widow's black."

"Can you make out what she is doing?"

"It looks like she is pleading with him," Rachel said. "She is wasting her breath. He has a heart as cold as stone."

"Look! She collapsed next to his horse. Is that her mother comforting her?"

"I can't see well enough to tell."

"He has four children, the youngest of whom is dreadfully ill," Eugenia said, drying her eyes with her handkerchief.

"I heard he was a gambler," Rachel said, already speaking of him in the past tense.

"A professional gambler," Philip added. "Planters from as far away as Baton Rouge traveled to New Orleans to bankroll his card playing and split the gains. I recognize a few of their faces in the crowd."

"Thank goodness. At least his widow has the means to support his family," Rachel said.

"Unfortunately, not," Philip said with a sad countenance. "Over time, he managed to gamble away all of his winnings as well as his wife's considerable inheritance."

"How will his family ever survive?" Eugenia asked.

"Some say that Butler promised Mrs. Mumford gainful employment."

Eugenia's face reddened. "Doing what, pray tell? Clearing the streets of horse manure? I must see what I can do to raise a subscription for his family's care."

"I will join you," Rachel said. "Sarah tells me that no one in her sewing circle has talked about anything else since the Beast tried the poor man."

"From what I hear, this is the second time that Mrs. Mumford has implored Butler to spare her husband's life," Eugenia said. "Phebe shared that someone from her church stopped by our house this morning and told her over coffee that the Beast agreed to meet Mrs. Mumford and her family in their home last night to hear their pleas. Afterward, he left her and the children wailing on the floor. As soon as he left, he publicly mocked her entreaties as insincere and not worthy of his consideration."

"Look!" Eugenia exclaimed. "Mrs. Mumford is still on the ground."

"The poor dear is prostrate with grief," Rachel said softly. "Perhaps it is a mercy she may not awaken in time to witness her husband's hanging."

Eugenia's voice rose with quiet fervor as she quoted from *Measure for Measure*:

> Man, proud man,
> Dressed in a little brief authority,
> Plays such fantastic tricks before high heaven
> As make the angels weep.

On the scaffold, Mumford stood as erect as a statue with his hands bound behind his back, alongside a military chaplain, two physicians, and his executioner.

Butler shouted, "I am giving you one last chance to denounce your actions, repent for what you have done, and swear your allegiance to the Union. Otherwise, I shall order the hangman to proceed. What do you say now, sir?"

"I say God Bless the South, sir!" Mumford shouted back, followed by the deafening cheers of the crowd. "When I fought in the war with Mexico under the command of General Twiggs, I was proud of the Stars and Stripes. Now that your army has invaded our land, dishonoring that flag, disrespecting our women, and bringing death and destruction upon us, I will gladly give my life for the Stars and Bars."

"Then may God have mercy upon your soul," Butler bellowed, raising his sword, "For I shall have none."

The military chaplain approached the condemned man, prayer book in hand.

"I don't need a chaplain," Mumford said.

"But you *do* need to confess your sins to save your soul, son," the chaplain pleaded.

"Preacher, I mean no disrespect. But I have seen soldiers ripped open and their insides spill out upon the ground, and I have looked into their dying eyes as they breathed their last breath, but I have yet to see a soul."

Despite Mumford's protest, the disconcerted chaplain managed a hurried blessing, and the black hood of death was pulled over the head of the man who would die a hero but forever live a martyr in the hearts of Southerners.

General Butler's sword slashed through the air with a swift descent, whereupon General Shepley signaled the executioner, who released the trap door.

When Mumford's body dropped, audible gasps erupted from the front of the otherwise silent crowd at the sound of his neck snapping and the violent convulsions that followed.

Eugenia and Rachel averted their tearful eyes and retrieved their handkerchiefs.

Eugenia, appalled at the execution, asked, "How long do you think they'll allow his body to hang there shaking like that?"

"Until he is still, and the doctors determine that he has no heartbeat," Philip returned dispassionately.

Immediately responding to the emotionally detached answer to her question, she said, "Philip, I'd like to leave now. I cannot bear any more of this dreadful scene."

Philip grabbed the stallion's reins to ease the phaeton out of the crowd.

"Do you think the family has a tomb for him?" Rachel asked, drying her eyes.

"He was a volunteer fireman," Philip said. "Even with his war injuries, I'm told he managed to help maintain the equipment and feed the horses. I'm sure he will be provided a vault in Cypress Grove Cemetery for firemen."

"Isn't that the one at the end of Canal Street?" Eugenia asked.

"Yes, it is."

Eugenia cleared her throat. "I understand that the viewing will be at Christ's Church."

Rachel nodded.

"The Confederate roses in my garden are blooming splendidly now, Rachel," Eugenia said softly. "Would you join me after the memorial service to place several of them at his grave?"

Rachel clasped Eugenia's hand, recalling the gardenias she had given her from her garden for Levi's funeral. "It would be my pleasure to accompany you, just as I did today. Even though custom demands that I remain in isolation during my period of mourning, I cannot stay confined to my parlor while such an injustice occurs."

"Some customs need to be changed," Eugenia said. "Levi would have certainly approved of you honoring this hero's martyrdom and visiting his grave."

Suddenly, a sharp crack tore through the air—then another, and another. *Bang! Bang! Bang!* The reports echoed down the narrow streets in deliberate succession, swelling into a thunderous cadence that rolled across the city like distant cannon fire. Twenty-one shots in all.

Eugenia flinched. "Philip, what on earth is that?" she asked, her hand instinctively rising to her throat.

Philip hesitated. "It's probably just Butler's men practicing their aim," he said.

In truth, while Mumford's body twisted at the end of the rope, Butler's soldiers were firing a twenty-one-gun salute in honor of the Union flag rising over City Hall. The timing was no accident. Butler had orchestrated the spectacle to send a clear message: insurrection would be met not just with punishment, but also with patriotic pageantry.

RED STORE
DRY GOODS & CLOTHING
BOOTS & SHOES HATS & CAPS

8

THE FRENCH MARKET

A freedman driver descended from his perch to assist Rachel with disembarking from his hansom cab at the French Market.

Sarah, struggling to maneuver with her near-term baby, needed extra help. Once she was safely on the sidewalk, she reached into her purse to grab a shinplaster.

The driver took the fare with a smile. "Thank you, ma'am." He grasped the chain of his pocket watch, flipped open the cover, and squinted at the dial. "Y'all say be back in 'bout an hour?"

"Yes, thank you, driver," Rachel replied, holding her wicker shopping basket and taking Sarah's arm. The sisters had agreed this would be Sarah's final outing, in keeping with their family physician's orders that she begin her period of confinement before her *accouchement*.

"Enjoy y'all's shoppin'," the driver called after them, already returning to his seat and gathering the reins of his swayback chestnut.

Rachel stood for a moment, taking in the vibrant array of colors and scents.

The warm, humid morning air carried a heady perfume of the dark, bitter tang of roasted coffee drifting from iron pots, blending with the powdery sweetness of beignets dusted in sugar. Steam curled around the stalls, mingling with the sharper, briny scent of fish laid out on glistening beds of ice—red snapper, catfish, eels coiled like sleeping ser-pents—all glinting beneath the cleavers of the shouting butchers.

The air was heavy with humanity. A Choctaw woman, her dark braid falling over a faded shawl embroidered with colorful beadwork, stood beside baskets woven from palmetto and straw, small enough to hold herbs. She held up an Arabi basket, broad, flat-bottomed, and deep, its reeds dyed ochre and brown, her voice low but firm as she named her price in French. Beside her, an elder crouched over a plain wooden box filled with sachets of dried sassafras, bay leaf, and filé, the pungent green dust that thickened gumbo.

Vendors called over one another like competing choirs: Creole butchers, Sicilian fishmongers, Irish flower girls in faded bonnets pinning dahlias and jasmine into bunches with twine. A toothless Negro organ grinder, his monkey in a tasseled vest perched dutifully at his shoulder, turned the crank with tireless devotion, causing a wheezing tune to warble into the din. Not far away, a fortune teller in a velvet headscarf read palms with a solemn nod.

Rachel enjoyed the familiar chaos. Here was the soul of New Orleans. The French Market was not merely a place of commerce; it was a celebration of the senses. And for the hour she had promised the driver, it belonged to her and Sarah.

"Where should we begin?" Rachel asked, encouraged by the sight of a new shipment of produce.

"You decide," Sarah said, a hint of irritation in her voice. "You'll be making this trip on your own next time. Prudence is going to be a very big girl."

"I'm happy to do that. You and Prudence can wait at home, snuggled comfortably in bed after I've propped you up with pillows."

"Quite frankly, sister," Sarah said, "neither of us should be out nor about. I should be resting while expecting, and you should be confined during your period of mourning. If the Yankees hadn't taken our servants, neither of us would be in this position."

Sarah and Rachel made their way through the crowd to a stall manned by a gaunt old fishmonger whose tooled, leathery face bore the portrait of a lifetime of hardship. Noticing the women take an interest in his wares, he set his pipe aside to wave an inviting hand over dozens of catfish filets neatly displayed on a bed of ice.

"Caught em fresh at sunrise up on Lake Pontchartrain, ladies," the old man assured them. "Won't find no sweeter fish in the market."

Sarah pointed to the largest filet, prompting the vendor to retrieve it for wrapping.

"I put a bit of ice in with it, ma'am," he said, handing her the package. "Best make it home to your cooling chest as soon as you can."

"Thank you, sir," Rachel said, exchanging a nickel for the neatly wrapped catfish filet and placing it in her basket.

"Notice anything different today, sister?" Rachel asked as they walked to the next vendor, suddenly realizing that her sister hadn't requested her nosegay sachet from their shopping basket as she usually did on their trips to the French Market.

"Yes," Sarah said. "It's as crowded as ever, but there are no rotten fish heads beneath the butcher's feet, nor that dreadful slime spilling over onto the walkway." Seeing a vendor selling balloons, she said, "Children can even play on the street now."

"And it *smells* much better," Rachel said. When she received no response, she ventured, "I suppose we must give the devil his due. The city's street workers started only a few days ago, but the market is already much cleaner."

Sarah raised an eyebrow as she moved on to the next stall, which displayed summer squash. However, she decided to pass it by because the squash was caked with dirt and had brown spots. "You might give the Beast some credit, but I don't. I've grown accustomed to the stench."

"Word has it he believes cleaning up French Town and establishing a quarantine for incoming ships will stop the fever this year."

"Why should we care? It's only the Union soldiers who'll die because they're not accustomed to our clime. Most of the rest of us will survive, thank Heavens."

Rachel understood Sarah's bitterness with the occupation, which was shared by most people in town who wished nothing but harm upon their invaders. She had her own reasons to be bitter, but decided to maintain her composure for the sake of her sister and her unborn child.

"Did you notice that there was a bakery open along our route here today?" Rachel asked, "I saw a sign on the window. Pity the price of bread is still high, though. Can you believe it's now a dime for what used to cost three cents before the occupation?"

"If you want bread, you'll have to remember where it was and tell the driver where to stop on our way home. I was too busy looking at all the boarded-up businesses to notice any bakery."

Rachel nodded. "I miss my warm, buttered French bread with its deliciously crisp crust!"

"So do I," Sarah agreed, "but it's been difficult to find because of the shortage of lard and flour." She paused, looking at Rachel to see how loose her dress was. "I haven't said anything, but you've lost too much weight."

"We must remember to buy some butter," Rachel said, choosing not to speak about her loss of appetite during her grief over the past two months. She had only recently begun to look forward to enjoying some of her favorite dishes.

"There's a lady down yonder who still has a little butter left," a nearby vendor said, pointing to a woman toward the end of the market. "Better hurry along. She ain't got much left last time I checked."

"Thank you," Rachel said. "We'll go straight away."

"Don't be fooled by her blarney," the woman warned sotto voce. "Ask her to cut into it. Sometimes, she stuffs a little potato in the middle to stretch it out to make more butterballs. 'Specially when she ain't churned that much."

"Thank you for warning us," Rachel whispered.

"Do you think that we can find any plantains?" Sarah asked Rachel.

"Eugenia mentioned that Phebe found some at the Poydras market. They just received a shipment from Cuba."

"Poydras is so far away," Sarah said.

"Yes," Rachel agreed, "We wouldn't want to cross over Canal Street for a few plantains."

"Look, Rachel!" Sarah exclaimed, excited as they approached the next stall. "Fresh greens!"

"Oh my!" Rachel said, admiring a basket of spinach. "We haven't had fresh greens since the blockade. And look! They also have a few carrots. Thank goodness the Beast allows safe passage to ships bringing in produce from Mobile and Matamoros."

Sarah sorted through the spinach. "The leaves are terribly wilted from the ship having to sit so long in quarantine."

"Not to worry. Try to pick out the best batch, and I'll freshen it up with a little cold water from the drip pan of the ice chest, dear. And buy a carrot while you're at it. Our driver's horse would appreciate one when he returns."

"You're such a fool for horses," Sarah said.

Rachel's expression brightened. "While you're doing that, I'll fetch us some butter before it's all gone. Would you like to hold the basket?"

"Yes," she said, taking the shopping basket. "How much is the spinach?" Sarah asked the vendor while her sister stepped away for the butter.

"A dime, ma'am."

"That much?"

"Hard to get fresh spinach, ma'am, and them paper baskets ain't cheap."

Sarah retrieved a dime from her handbag.

"Tell your sister here's a carrot for the horse," the woman said with a smile, handing her a large one with the spinach.

"That's kind of you," Sarah said, placing the vegetables in her basket and feeling better about the price.

Approaching her sister, who was standing in front of the butter vendor, Sarah stopped short, terrified by what she saw. The vendor—a stout, freckled Irish woman with fiery red hair and an angry face to match—was gripping a butcher knife high above her head with thick, mannish hands. Suddenly, she swung it down like an executioner's axe to cleave a butterball in twain on the massive butcherblock table.

"See! There ain't no potato!" the angry vendor snarled, still brandishing the butcher knife. "It's all pure Irish butter churned by me own hands just this mornin'," she said, pointing to a row of churns behind her. "I don't know who in tarnation put that nonsense into that pretty head of yours. I've half a mind to give it to you for free if you be willin' to point out the sleeveen who done me dirty. I'd love to tear a strip from her hide."

Unfamiliar with the meaning of "sleeveen" and reluctant to be schooled in the Irish tongue by a butcher knife-wielding mad woman who seemed eager to flay her fellow vendor, Rachel tactfully placed a dime on the table for the split butter ball, along with a nickel as a peace offering. "Forgive me, madam. I fear that someone's slander has caused me to suspect you wrongly. Please accept a little extra as a token of my apology."

The butter assassin's demeanor changed instantly. "Thank you kindly, ma'am," she returned in a sweet voice while deftly combining the cloven halves of butter into a single ball for wrapping. "You're a true lady," she gushed, handing the hastily wrapped ball of butter to Rachel.

Relieved that she had appeased the woman without sustaining bodily harm, Rachel noticed that Sarah was approaching, so she swiftly took the restored butterball.

As Rachel grabbed her sister's arm to make their escape, she accidentally stubbed her toe. Glancing down, she saw a basket of small potatoes beneath the vendor's table.

9

THE FUNERAL OF LIEUTENANT DeKay

French Town abounded with drunken souls, dancing to music and singing "The Bonnie Blue Flag." Celebrants transformed every street corner into a festival. The traditional *Farineaux*, or "Flour Festival," popular among Cajuns and Creoles at Mardi Gras, made sporadic appearances. Still, a scarcity of flour compelled responsible revelers to save it for bread-making instead of flinging it playfully at one another.

The cause of the festivities outside of Mardi Gras season was the recent good word from Richmond. The "grapevine," a network consisting of improvised telegraph lines and messengers, had transmitted the news from the Confederate capital to a point within forty miles of New Orleans on the northeastern shore of Lake Pontchartrain. The last tendril of the grapevine was Confederate "fishermen" in rowboats who memorized the information to avoid committing anything to writing and then relayed it in person to various agents in the city.

The news was that General Lee had captured McClellan's army and was parading the Union general and his soldiers as prisoners of war through the streets of downtown Richmond. After the reputed Confederate victory, Beauregard's troops were said to be bound for New Orleans, where they would arrive any day now.

Everyone deemed the news credible since McClellan, unlike Lee, was a young, untried general without real military experience. He was widely mocked in the Confederacy as being deficient in the necessary confidence to mount a campaign. Like Shakespeare's conflicted Prince Hamlet, McClellan's thoughts were bloody, but his hands remained clean.

As jubilant Confederate supporters in French Town celebrated one of their best days since the victory at Manassas last year, blocks away on the English side of Canal Street, Union soldiers and loyalists mourned the loss of Lieutenant DeKay during a funeral procession along St. Charles Avenue. They regarded this day as one of their worst in occupied New Orleans.

Union officers, mounted on magnificently groomed midnight-black stallions, led the solemn procession. Next came two open barouches bearing Lieutenant DeKay's relatives and a Union chaplain, followed by the closed funeral carriage with curtained windows transporting the body of the deceased. Fifteen empty carriages with closed window curtains were the last of the vehicles. A Union brass band playing various hymns and a phalanx of armed soldiers in dress uniforms brought up the rear of the procession.

The funeral march encountered horse-drawn streetcars headed to French Town, with ladies in their finery holding their heads high, wearing Confederate cockade hat pins featuring red, white, and blue ribbons that framed images of the Stars and Bars. The silent protesters in bonnets exhibited manifest contempt for their invaders' grief with disdainful smirks. Still, they stopped short of mouthing their defiance to avoid being charged by Butler's Woman Order as women of the town, plying their avocation.

Enjoying the sporadic protests on St. Charles Avenue from her balcony, Eugenia celebrated General Lee's reported success as best she could. She was pleased to hear a few defiant citizens on the street singing "God Save the South" before soldiers chased them away.

It was a bright and clear Sabbath afternoon, so she had invited Rachel to join her and her two younger children, William and Emma. The children were eager to play games on the balcony, as their father had forbidden them from leaving the house except to attend school during the week and synagogue with their family on the eve of the Sabbath.

Eugenia decided that having a birthday celebration for Clavius, her oldest son, and Fannie, her oldest daughter, would be the perfect way to disguise her happiness over the Confederate victory outside Richmond. It was irrelevant that their birthdays had passed earlier in the month. Both were now married and settled safely in LaGrange, Georgia, as were her other adult children.

Turning to her two youngest children, Eugenia said, "While John and Eugene are in the parlor playing chess, why don't you two play a game out here on the balcony so we can enjoy this lovely day?"

"Charades!" shouted William.

"Yay! Charades!" Emma exclaimed.

"That's grand," Eugenia said, delighted that the siblings had settled upon the same game without engaging in their usual bickering. "Tonight, when your father comes home from work, we'll have a birthday party for Clavius and Fannie. I baked a cake last night."

"Oh, goody! What kind of cake?" William asked.

"White cake with chocolate icing topped with butter-toasted pecans."

"Yum!" William said, rubbing his stomach. "My favorite. Will it have lots of candles?"

Eugenia laughed. "Heaven forbid, William! We might set the parlor aflame with that many candles."

Emma pursed her lips in a fulsome pout. "I wish Father didn't have to work on the Sabbath."

"Father wants to provide his family with a roof over their heads, darling, and the occupation has made it hard for him to do so. He promised me that he'd be home before sunset for the lighting of the Sabbath candles. Until then, let's have fun and enjoy the rest of the day."

"I'll go first," William said, immediately falling on all fours, then swinging on the black wrought-iron rails and cavorting about the balcony. Finally, he stood to scratch under his arms.

Eugenia and Rachel, seated comfortably in their chairs, joined Emma in laughing at his antics.

"I know! I know!" Emma exclaimed, "You're a monkey. That was simple enough."

"Fiddlesticks! Your turn."

Moments later, Eugenia noticed Lieutenant DeKay's funeral procession passing along the street in front of the house and stood to walk over to the balcony railing.

"What is that, Eugenia?" Rachel asked, rising to join her.

"It's a Union funeral, from what I can see."

From the street below, a member of the procession spotted Rachel standing on the balcony in her mourning attire and saluted.

"Look at that," Eugenia scoffed. "That old man thinks that you're mourning the death of the Yankee."

"Do you suppose we should all go inside until they pass?" Rachel asked. "They might notice the children laughing and playing up here while they are mourning."

"Why should I honor the death of a Union soldier? After all, Beast Butler tried that brave Mumford in a sham trial and hung him in short order. I still remember his poor widow and children at his funeral." Then she thought of all the trains that had only recently stopped running from Shiloh, filled with wounded soldiers and crude coffins hastily nailed together, but she remained silent out of respect for Rachel's loss.

Rachel returned to her seat, appearing distressed.

Turning back to join the game with her children, Eugenia saw Emma flapping her arms flexed at the elbows, her hands held to her armpits, and yelling, "Pock, Pock, P-o-o-o-ck!"

"I know," William yelled, laughing with his mother. "You're a chicken."

Emma pouted. "I'll fool you next time."

"Remember that making any noise is against the rules," William coached her.

Emma crossed her arms and scowled. "It's a silly rule."

Eugenia looked at her fondly, thinking how much Emma reminded her of herself at the same age.

Watching mourners march along the street, Eugenia noticed several people looking up to the balcony and frowning, but she ignored them. After all, what was happening in the confines of her private dwelling was her own business. Her privacy was the last of her remaining freedoms.

Then she noticed the carriages following the hearse and wondered why the curtains on their windows were drawn. Her curiosity was piqued, so she leaned over the railing for a closer look. "Rachel," she called over her shoulder, "look at all those carriages with the curtains drawn. It seems strange. Do you think they're empty?"

Rachel stood and stepped to the railing with Eugenia. "Why on earth would they do such a thing?"

"For appearances," Eugenia said. "Butler is quite the showman. He would go to great lengths to glorify a Union hero, even orchestrating a procession of empty carriages."

"Do you see that elderly man with the cane, pointing up here and talking to an officer? He looks distraught. Should we take the children inside?"

"What's it to me?" Eugenia asked, but upon noticing Rachel's discomfort, she added, "Why don't you go inside, my dear, until they've gone by? It seems to be distressing you."

"I need to head back home, anyway," Rachel said. "I told Sarah I would visit for only an hour or so before helping her with the laundry."

"Why don't you hire a maid?" Eugenia asked. She immediately regretted her question, aware that Rachael and Sarah were living off the small savings they had managed to keep, whereas Philip continued to earn a comfortable income.

Rachel blushed. "At the moment, we must fend for ourselves, Eugenia. Perhaps when Jacob comes home and returns to work, things will be better."

Eugenia embraced Rachel. "I'm certain that all will be well. Let me walk you to the back door while the children enjoy their games."

After Eugenia and Rachel left the balcony, the procession continued down Canal Street toward Christ Church.

Confederate bystanders along the route whispered among themselves, noting that it was the same church where William Mumford's funeral had been held just over a fortnight ago. Someone cited Matthew 5:45—"He maketh His sun rise on the evil and on the good, and sendeth rain on the just and on the unjust"—implying that their hero, Mumford, was among the "good" and the "just," while Lieutenant DeKay was among the "evil," and the "unjust."

Similarly, Union sympathizers, who also recited the same biblical passage along the way, reinterpreted the concepts of good and just versus evil and unjust, seamlessly swapping the names of Mumford and DeKay in their viewpoints.

Blocks later, Christ's Church, a towering Gothic-style cathedral, appeared in the distance. It was the first Protestant congregation established in the predominantly Catholic city.

Since the church's bishop, Dr. Lealock, had received anonymous death threats warning him not to officiate at the ceremony, General Butler had appointed Union Chaplain Chubbuck to serve in his stead.

A Union officer opened the massive carved wooden doors of the church and was appalled to find the sanctuary filled with ordinary citizens joined by former slaves, who eagerly accepted an invitation from Confederate sympathizers to sit wherever they pleased. Upon seeing the officer, the White people in the crowd burst into singing, "God Save the South."

"Clear the church! Now!" the officer bellowed.

The motley congregation reluctantly filed out of the sanctuary, cowed by the stentorian command of the armed Union officer, flanked by a dozen soldiers with bayonets.

Once the sanctuary was cleared, the pallbearers wheeled the cart bearing Lieutenant DeKay's flag-draped casket down the center aisle. After the soldiers situated the coffin in front of the altar, they carefully adjusted the Union flag, saluted it, and then executed a precision about-face, marching in lockstep to usher in the DeKay family.

Reaching the front of the sanctuary, the DeKay family took their seats along the center pew while the other mourners stood respectfully until they were seated.

Chaplain Chubbuck marched solemnly to the pulpit to address the congregation. "Brothers and sisters, we are gathered here today to mourn the loss of our friend, the recently departed and most honorable Lieutenant George Coleman DeKay, aide-de-camp to General Williams. Lieutenant DeKay was shot in the back by a cowardly Confederate bushwhacker in Orleans Parish just two days ago while attempting to prevent a farmer from burning his cotton to keep it from the Union. Since my own words would not be worthy of the valor of this eighteen-year-old man cut down in his youth, I shall quote from the

Gospel of John, chapter 15, verse 13. 'Greater love hath no man than this, that a man lay down his life for his friends.'"

The keening and wailing of a young woman in the family pew prompted Chaplain Chubbuck to pause the service, allowing an older woman to step forward and offer comfort.

The chaplain waited patiently, allowing the young woman time to weep. When her sobs at last began to quiet, he opened the *Book of Common Prayer* and prepared to resume the liturgy.

10

EUGENIA'S ARREST

Eugenia struggled with her sewing machine's bobbin while Rachel, seated nearby, moistened her fingertips to flip through her fashion plate booklet, considering choices for a fall outfit.

"I wish Sarah could have joined us," Rachel said. "She has a real talent for threading bobbins on those Singer contraptions."

"Yes," Eugenia replied, her frustration mounting as the bobbin refused to cooperate. "But it's probably best she stays home, given her condition. The ladies in her sewing circle will keep her entertained."

Rachel chuckled. "Indeed. Beast Butler never fails to be the subject of whispers at every salon and supper table. I believe he has them all Butlerized by some wizardry."

Suddenly, Eugenia's rotund Irish maid, Phebe, burst into the dressmaking room. Wiping her forehead with her apron and pausing to catch her breath, she exclaimed, "Miss Eugenia, a Yankee soldier is waiting downstairs at the front door. He says he has a message for you."

"Control yourself, Phebe," Eugenia said, a hint of irritation in her voice. "You know how I despise being interrupted when I'm working. Ask him if you may deliver his message to me. Inform him that I'm indisposed."

"I've told him that several times, ma'am," Phebe fretted, "but he won't give it to me, and he refuses to leave. He keeps saying that General Butler ordered him to deliver the message directly to Mrs. Eugenia Phillips."

Realizing she had no choice, Eugenia abandoned fumbling with her bobbin and rose from her sewing machine. She paused momentarily before reaching the hallway door, recalling her ordeal in Washington when she and her entire household had been detained in a dismal attic.

Rachel stood and said, "I'll go with you."

"No, Rachel," Eugenia said firmly. "I want you to follow me into the hallway, take the back stairs to the kitchen, exit through the courtyard gate, and catch the next streetcar home."

"Please be careful, Eugenia," Rachel urged, embracing her friend in the hallway. "Let me know what happens."

"I'm certain it's nothing," Eugenia said, though she inwardly acknowledged the potential danger, given that the city was under martial law. She had learned from her detention in Washington what it could be like when the writ of habeas corpus was suspended.

Rachel hurried down the hallway and descended the back stairs to leave.

Eugenia followed her anxious maid downstairs to the front door, where a young Union Army sergeant stood patiently on her stoop. "This is for you, ma'am," he said, handing her a strip of ruled paper with a ragged edge that appeared to have been hastily torn from a bound ledger. On it was scrawled, "Bring me Mrs. Eugenia Phillips." It was signed "B. F. Butler."

Eugenia was shocked to see Butler's hastily scribbled note, which she knew amounted to nothing less than a warrant for her detainment under martial law. "This is a mistake, sir," she protested while trying to recollect any offense that would have led him to write the note. The only incriminating thought that occurred to her was that she had been zealous in raising a subscription for the widow of the murdered Mumford. She wondered if this charitable act was her supposed crime.

She turned to her servant, who had begun to wring her hands. "Phebe, please go back upstairs and summon Mr. P. to accompany me to the Customs House with this officer."

"Yes, ma'am," Phebe said and hurried to comply.

"Officer," Eugenia asked respectfully, "may I go upstairs and dress suitably for my audience with General Butler?"

The officer reluctantly nodded his assent. "You best not keep the General waiting long, ma'am. He is most anxious for your arrival."

On her way up the staircase, she reflected, *Most anxious for my arrival? What charge would his twisted brain contrive? What cruelty could he possibly have in mind for me?* She then imagined a thousand ways in which Beast Butler, who had sentenced dozens of citizens to hard labor for the most trivial offenses, might punish her for her supposed crime.

Yet, she felt curious about what all of this meant. In an oddly intriguing manner, she looked forward to an audience with the most hated man in New Orleans.

Upstairs in her bedroom, she sat at her dressing table and hurriedly applied her makeup while considering what she would tell her husband. When satisfied with her appearance, she went to her cedar armoire and selected a suitable costume to engage her enemy.

"Eugenia, what is this all about?" her husband inquired, entering the bedroom in a frenzy. "Phebe just informed me that General Butler has summoned you to the Customs House."

His concern elicited a disingenuous laugh as she casually disrobed and put on her fresh dress. "This is all a huge mistake, dearest. As soon as I see the general, the matter, whatever it is, will be settled shortly without any consequence. Frankly, I am quite eager to meet the Beast." She selected a necklace. "Would you mind buttoning me up and fastening this for me?"

"Of course."

After Philip finished buttoning up her dress and fastening her necklace, she turned around and asked, "How do I look, dear?"

"You look lovely, my darling," he said, leaning down to give her a peck on the cheek. "I will only take a moment to prepare myself to go with you."

Eugenia gauged by his smile that her performance had assuaged his fears.

The arresting officer led Eugenia and Philip outside to a polished black military carriage that shone like his shoes. It was adorned with radiant brass lanterns that harmonized with the gleaming buttons of his uniform.

Watching Eugenia and Philip leave, Phebe positioned herself at the front door, observing the neighbors on the street engaging in hushed conversations. A woman within earshot confidently asserted to her companion that Eugenia would undoubtedly join the ranks of those contemptuous women that Butler had already exiled to Ship Island.

Once Eugenia and Philip took their seats in the carriage, the officer stepped inside and sat on the bench facing them, nervously drumming his fingers on his leg. She surmised that he was not pleased with his assignment.

In the intimate interior of the carriage, Eugenia took the opportunity to probe her jailer about the circumstances of her arrest.

"Officer, might I ask as to the nature of General Butler's interest in my person?"

"I'm sorry, ma'am, I only have my orders. I know nothing aside from that."

"Rumor has it that the General is out of town, escorting Confederate prisoners from Baton Rouge."

"He returned to the city earlier this morning, ma'am. As I informed you, he awaits your arrival at the Customs House, where he presides over civil matters."

"Do you know what provoked him to command my presence?"

"No, ma'am."

Convinced that this courteous soldier was simply a functionary of the general, Eugenia ceased her interrogation and resolved herself to the inevitability of a confrontation with the Beast.

In the ensuing silence, she imagined herself trapped alive in a coffin, traveling to her funeral in a hearse. But unlike a coffin, there was no grave alarm in the carriage, no string to ring a bell to signal someone outside to free her.

She was thankful it would be a short ride since her house was just across from City Hall on St. Charles Avenue, and Butler's headquarters in the Customs House on Canal Street was only about six blocks east and a block north.

Minutes later, the carriage reached the massive gray stone Customs House, and Eugenia took the officer's hand to step out of the carriage. A shiver ran down her spine when she stood facing the massive granite stairs leading into the towering building that reminded her of the Bastille. Inside, she had heard that the self-righteous Butler had styled himself "Christ's vice-gerent" and reigned in his Hall of Justice under martial law as both judge and jury.

After the officer opened the heavy door of the imposing edifice, he led the couple through a crowd of Negroes in a grand marble hall with banks of windows admitting the morning sunlight. The stench of the fugitive slaves' sweaty bodies packed tightly together in the heat of late June nearly overwhelmed her, and she regretted not bringing her nosegay.

Toward one end of the many-columned hall, she pitied a manacled young Confederate officer being led limping up a massive stairway by two Union soldiers. She knew he would be incarcerated on one of the upper floors where Butler had created a prison for his recent captives.

Suddenly, a disembodied voice called, "Has Mrs. Phillips yet arrived?"

Eugenia looked up to see an officer. "Yes, sir, here she is."

She noticed he was an older soldier, and his epaulets indicated a superior rank to the young officer who had arrested her. She considered it curious that he blushed when she approached.

"General Butler is waiting, ma'am. Follow me," he ordered, executing an abrupt about-face to march briskly through an open doorway leading into another room.

Eugenia and Philip were subsequently escorted through several rooms crowded with a strikingly diverse assembly of people. She observed Black men in coarse work shirts, women of mixed ancestry in faded calico dresses, and White men, some in threadbare coats and some in fine frock jackets. From their varied attire and grooming, she discerned a broad spectrum of social standing, ranging from the destitute to the well-heeled. It seemed to her that injustice made no distinction of color or class in the general's court.

Finally, the couple reached a mysterious, padded door, upholstered with a green baize material that resembled the coarse woolen surface of a billiard table.

Seeing the Phillips couple standing behind the older officer at the door, a younger officer approached Eugenia's husband and whispered, "Sir, General Butler wishes you to remain outside."

Hearing the whispered message, Eugenia immediately seated herself on a nearby sofa, crossed her arms, and declared, "None but physical force can make me go alone into that room. So, I advise you, valiant men, to get a rope, wrap a noose around my neck, and pull my corpse inside."

The two officers stood in dismayed silence. After a brief whispered conference, one said, "I will see what can be done, ma'am." He then briefly entered Butler's sanctuary, closing the door behind him.

"Be careful, Eugenia," her husband whispered nervously. "You don't want to upset the general."

The officer returned shortly and announced, "I have obtained consent for your husband to accompany you, ma'am."

The two officers opened the mysterious baize door and escorted the couple inside. There, General Butler sat behind a large mahogany writing table elevated on a dais surrounded by armed officers. On top of his desk, near his right hand, lay a Colt revolver, and a holstered pistol was strapped around his waist.

Eugenia found Butler's stagecraft amusing, but a chill ran down her spine when she gazed upon his grotesque countenance. Balding and bloated, with crooked, squinty eyes, he had a face that would sink a thousand ships.

When the couple approached him, he rose and leaned over his writing table to thrust an accusatory finger toward Eugenia's face, his countenance contorted with rage. "You were seen laughing and mocking at the remains of a federal officer during his funeral procession," he bellowed, "a man who served as my personal guard when I first came ashore in this rebellious city. And you were doing so in the presence of a mourner standing on the same balcony as you were. I do not call you a common woman of the town but an uncommonly vulgar one, and I sentence you to Ship Island for the duration of the War."

Eugenia considered that his special branding distinguished her from all the other ladies referred to as common women of the town by his "Woman Order." But she dared not tell him she was flattered by his characterization of her for fear of being summarily sentenced to the gallows.

She could see that Mr. P. was angered by her treatment at the hands of the Beast, so she took his arm to try to restrain him.

Ignoring her, he protested, "General Butler. I have known you before you came here, and you know me. I will not allow this language to be spoken to my wife."

Butler's face contorted with rage once more. "Gag this man! Arrest him and shackle him upstairs with the Rebel soldiers."

Eugenia felt a wave of guilt. Her Confederate loyalty was harming her husband again, just as it had ruined his successful law practice in Washington. Could it be that Butler was aware of her past involvement in spying activities? Was this the reason for his anger and not her alleged disrespect for DeKay's funeral procession? After all, hundreds of women crowding the streetcars adorned with Confederate symbols were just as guilty of disrespect for the Union soldier as she was, and, to her knowledge, not one of them had been detained.

Regardless of the past, she was horrified at the idea of her husband being shackled with the Confederate prisoners upstairs, so she calmly turned to him and said, "Mr. P., please go out and leave this man to me."

An officer bent down to whisper something in Butler's ear, which caused him to relent. She strongly suspected that the man had informed the general of her husband's service in the U. S. Congress as a representative from Alabama and later as an accomplished attorney in Washington who had argued before the Supreme Court. There were also his recent business transactions in town since they arrived from Washington, some of which most likely kept the general's textile mill in Massachusetts supplied with cotton.

She was pleased to see that whatever the officer had whispered in Butler's ear had caused him to allow Philip to remain at her side. With a saddened countenance, he sat quietly and offered no further resistance.

But she was horrified by the general's mention of Ship Island, the dreaded, desolate strip of land off the coast of Mississippi that was a quarantine station for yellow fever victims.

"General Butler," she said calmly, "I was in good spirits on the day of the funeral, and my laughter had nothing to do with the procession passing beneath my balcony. My children and I were having a belated birthday party for two of my older children, who are now living independently. We were enjoying ourselves, and I received some good news about another matter. I did not think that my behavior in my private dwelling could offer anyone any offense."

Eugenia chose not to incite the Beast further by letting him know of her good cheer upon hearing of the success of Confederate troops defending Richmond.

Butler ignored her defense and began writing intently upon sheet after sheet of paper. She assumed that he had determined her guilt and was penning the details of her sentence and terms of imprisonment.

Eugenia sat patiently for about half an hour, trying to remain calm. Her thoughts turned to Butler's cruelty. After he hanged Mumford, he censored local presses for daring to point out this and other misdeeds. He had even confiscated the *Commercial Bulletin* and sentenced its owner, William Seymour, to three months in prison without a trial.

Seymour's offense was to suggest that his deceased father, Colonel Isaac Seymour, was a patriot after he had fallen in action at the Battle of Gaines' Mill in Virginia just this last Friday. His father had also fought in three wars on behalf of the nation. Seymour later told friends that Butler had accused him of supporting the rebellion, roaring, "I am the military governor of this state—the supreme power—you cannot disregard my order, sir. By God, he that sins against me, sins against the Holy Ghost."

Eugenia called her husband's attention to the large placard over the general's desk to break the stressful silence. "There is no difference between a He and a She adder in their venom," she whispered.

"That may be so," he replied, "but from his degree of agitation, I sense that 'She adders better than He adders' would have been a better expression of his sentiments."

Smiling at her husband's take on the general's placard, Eugenia fell silent.

Appearing satisfied with his order, General Butler looked up and cleared his throat to read. "I hereby issue General Order 150, sentencing you to Ship Island for the duration of the war...."

Noting that hers was number 150 issued in only two months of his reign in New Orleans — amounting to over two orders a day — she listened intently as he read aloud his rambling decree banishing her to the dreaded quarantine island. There, he ordered that she was to be held in isolation, fed soldiers' rations, and denied communication with her family. In what she considered an attempt to appear humane, he allowed her one servant in her employ to cook her rations and a few other amenities she deemed unworthy of consideration.

When he finished, he hesitated and stared at her, which she interpreted as an invitation to fall to her knees and tearfully beg for mercy. When she did not, she noticed a nervous twitch in his right eye and concluded that he was particularly vexed.

Instead of begging for mercy, she taunted, "The only good thing about Ship Island, sir, is that when I step ashore, you will not be on it."

The general's jaw dropped.

"Is that all?" she asked calmly, managing a trace of a smirk at a man whose countenance was so disfigured that he could not even look her straight in the eye.

"Major!" he growled, the veins in his face distending as if they were about to pop. "Remove this she-adder from my presence!"

After she was escorted from the room, Butler continued to seethe, gritting his teeth. "Another damned Jew who betrayed our Savior. They're interested in nothing but filthy lucre and aiding and comforting the enemy in the cotton trade."

Just outside, an officer swung open the door to a small chamber and gestured for her to enter. As the heavy metal door clanged shut behind her, the jangle of keys and the sharp click of the lock echoed through the room, carrying her back to the cold confines of her detention in Washington.

Shortly after her confinement, she noticed a barred window, so she looked outside to see her husband stepping into the carriage that had conveyed them to her tribunal. She knew then that it was left to him to say her goodbyes to her family and friends since Butler's order forbade any communication during her exile.

Standing at the window, she no longer felt the necessity to act composed as she had felt in the presence of her husband. Terrified by the thought of being banished to Ship Island, she tried to calm her racing heart, which she was convinced would leap from her chest at any moment.

Then, the terror gave way to indignation at the injustice just meted out to her by a despicable and coldhearted man. *"Bâtard! Bête!"* she raged, watching her husband being spirited away in the military carriage.

Drying her eyes with her handkerchief, she turned around and sat at the small writing desk.

In her imagination, she returned to her youth when her mother, a British actress, would coach her in bit parts. She stepped upon the stage and fancied herself a man, crazy for a duel with the Beast. But the limelight dimmed because she had no lines to deliver. She was only a wretched, weak woman, deprived even of the privilege of protesting her fate.

Then she noticed a pen, ink, and paper on the desk and decided to write about her tragedy, giving vent to her sorrows.

She dried her damp palms on her sleeves and then feverishly wrote of her crimes and rebellious spirit. She trembled as she appealed to the souls of martyred heroines of ancient lore, whose wrongs paled when compared to those of her own.

Armed with her newly penned lines, she returned to the limelight of her imaginary stage to assume the role of her prosecutor, who protested that it was beyond human nature for anyone, much less a general, to have to be kept from his Champagne and ice on a summer day by a vile "She-Adder." Her character raged in a prosecutorial tone, "Of course, Eugenia Phillips deserved her fate; why, it was mild! Consider the fate of that fellow Mumford."

The limelight faded once again when the door opened abruptly without the courtesy of a knock. In the doorway's dim light, she beheld the face of an uncommonly handsome man of noble bearing who stood staring at her. Was he a fan waiting breathlessly at the stage door for her autograph?

Suddenly, the handsome visage of the imagined admirer morphed into that of the detested Union soldier, Stafford, Mumford's hangman. She reflexively pointed a finger of condemnation. *"J'accuse!"*

Abruptly returning to the present, she regretted her lack of discretion. However, upon noticing the man's blank expression, she realized that she had been spared from Mumford's hangman by his apparent ignorance of the French language.

11

An Incident Involving Madame Larue

On the morning of the Fourth of July, the bread line at Monsieur Duplantier's bakery stretched along the banquette, its length a testament to wartime scarcity. Rachel waited patiently, her eyes fixed on the diminishing stack of loaves, when a sudden commotion farther up the street broke her reverie.

She shaded her eyes to see a woman parading down Canal Street in a flowing white gown cinched with bold Secessionist red and white sashes, as though she were the star of some midsummer comedy. The woman's fair hair cascaded over her shoulders in theatrical waves, and a well-groomed miniature snow-white poodle pranced at her side, adorned with ribbons and a miniature Beauregarde cockade. Rachel recognized her at once as Madame Larue, a familiar figure on the New Orleans stage and no stranger to spectacle.

In the heavy July heat, Madame Larue moved with practiced flair, distributing handbills to passersby from a wicker basket on her arm. She paused after each delivery to offer a deep, dramatic bow, drawing cheers from a small but growing crowd. A swell of voices rose as she launched into a defiant rendition of "The Bonnie Blue Flag," her voice clear above the clatter of carts and the barking of her little dog.

Rachel's heart pounded, torn between alarm and fascination. She knew that she should turn away since sensible women did not linger at the edges of trouble, but her feet refused to carry her onward. She watched Union soldiers nearby laugh at the spectacle, their mirth carrying across the sunbaked street, until an officer's sharp command cut through the revelry like a saber. "Arrest that woman and disperse her followers!"

Madame Larue let out a startled cry, her basket of handbills tipping, while her poodle Pierre yelped and bolted down the street, his ribbons flying behind him like battle streamers caught in retreat.

A man burst from the doorway of a nearby shop, pistol in hand and trembling with urgency. "Drop that sword!" he yelled, the words echoing in Rachel's ears. Her stomach tightened as the officer held his ground, refusing the demand of a Southern gentleman rushing to defend a lady. A crack of gunfire split the air.

Rachel flinched as the officer collapsed onto his sword. Madame Larue's' pamphlets, once waved so triumphantly, rained down over his body, their proclamations of Confederate victories now stained with blood.

Cries of "Murder!" pierced the uproar. Another voice loosed a rebel yell, sharp and wild, before vanishing into the gathering chaos. Soldiers swarmed the scene, seizing the gunman and dragging Madame Larue, wailing for her lost poodle, toward a waiting police cart. Her cries of *"Pierre! Reviens, mon chéri!"* rang out, a pitiful counterpoint to the heavy thud of shoes and the clatter of wagon wheels.

Rachel pressed back against the rough brick of the bakery wall, her chest tightening. At that moment, her desire for bread paled in comparison to a deeper, gnawing hunger for order and safety, an end to the madness that had gripped her city.

As the police wagon rumbled away with Madame Larue, a cloud of dust curling in its wake, Rachel stood alone. Though her knees felt unsteady beneath her, she steeled herself and stepped forward to open the bakery door. Crossing the threshold, she left the street behind, yet the defiant image of Madame Larue and the fading echoes of her poodle's frantic yelps clung to her mind.

The next morning, a somber-faced Madame Larue stood before General Butler, her exhaustion etched upon her face, and her belly ached from hunger. Last evening, she had been served a soldier's meager fare of salted beef and stale hardtack after her arrest. Confined to the Customs House, she and several other women had been segregated from the Confederate soldiers awaiting the next prisoner exchange. Her sleeping arrangement consisted of a thin mat on a hard wooden floor. To her chagrin, she found herself sharing a single chamber pot with her fellow inmates, some of whom she recognized as women of the streets.

She appeared before Butler's military hearing in the same dress she wore when she was arrested, without the colorful sashes seized by the arresting officials without explanation. Standing beside the seated general, an officer leaned down to whisper something in his ear.

"Haven't I seen you before, Madame?" Butler asked quizzically.

Madame Larue glanced at his face with a sudden look of recognition. "You were in the audience at my last performance. I played Suzanne in *Le Mariage de Figaro.*"

He smirked. "Was that before or after I fell asleep?"

Despite the sting of her tormentor's insult, Madame Larue, experienced in verbal sparring from her sharp repartee in French farces, retorted, "At no time did I hear you snoring, sir. Nor did I see an usher prod you with a wakeup stick."

"That, Madame, is because my wife, who dragged me to your boring play, kept elbowing me when I nodded."

"I demand an explanation of the charges being levied against me," she said, tiring of his abuse.

"Disturbing the peace, distributing treasonous statements, and inciting a man to murder one of my officers, Madam." Seemingly out of nowhere, he produced her confiscated red and white sashes and threw them across his desk at her. "Not to mention desecrating a Union flag."

While recognizing the sashes she had cut from the Union flag stolen by her husband and his companions after a drunken night of poker, Madame Larue decided not to respond to his last accusations.

"On the first charge," Madame Larue declared, "I maintain that there must *ipso facto* be a peaceful state to charge me with disturbing the peace."

"You, Madam, are no Portia," he snarled. "You are at my mercy now, not prosecuting a bloodthirsty Shylock in one of Shakespeare's plays. I would advise you to conduct yourself accordingly."

Madame Larue stood firm, shifting her approach. "My sources inform me that General Beauregard is approaching our city, and General Lee has issued a warrant for your arrest as a war criminal for hanging that poor Mumford fellow. I suggest you abandon this pretense of a trial and set me free to go about my business."

Butler's face turned crimson, veins bulging in his neck, while frothy saliva gathered at the corners of his mouth, betraying his seething rage. "I've had enough of this boorish performance!" he yelled. "I sentence you, Madame, to Ship Island for the duration of the War." He motioned to an armed soldier standing at the door. "Guard! Take this traitorous she-adder from my presence. Prepare her to sail to Ship Island on the next transport."

The guard snapped to attention and saluted. "Yes, sir!"

"What about my Pierre, my dear, sweet, little poodle?" Larue wailed pitifully while she was being escorted from the room.

"Not to fear, Madame. Pierre is safe," Butler said, mocking her with feigned compassion. "My men reported that they fed him some of their rations last evening after your arrest. They informed me that little Pierre performs tricks like a circus dog."

"When will I get to see him?" she called from the hallway, her spirit broken.

"Never!" he yelled after her. "I wouldn't send my *own* dog to a God-forsaken place like Ship Island. I'll send Pierre to Boston with the finest accommodation on the next outbound vessel. My favorite niece's sixteenth birthday is next month, and she's always wanted a dainty French poodle. Now she'll have one."

12

SHOULD AULD ACQUAINTANCE BE FORGOT?

Eugenia's husband, Philip Phillips, wiped the beads of sweat from his tanned brow with his handkerchief as he descended from his phaeton, tying his horse's reins to the hitching post in front of the St. Charles Hotel. A uniformed ostler promptly stepped forward to greet him.

"Will you be lodging with us, sir?" asked the silver-haired man.

"No, I'm just visiting a friend," Philip said.

"Very well, sir," the ostler responded, handing him a numbered token. "After your visit, please return here, and I will fetch your phaeton. In the meantime, we will take good care of your horse and keep him in the shade with plenty of water."

"Thank you," Philip said with a smile, handing the aging gentleman a silver coin before stepping onto the curb to approach the hotel's grand entrance.

Inside the lobby, the atmosphere pulsed with the presence of businessmen donned in top hats and coats, their attire accentuated by the glint of gold pocket watch chains. Philip recognized several of them as his affluent planter clients who, having signed the Oath of Allegiance, were able to temporarily retain their slaves under terms negotiated with Butler.

Animated conversations filled the space, and a discernible tension mounted as one man appeared red-faced, struggling to contain his anger. Catching fragments of the man's conversation, Philip deduced that his reaction likely stemmed from an encounter with the general.

Philip's clients often remarked on the irony of General Butler's two-faced dealings. On the one hand, he was likened to Robin Hood, robbing the rich to aid the poor. On the other hand, those same clients claimed he favored the wealthy, so long as their bribes were generous enough.

As he reached the check-in desk, Philip's eyes were drawn to the large regulator clock on the wall behind the clerk. Its glass face caught the gaslight as the hands moved toward a quarter to nine.

"May I help you, sir?" the uniformed clerk asked, adjusting his waistcoat.

"My name is Philip Phillips, and I am here to see one of your guests, Mr. Reverdy Johnson."

"Is Mr. Johnson expecting you?"

"Yes," Philip said, handing the clerk Johnson's *carte de visite*. "I sent him a note yesterday, and he responded with his room number here and our appointment time."

"Very well, sir," the clerk said after inspecting the calling card and glancing at the clock on the wall behind him. "Since he expects you momentarily, you may proceed to his room. The elevator is just a few steps to our right and then a sharp turn to your left."

Philip blinked. "Did you say elevator?"

"Yes, sir. Just recently installed. One of the few of its kind in the South."

"Thank you," Philip said, retrieving Reverdy's card and walking to the brightly polished brass doors of the elevator just as they were opening.

The elevator operator asked, "Floor, please?"

"Third floor, please," Philip replied as he stepped to the back of the elevator to organize his thoughts for the meeting. He wondered if Reverdy would still remember him. They had once been friends, sharing similar views on most political issues. Both men had served in Congress, albeit during different periods and in different chambers.

Each had also received the prestigious honor of being allowed to argue cases before the U.S. Supreme Court. Through these legal pursuits, Philip had formed a close bond with Reverdy, who had represented Dred Scott in the infamous 1857 case that bore his name. In that case, Scott, an enslaved man, was denied legal standing because he was not recognized as a citizen. Together, Philip and Reverdy mourned the devastating 7-2 decision, which included Chief Justice Roger Taney's opinion that not only denied Scott his freedom but also set the precedent that enslaved individuals had no standing in court and no right to representation by an attorney.

Philip's mind raced through the key points he needed to discuss with Reverdy until the operator opened the elevator door. He entered the hallway, scanned the room numbers, and saw that Reverdy's was the third room on his right.

Lightly tapping on the door marked 312, Philip awaited a response.

As soon as the door creaked open, Philip came face to face with his old friend.

"Philip!" the silver-haired Reverdy said, his sagging face drooping like a hound dog's, his one good eye sparkling with intelligence. "Look at you! You're a sight for sore eyes, my boy. You're as handsome as ever, but you could stand to put a few more pounds on your bones."

"Reverdy," Philip returned, entering the room to embrace his old friend. "I was hoping that you had not forgotten me."

"Forgotten you? How could I? We enjoyed such marvelous conversations when you were in Washington. And your lovely wife is the perfect hostess." Reverdy gestured toward one of two high-backed chairs facing the window. "Please have a seat, my friend. May I offer you something to drink? Something cold, perhaps? This New Orleans heat is stifling."

Philip approached a leather-upholstered, high-backed chair and sat down. "I don't want to impose."

"It's nothing, Philip. I have some fresh-squeezed lemonade in the cooling chest. I had room service deliver it earlier this morning."

"That does sound delightful."

"My maid came in sick this morning, so I sent her home. A terrible case of the ague. Please excuse me while I go into the kitchen to fetch a drink for both of us."

"Thank you, Reverdy."

Looking out the window, Philip stared at the levee, recalling the day Eugenia was taken aboard a transport under guard, destined for Ship Island. His eyes filled with tears, and he took out a handkerchief to wipe away the evidence of his grief before his friend could return with the lemonade.

"Here we are," Reverdy said, setting a silver tray with two glasses and a pitcher of lemonade on the table between the high-backed chairs. Leaning down, he poured the drinks.

"Thank you," Philip said, taking his glass and waiting for Reverdy to take his seat. "Forgive me for not having asked how you are faring."

Reverdy took a sip of his lemonade. "I'm faring well, Philip…for a man my age."

"You're only a decade older than me," Philip remarked, inwardly marveling at how much difference a decade could make. He mused that the ricocheting bullet, which had blinded Reverdy in one eye, did not help matters. So much for his coaching a friend in preparation for a duel.

"That may be, but the plumbing is not the same as it used to be. Takes a lot longer for me to piss in the pot, and I can never fill it up in one session."

Philip nearly choked on his lemonade. "Sorry to hear that, Reverdy. And how are your lovely wife and children?"

"My wife and all fifteen of my children are faring well. How is your family, Philip? I believe you and Eugenia had nine children when we last spoke."

"The children are fine, all nine of them. Several of the older ones are married and starting their own families. The four younger ones…" The words caught in Philip's throat as he recalled sending all four of his younger children to live with relatives in LaGrange, Georgia.

Reverdy leaned in. "There, there, Philip. Is there anything I can do?"

Philip fought to regain his composure. "When Butler sent Eugenia to Ship Island, I wrote my daughter, Fannie, and she came to stay with me."

"Ship Island?" Reverdy asked incredulously.

"Yes," Philip nodded sadly. "And she is still there."

"I've heard the complaints of a dozen families whose members were sent there, some for the most trivial offenses, but I had not heard about Eugenia. Please tell me she didn't get involved in espionage again. It was all the buzz when she was detained in Washington."

"Nothing of the sort. Butler accused her of disrespecting a funeral procession for a Union soldier. I know the accusation wasn't true since she told me she was having a birthday party and playing games with two of our younger children on our balcony while I was at work."

"I see," Reverdy said, stroking his chin.

"Is there anything you can do to obtain her release?" Philip asked, knowing that his old friend was his last hope.

"Not directly, I fear, since I have no authority over the general. But I have been asked to hear the complaints of the embassies and the citizens of New Orleans, write a report, and submit it to President Lincoln for his intervention as he deems appropriate."

"I don't know what you've found so far, but Butler has appointed himself Christ's regent here in the city. Through his brother, Andrew, he has arranged to buy cotton below auction price to supply a mill in Massachusetts in which he holds considerable interest."

Reverdy nodded. "Several merchants have so informed me."

"Also, Chase's nephew, Denison, has benefited handsomely from his post as a customs agent, which is no surprise, given that his Uncle, Chase, the Secretary of the Treasury, sent him there. I've spoken to many of my clients who have complained about having to bribe him to do business."

Reverdy chuckled. "Butler informed me of Denison's indiscretion to throw me off the scent of his brother's corruption."

Philip was confused by his friend's seeming indifference to the rampant corruption in the city. "Did you also discover that Denison authorized Senator Sprague, Chase's son-in-law, who owns a mill, to engage in arms trade with the Confederacy in return for cotton?"

Reverdy's face grew solemn. "I fear that the President was correct when he told me, in so many words, that an intelligent angel looking down from heaven would conclude that this war is being prosecuted for obtaining cotton from the South for Northern cotton mills."

"The President is aware of all this?" Philip asked.

"Philip, my friend, the reign of King Cotton stretches far beyond the confines of New Orleans. It is not just Butler who is stained by corrupt dealings, though he has perfected the craft. Corruption will continue so long as there's profit to be gained. The President has chosen to pass these matters on to Congress for investigation after the war. For now, his main concerns are avoiding the anger of foreign embassies and preventing local tensions from escalating among the citizens. The last thing he wants is foreign intervention in our war or having the populace resist efforts to reunite with the Union."

"I understand," Philip said, feeling a profound sense of relief that his friend's mission included addressing the concerns of local citizens. So many of them, like his wife, had been treated unjustly by Butler without an opportunity to defend themselves.

Leaning in, Reverdy spoke earnestly. "Rest assured, my friend, that upon my return to Washington, I will exert every effort to plead Eugenia's case. I will be your best advocate before the President, but I cannot guarantee the outcome. Once she is eventually freed, though, I strongly recommend that you seriously consider relocating beyond the reach of this man they call 'the Beast.' Philip, you're still a young man. And you are among the most talented attorneys I know. You will prosper wherever you settle."

Philip reciprocated by leaning in to express his gratitude. "You don't know how much this means to me, my friend."

13

Eugenia's Return

Under the cover of darkness, Butler's soldiers led Eugenia to the carriage step outside her home. Her hair was matted, her frame gaunt, and her skin streaked with grime. It was not from neglect, but because a bath had been denied her throughout her confinement. She stood next to her loyal servant Phebe, whose appearance was hardly better.

Eugenia's hand trembled as she reached to turn the brass knob of the doorbell. Her heart pounded at the sound of the ringing bell, fearing that Butler had confiscated their house and banished her family further into the Confederacy during her exile.

Aside from passing on dozens of baskets of picked-over fruit with nothing to identify who sent them, the guards on Ship Island followed Butler's orders and denied her any communication with her family. Keeping her incommunicado deprived her of their words of comfort and compounded her misery.

She rang the doorbell again, and the front door creaked open. In its frame stood a gray-haired Negro manservant she did not recognize, clad in his nightgown, holding a whale oil lamp. By the dim light, he caught sight of the two emaciated women, let out a startled scream, and slammed the door shut.

Not recognizing the manservant, Eugenia was terrified that another family had taken up residence. Then she heard the man rousing her household with frantic cries of, "Mr. Phillips! Mr. Phillips! There be two haints at the front doh."

"I know him, Miss Eugenia. That's Elijah," Phebe said. "He's an old Gullah man from

Savannah who used to help me in the kitchen when you held soirées. I fear he believes we are ghosts."

"Let us hope that his cries summon someone less superstitious to let us in. I'm exhausted and cannot for the life of me remember the last time I was able to walk through a closed door."

Moments later, the door opened again, but this time, Eugenia's daughter, Fannie, stood at the entrance holding a lamp. Fannie placed the lamp on the foyer table and rushed to embrace her mother and Phebe in a tearful reunion as they entered.

"Elijah claimed to have seen your ghost at the door, Mother," Fannie said. She turned and called upstairs, "Elijah! Light the lamps in the hallway so we can see our way up the stairs. Mother and Phebe are home. Tell Father!"

"Elijah was not entirely mistaken, my dear," Eugenia said, feeling uneasy in her home after her extended absence. Glancing into the parlor, nothing looked quite the same. "I have the strangest sense that I *have* returned from the dead. Where is your father?"

"He remains upstairs in his room as always, with the curtains drawn, sequestering himself in continual darkness. He has been in a state of grief since your banishment and wakes in the middle of the night with sweat on his brow, crying out your name. In his impressionable state, I fear Elijah's news of seeing your ghosts at the front door has overwhelmed him."

Eugenia's heart ached, leaving her incapable of articulating the anguish she felt for her husband's mental state.

"When Father wrote to me of your situation, I traveled here and found him emaciated and in despair. My husband and the rest of our family have provided financial support for the past several months, as Father has been unable to work in his present state. He used what little energy he had left to summon his old friend, Reverdy Johnson, to intercede with Lincoln. Unfortunately, it took weeks for you and Phebe to be released. He was beginning to abandon hope, and I feared for his life."

Hearing of her husband's condition, Eugenia rushed up the staircase as quickly as her frail body allowed and burst into their bedroom. There she stood motionless, staring at her unshaven and disheveled husband, sitting on his side of the bed, slouched over in grief.

As she approached, tears welled up in his disbelieving eyes, and the sight of his emaciated figure overwhelmed her. She screamed, then collapsed at his feet.

When Eugenia regained consciousness, she caught the pleasant scent of lavender. Then she noticed that someone had cut off her filthy clothing and had given her a sponge bath before putting her in bed. She was relieved to find herself enveloped in clean linens, with two bearded family physicians standing over her like guardian angels, accompanied by her daughter, Fannie.

"Welcome back, Mrs. Phillips," a rotund Dr. Horn greeted warmly. "Everyone has missed you."

"As I have them, my dear Doctor." She then bolted upright in a panic. "Where are William and Emma?"

Dr. Brown, a tall, thin man, smiled warmly. "Fannie sent them to be with the rest of your family in LaGrange."

"Thank goodness. They will be safe there, so near Atlanta. What about Philip and Phebe?"

"Phebe is doing well," Dr. Horn assured her, "and your husband is much relieved now that you are home. I insisted he have a draught of whisky to calm his nerves."

Dr. Brown said, "Phebe is young and has a strong constitution. She has baked a fresh loaf of bread with butter, strawberry jam, and a warm glass of milk. I told her I would let her know when you could partake."

Eugenia felt a smile come to her face for the first time since her exile. "Phebe is a treasure. She willingly gave up her freedom to accompany me to that hellish island."

Dr. Brown offered a nod, gently patting Eugenia's hand. "Phebe is a blessing. I'll inform her that you're ready to see her. However, I'll caution her to be mindful of how much she initially encourages you to eat despite her eagerness to help you regain weight. I'll provide her with a list of foods and beverages to aid in your recovery, along with cod liver oil and tonics to support your constitution. Additionally, given your weakened state, you may need assistance with stairs to prevent any mishaps. Rest is paramount now. And you need not worry about Philip's melancholy. He is in much better spirits now that you are home. The color is already returning to his cheeks."

"Thank you, Doctor," Eugenia said, finding solace in his reassuring words.

The two physicians took their leave to step into the hallway, where they conferred with her family. She could judge by their hushed tones and her husband's demeanor that they were being informed of her condition.

After the hallway conference, Fannie entered the bedroom and said, "I've picked out a pattern and material to sew a new dress for you, Mother." With that, she laid a piece of material on the bedside table and then settled on the edge of the bed beside her.

Eugenia clasped her daughter's hand. "So, you noticed that my filthy dress shunned the gauntness of my body?"

Fannie gently kissed her mother on the forehead. "That old dress has served its time, Mother. Your new dress will adore your slender form. Notice that I chose your favorite shade of green to complement your amber collier." She turned to the dresser to pick up a piece of the cotton dress material and the collier with its carved amber pendant.

Receiving the fabric from her daughter, Eugenia ran her fingers along the silky softness of the satin, but her gaze remained fixed on her cherished amber necklace. "Please take the material, Fannie. I want to hold my collier."

Fannie took the dress material and offered her the necklace. She observed her mother's gentle caress of the golden amber, savoring its preternatural warmth. The gesture reminded her of Phebe's reverent handling of her novena beads during daily prayers.

"There's something mystical about amber, don't you think?" Eugenia asked. "It has a certain *je ne sais quoi*, particularly when it captures an ant, like my little friend in this pendant." Her eyes remained locked on the tiny creature. "Alas, my little soulmate," she whispered. "Your sole transgression was navigating life's shifting fortunes. You were in the wrong place at the wrong time when the golden resin imprisoned you for eternity."

Eugenia returned the treasured piece to Fannie, wondering what marvelous events her trapped six-legged friend had witnessed over the millennia.

Shortly after Eugenia's and Phebe's return to New Orleans, news of their release spread like wildfire. When Eugenia's physicians allowed her to receive visitors, their house was besieged by well-wishers: Rabbi Gutheim, Phebe's priest, their friends, curious neighbors, numerous strangers whom she suspected were Butler's spies, and admirers of Madame Larue, who was still suffering on Ship Island. They all wanted to know more about the conditions in the dreaded place.

There were so many visitors that her husband had to station someone at the front door to welcome everyone without allowing a crowd to rush upstairs to her bedroom all at once. She asked Fannie to keep a register of callers to preserve the fond sentiments everyone shared and the many heartfelt prayers for her speedy recovery.

That register meant even more to her since it was stationed on the secretary she had purchased from her dear friend, Mrs. Jefferson Davis. After leaving Washington, she insisted that her husband ship it to the various stopping points along their journey to New Orleans. It was the only piece of furniture she refused to abandon, and seeing how much comfort the small writing desk brought her, he complied.

Some of her well-wishers had heard that she was dead; others, that she was driven mad on the dreaded island; still others came to satisfy their curiosity regarding Beast Butler's scurrilous announcement that, well into her forties and being forcibly separated from her husband, she had seduced one of her guards for special treatment and was with child.

A few days into her convalescence, she received her friends Rachel and Sarah with Sarah's newborn son, Noah. The three friends sat in the parlor, Rachel and Sarah in high-backed chairs, while Eugenia sat on the sofa holding Sarah's baby.

"Thank you, Phebe," Sarah said, holding her cup up for more tea.

"Noah is such a beautiful baby boy. He has his father's blue eyes," Eugenia cooed, holding him in her lap. "Sarah, I thought that old voodoo woman told you your baby would be a girl."

Rachel's eyes darted toward her sister, then back to Eugenia. "So much for witchcraft and sorcery."

"Phebe," Eugenia said, "would you fetch me the brooch I had made for Rachel?"

"Yes, ma'am," Phebe said, leaving the parlor.

"Brooch?" Rachel echoed, her eyes widening with curiosity.

"You'll see," Eugenia returned with a warm smile. "It's a surprise."

"Now you have me on pins and needles!" Rachel exclaimed, a delighted grin spreading across her face.

"We so missed you, Eugenia," Sarah said. "Rachel and I spoke of you almost daily. We visited your house several times to speak with Fannie, but she had not heard from you, and Mr. P. was always indisposed."

"And I thought of you as well," Eugenia said. "Thinking of the two of you and my family gave me hope on that desolate island."

"Here it is, Miss Eugenia," Phebe said, returning to the parlor to hand Eugenia a gold brooch.

Eugenia passed it to Rachel. "I had this made from a lock of Levi's hair. The brooch itself is from England."

"It's beautiful!" Rachel exclaimed, cradling the gold mourning brooch in her hand. "Where on earth did you get a lock of Levi's hair?"

"Do you remember the day he asked you to trim his hair before he left for Shiloh?"

Rachel's face lit up. "Yes. It was getting long. He always hated going to a barber."

"Well, as you recall, hair was flying everywhere."

"It certainly was," Sarah added with a smile. "I found several pieces of his locks in the folds of my dress after we all cleaned up."

"As did I," Eugenia said. "When I returned home, I thought of throwing it away, but had a sudden twinge and saved it. Then, shortly after, before my encounter with the Beast, I decided to have it encased in a brooch for you."

"I'm so glad you did," Rachel said, her voice soft with emotion.

"Here," Eugenia said, taking the brooch from Rachel and carefully pinning it on her mourning dress.

"It's lovely," Rachel whispered, tears welling in her eyes.

"I'm so pleased it makes you happy," Eugenia said, leaning in to kiss her on the cheek. "I wanted to give it to you earlier, but my little sojourn to Ship Island interfered."

"I will always treasure it," Rachel said, gazing at the brooch.

"Do we know about Noah's father, Sarah?" Eugenia asked cautiously.

"Oh, yes!" Sarah exclaimed, her face radiating joy. "The Union released Jacob under the Dix-Hill Cartel prisoner exchange agreement. He's still in a federal hospital. I don't know exactly where, but the paperwork for his exchange has already been signed."

"Sarah! That is wonderful news!" Eugenia said, reaching up to hold Sarah's hand. "I know you can't wait to feel his arms around you again."

"Oh, yes!" Sarah cried, her eyes sparkling with joy. "Can you imagine Jacob's happiness when he cuddles Noah and kisses his chubby little cheeks?"

Eugenia's eyes filled with tears, already envisioning their reunion.

"After so long and all the worry, I'll finally see him again. Lately, I've been imagining him everywhere. I see him in the faces of strangers on the street, reflections in shop windows, shadows on the bedroom wall at night. It's like every glimpse taunted me with a resemblance."

Eugenia wiped away her tears, but her gaze drifted to Rachel, who sat unmoved, her expression unreadable as her sister shared the news that had lifted such a burden from her heart.

Just then, Phebe entered the room, breaking the emotional moment. "Would you ladies like me to bring a plate of madeleines fresh from the oven?"

"Thank you, Phebe," Rachel said. "Let me go to the kitchen with you.

"Much obliged, ma'am, but I can manage by myself."

"I must insist, Phebe," Rachel said, following her out of the parlor.

Rachel sat at the kitchen table while Phebe set a water kettle on the wood cookstove.

"Sarah only knows part of the truth about her husband," Rachel confided.

"Ma'am?" Phebe asked, taking a seat at the table.

"She received a dispatch concerning his confinement in the hospital, but it was the first of two." Rachel pulled a letter from her handbag and passed it across the table.

Phebe read the letter, then handed it back. "So, he's here in town now, is he?"

"Yes. A Union officer informed me that he's at the St. Louis Hotel, which Butler converted into a hospital."

"Will you be able to visit him?"

"I will do everything within my power if he is still there. I need to know his condition before breaking the news to Sarah. There must be a reason they've kept him in the hospital for so long."

"I understand," Phebe said, her concerned look reflecting her compassion. "I will say a novena for his speedy recovery."

"May I rely on you to keep this information in confidence?" Rachel asked, gently taking her hand.

"Of course, my dear," Phebe said. "And as the Good Lord would have it, Miss Fannie asked me to speak with you in confidence about another matter."

"Oh?"

"Yes. She has a mission for you if you will agree to it."

"I will do anything within my power to fulfill her wishes."

The tea kettle hissed on the stove.

"Teatime!" Phebe announced cheerfully, jumping up to attend to the insistent kettle.

Bad spirits attend you wherever you go,

For you murdered poor Mumford a long time ago;

But the widow yet lives, and her brave orphan boy

United will mix all your gold with alloy.

Thou art weighed in the balance with Bill No. 2,

Long used to foul deeds, he is nothing to you.

E 'en now the handwriting appears on the wall,

Reverdy surely peeped in at that ball!

14

Eugenia's Diary

Fannie, now accustomed to the nightly ritual of bestowing goodnight kisses and tucking her parents into bed, extinguished their kerosene lamps before tenderly closing the bedroom door.

Standing in the hallway, she reflected on the role reversal in her life: the little girl who had once been kissed and tucked into bed was now the nurturing presence, gently kissing and tucking in her parents as they had once done for her.

She recalled the line, "The Child is Father of the Man," from William Wordsworth's "My Heart Leaps Up" that she had once dismissed as the meaningless drivel of a romantic poet.

Wordsworth's words now held new meaning for her. She had come to realize how her childhood experiences had shaped her. In this sense, that little girl in the past was the nurturing mother of the woman she had become in the present, performing the nightly ritual of kissing and tucking in her parents.

She turned off the gas sconces along the hallway on her way to bed but paused at the last one outside her bedroom door. Although she was already in her nightgown and it was getting late, she decided against carrying her unsettled mind to bed, knowing that she would never fall asleep, regardless of how many sheep she counted.

Retracing her steps past her parents' bedroom, she went downstairs to the parlor. The soft glow of streetlamps outside, filtering through the lace curtains, provided enough light to illuminate the brass reading lamp.

Settling into the curved arm of the velvet sofa facing the fireplace, she contemplated the horrors of her mother's banishment to Ship Island. She remembered that the first thing her father did after the incident was to pen a letter, asking her to help relocate her younger siblings to Georgia.

She responded by immediately coming to New Orleans, escorting her siblings to safety, and then returning to help her father. She found him alone and despondent, despairing of any hope of freeing her mother since all his political connections were back in Washington, and he had no influence in New Orleans.

Later, he was heartened to find that President Lincoln had appointed Reverdy Johnson, a former senator from Maryland, to investigate firsthand the outcry of foreign embassies in New Orleans when he violated their sovereignty and confiscated Confederate gold held in their safekeeping. Fortunately, Johnson had been her father's friend when he lived in Washington.

Her father had told her how, after settling in New Orleans, he had sought Johnson's help. Johnson had heard him out and promised to report the incident to the President. Unfortunately, weeks passed before the President countermanded Butler's sentence, and by then, her father had already fallen into despair.

For his acts of kindness in reversing dozens of Butler's orders, including the infamous Woman Order, the ladies of the town immortalized Johnson in a popular parlor game of acrostics using the first letters of Benjamin Franklin Butler's name as the initial letters of each line.

Fannie looked above the fireplace mantel to see her favorite acrostic lambasting the Beast in a framed sampler. She never seemed to tire of reading it:

> **B**ad spirits attend you wherever you go,
> **F**or you murdered poor Mumford a long time ago.
> **B**ut the widow yet lives, and her brave orphan boy
> **U**nited will mix all your gold with alloy.
> **T**hou art weighed in the balance with Bill No. 2,
> **L**ong used to foul deeds, he is nothing to you.
> **E**'en now the handwriting appears on the wall,
> **R**everdy surely peeped in at that ball!

Fannie reflected that the unique charm of this sampler lay in its origin as a gift from Sarah's sewing circle. It portrayed Butler as a figure more sinister than even one of New Orleans' notorious tough guys, nicknamed Red Bill No. 2. Departing from their customary sewing of Confederate flags to be secreted to school classrooms, the circle had created this acrostic to celebrate Eugenia's homecoming.

Fannie considered Butler a coward for not owning up to the enormity of what he had done to her mother. Instead, he spread false rumors claiming she was with child and piously announced that, out of an act of Christian charity, he did not wish to inflict suffering upon an unborn innocent.

She realized that his hypocritical invocation of faith to cover his misdeeds should have come as no surprise. He had already labeled her mother an "uncommonly vulgar woman," implying she would naturally seek favors by wantonly inviting guards into her squalid prison to take pleasure in her company.

In a sudden revelation, Fannie understood that Butler had explicitly targeted her mother for harsh punishment and labeled her a harlot due to her Jewish heritage, even though many other women had shown disrespect for DeKay's funeral procession with their Beauregard cockades, haughty looks, and concealed smiles. Yet it was her mother whom Butler branded a harlot and made into a public example.

Setting these thoughts aside, Fannie was grateful that Phebe had cleverly secured her mother's diary. Now, she was ready to read it after having avoided it earlier out of fear of what she might learn. Rising from the sofa, she approached her mother's cherished secretary and opened a side drawer.

Holding the diary tenderly, she leafed through the pages that recounted the events of the early Union occupation. One of Butler's maneuvers during the early days of his occupation caught her attention.

According to Eugenia's telling, Butler devised a scheme as ruthless as it was ingenious. First, using funds drawn from the army chest, he quietly purchased the nearly worthless Confederate currency that still lingered in the city. Then, through a compliant newspaper, he planted the fabrication that England stood ready to recognize the Confederacy and that Congress itself was weary of the struggle and near to acknowledging Southern independence. Hope took fire among the city's secessionists. Believing their paper money on the verge of revival, they hastened to exchange it for gold to avoid any further fluctuations in the value of the currency and have something more negotiable in hand for the future. At that moment Butler released his hoarded notes back into circulation, reaping a fortune in hard coin with which he repaid his so-called "loan" to the war fund.

Yet the blow did not end there. The general permitted Northern speculators to advertise counterfeit Confederate bills in his newspapers at the rate of five Union dollars for ten thousand. Soon, the city swarmed with false notes, and the same currency Butler had just sold for gold collapsed again into worthlessness. Families who had trusted in its value were left destitute, forced to beg sustenance from the very hand that had robbed them.

Reaching the part of the journal that described her mother's inhumane treatment on the first day of her imprisonment, her eyes welled up with tears, making it difficult for her to continue reading, but she persevered.

Fannie was horrified when she read that guards had locked Phebe and her mother inside an unfurnished wooden shipping crate that barely allowed enough room to sleep on the floor. The absence of a single shade tree exacerbated the island's sweltering climate, and swarms of mosquitoes infested their tent since it had no netting.

Then, there was the matter of food and water, which had been initially denied. Reading on, she found that when a kind physician attempted to send them sustenance, the guards arrested him, even though he was a Union officer.

Unable to turn another page, Fannie wiped away her tears and closed the diary. She was glad that she had entered a pact with Phebe to inform her mother that it had gone missing while assuring her that they would continue to search for it. For now, they both agreed that recalling the horrors of her imprisonment could lead Eugenia to sink deeper into melancholy.

Concealing the diary from her mother was not the only way the family sought to protect her. During her recovery under Phebe's careful watch, the family kept her mother isolated from the outside world. They did, however, share the occasional good news. For one, they told her that the Confederacy had prevailed at the Second Battle of Manassas just weeks before her release from Ship Island. Upon hearing of the victory, she was pleased and said her mentor, Rosie Greenhow, would be proud of her contribution to the campaign.

What the family did not share was that Confederate efforts to retake Baton Rouge had failed while she was away, and that it was shelled, destroying many buildings. Nor did they relate news of the bloody Confederate stalemate at Sharpsburg, Maryland, that had just reached the city through the grapevine telegraph. It would be weeks before wounded New Orleans natives made the thousand-mile journey home, so keeping the devastating news from her mother for a while would not be difficult.

The family also discussed their plans to leave New Orleans. Everyone agreed that Atlanta was far enough inland to be safe from the Yankees since Confederate strongholds in the East defended it. Confederate troops in the West also guarded the railroad from Chattanooga to Atlanta to prevent the Union from using it to advance their forces.

Eugenia and Philip had settled on LaGrange, just south of Atlanta, as their favored destination, since they already had family there. The plan was to take a steamer to Mobile for the first leg of their journey. Overland travel would be less harrowing from there, as it would be through Confederate territory.

That much was settled. But the matter of her mother's mysterious trunk remained, and she had requested that it be shipped separately, "by some secure means." She remembered seeing her mother visit it now and then in the attic before her exile: always alone, always quiet. No one was permitted to glimpse at what lay inside. More than once, she had watched her mother abruptly close the lid at the sound of footsteps, snapping the iron padlock into place before anyone could draw near.

Her father, too, had seemed wary of the trunk's contents, though he never challenged her about it. Whatever secrets it held, he chose to honor them, allowing it to remain her private domain.

Now, with Phebe having spoken to Rachel on her mother's behalf just days earlier, she felt assured the trunk would soon find its way to her mother's waiting hands in LaGrange.

15

RACHEL'S MISSION

Rachel gathered her skirt and stepped down from the St. Charles Avenue streetcar. Aware of her friend Eugenia's reputation for espionage in Washington and for boldly confronting General Butler in New Orleans, she remained watchful, making several careful transfers before finally arriving at her destination.

Standing at the St. Peter Street intersection, she paused to take in the surroundings, marveling at the transformation. It was as though she had stepped into an entirely different city, a place that bore little resemblance to her hometown.

Dozens of sanitation workers moved along the uneven stone block pavers in the damp early morning fog, sweeping up garbage and shoveling it onto mule-drawn carts. Several fire pumpers trailed behind, each with two men powering the pumps to flush away horse and mule manure into the gutters that drained into the canals. Other workers emptied refuse containers sitting in front of houses onto other carts.

She knew the Beast had forced Mayor Monroe to keep Frenchtown clean since his arrival, yet she had remained unaware of the full scope of his sanitation efforts until now.

As she strolled down the street, she saw workers with black paint covering the gold-lettered initials of the shop owners who had fled the Union occupation and marked their once-thriving businesses closed. The rows of columns resembled mourners donning black armbands, marching in an endless funeral procession.

Much like pallbearers in their solemn duty, workers on ladders diligently took down the painted signs depicting shoes and other merchandise, poignant reminders of items once sold in the shops below. The workers then carefully wrapped the signs and transported them on mule carts to storage, preserving the landlords' hope that they would be resurrected with the influx of Northern merchants.

After walking four blocks, Rachel reached Rampart Street, where she stopped to catch her breath. Leaning against a lamppost, she retrieved a scrap of paper from her bag to remind herself of the address Phebe had given her. Spotting a Union soldier standing in front of her destination, she hesitated.

Out of nowhere, two young boys delivering newspapers turned the corner and stopped short of the soldier to engage in a loud, staged exchange.

"Jack, have you heard the news?"

"No, Tom, what is it?"

Tom waved a newspaper at the soldier. "Read all about it! Got the yellow fever prime right here in Frenchtown; two Yanks dead already."

"Run along, boys, or I'll box the ears off the both of you," the soldier barked, his jaw clenched in irritation at their antics. As they scurried away, he exhaled, the tension easing from his face. He touched the brim of his hat and smiled at Rachel. "Mornin', ma'am."

"Mornin', sir," she said, managing a curtsy while hurrying past him. The news of the two dead Yankees surprised her since she had not heard of any deaths from yellow fever this year.

When the soldier departed, she turned the doorknob on the boarding house's front door and entered an unadorned foyer. Floral-printed wallpaper covered the walls, its once vibrant hues muted and yellowed by time. Beyond this dreary entrance, a lengthy hallway unfolded, its perimeter marked by doors, each labeled with tarnished brass numbers ranging from one to four. Lifting her eyes, she discovered an oak staircase.

As she ascended the stairs, her footsteps silenced by the frayed carpet runner, she spotted the number six on a door, her ultimate destination. She pondered whether the woman she had come to meet would receive her.

According to Phebe, the lady's name was Madame Loreta Velazquez. She was a Cuban native who had once lived in New Orleans, where she had married a soldier and given birth to two children. However, tragedy struck after she moved, and she lost her husband to the ravages of war and both her children to disease. Bereft of her family, Fannie said that Madame Velazquez had adopted the clandestine life of a spy, assuming multiple identities and disguises, even masquerading as a man to fight for the Confederacy.

Controlling her trembling hand, Rachel removed her gloves and knocked on the door bearing the number six.

"Who's calling?" came a muffled voice through the door.

"My name is Rachel, ma'am. A friend of Mrs. Eugenia Phillips."

The door opened a crack, revealing the face of a diminutive young woman with dark hair, striking brown eyes, and smooth olive skin.

Rachel passed Eugenia's *carte de visite* to the woman, who glanced at it and then at her widow's attire, returning a faint, enigmatic smile. "Please come in."

Rachel sat uneasily on a tattered horse-hair-upholstered armchair facing a low sofa table, while Loreta, attired in a gentleman's dressing gown, poured hot tea into an unadorned porcelain cup, offering neither cream nor sugar.

Rachel observed that the cramped room was devoid of ornamentation. The only embellishments were the peeling floral-print French wallpaper, a tarnished silvered mirror on the wall, and a solitary kerosene lamp that flickered dimly when she entered. It seemed like a fitting refuge for a fugitive who might need to vanish suddenly in the dead of night.

Rachel took a sip of the proffered tea, steadying her cup with both hands to conceal her trembling.

"Did you have any difficulty finding me?" Loreta asked pleasantly.

"No, ma'am. Eugenia's servant, Phebe, provided good directions."

"Good. I tried to find a place away from the hubbub of French Town. Congo Square, right across the street, offers little to attract attention from the soldiers since it is a haven for freed slaves to practice their native religions. Besides, few Union soldiers are fluent in the French or Spanish tongue. Fortunately, they're more interested in congregating in the coffee houses and bordellos when off duty."

"They're men, after all," Rachel said, "separated from their wives and family."

"Yes, they are…incredibly lonely. Speaking of which, we both have lost our husbands to the Cause."

Loreta's unexpected revelation caught Rachel off guard.

"Your husband and I both fought at the battle of Shiloh," Loreta explained.

Rachel gasped, confused by the incongruity of a woman in battle, let alone one who might have fought alongside her husband. "You knew my Levi?"

"I met him briefly around our campfire. He spoke of you."

Rachel gasped. "What did he say?"

"That he loved you and couldn't wait until he could see you again. He showed me a gold watch engraved with both of your names, which he had kept with him since he left New Orleans. Only after I arrived here did I learn more about you from Eugenia."

Rachel began quietly sobbing, holding her face in her hands.

Loreta leaned over to place her hand on Rachel's shoulder. "I'm sorry, my dear. I wish I could tell you more. That was the only time I spoke with him."

"I understand," Rachel said, struggling to contain her grief. She found Loreta's attempt to comfort her unsettling for some inexplicable reason, perhaps because it struck her as strangely masculine.

"It's good that you have a sister as a companion," Loreta said, responding to Rachel's almost imperceptible recoil from her touch. "I never had anyone close to me as an adult... except for my husband and children."

"Sarah is all I have left since I lost my husband," Rachel said. "She has her own husband to worry about now that she has learned he is coming home wounded."

"I, of all people, can understand your grief, my dear. After I lost my children and learned of my husband's death, there were no tears left to shed. Later, I received his uniform by special dispatch."

"At least you had that," Rachel said, trying not to recall the horror of learning about her husband's mutilated body at the mortuary.

"I had a great deal more than that uniform," Loreta declared, her face hardening and her voice taking on a mannish air of confidence. "I had my own personal cause. Something that gave meaning to my life at a time when I had abandoned all hope. It struck me like a lightning bolt when I touched that uniform. Suddenly, I became Joan of Arc, my childhood heroine. But my epiphany, unlike my martyr's, came to me without an Archangel and two saints guiding me. Once again, as when I was a child pretending to be her, I practiced walking and gesturing like a man."

Loreta stood and stepped to the looking glass on the wall. As she gazed into it, Rachel, watching from behind, saw their eyes meeting momentarily in their reflections.

"After I lost my family, I decided that my world was too expansive to be confined to a woman's body. I grabbed a pair of sewing shears, hacked off most of my hair, and donned my dead husband's uniform. I had to take it up a bit and bind my breasts, but I managed to fit into it well. Thus began my transformation into a soldier. I became a warrior who wielded the sword of righteousness to avenge the death of my husband. For my noble task, I chose the name of Buford."

"You see, Rachel, I served my time wearing the petticoats, the gloves, the little lace collars. I bore children and buried them. I made soup for a man who never returned from battle. And I wept, like a woman is expected to do."

"But when I cut my hair and took up arms, I ceased to be a thing to be pitied or protected. No one told me to hush or stay in my place. No one warned me that I might faint at the sight of blood. I was a man, and so I was listened to and respected."

Rachel said nothing, only watched, absorbed in Loreta's story.

Loreta gave a faint, sardonic smile. "The strangest thing, Rachel? I did not feel like I had become a man. I felt like I had finally become myself. And it sickened me to know that to be heard, to be feared, to be free, one must wear trousers and bear arms."

She looked back at Rachel, her voice softening. "And once you've tasted true liberty, you cannot return to the silence the world demands of us."

Rachel sat in awe. The woman gazing back through the looking glass at her had undergone a remarkable metamorphosis, transforming entirely from Loreta, a petite female, into Buford, a figure of strength and courage. This change extended beyond physical appearance, encompassing mannerisms that exuded powerful masculinity. A disconcerting sensation accompanied the shiver that ran down Rachel's spine, evoking the unsettling thought of a masculine spirit taking possession of the woman who stood before her.

The figure in the looking glass transformed again, shifting from Buford to Loreta. Without a pause, Loreta turned around and asked, "Are you acquainted with the tale of Clytemnestra?"

"Yes," Rachel said, impressed by Loreta's familiarity with the classics. "My father, a professor in the field, would share bedtime stories drawn from Greek myths and plays. You're referring to Aeschylus' *Oresteia*."

"Then you may recall Clytemnestra's vow after her husband was killed:

> By no female lot,
> Nor birthright of womanhood possessed,
> Doth she this daring feat,
> But with a man's bold heart,
> She hath vowed a manlike vow,
> To meet a husband's death
> With a vengeful manlike hand.

"I always felt that Aeschylus, who wrote over two thousand years ago, understood women like no other man has since," Loreta said.

Loreta returned to her seat, crossing her bare, unshaven legs in a masculine ankle-over-knee manner. "So much for my past. I'm certain you're curious about how I managed to evade Ship Island, unlike our friend Eugenia, the poor dear."

Rachel nodded, still stunned by what she had just witnessed, hoping she did not betray her uneasiness. "There were whispers of your arrest and transport to the Customs House," she said, "but no word as to how you avoided the Beast's usual sentence for anyone who defied him."

Loreta gave a knowing smile. "You see, my dear, your friend's battle tactics are frontal while mine are evasive. I have always maintained that it is better to keep the enemy off guard, outflank him if possible, and live to fight another day."

"Eugenia can be quite direct."

"Not the most effective survival tactic with this particular breed of Yankee general," her hostess said, pausing to enjoy a sip of her tea.

Rachel sat on the edge of her chair, leaning forward in anticipation of the story she was about to hear.

"My encounter with Butler was recent. Ironically, his men had issued me countless passes to cross the lines without suspecting anything. I was able to communicate freely with Confederate agents once I was there and transported my usual contraband of laudanum to ease the pain of the wounded. The Confederate officers were generous with their gold, which helped me finance my endeavors. In Mobile, I was even issued a pass to visit my home country of Cuba, where I trained with Confederate agents headquartered there and learned how to code. Not long after my return to New Orleans, I was accused of sending dispatches to Confederate forces at Camp Moore across Lake Pontchartrain. It was one of my lesser missions, I might add."

Rachel found herself sitting on the edge of her chair again.

"When I approached the bald vulture in his inner sanctum at the St. Charles, he was ensconced upon his throne, surrounded by his minions standing stiffly like so many toy soldiers. His countenance was most threatening. I tried to look him directly in the eye as I came closer, but my efforts were useless. With his crooked eyes, he couldn't lock eyes with anyone else."

Rachel joined in Loreta's laughter, amused by the mention of Butler's unevenly positioned eyes, features that appeared as if a child had whimsically molded his visage from a lump of damp clay.

"I failed to mention," Loreta continued, "that I had taken precautions against precisely such an encounter by cultivating friendships with various Union officers, ready to seek their aid when needed. The task proved to be quite effortless. They were often lonely and delighted to have a companion for dinner and an evening at the theatre, so long as the conversation avoided politics and offered them the solace of feminine companionship."

"I can understand how they would be attracted to a show of kindness after so many of them were spat upon after they arrived," Rachel said, surprising herself with the note of compassion in her remark.

"Many of the city's theatres have gone dark since locals have shunned mixing with the Yankee audience, unwilling to endure the mandated patriotic songs during intermission."

Rachel nodded. "Sadly, they have."

"But I must give the Yankees credit for being creative. Last evening, I attended a farce—*Servants by Legacy*, if memory serves—on the *U.S.S. Pensacola*. The Federals had ingeniously transformed the warship into a showboat to entertain their officers and lady friends. It was amusing to witness the entire female cast played by the ship's crew."

Rachel joined Loreta in laughter, finding irony in her hostess's enjoyment of the cross-dressed crew, given her experience of crossing genders as Buford.

"I've often wondered what my dashing young officer would have thought if he had discovered that I was one of the 'men' who had fired upon his comrades at one battle or another."

Rachel marveled at how much Eugenia differed from this person, who seemed to have a unique talent for living in the shadows as a woman and fighting in the daylight as a man.

"I found myself engrossed in captivating conversations with several of Farragut's officers," Loreta continued. "I learned that, after the military mayor of Vicksburg rebuffed the Union's initial demand that he surrender the city, it seems that Farragut abandoned the idea of launching an assault on its formidable defenses perched atop towering bluffs." She indulged in a sardonic smile. "He came back to New Orleans vexed by the challenges posed by navigating the diminishing waters of the Mississippi with his deep-draft ships, grumbling that he was not equipped with a 'brown water navy.'"

"Some officers on the *Pensacola* shared rumors that Secretary of the Navy, Welles, and President Lincoln were greatly displeased with the failure and urged Farragut to reconsider his strategy. Subsequent orders from top brass directed Porter to rendezvous with Farragut in New Orleans, abandoning his original plan to use Ship Island for an attack on Mobile. Despite combining their forces for a second attempt on Vicksburg, Porter and Farragut are back in New Orleans, acknowledging that the heavily fortified city cannot be subdued solely through a river assault."

"But let's set aside the naiveté of the men I escorted," she said with a sly smile. "Now, back to my version of 'Beauty and the Beast.' As soon as I was brought into his presence, he pointed an accusatory finger at me and brandished a letter he had received from one of his officers. Allegedly, it had been confiscated from a Confederate apprehended at the lines north of Lake Pontchartrain. He then presented a pitiful, elderly Negro man who asserted that I was the woman who handed the incriminating note to the same Confederate on the south side of the lake before he rowed across."

"Oh my!" Rachel gasped. "What did you say?"

"I denied that I had written the letter and told him that I was being accused falsely. Then I stared at the Negro man until he lowered his eyes and shuffled his feet. 'Sorry, ma'am,' he whined. 'I ain't so shore now it wuz you I seen.'"

"Butler abruptly dismissed the old man and bellowed at me, 'What do you say to these charges?'"

"I deny everything," I said. "Under the law, you must present evidence. I did not write this letter. You can see that it bears the name of someone else. The old Negro man you produced has cloudy eyes and is an unreliable witness, as you have just seen."

Rachel admired Eugenia and looked up to her as a tower of strength, but this woman was of another order.

"The theatrical tyrant was undaunted," Loretta said. "He bellowed, 'I'm confining you to the Customs House with the Confederate prisoners until I have additional evidence of your guilt.' I said nothing, but my silence appeared to anger him even more. 'Take this woman out of my sight,' he roared, whereupon I was promptly removed, but not before noting a placard on the wall behind his desk which read something along the lines of, 'She adders better than He adders.'"

Rachel was amused at Loreta's reference to she-adders, an ophidian term Eugenia had told her the Beast used to brand women who dared defy him.

"Fortunately, since I had befriended his officers, my jailer was kind enough to slip a word to one of them, asking him to visit me. When he arrived, I convinced the man to pass a note to the British consulate requesting an ambassador to enter my room and find proof of my British citizenship in my steamer trunk. Inside, I had hidden a pass I had purchased from a British woman stranded in the city and in dire need of specie. Since foreign nationals were exempt, I had originally procured the pass to avoid taking Butler's Oath of Allegiance. Now, however, I needed it for an entirely different purpose."

"Did the ambassador find your pass?"

"Yes, he did. With my pass in hand, he showed up quickly, and I was free to leave the Customs House as a British citizen."

Rachel admired the cleverness and courage of this mysterious manwoman. "So, will Butler leave you alone now?"

Loreta laughed. "*Al contrario.* He won't rest until he finds someone willing to be bribed into bearing false witness. I now have no choice but to leave the city, the same as Eugenia must do. This man is nothing if not vindictive, and he's not finished with either of us."

"My neighbors were gossiping yesterday that Butler had headed north of town with many of his troops."

"My sources confirmed that he intercepted General Ruggles' forces at Manchac Pass, just north of Lake Pontchartrain. Ruggles certainly wasn't expecting Butler to meet him at the bridge."

"At least we know our troops haven't forsaken us."

Loreta remained silent.

"When do you plan to leave New Orleans?" Rachel asked.

"I have a few loose ends to tidy up before I can leave. And may I ask, what are Eugenia's plans?"

"Eugenia took the oath to the Union just a few days ago as a condition of her release from Ship Island."

"Poor dear. I'm sure she'd rather walk on hot coals."

Rachel's face softened, a somber expression settling into her features. "Mr. Phillips expects the family will be issued passes to Mobile soon. They plan to spend Rosh Hashanah with their family in LaGrange."

"And when is Rosh Hashanah this year?"

"The Jewish New Year falls next Wednesday, the 24th."

Loreta nodded. "I must say, I admire Eugenia's servant, Phebe. Not many would follow their mistress through such trials. My manservant deserted me on the battlefield. Can't say I blame him. He was my slave and saw his chance for freedom." She added wryly, "A popular notion these days."

"Phebe goes wherever Eugenia goes," Rachel said. "Even to Ship Island."

"Ship Island," Loreta echoed, her eyes distant. "It's a low sandbank about nine miles long and one mile wide, sixty miles from New Orleans and fifty from Mobile. A military station with a brick fort, machine shop, and sundry small buildings is at the western end. The eastern end is scraggly with pines, and in between, a sandbar rises just above the water. There is no shade, just relentless sun baking the white sand. Then there are the mosquitoes. That's where they must have kept Eugenia and Phebe."

"You describe it as if you've been there," Rachel remarked, imagining the desolation from Loreta's vivid description.

Loreta smiled as though holding back a secret. "I learned it from the Union officers who were stationed there while they planned their attack on our city. I make it a point to understand the terrain wherever I might be. It's been useful for planning my escapes."

Rachel sighed. "If only Eugenia had left New Orleans before her ordeal."

"How is she faring now?" Loreta asked. "I wanted to visit and compare notes on our adventures, but I feared Butler would hang us both as spies. The man has eyes everywhere, and no corner of this city is safe from his reach."

Rachel instinctively recoiled at the mention of spies, unsettled by the thought of being drawn into that dangerous world, but quickly regained her composure. "She's better now. Phebe told me she nearly died from heat exhaustion. She fainted so often that she came home bruised and in pain from head to toe."

"I have a remedy for that."

"Oh?"

"Yes, and I promise it works. I volunteer at the hospital in the old St. Louis Hotel.

Laudanum flows liberally there. I've mixed it with sweet red wine. It's potent. A few sips throughout the day, especially before bed, should help her immensely. Before you leave, remind me to give you a bottle for her."

"Eugenia will be grateful," Rachel said, touched by Loreta's unexpected kindness. "Things will be better once she's back with her family in LaGrange."

"That's near Atlanta, isn't it?"

"Yes. Philip believes it's safe."

Loreta's face softened, and her demeanor shifted. "I once considered this city my home," she said wistfully. "It, too, felt safe. President Davis and Judah Benjamin swore New Orleans was untouchable and safer than Timbuktu when the war began. They said any Yankee attack would come from upriver, and Port Hudson and Vicksburg would hold firm."

"They were wrong," Rachel said quietly. "As Secretary of War, Benjamin should have known better and left more troops to defend us."

Loreta fell silent, and her expression grew nostalgic. "Do you know what I miss most about the streets of New Orleans?"

Rachel shook her head.

"The organ grinders," Loreta said softly. "I remember walking along Carondelet Street as a child, watching the little barefoot Negro boy struggling to turn the organ's crank. I can still hear that tune and the clink of coins my mother tossed into his tin can. And that wide, ivory-white grin on his ebony-black face."

Rachel's lips moved into a fragile smile, as though remembering something lost. "I'd forgotten what that was like. Let's pray we return to those days again."

Loreta nodded, pulling herself from her reverie. "I've enjoyed this conversation, Rachel. I rarely get to speak so freely with someone I trust."

"I've enjoyed it as well," Rachel said sincerely.

"Now," Loreta began, her tone shifting, "why did Eugenia send you to me?"

Rachel hesitated. "Actually, it was her daughter, Fannie, who wanted me to ask for your help to ship one of Eugenia's trunks ahead secretly."

Loreta offered nothing but a sly, inscrutable smile.

"Fannie said that Eugenia had considered bribing a soldier to smuggle it on board a steamer, but she thought it was too risky."

"With good reason," Loreta said. "After Ship Island, I don't blame her for not risking further consequences." Her expression hardened, focused on the task. "I might be able to help. Listen carefully."

Rachel nodded.

"Are you familiar with Butler's order demanding that residents remove water closets from their courtyards?"

"Yes. It's almost impossible to find someone to do it now that the Union confiscated most of the horses and carts for their sanitation efforts."

"Tell Eugenia to order two new water closets, then unpack the trunk and transfer its contents into them. On a day I specify, a man with a mule cart will come to haul them away. He'll identify himself by handing her a paid receipt. No further compensation is needed."

"But doesn't her house have a cesspool?"

"In her neighborhood, most do," Loreta said with a sly smile, "but Butler's men won't be keeping track of cesspools."

"And what happens after they're hauled away?"

"When she reaches Mobile, my contacts will restore her belongings."

"Should I give her any names?"

"There's an old Cuban saying," Loreta replied. "*'En boca cerrada, no entran moscas'* — 'In a closed mouth, no flies enter.'"

Rachel was pleased she had accomplished her mission. But something held her back from leaving. A vague feeling, a need for understanding. "There's one more thing," she said, hesitating. "Can you tell me what it was like at Shiloh?"

Loreta's expression turned serious. "Are you certain you want me to tell you? It won't be pleasant."

"Yes," Rachel replied, bracing herself. She needed to know what her husband had faced for his country and her.

Loreta spoke in a hushed tone, her words casting a spell like a shaman conjuring visions from another world. Rachel leaned in, her eyes wide and unblinking.

"After a day of fierce battle, I strained to discern whether the enemy had withdrawn. A haunting stillness had settled over the wooded battlefield; the air was choked with smoke, and every breath was difficult. My eyes burned so badly I could scarcely see my hand before me. All around me lay a grim tableau: bodies twisted in grotesque poses, some propped upright against tree trunks, their mouths agape in bloodied silence, frozen mid-gasp. Death had made its art here."

"I told myself I had a duty to the fallen, if to no one else. Someone had to see them buried. I began turning over bodies, rifling through haversacks and the occasional knapsack, searching for anything I could use to dig graves. At last, my fingers closed around the handle of an entrenching tool."

"Digging that first grave was a miserable business. The soil, mercifully loose and free of stone, still fought me with every thrust. Sweat dripped from my brow, mingling with soot and blood as I heaved the dirt over my shoulder. Then, there was a crack of gunfire from a nearby ravine. A flash of white-hot pain tore through my arm, and the world collapsed into darkness."

"I don't know how long I lay there unconscious. But when I came to, I was suffocating beneath a tangle of dead weight. Warm blood soaked through my uniform and ran across my face. I could taste it: salty, metallic, not my own. I gagged, coughed, spat it out."

"Summoning what little strength remained, I shoved at the bodies atop me, clawing free, wiping blood from my eyes with a trembling sleeve. Then it hit me with the force of a thunderclap: my comrades had mistaken me for dead. They'd dug the grave deeper and tossed more bodies in, entombing me alive."

"I clawed my way out over the corpses, gasping for breath. The scene had changed while I was buried. The gun smoke had lifted, only to be replaced by a heavy fog that clung to everything."

"Out of that whiteness came the sound of moaning. Desperate cries for water. Outstretched hands reached toward empty air. The woods had become a living nightmare. Voices cried out, echoing like discordant notes in a hellish symphony."

"Gripped by dread, I stumbled along, slipping on severed limbs and shattered faces, falling repeatedly. Each time I hit the ground, I landed beside yet another man who'd already crossed the veil."

"Eventually, I reached a tent in a clearing. I didn't care who it belonged to. Rebels or Yankees, it didn't matter anymore. I was bleeding badly, and without help, I knew I'd be the next one lying in the dirt."

"Inside was blood and screams, men in gray and blue side by side, caught between life and death. All was chaos. Doctors from both sides worked shoulder to shoulder, binding wounds, sawing limbs, and cauterizing flesh. The stench of burning meat turned my stomach."

"A Union doctor knelt beside me, tore a blood-soaked strip of cloth from a dead man's uniform, and wrapped it tightly around my arm, telling me the poor boy didn't need it anymore."

"His voice was oddly kind. I opened my mouth to thank him, but my knees buckled. I collapsed before I could utter a word."

"When I woke again, the scent of coffee greeted me. A Yankee soldier knelt beside me, offering a tin cup. 'Here,' he said. 'Found a pack of coffee in a haversack out there. The poor devil never got to taste it.'"

"I took it with trembling hands and drank. The warmth was comforting, though the irony did not escape me: a Union doctor had saved my life; a Union soldier had brought me relief."

"As I finished the cup, the soldier helped me to my feet and told me I'd be on a wagon in the morning, then a train to New Orleans with the rest of the wounded."

"I stepped outside the tent into a world transformed. Mars had abandoned his post, and in his place stood Beelzebub, the Lord of the Flies."

"The heat was suffocating, thick with the stench of death. Flies swarmed in maddening clouds, their droning a chorus of decay. I recoiled as I saw a pack of half-starved dogs, wild-eyed and snarling, tearing at the corpses."

"Please stop!" Rachel cried, tears welling up in her eyes at the horrific memory of her visit to Casanave's funeral home.

"I'm sorry, my dear," Loreta said, leaning forward to comfort her. "I tried to warn you."

"No! Please don't," Rachel exclaimed, abruptly standing. "I must leave at once."

Loreta stood to open the door for her guest to retreat from the apocalyptic scene she had conjured up.

Rachel stepped outside the room, her stomach in knots, her steps unsteady. Pausing in the hallway, she remembered Loreta mentioning her work in a hospital, tending to wounded soldiers. With undried tears on her grief-stricken face, she turned back. "I've been informed that my brother-in-law is a patient at the hospital that was once the St. Louis Hotel."

"That is where I volunteer," Loreta said, still standing in the doorway. "I assist the Sisters of Charity with various tasks as needed."

"Would it be possible for me to visit tomorrow and see if I can find Jacob?"

"What is Jacob's family name?" Loreta asked.

"Mercier."

Loreta noted the painful expression on Rachel's face. "I will be at the hospital by nine in the morning. Every admission is entered in the patient roster with their name, hair and eye color, and height, just as in their original enrollment records."

"Thank you. I will meet you there," Rachel replied softly, adding, "Jacob has auburn hair and blue eyes and stands about five feet eight inches tall."

"If you will stay for a moment, I'll fetch you that bottle of elixir for Eugenia."

Rachel stood at the door until Loreta returned with the bottle she had promised.

With a quiet nod, Rachel took it and turned to leave. A guilty silence settled over her as she descended the stairs, gripping the railing tightly for balance. She was unsure whether truth or discretion would prove more righteous. Sarah was Jacob's wife. She had every right to know about him as soon as possible. Yet she was unable to shake the feeling that keeping the truth about Jacob's injuries from her sister until she knew more about the extent of his injuries and his chances of recovery was the wiser choice, even if she had to live with it on her conscience.

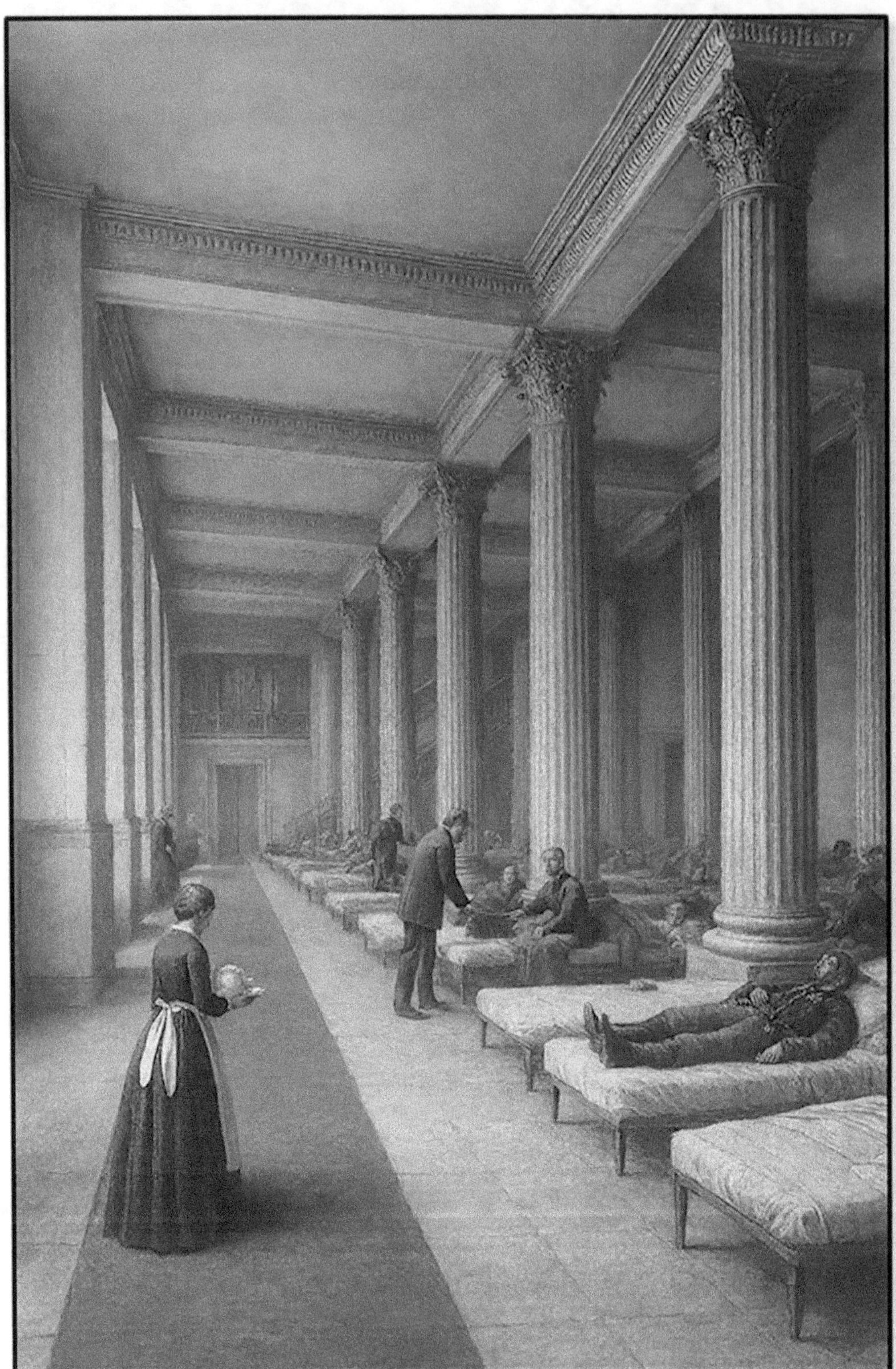

16

An Army of Shadows

With a heavy heart, Rachel stepped off the St. Charles streetcar at the bustling intersection of St. Louis and Chartres Streets, just a stone's throw from the St. Louis Hotel. Her mission was to locate her brother-in-law, whose health was uncertain, and to prepare for the difficult task of delivering potentially bad news to her sister. Each step she took echoed with the weight of unspoken sorrow amidst the splendor of autumn leaves surrounding her.

A prominent landmark in Frenchtown, the St. Louis Hotel stood a proud four stories tall and was topped by an impressive 80-foot dome. Before the occupation, it was the Creole counterpart to the Anglo St. Charles Hotel across Canal Street, rivaling its elegance.

Unlike the St. Charles, which Butler had preserved in its original Anglo elegance to serve as his headquarters, he had ordered the St. Louis closed to the public after the occupation and transformed it into a hospital. Its once-grand halls now echoed with groans and the shuffling of orderlies, filled not with guests in evening attire but with the wounded bodies of soldiers, most of them Union.

Approaching the armed guards at the hospital's entrance, Rachel struggled to stay calm, reminding herself of her mission to find her brother-in-law. The younger guard, tipping his hat, greeted her. "Yes, ma'am. May we be of assistance?"

"Pardon me, sir. My name is Rachel Durand, and I've come to inquire about my brother-in-law." She paused, cautious not to disclose that he was a Confederate. "Nurse Loreta told me that he is a patient here. He was wounded at Shiloh."

"I'm sorry to tell you, ma'am," the guard said gently, "that most of our soldiers from Shiloh have been discharged. Now, we're getting boys back from Antietam."

Undeterred, Rachel pressed on. "Might I have a word with Nurse Loreta, please?"

Apparently admiring her persistence, the guard said, "I'll ask her if she can spare a moment, ma'am. It's quite hectic in there today."

"Thank you," Rachel said, appreciating his politeness while positioning herself at a cautious distance from the second guard, an older man whose smile, bordering on a leer, was unsettling.

After a few tense minutes of silence, the first guard reappeared. "Ma'am, Nurse Loreta told me she's expecting you."

"Thank you, sir," Rachel said, stepping into the massive lobby as he held the door open for her.

"Good morning, Rachel," Loreta greeted, standing at the foot of the lobby's winding staircase.

"Good morning, Loreta," Rachel said, recognizing the woman but challenged by her transformation: a crisp white cotton apron adorned her modest gray dress, and her hair was neatly arranged in a bun.

"After discovering your brother-in-law's name on the roster, I looked for him last evening while tending to patients," Loreta said. "I finally found him."

"Are you certain it is Jacob?" Rachel asked, her face lighting up with anticipation.

"He is the only patient with the surname Mercier, with auburn hair and blue eyes. Besides, I found this by his pillow when I changed his linens," Loreta said, handing Rachel a lace-fringed handkerchief.

Rachel recognized the delicate looping S monogram entwined with a threadbare vine. The linen still carried the faintest trace of rose water, her sister's favorite perfume, softened now by time. Sarah had given it to him to send him off with the scent of home, of love, of memory. Nestling it securely into her bosom, she resolved that, when the time was right, this would serve as a meaningful way to convey to Sarah that she had found Jacob.

"We'll need to navigate through the lobby and down the main hallway to the dome where Dr. Smith is attending to him."

"Dr. Smith?" Rachel asked, surprised to hear his name.

"Yes, Dr. Smith. The men are fortunate to have him here. He came out of retirement to attend to the wounded. I honestly don't know if the man ever sleeps."

Rachel struggled to reconcile the memory of the physician who had delivered her in the front bedroom of her parents' home with the notion that he was still practicing medicine. She also remembered his political involvement, particularly his unsuccessful efforts with the

Sanitation Commission to convince the government to clean up the streets and establish a quarantine to prevent recurring outbreaks of Yellow Fever.

Rachel followed Loreta through the vast lobby, lined with majestic columns and rows of cots occupied by men bearing the scars of battle. She saw portraits of shattered dreams in their sunburned faces and a deep longing for the homes and families they had left behind. Her heart pounded as a tightness grew in her throat; confusion set in, and her vision blurred as her mind faltered, unwilling to fully face the anguish before her.

Struggling to keep pace with Loreta, Rachel followed her down the corridor, carefully stepping over bloodstains on the rug as she navigated through a sea of patients. Some men recognized Loreta as their nurse, while others, delirious and calling for water, reached out, mistaking the two women for their sisters, wives, or mothers.

As she moved along, Rachel passed rows of rooms with closed doors, yet the muffled sounds of anguished cries and moans seeped through, a chilling reminder of the amputations being performed within. The air was thick with the scent of seared flesh from cauterized wounds mixed with the lingering sweetness of ether, clashing against the sharp, acrid smell of carbolic acid used to clean the bone saws. She braced herself, steeling her mind and body against the overwhelming assault on her senses.

In the sea of suffering, she witnessed the haunting image of hands clutching worn Bibles and lips whispering frantic prayers, tortured souls desperately clinging to life.

Without their uniforms, it was impossible to distinguish Union from Confederate or between blue and gray. The once-distinguished colors blurred in her mind, merging into an indistinct army of shadows.

Amid this fetid atmosphere, Rachel's curiosity compelled her to ask her guide, "How can you tell the Confederates from the Union soldiers in all this chaos?"

Loreta halted abruptly, turning to face Rachel amid the grim surroundings. "In their condition, my dear, it matters little. None of them will return to the battlefield, even if they are fortunate enough to survive."

Rachel paused, sensing a subtle rebuke in Loreta's tone even though she had expressed no animosity toward the wounded, regardless of their loyalty. "I understand," she said softly, her voice tinged with contrition.

At the end of the hallway, they entered a grand arena beneath a towering dome supported by majestic Ionic columns reminiscent of an ancient Greek temple. Once, this vast space had been the City Exchange, a bustling center of commerce where every imaginable form of property, including slaves, was auctioned beneath an archway framed by two columns.

Suddenly, memories came rushing back. It was here that Sarah and Jacob had surprised her on her birthday. The backdrop had been a slave auction. She could still see the young woman, barefoot and shabbily attired, her wide eyes filled with terror as she climbed onto the auction block.

"Here we have a fine young specimen," the auctioneer proclaimed. "Look at the size of her hips. She'll make good breeding stock."

Jacob shouted, "Eight hundred!" sharing a furtive smile with her. From behind, another voice countered, "Nine hundred." Unshaken, Jacob immediately raised his bid: "A thousand!" The bidding war continued until Jacob confidently declared, "Twelve hundred," sealing the deal with the auctioneer's final gavel.

"Happy birthday, Sis. You're now the proud owner of your very own personal servant," Jacob had said, wrapping her in a warm embrace.

Rachel looked at him fondly, her eyes betraying tears she struggled to suppress. "Thank you, Jacob. Thank you, Sarah. Would you mind holding her here for me? I'll need to buy her some new clothes to replace those rags. I want her to look presentable for Levi when he comes home this evening."

"What will you name her?" Sarah had asked.

"I've always liked the name Rebecca. Yes, that's it. I'll name her Rebecca."

Her thoughts returned to the present as Loreta gestured toward a soldier near the auction block of her memories. He was propped up in bed on a pillow with his eyes closed, wearing a long-sleeved, brown suede shirt.

The sight unsettled her in ways she hadn't anticipated. It was here that she had once been given a slave for her birthday. She had accepted the gift without hesitation, offering polite thanks, as though it were no more remarkable than any other birthday present. At the time, it had seemed only the natural order of things. But what she had once received with unquestioning grace now filled her with quiet shame. She could not say precisely when the change had begun, only that it had, and that it had taken root deep within her, reshaping the way she saw the world.

Loreta approached the man, gently placing her hand on his forehead. "Jacob? Can you hear me?"

Jacob opened his blue eyes and asked, "Can I have a drink of water, nurse?"

Loreta turned to the bedside table, poured a glass, and handed it to Rachel.

Trembling, she carefully extended the glass toward the delirious Jacob, leaning gently over him. To her surprise, he did not attempt to reach for it. Only then did she notice the long, empty sleeves lying motionless against the bed sheets.

"Oh!" she gasped, gripping the glass tightly to avoid spilling it on him.

"Sarah?" Jacob murmured.

"No, Jacob, it's me, Rachel. I've come to visit," she replied, her voice trembling under the weight of her grief.

Jacob's eyes filled with tears as he looked down at the glass Rachel lifted to his lips, her hands trembling. He met her gaze for a moment, then drank.

"Oh, Dr. Smith!" Loreta exclaimed, noticing the elderly physician hobbling toward them with his cane, its intricately carved silver handle adorned with delicate engravings that bespoke his status.

Relieved by the sight of a familiar face, Rachel placed the empty glass on the bedside table. "Dr. Smith. Such a pleasure to see you again."

"Rachel, my dear, it's good to see you as well," the doctor said warmly, taking her extended hand. "I'm glad you came to see Jacob. Since we broke his fever, he's been talking about his family. Perhaps your visit will lift his melancholy."

"How is Sarah?" Jacob asked, interrupting the conversation.

"She's fine... and so is your son," Rachel said, noting that Jacob was becoming more alert.

"My son?" His eyes widened in disbelief.

"Yes, Jacob. You have a beautiful baby boy. He has your blue eyes."

Jacob looked perplexed. "I didn't know..."

"Sarah wanted to tell you she was with child before you left, but she didn't want you to worry about her and the baby while you were off to battle."

"What's his name? Sarah and I always said we'd name our first son Noah. We've always loved the name."

"Noah, it is."

"Noah Mercier," Jacob whispered with a contented smile. He turned to Dr. Smith and asked, "When can I go home, Doctor?"

"Very soon, Jacob. I must ensure your fever is fully resolved and your wounds have healed."

Rachel reached for Jacob's hand but hesitated, remembering he no longer had one to hold. "Nurse Loreta gave me Sarah's handkerchief, Jacob. May I keep it to give to her so that she knows I've found you?"

A soft smile touched his lips. "Please do. I won't need it anymore now that I'm home."

Suddenly, his expression shifted with concern. "Rachel, why are you wearing black? Has something happened to Levi?"

Rachel felt her heart tighten, but she braced herself, unwilling to burden him in his fragile state. Forcing a steady tone, she replied, "Levi is fine, Jacob. I wore black for a funeral earlier today."

The lie weighed heavily on her heart, but she knew it was kinder than revealing the heartbreaking truth about her husband, Jacob's best friend, while he remained in such a fragile state.

Dr. Smith intervened, speaking softly. "Rachel, may I have a word with you? Jacob needs his rest. Your visit has been exciting enough for one day."

Rachel leaned down, placing a tender kiss on her brother-in-law's forehead. "I'll be back to see you soon."

As she followed Loreta and Dr. Smith back to the corridor, the doctor halted, his expression turning solemn. "Rachel, my dear, Jacob has been very ill. It's a miracle that he survived a double amputation above the elbows. Very few men do. While his wounds are closed, and I've kept the infection under control, his fever returns from time to time. I'll need to keep him a little longer to watch him closely."

"I understand, Doctor," Rachel said. "When might I see him again?"

"Come back next week. If he's improved by then, we'll discuss his care. In the meantime, you may want to consider acquiring a wheeled invalid chair. They're in short supply, but General Butler has allowed some to be shipped from Mobile. They should be arriving soon."

"Thank you, Dr. Smith. You're very kind."

"You're most welcome, my dear," the doctor said, his gaze shifting to Loreta. "Might I have a word with my nurse?"

"Of course," Rachel said, stepping aside to allow them privacy.

"Yes, Doctor?" Loreta asked.

"I see you dressed him in that shirt to make him decent for visitors, but please take it off after Rachel leaves. I need to examine his wounds."

"Yes, Doctor," she replied.

Dr. Smith nodded and turned away to continue his morning visits.

Following Loreta down the corridor to the lobby, Rachel allowed herself to feel the shock of seeing what was left of Jacob and the burden of lying about Levi's death to spare him the pain of losing his best friend.

"Are you all right, my dear?" Loreta asked gently, her concern deepening as she saw the dazed look in Rachel's eyes.

"I'll be fine," Rachel said, though her thoughts swirled with the urge to ask for divine intervention. She quickly recalled the fate of those who dared to seek mercy from the Fates, only to meet cruel twists of destiny. Retreating into the protective web of language she often spun to shield herself from unbearable stress, she whispered, "Oh, Clotho, weaver of mankind's destiny. Cruelest of the Fates, where do you hide? I beg of you, please unravel the threads of Jacob's fate and return him to the man he once was. And bring Levi back from the land of shadows."

Tears streamed down her cheeks as she proceeded past numerous sick and injured soldiers. Her heart ached to see that many appeared to be little more than schoolboys, scarcely old enough to have ventured far from their mothers' care. The subtle aroma of antiseptic intertwined with the metallic scent of blood, while the low murmur of pain swelled into a grim symphony of suffering.

Her mind raced with a flurry of thoughts. Was she truly morally superior to these men, regardless of which side they fought for? How could she, in good conscience, wish ill upon these broken souls, desperately clinging to their mangled bodies?

With tomorrow evening's sunset marking the start of Rosh Hashanah, the Jewish New Year, Rachel felt especially reflective. The day's events had created an indelible memory. However, she recognized that the war's trajectory was beyond her control: only the powers in Washington and Richmond could determine its outcome.

17

GENERALS, SPIES, AND A WAR ON THE RAILS

President Lincoln stood at the window of his office in the Executive Mansion, gazing at the sprawling expanse of Army tents. The sky had grown dusky, casting long shadows over the encampment, and the ground was still muddy from recent rains. The sight weighed on him, a stark and inescapable reminder of a nation at war.

Lincoln's thoughts shifted to strategy and hope. Although recent months had weighed heavily on him with a continuous toll of defeats, the Union's occupation of New Orleans, the South's crucial seaport, had initiated the effort to open the Mississippi, that great artery of the nation. Yet much of the river above Baton Rouge remained firmly under Confederate control, and even as Union forces advanced, the route to victory twisted like the river itself.

Turning away from the window, his gaze fell upon a small, ornate brass kaleidoscope resting on a side table. It once belonged to his beloved son Willie, whose bright spirit had been extinguished too soon, leaving an emptiness that the passage of time had yet to fill.

With a heavy sigh, Lincoln picked up the instrument and held it to his eye. As he slowly turned the cylinder, shards of colored glass clicked into motion, breaking apart and reassembling into fleeting geometries, brief flashes of order spiraling back into chaos. In the dance of light and glass, he saw not a child's toy, but a nation fractured.

Another twist.

The shifting fragments whirled and fused into ever-changing patterns, like stained glass shattered by cannon fire, then caught in the light again, creating a mosaic of fractured brilliance that mirrored the turmoil consuming the nation. In its delicate prism of glass and light, he caught fleeting visions: battlefields shrouded in smoke, shattered limbs, the hollow eyes of exhausted soldiers, and a land divided by invisible fault lines.

Another twist.

The Mississippi slithered like a great serpent through the mud, its waters choked with gunboats, torpedoes, and fallen men. Along its banks, enslaved families emerged from the shadows of the cane and cotton fields, their voices rising in desperate pleas to be taken aboard the Union ships. Some waded chest-deep into the current, clutching children, waving rags, and calling out, with raw hope shining in their eyes as freedom floated just beyond their reach.

Another twist.

A mother reached for her child, torn from her arms at auction, her scream silent in the cold metal and glass of the kaleidoscope.

Another twist.

Faces emerged next, those of his generals, each shifting within the ever-turning mosaic of war. First, there was his new military advisor, Halleck, "Old Brains," who had been brought to Washington after his supposed victories in the west, even though Grant and Buell had won the battles at Forts Donelson and Henry. Then there was Sherman, who had redeemed himself at Shiloh after his "insanity" in Kentucky, demanding two hundred thousand men to defend the region.

The most glaring image of all was McClellan, disgraced on the Peninsula despite commanding the largest army in the nation's history, yet now praised by some as the savior of the Union after the Battle of Antietam. It was a horrific, inconclusive slaughter, but because Lee's bloodied army had retreated across the Potomac in its aftermath, the North was allowed the illusion of victory. The river, once a boundary, now became a veil through which a battered Confederacy slipped back into its own territory. McClellan, cautious as ever, claimed enough success to maintain his legend — for a time.

With a final twist, the figure of Allan Pinkerton emerged as a quiet sentinel of security. Lincoln reflected on Pinkerton's invaluable intelligence network, whose spies had thwarted the Baltimore Plot and ensured his safe passage from Illinois to Washington for his inauguration.

Each vivid and weighty image that swirled in the kaleidoscope seemed to mirror the intricate web of decisions he faced as President, each turn of the cylinder representing a path not yet taken that would alter the course of history.

He lowered the kaleidoscope and placed it gently back on the table, the memory of his son lingering in his thoughts. With renewed determination, he sighed deeply, rubbing his temples as he pondered his next course of action.

Years before the war, he, Pinkerton, and McClellan had worked for the Illinois Central Railroad. Friendships had formed over shared experiences and mutual respect, especially between Pinkerton and McClellan. After winning the presidency and appointing McClellan to rebuild the Army of the Potomac following the Union's defeat at First Bull Run, Lincoln supported his decision to enlist Allan Pinkerton for war intelligence. Since he was now considering dismissing McClellan, these connections only complicated the situation and risked alienating Pinkerton.

Also, replacing the high-handed General Butler would be no easy task. Who could take his place in the Western Theatre? General Nathaniel Banks, perhaps? Known for a more diplomatic approach, he stood in stark contrast to Butler.

It was a consideration fraught with its complexities. However, in the maelstrom of war, a steady and compassionate leader might be precisely what was needed to shepherd New Orleans, the first major occupied city in the South, back into the Union's fold.

He knew the road ahead was fraught with difficult choices and uncertain outcomes. The Union's survival depended on his leadership, and he would continue to shoulder the burden, no matter how heavy it became.

As much as the weight of the nation burdened him, his aching feet were a nagging reminder of the ills that flesh is heir to. Corns, bunions, and shoes that rubbed sores on them had become a constant agony.

At least there was some solace in knowing that Dr. Issachar Zacharie, the famed chiropodist, would soon arrive to treat his ailments.

For now, Lincoln leaned back in his chair, glancing at a small furry form curled on a cushion beside his writing desk. The soft, rhythmic purring of Tabby, asleep and content, was a quiet comfort in the stillness of the hour.

President Lincoln retrieved his spectacles from a cubbyhole in his cluttered oak desk, which Mary Todd often urged him to replace in her relentless efforts to refurbish his office.

Before him rested three items: a letter written in elegant cursive on fine parchment, an editorial clipped from the *New York Evening Post*, and a scrapbook with brown-tooled leather covers secured with matching leather boot laces. The scrapbook cover boasted "Dr. Zacharie, Chiropodist: Testimonials" in gold-stamped lettering.

In an upholstered armchair facing the President sat Dr. Issachar Zacharie, a dapperly dressed, short, rotund, bearded man in his late thirties. The most striking aspect of his appearance was his commanding Roman nose and sparkling diamond stickpin that adorned his impeccably tied silk ascot.

Of the three objects presented to him by his visitor, Lincoln picked up the letter first. He saw that it was from his friend, William Cullen Bryant, and read it silently.

To Mr. Lincoln

The bearer of this note, Dr. I. Zacharie, a chiropodist of marvelous skill, as I have occasion to experience, has desired I would say to you what I know of him. He is a regularly educated surgeon whose operations on the feet are performed with nicety and delicacy, which is truly surprising. If you or any of your family are incommoded with any disease whatever of the feet, he will be happy to give proof of his skill.

Yours Very Truly,
W.C. Bryant

After carefully placing the letter aside, he picked up the second item. It was a newspaper editorial entitled "Chiropody in the Army," also written by Bryant, clipped from the August 22 edition of the *New York Evening Post*.

Bryant outlined in the editorial why the Union Army should establish a Chiropody Corps. He noted that while Napoleon famously declared that an army travels on its stomach, he seemed to have overlooked that it also marches on its feet. He pointed out that Frederick the Great's Prussian army had a chiropody corps, contributing significantly to its effectiveness.

While the President examined the three items in front of him, the doctor sat quietly, his fingers tapping a silent rhythm against his pant leg. His gaze wandered over the walls, where maps were arranged in neat rows, with hand-colored, intricate legends and markings connecting each position to the locations of various generals relayed to him by the War Department Telegraph Office across the street via messenger each day.

At length, his eyes turned to the window. Beyond the pane, a sprawling encampment stretched across the hills of the burgeoning capital. Soldiers bustled through the chaos like ants in a vast colony.

On Capitol Hill, a ring of shanties and makeshift tents encircled the unfinished Capitol building, its dome yet to crown the rising structure. Enslaved laborers, leased from nearby plantations, toiled as stonemasons, bricklayers, and carpenters, their steady movements mirroring the organized tumult of Union soldiers encamped below.

The stark juxtaposition of soldiers and slaves created a haunting tableau, where war and bondage stood inextricably bound within the young nation's agonizing struggle for survival and its search to define itself.

The partially constructed Washington Monument stood in the distance, reaching toward the sky. Its shadow stretched across the ground like a giant sundial, quietly marking the passing days of internecine conflict.

Even though Zacharie was inwardly terrified that the President would politely dismiss his grand idea before he could fully present it, he maintained a calm demeanor. Today was his only chance to win the confidence of the most powerful man in the United States.

Lincoln cocked an eyebrow as he held up Bryant's editorial. "Quite impressive, Dr. Zacharie. William's a talented newspaperman. He's also my favorite homegrown poet."

The President carefully set the letter aside, aware of its significance since Bryant had introduced him at his 1860 speech at the Cooper Union in New York, which had launched his bid for the presidency.

A slight half-smile formed as he leafed through Zacharie's extensive collection of testimonials. "Was it your intention to cut all my generals' corns?"

Zacharie grinned, welcoming the opening. "Several told me you also have problems with your feet, Mr. President."

Lincoln winced. "Indeed, I do. Even with custom shoes from Dr. Kahler, nothing seems to prevent my feet from developing corns. I have to grit my teeth to avoid limping in public. I've resorted to goatskin slippers around the Executive Mansion to feel comfortable enough to carry out my duties."

The President motioned to the oak table in the center of his office beneath a polished brass gasolier. "My Cabinet meets around that table twice a week — or at least as many of them as can manage to fit around it given their girth. At our last meeting, they were so irascible that I informed them they needed to see a chiropodist. From your book of testimonials, it seems a few of them took my advice."

Seizing the moment, Zacharie offered, "May I remove your corns, Mr. President? I promise the procedure will be painless, as the testimonials attest."

Without hesitation, Lincoln rose and crossed the room with his characteristic loping gait. He sat before the fireplace and propped a bony size 14 foot on a stool. "Is this acceptable, Doctor?'

Zacharie, setting aside his jacket, examined Lincoln's foot. The thickened corns and bunions were evidence of years of poorly fitted footwear. Dr. Kahler's work, it seemed, left much to be desired.

Opening his instrument bag, Zacharie began scraping away the hardened skin with practiced precision.

Lincoln exhaled and smiled, the tension fading from his brow. "My generals were right. It's painless. Your skill is evident."

"I appreciate that, sir," Zacharie said, pleased to see that he was gaining the President's trust.

After the procedure, Lincoln pulled on his slippers.

As Zacharie packed his instruments, his eyes caught a newspaper headline that had fallen to the floor. The lead article described the development of a military surveillance balloon, complete with a massive hydrogen generator, which had been demonstrated to the President the year before.

"Mr. President, may I ask about the balloon launching on the grounds behind the Executive Mansion last year?"

Lincoln nodded. "That was Thaddeus Lowe's work. His aerial surveillance balloon seemed invaluable for assessing Confederate positions and reinforcements, providing a vantage point over the battlefield that few commanders could dream of. That's why I appointed him to create the Balloon Corps."

Zacharie took a deep breath. "With your permission, Mr. President, I propose forming a Corps of Chiropodists for the Union. After all, an army marches not only on its stomach but also on its feet. European monarchs have long relied on men like me for such services."

Lincoln's face remained unreadable as he stood. "Yours is an intriguing idea, Dr.

Zacharie. I'll need time to mull it over. I'll have an answer for you when we next meet," he said.

Zacharie's spirits lifted when he realized his proposal had not been dismissed outright. "I would be honored, Mr. President. I must follow up in a few days to ensure your feet heal properly. In the meantime, please wear clean white cotton socks to prevent your feet from being rubbed by your shoes."

"I rarely wear socks," Lincoln said casually. "Never saw the need, unless Mary insists."

Zacharie flinched but decided to let it go. "Shall we discuss my proposal the day after tomorrow?"

"I'll need a few more days," Lincoln replied, shaking his hand. "When I'm ready, I'll send word and dispatch a carriage to fetch you."

18

Dr. Zacharie's Follow-Up Visit

r. Zacharie gently released the President's wrist as the oak fire logs crackled softly in the hearth. "Does that feel any better?" he asked, his eyes attentive to Lincoln's response.

"A remarkable improvement," Lincoln replied, flexing his wrist with a thoughtful nod. "Do you think you might be able to relieve my back pain as well? My rheumatism always flares up with the change of weather."

"Another of my specialities," Zacharie assured him, inadvertently slipping into his native British English. He pointed across the President's office to the wooden chairs around the Cabinet table. "I will need you to remove your coat and straddle one of those chairs, face the back, and lean forward."

Once Lincoln had settled into position for the procedure, Zacharie began his work, massaging the muscles along the President's spine while anxiously awaiting a response to the proposal he had made during their previous meeting.

Moments later, Lincoln spoke with measured deliberation. "I have considered your proposal, Dr. Zacharie, and concluded that your skills would be a valuable contribution to our war efforts. However, before establishing a Chiropody Corps, I propose conducting a field trial to assess how well you can function in a military setting. Would you be willing to travel to Fort Monroe and report to General Dix?"

Before Zacharie could respond, the President interjected, "I should warn you, Fort

Monroe is about two hundred miles south by steamer. It's a good two-day journey. The overland route is shorter, but perilous since you'd have to pass through the Confederate capital of Richmond."

Zacharie struggled to contain his enthusiasm. "I would be honored, sir," he said, thrilled at the prospect of being assigned to the fort renowned for launching General Scott's Anaconda Plan to blockade the South's seaports.

A trace of a smile crossed Lincoln's face. "I will provide you with a personal testimonial and the necessary funds for your travel. Additionally, I'll telegraph a request to General Dix to offer you his hospitality, allowing you to treat his soldiers. You'll be provided shelter and food in the officers' mess hall."

"Your generosity is greatly appreciated, sir. How is your back feeling now?"

"Much relieved, Doctor," Lincoln replied, standing and turning to face Zacharie. With a wink, he added, "I am also told General Dix has a fine wine cellar, including a few bottles from the Napa region."

"That would be much appreciated," Zacharie grinned. "I seem to recall General Dix negotiated the Dix-Hill Cartel."

"Yes," Lincoln confirmed. "He's quite the diplomat. He navigated the treacherous waters of prisoner exchanges where many before him had hesitated."

"I'm certain I could learn a great deal from him."

"He's a man of ingenuity and integrity. We share an interest in the future of railroads in this country. In fact, he served as president of the Mississippi and Missouri Railroad before the war. Given your business background, I expect you two will find much to discuss around the fire with winter approaching."

"Indeed."

"I've heard that you are a British citizen," Lincoln said, cutting through the pleasantries.

"Yes," Zacharie said, uneasy at the mention of his citizenship.

"I've made inquiries about your background. Two matters were raised. First, your British citizenship is a concern, given the Confederacy's efforts to secure British support. Some have even suggested you might be one of their agents. Second, I'm told some of your wife's kin lean Southern in their loyalties."

The suspicion in Lincoln's tone unsettled Zacharie. "My loyalty to the Union is unwavering, Mr. President, regardless of my citizenship or in-laws. I would swear an oath to that before my Maker, sir."

Lincoln met his gaze, his expression softening. "I understand, Doctor. My wife's Southern roots have raised similar concerns from certain members of Congress. But I must remain cautious in whom I place my trust."

He paused. "I've weighed my advisors' concerns and trust your loyalty. But you'll need the proper documents to move freely in Union territory. Secretary Stanton will issue you a pass. Without it, you'll face suspicion from our commanders."

"I appreciate that, sir, and I would be grateful for a letter of introduction."

"I'll inform Secretary Stanton, and the pass and a letter will be issued."

"Thank you, sir."

"After a month at Fort Monroe, I'd like you to report on any refinements to your plan or any new ideas that could benefit our war effort, especially after collaborating with General Dix. When we meet again, we'll discuss where your talents might be best utilized."

"Understood, sir."

Lincoln rose and extended his hand. "Dr. Zacharie, I'm grateful for your exceptional treatments and look forward to our next meeting."

"The honor is mine, Mr. President," Zacharie said as he stood, grasping Lincoln's large hand in a firm handshake. "I am deeply honored by your trust."

Lincoln walked Zacharie to the door. "I expect my Cabinet will arrive shortly since I sent for them earlier this morning." He patted his vest pocket. "No need for my watch when our neighborhood Chanticleer reports for duty at sunrise."

Zacharie smiled, offering a slight bow. "I'll do my best not to disappoint, sir."

After Zacharie left, Lincoln glanced at his gold railroad pocket watch to see that he had less than thirty minutes to prepare for the impromptu Cabinet meeting.

19

LINCOLN'S CABINET MEETING

Following his meeting with Dr. Zacharie, President Lincoln assumed his usual position at the head of the rectangular conference table in his office just before noon to begin his Cabinet meeting. Only five seats were available, so some of the seven members had to slide their chairs out to sit together while others stood.

Nicolay and Hay, his dapper personal secretaries, were seated at a side table. Each young man had pens, inkwells, and stacks of stationery at his disposal.

Lincoln's Cabinet consisted of seven fiercely independent men, many of whom considered the President a political rival. Believing that disarming enemies by making them allies was the most effective strategy, Lincoln assembled this group of political rivals to serve as his advisors. The outcome was a formidable group of the era's most prominent political figures, each contributing unique experiences and unparalleled expertise to the Cabinet.

Some in the press suggested that the President deliberately chose the men because of their proclivity to bicker so that he could stay out of the fray and make decisions unimpeded by their differences.

Lincoln's Cabinet gathered around the long table, many of whom were former political rivals. At his side sat William H. Seward of New York, once a presidential contender and now Secretary of State. Beside him was Edwin Stanton, the iron-willed Secretary of War. Salmon P. Chase, the ambitious Treasury Secretary from Ohio, leaned forward in quiet intensity, while Edward Bates of Missouri, now Attorney General, carried the air of an elder statesman. To Lincoln's left was Gideon Welles, the bearded Secretary of the Navy, and at the far end stood Montgomery Blair, Postmaster General, remembered for his brilliant yet unsuccessful defense in the Dred Scott case. Caleb Smith of Indiana, now Secretary of the Interior, filled out the circle, a reminder that even his small role of seconding Lincoln's nomination at the 1860 Chicago Republican National Convention earned him a seat at the table.

In a jovial mood following Dr. Zacharie's recent chiropody treatment, the President addressed his Cabinet with a smile. "Gentlemen, I apologize for the short notice, but perhaps I can make it up to you with a bit of humor. You are all familiar with Mr. Artemus Ward's satirical work in *Vanity Fair* and *Punch*, not to mention his popular exhibitions of wax menageries and famous figures, including one depicting the Last Supper. Some of you know I've been an eager follower since he published an imagined interview with me back in Illinois before I came to Washington."

The President held up a book. "Mr. Ward just sent me this autographed copy of his latest work. I was particularly amused by the passage, 'Highhanded Outrage at Utica.' Before delving into the gravitas of our meeting today, I thought it fitting to preface our formal agenda by reading that passage aloud."

Lincoln adjusted his spectacles and turned to the marked page, beginning his expressive narration with his familiar folksy twang.

"'High-Handed Outrage at Utica,'" he read. "In the faul of 1856, I showed my show in Utiky, a trooly grate sitty in the State of New York.'"

"'The people gave me a cordial recepshun. The press was loud in her prases.'"

"'1 day as I ws givin a descripshun of my Beests and Snaiks in my usual flowry stile what was my skorn & disgust to see a big burly feller walk up the the cage containin my wax figgers of the Lord's Las Supper and cease Judas Iscarrot by the feet and drag him out on the ground. He then commenced fur to pound him as hard as he cood.'"

After finishing his theatrical performance of Ward's satire, which depicted a burly man destroying a wax figure of Judas because he was offended by the traitor's appearance in his city, he concluded with an account of the vandal being arrested. He then chuckled with self-satisfaction and peered over his spectacles to gauge the reaction of his Cabinet.

His observation revealed a wide spectrum of expressions, from Seward's broad grin to Stanton's stoic countenance, a product of his strict Methodist convictions.

The President closed Ward's book and cleared his throat. "Now for more serious matters. Gentlemen, as you know, I have thought a great deal about the relation of this war to slavery. You all remember that some time ago, back in July, I read to you a Proclamation I had prepared on this subject. I decided not to issue it then because some of you objected that the Rebel army had been victorious on the Peninsula. Since then, it has reached Frederick County in Maryland, attempting to isolate Washington, and some might have seen the Proclamation as an act of weakness."

"Now, the Rebel army is expelled from Maryland, the threat to the capital has been neutralized, and Pennsylvania is no longer in danger of invasion. Therefore, I consider the Proclamation to be a strategically sound military decision whose time has arrived. I emphasize *military* decision since some of you know that my intent in issuing the Proclamation is to preserve the Union, not to make a moral statement about the issue of slavery since that institution is embodied in the Constitution."

Lincoln scanned the room, gauging the reactions to his words. He was aware that Bates, a slaveowner, had already expressed his disapproval, even though he hailed from Missouri, which was exempt from the Proclamation since it was a border state that chose to remain neutral in the conflict.

Smith, who remained, at best, lukewarm, appeared inclined to withhold any comments.

The President knew that Seward was his strongest advocate, a man who believed that slavery was morally wrong. In his tenure as Governor of New York, Seward had fallen just short of openly siding with abolitionists. In his current position, he was the one who had urged him to wait until the Union had achieved a decided victory. Otherwise, he advised, the Proclamation might be interpreted as the desperate act of a failing Union anxious to weaken the Confederacy by what they would claim was trickery and a violation of the Constitution.

Stanton could be relied upon, as he had advocated for a provision permitting former slaves to serve in the Union army, primarily in supportive roles that did not involve bearing arms. His rationale emphasized a dual military advantage: not only would it deplete the Confederacy's labor force, it would also provide essential manual labor and valuable intelligence for the North. His reasoning was supported in the field by General Butler, who had suggested that runaway slaves be treated as contraband of war and deployed for military purposes.

Satisfied that there were no immediate objections, Lincoln continued, "What I have now written and have assembled all of you here today to consider is what my reflections have determined me to say. If there is anything any one of you thinks had best be changed, I shall be glad to receive suggestions."

Lincoln waited, but none of the Cabinet members objected to his reading the draft Proclamation. Adjusting his spectacles, he proceeded deliberately, punctuating the narrative with marginalia to highlight sections he had altered based on the suggestions and objections raised by each Cabinet member.

Seward, whose signature on the document as Secretary of State would appear underneath Lincoln's, was the first to speak after the President finished his reading. "Mr. President, would it not make the Proclamation clearer and more decided to not merely say that the government 'recognizes,' but that it will 'maintain,' the freedom it proclaims?"

Chase spoke next. "The Proclamation does not mark out exactly the course I prefer, but I am ready to take it just as written and to stand by it with all my heart. I think, however, the suggestion of the Secretary of State is judicious, and I shall be glad to have it adopted."

Postmaster General Montgomery Blair objected, "Mr. President, I, for one, am concerned that this proclamation could cause rebellion in the loyal slave states, demoralize the army, and give the Democrats a club with which to pummel the administration in the upcoming midterm elections."

Recognizing the Blair family's tremendous wealth and political influence, Lincoln met this objection with thoughtful silence before responding. "Sir, I have exhausted every effort to persuade the loyal slave states to begin their own voluntary emancipation programs. Since they have unanimously refused, we must proceed without them. I am convinced that they will acquiesce, if not immediately, soon, if for no other reason than to take advantage of my offer of compensated emancipation to avoid entering the conflict. As for the elections, I have not much concern because the Democrats will use their club against us, take whatever course we might."

Hearing no further objections, Lincoln said, "Gentlemen, I want to express my deepest regard for your support for the modification proposed by Secretary Seward. As I had previously stated, I felt certain expressions in the Proclamation could be improved, and I will attend to making the suggested changes. I know very well that many others might, in this matter, as in others, do better than I can. However, I am the man currently holding the office of President. Therefore, I must do my best and bear the responsibility of taking the course I feel I ought to take."

The room remained silent.

"That is all that I have to discuss, gentlemen. I appreciate your coming on such short notice and bid you a pleasant remainder of your day."

As the Cabinet members filed soberly out of the room, Lincoln addressed Chase and Seward. "Secretary Chase, Secretary Seward, I would appreciate a word with you, gentlemen, in private."

Following the other Cabinet members' departure, Lincoln closed his office door and began his conference with Chase and Seward.

"Gentlemen, I know you are prepared to discuss the two topics I presented to you only last week: financing the conflict and the recent reports regarding General Butler's course of conduct in New Orleans. We do not have all the facts before us, so I expect we will meet many times until certain of these matters are resolved to our satisfaction."

"On the subject of financing this conflict," Lincoln continued, "we have lost both our tariffs paid by purchasers on goods heretofore imported from Europe through the port of New York and shipped by our railroads deep into the South, as well as on the usual profit made by the Northern textile mills for want of cotton. And so, it has come to imposing a federal income tax, a tax as distasteful to the conquered Confederate populace as the British tax was on tea and similarly impressed upon them — at least in their minds, and probably with some merit — without allowing them representation."

Chase leaned forward in his chair. "With all due respect, sir, the Confederate populace assumed responsibility for this conflict when they seceded from the Union and fired upon Fort Sumter. If they desire representation, they can lay down their arms and return to speak their minds in Congress."

Lincoln said, "I agree that the only lasting solution is to cease hostilities and reunite as a nation since the North and the South are geographically inseparable despite their disagreements. We cannot simply erase our territories' boundaries and create two independent nations. We are destined to coexist, whether that coexistence is harmonious or contentious."

Chase gathered his notes and began his presentation. "Mr. President, regarding the matter of trade and finance, after much consultation with various merchants and several of our generals, I would recommend that all needed cotton, sugar, tobacco, and rice should henceforward be purchased only by government officers. The commodities should be paid in gold to the owners, loyal or disloyal. The payment amount should be a certain proportion of the price in New York, and a certificate would entitle the owner to the remainder of the proceeds, after deducting taxes and charges, at the end of the rebellion, provided they remained loyal to the Union. Doing so will remove the rebels' advantage with Europe in the cotton trade."

"Secretary Seward, do you have any comments on the issue?" Lincoln asked.

"Yes, Mr. President. I have communicated with Generals Sherman and Grant, who agreed that trading with the enemy would prolong the war by funding the rebellious states with gold to purchase weapons through foreign and domestic channels. We have already seen foreign trade originating from the neutral ports of Matamoros and Cuba. Domestically, Sherman reports that clandestine sales are being made through Memphis, and Grant has confirmed it. Secretary Stanton is also informed of the generals' sentiments."

The President stated, "I fear I must differ with Generals Grant and Sherman on domestic trade with the enemy. As you are well aware, I have provided numerous examples to support my position. Trade between the Southern states and Europe, particularly when it involves ships and munitions, is another matter entirely."

Seward leaned forward, a wry expression on his face. "There's a particular irony in all this. John Slidell, once a senator from Louisiana and now the Confederacy's envoy to

France, made his way across the Atlantic following the Trent affair. His mission was to woo Napoleon Bonaparte's nephew with promises of renewed French influence in the Western Hemisphere. It was a curious ambition, considering that his uncle was once compelled to sell the Louisiana Territory to us. Slidell pledged Confederate support for placing France's Austrian puppet, Maximilian, on the throne in Mexico. More immediately, he promised a steady stream of cotton from New Orleans. But that pledge is empty with the city now in our hands."

Chase nodded in agreement. "The capture of New Orleans couldn't have come at a better time. Cotton trade was the Confederacy's lifeblood, and now the richest rebel port lies securely in the belly of the Anaconda."

"As for the European implications," Lincoln added, "Secretary Seward, you pointed out that with New Orleans under our control, European nations will soon see the Union as their only reliable source of cotton. Their interest in the Confederacy will fade as they deem the rebellion a domestic issue, not worthy of their involvement. Soon enough, the remaining cotton crops in the rebellious states will be depleted or destroyed, and they won't be replenished without the labor of the slaves we will be emancipating. The tyranny of King Cotton is ending."

Seward spoke next. "Regarding the blockade runners acquiring weapons for the Confederacy, Secretary Welles continues to strengthen our navy and has made significant progress."

"Nevertheless, gentlemen," Lincoln interjected, "there is still the matter of appearances, both at home and abroad. If an intelligent angel were to observe our discussions since the start of this conflict, he might conclude that this war is being waged for the sole purpose of securing cotton from the South for Northern mills."

"On that point, Mr. President," Chase said, "Reverdy Johnson's report suggests that General Butler has reinforced the conclusion of your intelligent angel."

"I have other concerns about General Butler," Lincoln replied, his tone sharpening with irritation, aware that Chase's agent was also implicated in Johnson's findings. "Secretary Seward, have you communicated with the Dutch consulate regarding the return of their assets after General Butler confiscated the Confederate gold they were safeguarding?"

Seward nodded. "Yes, sir. General Butler has returned all the gold, and we've assured the Dutch Ambassador that the sovereignty of their embassy will be respected moving forward."

"Good," Lincoln said. "And have you reviewed Reverdy Johnson's full report?"

"I have, Mr. President," Seward replied. "He has also briefed me personally about his time in New Orleans. The report raises significant concerns, particularly the growing animosity of local citizens toward the Union. Johnson attributes much of this to General

Butler's heavy-handed and, some might say, retaliatory orders. This is troubling, given your vision for New Orleans as a model of goodwill to help reunite our adversaries and bring Louisiana back into the Union. With all this unrest, it seems unlikely Butler will be able to manage a Congressional election by your deadline of next month."

Lincoln nodded, his expression turning somber. "Broken eggs cannot be mended, but I intend to ensure the safety of what's left in the nest by finding a better guardian."

20

BUTLER'S FAREWELL

General Butler stood on the portico of the Custom House, arms crossed with resolute authority, his dress uniform crisp against the damp morning fog. Above him, a colossal U.S. flag flapped in the brisk December wind. Beyond the levee, the ship awaiting his departure loomed in the mist, its silhouette a ghostly presence on the water.

An assembly of agitated spectators, their mood oscillating between ire and elation, gathered to hear his parting words and express their good riddance. It was a day they had long prayed for, and now it had arrived, following his sudden replacement by General Banks just ten days ago.

Even though his departure was imminent, he understood that his legacy as a despot would be immortalized in poetry and song. Today represented his final chance to redefine that legacy, highlighting the challenges he had overcome during his tenure and the significant progress he had achieved for the benefit of the citizenry.

"Citizens of New Orleans," he began, in a stentorian voice that stilled the rowdy crowd, "it may not be inappropriate, as it is not inopportune in occasion, that there should be addressed to you a few words at parting, by one whose name is to be hereafter indissolubly connected with your city."

"Commanding the Army of the Gulf, I found you captured but not surrendered; conquered but not orderly; relieved from the presence of an army but incapable of taking care of yourselves. I restored order, punished crime, opened commerce, brought provisions to your starving people, reformed your currency, and gave you quiet protection, such as you had not enjoyed for many years."

"The men who had assumed to govern you and to defend your city in arms having fled, some of your women flouted at the presence of those who came to protect them. My soldiers were subjected to obloquy, reproach, and insult."

"By a simple order, Number 28, I called upon every soldier of this army to treat the women of New Orleans as gentlemen should deal with the sex, with such effect that I now call upon the just-minded ladies of New Orleans to say whether they have ever enjoyed such complete protection and calm quiet for themselves and their families as since the advent of the United States troops."

"The enemies of my country, unrepentant and implacable, I have treated with merited severity. I hold that rebellion is treason. Upon this thesis, I have administered the authority of the United States."

"To be sure, I might have regaled you with the amenities of British civilization and yet been within the supposed rules of civilized warfare. You might have been smoked to death in caverns, as were the Covenanters of Scotland by the command of a general of the royal house of England, or roasted, like the inhabitants of Algiers during the French campaign; your wives and daughters might have been given over to the ravisher, as were the unfortunate dames of Spain in the Peninsular War; or you might have been scalped and tomahawked as our mothers were in Wyoming by the savage allies of Great Britain in our own Revolution."

"But I have not so conducted. On the contrary, the worst punishment inflicted, except for criminal acts punishable by every law, has been banishment with labor to a barren island, where I encamped my own soldiers before marching here."

"It is true. I have levied upon the wealthy rebels. I saw that this Rebellion was a war of the aristocrats against the middling men, of the rich against the poor, a war of the land-owner against the laborer, and a struggle for the retention of power in the hands of the few against the many. I therefore felt no hesitation in taking the substance of the wealthy, who had caused the war, to feed the innocent poor, who had suffered by the war."

"I have found you trembling at the terrors of servile insurrection. I found the dungeon, the chain, and the lash your only means of enforcing obedience in your servants. I leave them peaceful, laborious, controlled by the laws of kindness and justice."

"And I shall now leave you with the proud consciousness that I carry with me the blessings of the humble and loyal, under the roof of the cottage and in the cabin of the slave, and so am quite content to incur the sneers of the salon or the curses of the rich."

"I have demonstrated that the pestilence can be kept from your borders. I have cleansed and improved your streets, canals, and public squares and opened new avenues to unoc-cupied land."

"I have given you freedom of elections greater than you have ever enjoyed before."

"I have caused justice to be administered so impartially that your own advocates have unanimously complimented the judges of my appointment."

"You have seen, therefore, the benefit of the laws and justice of the government against which you have rebelled."

"Let me conjure you, if you desire ever to see renewed prosperity, giving business to your streets and wharves, if you hope to see your city become again the mart of the western world, fed by its rivers for more than three thousand miles, draining the commerce of a country greater than the mind of man hath ever conceived, return to your allegiance."

"There is but one thing that at this hour stands between you and the government, and that is slavery. The existence of slavery is incompatible with the safety either of yourselves or of the Union. I am speaking with no philanthropic views as regards the slave, but simply of the effect of slavery on the master. See for yourselves."

"Look around you and say whether this saddening, deadening influence has not all but destroyed the very framework of your society?"

"I am speaking the farewell words of one who has shown his devotion to his country at the peril of his life and fortune, who in these words can have neither hope nor interest, save the good of those whom he addresses."

"Take into your own hands your own institutions; remodel them according to the laws of nations and of God, and thus attain that great prosperity assured to you by geographical position."

The audience remained silent, not because Butler's words swayed them, but because no one among them was ready to sacrifice their freedom for vengeance at this late hour when their tormentor was being expelled in disgrace by his own government.

Executing a swift about-face, Butler retreated into the Customs House to receive a farewell from his officers.

Standing toward the front of the crowd, Dr. Smith knew the truth of the general's words regarding his keeping the "pestilence" from the city's borders, an accomplishment no one had achieved before him. He also knew that the man despised as the Beast had opened the shipping lanes to Mobile, Cuba, and Matamoros, ending the blockade that had been starving the population of a once-thriving city.

The doctor decided that Butler's expressed political philosophy was decidedly Marxist. He spoke against the social structure of the South as "the struggle for the retention of power in the hands of the few against the many." Such was his justification for styling himself the Robin Hood of New Orleans, confiscating the riches of the plantation owners and wealthy merchants to feed the starving masses.

Yet he could not ignore the fact that this was the same man who had hanged Mumford without a fair trial and threatened the condemned man's elderly physician friend, who had pleaded for his life. Regardless of his justifications, he was also the same man who issued the infamous Woman Order, banishing women to Ship Island for petty offenses, and cast a shadow over the holidays by marching his troops with their bayonets through downtown New Orleans in late November to display his military might.

Leaning on his silver-tipped cane, the doctor savored a lengthy draw from his beloved briar pipe and squinted through the fog at the *U.S.S. Mississippi.* Butler would leave New Orleans on it, with its only ballast being what he considered his share of the spoils of war.

Bending down to take a handful of sand, the doctor watched it trickle through his fingers, returning to the earth below. In that reflective moment, he pondered how the same soil had a history of passing through many hands with the rise and fall of empires. The Spanish claimed it from the Native Americans in 1762, and the French claimed it from the Spanish in 1802. In 1803, during his youth, the United States acquired the territory from financially troubled France in the historic Louisiana Purchase. It joined the Union in 1812 but was attacked by the British in 1814. Then, it seceded from the Union in 1861, only to be reclaimed just a year later.

If history had taught him anything, it was that the fate of New Orleans remained uncertain.

As he revisited the moment, he contemplated a man who might qualify as an Aristotelian tragic hero due to his fall from power. While the general displayed fatal flaws and considerable hubris, aligning with Aristotle's criteria, he lacked the fundamental traits of noble birth and self-awareness of his shortcomings, both essential for a tragic figure in Aristotelian terms.

Yet even though Butler's actions did not strictly meet these Aristotelian criteria, the eulogy for another fallen hero found in a Shakespearean tragedy remained in the back of his mind as a more fitting farewell for the general.

"Hail, Caesar!" he declared, recalling the words Shakespeare gave to Mark Anthony. "I come to bury Caesar, not to praise him. The evil that men do lives after them; the good is oft interred with their bones; so, let it be with Caesar."

After delivering his eulogy for a man he regarded as a paradox—a self-fashioned hero and a scorned villain—who had fed the starving, championed the poor, and battled disease; yet also exiled women to Ship Island, seized private property, and hanged a man for tearing down a Union flag, the elderly physician made his way toward the St. Charles streetcar that would carry him home.

Watching her beloved childhood physician's departure, Rachel stood for a moment, reflecting on a passage in Butler's speech that resonated in her mind: "I saw that this Rebellion was a war of the aristocrats against the middling men…that it was a struggle for the retention of power in the hands of the few against the many."

On her walk home, Rachel's thoughts were ensnared by those words. She questioned what she and her family had gained through their loyalty to the Confederacy, but could not come up with anything. On the contrary, her family's prospects had never been bleaker.

She had lost her husband, the family wealth had been decimated, her silverware and jewelry had been confiscated, the household servants had fled, and she alone bore the burden of sustaining a family of four with dwindling savings. Not a single able-bodied man remained to defend their home or earn their daily bread.

Might it be possible that the words of the despised general, who would forever be branded "The Beast," rang true?

21

OUR MARYLAND

As the sultry months of spring and summer gave way to the crisp coolness of December, New Orleans embraced the return of its traditional theatre season. The oppressive heat and heavy humidity of the warmer days, made more stifling by the fierce blaze of footlights and the shimmering glare of jet-fed house lamps, had kept many theatergoers away. But with the arrival of cooler evenings, the city's grand playhouses once again beckoned eager audiences through their doors.

Just before his departure, Butler presented a farewell Christmas gift to the citizens of New Orleans: an evening performance at the grand St. Charles Theatre of *Our Maryland*, a hastily written patriotic Union play penned by a local playwright. The production was staged as part of his so-called "Grand Union Dramatic Festival."

News of the play at the city's only theatre that staged performances exclusively in English hung over the city like a gathering storm, its dark clouds thick with tension.

The production's provocative theme, celebrating a bloody Union victory at Antietam in mid-September, struck a raw nerve as many men of the city had died or been wounded in the war. The outrage only deepened when it was revealed that the proceeds from ticket sales would support the Northern war effort. Unsurprisingly, no Confederate sympathizers attended, save for a few spies lurking in the shadows.

As a result, Union soldiers had to choose between seeking the company of a small group of honorable ladies who stayed loyal to the Union or opting for companions from a broader selection that included prostitutes, spies pretending to be Union loyalists, or a mix of both. The common saying went that a Gold Eagle could buy an evening with a lady of the night, while a Double Eagle could provide the company of the establishment's Madame. The difference in value came from the fact that the Double Eagle secured the company of a more refined escort, one who could afford an exquisite gown and a finer fragrance and who excelled at portraying the role of a sophisticated lady deserving of an officer's rank.

In anticipation of the rising curtain, the Union military band burst into a rousing rendition of "Hail Columbia," following General Butler's directive for all public performances. The audience rose to their feet to sing along with the patriotic closing chorus:

> Firm, united, let us be,
> Rallying round our liberty,
> As a band of brothers joined,
> Peace and safety we shall find.

Comfortably seated in her front-row place on the first-level balcony, Loreta, in her role as confidante and spy, turned a radiant smile upon her young companion, John, a colonel in the Union army, whose handsome features and broad shoulders drew admiring glances from those nearby. As the singing concluded amid thunderous applause and enthusiastic "Hurrahs," she settled back into her plush opera seat, looking down on the theatre's main floor where the audience had to contend with less comfortable, unpadded wooden seating.

"My brother is in the band," John said proudly, pulling her from her reverie. "He's the drummer. Can you see him just there?" he asked, using his best manners to nod toward the orchestra pit rather than raise his hand to point.

Loreta looked through her opera glasses at the band, whose backs were to the audience. "Ah, yes," she returned with a coy smile. "I can see him. Such a nice, fulsome head of black hair."

Grinning proudly, John ran his fingers through his own thick head of hair. "Yes, he does. It runs in the family."

Men are such imbeciles, Loreta thought, reminding herself to smile sweetly and hang on to her escort's every word, just as she had trained herself to do. *He sits beside me, my fool for the evening, paying a dollar for the best seating, fancying that I am a British lady of some distinction. He remains completely oblivious that I harbor not a shred of attraction for him and would readily engage him in combat as Buford.*

Her reverie was interrupted by an imposing actor clad in a lieutenant's deep blue uniform, entering from the left wing and halting center stage in front of the closed curtain.

"Good evening, ladies and gentlemen," he announced in a Boston accent while managing a crisp salute. "Tonight, you will witness a glorious Union victory at the Battle of Antietam, where the Union Army of the Potomac met the Confederate Army of Northern Virginia. Therefore, tonight, on this stage, there will be the roar of cannon fire and the sharp report of many rifles. Let me assure you, gentle ladies, that our weaponry consists solely of gunpowder. There is not a single bullet, shell, or cannonball on the stage. Moreover, you have your protector seated beside you."

"How comforting," Loreta whispered beneath her breath, entertained by the farcical character and his reprehensible display of condescension.

"You needn't fret, my dear," her colonel chivalrously reassured her, softly extending his strong hand to grasp her dainty, gloved one.

With a flourish, the emcee dramatically drew his sword and raised it above his head. "Let the battle begin," he cried.

The resounding blare of trumpets accompanied the curtain's slow ascent. The spectators sat at the edges of their seats, captivated by the detailed depiction of the Antietam battlefield, with soldiers discharging volleys of gunfire. The intense tableau, enveloped in the thick haze of gun smoke, unfolded against a painted scrim backdrop portraying a cornfield beneath the peaks of South Mountain.

In a sudden scenic *deus ex machina*, a dashing General George McClellan, astride a magnificent mechanical replica of his horse, Daniel Webster, made his grand entrance. The exuberant audience erupted in a resounding standing ovation to greet their hero of the moment.

Beneath the pale light of a waning crescent moon, Loreta sat in the backseat of their cab, enduring John's ceaseless chatter about the play's most memorable scenes as they made their way to his favorite coffeehouse on Tchoupitoulas Landing.

Directly ahead at the levee, illuminated by streetlamps, a group of animated Negro men sang and danced as they marched along.

"Pull over, driver!" Colonel John shouted. He turned to Loreta. "I should see what this is all about."

As the group of about twenty Negroes drew nearer, clad in tattered attire, Loreta and John could discern the lyrics of their song, delivered in the Creole dialect of plantation slaves.

Say, darkies, hab you seen de massa, wid de muffstash on his face,

Go long de road some time dis mornin', like he gwine to leab de place?

He seen a smoke way up de ribber, whar de Linkum gunboats lay;

He took his hat, and lef' berry sudden, and I spec' he's run away!

De massa run, ha, ha! De darkey stay, ho, ho!

'It mus' be now de kingdom comin', an' de year ob Jubilo!

He six foot one way, two foot tudder, and he weigh tree hundred pound,

His coat so big, he couldn't pay the tailor, an' it won't go halfway round.

He drill so much dey call him Cap'n, a' he got so dreful tanned,

I spec' he try an' fool dem Yankees for to tink he's contraband.

De darkeys feel so lonesome libbing in de loghouse on de lawn,

Dey move dar tings into massa's parlor for to keep it while he's gone.

Dar's wine an' cider in de kitchen, an' de darkeys dey'll have some;

I s'pose dey'll all be cornfiscated when de Linkum sojers come.

De obserseer he make us trouble, an' he dribe us round a spell;

We lock him up in de smokehouse cellar, wid de key trown in de well.

De whip is lost, de han'cuff broken, but de massa'll hab his pay;

He's ole enuff, big enuff, ought to known better dan to went an' run away.

Moving past the cab, the jubilant men offered bows and grins to the colonel. Two of them saluted, exclaiming, "Say Merry Chrismus to Pres'dent Linkum!"

"I'll do just that," John replied, still chuckling at the innocent merriment.

Once the brief parade of fugitive slaves had passed, John signaled the driver, "You can proceed now."

As the cab moved along the street, John flashed a grin. "Guess they got the news of the President's preliminary proclamation freeing them. It's high time they had their fun!" Recalling the song's lyrics, he declared, "I can imagine the slaves locking up their overseer in the smokehouse cellar, moving into their master's abandoned mansion, and guzzling his cider to celebrate their newfound freedom from the whip and shackles."

Loreta forced a laugh, mirroring John's, although the moment didn't tickle her fancy. "Quite a catchy tune, I must say. I found it amusing when they sang about their master being a Confederate captain, drilling in the sun for so long that he got dark enough to pass for contraband when he skedaddled. I can picture that paunchy Southern planter digging ditches for the Union!"

"Guess I missed that part," he admitted with a chuckle.

Deep down, Loreta felt her colonel deserved to savor the moment's joy before learning the inevitable news of Sherman's setback near Vicksburg, along the cliffs of the Yazoo River. She had received word of the Union general's tactical defeat by Pemberton earlier that afternoon, relayed by her grapevine connections, the fisherman spies who had crossed Lake Pontchartrain from Camp Moore. The crowning glory was the news that Confederate torpedoes had sunk the Yankee ship *Cairo* on the Yazoo River earlier in the month. She was delighted to hear of the victory, as *Cairo* had been the lead ship of the Union ironclad gunboats and the first vessel in the war's history to be destroyed by torpedoes anchored in the river, detonated by wires from onshore. This was in addition to the great victory in the East, where Robert E. Lee had defeated Burnside's army at Fredericksburg, with Union casualties more than double those of the Confederacy.

While the two continued to enjoy the light-heartedness provided by the jubilant slaves, they noticed an eerie glow emanating from an alley just ahead. As they approached, a blazing bonfire came into view.

"Halt, driver!" the colonel ordered, "Pull over!"

Startled, the driver quickly steered his horse to the side of the street. Before the cab had entirely halted, Loreta's valiant colonel threw off his coat and leaped out. With a swift motion, he unsheathed his sword and charged toward a shadowy figure looming behind what appeared to be a pyre of burning corpses.

"Murderer! Put out the fire, now!" John shouted.

"I ain't burnin' nobody, mister," a man standing in the shadows assured him, tipping his hat respectfully as he cautiously stepped into the warm glow of the firelight. In the pale light, the middle-aged Negro man looked visibly shaken at the sight of the unsheathed sword. "Them's jest the dolls that Gen'ral Butler had me carve out of wood and paint black to look like darkies."

"No one informed me of this," John replied, sheathing his sword. "I would appreciate an explanation."

The man was visibly relieved that the soldier accepted his story and put away his sword. "Genral Butler tole me he wuz plannin' on havin' his soldiers carry 'em on sticks like puppets in some sortah parade so they'd look like they was walkin' all shackuled up like. Then he planned for sumboddy dressed up like a Lady Liburty with a great big sword to come 'long and cut off the shackuls, just for show, you know. Sumboddy said it was 'bout that Emsupashun Procluhmashun Linculn signed to free thuh slaves."

"So, who told you to burn them?"

"Nobody," the man said, busily stirring the ashes at the fire's edge. "The genral's leavin' town without payin' me a nickel." He placed his hat back on and grabbed a pitchfork to poke at the fire. "Shame they ain't good for nothin' 'cept fur keepin' me warm tonight."

Loreta sympathized with the man cheated by Butler but found the scene amusing: her fearless colonel confronting a Negro man burning a pile of wooden dummies. Suppressing a condescending laugh at the absurdity of it all, she contemplated how to assuage her valiant hero's wounded pride, especially given that his escort for the evening had witnessed the event.

Pretending not to hear the man's explanation and the colonel's embarrassed apology, she cried out in distress, "Oh! John! I feel faint," and waited for him to dash to her side.

John rushed to her rescue on cue and vaulted into the cab beside her. He covered her with his coat, reassuring her affectionately, "There, there, my dear. I've taken care of everything. All was not as it seemed."

"Thank heaven," she sighed softly, her delight hidden behind a demure smile as her ploy succeeded. She gently caressed his cheek with her gloved hand. "I feel so safe with you, John," she whispered. "You're the strongest, bravest man I've ever known."

John's chest swelled with pride as she expertly conjured a trembling lip and endured his embrace. Pulling back, she met his pleading gaze with a rush of well-practiced tears, radiating feminine submission. He responded with the same helpless look of frustrated passion she had seen countless times when she wielded her charms against unsuspecting adversaries.

Pleased with the triumph of her feminine wiles, she mused, *Has another knight fallen on my chessboard?*

1863

ROMANCE, RIVERS, AND ESPIONAGE

HYDE & GOODRICH

22

THE POISON PEN

On a brisk January morning, Rachel strolled along Canal Street, tilting her parasol to shield her face from the sun's sharp glare. As she passed a shopfront, her reflection caught her eye, and she paused before the glass. Her dark silhouette seemed to merge with the colorfully dressed display forms beyond, arranged in a fanciful garden tableau beneath a wooden trellis draped with climbing silk roses. Her spectral figure, cloaked in winter's chill, starkly contrasted with the vibrant promise of spring just beyond her reach. Each vivid blossom mocked her, reminding her of the life she had lost and the pain she continued to endure.

She had grown accustomed to the accoutrements of mourning: the weight of dark fabrics and her somber silhouette in the mirror. But a strange sensation stirred within her as she gazed at the shopfront glass. Grieving for Levi, she realized, might soon become a luxury she could no longer afford. With no man to provide for the household and four mouths to feed—five, counting Jacob's caretaker—her widow's weeds would have to be set aside, not for lack of sorrow, but out of necessity. If she hoped to find any gainful work, she would have to cast off the garments of grief and step into the world as something other than a widow.

Setting these troubling thoughts aside, she decided there was much to be thankful for in the New Year, so she resolved to allow herself a slight reprieve from her usual worries and indulge in a brief escape.

She resumed her window shopping, pleased that more merchants were open today than during her last stroll. The freshly painted, vibrant signs on the storefronts, where many new owners stood at their doors greeting customers with clipped Northern accents, rekindled her hopes of finding a milliner's shop.

Almost a year ago, she had spent days poring over patterns in the spring issue of *Godey's Lady's Book,* carefully selecting a design for her new dress. Since the war had brought much of life to a standstill, she knew that last year's fashions remained the *dernier cri.*

By April, Passover had come and gone, and she had abandoned her project, leaving the dress unfinished and still without a matching hat. The relentless Union blockade, the painful duty of burying her husband's remains after Shiloh, and the growing fear of occupation had left her no heart for celebration.

Despite these devastating events and the Union occupation of New Orleans last Passover, she was grateful for the news from Virginia that General Lee had been victorious again.

Closer to home, General Pemberton had repelled General Sherman's assault at Chickasaw Bayou just north of Vicksburg, delivering a temporary check to Union forces. This maintained the Confederate hold on the Mississippi, extending southward from Vicksburg to the fortifications on the bluffs at Port Hudson. These strategically vital defenses protected the area where the Red River, flowing from Texas, joined the Mississippi, ensuring a steady supply of western beef and grain for the troops while denying the same to the federals.

Buoyed by these successes, Confederate loyalists fervently prayed for their beloved General Beauregard to liberate New Orleans, restoring Confederate dominance over the river down to the Gulf.

Amidst these turbulent times, she prepared to commemorate Passover with Sarah and Jacob, welcoming Noah, the newest member of their household. If Jacob felt up to it by April, this would be his first outing since his illness. It would be a chance to join with friends in prayer, reflecting on their struggles for deliverance, just as their ancestors did during their captivity in Egypt.

Resolving to shed her mourning clothes, Rachel decided to find the perfect hat to complete her outfit and signify her return to the world. With three months until Passover, she had plenty of time to make an exchange if it wasn't the ideal match.

However, the real challenge would be finding enough lace to trim her new hat. Her supply had already been depleted, embellishing the dress. Yet, an elderly woman from her synagogue, renowned for tatting delicate Queen Anne-style lace, might have just what she needed. The woman spent her days creating intricate designs, pricing them reasonably to raise money for wounded soldiers.

Approaching the intersection of Canal and Royal, she noticed two Union soldiers bearing rifles — one White and one Negro — stationed at the entrance to Hyde & Goodrich's establishment. Above them perched the Golden Pelican, featured on Louisiana's state flag. Once a symbol of the state's pride and resilience, it had been tested under Union control.

The Negro man was undoubtedly a member of Banks's Louisiana Colored Troops. The sight of a former slave in uniform, wielding a firearm, was a reminder of how drastically the world was changing.

Should she walk past the soldiers as if they weren't there or cross to the other side of the street? Curiosity won out, so she gathered her courage and walked straight ahead until she reached the store's display.

Startled by what she saw, she froze, mesmerized by the beautiful, multitiered chandelier that appeared to float weightlessly in mid-air, framed by luxurious gold velvet curtains. The crystal pendants caught the sunlight, scattering it into vibrant rainbow hues that danced across the polished silver serving pieces below.

But what made *this* chandelier so special that it required protection by armed soldiers? Hyde & Goodrich was known for offering the finest and most expensive European art south of New York City, yet she had never seen guards stationed there until today.

Her curiosity piqued, she moved closer to the display window and glanced at the sign beneath the chandelier. The words stopped her in her tracks, and before she could stifle her reaction, she gasped, "It holds the pen Lincoln used to sign the Emancipation Proclamation!"

Hearing her, the Negro soldier flashed a toothy grin. "Yes ma'am. President Lincun used that pen to free us black folks like Moses did with his staff when Is'rl was in Egypt land."

Rachel was startled by the man's remark, which referenced a slave song once banned on plantations before the occupation. Could the slaves see Moses as their deliverer, much like they revered Jesus as their savior? If they were drawing parallels between their plight and the Israelites' exodus from bondage, as this man did, it exposed a striking irony: the same Bible that planters had long used to cite the so-called curse of Ham as divine sanction for enslaving Africans could just as easily inspire hope for freedom.

The White soldier turned toward the window, pointing up to the chandelier. "Look in the middle at that glass tube, ma'am, where all the parts come together. It's a little hard to see since it's so small."

Rachel's gaze fixated on the unassuming ink pen encased within the chandelier's central glass column. It was just a wooden shaft with a steel nib. In disbelief, she reasoned it had to be a replica. Surely, no one in their right mind would openly display the original pen used to sign such a reviled document in an occupied Confederate city.

Regardless of its authenticity, her thoughts raced to understand why the proprietors would display such an item. Perhaps they were trying to curry favor with General Banks. Then again, maybe he had coerced them. Whatever the reason, she was certain that no one would set foot in Hyde & Goodrich after this.

Convinced that the display would soon be taken down, she turned and continued along the street, though her thoughts remained fixed on the pen. What other reason could there be for displaying it so prominently in the window of such a prestigious shop on the busiest street in downtown New Orleans if not to provoke the city's citizens? But that seemed like something Butler would have done, not Banks.

Then she recalled the rumors of a planned insurrection that had swept through the city if Lincoln didn't keep his promise to free the slaves by the New Year. Tensions had started to rise in the fall of '62, especially when crowds of freed slaves began boarding streetcars and refusing to give up their seats to White passengers. At the time, she hadn't noticed, as she had always hired a cab for her trips to the French Market while Sarah was confined with child.

Even more troubling were the reports of rogue slaves roaming the streets, kidnapping and binding several White men to stage mock trials, judging them for the crime of enslavement. Though no casualties had been reported, the audacity of these unrestrained former slaves had sent a wave of alarm through the White community. Outrage grew as Union soldiers brushed aside the concerns of White victims, ignoring what many citizens viewed as bold and dangerous transgressions.

To further complicate matters, she had heard that one of Butler's soldiers, knowing the general's satisfaction in seeing freed slaves taunt their former masters, confronted a particularly outspoken White man. The soldier brazenly remarked that if Southern men could share their beds with slaves, then slaves should be allowed to share the same streetcars. Adding insult to injury, the soldier remarked that many light-skinned Negroes carried the surnames of New Orleans' most prominent families.

Amidst this social upheaval, rumors circulated that General Banks had feared a slave revolt. Supposedly, this fear had led him to reposition Union troops from Baton Rouge to New Orleans shortly after his arrival and return many of the weapons Butler had confiscated from citizens. These moves only fueled Rachel's suspicion that Banks was silently preparing for an uprising. Yet she knew she could never fully grasp his motives since he made no public statements on the matter, and the newspapers remained heavily censored.

A single tear traced a slow path down her cheek. It was a bittersweet symbol of sorrow fighting against her resolve to persevere in a changing world.

Her father's words echoed in her mind, reminding her she was strong enough to face any challenge.

"Oh, Papa," she whispered, "if only you had known the insurmountable obstacles that would stand in my way."

Reminding herself that her family was the most important thing in her life, Rachel continued down the street, offering a silent prayer for peace and some way to provide for her family.

23

THE GENERAL AND THE DOCTOR

Dr. Issachar Zacharie stood outside the St. Charles Hotel, eager to meet General Banks at his headquarters, yet travel-weary and desperate for a bath after the long, dusty journey from Fort Monroe to New Orleans.

Standing before the imposing new structure that had risen from the ashes of the one lost to the fire of 1851, he marveled at its grandeur. Despite the years since his brief business venture in the city, the hotel exuded the same timeless elegance as the original. However, the new structure lacked the 180-foot-tall dome, a feature that reminded him of the Capitol building dome in Washington, which remained a work in progress.

Zacharie entered the hotel lobby, admiring the towering Corinthian columns, the imported Carrara marble floors, and the storied balconies. The stucco walls glowed from the amber light of the massive crystal gasolier, which had been recently illuminated before the approaching sunset.

Hearing New England accents, his gaze shifted to the balconies, where he saw uniformed Union soldiers strolling casually. If not for their uniforms and accents, their relaxed conversations reminded him of the hotel's previous civilian clientele.

The doctor recognized St. Charles's reputation for fine dining from his short chiropody practice in the Crescent City. He remembered elegantly dressed guests, many of whom were planters, indulging in lavish meals. The beautiful sounds of a Steinway grand and occasional appearances by a wandering violinist each night elevated their dining experience.

He remembered the seven-course feasts, complete with skilled sommeliers decanting a thoughtfully curated array of wines from France's most esteemed vintners, alongside

California wines for guests of more modest means who aspired to genteel tastes. The meal culminated in such artistic delights as flambéed peaches in brandy, featuring an aromatic blend of rum and banana liqueur that was dramatically prepared tableside in a blaze of dancing blue flames.

For the gentlemen, the evening concluded in a grand finale of Cuba's finest hand-rolled cigars, perfectly paired with a soothing cognac nightcap, elegantly served in a gleaming snifter.

The unparalleled elegance of the dining experience at St. Charles drew the city's Anglo socialites into a friendly competition, each striving to host the most extravagant parties. Newspaper reporters eagerly sought invitations to capture the essence of these elegant soirées for the vicarious enjoyment of their less well-to-do subscribers.

But when Farragut's ships approached, the hotel's owners packed up their famous solid gold tableware, withdrew their gold from the banks, gathered their horses and buggies, and fled with their families deeper into the Confederacy.

As Dr. Zacharie strolled through the lobby, he passed several gentlemen clad in tailcoats and topped with silk hats. Their conversations centered on acquiring abandoned shops and crafting strategies to sell goods to the occupying army. From their accents, he surmised that they were part of the wave of New York businessmen eager to seize opportunities created by merchants who had fled the occupation.

New Orleans landlords, who owned the shops along Canal Street and had signed the Oath of Allegiance to maintain their properties, eagerly mingled with businessmen to secure new tenants. Zacharie was intrigued by the landlords' business practices, particularly their strategy of renovating the signs from closed shops for free advertising and offering a month of complimentary rent in exchange for extended lease agreements.

Raucous laughter echoed through the hall, drawing him past the check-in desk and toward a broad archway. As he stepped closer and glanced inside, an extraordinary scene appeared.

Through some strange act of prestidigitation, the elite audience that once filled the hotel's grand dining room seemed to have vanished into thin air. In its place, a sea of blue uniforms, adorned with shiny brass buttons and shimmering gold braids, materialized.

In what seemed like an alternate reality, he saw what appeared to be recently escaped Negro plantation house servants waiting tables, decanting liberal portions of whiskey from the hotel's pre-war stock to quell complaints about occasional maggots in the salt-preserved steak shipped from Matamoros. Fresh steak, which was occasionally available in local markets at the exorbitant price of forty cents a pound, was not to be had.

The scarcity resulted from the Confederacy's control of a crucial supply line that started in Texas and followed the Red River to its junction with the Mississippi at Shreveport, the newly declared Confederate capital of Louisiana. This was a strategic move to safeguard this vital route that channeled supplies from Texas to the lower Mississippi region.

Zacharie's attention was drawn to a nearby supper plate. He noticed that the steak tips were drenched in butter and roasted garlic, accompanied by several sautéed tender spring potatoes.

Although the dish was served on the exquisite hand-painted china, he remembered from his last visit, the distinctive solid gold service of the St. Charles, adorned with its opulent French Rococo pattern, had now been replaced by tin utensils taken from mess kits. The stark contrast between the elegant china and goldware and the crude mess kit utensils was striking.

Then he caught wind of a conversation at a nearby table. An officer with a French accent explained that the gourmet dish was meant to be *"steak au beurre d'ail,"* which he translated for those at the table who were not fluent in the language of fine cuisine as "steak with garlic butter." However, he playfully suggested that it could also be dubbed *"escargot sur sabots"* or "snails on hooves," owing to the snail-like consistency of the petite steak portions prepared similarly to the familiar French delicacy.

Amid the laughter circulating the table, a well-schooled officer with an English accent, not to be outdone by a Frenchman, cheekily referred to escargot as the "French solution," insisting that it involved harvesting otherwise unpalatable gastropod mollusks for the supper table, drowning them in a sea of sizzling butter and roasted garlic, and then bestowing the elaborately prepared rasp-tongued garden pests with a fancy French name.

"C'est vrai," his jovial French comrade agreed, toasting the observation with his glass of Merlot, graciously acknowledging his English-speaking companion's vivid portrayal of French cuisine. *"Le même chose que vous servez ici, mon ami, avec l'Étouffee de Crawfish. Mais nous, Les Française, sommes assez sages pour server un vin de qualité afin de le render plus agréable."*

"What'd you say?" came the response. "Damn it, Frenchie! Speak English."

"I said, *Le Rosbif,* the same goes for your Crawfish Étouffée. But we Frenchmen are at least wise enough to serve fine wine with it to make it more agreeable!"

The table again erupted in hearty laughter at the jovial Frenchman's use of the term "Roast Beef" to playfully refer to the Englishman and his clever remark, drawing a humorous comparison between unwanted French garden snails and Louisiana crawfish, which ravaged local rice crops. The implication was clear that, just as the French had perfected the art of preparing escargot, Louisianans had borrowed the technique for their beloved crawfish étouffée.

At the next table, an officer with a thick German accent boasted about his eagerness to join General Banks's much-anticipated campaign up the Red River. He excitedly explained that the expedition would open a vital route from Texas to Shreveport, allowing live cattle shipments to reach New Orleans again. However, he conveniently overlooked the Confederate fortifications between Shreveport and New Orleans along the Mississippi. With a grin, he added that he couldn't wait to savor a fresh steak cooked so rare he could still hear it moo.

Turning away from the surreal scene in the dining room, Dr. Zacharie approached the elevator, noting that the old St. Charles never had one. He stood for a moment admiring the gleaming brass doors, then he pressed the button of the small brass mechanical bell embedded in the wall. Stepping back, he watched the dial above the elevator door, tracing the lift's gradual descent like the minute hand of a clock turning backward through time.

When the elevator reached the main floor, the doors creaked open, revealing an elderly Negro in a smartly tailored elevator operator's uniform. The man made a welcoming gesture for Zacharie to enter.

"Good evenin', suh," the operator greeted in a syrupy Southern accent. "What floor, please?"

"I'd like to go to the top floor," Zacharie said, stepping to the back of the empty chamber.

"Yassuh," the man replied, smoothly pulling the lever to shut the heavy brass doors. He then turned the crank to the marker for the top floor. "Guess you be off to see the Gen'ral," he added, as if privy to some unspoken secret.

Zacharie did not respond, letting the old man's remark hang in the air.

The attendant's eyes lingered on Zacharie's diamond stickpin. "That's a mighty fine di'mon you got there, mistuh. You one of them Yankees come down to do business in New Or-leans?"

Zacharie returned a polite smile, although the man's curiosity felt a bit too familiar for his taste. "Thank you, it is. But no, I'm not a Yankee. I hail from England."

The old man nodded silently, seemingly satisfied with the answer.

When the elevator began its ascent, the creaking and popping of the cables made the doctor slightly uneasy. Seeing no manufacturer's nameplate, he recognized it as a "rope-and-pully" model, not Otis's revolutionary "safety elevator," which was first installed in New York City in 1857 at Haughwout's emporium, one of Mary Todd Lincoln's favorite stores for purchasing decorative items for the Executive Mansion.

Attempting to distract himself from concern about the cable snapping and falling to an untimely death, he turned to focus on the elevator's interior. Despite its compact size, it exuded a charming coziness, with rich mahogany paneling, brass appointments, spotlessly polished marble flooring, and two kerosene sconces casting a warm glow over the entire space. The amalgamation of scents—polished mahogany with a soothing hint of sandalwood oil, complemented by polished brass bearing the nostalgic scent of mothballs, which his wife used in her fur coat closet—created an unexpected yet calming atmosphere that distracted him from his fear of plummeting to his demise.

Feeling more at ease, he allowed his thoughts to drift back to his time at Fort Monroe, where he had tended to the aching feet of nearly five thousand soldiers, treating corns and bunions with tireless precision. Yet despite the scope of his work, no official Chiropody Corps was ever authorized. The reason was plain enough: Surgeon General William Hammond had taken umbrage at his decision to bypass the chain of command in proposing it.

Undeterred, he turned his attention to other means of serving the cause. He had been intrigued by General Dix's successful use of peddlers disguised as spies who wandered into enemy territory under the guise of trade to gather critical intelligence. So, when word reached him that General Banks had been appointed to command the Department of the Gulf, he seized the opportunity. He wrote at once to offer his services in a similar capacity.

Banks, ever hungry for intelligence to bolster his campaign, had received glowing endorsements of the doctor's talents from no less a source than the President himself. Wasting no time, Banks urged him to proceed to New Orleans—and to "spare no expense."

The metallic jolt of the elevator reaching its stop broke his reverie.

"Top floor," the attendant said, opening the door for Zacharie to exit. "You have yourself a nice day, mistuh."

"You as well," Zacharie said, relieved that his feet were safely planted on the luxuriously carpeted hallway.

Walking along the lengthy corridor, Zacharie considered that the much-despised General Butler had favored the St. Charles as his headquarters, sparing it the fate of the St. Louis, which had been stripped of its luxurious appointments and converted into a military hospital.

As the sun dipped toward the horizon, young Negro women in neatly pressed uniforms moved along the corridor, opening the gas valves of the gleaming brass wall sconces and lighting them with long lamplighter matchsticks. Come sunrise, these same women would return to extinguish the flames and polish the fixtures to a lustrous shine. Though now earning wages, their days still stretched from "can't see to can't see," echoing the unbroken rhythm of toil they had once known in the fields but now within walls gilded by refinement rather than ruled by the lash.

Approaching the end of the long corridor, with the laughter of the supper conversation still ringing in his ears, Zacharie encountered two armed, swarthy soldiers. They were flanking carved Honduran mahogany double doors that marked the end of the hallway. He was impressed by how proudly New Orleans' beloved Zouave soldiers, formed initially as the Tiger Rifles and trained at Ft. Moore, stood stoically while guarding their posts. Though he had long been aware of their reputation in battles from the First Manassas onward, he had never seen their exotic French uniforms up close. The distinctive blue jackets with intricate red embroidery, billowy red trousers, and matching fezzes crowned with golden braided tassels were genuinely captivating. It intrigued him how these soldiers had earned their place as some of the most feared fighters on the battlefield despite the burden of such cumbersome attire.

Zacharie halted in front of the soldiers before the massive doors. One of the men silently glanced at his pass, opened the right-hand door, and gestured for the distinguished visitor to enter.

In an office where military maps papered the walls, General Nathaniel Prentiss Banks, an impeccably groomed man in his forties, sat bolt upright in his chair behind an imposing mahogany desk. Clad in the authoritative uniform of a U.S. Army major general, complete with golden epaulets, he was framed by windows draped with royal blue velvet curtains. Behind him, the backdrop of a breathtaking sunset presaged a grand city nightscape, brought to life by the warm glow of flickering gas streetlamps.

When Banks stood, he seemed to be of average height, yet he was imposing. He boasted a full head of lustrous brown hair that cascaded over his ears. His skin was bronze-toned, his thick mustache was well-groomed, and his captivating gray eyes complemented an unusually handsome face.

The general carried himself with a regal demeanor that hinted at aristocratic lineage and formal military training. Truth be told, he had neither. But rather than feeling ashamed of his background, he took pride in the nickname "Bobbin Boy" he had earned during his impoverished youth. He had assisted his father, a mill foreman, by tirelessly refilling empty bobbins six days a week, twelve hours a day, to support his family.

What Banks lacked in heritage and training, he made up for in political savvy and social skills. He was one of Lincoln's chosen "political" generals, a term reserved for those accomplished politicians like himself and General Butler who did not graduate from West Point or have any formal military training. Instead, Banks's résumé boasted stints as Speaker of the U.S. House of Representatives and later as Governor of Massachusetts. He had even aspired to secure the Republican presidential nomination in the last election but failed early on.

Banks stood to extend a hand across his desk. "I've been looking forward to your arrival, Dr. Zacharie. I was expecting you some weeks ago."

Zacharie reached out to receive a handshake from the man who had written him to "spare no expense" in traveling posthaste to New Orleans upon the President's recommendation. "I would have arrived considerably earlier if not for General Grant's order prohibiting Jews from traveling through his command, including the railroad that connects to your Department of the Gulf."

Banks flinched, sensing a touch of irritation in his guest's voice. He took a slow breath, softening his posture as he shifted into a more hospitable tone. "General Order 11 against Israelites was most unfortunate. As you are aware, the President promptly countermanded it. Please have a seat, Dr. Zacharie. May I get you something to drink? A glass of California Merlot, perhaps?"

"Thank you. A glass of Merlot would be splendid," Zacharie replied, easing into the armchair before Banks's desk. As he reflected on the general's disarming charm, a thought struck him: someone must have informed Banks of his fondness for California Merlot.

He paused, considering ways to initiate a conversation with a man he knew to be deceptively charming, yet deep down, somewhat cold and withdrawn, with no intimate friends apart from his wife. "How are your feet?" he blurted out, immediately feeling self-conscious as soon as the words escaped his lips.

A subtle curl at the corners of Banks's lips betrayed his amusement at the doctor's social awkwardness. He stood from his desk, decanted a glass of Merlot from his liquor cabinet, and then handed it to his guest. "I have been well. Thank you for asking, Dr. Zacharie."

"Oh, thank you," he said, sipping the wine while admiring the beautifully etched Waterford lead crystal. "Nice body," he said, gently swirling the wine to watch the streaks trickling down the glass.

Banks looked confused.

Zacharie laughed. "I meant the Merlot has a good feel upon the tongue—sturdy yet refined. You say it's from California?"

"Yes, actually it is," Banks replied, pouring a glass of water for himself. Taking his seat, he looked embarrassed by his unfamiliarity with the lexicon of wine connoisseurs, having been the abstinent son of an alcoholic father.

Zacharie leaned back in his chair. "I enjoyed the wines near Stockton when I opened a general store for the miners during the gold rush in '49. I even ventured into fermenting with a batch or two myself. I must admit, California life was good to me and my family."

Zacharie quickly changed the conversation, noting Banks's disinterest in his business affairs. "If it suits you, I'll bring my instruments and examine your feet first thing in the morning. After that, we can discuss how I might be of further service."

Banks flashed his signature smile, revealing a perfect set of dazzling white teeth. "That would be much appreciated."

"My pleasure," Zacharie said, noting that the general engaged best when the conversation turned transactional.

Banks leaned back in his chair. "The President seems quite impressed with your medical expertise and loyalty to the Union."

"Thank you, sir. And he has a very high regard for you as well."

The general gave a brief, sardonic nod. "The President has a way of befriending his political rivals."

"Yes, he does," Zacharie agreed, aware that Banks had failed to secure a place on the same presidential ballot that elected Lincoln. Yet the President had appointed him to the Department of the Gulf and entrusted him with matters of great consequence.

"I appreciate his allowing you to assist me, especially given the situation here in New Orleans after General Butler's command." Banks opened the center drawer of his desk, pulled out an envelope, and handed it to Zacharie. "Take a gander."

Zacharie stood, took the envelope, and resumed his seat to open it and unfold a letter offering a $100,000 bribe to General Banks, urging him to permit business to continue as usual. "That's more money than most men see in a lifetime," he murmured.

Banks shifted uncomfortably. "It's an embarrassment, especially considering it was posted by General Butler's brother, Andrew. George Denison, Chase's nephew and the customs agent here, informed me that Butler had been using Andrew to supply cotton for his interests in the Middlesex Mill up in Lowell, Massachusetts."

Zacharie shrugged. "From what I've heard since arriving in town, that sounds like how business is conducted here."

"I recently wrote to my wife, telling her how disheartened I've been by what I've found upon my arrival. Nearly everyone tied to the occupied government has been busy stealing anything they can get their hands on: sugar, silver, and gold coins, tableware, horses, and carriages. I even heard that Butler confiscated a woman's poodle."

Zacharie blinked, trying to process what he'd just heard. "I'm sorry. Did you say he confiscated her dog?"

"Yes. The poor woman's name was Madame Larue. She's an actress here in New Orleans and quite the patron of the fire department's annual fundraiser, where people dress up their dogs for a grand parade down Canal Street. Anyway, the firemen were furious when Butler had her sent off to Ship Island for spreading Confederate disinformation. I don't know if they were angrier about her treatment or losing her and her little poodle from the parade lineup."

"I'd think twice before crossing firemen," Zacharie said with a wry smile. "A man never knows when he might need them."

Banks gave a knowing nod. "Butler excelled in pettiness. He was always confiscating small things just to needle folks."

"The spoils of war," Zacharie mused. "And no spoils richer than those found in the South's busiest seaport."

"Butler is no longer a factor," Banks said, his voice tight with tension. Turning the conversation to business, he gestured to the maps lining the walls. "At the moment, I'm balancing military duties with the complexities of civil governance."

"Quite a task," Zacharie said.

"First, I had to rearm citizens to defend themselves against an impending riot when slaves were pouring downriver into the city, demanding proof that the Union would uphold Lincoln's Proclamation. They even took over the streetcars and staged mock trials of White men for enslaving them. With the help of a friend from Massachusetts, I made quite the spectacle by placing the pen used to sign the Emancipation Proclamation in the planters' favorite downtown storefront. It still hangs there, a simple pen showcased in an ornate crystal gasolier, serving as the centerpiece among the luxury goods displayed in the window. Somewhat ironic, wouldn't you say? That pen of Emancipation poised above all the sterling dinnerware that only the wealthiest planters can afford?"

"Yes," Zacharie said. "I saw that. It was a stroke of genius." He noted that the "Bobbin Boy" seemed to take a quiet satisfaction in the aristocratic planters' reaction to the display.

"I further managed to defuse the situation by offering the freedmen paying jobs, free food, and shelter in houses left behind by Confederates who fled the occupation. I also kept a few of Butler's sanitation workers for maintenance after the streets and gutters were cleared. The others I employed for jobs germane to our mission, including working as longshoremen and reinforcing the levees."

"That sounds pragmatic," Zacharie said. "It expands your labor force and frees up your troops for other matters."

"I then had to quell another potential uprising," Banks continued, "this time from the White population objecting to Butler's decrees on freedom of speech and religion, which are always volatile issues, especially under martial law. Even though the President sent Reverdy Johnson here last year to investigate, you can see by the letter I showed you that I'm still dealing with the aftermath."

Zacharie remained silent, giving the general a chance to vent his frustrations.

Banks gestured toward the bustling streets below, where the clamor of New Orleans never truly ceased. "I must govern this occupied city, oversee public services, maintain order, and somehow facilitate the Union's reconstruction policies all at once. Do you know how complex that is? It means balancing the demands of freedmen seeking justice, Unionists clinging to loyalty, and Southern elites desperate to preserve what remains of their world." His voice grew firmer, the frustration evident. "They call Grant a great general. I am the first to admit that. But his responsibilities are clear-cut. March. Fight. Conquer. I, on the other hand, am tasked with stitching together the frayed fabric of this city while the war rages around us."

Banks turned back to Zacharie, his gaze resigned. "This city," he said, his tone softening slightly, "is not just another strategic location. It is the heart of the South's trade, the gateway to the Mississippi, and a crucible for everything this war is about: economics, freedom, and power. That's what makes this job more than just a command. It makes me, for better or worse, one of the most prominent military administrators of this entire war."

Zacharie was struck by Banks's sharp grasp of the complexities of occupying the South's largest seaport and his ability to adapt to its shifting challenges. Yet, it was equally clear that the general harbored a lingering bitterness about the weight of his responsibilities, particularly when contrasted with Grant, his potential rival for a future presidential bid.

"The President tells me you've made remarkable progress in addressing critical issues during your short tenure," Zacharie remarked.

Banks allowed himself a faint, satisfied smile, his eyes gleaming with quiet accomplishment.

Zacharie leaned forward and said, "You may not realize that I had planned to create a Chiropody Corps when the President sent me to Fort Monroe. However, after staying there and learning about the success of General Dix's deployment of peddler spies, I decided that using my business skills to do the same would be a greater advantage for the Union. I then discussed my changes of plans with the President."

"Yes. He informed me of your decision. That's why I invited you here."

"In preparation for my mission, I've written ahead to one of my fellow Israelites in New Orleans, a Union loyalist, who has agreed to assist me by providing a list of potential peddler spies.

"Excellent."

"I can also mix with the locals to gauge how your policies are being received, giving you a clear sense of what's working and what isn't. From what I've gathered, about a third of the population is open to cooperation with the Union, primarily for economic reasons, especially the ones you employ to work on your projects, like shoring up the levees. Additionally, I can help foster goodwill within the Jewish community, which holds considerable influence among merchants and bankers."

"The President informed me of your ties with the Jewish community, and I could certainly use your help in gathering intelligence," Banks returned with sober acknowledgment. "On a related issue, I've had my eyes on the Judah Touro Building to domicile my colored troops temporarily. I haven't mentioned it yet to my friend, Rabbi Illowy."

"I can certainly reach out to Touro's foundation through Rabbi Gutheim," Zacharie assured him. "As far as I know, the two rabbis have collaborated effectively in the past." He paused, a wry smile curling his lips. "Well, as effectively as any two rabbis ever manage to work together."

Banks chuckled knowingly. "Christian ministers are no different. Otherwise, there would have been no Protestant Reformation, and they'd all still be priests. Cooperation comes with a healthy dose of debate, regardless of faith."

Banks turned to look at the softly ticking tall-case clock. "We have much to discuss, Dr. Zacharie, and I'm eager to hear more. But given your long journey and my upcoming meeting with my adjutant, let's continue this tomorrow morning. Would you like to join me for breakfast after a good night's rest?"

"That would be splendid, General."

"Then I'll see you at 8:00 sharp. My schedule for the rest of the day is quite crowded. You'll find the guards stationed outside my private dining room just down the hall. We can continue our discussion, and I'll have more information that may assist your mission."

"I look forward to our meeting, General."

"And feel free to bring your secretary, Charles, along," Banks added, standing to accompany Zacharie to the door.

The doctor stood up and offered his goodbyes.

As he walked down the hallway, he reflected on the conversation. Banks's familiarity with his secretary's name and the casual mention of his fondness for California Merlot struck him as curious, leaving him to wonder what else Banks knew.

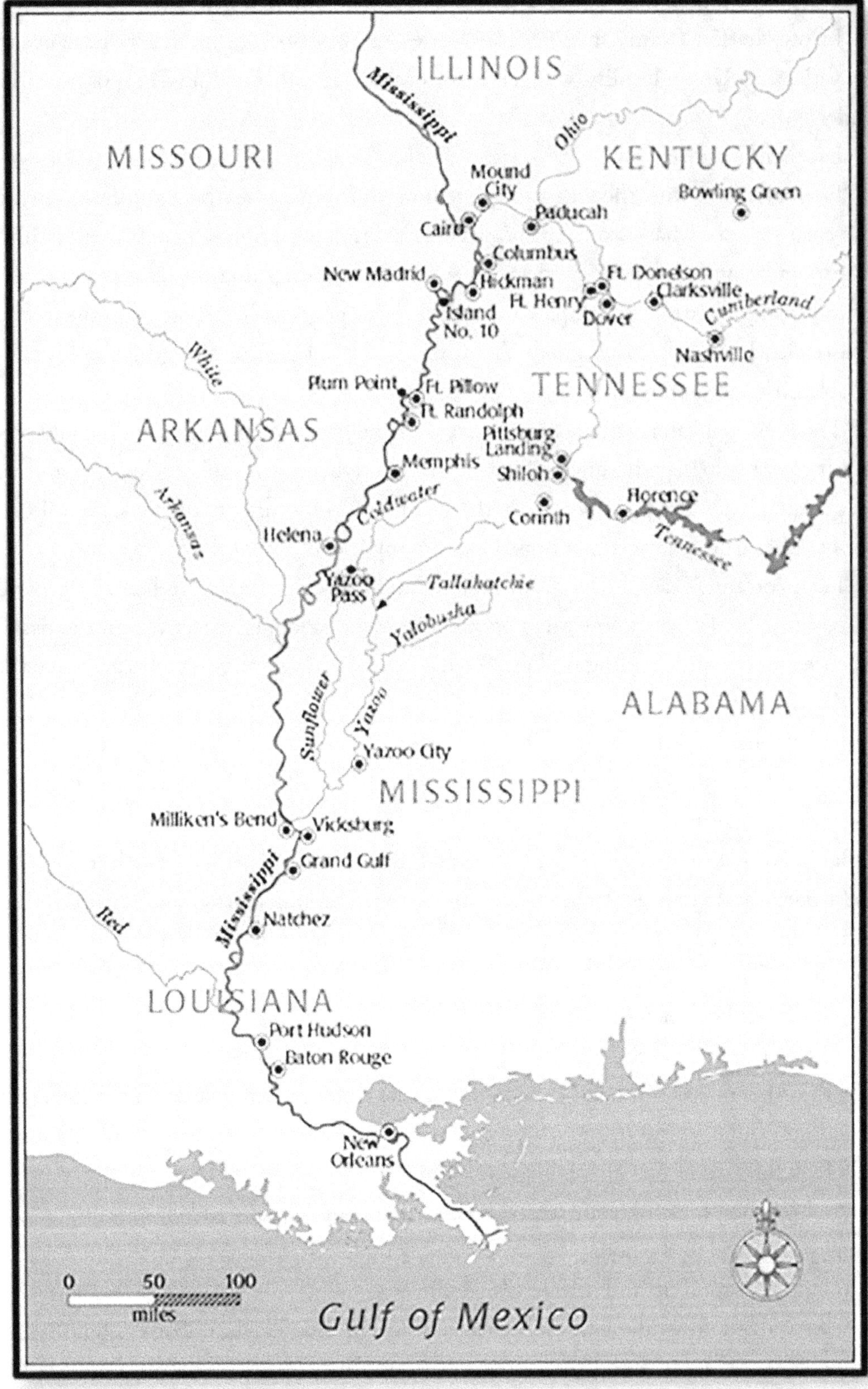

ILLINOIS
MISSOURI
KENTUCKY
Mississippi
Ohio
Mound City
Bowling Green
Cairo
Paducah
Columbus
New Madrid
Hickman
Ft. Donelson
Clarksville
Ft. Henry
Cumberland
Island No. 10
Dover
Nashville
Plum Point
Ft. Pillow
TENNESSEE
Ft. Randolph
Pittsburg Landing
ARKANSAS
Memphis
Shiloh
White
Coldwater
Florence
Corinth
Tennessee
Arkansas
Helena
Yazoo Pass
Tallahatchie
Yalobusha
ALABAMA
Sunflower
Yazoo
Yazoo City
MISSISSIPPI
Milliken's Bend
Vicksburg
Mississippi
Grand Gulf
Red
Natchez
LOUISIANA
Port Hudson
Baton Rouge
New Orleans
0   50   100
miles
Gulf of Mexico

24

Dr. Zacharie's Peddler Spies

General Banks sat in his private dining room at the St. Charles, facing Dr. Zacharie across a small round table covered with crisp white linen and a plentiful spread of traditional New Orleans petit-déjeuner. At the center, a woven straw cornucopia overflowed with bananas, persimmons, and quinces, while Zacharie's gift of a large, ripe pineapple added a tropical touch to the wintry atmosphere.

Zacharie admired the gold-trimmed chinaware, noting its striking resemblance to the handcrafted pieces commissioned by Mrs. Lincoln from Haviland & Company. His first encounter with this exquisite set had been at the Executive Mansion, where the President had shared its backstory.

The President had explained that the chinaware was imported as bisque ware and sent to E. V. Haughwout & Company in New York, where artists meticulously hand-painted Mrs. Lincoln's design on each piece before it was fired. The intricate pattern featured a wide, gilded purple border surrounding a central medallion depicting a majestic bald eagle with outstretched wings, clutching arrows in one talon and an olive branch in the other, poised between war and peace.

Doubting the authenticity of Banks's chinaware, since imitation sets with printed transfers were typical souvenirs on the streets of Washington, Zacharie remarked, "I was admiring the chinaware. I've seen it at the Executive Mansion. The President told me his wife designed it."

"Yes, it is magnificent," Banks replied. "My wife sent a set of it to me shortly after I arrived in New Orleans. She had admired it at the Executive Mansion when Mrs. Lincoln hosted the opening of the East Room last year after she had it refurbished."

Zacharie, ever perceptive of the significance behind the objects people choose to surround themselves with, couldn't help but reflect on the Banks's desire for the Executive Mansion chinaware. It hinted at aspirations beyond the roles of a general and his wife, suggesting the couple's quiet ambition for elevated social standing.

"What a splendid gift," Zacharie said. He turned his attention to the dining room's décor, the intricately carved American walnut liquor cabinet, and the side buffet. "It appears that this room has been recently refurbished."

"Yes. And the hotel concierge has extended lavish hospitality. Upon our arrival, a fruit basket and a chilled Champagne were waiting in each officer's room."

Zacharie had little doubt that Butler's departure was greeted with Champagne corks popping and toasts raised in relieved anticipation. The promise of continued full occupancy and rent reliably paid by the Union on the first of each month only enhanced the festive mood.

"I trust you had a good night's sleep," Banks said.

"It was very restful. I had forgotten just how incredibly comfortable the hotel's beds are," Zacharie replied, grateful that St. Charles's high standards had been preserved.

"That's good to hear. I forgot to ask about Charles. I see he's not with you today."

Zacharie responded nonchalantly, still inwardly surprised that Banks knew about his secretary. "He woke up coughing this morning, feeling feverish, with aches and pains in his joints. Hopefully, it's just a case of the grippe that will resolve on its own."

"Sorry to hear that," Banks replied with a trace of indifference. "Would you care for some coffee? A shipment just arrived from Havana."

"Thank you," Zacharie said, pleasantly surprised that his host had secured coffee, especially since it was so scarce in the shops, which typically supplemented it with chicory root. No sooner had he spoken than a Negro servant appeared, seemingly from nowhere, to pour his cup.

Banks gestured to the man and nodded toward the pineapple. "Zeb, please take the pineapple Dr. Zacharie brought and prepare it for us."

The servant collected the fruit with a subtle bow and disappeared through a side door that led to the kitchen.

Though hunger gnawed at him, Zacharie patiently stirred cream and sugar into his coffee, following the timeless etiquette of waiting for the host to start the meal.

Once Banks spread butter over his croissant and topped it with a thick layer of orange marmalade, Zacharie reached for the butter, relieved by the tacit permission to begin eating.

Before Banks took a bite of his croissant, he asked, "Do you remember yesterday when I mentioned Butler's brother, Andrew, and his proposal to carry on his usual business practices here after I arrived?"

"Yes, I remember."

"What I neglected to mention," Banks continued between bites, "was that Andrew provided cover for Butler's commercial ventures early in the occupation with a rather ingenious plan."

"Oh?" Zacharie prompted.

Banks took a bite of his croissant and chewed it slowly as if deliberating on what he would say next. He finally added, "It began with a shortage of ballast for ships transporting cotton to New York. To address this, Butler first confiscated bells that the Confederates had collected from plantations and churches at General Beauregard's request. Beauregard intended to melt them down for cannons, but under Union occupation, Butler used them as ballast, shipping the bells to New York for auction to aid our war effort. Once the bells were all shipped, Butler claimed the only remaining option for ballast was importing sand from Ship Island, but the cost would have been prohibitive. That's when his brother came up with the idea of using barrels of sugar as ballast."

"That was smart," Zacharie remarked.

"More like *clever*, since it wasn't as straightforward as it appeared. Andrew secured Seward's permission to buy the sugar, claiming it was at his own expense and intended for use as ballast. He argued that his plan cost the Union nothing and saved money, as it avoided the expense of transporting sand from Ship Island and dumping it in New York.

What no one realized, though, was that this arrangement allowed him to ship the sugar for free, have it brokered by his agents in New York, and pocket a considerable profit."

"Very clever, indeed," Zacharie replied, impressed by Butler's cunning.

Zeb returned quietly, setting down a tray of sliced pineapple rings and a serving fork in front of Banks before disappearing once more through the door beside the buffet.

"Thank you, Zeb," Banks said, casually stabbing a slice of pineapple with the serving fork and placing it on his plate to slice it into small chunks with his knife. "I'm told that Butler even waved around a letter from Seward to his officers, congratulating him on the plan. After that, no one questioned his other business dealings in New Orleans. And no one paid much attention to his brother's ventures that benefited the Confederates. At least not until his scheme was uncovered when Lincoln sent Reverdy Johnson to look into complaints from the foreign embassies."

"I heard about Johnson," Zacharie said, taking the serving fork to help himself to a slice of pineapple. "The President relied heavily on that report to justify reassigning General Butler."

"And that's when I was sent to the Department of the Gulf," Banks said after swallowing a bite.

Zacharie understood why the President would be concerned about complaints from European embassies, knowing that intervention by England or France would be disastrous. Yet, he did not seem worried about domestic trade with the rebels. "I've overheard the President say that trade between the North and the South must go on, whether as enemies or friends."

"I've heard the same," Banks replied. "Of course, he was referring to trade for essential goods, not munitions. So, when Butler organized safe passage to the Confederate port of Mobile to provide food for the population, no one in the administration objected."

"It bodes well for commerce," Zacharie noted. "It should help rally support for the Union among the local merchants."

"Yes," Banks agreed. "One would hope. At least that's one positive note the man left on."

"Speaking of merchants," Zacharie said, "I took my morning constitutional past Hyde and Goodrich on the corner of Canal and Royal to look at that pen you had encased in the chandelier."

Banks grinned. "What did you think of it?"

"I found the symbolism of light representing freedom to be a stroke of genius."

"Unfortunately, I can't take credit for that. One of my officers came up with this notion. However, as I mentioned yesterday, I did have the idea to display it in the planters' favorite luxury shop alongside European finery."

"I'm curious," Zacharie said, "How did you come to possess that pen?"

"At the request of Senator Sumner, the President gave it to George Livermore, an ardent Massachusetts abolitionist and supporter of the Emancipation Proclamation. When Sumner approached Lincoln to make his request, he said, 'Do as you wish. I signed it, but you earned it,' and handed him the pen."

Zacharie was aware of the President's modesty and his deep respect for Senator Sumner, who had been brutally beaten with a walking cane on the Senate floor by Representative Preston Brooks of South Carolina after delivering a fiery anti-slavery speech that condemned a relative of Brooks.

Banks continued, "When I came up with the idea to display the pen here, Sumner had already sent the pen to Livermore to add to his collection. I contacted Livermore, and he agreed to lend it to me, provided I guaranteed its safe return. When it arrived under armed guard, one of my officers suggested placing it in a chandelier and calling it a beacon of light, symbolizing freedom for the slaves. I agree with you that it was a nice touch."

"But how did you convince the proprietor to display something so controversial, given his planter clientele?"

"At first, Mr. Hyde was worried he'd lose his customers and be forced to close if he displayed the chandelier, but I persuaded him. But I discovered that he hadn't signed the Oath of Allegiance; somehow, Butler had overlooked that. So, I agreed not to confiscate his inventory if he allowed the chandelier to be prominently displayed in his window for the entire month of January."

"I see why you stationed armed guards there to protect it," Zacharie said.

"It caused quite a stir among the hostiles when it was first displayed," Banks admitted, "but I felt it was necessary. The slaves had threatened to revolt if the Emancipation Proclamation wasn't enforced by January 1st as promised. I thought displaying the pen in downtown New Orleans would underscore the President's commitment."

"It seems to have done the job," Zacharie noted. "I've seen most freedmen going about their lives peacefully."

Banks finished his coffee, set the cup down, and wiped his mustache with his napkin. "I must give the President credit for navigating the political complexities of the Proclamation. I've always considered him a political genius with his ear to the ground. Few know him as I do since he was an attorney for the Illinois Central Railroad when I was its vice president."

"I agree with you about his acumen," Zacharie replied, catching in Banks's tone not only admiration but also a faint tinge of envy, as though he begrudged Lincoln the glory that had eluded him.

Banks poured another cup of coffee. "I've never met anyone who reads as voraciously as the President. He scours every major newspaper daily to understand the political climate."

"I had the feeling he'd already read the article I gave him during our first meeting."

"Rest assured, he had," Banks said. "Did you know he published a book?"

"I knew he published his debates with Douglas. It was a bestseller."

"Exactly. Decorum and tradition kept him from campaigning for himself, but letting the debates speak for him was fair game. It catapulted him to the top for the Republican nomination."

"A brilliant move," Zacharie remarked, sensing a hint of envy in Banks's praise.

Banks's smile turned sardonic. "And did you know he bought a newspaper business?"

"No, I wasn't aware of that."

"It was the *Staats-Anzeiger*, a German newspaper based in Illinois."

"A German paper?"

"Yes, printed in archaic type that most young Germans can't read."

"What possessed him to buy such an obscure paper?"

"He recognized that the older German immigrant population was growing rapidly, and the Democrats were ignoring them. Knowing the race would be close, he directed his newly acquired *Staats-Anzeiger* to publish articles exclusively in support of the Republican Party and his own candidacy."

Zacharie stroked his beard thoughtfully. "I've noticed that the German Coast in New Orleans supported him in the election. It always puzzled me, considering the President was a Whig before becoming a Republican, and the Whigs up North were infamous for railing against German Catholics."

"And the Irish Catholics as well," Banks added casually, picking up another croissant and offering the plate to Zacharie. "Through articles in his German newspaper, he managed to convince them he was different from the rest."

"Apparently so," Zacharie agreed, taking the croissant.

"And his plan for the transcontinental railroad is all over the papers," Banks continued, now buttering his croissant. "Much like the articles in his German newspaper, it helped sway key voters. Lincoln knew how to appeal to various minorities, whether through his promises of improved transportation or by convincing them he was different from other politicians. He always knew how to turn the press to his advantage."

"Yes, I've read several articles," Zacharie said, taking up the butter knife.

"I've always maintained that the real reason he wants the transcontinental railroad built is so he can put his ear to the rail and hear what's happening across the country."

"That certainly fits with what I know of him," Zacharie agreed, though by now he recognized that Banks's extended praise of the President, tinged with envy, revealed more about Banks's own unfulfilled ambitions than Lincoln's genius.

"When we spoke yesterday, we touched on deploying peddler spies. Would you care to elaborate?" Banks deftly spread marmalade on his buttered croissant while he awaited Zacharie's response.

Zacharie was pleased with the shift in conversation. "As you know, I plan to recruit several peddlers. You would supply them with goods to sell in Confederate territory, and in return, they'd provide intelligence on enemy movements. The intelligence we'd gain would far outweigh any benefits the enemy might see from the goods. General Dix at Fort Monroe has had considerable success with this tactic."

Banks stroked his chin. "I can arrange that, doctor, provided no arms are involved. What items did you have in mind?"

"Confederate sympathizers here struggle to supply footwear to their soldiers. I'm told many of their soldiers are marching barefoot. I might convince local sympathizers to donate shoes, which my peddlers would deliver to the other side for a small fee."

"That wouldn't strain my budget. What else?"

"Nothing they could use in combat, of course. Other than used footwear, I thought I would take the basics: bandages, socks, and liniment. Perhaps even throw in a little quinine. Each peddler would need to carry an inventory valued between fifty and two hundred fifty dollars to make their mission look legitimate. The danger would be real: they could be executed as spies if caught."

Banks gave a measured nod, finishing his croissant. "I understand the risks," he replied. Then, a hint of a smile played at the corner of his mouth. "But your request is financially feasible. Selling them used shoes is good, but I must say, including quinine is brilliant. We've embargoed its shipment into the Confederacy, so smuggling a few bottles through the lines will go a long way toward earning the enemy's trust."

Zacharie felt a flicker of satisfaction. "I'm pleased you see the value in the strategy, General." After a pause, he added, "We'll also need horses and buggies, along with an expense account and salary for each peddler. Their cover must be convincing, and they'll need the means to move freely."

"The President has set aside funds for intelligence gathering. He appreciates the need for reconnaissance and supports any initiative that aids our campaigns. Submit a requisition with an itemized list of expenses to my paymaster at your earliest convenience."

"I'll have it to you within the week," Zacharie said, relieved that the general considered his plan feasible. He paused. "You also expressed interest in learning about the sentiments among the population in New Orleans and gaining the support of the Jewish community."

"Yes," Banks replied. "This is also critical. I've learned that the Jewish population is approaching five percent of the total in New Orleans, as Jews move in from the countryside for safety and relocate from the North to establish their businesses. Given the President's plan to hold an election supporting a return to the Union, requiring ten percent of the population to vote for it, this puts us in a good position. Also, I am working to encourage registered enemies to leave the city."

"I can help with all of that," Zacharie assured him. "I've already written to Gershom Kursheedt, the president of the Dispersed of Judah congregation, a Union loyalist, and he provided me with a list of loyal Jews, some willing to act as peddler spies. Additionally, Rabbi Gutheim of the same congregation, who is on the registered enemies list, is eager to assist congregants who wish to leave New Orleans."

"Excellent," Banks said. "Reducing the number of citizens opposing reunification will certainly help." He leaned back in his chair. "We can go over the details later. For now, let me give you an overview of our campaigns along the Mississippi." He wiped his mustache with his napkin, folded it neatly to place it beside his plate, and then stood and walked over to a map on the wall. "While we await updates on Rear Admiral Farragut's progress, I'll brief you on our strategy to reopen the Mississippi and cut the Confederacy in half."

Picking up a pointer, Banks continued, "General Grant and Flag Officer Foote first secured the mouths of the Tennessee and Cumberland Rivers at Fort Donelson and Fort Henry. This provided us with river access to Bridgeport and Nashville, which had previously protected essential Confederate supply lines. Railroads, like the junction at Corinth, are also crucial, but I'll save those details for later."

"Progressing southward on the Mississippi, Island Number 10, Fort Randolph, and Fort Pillow came under Acting Rear Admiral Porter's control, giving us Memphis and ensuring an open river down to Vicksburg," Banks explained, pointing to the map. "However, safe passage depends on reconnaissance along the White, Yazoo, and Arkansas rivers to identify any concealed gunboats and rebel sharpshooters. Additionally, there is the critical issue of submerged torpedoes anchored in the waterways, ready to be triggered by rebels onshore."

Zacharie nodded in understanding.

Banks pressed on. "Unfortunately, the stretch between Vicksburg and Port Hudson remains tightly held by Confederate forces and remains resistant to Farragut's assaults. Both cities have veritable fortresses on the riverside. Grant's troops, supported by naval forces, are tasked with taking Vicksburg. At the same time, with naval backing, I am responsible for clearing the Mississippi at Port Hudson and reopening trade on the Red River from Shreveport to its confluence with the Mississippi between Port Hudson and Vicksburg." He tapped the map with his pointer for emphasis. "For various reasons, there's some discussion about postponing a Red River campaign until Mobile is secured, so I won't discuss the issues of the Louisiana terrain. But I will share that it was much easier to maneuver back East."

Zacharie reflected that the battleground in Louisiana indeed presented unique challenges. Here, soldiers contended not only with the enemy but also with the relentless heat and humidity, dense swamps, tropical disease, venomous snakes, alligators, and the constant threat of ambush from guerrilla fighters lurking in the thick underbrush. The unpredictable waterways, often dotted with submerged torpedoes and rebel sharp shooters onshore, added another layer of complexity. This was a war fought not just against men and weapons, but against nature itself.

Banks laid down the pointer and crossed his arms. "More relevant to our conversation is my immediate need for intelligence covering the area from Baton Rouge to Port Hudson. My original plan was to dispatch several operatives for this mission." Banks returned to his seat. "But the journey is perilous, especially with rebel guerrillas patrolling the riverbanks. They tend to shoot first and ask questions later. And, of course, the Confederates have positioned sharpshooters armed with those damned British Whitworth rifles, which they obtain through blockade runners."

"I've heard of those rifles," Zacharie said. "Their range is incredible."

"Yes, and their accuracy is equally lethal. Who would have thought a square bore could outmatch the traditional rifled round one for long-range precision?"

Zacharie sensed the question was rhetorical and stayed quiet.

Banks leaned forward. "This is where I can see the value of your peddlers. They won't draw the same attention as uniformed soldiers or traditional spies." Banks paused. "And if you could manage for them to be mostly Jewish, that would fit in with what people are accustomed to seeing."

"Of course. That won't be a problem," Zacharie replied smoothly, eager to reassure Banks that he took no offense at the remark about peddling being predominantly associated with itinerant Jews. "I was wondering if you had someone with experience and knowledge of the area above New Orleans who could blend in with the Confederates.

Banks leaned back, stroking his mustache as he mulled it over. "I do have someone in mind. He's a young attorney from Baton Rouge who sought refuge in the North during the city's occupation. He spent six months under Pinkerton's tutelage. Though not as experienced as some, he's well-educated, well-spoken, and versatile. To top it off, he grew up a planter's son, so he can pass as one of them. He's particularly skilled in cartography. More importantly for this mission, he can memorize maps and redraw them weeks later, which reduces the risk of being caught with sensitive material while in the field. Dressed down and streaked with soot, he could easily pass as a peddler and, with some training, even a tinkerer."

"Tinkering is simple enough to teach," Zacharie said. "I could show him how to solder and supply him with the necessary tools. My main concern is whether he can defend himself if attacked."

"As I mentioned, he served with Pinkerton. His men are trained in handling sidearms and self-defense," Banks assured him.

"When would he be available?"

"I can deploy him whenever you're ready. He's no longer affiliated with the Union Secret Service since Pinkerton resigned following McClellan's removal by the President."

"He sounds like a good choice," Zacharie said. "So, Pinkerton no longer gathers intelligence for the government?"

"Stanton appointed Lafayette Baker to replace him as the head of the Union Intelligence Service."

"So, what about Pinkerton?"

"He's here in New Orleans."

Once more, Zacharie was taken by surprise. "The President never mentioned any of this to me."

"Pinkerton now works through his private agency in New Orleans to investigate contractors defrauding the government. As you can imagine, the ground has been fertile here for some time for war profiteers."

"I must ask you to forgive me, General, if all of this seems a bit overwhelming," Zacharie said.

"Not at all," Banks returned with a smile. "It's a lot to take in. I occasionally talk with Allan about his investigations when they cross into Confederate plots, which also find fertile ground here in New Orleans."

"So, is this man of yours available immediately?"

"Yes, although I'd like to give him time to gather intelligence on Port Hudson from my sources. He can study my maps, speak with Southerners dodging Confederate conscription, and tap into the information we've obtained from contrabands fleeing the plantations. Once he's fully briefed, I'll notify you."

"Thank you, General," Zacharie said, satisfied. "He sounds like just the man I need."

Banks regarded the doctor for a moment before nodding. "I will rely on your judgment."

"There is one more favor I'd like to ask," Zacharie said hesitantly.

"Go on, Doctor," Banks said, leaning back in his chair.

"I neglected to request that Rabbi Gutheim, though registered as an enemy as I mentioned earlier, be allowed to remain in New Orleans a while longer. He's been instrumental in assisting members of his congregation who refuse to sign the Oath of Allegiance and are preparing to leave the city."

Banks paused, considering the request. "I have already spoken with Rabbi Gutheim and know his Southern sympathies. I gave him a month to help his congregants before carrying out his own plans for deportation."

"Thank you, General," Zacharie replied with a respectful nod. "I truly appreciate the courtesy. It will serve us well with the portion of the Jewish population that remains."

25

Tête-à-Tête at Tujague's

Thursday, January 22

At eight o'clock in the morning, Dr. Zacharie and his secretary, Charles, strolled along the uneven cobblestones. The air buzzed with the promise of the day's commerce in the French Market, a vibrant blend of industry and camaraderie under the morning sun.

Vendors were setting up their stalls, their voices rising above the rhythmic thuds of wooden crates being unloaded from wagons. The scent of freshly cut herbs mingled with the earthy aroma of ripe vegetables while fishmongers displayed their shimmering catches on crushed ice, hawking their goods to early customers. A flower seller carefully arranged festive bundles of red camellias and delicate paperwhites with golden throats, their midwinter blooms drawing admiration from passersby.

The men's stroll brought them to the storied façade of Tujague's restaurant, its timeless exterior merging with the lively spirit of the market. At that moment, the juxtaposition of genteel tradition against commerce's raw, bustling energy painted a portrait of a vibrant city poised on the cusp of another promising day.

Inside Tujague's, bartenders worked briskly behind the tin-mirrored walnut bar, their busy hands a blur as they washed and polished glasses to a pristine shine. The soft clink of crystal punctuated the early morning preparations, a rhythmic prelude to the day's bustle.

"Bonjour, Messieurs," a uniformed waiter greeted them, his eyes briefly assessing Zacharie's ample frame. "Are you here for our Butcher's Breakfast? We are famous for the hearty fare we have served the butchers across the street for years."

Zacharie replied, "I lived in New Orleans in the late '40s when another establishment occupied this spot. I've yet to experience your cuisine."

The waiter flashed a well-practiced smile. *"Eh bien, alors, Bienvenu, Monsieur.* Tujague's has been serving guests since '56. Please allow me to show you and your companion to a table so you may order your drinks." Turning to Charles, he added, "We also offer lighter fare if that's more to your liking."

"Is there a secluded area where we could have a private conversation?" Zacharie asked, deliberately ignoring the waiter's thinly veiled assumptions about their dining preferences based on appearances. He had always felt that confronting waitstaff was rarely a wise move. In his experience, letting the tip express dissatisfaction was better.

"Oui, Monsieur," the waiter replied, glancing over his pince-nez glasses, the lenses nearly as thick as the bottoms of glass soda water bottles. "We have a private dining room available just beyond the bar. Please, follow me."

The waiter led them past a well-stocked stand-up bar into a cozy dining room. Inside, six tables, each covered with white linen, were carefully arranged and set with cut glass goblets and gleaming silverware.

Ushering his guests to a table at the far end of the room, the waiter pulled out their chairs with a practiced flourish. "Would you gentlemen care for a glass of Champagne or brandy? Or perhaps a cup of coffee?"

"I'll have a glass of California Merlot," Zacharie said.

"May I suggest a sample of our featured Bordeaux Merlot?" the waiter offered, barely masking a faint disapproving frown.

"That will be fine," Zacharie replied, sensing the waiter's subtle disdain for any Merlot that didn't originate from Bordeaux. As he watched the man retreat, Zacharie reflected on the French maxim *chacun à son goût,* a gentle reminder to respect individual tastes. Yet, when it came to wine, he mused, the sentiment seemed to carry little weight in French circles.

The waiter turned to Charles. "And for you, Monsieur?"

"I'll have coffee," Charles said. "Black and without chicory, please."

The waiter looked aghast. "Monsieur! We do not adulterate our coffee with ground weeds' roots."

"I certainly hope not," Charles quipped, growing weary of the waiter's arrogance.

"Très bien," the waiter replied, his smile faltering momentarily before he quickly regained his composure and moved on. "Please make yourselves comfortable while I bring your wine and *café noir—sans chicorée."*

When the waiter left, Charles remarked, "That fellow reminds me of a poodle I once owned. When he disapproved of my commands, he'd scurry under the table, let out a muffled bark, and glare at me. I've since called that behavior the 'poodle bark.'"

Zacharie quipped, "Well, they're both French, after all."

Charles chuckled. "Yes, I suppose they are."

"You hear that Butcher's Breakfast the waiter mentioned? It sounds hearty."

"We could share," Charles suggested.

"I think it might be too much even for the two of us," Zacharie chuckled, rubbing his belly.

"I'll have to ask if they serve crepes. Without a menu, I have no idea what else they have."

"Now, about my breakfast meeting with the general yesterday," Zachary began. "I'm eager to hear your thoughts on what I shared with you on our way here."

Charles leaned in and looked over his spectacles. "From what you've told me about Banks, he seems to embody the polish and refinement of a political general: impeccable table manners, skilled in conversation, and well-versed in diplomacy. Yet, as you pointed out, he lacks formal military training."

Zacharie nodded. "Exactly. As Stonewall Jackson showed us in the Shenandoah, General Banks is far more adept at politics than battlefield strategy."

"And based on what you've told me about his reaction to Butler's brother's letter, it sounds as though the general, even though he is transactional, as you noted, is also surprisingly naïve when it comes to business matters."

"Yes," Zacharie agreed. "He's a man of ethics. That's why I held back from suggesting that a few well-placed bribes would open doors to vital information without him needing to dirty his hands by pocketing any money."

Charles raised an eyebrow. "It's surprising he hasn't realized that pre-war ethical standards no longer apply."

"Precisely," Zacharie said, nodding. "On that note, I recently met a blockade runner named Betterton. He's well connected within the Confederacy and tried to smuggle British arms through Cuba to Mobile, hidden in hogsheads of sugar."

"Clever," Charles noted.

"It might have worked," Zacharie continued, "if the Confederates had held up their end of the deal. Betterton was furious when the shipment was returned, leaving him stuck with the costs."

"Do you think Butler caught wind of it?"

"No. New Orleans still trades openly with Cuba and Mobile for food. Smuggling arms amid such trade wouldn't have been easy to detect among the crates. If Betterton had been caught, he'd be on Ship Island by now. The real mystery is why the Confederates refused the delivery."

"That is odd," Charles agreed.

"*Voilà, Messieurs,*" the waiter announced grandly as he returned, expertly rolling a cart beside the table. With a flourish, he presented a bottle of wine to Zacharie. "A fine Merlot from Saint-Émilion." He carefully decanted a sample, then turned to pour Charles a cup of coffee. After serving them both, he asked, "How is the wine, Monsieur?"

"It is satisfactory," Zacharie replied, though he privately admired its richness.

The waiter, visibly disappointed, raised an eyebrow. "We do have a Château Ausone. It's priced at thirty dollars. Shall I bring a bottle?"

"Perhaps another time," Zacharie responded without hesitation, silently noting that the price of the wine was almost the same as the total of his train and steamboat tickets to New Orleans.

The waiter filled Zacharie's glass. "Please take your time with the menu, Messieurs. I'll return shortly."

Charles took a sip of his coffee.

"How is your coffee, Monsieur?" the waiter asked midstride.

"Fine. Thank you," he said.

"*Avec plaisir, Monsieur,*" the waiter replied, casting a final glance over his shoulder as he quipped, "And without chicory," then closed the door behind him.

Zacharie laughed, nearly spilling his wine. "The poodle bark!"

"Indeed," Charles said with a grin. "Impeccably delivered, and his timing was right on the mark. Though I wasn't about to admit this is the best coffee I've ever had."

"Nor was I going to tell him the wine is outstanding," Zacharie added, silently conceding that it surpassed his usual California Merlot.

Once the laughter subsided, Charles asked, "What's your endgame with this Betterton fellow?"

"I'm still working on that," Zacharie replied. "I've been weighing the idea of using his ties to the Confederacy to float a peace proposal through Judah Benjamin. He's a fellow Israelite and one of the few men who has Jefferson Davis's ear."

Charles looked stunned. "Richmond? A peace treaty? You haven't mentioned this before."

"My ideas are still forming, but any proposal must include compensated emancipation and return of property rights for their land. That might sweeten the deal for Judah and Davis since they lost their plantations and all their slaves when they fled to Richmond."

"The President has already tried that in the border states," Charles pointed out. "Even they refused. What else could you offer?"

"Settling the Confederacy's war debt with Europe. They're in desperate need of hard currency, as the blockade has severely diminished their cotton trade with England and France, despite the efforts of blockade runners."

"That's a tremendous economic undertaking," Charles said, "given how the war has drained federal resources."

"It pales compared to the cost of continuing the war," Zacharie countered. "Bonds could fund it and be paid off over time."

Charles shook his head, his expression thoughtful. "The Union's national debt is already skyrocketing. It's approaching a billion dollars now," he said, sipping his coffee. "I doubt that even a generous offer like that would work. In my opinion, Southern pride is what's driving this rebellion now. It's no longer about politics or economics. Now, it's about defending their honor. They're willing to fight and die for that to the last man."

"Pride goeth before destruction," Zacharie quoted from Proverbs. "Still, the recent French intervention in Mexico might offer another gambit to consider."

"Oh? How so?" Charles asked, intrigued.

"If the President proposes a temporary truce to deal with the French in Mexico, it could pause the fighting here, at least for a while."

"And after that?" Charles pressed, leaning forward.

Zacharie thought for a moment. "Our country has a history of territorial expansion. Maybe allowing the South to extend beyond Mexico to Cuba or Nicaragua could ease secessionist tensions."

Charles nodded slowly, carefully considering Zacharie's words. "Expanding southward has been a lingering dream of the Knights of the Golden Circle since the fifties."

"Exactly," Zacharie agreed. "It's unconventional, but it could be a solution. It would allow the South to save face and, at the same time, expand its empire."

Charles raised an eyebrow. "And how do you plan on contacting Confederate leadership?"

"That's where Betterton comes in with his ties. But first, I need to earn his trust. Meanwhile, I'm recruiting peddler spies to gather intelligence for General Banks while supplying the Confederates with shoes and medical supplies."

Charles smirked. "And you're confident the rebels won't suspect anything?"

"They'll see the familiar sight of Jewish peddlers with wagons full of supplies crossing enemy lines and believe what they see with their own eyes."

Charles chuckled. "Sounds like you're juggling a lot: negotiating peace with the Confederates while running a network of peddler spies and working in an occasional patient with aching feet."

Before Zacharie could respond, the waiter reappeared. "Your breakfast will be out shortly, messieurs."

"But you haven't given us menus to order," Zachary said.

"Monsieur, aside from the Butcher's Breakfast, we offer a set fare."

"In that case, bring everything but the grits."

The waiter rolled his eyes dramatically. "*Chacun à son goût.*"

Zacharie and Charles exchanged amused glances as the waiter departed, stifling their laughter until neither could hold it back. Their earlier tension melted away as they laughed together.

"*Chacun à son goût*, indeed," Zacharie quipped, raising his glass to Charles in a playful toast. "Though I daresay shunning grits in the South is nearly as unforgivable as ordering a California Merlot in a French restaurant."

26

DR. ZACHARIE GOES TO SHUL

fter walking a block from the St. Charles Hotel, Dr. Zacharie paused on the corner of Canal Street and St. Charles Avenue, drawing his coat tighter against the morning chill. A damp wind set him shivering as he weighed his options. Though he had intended to walk the remaining distance, the thought of braving three more blocks on foot lost its appeal. With a resigned glance toward the tracks, he stepped toward the approaching streetcar, deciding to ride the rest of the way to visit Rabbi Gutheim.

The clip-clop of hooves on the cobblestones grew louder as the streetcar approached, accompanied by the soft creak of the wooden car and the metallic clatter of steel wheels on the iron tracks. The car slowed to a stop with a smooth grind and a jolt.

Stepping aboard, he navigated his way down the narrow central aisle. Toward the back, he spotted a single empty seat beside an elderly Negro, who glanced up without speaking and shifted to make room for him.

The sight of a Negro man on a New Orleans streetcar struck Zacharie as peculiar. Such a scene would have been inconceivable when he lived in the city years ago, but it was clear that times were changing.

As the streetcar clattered away, Zacharie turned up his collar in a futile attempt to shield himself from the biting chill that swept through the open vehicle. He leaned forward, peering at the shops lining Canal Street. Some storefronts stood shuttered and silent, their windows boarded up. Others buzzed with the clamor of renovations, as the building was being refitted for new tenants who had recently arrived from the North.

When the driver reined in the streetcar's horses at Bourbon Street in front of the synagogue, Zacharie stepped onto the street, grateful he hadn't attempted to brave even the short three-block walk in the biting cold.

He paused to admire the neoclassical Greek elegance of the Dispersed of Judah synagogue, its towering white Ionic marble columns exuding timeless dignity. As he climbed the stairs to the portico, his eyes were drawn to the imposing carved mahogany doors, their craftsmanship a testament to the artisans who shaped them. Looking upward at the pediment, he marveled at the intricate golden depiction of the Burning Bush, an iconic scene from the story of the Exodus. With a quiet sense of reverence, he stepped forward to turn the doorknob and push open one of the massive double doors.

Inside, he discovered a warmly lit, mahogany-paneled vestibule. Approaching the *tzedakah* box for charitable donations, he pulled out his leather purse and retrieved a Gold Eagle, which he dropped into the slot. The coin landed with a resonating metallic clink, joining many of its kind. He reached for a yarmulke in a wicker basket hanging on the wall. Placing it awkwardly on the crown of his head, he tried to recall the last time he had worn one.

Entering the sanctuary, he sat at the aisle end of a back pew to wait for Rabbi Gutheim. While he waited, his eyes were drawn to the stunning stained-glass windows that lined the sanctuary. Each panel depicted symbols of Jewish tradition: the Tablets of the Law, a menorah with glowing candles, and a shofar. The sunlight streaming through the glass bathed the interior in a rainbow of colors — deep sapphire, ruby red, emerald green, and golden amber — creating a warm, reverent glow.

The flickering gas flame of the Eternal Light, suspended from the ceiling as a timeless symbol of God's presence and the enduring strength of the Jewish faith, cast a gentle, golden glow across the sacred carved wood of the Ark of the Covenant, which stood behind the bimah.

As he sat waiting, the delicate, sweet odor of lavender, lingering from the recently scrubbed pews, stirred memories of the days when he and his young friends had volunteered to clean the pews with the fragrant Kosher soap. He reflected on how different it was from the soap used in churches, made with pig lard. Although each had its distinctive pleasant scent, the difference was so pronounced that even blind congregants would be able to notice it immediately upon entering the house of worship.

His Jewish identity, he reflected, was rooted in birthright, derived from being born to a Jewish mother rather than from strict observance. Although he couldn't recall the last time he had stepped into a synagogue since marrying outside his faith, he felt that his absence from Sabbath services hadn't weakened his bond with the community, nor had it diminished his sense of duty to serve those less fortunate than himself.

Lost in reverie, he recalled attending Sabbath services with his family in England, the rhythmic cadence of Hebrew prayers filling the air. His mind drifted to his Bar Mitzvah, a defining moment on his thirteenth birthday when he came of age under Jewish law. It was a momentous occasion, the congregation watching as he stood before the Torah, his parents seated proudly in the front row.

He vividly remembered his trembling thirteen-year-old hand guiding the *Yad*, a silver pointer intricately shaped like a miniature hand with an outstretched index finger, across the hand-lettered Hebrew text. Moving carefully from right to left, he traced each sacred word in the Torah scroll, with the *Yad* ensuring no direct contact with the parchment. The memory of that day, filled with solemnity and pride, lingered like the echo of ancient prayers.

Throughout the ages, congregations remained tightly knit through participation in weekly Sabbath services, observance of holidays, and performance of rites of passage from birth to death. This spiritual connection endured the challenges of plagues, famines, persecutions, wars, and periods of bitter captivity.

Echoing like voices of ghosts from the past, he recalled a sorrowful chorus reciting the Mourner's *Kaddish*, honoring the loss of their loved ones. He could still hear their chant, "יִתְגַּדַּל וְיִתְקַדַּשׁ שְׁמֵהּ רַבָּא בְּעָלְמָא דִּי בְרָא כִרְעוּתֵהּ," with the distinctive cadence of Hebrew poetry, which relied on alliteration, wordplay, and chiasmus to emphasize thought, emotion, and meaning through its structure, rather than the rhyme and strict meter typical of Christian liturgy.

He always marveled at the words of the *Kaddish*. He found it paradoxical that, while the mourner's faith was often shaken by their loss, they recited a prayer that purposefully omitted any mention of death or dying. Instead, their chant exalted the greatness of God, signifying that even in their time of grief, they acknowledged the unspeakable majesty of their Creator.

When he was young, he recited the *Kaddish*, his voice high and wavering with the fragile tone of adolescence, tearful with grief as he mourned his grandparents, honoring their memory year by year. As time passed, his voice deepened with age, steady as he spoke it again for his parents, their names carried on his lips with solemn resolve. He knew that someday, his children would recite the *Kaddish* for him, and their children would do the same for their parents, forming an unbroken chain that linked the living to the dead, generation to generation, through the ages.

Tonight, after offering a prayer while lighting the Sabbath candles to welcome Shabbat, congregants would recite a solemn memorial for loved ones recently lost on the battlefield. At the back of the sanctuary stood a long table beneath the Yahrzeit memorial wall, where plaques honored those who had fallen. New names lay waiting there, yearning to join the ranks of brothers already enshrined on the wall above.

"Rabbi Gutheim!" Zacharie called cheerfully, rising to greet the spiritual leader as he entered a side door near the bimah.

"Shalom, Dr. Zacharie," greeted the distinguished man in his late forties, his wire-rimmed glasses catching the light as he approached with deliberate steps. His neatly trimmed beard and wavy hair gave him an air of refinement, while the clipped precision of his German accent spoke of his upbringing. "Welcome to our shul. It has been a while. When I received your letter, I remembered you coming to New Orleans in the late '40s and leaving shortly after." He stroked his beard thoughtfully. "I can't seem to recall why you left."

Zacharie had hoped to avoid discussing his departure from New Orleans, which involved some allegedly shady business transactions for which he was never formally charged.

"Rabbi, the opportunities in California were far better in '49," Zacharie said, shaking Rabbi Gutheim's hand, carefully omitting any mention of the fortune he'd amassed selling supplies to miners during the gold rush. Boasting of wealth to a rabbi would spark a conversation about a sizeable charitable contribution. "I was admiring your synagogue."

The rabbi graciously nodded, steering the conversation toward his synagogue rather than delving into the doctor's past. "Much has changed. A year or so after you left New Orleans, my associate Gershom Kursheedt and I convinced our city's most successful businessman, Judah Touro, to acquire the old Christ's church building and renovate it for our Dispersed of Judah synagogue. Its Greek architectural design, lacking a steeple, made it a suitable structure. Judah purchased the building and allowed the congregation to take their Christian-themed stained-glass windows, Jesus and all. He also generously provided them with a piece of land for their new church. As a result, our congregation experienced significant growth, leading us to consider moving. About six years later, we constructed the edifice you see now."

"It is certainly magnificent."

"Thank you. We are very proud of it. It's a shame Judah passed in '54 before he could see the full impact of his generosity. Why don't we take our conversation into my office, Doctor? I think that you would find it more comfortable." The rabbi winked at Zacharie. "When I met with the building committee, I insisted that there be no padding on these miserable hardwood pews. I wanted to keep the congregation awake during the service."

The rabbi and the doctor sat facing each other in comfortable, high-backed leather chairs. Shelves heavy with worn volumes lined the modest office, their spines catching what little remained of the day's light filtered through a single window. In deference to the Sabbath, the rabbi had not lit the gas wall sconces or the kerosene lamp on his desk, honoring the sacred prohibition against kindling flame after sundown.

The rabbi recited the *Kiddush* over wine, praising God for the gift of the fruit of the vine. "How is your wine?" the rabbi asked after Zacharie took a sip from the ornately crafted silver *Kiddush* cup, its surface adorned with raised embellishments of grapevines, leaves, and clusters of grapes.

"It has a pleasant bouquet," Zacharie said, choosing his words diplomatically to avoid mentioning his preference for the drier, more expensive Merlot from his favorite California vintner over regionally made kosher wines. He also preferred sipping his wine from a crystal glass, where he could fully appreciate its rich, deep color and clarity, rather than from a silver cup that concealed it. The silver cup, he felt, also interfered with the delicate kiss of the wine like an unwanted chaperone.

"Will you be staying for Shabbat services, Doctor?" the rabbi asked.

Zacharie shifted uncomfortably. It had been quite a while since he had attended services, and the rabbi's inquiry felt more like an invitation than a question. "I'm sorry, Rabbi. I appreciate your hospitality, but I am already engaged for the evening."

"So, how was your sojourn to New Orleans?" the rabbi asked, setting his wine on a side table, smoothly moving the conversation forward as if his invitation had not been declined with what seemed like a thinly veiled excuse.

"Once President Lincoln overturned General Grant's General Order 11, I could take the train here without delay."

The rabbi's expression darkened. "Ah, yes. General Order 11. What do you know of the Jewish delegation that traveled to Washington to petition the President to rescind that despicable order?"

"I was not aware of that. I only knew that Grant issued his order sometime in December last year."

"That day is etched in my memory. It was the second night of Chanukah when the celebration of light was eclipsed by the decree that fell like a shadow over every Jewish household."

"I have to admit, I was unaware of the actual date," Zacharie said. "I only found out later when I read an article in *The Jewish Messenger*."

"Grant's decree caused quite a stir among our Southern brothers and sisters in the areas under Grant's command. The word spread quickly. Entire communities feared banishment and the loss of their homes and businesses. Paducah's Jewish delegation of businessmen, led by Cesar Kaskel, arrived in Washington on Friday, January 3rd. When he met with the president, he spoke eloquently and presented numerous letters of introduction from Cincinnati's Jewish leaders."

Zacharie listened intently, wondering why the President had never informed him of this delegation.

"The president sent General Grant a telegram the same day ordering the revocation of General Order 11."

"So, that explains why my pass was issued the following Monday," Zacharie said.

The rabbi chuckled, leaning into the conversation with a mischievous expression. "Let me share something I found humorous about the whole affair. Grant's antipathy toward the Jews was bad enough, but what got his dander up was when his father approached him privately at his headquarters, pleading for a permit on behalf of the Mack brothers of New York to buy confiscated cotton in occupied Union territory. Ironically, the Mack brothers are Jews and happen to be the largest suppliers of Union uniforms."

Zacharie slapped his thigh and burst out laughing. "Of all the twists of fate! Grant's own father was doing business with Jews to make the uniforms he and his men were wearing."

"What I would give to have been a fly in his tent!" the rabbi said. "When the General refused to issue the permit to the Mack brothers simply because they were Jews, his father stomped out of his tent cursing and yelling, 'I hope you wear a hole in your breeches big enough to show your ass! And when you do, don't expect a new pair anytime soon!'"

Zacharie reached for his handkerchief to wipe the tears from his eyes. "Rabbi, I can't recall the last time I had such a good laugh. Your story certainly takes some of the sting out of Grant's order."

"His hatred of Jews had blinded him," the rabbi said. "Only a blind man would think that trade between the Confederacy and the Union ended when the conflict began. And it's not just Jews who are involved in the transactions. Just keep your eyes open and look around right here in New Orleans. Last year, it was Butler and his brother Andrew, and now it's that treasury agent, Denison, Salmon Chase's nephew, taking the lead. But they are not alone. It's everywhere, on every street. Fortunes are being made daily. Sign the Oath of Allegiance, drop a few gold coins here and there, point your finger at the Jews, and anything is possible."

Zacharie smiled, appreciating the rabbi's candor and the shift in the conversation toward his mission. "Rabbi, one of the reasons for my extended stay in New Orleans is to assist our people who wish to travel into the Confederacy but lack the means to do so. To accomplish that, I have had to forge some unusual alliances, including a relationship with General Banks."

The rabbi's expression turned solemn. "I will share with you what I tell all my members: in all things, you must follow your heart. In this case, I understand that you are better positioned to help your fellow Israelites if you have permission from the enemy. As you may have heard, Dr. Zacharie, I have refused to sign the mandatory Oath of Allegiance. Consequently, at some point, probably sooner rather than later, I will have to leave New Orleans with the other registered enemies. It's like the sword of Damocles hanging over my head, never knowing when it will drop. However, I can share the names of some fellow Israelites who have sought my assistance in leaving."

"I promise that I will work towards ensuring safe passage for our people who want to reunite with their families deeper into the Confederacy," Zacharie assured the rabbi. "Under occupation, I understand that some of them have faced near starvation for refusing to sign the Oath of Allegiance."

"That is true," the rabbi said, his tone tinged with sorrow. "Under General Butler's command, the Free Market callously withheld even the most basic necessities from those who maintained allegiance to the Confederacy. Although General Banks has taken a more tempered approach, especially concerning the impoverished masses regardless of their loyalties, challenges persist for those on the registered enemies list. It's a perilous position, casting a perpetual shadow over their lives. Fortunately, despite their differences, Rabbi Illowy and General Banks get along quite well. After I've left, you can be a good point of communication between them."

"That's good to know," Zacharie said, pleased to hear that the rabbinical community shared Banks's view that they worked well together. "General Banks shows promise in addressing the city's poverty without the severity of his predecessor." He paused, then added, "When I met with him recently, he mentioned his desire to house Colored Troops on a Touro property. If that could be arranged, I believe it would serve our community well."

"I'm certain Rabbi Illowy and I can arrange to accommodate the general's needs," the rabbi said. He fell silent, a look of concern crossing his face. "May I ask you another favor, Doctor?"

"Anything within my power, Rabbi," Zacharie said, with a trace of guilt clouding his conscience as he couldn't fully disclose his plans of recruiting peddler spies.

"Shortly after the occupation, Judah Touro's trust endowed us with our version of the Free Market, enabling us to distribute food to needy people. We've also offered clothing and, in certain instances, limited shelter in some of his storefronts that have been vacated along Canal Street."

"I'm heartened to learn that our people are receiving at least some support."

"However, some face more pressing needs than others, and our resources are limited."

Zacharie braced himself, anticipating the rabbi's request.

"There is a young lady in our congregation who deeply concerns me," the rabbi said. "She is a beautiful woman with one of the fairest souls I have ever known. Tragically, she lost her husband at Shiloh last year. I officiated at his funeral. Last fall, her sister, who lives with her, was blessed with a son, Noah, and I was honored to perform his bris. Regrettably, the baby's father returned from Shiloh without both arms. Before the war, both her brother-in-law and her husband were attorneys and provided well for their families. Now, the brother-in-law requires constant care, and there is no family income."

"That is indeed most unfortunate," Zacharie said, a note of empathy in his voice. "Is there any way I might assist?"

"I'm glad you asked," the rabbi said with a smile. "Regarding the peddlers you plan to employ for travel into the Confederacy, are you willing to compensate them generously for their efforts, considering the dangerous nature of their work?"

"Quite well, Rabbi. I've arranged to supply each of them with a wagon load of goods, a travel allowance, and a salary for their families while they're away. As a bonus, they keep the money from their sales."

"Excellent," the rabbi said. "And would you consider choosing a woman?"

Zacharie paused, considering the perils of the mission. "Yes. Given the right one."

"Could you speak with the woman I mentioned? See if she might be someone you could employ?"

"I'd be happy to speak with her, Rabbi. I'll certainly retain her if she's suitable for the mission."

"Good. I'll jot down her name and the address where you will find her tomorrow. When she spoke with me, it was clear she was desperate for money, mentioning her intention to seek employment in the morning."

"What kind of employment is she looking for?"

"The kind that many decent women throughout the ages have turned to when they have exhausted all other options to support themselves and their family."

"I see," Zacharie said thoughtfully, grasping the delicate nature of the situation as he pondered how best to approach General Banks about involving a woman in the mission. Then, he recalled that Allan Pinkerton had credited one of his female spies with infiltrating the conspirators in the Baltimore Plot.

The rabbi stood and walked over to his desk, where he retrieved a pen and paper. After jotting down the address of *La Maison du Soleil Levant*, he handed it to Zacharie.

Zacharie folded the paper and placed it in his vest pocket. He hesitated, deliberating the wisdom of his next question, considering the rabbi's loyalties to the Confederacy. However, driven by curiosity, he decided to ask anyway.

"Rabbi, I have always wondered how Jews, like Judah Benjamin, who left his plantation here in New Orleans to join Jefferson Davis as a member of his Cabinet, could bring himself to own slaves, given our people's history."

"Ah, yes. Judah Benjamin, the brains of the Confederacy," Rabbi Gutheim said, stepping to his bookshelf to retrieve a volume of the teachings of Maimonides. Returning to his seat, he reverently leafed through the pages. "In ancient times, following the Exodus, we read that God spoke to the Israelites and set forth the laws of enslaving both Israelites and prisoners of war from other tribes. At that time in history, chattel slavery, such as we have here in the South, was forbidden for Israelite slaves but sanctioned for slaves taken from other tribes."

Zacharie nodded, reminiscing about his readings from the Torah during his youth.

"However," the rabbi said, "by the time of Maimonides in the 12th century, this esteemed rabbi proclaimed that slavery, in the sense of owning other human beings as property, is nothing short of idolatry. He argued that believing one person could own another is akin to playing God."

"I did not know that," Zacharie said, appreciating the rabbi's knowledge of Jewish history.

"Few Jews do," the rabbi said, carefully placing the book of Maimonides's teachings on the table beside his chair. "And it's not a popular topic for me to discuss here in New Orleans, especially considering the daily slave auctions that were held under the dome at the St. Louis Hotel before the occupation."

Zacharie nodded in understanding.

The rabbi continued, "Even so, I doubt discussing it would make much difference. Jews here, like many in the diaspora throughout history, have assimilated, adopting the customs of those around them. In New Orleans, many proudly identify as devout Jews, just as others see themselves as devout Christians, yet have no qualms about owning slaves to advance their economic interests. I'm certain you've noticed how easily most people, regardless of faith, can compartmentalize their religious beliefs from their business practices."

Zacharie paused, considering the rabbi's words. "It's true; people often set aside their morals when profit is involved. What I've found even more troubling, though, is how Christians sometimes turn to the Bible itself, citing Noah's curse on his son, Ham, to justify slavery."

"That story is found in Genesis," the rabbi explained. "The King James Version, which Christians often cite, quotes Noah saying, 'Cursed be Canaan; a servant of servants shall he be unto his brethren.' However, the passage says nothing about Ham's skin color changing due to the curse. In Jewish tradition, Noah's curse is understood as a punishment for Ham's failure to honor his father, even when he was naked and drunk after too much wine. The curse condemned Ham, not his progeny, to servitude, specifically to serve his brothers."

The rabbi gave a playful grin. "I've always believed the world's first vintner deserved a reprieve. After all, Noah was a good provider and walked with God. Besides, his singular indiscretion was being drunk and naked in his own tent, not riding a camel through the desert while drinking and naked."

Zacharie was amused by the rabbi's absurdist humor and remembered it was a frequent rabbinical practice to reinforce important moral truths with humor.

The rabbi continued his Torah lesson. "The moral of the story is that a dutiful son would have respected his father's dignity by covering his nakedness and allowing him to sleep undisturbed. Instead, by spreading gossip about the incident to shame him, he brought dishonor to himself. It is challenging to see how this story could be construed to justify slavery since, as I mentioned, neither race nor slavery is mentioned."

Zacharie said, "Perhaps it's because so much gets lost in translation."

"Don't get me started on corrupt translations and the motivations behind those who make them!" the rabbi exclaimed, throwing up his hands. "How Christian philosophers derive their concept of the Trinity from the Creation story is beyond me. I've never known a better example of *petitio principii*. The Hebrew text uses the word *na'aseh* for the Godhead, which is indeed the first-person plural, causing some confusion. Yet we have no trouble accepting the 'royal we' of British monarchs. Besides, the *Shema* proclaims, 'Hear, O Israel, the Lord is our God, the Lord is One.'"

While theological debates weren't his strong suit, Zacharie admired the rabbi's expertise. He was particularly impressed by his use of the Latin term *petitio principii* for "begging the question," which cleverly referenced the logical fallacy of assuming the conclusion within one of the premises.

The rabbi finished his lesson by opening a drawer in his desk and producing a list, which he handed to Zacharie. "Rabbi Illowy has worked with me to compile this list of families from all the congregations in New Orleans who are seeking to leave the city and reunite with their relatives deeper within the Confederacy. I will be joining them eventually. Can I trust it to your safekeeping?"

Zacharie took the list and spoke sincerely. "Rabbi, I am truly honored by your trust. I will do everything in my power to assist these families."

"It is a great mitzvah, Doctor. Many of them will need provisions for their journey."

"I am happy to perform it, Rabbi."

"My blessings go with them. It is not as though I am losing my congregation," the rabbi assured him. "You must understand that I've witnessed a considerable influx of Jewish bankers and merchants from New York, starting not long after Butler's arrival and continuing once Grant's order was lifted. The entire nature of commerce in the city is evolving as Union supporters take the place of Confederate loyalists."

"I am pleased to hear that the congregation remains robust," Zacharie said.

"Much more so than it was. It's a surprising twist in the war. New York Jews tend to be more observant than Jews in New Orleans. In New York, they live within their communities, marry within their faith, and bring up their families within the synagogue's embrace. Here in New Orleans, the Jewish community isn't as tightly knit, interfaith marriages are common, and there is little concern about keeping kosher where shellfish are abundant..."

Rabbi Gutheim halted midsentence, his words giving him pause. "I suppose, in a way, I should be content to have a more observant congregation now, but I am not." He chuckled, his laughter tinged with a sardonic edge. "The transgressors in the extreme Reform camp used to give me something to kvetch about. Though truth be told, I lean far more Reform than Orthodox myself."

Zacharie sat quietly, listening to the rabbi's genuine affection for old New Orleans, with its nonobservant congregation and all its imperfections revealed by the tears he seemed to be fighting back. Perhaps, he reflected, silent acceptance was the wiser response.

"Well, Dr. Zacharie," the rabbi said as he rose, slipping a hand into his vest to draw out his pocket watch, "as my Cuban congregants say in these trying times, *'Al pan, pan, y al vino, vino.'* Bread is bread, and wine is wine. Simply put, it is what it is, and there's no need to embellish the simple truth."

"It's a pleasure to see you again, Rabbi," Zacharie replied, rising with him. "I will return as soon as I have something to report from my meeting with General Banks."

"*Shabbat Shalom*, Dr. Zacharie," the rabbi said. "We have enjoyed our wine and conversed candidly, my friend. Please come and visit me anytime. Now, I must make my preparations to welcome our Sabbath Queen."

"*Shabbat Shalom*, Rabbi," the doctor said, following closely as they headed toward a side door leading to the street.

27

THE HOUSE OF THE RISING SUN

SATURDAY, JANUARY 31

Sunday afternoons were always bustling in "The Bottoms," the bawdy district of the lower French Quarter, stretching along Decatur and Chartres Streets. Today was no exception. Male churchgoers, still basking in their newfound absolution and sated by a Sunday dinner with their families, filled the taverns, priming themselves for another round of carnal delights.

Half-drunk and feeling absolved, the men were primed to open their purses more freely, living proof of the saying, "A fool and his money are soon parted."

Meanwhile, the women preparing to sell their charms and company lounged near the brothel's hearth, bundled in warm shawls as they counted the week's earnings with knowing smiles. Awaiting a new round of customers, they indulged in playful rivalry, debating who had entertained the most prominent gentlemen in town and who had earned the heaviest purse of gold.

Rachel, attired in an attractive, colorful dress and stylish *paletot* coat, strolled down the street of shattered dreams, a path well-trodden by countless desperate young women before her. Her heart raced, and with each step, her palms grew damper. She paused briefly to catch her breath, retrieving a handkerchief from her handbag to dry the tears from her cheeks.

"You are better than this, Rachel," she whispered to herself. The words, laden with self-reproach, cut deeply. "But what other choice do I have?" she asked with a sense of resignation.

She wrestled with her conflicting thoughts, attempting to console herself with the knowledge that she had chosen the most reputable establishment of its kind in town. It was said to be furnished with the finest imported French pieces and designed to attract only the most esteemed gentlemen from New Orleans and the nearby plantations who could afford its discreet, forbidden pleasures.

She took solace in knowing that Union soldiers, constrained by their meager pay, couldn't afford the establishment's luxury. Still, the fear nagged her that its reputation might catch the eye of their superiors. Her thoughts drifted to the St. Louis Hotel hospital, where she had been struck by the sight of soldiers stripped of their uniforms, indistinguishable in their vulnerability. It seemed ironic that the men patronizing *La Maison du Soleil Levant* similarly lacked uniforms. There, in the privacy of the elegant boudoirs, they were no different from the nude women who entertained them. At that moment, everyone was reduced to their common humanity regardless of their side in the conflict or their station in life.

She recalled Isabella from Shakespeare's *Measure for Measure.* In the play, when Isabella faces a corrupt official's proposition to yield to his lust in exchange for her brother's life or resist and witness his execution, she decides to maintain her chastity.

But, unlike Shakespeare's Isabella, she made the selfless choice, ensuring her family's survival over her chastity.

Just ahead on Decatur Street, she saw the sign of *Le Maison du Soleil Levant,* bearing a gilded sunburst emblem harkening to the era of Louis XIV, the "Sun King."

The emblem, a cherished relic of Louisiana's French colonial days, was initially imported by early settlers who longed for feminine companionship in the town, which was nostalgically named for the Duke of Orléans. In 1721, after the death of the Sun King, their prayers were answered when the French government closed *La Salpêtrière* hospital, which housed poor and mentally ill women driven to prostitution, and shipped them to the colony to earn a recumbent income.

Famous for decades, the establishment underwent a change in management after its owner fled to Baton Rouge with her employees on the first day of the occupation. Little did the madame know she would be forced to flee further north to Shreveport when Farragut continued upriver from New Orleans to claim Baton Rouge.

With these thoughts racing through her mind, Rachel was not looking forward to her interview with the house madame. But she now had a sister, a brother-in-law, his caretaker, and an infant nephew to support.

Approaching the door beneath the iconic sign, Rachel reluctantly twisted the doorbell knob and waited. The door creaked open, revealing a grand stairwell in a softly gaslit foyer adorned with rich burgundy wallpaper embossed with fleur-de-lis. Inside stood a svelte young Black man, impeccably dressed in a red velvet waistcoat and embroidered silk vest.

His high, starched collar framed a lace cravat, and his black patent leather shoes gleamed in the dim light.

The man executed a graceful bow, his movements almost theatrical. *"Bienvenue, Mademoiselle,"* he said in a high, clear tenor voice, holding the door open wide.

Rachel hesitated, her palms damp as she clutched her coat. She took a deep breath as she stepped inside, lowering her eyes modestly.

The man bowed once more before vanishing through a side door. Rachel's gaze darted around the lavish foyer, where a magnificent crystal gasolier glittered overhead. Plush floral rugs softened dark oak floors.

Beyond the archway, the expansive living room beckoned. Scarlet drapes with gold tassels framed towering windows overlooking a private courtyard garden. A tiered cast iron fountain stood at its center, surrounded by green benches adorned with fleur-de-lis motifs and interspersed camellias. Their winter-blooming flowers added vibrant accents of red, pink, and white.

Gilded mirrors and paintings of voluptuous ladies adorned the burgundy walls, and marble-topped tables stood between clusters of gilded sofas and chairs in the Napoleonic Second Empire style.

In front of a carved pink marble fireplace, a pianiste played softly while a lone elderly gentleman reclined in a chair, a scantily clad young woman perched on its arm. She stroked his thinning hair and peppered him with feigned kisses, but he seemed indifferent, savoring his whiskey and puffing on a cigar with quiet ennui.

The faint scent of gardenia reached Rachel as a rich feminine voice spoke behind her. *"Bonjour, Mademoiselle."*

She turned to find an elegantly dressed middle-aged woman adorned with jewels, her face painted and cheeks heavily rouged. *"Bienvenue à La Maison du Soleil Levant. Je m'appelle Madame Félicité."*

"Je m'appelle…my name is Rachel," she stammered.

"Enchantée," the Madame replied, noting the refinement in Rachel's French accent as she extended her hand with a gracious smile. Her gaze lingered on Rachel's reddened eyes. "Let's speak in my office, shall we, dear?"

Inside the lavishly appointed, windowless office softly illuminated by the warm glow of gas wall sconces, Rachel sat stiffly on a plush red velvet sofa, her hands clasped tightly in her lap, betraying her unease.

Madame Félicité seated herself opposite, gazing into Rachel's eyes. "I see you're new to the profession," she began gently.

Rachel's voice quivered as she replied. "I've never done anything like this before. I feel so guilty. Truthfully, I don't even know if I can. But… I have no other way to feed my family."

The Madame's expression softened, though her tone remained firm. "Do you honestly think you're the first woman to sit where you are, trembling, doubting herself? You're not, my child. Life doesn't always give us easy choices."

Rachel hesitated, tears brimming in her eyes. "My husband… he died at Shiloh. My brother-in-law came home maimed and needed an attendant to care for him. There's no one left to provide for us but me since my sister has a baby."

Madame Félicité leaned closer, her voice steady. "War takes so much from us. The men fight, they die, and we're left to pick up the pieces and continue our lives. And still, we're called the 'weaker sex.' Tell me, Rachel, when a wife gives herself to her husband, does she always love him?"

Rachel looked down. "No… but that's different."

"Is it?" the Madame pressed. "A wife depends on her husband for her livelihood. She pleases him even when it displeases her, bears his children, cooks and keeps his house, and mends his socks, all for the money he provides. Here, the money you earn is yours. No man beats you for letting dinner get cold, claiming you look at other men, or for not giving him enough attention. Here, you answer only to yourself."

Rachel's voice broke as she whispered, "But what will people say?"

Madame Félicité let out a throaty laugh. "People will always judge women who step outside the roles they've laid out for us. The washerwoman, the maid, the spinster. Each one is scorned just the same, my dear. The question is, will you let their judgment starve your family?"

Rachel wiped her tears. "I'll try. For them, I'll do what I must."

The Madame offered a tender smile. "That's all you can do, child. You're stronger than you think."

The madame stood and said, "Now, why don't you go back into the receiving area and speak with some of the gentlemen while I have a room prepared for you to entertain them?"

Dr. Zacharie stepped down from his cab, handed the driver a silver coin, and adjusted his silk cravat as he approached the door beneath the *Maison du Soleil Levant* sign. Turning the doorbell knob, he waited.

The door opened onto the grand stairwell. Standing before him was a Negro man-servant, impeccably dressed, who bowed with practiced grace. *"Bienvenue, Monsieur, à la Maison du Soleil Levant. Veuillez entrer."*

"Merci," Zacharie said, stepping into the marble-floored foyer and handing off his coat. The man bowed again and disappeared with the coat folded over his arm.

Zacharie paused, taking in the opulence of the décor when a feminine voice behind called, "*Bonjour, Monsieur.*"

Turning, he found Madame Félicité, who smiled with practiced charm. "*Bienvenue à La Maison du Soleil Levant. Comment puis-je vous aider?*"

"*Bonjour, Madame,*" he greeted with a gallant bow. He was painfully conscious that it had been a while since he had spoken French.

The proprietor offered a political smile. "I see that you are English."

"Yes," he said, relieved to revert to his native language.

"Welcome to The House of the Rising Sun, Monsieur. My name is Madame Félicité. How may I be of service?"

"My name is Doctor Zacharie. I am here to see a certain lady."

"Dr. Zacharie. *Quel plaisir.* And may I inquire as to her name?"

"Her name is Rachel."

The madame's countenance mirrored her concern. "Are you here from the Department of Sanitation?'

"No, Madame. I am here as a private citizen."

"She is not ill, is she, Doctor? I have very strict guidelines."

"Not to my knowledge."

She appeared relieved, and then curiosity crossed her face. "Pardon me for asking, Doctor, but are you her father?"

Zacharie was caught off guard. "No. I am of no relation. I have never met her. A friend recommended her to me."

"*Bien,*" she said, her eyebrows lifting in a subtle betrayal of perplexity since Rachel appeared naïve and had not disclosed any prior work history.

"Is she available?"

"Do you see that young dandy sitting in the corner smoking a cigar and eyeing all my girls?"

"Yes."

"He's the son of one of the planters upriver, jaded beyond hope," she said with disdain. "He spends money like the spoiled little boy he is. He spoke with her for a few minutes, and I could have sworn he looked as though he had seen her before. I've already told her to get ready to receive him."

"Would you consider allowing me to see her first?" he asked, retrieving a gold Double Eagle from his vest pocket.

She gave a knowing smile. "I think that can be arranged," she said, taking the coin. "I'll tell him she is indisposed and send one of my other girls over to entertain him."

"Thank you, Madame."

"However, I must first go over the house rules with you," she said firmly, gesturing to the sitting area. "*S'il vous plaît.*"

Zacharie followed Madame Felicité to the first table and pulled out a chair for her.

"May I offer you something to drink?" she asked as she sat across from him.

"A glass of Merlot would be grand."

"French or Californian?"

"Californian," he said, noting her keen discernment. He saw in her the practiced finesse of a madame who could read her clients and cater to their desires without judgment.

Madame Felicité rang the tiny brass bell on the table, and the young man who had first greeted him approached. "*Oui, Madame. Quel est votre plaisir?*"

"*Nous prendrons deux verres de Merlot, s'il vous plaît, Beaux. Prenez un Merlot californien pour le monsieur, et un Merlot français pour moi.*"

"*Oui, Madame,*" the servant said, leaving the table.

"Beau's such a sweet young man," Madame Felicité said with a smile. She lowered her voice to a whisper. "But that's because he's a eunuch. I purchased him recently from one of the local plantations. In my position, one must protect the ladies of the house."

While he knew about planters castrating their male house slaves to protect their women, Zacharie was surprised by her casual approach to the topic. Despite his deep disgust, he hid his reaction, taking twisted satisfaction in her ignorance. She did not realize that castrated males could still perform sexually, even though they could not father children, which some planters' wives had learned firsthand during discreet affairs, emboldened by the absence of consequence.

"Now for the house rules," the madame said, assuming her professional demeanor. "First, clients are required to take a bath before enjoying the company of our ladies. Rachel will assist you with this. You may drink in the room, but please refrain from smoking due to the risk of fire. You may not strike Rachel. You must leave if Rachel notices signs of disease on any part of your person. If at any point she asks you to leave for any other reason, you must also leave. In all instances where you fail to comply with house rules, you will forfeit your payment. Finally, we have a strict two-hour time limit so our ladies can prepare for their next client. Do you understand?"

"Yes," Zacharie said, thinking how "prepare themselves for the next client" alluded to the practice of taking a douche to prevent conception, though it was not entirely effective.

"The fee is twenty dollars per hour, payable in advance in gold."

Zacharie reached into his pocket and retrieved a Double Eagle. "Here," he said, extending his hand with the gold coin.

"Are you certain that you wish to stay for only an hour?" she asked, placing the coin in her handbag with the one he had given her earlier. "The girl you've chosen is a lovely young lady."

"Yes, Madame. I am certain that an hour is all I will require."

Beau reappeared, gracefully balancing a silver tray that bore two cut-crystal glasses of Merlot and an assortment of canapés arranged on two china plates. After carefully placing the tray on the table, he draped crisp white linen napkins across their laps.

Madame Félicité and Dr. Zacharie stood in the upstairs hallway outside of a closed green door adorned with a brass numeral "2."

Madame Felicité tapped on the door. "Rachel?"

"Yes," came a faint voice through the door.

"*Madame Félicité ici.* You have a guest."

Rachel tentatively opened the door.

"This gentleman is a physician," Madame said. "He is a very kind man and quite generous."

Rachel greeted Zacharie and stood aside so he could enter.

Zacharie shut the door behind him and approached the window, sinking into a plush chair draped with crocheted throws. The heavy red velvet curtains were closed, restricting the light from flowing into the room. Still, there was enough illumination to make out a polished brass headboard against one wall and a door suggesting a bathroom beyond.

"Don't be afraid, Rachel," he said. "I am here to help you, not to take advantage of your situation."

Rachel felt confused. Who was this strange, round little man?

"Rabbi Gutheim sent me."

"Rabbi Gutheim?" she asked incredulously, sitting on the edge of the bed.

"Yes. He asked me if I could assist you with your financial problems."

"I don't understand."

"I am here to offer you employment."

"What kind of employment?" she asked incredulously.

"I need peddlers to carry goods into the Confederacy for the troops: shoes, boots, belts, canteens, and the like. I can pay your salary to your family, supply you with money to travel, and allow you to keep the income from your sales."

Rachel was skeptical. What this man was offering seemed too good to be true. "Why me?" she asked.

"As I mentioned, Rabbi Gutheim told me you were in desperate straits. He shared that you had a family to support, including your sister, a crippled brother-in-law, and his caregiver. I believe he also spoke of a little nephew."

"Yes," she said, "That is true. However, Jacob is an attorney, and his old law firm will provide him with an amanuensis and a private office to prepare briefs. Soon, he will be earning an income. Right now, though…"

"'Right now' is precisely why you're here," Zacharie said, slicing cleanly through her protest. He reached into his coat pocket and withdrew three gleaming Double Eagles. He extended his hand and placed the heavy coins—nearly three ounces of gold—into her palm.

"Consider this your first month's wages in advance. I'll see to your family's needs, provide you with a wagon and trade goods, and arrange for a business partner so you won't be forced to make the journey alone."

Clutching the gold coins, she thought of how much food they could buy for her family. "What should I say to Madame Félicité?"

"Tell her whatever you wish," he said, appearing to regard her comment as remarkably naïve. "Inform her that I told you your mother is dying and that you must visit her. To Madame Félicité, you're nothing more than an entry in a ledger. The moment you leave, she will have a replacement ready."

"How shall I find you?"

"You do not have to find me. I will send word when I'm ready to deploy you on your mission."

Rachel remained seated, her hand nervously tracing the richly textured pattern of the imported silk *matelassé* bedspread while her heart wrestled with a complex mix of emotions. Feeling the weight of the gold coins in her hand, she felt a strange sensation coursing through her veins. Was it relief at the prospect of escaping destitution? Or was it fear of leaving home with a man she did not know?

Perhaps it was both.

28

THE BATTLE OF THE HANDKERCHIEFS

Rachel had set out for the St. Charles Hotel to meet with Dr. Zachary, but without warning, she was swept into the tide of fervent well-wishers gathered at the levee to send off their soldiers bound for Union prisons. Draped in warm clothing and shielding themselves with parasols from the bright noon sun, women with children in tow waved their handkerchiefs with fervor, their excitement cutting through the chill of the breeze.

"Look yonder, Joscelyn!" Rachel called to her friend. "It's Xariffa! See how bravely she stands at the front of the crowd, proudly waving her handkerchief."

"Oh, I do so admire her poetry!" Joscelyn said with a dreamy expression in her eyes. "Especially the lines from 'Lake Pontchartrain.'" She struck a dramatic pose, extending her arm as she recited:

> Into thy sapphire water, fair Pontchartrain,
> Slow sinks the setting sun; the distant sail,
> On far horizon's edge, glides hushed and pale,
> Like some escaping spirit o'er the main…

Joscelyn, please desist!" Rachel pleaded, not in the mood for poetry. "Here we are, shivering in the winter's cold, at risk of being trampled, yet you indulge in poetic musings."

Unfazed by her friend's rebuke, Joscelyn said, "Indeed, we are an enthusiastic lot. But what of the crowds and the cold? I don't give a fig! Here we stand, all sisters, stay

ing warm in our wraps as we bid our heartfelt farewells to our beloved soldiers. The St. Charles streetcar was so crowded, I feared I might be struck with apoplexy, crushed between bustling passengers, and chilled to the bone."

Rachel's face fell as she realized the futility of trying to quell her friend's histrionics. Yet, she felt relieved that Jocelyn hadn't noticed that she was no longer dressed in mourning attire less than a year after losing Levi.

Joscelyn paused, her expression softening with concern. "I'm surprised to see you here today, Rachel, with everything you have to attend to at home now, with Jacob returning crippled, and your sister with little Noah to mind."

"Oh," Rachel replied, concealing the reason for her outing, "I had my usual errands to run, and when I saw the crowd gathering at the levee, curiosity got the better of me. That's when I spotted you."

"Didn't you read about this in the papers?" Joscelyn asked incredulously. "This is one of the largest prisoner exchanges of the war. The Federals denied us our Mardi Gras this year, but they can't deny us the chance to see off our heroes. We are a veritable river of women flowing toward the Mississippi, and neither a levee nor a battalion of soldiers can hold us back." She proudly straightened her cockade of red and white satin ribbons, which framed a portrait of New Orleans's beloved native son, General P. T. Beauregard. "Yet one could hardly call us a mob, with so many ladies prominent in culture and social position gathered to wave their handkerchiefs and send our boys off with our heartfelt 'God bless you' and goodbyes.'"

Rachel and Joscelyn braced themselves against several ladies trying to push their way forward to the dock. "Please! I must see my son off!" one of them cried.

"God bless!" Rachel said, struggling to step aside to make way for her fellow citizens. *So many broken bonds*, she mused, *so many families torn apart. What had any of it truly gained them?*

"And to think," Joscelyn said, "this began with only a whisper of the news."

As the two friends reached the front of the teeming crowd, armed Union guards blocked their path. A phalanx of ladies adorned with Confederate cockades confronted them, waving white lace handkerchiefs and shouting, "God bless President Davis! God bless General Beauregard!" and "Hurrah for the Confederacy!"

Others waved palmetto fronds as a tribute to their unyielding spirit. The gesture conveyed a deep sense of solidarity and determination, reflecting the South's historical connection to the palmetto as a symbol of resilience, harkening back to 1776, when palmetto logs at the fort on Sullivan's Island in South Carolina absorbed the force of British cannonballs during the Revolutionary War, securing a crucial American victory.

Rachel pointed to the crowd. "Look, Joscelyn, that lady over there is using the deaf and dumb language to converse with a prisoner onboard the *Empire Parish*."

"Such a marvelous telegraph of the hands!" Joscelyn exclaimed. She cupped her hands around her mouth, amplifying her voice, and asked the lady, "What did your loved one say?"

The lady called back, "My brother told me that the federals taunted them by consuming the fruit and sweets from the baskets all of us sent to our brave soldiers this morning!"

"How disgraceful!" Joscelyn exclaimed. "The good Lord surely has a special place for them in the ninth level of perdition."

News of the stolen fruit and delicacies spread through the crowd like wildfire, sending the women into a frenzy. Suddenly, Union soldiers armed with bayonets marched into their midst, trying to halt their advance toward the ships in the harbor.

"Help! I'm wounded," a woman cried out, tossing a blood-stained handkerchief into the air to signal her distress. Without hesitation, her sister comrades rushed to her aid, using their handkerchiefs to stem the flow of blood from the gash in her hand. Other women hastily pulled their children away from the gruesome sight, the little ones still waving their tiny handkerchiefs.

"Beasts!" one woman shouted. "Murderers!" cried another as the crowd surged forward undaunted, striking at the soldiers and trying to wrench their weapons away. The soldiers hesitated, unwilling to fire on them.

Suddenly, the gate at the top of the gangplank to the *Laurel Hill*, an empty steamer moored beside the *Empire Parish*, gave way to the weight of the masses. Protestors were swept aboard, ignoring the loud warnings of the armed soldiers attempting to guard the gangplank. "Halt! Halt!" they shouted in vain. "There's no captain aboard! You'll either be wrecked or carried out to sea."

"Rachel, look!" Joscelyn shouted at the top of her voice, "Isn't that Xariffa being swept aboard the *Laurel Hill*?"

"Goodness, it is!" Rachel gasped, her eyes widening with alarm. "She looks so helpless."

"Did you hear that soldier shouting that there's no captain aboard?" Joscelyn exclaimed, gripping Rachel's sleeve. "Hold onto something, Rachel! We don't want to be swept away with them."

From ashore, the rustling of countless silk crinolines filled the air, mingling with a chorus of cheers that swelled with excitement at the fearless women who were now taking the helm.

Onboard, Xariffa shivered as the atmosphere surged around her, like the creature in Mary Shelley's *Frankenstein*, jolted to life, brimming with energy and invincibility.

"The ship has broken free of its moorings!" someone shouted. "We're floating downriver without a pilot!"

Cheers erupted as a sense of triumph swept over the crowd. Women surged to the edge of the deck, defying Union soldiers with shouts and raised fists.

"Hallelujah!" the bardess exclaimed, her voice soaring above the din. "The Battle of the Handkerchiefs has begun!"

29

THE SERENDIPITOUS SPY

Having forced their way aboard the *Laurel Hill*, the women had somehow un-moored the vessel amid the frenzy. As shouts echoed from the levee and the ship drifted awkwardly into the current, Rachel broke free of the crowd and reached the curb in front of the St. Charles Hotel. A quick glance over her shoulder sent a shiver down her spine as she saw Union soldiers escalating the violence, towing a cannon toward the levee and aiming it threateningly at the women.

Taking a deep breath, Rachel forced herself to focus. The sight of the cannon gnawed at her nerves, but her mission loomed larger. Then she asked herself what she had gotten herself into by agreeing to meet the doctor. What if she could not agree with his terms after learning all the details? Would he demand his advance back if she had cold feet at the last minute? Much of that money had already been spent feeding her family and paying Jacob's caretaker. And what if one of the prerequisites for the job was signing the Oath of Allegiance? How could she explain that to Sarah?

As Rachel stepped into the hotel lobby, the welcoming warmth helped her regain her composure. Nothing must stop her now. She let her gaze drift across the towering Corinthian columns and storied balconies, unchanged from the days before the occupation. The massive crystal gasolier caught her eye, igniting a flood of memories. She lingered in the reverie, recalling the joyous toasts and the grand celebration of her wedding reception in the St. Charles.

Her eyes lifted beyond the gasolier to the balconies above, where many of General

Banks's officers conversed in lively tones, a reminder of how much had changed since those happier days.

She turned her attention to the conversations surrounding her in the lobby. Union officers were discussing the departure of Confederate prisoners on ships bound for Mobile to be reunited with their families. Two of the men deliberated on the wisdom of the exchange. Despite signing pledges to abandon the fight in exchange for freedom, they doubted that the Confederates would truly forsake their cause.

A third officer agreed, recounting a conversation he had overheard in which a Confederate, identifying himself as an attorney, claimed the pledge was invalid since it had been signed under duress. The man further explained that it held no weight under *lex loci contractus,* which stipulates that a contract's enforceability depends on the jurisdiction's laws where it was executed. Therefore, the agreement would be null and void once outside Union-occupied territory.

Rachel felt a deep sense of pride listening to the officers express their concerns about the tenacity and intelligence of their Confederate adversaries. They also freely admired the courage of the women outside, who had gathered to honor their men and confront the armed soldiers General Shepley had sent to restrain them. This unexpected revelation transcended the usual animosity that defined the relationship between the two sides, prompting her to reevaluate the complexity of the conflict's dynamics.

She recalled other recent experiences that had shattered her preconceived notions about Union soldiers. At the St. Louis Hotel hospital, for instance, she found her maimed brother-in-law among the wounded, indistinguishable from the very men he had once fought. In that moment, human suffering became a shared reality, transcending the divide between Blue and Gray.

Setting her thoughts aside, she sought comfort in the timeless elegance of one of the city's most prestigious hotels. Yet, something felt amiss: an indescribable change had taken place. It appeared as if the illustrious old dame had lost her charm.

Crossing the lobby to summon the elevator, myriad questions flooded her mind. Chief among them was the puzzling presence of Dr. Zacharie in a Union stronghold, the same hotel that once accommodated Beast Butler and his wife. Something didn't quite add up. Yet he did seem to be a man of honor.

"Which floor, ma'am?" asked the young Negro operator, his tone polite just as she reached the open elevator.

"Third floor," she replied, stepping into the car and positioning herself at its center.

"Yes, ma'am," he said, closing the doors. He reached for the lever and turned the crank to number three.

The elevator jolted to a stop on the second floor, and the operator opened the doors.

Standing in the hallway was a woman garishly dressed in a crimson gown, draped in gaudy jewelry, her cheeks caked with rouge. She cast a scornful glance at Rachel as though she were the girl who had stolen her wealthy mark at a plantation ball. She then stepped into the elevator, trailed by a cloud of perfume.

"Which floor, ma'am?" the operator asked, keeping his gaze averted.

Such an appearance, openly suggestive of the world's oldest profession, would never have been tolerated in the hotel's more genteel era. But now, such sights passed uncensored in a hotel teeming with lonely soldiers.

"Third floor, boy," she replied haughtily.

Moments later, the elevator jolted to a stop, and the operator opened the doors. A Union officer stood waiting outside, his face breaking into a broad grin. "I thought you'd lost your way, Belle."

"No, soldier boy," she replied in a throaty, liquor-laced voice, a mischievous smirk curling her lips. "I was otherwise engaged."

The officer chuckled, pulling her closer and giving her a playful slap on the derrière.

A flush rose to Rachel's cheeks. The image of the woman and the ache of her troubling past propelled her to a quiet resolve. She would accept the job Zacharie had offered, whatever the risk.

Exiting the elevator, Rachel walked down the hallway and stopped at 306. She knocked softly to announce her presence.

A voice from within inquired, "Who calls?"

"Mrs. Durand," she replied.

The door opened, and a dapperly attired Dr. Zacharie stepped back to usher her in. "It is good to see you again, my dear," he said, offering a slight bow.

Rachel stepped inside, catching the faint sweetness of the doctor's sandalwood cologne and the sheen of his neatly pomaded hair. Seated at a desk at the far end of the room was a plain but meticulously groomed young man, his wire-rimmed spectacles perched firmly on his nose as he busily crunched numbers and jotted them into a hefty accounting ledger.

"This is my secretary, Mr. Charles Smith," Zacharie said. "Charles, "I'd like you to meet Mrs. Rachel Durand."

"A pleasure," Charles said, standing and crossing the room to gently take her outstretched hand.

"The pleasure is mine," Rachel returned, noting the bespectacled man's diminutive stature.

Zacharie gestured to an upholstered armchair for her to sit. "I was rather concerned about you today," he offered, "considering the enthusiasm of that sizeable crowd outside."

"Thank you," she said, appreciating his concern. "It was quite a whirlwind, but I arrived safely."

"May I offer you a glass of wine?" Zacharie asked. "It would help to calm your nerves."

Still chilled from the cold, Rachel settled comfortably into the chair facing the window and asked, "Would it be an imposition to request a cup of hot tea?"

"Is Gray's to your liking?" he said.

"That would be delightful," she said.

Turning to Charles, still standing, Zacharie asked, "Charles, please serve our guest some tea. And bring some cream and sugar if you would."

"Yes, sir," Charles said, disappearing through the swinging door adjacent to the buffet.

"How is your family, Rachel?" Zacharie asked, breaking the uncomfortable silence after the secretary's departure.

"They are faring well," she said, choosing not to share her brother-in-law's melancholy.

Zacharie nodded compassionately. "I know you are doing everything possible to support your family until your brother-in-law recovers."

Charles returned with a large sterling silver tray bearing a Blue Willow china teapot and silver tea service, which he placed on the table before Zacharie and Rachel. Turning to Rachel, he said, "I have sugar and cream for the tea. It will take a moment to brew. Would you care for some honey or cinnamon?"

"Thank you, no," Rachel said, wondering how he had acquired such extravagant serving pieces and rarities like honey and cinnamon.

Shifting his attention to the doctor, Charles asked, "Is there anything else I can get for you?"

"No, Charles, that will be all, thank you. If you can cipher while we talk, I'd appreciate you finalizing the week's bookkeeping so I can be paid."

"Yes, sir," he said, turning to cross the room. But before he sat down, he turned back and asked, "Do you mind the sound of my arithmometer while you are talking?"

"No, Charles," Zacharie said, glancing at Rachel for confirmation. "I think we can manage to ignore it."

A nostalgic smile crossed Rachel's face. "I'm accustomed to the sound. My husband often brought work home and used his noisy old machine to calculate monthly expenses. Oddly enough, I found it comforting."

"Thank you," Charles replied, already focused on the ledger sheet, tapping out numbers.

Zacharie chuckled. "I find it comforting as well. It's the sound of getting my expenses reimbursed."

Rachel poured herself a cup of tea, amused by the doctor's remark.

The lightness of their conversation lingered for a moment before Dr. Zacharie's tone shifted, growing more focused and deliberate. "I have given your assignment considerable thought since we last spoke. My greatest challenge was selecting a suitable business partner for you, given the extensive and varied nature of the travel required. I plan to send you to Baton Rouge and then to Port Hudson. Arrangements have been made for you to stay at a plantation along the way, where you will be furnished lodging and provisions."

The mention of a business partner caught Rachel's attention. "Dr. Zacharie, may I ask about this person you have chosen as my partner?"

"His name is Thomas Manget, and he should be arriving any moment now. He is about your age, maybe a few years older, and is Jewish. He is an attorney by profession, but has acquired some trade skills that will facilitate your mission."

"He sounds well-suited for the assignment," she said, wondering if the man and Levi had ever crossed paths. With so many planters transferring ownership of their plantations to their wives, who could then take the Oath of Allegiance to save the property and spare their husbands the social stigma of having to do so, their paths had likely crossed.

"I trust you shall feel secure in his company," Zacharie said. "Your pretext is that he is your brother, and together, you earn a living by selling goods and mending pots and pans whilst searching for your parents, who fled into the Confederacy from Baton Rouge. Being a city native, Thomas can undertake most of the talking and convincingly portray his background."

Zacharie omitted the crucial detail of Thomas being a Union loyalist and one of Banks's spies.

"That should be easy for me," Rachel said. "I have no qualms about selling goods to the Confederates." She felt a wave of relief, thankful that, at least at this point in the conversation, there was no mention of signing the Oath of Allegiance.

Charles responded to a knock on the door and greeted a tall young man standing in the hallway. "Good morning, Thomas. Please come in. Dr. Zacharie is expecting you."

Rachel was struck by the commanding figure looming over Charles in the doorway. Sporting a meticulously groomed mustache and beard, she had never encountered such a striking man. He exuded an air of distinction with bronzed skin and auburn hair that had a slight wave. He was dressed in a silky, mahogany-brown broadcloth suit accented with a fashionable crimson cravat. What captivated her most was the discerning gleam in his gray-brown eyes, as if they possessed the power to penetrate the depths of her innermost thoughts.

"Thomas, it's a pleasure to see you again," Zacharie said, standing to extend a handshake. "Allow me to introduce you to Rachel Durand. Rachel, this is Thomas Manget."

The subtle fragrance of bay rum aftershave, the scent Levi always wore, wafted toward Rachel as she rose to meet the stranger and extend her hand.

"Durand. That's an old French family name," Thomas said, taking her hand gently.

"Yes," Rachel said, my parents emigrated from Paris when I was young." Feeling the tempered strength in his grip, firm yet gentle as befitted greeting a lady, she couldn't help but wonder how much more forceful it might be when he clasped hands with a man.

"Enchanté, Madame. C'est un plaisir de vous rencontrer. Mes parents sont d'Amiens. Il semble que nos ancêtres étaient pratiquement voisins."

As Thomas revealed that his parents were from Amiens and had been practically neighbors to her parents in Paris, a sense of shared connection blossomed between them. For a fleeting moment, she felt Levi's presence, a bittersweet echo of her lost love.

Rachel's mind swirled, consumed by memories. Thomas's voice, with its French cadence, echoed Levi's so closely that it resonated deep within her, awakening a longing she had struggled to repress. It was as if he were writing her life story with his words, unearthing feelings she thought were forever lost. How could this stranger ignite a passion within her, even stronger and more intense than anything she remembered with Levi?

Struggling to keep her emotions in check, Rachel pressed her fingers against Levi's pocket watch, still hanging around her neck. She gripped it tightly, grounding herself, fighting the intoxicating allure of this stranger.

Reste tranquille, mon cœur, she silently pleaded, willing her heart to steady itself against the passion that stirred within her bosom.

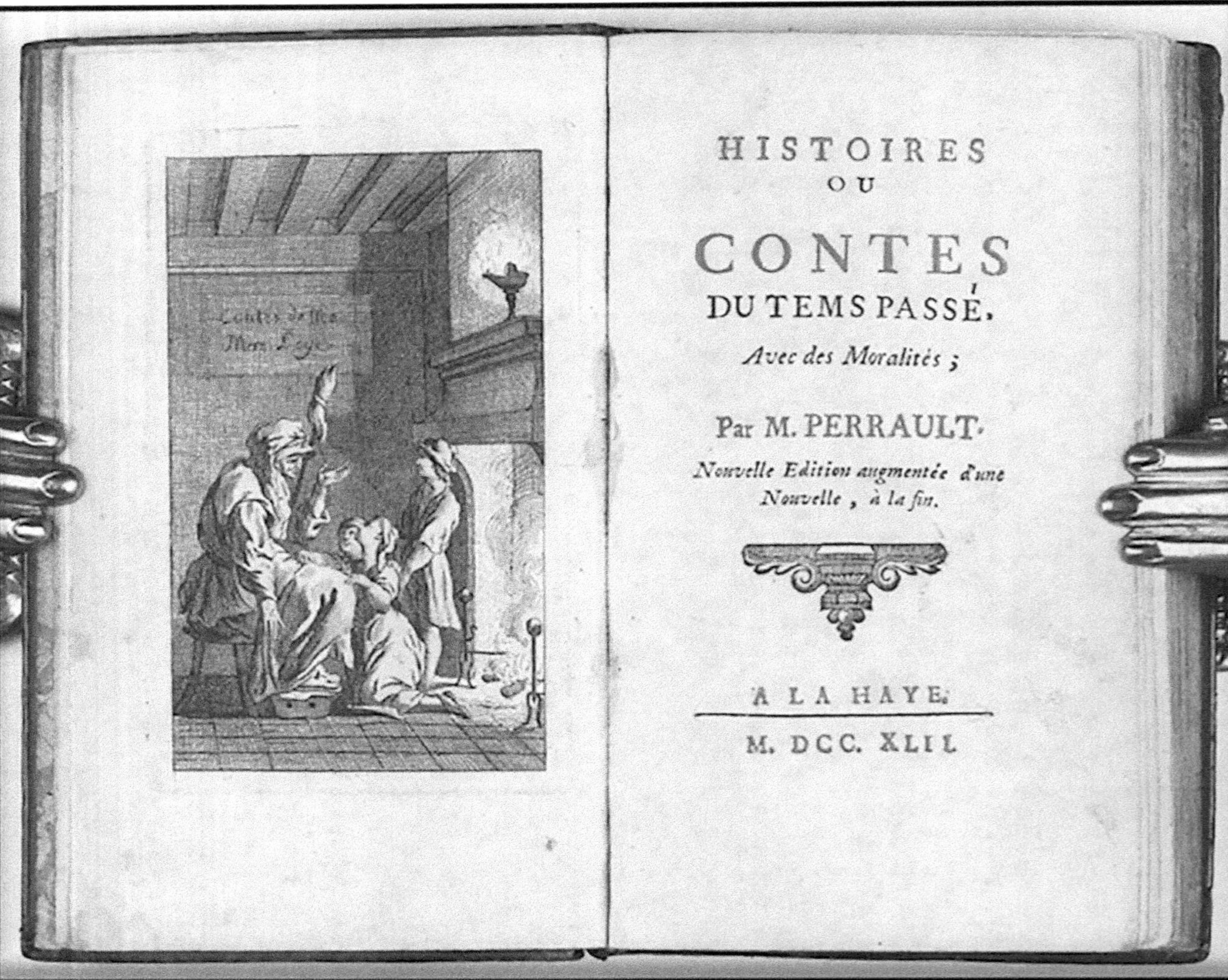

HISTOIRES
OU
CONTES
DU TEMS PASSÉ.

Avec des Moralités ;

Par M. PERRAULT.

Nouvelle Edition augmentée d'une
Nouvelle , à la fin.

A LA HAYE.

M. DCC. XLII.

30

RACHEL'S FAREWELL

Sarah eased onto the warmth of the library sofa, where Noah, now six months old, rested comfortably against Jacob's side, and Rachel worked quietly at her knitting.

Two golden brass hands, one on either side of a music stand set in front of Jacob, held an exquisitely illustrated copy of Charles Perrault's *Histoires ou Contes du Tems Passé Avec des Moralités*. The antiquated spelling of its title belied its age.

Perrault's *Stories or Tales of Past Times with Morals*, first published in Paris in 1697, emerged when fairy tales were popular among aristocrats in Parisian literary salons. Perrault subtly modified the tales to reflect his belief in the superiority and good breeding of the nobility over the peasant class, reinforcing their supposed right to rule.

As Jacob theatrically translated Little Red Riding Hood's escapades into English, Sarah leaned forward to delicately turn the vibrantly illustrated pages, captivating their young son with part where the wolf threw off grandma's nightcap and leaped out of bed, snarling, "The better to eat you with, my dear!" Noah playfully lunged toward his father's spectacles, sending them flying off his face.

"Goodness, Noah!" Sarah exclaimed as she stood up, bent down to pick them up, and returned them to Jacob's face. "What did you do to Daddy's glasses?"

Jacob joined in Noah's contagious laughter. "My boy's not afraid of the Big Bad Wolf," he said, beaming with pride at his son's antics. "That was a sound strike, Noah. At least my glasses aren't broken."

Sarah chuckled. "I suppose you'll just have to come up with a scarier wolf, Daddy. Noah's not convinced."

Enjoying Noah's enthusiasm, Rachel inadvertently dropped a stitch in her knitting, prompting a pause to correct the error. "He's such a big boy," she said proudly, enjoying Noah's playfulness. "It's the first time he's been able to do that!" she said, yet her thoughts revolved around how to broach the delicate subject of her upcoming journey.

Rachel knew that explaining her planned absence for weeks, if not months, would be a challenge. How could she justify starting a venture with a man, much less one she had only recently met? But even though she was an adult capable of making her own decisions, she felt compelled to tell them.

"There's something I need to speak with you both about, Sarah," Rachel said, her tone conveying the seriousness of her topic.

"If it's about you letting go of your mourning clothes," Sarah said, "I support your decision. Jacob and I know how much you loved Levi."

"No, it's not that," Rachel said. "It's something that I've been struggling to tell you."

"What is it, sister?" Sarah asked, a concerned look crossing her face. "Whatever it is, Jacob and I are here to help."

Rachel set her knitting aside on the side table. "I've recently met a man who asked me to work with him to deliver much-needed goods through the lines to our soldiers."

Sarah gasped. "How is that possible? No one can travel through the lines without a pass from General Banks."

Jacob's eyes widened. "Rachel, you must be careful. What you describe could be considered providing aid and comfort to the enemy. Do you know what happened to people who smuggled quinine to our troops? Some of them were hanged."

Anticipating her brother-in-law's inevitable legal objections, she reached for her handbag beside the chair. From it, she withdrew a letter of safe passage bearing General Banks's signature. "I have this," she said.

While Rachel held the pass for Jacob to read, Sarah appeared worried. "Why would General Banks issue a pass to someone delivering aid to his enemy? Something feels off about this, Rachel. Besides, traveling through the lines is extremely dangerous."

"Peddlers make these crossings routinely," Rachel said.

"Yes, but..."

Rachel raised her hand, halting Sarah midsentence. "No one has tasked me with reporting back on what I witness."

"Who is accompanying you?" Jacob asked. "I understand the road north of Baton Rouge is lined with bushwhackers."

"His name is Thomas Manget. I've already met him. He's an attorney from Baton Rouge and seems quite the gentleman." She blushed, choosing not to share how handsome

Thomas was or the feelings that possessed her when they met. "I'm told that he knows how to defend himself."

"I don't believe I've ever heard of the man," Jacob said.

"You're embarking on this journey alone with a man you just met?" Sarah asked, clearly bewildered by her sister's unexpected revelation.

"Yes," Rachel said. "Besides, I will be paid well, and we need the money."

"Don't go, sister!" Sarah pleaded, sinking to the floor beside her. "I can take in sewing," she insisted, her voice trembling. "Some planters have signed the Oath and still manage to prosper. They have money to spend on their wives' gowns...."

Sarah stopped midsentence, and Rachel intuitively knew why. Once a prominent lawyer, Jacob had worked with these planters and mingled in the same social circles. Now, he was a cripple. If she took in sewing, they would gossip about him having to rely on his wife for an income, and that would plunge him deeper into depression.

Aside from this, Rachel knew that the amount Sarah could earn from taking in sewing would pale compared to what Dr. Zacharie offered her. "Sarah, my dear," Rachel said, attempting to assuage her sister's concerns, "I will be doing something to help our men. We're carrying supplies through the lines where they are sorely needed. As Jacob has told us, many soldiers are forced to wear shoes with soles that have holes in them or, even worse, are falling apart. Consider what this would mean for them."

"I can vouch for that," Jacob said as Sarah returned to the sofa, appearing chagrined. "The Confederacy struggles to supply its troops with even the most meager essentials."

"Besides," Rachel said, "I have arranged for you and Jacob to receive a portion of my pay to support the family. It should meet your needs until Jacob can return to work."

Sarah's shoulders slumped, and she let out a sigh of resignation as she returned to sit beside Jacob on the sofa. "I know you too well to think arguing with you will change your mind. You're just like our mother in that regard. But you must promise to write to us often, sharing your current location on your journey and letting us know how you're faring. I'll worry about you every day you're away."

"I will," Rachel assured her, pleased that her sister had finally come to terms with her mission.

"You may have my old shoes," Jacob said. "I won't be needing them anymore."

"I'll polish them before you go," Sarah offered.

"Thank you, Jacob and Sarah," Rachel replied warmly, relieved that her family had embraced her mission.

Sarah rose from her seat and stepped to the table beside the French doors leading to the balcony. She carefully opened a small box and retrieved her mother's gold brooch set with garnets. Offering it to Rachel, she spoke softly, "Mother gave this to me before she passed. You know that it was Father's wedding gift to her."

Rachel nodded. "Yes, I remember the day she gave it to you."

Sarah carefully pinned the heirloom on Rachel's dress, then kissed her fingertips and gently touched it as if sealing it with love. "I know you've always admired Mama's brooch, and since the Yankees took your pearls, I want you to have it. Let it remind you that no matter where you go, you have a family who loves you." She added with a playful wink, "And don't forget, young Noah needs his favorite aunt."

Rachel's eyes sparkled through her tears as she rose and crossed to the sofa to scoop up Noah and cradle him. Gazing into his deep blue eyes, she covered his cheeks with soft kisses until his laughter filled the room. "I love you, Noah," she whispered. "Auntie Rachel will never leave you. Never."

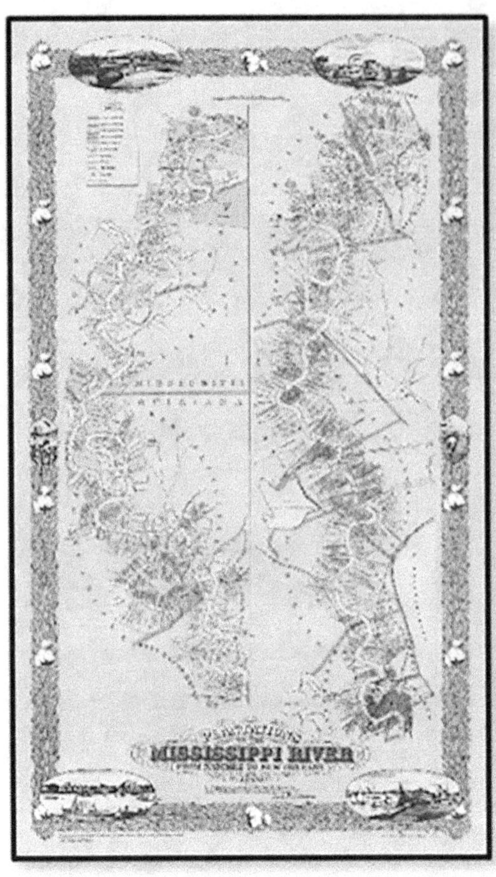

31

HIGH NOON AT THE ST. CHARLES

Cigar smoke billowed through the St. Charles Hotel Grand Ballroom like gathering storm clouds. Beneath the crystal gasoliers, planters from along the Mississippi, stretching north to the embattled Confederate lines at Port Hudson, had gathered in solemn defiance. They wore frock coats, shoes burnished to a mirror shine, and tall hats indicative of old wealth.

Their cane tips tapped against the marble floor in a disjointed cadence like a field of tiny snare drums as they mingled and conferred in low, angry tones. Each man had come prepared to confront General Banks, whose authority under martial law made him both magistrate and executioner of their way of life.

Beautifully framed landscapes by Marie Adrien Persac lined the ballroom walls, their delicate brushwork capturing plantations that lined the tranquil Mississippi River, and sailboats that drifted with ease across the placid expanse of Lake Pontchartrain. The serenity of his painted vistas stood in sharp relief against the present scene, where smoke curled through the room and the air itself seemed charged with unease.

Toward the back of the room, two freedmen planters stood apart, dark figures in a sea of white faces, discreetly maintaining their distance. Their presence silently underscored the paradox of former slaves now navigating the same system that still ensnared their kin.

Dressed as a planter, Thomas Manget, in a tan suit, moved with ease among the crowd, drawing the occasional nod of recognition from those who knew him as the son of a fellow planter and the attorney who had managed their real estate transactions. His familiarity with their world was the perfect disguise, allowing him to blend in seamlessly.

General Banks had specifically tasked him with attending this meeting, not as a mere observer, but as an undercover agent trained by the Pinkerton detective service. Banks had received disturbing reports. There were rumors of bushwhackers along the Mississippi, allegedly acting as proxies for the planters. These insurgents, though few, posed a significant threat to the Union's efforts to stabilize the region, armed as they were with British Whitworth rifles and specializing in ambushes and sharpshooting along the riverbanks.

Thomas's mission was clear: gather intelligence, identify potential sympathizers, and report any signs of organized resistance. As he listened to the bitter tone of the conversations around him, he stayed alert, knowing that even a casual remark could reveal dangerous sentiments.

Although cane cutting was winding down this month, the work was far from over. The fields required plowing and fertilizing. Drainage systems needed repair, and levees demanded maintenance. Additionally, the arduous task of boiling down the cane into syrup and processing it into sugar fell to the workers, and blacksmiths were busy shoeing horses and repairing and maintaining the equipment for the upcoming planting season.

The planters knew all too well that the loss of their slave labor at such a critical moment would be devastating. Yet the rumor that Banks planned to demand that planters engage their former slaves as contracted workers threatened to slash their profits, jeopardizing both their opulent lifestyles and their ability to reinvest in next year's crop.

"I don't see why I have to be here," an older planter grumbled to his companion.

"I hear he's got a contract for us to sign if we want to keep our slaves."

"What kind of contract?"

"Nobody knows for sure, but some folks say he's goin' to make us pay our slaves."

"What?" his friend exclaimed, his jaw dropping. "Zeke, you know as well as I do that when those savages got off the ship, they were naked, except for a filthy loincloth. Now they have clothes, shoes, and their own house. We even give them a chicken from time to time. What do they want now? Wages?"

"The Yanks have been fillin' their heads with ideas," Zeke replied. "They ain't got none of their own."

"Reckon so. I hear a lottah the runaways ended up in Yankee camps, diggin' trenches and eatin' gruel. Won't be long 'fore they come runnin' home, beggin' us to take 'em back."

"John," Zeke said, shifting the conversation, "I ain't seen you in a month of Sundays. How's the wife and grandkids?"

"They're all fine, thanks. My daughter Mary just got back from Paris with the kids. She was itchin' to pick up this year's ballgowns 'fore fall sets in. You know how women are 'bout them things."

"Women will be women," Zeke chuckled. "Mine's been stayin' with kin in London since the war started. Says she shipped home a surprise. Lord knows what it is. But my shipping agent in New York sent word to my place asking for my signature on a sizable draft she had requested. Had her surprise routed through Havana and forwarded by neutral traders. Must be somethin' mighty fine if she went to all that trouble to get it past the blockade."

"Any idea what it is?"

"She's always dreamed of havin' one of them Broadwood grand pianos for the ballroom," Zeke said. "Swears it was Beethoven's favorite."

General Banks, impeccably groomed and resplendent in full Union regalia, entered the room to stand tall and confident behind a sturdy oak table. As his stern gaze swept the room, methodically assessing the mood of the assembled crowd, his eyes landed on Thomas, diligently mingling among the planters.

His attention then shifted to the armed guards stationed discreetly near the entrance at the rear of the room. Their presence was a silent acknowledgment of the tension in the air and the need to maintain control. The general understood the volatility of the situation, and his every movement was a calculated effort to project authority and readiness for whatever might unfold.

"Gentlemen," Banks began, his voice carrying authority, "I've invited y'all here today to address the many questions and concerns surrounding President Lincoln's Emancipation Proclamation, issued just last month." He paused, surprised that the word "y'all" had slipped out. It seemed that even he wasn't immune to the contagious drawl of the South, but he swiftly decided it was fitting for his audience. "Rumors have been circulating that you may maintain ownership of your slaves simply by signing the Oath of Allegiance. Let me be clear: this is not the case. I am here to delineate the requirements that must be fulfilled should you wish to retain your labor force under my new mandates."

A wave of angry murmurs rippled through the crowd. Banks lifted his hand, commanding silence. "I understand you're eager to resolve this matter quickly, but I must insist that you refrain from speaking amongst yourselves while I address you. We'll have time for questions after I've finished."

The room fell into an uneasy silence, every eye fixed on the general.

"I have spent considerable time reviewing the implications of the Emancipation Proclamation in my military district," Banks continued. "And after careful deliberation and in consultation with other attorneys on my staff, I have drafted General Orders 11 and 12, which address the management of plantations under Union occupation."

"These Orders, gentlemen, will govern the relationship between you and the formerly enslaved people working your land and harvesting your crops. Allow me to outline the key provisions."

He paused, letting the significance of his words settle over the room. "First, after my staff has confirmed that planters have signed the Oath of Allegiance, they will be required to enter formal labor contracts with their employees. I have printed pro forma contracts for you to take with you today. I strongly recommend that you review them thoroughly. Once you have done so, you will inform one of my designated officials, who will visit your plantation and witness your signature and each of your contract laborers."

"What if our slaves can't read or write?" one of the planters called out.

"My men will explain the provision of the contract to them," Banks replied, his tone unwavering. "I'm glad you brought up the issue of education. I will address that later. Suffice it to say that an 'X' will serve as a signature. My representative will print their name for them."

A man in the back of the room, flushed with frustration, abruptly interrupted. "I have a question."

Banks raised his voice slightly, maintaining control. "I ask that you hold any further questions until I have finished presenting the orders. If we allow interruptions, we may well be here until nightfall."

The crowd shifted uneasily, but the man relented, grumbling under his breath.

"Regarding compensation," Banks continued, "the formerly enslaved, now to be regarded as contract laborers, will be paid wages for their work. The amount will be determined and regulated by the Union authorities, and it will vary depending on the nature of the work and the daily hours required."

Banks observed the men shifting their weight, their postures stiffening as their interest piqued. "Furthermore, as employers, you must provide these workers adequate housing, food, and medical care. The Union will oversee and enforce these provisions to ensure compliance with standards set forth."

The General's eyes swept the room, sharp and intent, like a hawk hovering above its prey, locking gazes with several planters whose expressions shifted from disbelief to outright hostility. "The freedmen will have two options. They may choose to stay on the plantation where they are currently working, or work for the Union in a capacity that we deem appropriate during their transition to a free labor system. However, let me make one point abundantly clear: as far as the Union is concerned, it is preferable that they remain where they are. But make no mistake. These individuals are no longer property. All claims to ownership are hereby nullified."

The room erupted.

"That's theft!" one man shouted, his voice rising above the others. "We've pledged our slaves as collateral to the banks to finance our crops. If you take away our collateral, we'll go bankrupt!"

"Hear, hear!" someone else chimed in. "It's a violation of our Constitutional rights!"

Soon, a cacophony of angry voices filled the room.

Banks remained still, allowing the uproar to run its course. When the noise finally began to subside, he raised his hand. His voice was calm, but it cut cleanly through the lingering outrage.

"As for the banks," he said, "I can assure you they have no interest in repossessing land that will lie fallow without labor to farm it. You forfeited your Constitutional rights when your state seceded. Still, each of you is free to accept or reject this arrangement. But understand this: if you refuse, I will dispatch an armed company to escort the formerly enslaved from your property, and you will not see them again. The choice is yours."

The room quieted, the gravity of his words settling heavily on the assembled men like a death sentence. Low murmurs spread among the crowd, but no one dared speak out of turn again.

Banks continued, consulting his notes. "Freedmen will be required to carry passes issued by Union authorities if they travel, particularly if they move between plantations or outside the area. Should they be found without such a pass, they will be detained and returned to fulfill their labor contract."

He paused for effect, letting the implications of this stipulation sink in. "Additionally, you will be required to educate these individuals at your own expense. They are to be taught to read, write, and do arithmetic. Should you fail to do so, the Union will assign one or more teachers to your plantation, and you will bear the cost. This education is not optional."

A rustle of discontent swept through the room, but no one spoke.

"Finally, planters will designate a time and place for weekly worship for the freedmen, which will not be supervised or controlled. This, too, is not up for negotiation."

Banks exhaled slowly, surveying the room before concluding. "This, gentlemen, is the gist of General Orders 11 and 12. Copies of the Orders and labor contracts are available as you leave. Should you have any questions, now is the time."

A grizzled planter near the front, known for his cruelty as both the owner and overseer of one of the larger plantations, raised his hand. "What if we refuse to sign the contract? What happens then?"

Banks fixed him with a steady gaze. "I believe I addressed that already, sir. To repeat, if you refuse, an armed unit will be dispatched to remove your former slaves, and they will not be returned."

"I'm an attorney like you, general," another man said. "How is your plan any different from indentured labor?"

"You have a point," Banks agreed. "Treating runaway contract laborers as vagrants who can be arrested and compelled to return to work aligns with the generally held definition of indentured labor. The difference is that General Orders 11 and 12 will expire with the end of the occupation when the war is over. Congress will have to address the status of the former slaves at that point."

A younger man, his face flushed with anger, yelled, "And what if I agree with some of the terms but not others?"

Banks's expression hardened. "Perhaps I wasn't clear that this is not a negotiation. That ended the moment the Confederacy fired on Fort Sumter, and the war began. You will comply with the terms set forth or lose your workforce."

The young planter raised a clenched fist, his face contorted with rage as he shouted, "This is tyranny! We have our property rights! I will not tolerate it!"

Banks calmly turned to one of the guards flanking the door. "Sergeant, arrest this man and take him to the Customs House with the other rebels. Shackle him if he offers any resistance."

The sergeant snapped a crisp salute. "Yes, sir."

The young man attempted to dash for the exit, but the guards quickly intercepted and restrained him. A tense silence followed as the other planters watched him being escorted out of the room, his arms twisted behind his back.

Banks, standing tall, turned back to the crowd. "Any more questions, gentlemen?"

Thomas watched in silence as General Banks dismantled the illusion of planter supremacy clause by clause. Around him, men who once wielded unchecked power now looked stricken, bewildered.

Marx's words floated unbidden through his mind:" The ruling ideas of each age have ever been the ideas of its ruling class." But not anymore, Thomas thought. He had no sympathy for privileged men decrying tyranny, the moment the people they exploited had to be paid wages.

ANTOINE'S RESTAURA

32

ANTOINE'S

Antoine's. The very name evoked enchantment and romance in the heart of New Orleans, conjuring visions of exquisite cuisine, a wide selection of French wines, and the charm of intimate, candlelit dining. Artfully crafted Mardi Gras masks adorned the walls, catching the flickering candlelight to create an atmosphere of mystery and celebration.

Thomas stepped out of the cab in front of Antoine's and closed the door behind him. "Thank you, driver," he said, extending a generous gratuity. He then circled the vehicle and took Rachel's gloved hand to help her disembark.

As Rachel descended from the vehicle, she caught Thomas's gaze, gently following her movements. What was that look? It wasn't a leer, and it wasn't a stare. Instead, it conveyed admiration and gentlemanly respect for her as a lady. She had not felt that for a long time.

As the two entered the restaurant, the driver tipped his top hat and gently pulled on the reins. The horse obeyed with a rhythmic clippity-clop, its hooves striking the glistening cobblestones as the cab rolled into the misty evening.

"*Bonsoir, Monsieur, Madame,*" the white-waistcoated waiter greeted the couple as they entered.

"*Bonsoir, Monsieur,*" Thomas replied. "*Mademoiselle et moi préférerions un coin privé, si vous pouvez nous accommoder.*"

"*Bien sûr, Monsieur,*" the waiter replied with a hint of a bow. "*Par ici, s'il vous plaît,*" he gestured straight ahead, leading them through a door that opened into a corridor. When they reached the third door in the hallway, he swung it open and nodded for them to enter a small, private dining room, just as Thomas had requested.

The intimate room featured four small tables elegantly draped with crisp white linen and set with bone china, and on top of the larger dinner plates, decorated with a gold fleur-de-lis pattern and edged in royal blue, rested smaller, matching salad plates.

The meticulously aligned silverware indicated the order in which the courses would be served. To the left of the plate, the salad fork was placed on the outside, with the dinner fork positioned closest to the plate. The teaspoon was set furthest out on the right side, followed by the dinner knife, its blade facing inward toward the plate. The dessert fork rested horizontally above the plate, ready for the final course.

The elegant table arrangement showcased long-stem Baccarat crystal wine glasses and water goblets, each gleaming from meticulous polishing. The water glass was positioned closest to the diner, above the knives and spoons to the right of the plate, with the wine glasses arranged just beyond.

Thomas seated Rachel, then circled to his side of the table, where the waiter pulled out a chair for him to join her.

The waiter then turned to a side table against the wall, retrieved two menus, and handed them to the couple.

Rachel observed that the entire menu was exclusively in French, unlike the usual practice in New Orleans' restaurants, where they were typically presented in French and English.

Thomas glanced at an abundance of seafood dishes. "I'm in trouble if you're trying to keep kosher," he said uneasily.

Rachel grinned. "I try not to bother Rabbi Gutheim with my dietary choices. One could starve trying to keep kosher in a city like New Orleans with all the shellfish on restaurant menus."

Thomas smiled playfully, "I promise not to tell the rabbi. Does anything look good to you?"

"I'm considering the seafood gumbo. It comes with a loaf of French bread and butter, my favorite." Rachel said.

"Would you like me to order?"

"Yes, please. I usually enjoy my rice on a separate dish rather than in the gumbo."

The waiter entered the room again and asked, "Have Monsieur and Madame decided what they want to order?"

"We will have two bowls of gumbo with French bread," Thomas said, "and extra butter. And please serve the rice separately from the gumbo."

"*Oui, monsieur.* Would you care for a white wine with your meal?"

Thomas turned to Rachel. "Would you care for wine?"

"A glass would be nice."

"We have an excellent white wine at the moment," the waiter said. "It pairs nicely with the seafood gumbo."

Thomas gave a small nod. "That will be fine." He turned to Rachel and said, "Though I should say I only indulge in a glass of wine when I'm not working. And this evening, I'm not."

"*Bon*," the waiter said with a nod before leaving the room.

Rachel offered a faint smile, appreciating his restraint. Thomas's conservative approach to drinking stood in quiet contrast to Levi, whose rare but unpredictable indulgences had cast long shadows over otherwise peaceful evenings. It was a small thing, perhaps, but it mattered more than she cared to admit.

"Are you excited about our trip?" Thomas asked.

Rachel shifted her weight in her chair. "I must admit that I am a bit apprehensive."

"Oh?"

"Yes. I have no idea exactly where we're going or how we'll get there. I was told we were headed to Baton Rouge and then to Port Hudson."

"Dr. Zacharie gave me precise instructions. I've arranged for us to take a steamer to Baton Rouge, as it's much faster than making the journey by wagon along the Poydras and Port Hudson Road. Once we reach Baton Rouge, I'll secure a horse, wagon, and our inventory. From there, we'll head north on the same road, traveling through the outskirts of plantations lining the Mississippi. Along the way, I arranged for us to stay overnight at a plantation owned by one of my father's former clients."

"How long will it take the steamer to reach Baton Rouge?"

"Since the river meanders quite a bit and we're traveling against the current, it'll take more than a day. If we start early Sunday morning and travel overnight, we'll arrive in Baton Rouge on Monday."

"I've never been on a steamer," Rachel said. "I've heard that some of them are palatial."

"The steamer we're boarding isn't exactly top-tier luxury. It's an iteration of the original *Natchez*, a sternwheeler, not a sidewheeler, and while it was once luxurious, it never rivaled the opulence of some grander vessels. These days, it's a Union transport primarily tasked with ferrying soldiers, supplies, and livestock along the Mississippi River."

"Livestock?" she asked.

Thomas chuckled. "You know, horses, mules, cows, pigs, chickens... the whole barnyard."

"Sounds more like Noah's ark," she quipped, amused at the image it brought to her mind.

"Yes, it does. From our end of the trip, though, it'll be mostly horses and mules."

"You're right. It sounds nothing like what my friends described as a 'floating palace' with a carpeted ballroom, chandeliers, and fine dining."

"Does that concern you?" he asked, a serious look crossing his face.

"Not in the slightest," she assured him, eager to dispel any notion of herself as a spoiled aristocrat. "I see it as merely a means to an end. A buggy ride to Baton Rouge would be utterly exhausting. My father traveled there as a guest lecturer at the new university just before he passed. I recall him complaining about how tiresome the trip was."

"Good," he said, a smile returning to his face.

"Besides, I love horses. I'll have to remember to take carrots along. I have a bunch still left in the cooling chest."

"I'm rather fond of horses myself," Thomas said. "Do you ride often?"

"Before my husband left for Shiloh, we rode together on Sundays. Unfortunately, he perished in combat. My sister, Sarah, never cared for horses, so I have no one to ride with now." Her face fell as she added softly, "I thought it best to find new homes for Clementine and Thunder." Her face fell. "It broke my heart."

"I'm so sorry," Thomas said. "Why didn't you go riding by yourself?"

"I guess I never really thought about it," she said, pausing to reflect on his question. "It would be incredibly lonely. Half the enjoyment of riding comes from chatting with a friend. The sense of camaraderie always brought me so much joy."

"Yes," he said, gazing into her eyes. "I feel the same way."

"Do you have a riding partner?" Rachel asked.

"Not at the moment."

As their eyes connected, she couldn't shake the unsettling notion that Dr. Zacharie might have divulged the circumstances of their initial encounter when she had felt compelled to make ends meet through prostitution. She had mulled over how to broach that uncomfortable topic if it ever arose, but prayed it would remain buried.

"What did Dr. Zacharie tell you about me?" she asked.

"That you're a brilliant and resourceful young lady," he replied.

"Resourceful?" she echoed, caught off guard by his quick response.

"He told me that you were actively seeking ways to support your family, and that Rabbi Gutheim had recommended you. He also mentioned that convincing you to take on this mission wasn't easy. Apparently, he had to offer you more than he had originally planned because you'd already secured a well-paying position in town and were concerned about the dangers of crossing the lines."

Rachel blushed, making a mental note to thank Dr. Zacharie for his discretion. "Yes," she admitted. "I'm still somewhat concerned."

"I can ease your mind," he said. "General Banks met with the planters at the St. Louis Hotel earlier this week. He proposed a system where they could retain their labor force as contract laborers, not as slaves, with terms that would ensure their well-being. This should help reduce hostility among the slaves along our route to Port Hudson."

"That's reassuring," Rachel said, relieved at the thought of fewer dangers from slaves who might still harbor resentment, even after the Emancipation Proclamation. "And what about you?" she asked. "Dr. Zacharie didn't share much about you other than that you're an attorney from Baton Rouge."

"Yes, I am an attorney by profession..."

"May I present your Chablis, Monsieur, Madame?" interrupted the garçon. Holding the bottle in a white linen napkin, he awaited Thomas's approval of the label before uncorking the wine with a flourish and decanting a taste of the vintage for him to sample.

Thomas swirled his glass, admiring the body and bouquet of the wine, then took a sip. "Excellent. Decant a taste for the lady, please."

The garçon hesitated. "Monsieur?"

"A taste for the lady, please," Thomas reiterated.

Rachel was entertained by the waiter's hesitation to pour wine for a lady's approval, as it was not part of his routine.

With a reluctance that appeared to border on resentment, the waiter cocked an eyebrow and moved to Rachel's side of the table to decant a meager portion.

Rachel savored her wine, offering a contented smile. "Delightful," she remarked, glancing at Thomas across the rim of her glass. She sensed he found the waiter amusing.

The waiter peremptorily filled each of their glasses, set the bottle on the table, and left the room without further comment.

"He'll get over it," Thomas said when he was out of earshot.

"I certainly hope so," she said, charmed by Thomas's easy humor and thoughtful regard. It was a pleasure to share a table with a handsome and refined man who treated her not as someone expected to defer but as a woman worthy of being heard, even when it came to something as trivial as the choice of wine.

33

STEAMING TO BATON ROUGE

Rachel stepped out of the carriage wearing a gray traveling dress and black leather ankle boots, her straw hat tilted to shield her face from the bright sun. The freshness of the morning air made her cheeks glow as she tried to hide her excitement on her way to the levee to meet Thomas. Still, beneath the thrill of her upcoming journey, a hint of uncertainty quietly flickered in her mind.

Thomas greeted her with a warm smile and a cheerful "Good morning."

The levee bustled around them with the sounds of workers and the creak of ropes and pulleys, but for the moment, her world centered on the anticipation of the journey.

Standing shoulder to shoulder, they stepped into their roles as siblings, a ruse that would shield their true identities on the voyage up the river to Baton Rouge. The first leg required them to board the *Natchez V*, built in the 1850s.

With a gentle Gulf breeze rolling up the Mississippi, the warm spring day affirmed Rachel's decision to pack lightly. She had chosen practical cotton dresses and modest bonnets over the cumbersome silk gowns and elaborate hats that would have weighed her down. Still, a nagging thought lingered: she would need to find a way to wash her limited wardrobe along their journey.

Gazing at the *Natchez*, it struck her as peculiar that she had never set foot on a steamer despite growing up in New Orleans. In school, her girlfriends regaled her with stories of opulent ballrooms, lavish feasts, and exciting encounters with handsome sons of wealthy planters aboard the *Princess*. Now, she was embarking on a journey with the most strikingly handsome man she had ever encountered, whose manner was refreshingly free of the haughty arrogance often accompanying being a planter's son.

Her father, a conservative professor, had always harbored reservations about steamboats, primarily due to the frequent explosions of their boilers. The tragic demise of the luxurious *Princess* in '59, when all four boilers exploded simultaneously near Baton Rouge, had left a lasting impression on him. This incident caused the deaths of many New Orleans passengers and cast a shadow over that year's Mardi Gras. That same year, the *St. Nicholas* and the *Pennsylvania* met with similar fates farther upriver.

These successive tragedies led her father to firmly declare that steamboats were, in his words, "like devilish engines right out of *Paradise Lost*" and vow never to allow his family to travel on them.

During his orations of dire foreboding, she was tempted to point out that it was Satan's newly invented cannon, not the steamboat, that Milton referred to in his *Inferno* as the "devilish engine."

In a moment of reflection, Rachel realized how rare it was for her to indulge in even the smallest pleasures. She had always been the dutiful daughter, managing finances, excelling in her studies, marrying a practical man, and now, supporting her family. Even her brief involvement with *La Maison du Soleil Levant* had been a selfless act driven solely by the need for income to support her family.

Levi had been her anchor, a man of unwavering kindness and devotion. Though not dashing, he was generous and dedicated. His only flaw was the rare occasion when a few drinks led to a brief loss of temper, though rarely directed at her.

Rachel remembered the freedom she felt during Sunday outings with Levi, who encouraged her to ride her horse astride rather than adhering to the traditional riding position of sidesaddle. That sense of freedom and the security he had provided had vanished with his death.

Despite everything, she took solace in having discovered, by a recent turn of fate, a way to support her family that did not bring dishonor. Nearly a year had passed since Levi's death, yet her emotions still surged and receded like a restless tide, stirred further by last night's heartfelt conversation with Thomas over supper at Antoine's.

"Look, Rachel," Thomas beckoned, calling her attention to the ship's crew lowering the gangplank.

"Ready for me to take your bags on board?" a strapping young Irish porter with flaming red hair and freckles asked.

Rachel lowered her gaze, enchanted by his Irish brogue.

"You ready, sister?" Thomas teased, slipping into his sibling role.

"I'm ready, brother," Rachel said with a smile, amused by his playful attempt to act the part of her sibling. She eyed him more closely, noticing something different. "I see your beard is fuller." *And more handsome,* she admitted to herself, feeling a flutter she could not name. But she quickly brushed the thought aside, reminding herself of the role they had assumed to accomplish their mission.

"Yes," Thomas replied. "I thought it might make me less recognizable when we reach Baton Rouge. I prefer to avoid drawing attention from anyone in my hometown who knows me."

They ascended the gangplank slowly, blending seamlessly with the flow of other passengers. From her elevated vantage point, Rachel paused and glanced back, taking in the familiar New Orleans skyline. The towering spires of St. Louis Cathedral rose majestically above Jackson Square, flanked by the Cabildo, a testament to the city's Spanish heritage, and the Presbytère, a reflection of its French roots. Together, these structures stood as enduring symbols of a city born from a blend of cultures, their stately lines etched against a horizon of billowing white clouds.

It felt strange to leave her hometown, especially aboard a Union transport. Her mind wandered to recent memories of Xariffa, the poet, who had been stranded with all the women on the *Laurel Hill* when it came unmoored, leaving it drifting aimlessly downriver without a captain at the helm. Thankfully, it was retrieved before it reached the Gulf.

At the top of the gangplank, Rachel and Thomas presented their passes to one of the guards before stepping aboard the ship.

Rachel reached for her portmanteau to retrieve a coin for the young porter who was busy unloading their luggage into the cargo section.

Thomas stepped in swiftly. "Permit me," he said, pulling out a silver coin before she could react.

Rachel paused, reassessing the situation. *Of course,* she thought, recalling the age-old etiquette that dictated a gentleman never allowed a lady to pay while in his company. The principle seemed to apply even in this unusual scenario, where they posed as siblings in a business arrangement.

Together, they navigated through the cluttered deck, weaving past horses, wagons, and soldiers stacking crates destined for General Banks's troops that he had staged in Baton Rouge for his assault on Port Hudson. The barnyard scent of fresh straw and manure filled the air, mingling with gruff voices and the occasional clank of metal and clink of chains. Nearby, men in Army uniforms shoveled manure overboard, completing the vivid tableau of life aboard a wartime vessel.

"Shall we take a moment to look at the city from the railing?" Thomas suggested, making his way to the deck's edge.

"Oh, look!" Rachel exclaimed, feeling a nudge at her portmanteau. "Isn't she beautiful?"

Thomas chuckled as he observed the chestnut brown mare. "It seems you've made a new friend. She's a Mountain Pleasure if I'm not mistaken."

"Yes, she is. Such a beauty," Rachel said, feeding the insistent mare a carrot. "Just look at her sleek coat and gorgeous long tail."

Several other nearby horses tugged at their tethers, their eyes fixed on the treat in the mare's mouth, eager for their share. One released an impatient whinny, its nostrils flaring in anticipation.

"Goodness," Rachel said, retrieving several carrots. "Everyone will have to wait their turn."

Thomas tossed back his head and laughed. "Have you ever met a horse who waited his turn for food?"

Captivated by his laughter, she smiled and said, "No, I suppose I haven't."

They watched as the horses savored their carrots, flaring their nostrils and tossing their heads impatiently, eager for more.

"Sorry, girls and boys," Rachel said, opening her portmanteau with a playful pout as he held it open for the horses to see. "I'm fresh out."

Convinced that there were no more carrots, the horses soon lost interest and relaxed on their tethers.

Suddenly, the shrill sound of the ship's steam whistle reverberated across the water, accompanied by the engine's "chug, chug." Another three blasts followed shortly, and the slow splash of the giant paddle wheel powered the boat out into the river.

Jacob gestured toward the shoreline. "Say goodbye to New Orleans," he said. "We won't be seeing it again for a while."

Rachel offered the faintest trace of a smile to conceal her concern for the family she was leaving behind.

Intrigued by the steamer, Rachel's curiosity prompted Thomas to offer her a tour, going below deck to step into what had once been a ballroom.

"What a difference a war makes," Rachel observed, her gaze sweeping across the room, now stacked high with provisions.

Though she had never traveled by steamer before, her friends had enthusiastically described the elegance of the *Princess* before its tragic demise. Their words painted vivid scenes in her mind: a glittering ballroom adorned with white gingerbread trim framing stained-glass windows high above, an expansive floor illuminated by a dazzling crystal gasolier, and elegantly dressed couples swirling to the rhythm of a waltz.

Natchez's ballroom, much less imposing than her friends had described, was repurposed as a dingy storage area. Its plain glass windows cast just enough light for the workmen stacking crates. Only the skeletal remains of a worn bar and a cloakroom remained, resembling ghosts of the room's former grandeur.

Rachel's eyes were drawn to the tarnished brass gasolier, its once-glittering crystals now dusty and missing in places. She reflected that, not so long ago, it cast a warm glow over elegantly dressed aristocrats who filled the ballroom with laughter. It stood as the last symbol of a fallen gentry, now repurposed for utility.

Her gaze fell to the floor, where the frayed remnants of a once-luxurious carpet still stubbornly clung, its former opulence sacrificed to the relentless march of muddy shoes. Beneath it, the plain oak decking now lay exposed and dirty, a stark reminder of how the room's splendor had been stripped away in favor of raw practicality.

"So sad," Rachel murmured.

"It is," Thomas agreed. "I used to work summers as a porter on steamers up in Baton Rouge, helping passengers as they boarded and disembarked."

"You were a porter?" she asked.

"In another lifetime," Thomas replied with a smile. "The pay wasn't much, but the gentlemen were generous tippers. It helped me buy my first horse and save for law school."

"I'm certain your family supported you as well," Rachel said.

"Yes, my father did. I lived at home through my studies, but I wanted to have my own money and transportation. I've always had an independent streak," he added with a grin.

"Your father must have been proud of you," she said, fanning herself. "I'm sorry, Thomas. The air is stifling down here. Would you mind terribly if we went back up on deck where there's a bit of breeze?"

"I was about to suggest the same," Thomas said, wiping his forehead. "All this straw packing is generating heat."

"You don't think it'll catch fire, do you?" Rachel asked as they began climbing the stairs.

"Not likely," Thomas reassured her. "No smoking's allowed on board. I suppose you're thinking of spontaneous combustion."

"Yes," she said.

He grinned. "Plenty of water and buckets around if it does."

Rachel laughed softly as they stepped onto the deck, the balmy breeze instantly refreshing her. She took in the vast expanse of the muddy river and said, "Yes, I suppose there is plenty of water and plenty of men to haul it down there."

Just then, a soldier approached her. "Miss Manget?"

"Yes?" Rachel answered, surprised that the soldier addressed her by Thomas's last name.

"I saw that we had a lady on the passenger manifest, and I set up a place for you to sleep tonight," he explained, gesturing aft toward a small tent. "Seeing as you're the only lady onboard."

"How considerate!" Rachel exclaimed, following the soldier to the tent.

"I managed to gather some clean linens and a pillow. One of the officers said he had extra since he had his laundry done while we were ashore in New Orleans."

Rachel greeted his kindness with a warm smile. "My! That's very kind of you," she said, noticing his pronounced Northern accent.

As she bent to open the tent flap, she found neatly laid bedding and a fluffy pillow, with a lone loose feather suggesting it was filled with duck down, just like her pillow.

"Thank you, sir," Rachel said, standing to face the soldier. "All the comforts of home."

"Yes, ma'am," the soldier said with a shy grin. "Let me know if you need anything else."

"What about my brother?" she asked.

"Don't worry about me," Thomas interjected, stepping forward. "I'll gather some straw from one of the bales over yonder and bed down beside your tent."

"You folks are welcome to join us at mess tonight," the soldier offered.

"Thank you," Thomas said.

"It ain't much, just beans and salt pork, but it'll fill your belly."

"You've been very kind," Rachel said, touched by his thoughtfulness. Though a tent and a soldier's rations were far from the comforts she was used to, his kindness was refreshing in a world upended by war.

"Well, ma'am, have a good trip," the soldier said with the tip of his cap. "I'll bring you a wash basin in the morning."

After he left, Rachel turned to Thomas, her brows slightly lifted. "Why do you suppose he called me 'Miss Manget'?"

Thomas leaned back with an easy smile, a flicker of amusement dancing in his eyes. "Well, since we're listed as brother and sister on the manifest, and you're traveling without a husband, he likely assumed you're unmarried. That would explain the shared family name."

Rachel gave a thoughtful nod. "I suppose that makes sense," she said, though the sound of his last name linked to hers felt odd.

Thomas's smile deepened, his gaze lingering on her, clearly savoring her reaction.

34

BATON ROUGE

At first light, Rachela and Thomas stood silently at the railing of the *Natchez* as the steamer approached the Baton Rouge landing. Their attention was fixed on the iconic state Capitol, its charred remains still standing like a shell of a castle after a siege. On either side, the remnants of buildings that once graced the waterfront were recognizable only by their brick chimneys, now standing like silent, wounded sentinels.

Thomas appeared visibly shaken. "I knew that Farragut shelled Baton Rouge last May and that there was more damage inflicted when the rebels marched from Camp Moore to retake it in August, but I had no idea there would be so little left standing. Hardly any buildings I recall along the riverfront remain."

Rachel reached over and touched his arm. "It must be difficult for you since it's your hometown."

"Yes," he said, attempting to conceal a tear. "But what saddens me most is the sight of what remains of the Capitol. I know it was an accidental fire, but the result is the same."

"It still stands proudly. It appears to be made of stone. Maybe it can be rebuilt."

"Perhaps," he said. "It was constructed with an iron frame covered with plaster that was scored to look like stone. I remember seeing it built back in '49. Saw it from start to finish. Everyone was excited about the project. I remember when the taverns donated their spent oyster shells to make the lime plaster when the supply ran short. Many people donated their horses' shed hair from grooming as part of the mix."

"That's interesting," Rachel said. "I had no idea what went into making plaster."

"Seems they're lowering the gangplank," Thomas remarked. "I'll find a porter to fetch our bags."

"Did you sleep well, ma'am?" a voice came from behind Rachel.

"Oh," she said, turning to see the soldier who had arranged her tent for the night. "Yes, I did, thank you. You were most kind."

The man lowered his head. "It ain't nothing, ma'am. I was just trying to show some respect for a lady."

A warm flush crept into Rachel's cheeks. "What's your name?"

"My name's Clyde."

"Please call me Rachel. Where are you from, Clyde?"

"I was born in downstate New York, a small town called Waverly, on the Pennsylvania border. I worked as an engineer for the Delaware and Western Railroad before the war started. Where are you from?"

"I'm from New Orleans," Rachel said, her words tinged with a hint of awkwardness. Though she wasn't overtly identifying herself as a Confederate, she feared the assumption might be made. "That was my brother you saw with me. We've taken to peddling wares to get by."

"Where're you headed?" he asked, appearing to be encouraged.

"Here, for now."

"I noticed you have a pass."

"Yes," Rachel said, trying to think of how to change the topic.

The soldier shifted, anxiously working his hat between his hands. "Begging your pardon, ma'am. I don't mean to be forward, but I was wondering if I might have the honor of showing you the sights this evening if it pleases you. I'll only have a couple of hours ashore, but I could arrange for a carriage."

Rachel noticed the cautious courtesy reminiscent of a man steeped in Southern decorum, striving not to overstep the boundaries of propriety, yet he clearly hailed from the North.

"Everything's ready," Thomas interrupted.

Hearing Thomas's voice, Rachel felt a warm blush rise to her cheeks. She stole a glance at him, and the tension in his expression confirmed that he was jealous. Yet, his desire to protect her stirred something unexpected. She hadn't realized how deeply she yearned for that sense of safety.

"It looks like my brother is calling me," Rachel said with a kind smile, not intending to hurt the soldier's feelings. "I really must be going."

The soldier's shoulders slumped. "Godspeed to you, ma'am. Maybe I'll see you on your way home."

"You stay safe as well," Rachel replied with a polite nod, leaving the dejected soldier behind as she quickly crossed the deck to join Thomas.

"Thank you, brother," she whispered, sighing in quiet relief as she reached his side.

LYTLE
Photographist
ROSENFELD
DRY GOODS

35

SOUVENIR

After leaving the Verandah Hotel, where he and Rachel were staying, Thomas walked down Main Street toward the intersection at Church Street. His heart grew heavier with every step, passing the remains of once-familiar shops that lined the street. Many were now boarded up or under repair, with faint echoes of the busy businesses they had once been before the devastating Union shelling.

Union-employed contraband workers lined the street: carpenters hammering away, glaziers replacing war-torn windowpanes, and masons replacing bricks torn from buildings, rebuilding the town of his childhood memories.

His mind drifted through the city's scarred remnants. With each step, the streets of his youth flickered to life, first as fleeting impressions, then as vivid scenes rising from the ruins. The bustling clothing shops emerged in shimmering fragments, their windows, once bright with finery, now shattered or boarded. He passed the saddlery where he and his father frequented and recalled the faint clink of harness rings and the musky tang of neatsfoot oil, conjuring the steady rhythm of a world that no longer existed.

And yet, amid all that had vanished, the decadent aroma of warm chocolate curled through the air from the candy shop of his childhood memories, miraculously untouched. The sweet harmony of melted cocoa, butter, and sugar came from within. It stirred a deep and aching longing for the simpler days when fingers were sticky with syrup and children's laughter rang down the street.

As he neared the intersection with Church Street, the towering steeple of the Methodist Church came into view, a rare survivor of the shelling from Farragut's flagship the previous

May. Just beyond, St. Thomas's Cathedral remained largely intact, surrounded by barriers to keep trespassers away, awaiting restoration to its former glory.

Thomas soon arrived at Lytle's photography shop, its exterior showing recent signs of repair. As he opened the door, the cracked glass panel rattled as the soft chime of the bell announced his entry. Seeing no one behind the counter, he perused the countless photographs that adorned the studio walls, each image a frozen moment. Though this wasn't his destination, he felt drawn to linger briefly before continuing down the street to the telegraph office, where he would send Rachel's message to Sarah, assuring her of their safe arrival in Baton Rouge.

The collection of photographs predominantly featured portraits of Union soldiers, with additional displays highlighting drill formations, rows of tents, a variety of sailing ships, multideck sidewheeler steamboats, smaller transports, and the iconic grouping of brick military barracks shaped like a pentagon. Others included government buildings, churches, street vendors, local shops, and oak-lined streets with private residences. Some images were captured from elevated vantage points, adding a unique perspective to the montage.

Aware that the portraits of soldiers were posed since any movement would blur the photographs, he stumbled upon one that offered a glimpse of candid authenticity, revealing the reality of the Union occupation. It depicted several officers seated in front of a tent, with a soldier standing at rigid attention nearby. In the middle of the scene, one of the officers was sitting in a rocking chair, clearly appropriated from a local home, recalling the mumblings of residents on the streets, bitterly complaining of Union soldiers stripping their homes of valuables for personal use.

The camera's voyeuristic gaze extended into the tent, where a haphazard collection of furniture lay like trophies. In the foreground, etched into the sand, was a six-pointed star lined with standing pins and a nearby ball, indicating that the men had been engaging in a game of Aunt Sally as a diversion before their impending march to Port Hudson.

Transfixed by the images of familiar neighborhoods, Thomas was again transported back to his childhood, recalling strolls along these streets after the winter's chill had passed. He vividly remembered waving to smiling families sitting on their front porches, shaded by the sprawling branches of massive oak trees. At the foot of the trees, endless beds of bright pink King George azaleas in full bloom heralded the arrival of spring. He could almost feel the cool, early morning breeze on his face in his reverie.

But now the waterfront lay in ruins, with the once-iconic Capitol building standing gutted. Meanwhile, its magnificent gardens and moss-draped oak trees had been reduced to ash. For blocks inland, the devastation continued, where deserted homes lay shattered by Union shelling or ransacked by the invading army, leaving little of the town's grandeur in its wake.

Then, his attention was caught by a large, framed photograph mounted over the counter. It was a picture of Lytle's shop, with "Lytle Photographist" written across it in bold white lettering. The Methodist Church, with its towering steeple, loomed majestically in the background, a steadfast symbol of the town's resilience and hope for resurrection from the ravages of war.

In stark contrast, a blurred image of an old man with a walking cane occupied the foreground. The man's image, caught mid-stride, seemed to animate the photograph, highlighting the passage of time against the unchanging backdrop of the historic church.

"Do you like my work?" a cheerful voice behind the counter said. "I apologize for the delay in greeting you. I was in my darkroom developing photographs."

Thomas turned to see a thirtyish-year-old, dark-haired, bearded man with a jolly round face and rosy cheeks that reminded him of the Santa Claus in last year's Christmas issue of *Harper's Weekly*.

"I grew up here," Thomas said, still engrossed in the photographs. "Many of these places bring back memories, although I'm curious why your photo of the Methodist church is missing a row of benches out front where folks used to wait for their carriages."

Lytle stepped to the photograph, as if rediscovering the detail through Thomas's eyes. "Yes, I remember the benches. They removed them before I took that picture. You have a marvelous memory for detail."

"Thank you," Thomas said. "It's a skill I've found rather useful now and then."

"I was about to say that I moved down from Ohio and began my work here before the war, so I was fortunate to capture the images of structures before many of them were shelled by Farragut last year. I've always considered it my job to capture moments in time."

"I remember your shop when you first moved here. You've painted the front a different color, though."

Lytle raised his eyebrows. "Young man, your memory's almost as good as my photographs. After the shelling, I had to repair some minor damage to my shop, so I considered it a good time to give the place a fresh face."

Thomas stepped over to shake the proprietor's hand. "My name's Thomas Manget."

Lytle extended a soft, plump hand. "Andrew Lytle, photographist and proprietor. Pleased to meet you."

"Pleased to meet you as well. I remember seeing your ad in *The Advocate* in '61 just before my friends marched off to combat."

"Shame they can't print actual photographs in newspapers."

Thomas cracked a smile. "The engravers might disagree. They'd all be out on the street without their work rendering photographs for printing."

"I suppose they would," Lytle chuckled. "The copy is catchy, though, isn't it? 'Everybody and their wife go to Lytle's and get their picture taken before Old Abe is inaugurated. After that time, everyone will look blue, although a good many are blue in anticipation of the fact.'"

Thomas reflected that Lytle's pun-filled words had proven eerily prophetic.

"Pity," Lytle said. "There are now many more soldiers here than residents. Most of the hometown folks fled when the Union invaded. The soldiers took everything they wanted when the residents left. Walking past downtown, you'll see fields of tents, just like the ones on the wall. Before the Union invasion, I worked from sunup to sundown, taking photos of Confederate troops. As long as there was enough light, I kept photographing."

Upon revisiting the images of the soldiers, Thomas's gaze fell upon a recurring backdrop: an artist's romanticized painting of a classical Greek-columned structure set against a canvas of billowing clouds. In these photographs, the soldiers posed before a scene of timeless tranquility, a stark contrast to the harsh reality they would soon face as they marched north to confront the guns of Port Hudson.

Thomas thought of Coleridge's *Rime of the Ancient Mariner*. Like the mariner burdened by the slain albatross, these men moved through an eerie calm, adrift beneath a painted sky and painted sea, as if trapped in a tableau of stillness, waiting for the storm they knew must come.

"I see that all of the soldiers in these photographs are Union," Thomas observed.

"Yes, necessarily so," Lytle replied. "After the rebels cleared out, I removed all the Confederate portraits and signed a contract with the Feds to document their presence here. A soldier from New York once told me I'm as good as Brady." He chuckled, his belly shaking like a bowl of jelly. "I told him Brady wishes he were as good as I."

Thomas was amused, recognizing the man's pride in his craft, though he knew comparing himself to the renowned Brady was pure bravado.

"The enlisted men are another story," Lytle remarked, a trace of amusement in his voice. "They'll give up their last bit of tobacco and rolling paper for cigars just to send a photograph home to their loved ones." He paused, studying Thomas with casual interest. "So, you say you're from Baton Rouge?"

"Yes," Thomas replied.

"Were you wounded in combat?"

"I'd rather not discuss it," Thomas said, his tone firm but not unkind.

Lytle quickly backtracked. "Begging your pardon. I didn't mean to pry."

"I'm just passing through after a stay in New Orleans. Heading to Port Hudson with a wagonload of shoes and dry goods for the soldiers."

Lytle's eyes widened. "You're a peddler headed through the lines? And you managed to get a pass?"

"Yes," Thomas confirmed.

"Hmm," Lytle mused, pausing to stroke his beard, deep in thought. Without further questions, he reached beneath the counter and pulled out a large, thick envelope tied with twine. "Some of the local boys skedaddled before I could develop their photos. These are what they left behind. I considered asking for a pass to deliver them across the line, but decided against it. Didn't want to be suspected of being a spy or getting shot by bushwhackers along the way."

Thomas remained silent; his curiosity piqued at Lytle's mention of espionage. He continued inspecting the photographs on the wall.

"I don't suppose, since you've got a pass, you'd consider taking these with you?" Lytle asked.

"Mind if I take a look?" Thomas asked, reaching for the envelope.

Lytle hesitated, holding onto it. "I'd rather not if you don't mind. I packed them carefully to avoid damage, and they're sorted alphabetically by the soldiers' names."

"I understand," Thomas said, watching Lytle's eyes closely, detecting the unmistakable signs of deceit in his dilated pupils.

"Besides," Lytle continued, "You'd need to give them directly to an officer for inspection."

Thomas's suspicion grew. Was Lytle trying to use him as a mule to carry military intelligence hidden among the photographs?

"Are you giving them away?" Thomas asked, deciding to pursue the subject.

"If you take them to Port Hudson and sell them, I could use the money when you pass through again. You can keep half. I have no use for the prints now and still have the negatives." He let out a sardonic laugh. "Displaying photos of rebel soldiers wouldn't be the best thing for business these days. I wouldn't be able to keep up with quarterage on the shop."

Thomas grinned at Lytle's dry humor and honesty about struggling to pay his overhead. "Probably not. I'm sure the boys at Port Hudson would appreciate having their pictures to send home while they still can. I'd be glad to take them."

"Would you like your portrait made?" Lytle offered, changing gears. "I could print a few *cartes de visite* with your name and a motto on the back. Business is slow today so that I could have a dozen ready by tomorrow afternoon."

"Thanks, but no. I don't plan on staying in one place long enough to have folks come back for more."

"The life of a peddler," Lytle said with a knowing nod. "Well, take your time. If anything catches your eye, something that brings back memories, you're welcome to take a few prints as souvenirs. Gratis."

"Thanks," Thomas replied, noting how easily Lytle switched allegiances based on the economics of war.

36

POYDRAS & PORT HUDSON ROAD

Rachel and Thomas's wagon moved slowly along a marsh-fringed stretch commonly called the Poydras and Port Hudson Road, tracing the edge of the Mississippi as it wound through the landscape like a giant anaconda. With each turn of the wheels, startled crayfish scattered in every direction, their shells cracking beneath the wagon's weight, the sound sharp and brittle against the hush of the river road.

"Looks like the makings of a good étouffée," Thomas grinned.

"There are so many," Rachel remarked, observing the scurrying crustaceans with fascination and distaste. "It's unsettling. I'd much rather picture them smothered in a big pot of roux on a supper table than skittering across the road like oversized insects."

Rachel's gaze shifted to the horse pulling the wagon. "I'm so glad you arranged to hire Nellie," she said fondly. "We got on the moment we met on the *Natchez.*"

Thomas returned her smile. "I noticed. She's a fine horse."

"I don't know that I ever thanked you," Rachel said, her tone softening.

"We needed to hire a horse, didn't we? Besides, it was clear you and Nellie became fast friends when you met."

Rachel chose not to comment on his deflection. It was typical, she mused, a man skirting the genuine sentiment behind the gesture. He must have devoted some effort to securing Nellie for their journey.

As the moment stretched on, doubts swirled through her mind. Would she continuously be left seeking a hint of emotion beneath his practicality? Then again, why did she even care if he was merely a business partner?

"What's on your mind?" Thomas asked, his gaze steady.

"Oh, nothing," Rachel replied, a flicker of unease crossing her face. She knew instinctively that he had sensed more than she intended to show.

"Look," Thomas said, pointing to the marshy area along the riverbank. "See the alligators?"

Rachel shaded her eyes. "My, they're big!" she said. "I don't remember seeing so many in one place."

"Plenty of fish around here for them to feed on," Thomas said.

Ahead, drier ground stretched where levees protected endless rows of sugarcane, lining both sides of the road. A sea of vibrant green blades swayed and whispered in the breeze.

"I never thought much about why the houses are set so far back from the river," she said. "It seems like quite a trek from their front door to their dock."

"The Mississippi is like a living thing," he explained, "always shifting, carving new paths. Take False River that we passed earlier. It was part of the river until it changed course in the early 1700s. Now it's a lake."

"That's fascinating," Rachel remarked, her eyes lighting up.

"Planters have their slaves reinforce the levees to slow erosion and prevent floods," Thomas explained. "But the river doesn't always cooperate, so the planters build their houses far enough back to avoid the worst."

"The levees are really tall," Rachel said, looking at the towering embankments that obscured the river. "Who will tend the levees once all the slaves are freed, and what will become of the plantations when the river rises?"

"Great questions. Only time will reveal the outcome. The planters might sacrifice some of their profits to compensate the freedmen for their work. General Banks is instructing his men to collect signed contracts from the planters to make this happen."

Rachel stared at the levees, struck by the truth Thomas's words had revealed. A part of her held on to the familiarity of the world she knew, yet she understood deep down that it was falling apart, making room for something new. She wasn't as sad to see the old ways ending as she was worried about what would take their place.

Thomas sat beside Rachel in the wagon, his thoughts drifting back to how quickly the world had changed. The Financial Panic of 1857 had shaken the economy, forcing banks to consider repossessing plantations and slaves when loans went unpaid.

But with plantations faltering, the value of slaves dropped, leaving lenders to debate whether to sell their collateral to Cuba. Yet, competition from trans-Atlantic slave traders, who provided a cheaper and seemingly endless supply of fresh labor to the island, depreciated the market value of such collateral.

Lenders became convinced that if they wanted their loans repaid, they would have to allow the planters to keep their slaves to produce cash crops, so they decided to hold off on foreclosures and ride out the economic downturn, waiting for the market to turn in their favor.

By late 1860, just before Louisiana's secession in January 1861, crop yields had hit record highs, and most planters repaid their loans. Thomas had sold his inherited plantation at its financial peak, escaping the storm brewing on the horizon.

Fearing Union occupation after secession, some planters cashed out their crops and fled with their slaves along the Red River from Shreveport to Texas. A few had settled there, while others pushed further West and South, continuing to Mexico to find that slavery had been abolished years before.

Thomas broke his reverie and began humming "Oh! Susanna" to pass the time and fight off the soft, hypnotic clop of Nellie's hooves on the tightly packed dirt of the road through the sugarcane fields.

As Thomas fell silent, lost in thought, a quiet satisfaction settled over him. He had calculated every detail of the mission. The soldiers' shoes and boots bound for Port Hudson were stowed deep in the wagon bed, concealed beneath a layer of coarse gunnysacks. Above them, barrels brimmed with bolts of vibrant calico, paper patterns for shirts and blouses, trousers, spools of thread, and slender packets of needles. The careful arrangement completed their disguise, casting them as harmless peddlers plying their wares to plantation households and local laborers, many of them Irish Catholics.

Thomas tugged the reins gently, guiding his wagon to the side of the narrow dirt road next to the sugarcane to let a solitary rider pass. The young man, dapperly dressed, sat atop a well-bred chestnut American Quarter Horse, its golden mane catching the breeze.

"Mornin', folks," the rider greeted with a casual tip of his hat.

"Mornin'," Thomas returned, tipping his tattered felt hat in kind. He recognized the rider as the son of a nearby plantation owner but couldn't recall his name. Still, he asked courteously, "You folks need me to stop by your place?" The offer was superficial, made solely to seem engaged in peddling his services.

Without looking back, the young man continued on his way. "Can't hurt," he called over his shoulder. "My father owns the next plantation upriver. Slaves don't take care of the kitchenware no more, not since they got the notion the Yankees are comin' to set 'em free. Best you mend 'em to save us buyin' new ones."

Once the road was clear, Thomas noticed Nellie had taken advantage of the stop to snack on a stalk of sugarcane. "Come on, Nellie," he coaxed gently, tugging the reins. "I'll get you a treat when we reach Buttonwillow."

Nellie snorted in defiance, still enjoying her snack.

"Please, Nellie. Be a good girl," Rachel urged. "I'll get you some nice big apples in Baton Rouge, I promise."

At last, Nellie relented, leaving her sweet treat behind as she resumed pulling the wagon along the rutted road.

Rachel shot a playful, triumphant glance at Thomas. "She just needed a woman's gentle touch."

37

BUTTONWILLOW PLANTATION

THURSDAY EVENING, MARCH 5

Thomas and Rachel arrived at a clearing in a cane field. In the distance, the silhouette of an impressive white mansion with tall Greek columns appeared, set back a few hundred yards from the riverbank.

"There's Buttonwillow," Thomas said, gesturing towards the plantation. "That's our lodging for the night."

"It's stunning," Rachel remarked.

"A lady named Josephine owns the place. She's a quinteroon, the daughter of an octoroon and a white man," he explained. "Her mother inherited the plantation from a man who started as a peddler and built his fortune in real estate, acquiring several plantations over his lifetime."

"He certainly knew how to make his mark," she said.

"He certainly did. His name was Julien Poydras."

"You don't mean *the* Julien Poydras, the philanthropist who founded the Poydras schools and the Poydras Asylum for female orphans and widows in New Orleans?"

"The very same. In his will, he asked that all his slaves be set free. That included those on several plantations he left to relatives, as well as Buttonwillow. After he died, though, manumission became illegal in Louisiana, and his last wishes couldn't be honored."

Rachel fell into a thoughtful silence, humbled by the mention of the man credited with Louisiana's admission as a state. The irony was not lost on her: the owner of Buttonwillow now could not carry out Poydras's will to free the slaves on her plantation. It was a stark contradiction to the idea that slaves were mere chattel, subject to their owners' whims, while those same owners couldn't determine the fate of what the law considered their property. The Union wasn't the only force interfering with slaveowners' property rights.

"I'm certain you'll find Josephine an interesting conversationalist," Thomas said. "I met her some years ago when she visited my father on our plantation, and he handled sundry legal matters for her. She brought me presents and was very kind. I always thought I would have liked having a mother like her."

Rachel nodded, noting the hint of admiration in Thomas's voice when he spoke of the mistress of the plantation.

The two rode silently along the riverbank past rows of poorly maintained slave quarters, weathered over decades and abandoned through time. Past the older houses were newer ones that sported fresh coats of whitewash and new metal roofs. Beyond the slave quarters lay the sprawling sugar cane fields tended by hundreds of workers.

"Look over yonder," Thomas pointed. "Those workers are thinning out dead cane stalks to make way for new growth. Harvest time occurs in the fall, when the sugar content is at its highest. There's a lot of work between now and then to maintain the crop."

As Thomas neared the plantation's Big House, he could see the tiny, well-kept homes nearby.

"So many little houses," Rachel observed, thinking how the slave cottages and even these more upscale dwellings for tradesmen were a far cry from the grandeur of the mansion.

"The ones we just passed along the river are for the slaves," Thomas informed her. "The ones we're coming up to now are for the tradesmen."

"What do they do?" Rachel asked.

"Some are blacksmiths, coopers, carpenters, and the like. Most of them are Irish."

"Why is that?"

"They're inexpensive White labor," Thomas explained. "Planters often engage Irish tradesmen to train their slaves. That way, when the tradesmen fall ill or finish their indentures, the slaves are ready to step in and take over their job and reduce expenses even more."

Thomas turned left off the dirt road and onto the driveway in front of the plantation's mansion.

"My, what a lovely home," Rachel said, admiring the stately columns of the plantation's Big House.

"Yes," Thomas concurred, gesturing beyond the house. "Did you notice those twin chimneys past the Big House?"

Rachel followed his gaze and nodded toward the distant structures. "Over yonder?"

"That's the sugar house smokestacks. Later in the fall, the sugarcane will be taken there to grind out the juice and boil it down, then evaporate it to produce sugar."

Thomas guided the wagon past the sugar house and pulled it to a stop beside the front porch of a modest clapboard tradesman's home. Glancing up at the gathering clouds, he saw that the approaching storm would soon force him to seek shelter for Nellie and the wagon.

Then, he noticed a young black boy standing barefoot near the wagon, his eyes wide with curiosity. The boy lingered shyly for a moment before inching forward. When he moved closer, a protective bantam hen burst into a squawking protest, her peeping brood scattering in all directions. The boy paused, startled, but after a breath, he cautiously resumed his approach, his gaze fixed on Thomas.

"Mistuh," The boy said meekly, "You got any fancy candy from the city? I got a shiny new penny in my pocket."

"Reckon you might as well be the first customer of the day," Thomas replied with an amused smile, bending down to retrieve several pieces of paper-wrapped British toffee from a tin beneath his seat. The boy stood on his tiptoes, eagerly exchanging his penny for the candy.

"How'd you come by that penny, boy?" Thomas asked.

"Johnny, that's a big White boy lives just down the lane, throwed it at me this mornin'. He say, 'Pick it up, boy. Ain't nothin' but nigger money to me.'"

Thomas winced at the cruelty of the white boy but watched the pleased look on the boy's face as he worked the sticky toffee in his mouth. "Well, I guess you got the better end of that deal, son. Now he's down a penny, and you're up one to buy candy."

The boy broke into a wide smile, showing strings of toffee stuck to his crooked teeth. "Yassuh."

It struck Thomas as peculiar that a boy living on a sugarcane plantation would spend his penny on British toffee wrapped in beeswax paper and shipped across the Atlantic when most kids enjoyed making fresh, warm pull candy for free.

Thomas recalled his childhood, when pull candy parties were a rare instance of joyful equality. Black and white children would wash their hands together under the watchful eyes of their mothers before slathering them with melted butter. They would then pull the thick, warm molasses between their fingers, stretching it back and forth. As the syrup cooled and thickened, it would transform into a golden Jacob's ladder of sugary delight. A song or two would always quicken the process and fill the air with laughter.

"You like that toffee better than the pull candy you can make at home?"

The boy hung his head. "The big kids shove me off while they takes what they wants."

"You got a name, boy?"

"Name's Joshua."

"Got any notion why your mama named you Joshua, young man?"

"Nossuh."

"Did she tell you who Joshua was?"

"Yassuh. She say he a man in the Bible. Say he fit a big battle 'ginst someplace called Jerrrychoh."

Thomas smiled affectionately. "Yes, yes, he did. And he won," he said with a nod, "just like you did when you stood your ground against that boy who called you a bad name and threw that penny at you." His voice carried a note of quiet admiration as he reached into his bag of toffee, selecting several pieces. He handed the candy to Joshua with a grin. "Here you go, Joshua. The first customer always gets a little something extra."

Rachel sat still, her hands folded in her lap, watching the quiet exchange between Thomas and the boy. A warmth spread through her body as she observed them relate, not as master and slave, but as two human beings enjoying each other's company.

38

LE PETIT DEJEUNER

Like many plantations along the Mississippi, Buttonwillow's mansion was carefully crafted to serve as an elegant backdrop for the daily routines of Southern aristocracy. The opulent dining hall, an enclosed space devoid of windows, was a haven for lavish feasts, whether during winter's frosty grip or summer's abundant harvests. In striking contrast, the richly appointed drawing room, bathed in natural light from its many windows, adapted gracefully to the seasons. Heavy, warm drapes shielded against winter's chill, only to be replaced in spring by airy, gossamer fabrics that welcomed gentle breezes carrying the sweet fragrance of magnolia blossoms.

At the heart of this display of affluence was the grand ballroom, the estate's crown jewel, designed as the focal point of the plantation's most lavish gatherings filled with social intrigue. Here, swirling hooped skirts glided gracefully across polished floors to the tones of woodwinds and strings.

Yet, the grandeur of these mansions was more stagecraft than reality, carefully designed to uphold the illusion of nobility while concealing the brutal truth: their survival depended on a system of human bondage.

Thomas descended the broad staircase with these very thoughts pressing against him. Once, he had moved easily through such surroundings, taking the polish and opulence as a matter of course. Now, the sight of carved banisters and glittering chandeliers struck him differently, each ornament a reminder of the enslaved hands that had built and sustained this world. What had once seemed noble now felt suffocating.

Daniel, the servant who had earlier assisted with his bath and change of clothes, stood waiting in the foyer. As Thomas approached, Daniel gave a respectful nod and opened the dining room doors. Inside, an elegantly dressed woman of timeless beauty, her auburn hair neatly coiffed, stood before a portrait of Julien Poydras. The painting, framed in ornate gilding, hung prominently above the buffet table, nestled between two tall, curtain-draped windows that softened the morning light filtering into the room.

It took only a moment for Thomas to recognize the lady as Josephine, the plantation's owner and a client of his father. She appeared lost in thought, as though conversing silently with the distinguished figure in the painting. Respecting her moment of reverie, Thomas remained where he was, allowing himself a moment to take in the elegant room.

The round Duncan Phyfe dining room table accommodated an egalitarian seating arrangement for six, departing from the hierarchical power dynamics typically associated with the traditional rectangular shape, which often designated the head of the table for the master and the opposite end for the mistress. The table and dining chairs were painted a tasteful shade of green and adorned with a central ceramic tureen shaped like a large cabbage flanked by a pair of golden candelabras, all positioned beneath a magnificent crystal gasolier. The ambiance was further enhanced by a gilded mirror mounted above the fireplace mantel with crackling fire logs below. The room radiated elegant European sophistication, framed by painted soft green walls and an intricate, plush British Axminster carpet woven with floral patterns.

"Mademoiselle," Daniel called out to his mistress. "Monsieur Manget is here to join you."

"Oh," she responded softly, shifting her thoughts back to the moment. "Thank you, Daniel. While you're here, please turn off the gasolier and the sconces. The sunlight streaming through the windows should be adequate."

Daniel responded with a "Yes, mademoiselle," and then he closed the valves on the gas lights. He carefully pulled the heavy mahogany doors shut behind him as he departed.

Instinctively, Thomas looked down and froze, embarrassed at the sight of his muddy footprints on the plush carpet.

Josephine's lilting laughter gently assured him that everything was all right. "Don't worry, Thomas," she said with a smile. "Its only purpose is to be trodden upon."

He was relieved by the cadence of her laughter and her gracious attempt to make him feel welcome, even as warmth rushed to his face. He felt like a little boy again, soothed by a mother's voice telling him everything would be all right.

"Thomas, *mon ami*," Josephine greeted warmly as she approached to take his hand and give him a gentle kiss on the cheek. "*Ça fait longtemps*." Her hand was soft, untouched by the rigors of manual labor. Her gown of golden silk, with its elegantly sloped shoulders, featured wide pagoda sleeves that cascaded gracefully to petite cuffs trimmed with delicate white lace.

He grasped her hand gently. "A pleasure, Mademoiselle Josephine," he returned, catching the citrus aroma of Eau de Cologne. "Indeed, it has been a while."

She offered a demure smile. "The pleasure is mine, Thomas. My, how you've grown! I remember when you were just…." She trailed off, seemingly deciding against exploring the past.

With the gentle rustle of her silk skirt, Josephine circled to the far side of the table in front of the fireplace. Daniel courteously pulled out a chair for her. "Thank you, Daniel," she expressed warmly. Turning to Thomas, she said, "I see that Rachel is not a morning glory. Last evening, we enjoyed a delightful conversation while I ensured she was comfortably settled in her room, and Daniel assisted you."

Thomas chuckled. "A morning glory she is not. I'd say she's more of an evening primrose."

"I see," she replied with a pleasant smile. "She is as lovely as any flower, regardless of when she chooses to blossom." She paused, then added, "I don't seem to recall your having a sister, Thomas."

Daniel automatically circled to Thomas's side of the table and pulled out his chair.

"Thank you…uh…Daniel," Thomas said somewhat awkwardly while trying to explain why Josephine had not met Rachel when visiting his father. "Rachel was born after you knew me," he returned.

"I see," Josephine returned. Turning to Daniel, she said, "Please tell Emma that she may serve our *petit déjeuner.*"

"Yes, Mademoiselle," Daniel said, retrieving a small crystal dinner bell from the fireplace mantel. Crossing the room, he opened the double doors to the dining room and rang the bell. Once finished, he returned it carefully to its place on the mantel.

"Thank you, Daniel," Josephine said. "You may serve coffee while we await our meal. And please inform Emma to keep a plate warm for Miss Rachel."

"Yes, Mademoiselle," Daniel replied, departing the room and gently closing the doors behind him.

As they waited for their coffee, Thomas was struck by the polite, almost cordial exchange between Josephine and Daniel. It was unlike the rigid, often brusque interactions he had witnessed between master and servant on most plantations he had visited and his own when he was young. Here, there was a surprising dignity in how the orders were given and received.

Thomas was also intrigued by how Josephine had been captivated by the prominently placed painting of Julien Poydras when he first entered the room. He waited until she glanced his way, then turned his attention to the portrait. "I noticed you were looking at the portrait of Julien Poydras earlier," he said. "It seems he holds a special place in your memories."

She gently touched her napkin to her lips and folded it neatly beside her plate. She then stood to walk over to the portrait and beckoned him to join her.

Thomas stood to follow Josephine to the painting, noticing that when she gently touched the gilded frame of the portrait, her eyes sparkled like a little girl looking up at her father.

"I suppose I never explained our relationship to anyone," she began. "I called him Papi, though he wasn't my grandfather." She caught herself. "At least, not by blood. There was no marriage between him and my grandmother. My grandmother was a quadroon working as his maid when she bore my mother, supposedly fathered by a white man visiting the plantation. That made my mother an octoroon. Papi treated my grandmother kindly and raised my mother as his own, ensuring she had a good education. When my mother later became pregnant by a White man who died of yellow fever, Papi treated me like family from the day I was born."

"I see," Thomas said, although he found it difficult to reconcile her story with how easily he had perceived her as a White woman, not a quinteroon. People who were one part in sixteen Black often passed for White. What intrigued him more was her willingness to share such personal details with someone who was little more than a passing acquaintance from years ago. It left him curious and unsettled, as if she had opened a door he did not wish to enter.

"I never knew who my father was for certain because my mother never told me. Papi was the only grandfather I ever knew, and I adored him. He died when I was very young, and it broke my heart. I picked white dandelion heads for weeks, blew softly, and watched the seeds lift into the air like a thousand tiny parasols. They floated gently on the breeze, scattering as if carried by unseen hands. I always thought of those seeds as messengers, carrying my whispered prayers to my grandfather in Paradise."

Thomas listened intently, moved by Josephine's unwavering love for the man she cherished as a grandfather.

"I would even sit on the bench by his headstone and speak to him." She looked Thomas directly in the eyes. "Do you think I have taken leave of my senses, Thomas?"

"Not at all. I'm so sorry for your terrible loss," Thomas said. "I never knew my mother, either." He fought the instinct to offer a comforting touch, careful not to overstep, and instead offered only his words of solace. "You were so very young."

She raised her hand gently to her bosom, acknowledging his sympathy. "You caught me unawares, Thomas. Each morning, I come downstairs to enjoy my *petite dejeuner* as we are doing now, but I always pay my respects to Papi first. Then I say a silent prayer."

"You certainly loved him very much. I'm certain he felt the same way about you."

"My mother and I remained on his plantation until his attorney visited a week or so after the funeral. The attorney explained that Papi recorded the deed in trust, noting only its lot on the surveyor's map. He owned many plantations, so it was a trivial matter to him."

Thomas nodded in understanding, but his curiosity remained. Why had Poydras left this plantation to her mother, a woman who had served in his household? The secretive nature of this arrangement only deepened the mystery. But Thomas knew better than to voice these questions. Some things were best left unspoken in the South. "Did he have any relatives?"

"Yes, but no direct descendants that I know of."

A gentle tap sounded at the door, and Daniel entered, carrying a large silver tray with a matching coffee service. He set the tray on the table, unfolded napkins, and placed silver spoons before them. He then poured coffee into china cups. After arranging the cream pitcher and sugar dish with a serving spoon within easy reach of his mistress and her guest, Daniel gave a slight nod and slipped silently from the room.

"Thank you, Daniel," Josephine called as he left. Turning to Thomas, she sat up straight and said, "I think I've shared enough about myself. I'd like to learn more about you."

Thomas felt his body tense, and his mind swirled with the mission he dared not share. "There's not much to tell," he managed. He returned to his chair, observing her reaction.

"Come now, Thomas. Surely there is more," she urged, her tone gentle like a mother coaxing a child to confess a harmless secret.

He smiled, amused at her persistence. "Well, let me see. Where to begin? I've never married."

"Continue."

"And I probably never will."

Her contagious laughter prompted him to join in.

"Do you see yourself as Molière's misanthrope or merely a run-of-the-mill misogynist?" she inquired.

"Mademoiselle allows me no opportunity to defend my honor," he rejoined.

"Well," she offered, "Let me see if I can help you."

Her answer caught him off guard. What did she know?

"The lovely Rachel speaks highly of you," she said.

"My sister is generous with her praise," Thomas said.

"But perhaps she doesn't know you as well as she thinks?"

Thomas was surprised. He wondered if she knew the brother-sister cover was just a convenient façade.

"She also mentioned that she believes you disapprove of slavery," she continued.

"I do," he affirmed.

"She spoke little to me about her opinion on the issue. Does she share your sentiments?"

Thinking swiftly, Thomas chose to deflect the question. "She concurs with President Lincoln's perspective that the slavery issue is akin to grabbing a wolf by the ears. Neither continuing to hold onto it nor letting it go seems a viable option."

"Yet Louisiana's legislature has chosen to persist in holding onto the wolf's ears," she said. "The law does not allow for manumission under any circumstances. With the Emancipation Proclamation and Reconstruction on the horizon, the prospect of free Black men outnumbering Whites at the polls and potentially displacing poor Whites from paying work is terrifying to most people. It would mean the end of the Southern hierarchy."

"That is true," he said, relieved that his deflection had shifted the conversation away from Rachel.

Josephine's expression grew somber. "On her deathbed, my mother made me swear to follow Papi's will and set all the slaves free. But as I mentioned, Louisiana passed a law that prevented me from honoring that promise when I inherited the plantation. President Lincoln's Emancipation Proclamation frees them here in occupied Louisiana, but they have nowhere to go except the Union camps. So I offered them a choice of staying here and working for a wage. That was even before I signed a formal contract with them, as General Banks directed, and I pay them the same wages as the Irish families you might have encountered when you arrived."

"How many of them stayed?" Thomas asked, impressed that she had begun paying wages to her slaves even before it was mandated.

"All but one. John, an eighteen-year-old, decided to join General Banks's *Corps d'Afrique*." She sighed. "Such is the rashness of youth."

A gentle tap at the door announced Emma, a short, stout, middle-aged woman in a maid's uniform. She had light skin and Caucasian features, with graying hair neatly styled and nestled in a hairnet. Her overall demeanor suggested a refinement that belied her servile position.

Emma rolled in a tea cart laden with a serving dish of shrimp and grits, accompanied by flaky biscuits, a dish of fig preserves, and pats of butter. She placed the entrees on the table and arranged the china plates and the sterling silverware.

"Is there anything else I can fetch for you, Mademoiselle Josephine?" Emma asked in a voice as sweet as molasses.

"No, Emma. This is lovely. Thank you," Josephine said, dismissing her. Turning to Thomas, she said, "Please help yourself. Emma's shrimp and grits are divine. She brought the recipe with her from Savannah. She's one of that area's coastal Gullah people, slaves imported from Sierra Leone for their skills in rice-growing."

Thomas took a bite of the dish and called to Emma. "Mind if I have your recipe? I've become fairly handy in the kitchen, given I'm a bachelor."

Emma returned swiftly, "No, sir. I can bring it to you in a jiffy."

"Don't bother," he assured her. "I'd like to visit your kitchen if Mademoiselle Josephine will allow."

"Of course," Josephine said. "Emma's cooking rivals the best in Louisiana."

"Come visit me anytime, Mr. Manget," Emma invited, and then left the room.

"There is another matter I need to bring to your attention," Josephine said. "I hardly know how to put this delicately. Rachel is indisposed." She paused, seeing the questioning look on his face. "Women's matters, you understand."

Thomas blushed and set his fork down.

"I mention it only because I think she would be more comfortable resting here for a few days and eating healthy meals to restore her constitution until she has regained enough energy to continue your journey."

"I agree," Thomas said, still embarrassed.

"May I get you anything else to eat?" Josephine asked, seeing that Thomas had finished his dish. "You must be famished."

"No, thank you," Thomas returned with a smile, relieved that she had changed the subject.

"Since you are passing as a tinkerer, you will be provided with a workspace in the blacksmith shop to complete your mending, which Emma informs me is quite considerable."

"I appreciate your hospitality," he managed, taking note of her clear implication that tinkering was only a cover for his mission. "Thank you for the lovely meal. The fig preserves were delightful."

She nodded to Daniel and said, "Please see that our guests' clothes are laundered and pressed. And if they require any provisions, please see that you accommodate them."

"Yes, Mademoiselle," he said, leading Thomas out of the room.

After he left, Josephine returned to gaze at Poydras's portrait and gently stroke the gold crucifix on her necklace. "*C'est un espion parfait, Papi. Vos souhaits vont enfin se réaliser.*"

Having assured her dear Papi that Thomas was the perfect one to facilitate a victory for the Union at Port Hudson, Josephine returned to her chair to finish her coffee, steeling herself against secrets that Thomas could never know.

39

EMMA'S KITCHEN

As the sun dipped low on Friday afternoon, Rachel sat across from Emma in her modest cabin. The space functioned primarily as a kitchen, with little more than a cot pushed against the wall to indicate that she lived there.

Despite the early spring days, a roaring fire burned in the hearth, though only a small one was enough to chase away the morning chill. Above the mantel hung a large painting of President Lincoln, framed in pine, flanked by numerous pots, pans, and various cooking tools hanging on the brick wall. In front of the hearth sat a simple oak table for preparing food, accompanied by two oil lamps and an assortment of spices in handmade pottery containers.

Emma leaned forward in her creaking rocking chair, locking eyes with Rachel. "I enjoyed talking with your brother yesterday.

"He told me he had a pleasant conversation with you as well," Rachel replied. "He suggested I might like to sit and visit a spell this afternoon since he's busy in the blacksmith shop mending pots and pans."

Emma smiled. "That man's a sight for sore eyes. I was beginning to fret about all the mending they needed. It's hard to come by new pots and pans these days."

"Yes, I would imagine so," Rachel said, enjoying Emma's delight in what most would consider a small thing.

"Your brother told me he cooks for himself back home, but I told him he needs a good woman to feed him enough to fill him out. That recipe for shrimp and grits I gave him won't do the job by itself. Tell him to come back to visit before the two of you leave, and I'll give him some of that hoecake you just ate."

Rachel chuckled at Emma's materteral advice to Thomas — the kind only an aunt could give. However, her attention soon shifted to two books on a shelf behind her hostess. The first was Harriet Beecher Stowe's *Uncle Tom's Cabin*, published in 1852, a novel she knew to be immensely popular among Northern abolitionists. However, the book that captivated her was *Clotel or The President's Daughter: A Narrative of Slave Life in the United States* by William Wells Brown.

Published a year after Stowe's work, Brown's novel was the first written by an African who had been enslaved in the United States. It also boldly exposed the affair between President Thomas Jefferson and his slave, Sally Hemings.

Rachel was caught off guard. These books had not been available in New Orleans. She had ordered her own copies from New York in secret, fearing that even possessing such titles might draw unwanted scrutiny from her sister. That Emma not only possessed them but had clearly read and cherished them revealed that she was far more learned than most White women. Emma's presence challenged every assumption upon which the old order rested.

"Your hoecake tastes just like what Rebecca used to make for us," Rachel said, leaning over to the kitchen table to return the serving dish. "I always enjoyed sopping it in the pot liquor from black-eyed peas."

"I like mine with a good glass of buttermilk," Emma said. "Was Rebecca an aunt?"

"No," Rachel replied. "She was one of our servants."

"A slave?"

Rachel blushed. "Yes. She ran off to a Union camp when New Orleans was occupied."

Emma gracefully shifted away from the uncomfortable topic. "I'm sorry about the fire, especially now that it's warmer outside. I've got to burn that oak down to cook tomorrow's food for the Big House."

"How do you manage to keep the food from spoiling overnight?" Rachel asked, relieved to move on past the uncomfortable admission that she had once owned a slave.

"See that big oak box over yonder in the corner? That's my cooling chest."

"Goodness! That's the largest one I've ever seen. I thought it was an armoire!"

"It's hard to get enough ice these days to keep it cold. Ships can't come downriver from up North. Has to be shipped the long way around now."

The two women fell into a brief silence before Emma spoke. "Mr. Thomas told me you're a widow woman."

"Yes, I am. My husband, Levi, died at Shiloh over a year ago."

"I'm so sorry. You must miss him terribly."

Without thinking, Rachel's fingers found Levi's pocket watch hanging on a ribbon around her neck, and she stroked it gently.

"Was that his watch?" Emma asked softly.

"Yes," Rachel replied, realizing how observant Emma was.

"I imagine your brother must miss him, too, being his brother-in-law and all."

Rachel blinked, realizing that Thomas would have been Levi's brother-in-law. Sensing the need to shift the conversation, she quickly found her footing. "Actually, they never met. Thomas wasn't living in New Orleans when I married Levi. He was on an extended business trip to New York and had to miss the wedding."

"I see," Emma said.

The note of suspicion in Emma's voice left Rachel uneasy.

"It's good that you have your brother with you now. He seems to care about you," Emma continued, watching Rachel closely.

Rachel couldn't help but wonder how Emma had formed that impression and why she emphasized "brother" so deliberately.

"He does look out for you, doesn't he?" Emma added.

"Oh yes, he's a good big brother," Rachel said, keeping her tone light, though a flicker of discomfort lingered.

"You're still a young woman. Perhaps one day, you'll find someone as kind and handsome as him and fall in love again."

Rachel offered a small smile. "I'm in no hurry to marry."

Emma rose from her chair and made her way to a wall shelf, her steps marked by a slight limp.

"Are you all right?" Rachel asked, noticing the flicker of pain in Emma's expression.

Emma dismissed her concern with a faint smile. "Ain't nothin', honey. Like my husband always used to say, 'Emma, you got too little feet for too much woman.'"

Rachel couldn't help but smile. She admired Emma's self-deprecating humor, which seemed to embody her resilience and unwavering strength of character.

Emma picked up a large, roughly made clay jar decorated with buttons and small mementos on the outside and turned to show it to Rachel. "This is my memory jar for my late husband, Luke. I made it out of clay and baked it in the oven. I lost him last year when he was shot along the road to Baton Rouge while carrying messages for the Union."

"A memory jar?" Rachel asked. "I think I've heard of those."

"Yes, some folks from Africa, where they came from, still call them spirit jars. It's where you keep things that remind you of your loved one: a button, a scrap of cloth, little things like that," Emma explained with a distant look. "It keeps their memories close."

"That's a lovely idea," 'Rachel said, watching Emma place the jar back on the shelf with reverence.

"It's also a way to mark the end of mourning," Emma continued gently, returning to her rocker. "Sometimes, you need to lay things down to move on. Take that watch you're wearing around your neck. Someday, you might consider placing it in a memory jar. It'll still be there, safe as a memory. But carrying it with you might weigh you down, becoming more of a burden than a comfort."

Rachel touched the watch absently, her fingers brushing its smooth surface as Emma's words lingered.

"I'll think about that," Rachel murmured, realizing there might be more wisdom in the idea than she had initially thought.

"You know, Miss Rachel," Emma said, "you White women have the privilege of mourning your dead, dressing in black, sometimes for years. But for us Negro women, that's a luxury we don't have. On plantations, when we lose a loved one, the best we can do is slip away to a quiet spot in the woods for a funeral. We call it our 'hush harbor.' It has to be late at night when the master is asleep. Then, after the menfolk bury the body in the woods, it's right back to work washing clothes, caring for the White children, and all the rest. But our hearts are still aching."

Rachel felt uncomfortable as she listened to Emma's words, unsure how to respond. She realized she had no way to truly relate to the experiences of someone who had endured life as a slave.

"Besides," Emma said, "if a young man like your brother comes along and fancies you, having that reminder of your husband around your neck might discourage him."

Rachel regarded her momentarily, then said, "I appreciate your advice, Emma. At some point, I may consider acting on it."

Emma's face lit up with a knowing smile, apparently content that she had made her point.

"Josephine seems to be a fine woman," Rachel said, changing the subject.

"We all love her like she was one of us. She's a quinteroon, you know. She's run this place for years. She pays us the same as the Irish folks here and lets us grow our vegetables and raise our hogs and chickens." Emma chuckled, patting her stomach. "I always say we're the best-fed slaves along the Mississippi."

Emma's humor amused Rachel. "I understand that she plans to give all of you your freedom if the Union prevails."

"She told us that if the Confederates win, she'll take us to Texas and then to Mexico. Once we get there, she said she has enough money to get us on a ship in Matamoros to take us to New York. She even plans to give us a little gold to help us get settled."

"I'm sure you would rather the North win. It would be much easier on you than going through all that."

"Yes'm it would," Emma agreed, a thoughtful expression crossing her face. "Be bad for the rebels, though. They always told us Black folks we were inferior because we'd been captured, which made the White race superior. But if they lose to the North, wouldn't that mean Southerners are inferior to Northerners?" Emma's eyes twinkled at the irony of the twisted logic.

"I can't argue with your logic, Emma. If brute force implies superiority, that conclusion proceeds naturally from the premise."

Emma grinned. "You should be a schoolteacher, Miss Rachel."

"That's a compliment, Emma, but I doubt I have the patience."

"Looks like the sun's about to set," Emma remarked, noticing the last golden rays streaking across the worn oak planks of the cabin floor.

"Yes, it's my favorite time of day," Rachel said. "Twilight makes everything look so beautiful, almost like a painting."

"Yes'm. It's 'bout time I warm up some food and take it up to the Big House for supper."

"I should be running along as well. I need to check on my brother and our horse."

"What's your horse's name?"

"Nellie."

Emma stood, stepped over to her cooling chest, and returned with a carrot. "Do you think Nellie would like this?" she asked, offering the carrot to Rachel. "It's fresh from my garden."

"Oh, my goodness!" Rachel said. "Thank you so much. I promised her apples, but she loves carrots."

Emma's eyes sparkled with a warmth that needed no words. "You run along and do what you've got to do, honey. I'll see you and Mr. Thomas up at the Big House for supper."

Rachel left Emma's cabin and strolled along the path toward the Big House. Garlands of purple wisteria blossoms against a background of Spanish moss cascaded from the sprawling oak limbs, and a gentle evening breeze carried the sweet fragrance of gardenias.

The enchanting atmosphere evoked the lyrics from Stephen Foster's most beloved songs she had heard performed by Christy's Minstrels in New Orleans. Yet, she couldn't shake the feeling that his heartfelt lamentation in "Swanee River"—"Oh darkeys, how my heart grows weary/Far from de old folks at home"—would soon become a relic of the past.

As she approached the blacksmith's shop, she spotted Thomas hard at work mending a stack of pots and pans. Leaning through the open doorway, she greeted him with an affectionate smile. "You must be miserable in that heavy outfit, sitting so close to those red-hot coals."

Thomas grinned, wiping the sweat from his brow. "Come on in, sister. Have a seat. You get used to it after a while."

Rachel stayed outside, shaking her head. "Thanks, but I'll stay out here where it's cooler. Besides, we need to head to the Big House for supper. I just came from Emma's. She's warming everything up now."

Thomas sighed and stretched, removing his blacksmith's apron. "You're right about the heat. I'll need a good bath before I'm fit to pull a chair up at the table."

Rachel blushed, thinking that after her time near Emma's fire, she, too, could use a moment to freshen up. "Looks like you've gotten a lot done today."

"I'm beginning to get the hang of this tinkering business," Thomas said proudly. "The trick is getting the pot red-hot, just enough to melt the solder, then applying the dam and letting it harden nice and slow to hold the mend. I'm almost done," he said, wiping the sweat from his forehead. "I'll finish the rest tomorrow in time to pack and head out.

Rachel reflected on how easy it was to coax Thomas to supper, unlike her late husband, who would stay absorbed in his work no matter how often she called him. It always frustrated her to ask her servant to rewarm the food repeatedly, only for it to dry out.

As Thomas stepped outside to join Rachel, he cupped his hand to his ear. "Hear that?"

"Hear what?" Rachel asked.

"The call of a whippoorwill."

Rachel paused, listening to the mournful call. "It's such a haunting sound. My mother used to say that a whippoorwill calls out to a departing soul and guides it to the other side."

"With all the death around us, it's not hard to imagine," Thomas replied somberly.

Rachel nodded, her expression downcast. "Yes, you're right."

As they approached the stable where Nellie was housed, Thomas said, "I need to check on the old girl to see if she has enough food and water. She has a long journey ahead of her tomorrow."

Rachel watched Thomas grab a pitchfork, add fresh hay to Nellie's stall, and check the water trough. "That's a good girl," he murmured, stroking her face with a tenderness that warmed Rachel's heart. It was rare to see such gentleness in a man.

"She's all set for the night," Thomas said, securing the stall and rejoining Rachel.

"Almost," Rachel said, offering Nellie the carrot Emma had given her. "There you are, girl," she cooed as Nellie eagerly accepted the treat. "I promised you something special on the way here. You didn't think I had forgotten, did you?"

A gentle smile crossed his face as he watched the interchange between Rachel and Nellie.

With Nellie settled down for the night, they turned and left together.

40

Port Hudson

After setting out from Buttonwillow early Saturday morning, Thomas and Rachel reached the marshes below the Port Hudson encampment by midday. The waterlogged terrain weighed heavily on Nellie's progress, with each step becoming an increasing struggle as the thick mud clung stubbornly to the wagon wheels, slowing its advance.

"See those white bluffs just up there, at that sharp bend in the river?" Thomas asked, nodding toward the distant rise.

Rachel shaded her eyes with one hand, squinting against the sun. "They're unlike anything I've seen so far. With a few exceptions, the land on both sides of the river has been mostly flat until now."

Thomas gave a knowing smile. "Those bluffs offer a significant tactical advantage. The sharp bend in the river at the bluffs slows navigation, leaving Union ships vulnerable to artillery fire from above. From the perspective of the Union ships on the river, the Confederate artillery is perched nearly eighty feet above them, making it nearly impossible for the ships' cannons to elevate their barrels high enough to fire back effectively. Rear Admiral Farragut found that out the hard way."

Rachel tensed at the mention of Farragut's name, her thoughts rushing back to the day New Orleans fell. The long, mournful cry of the street evangelist's shofar echoed again in her mind.

Thomas's voice pulled her back from her thoughts. "Approaching by land is just as daunting. The ground is either dense pine forest or swamp crawling with snakes and alligators, and the ravines are choked with underbrush so thick it's nearly impossible for soldiers to pass."

Rachel was impressed by the depth of his military knowledge. She couldn't help but wonder how he had acquired it. It was also apparent that he had visited here before. "Why is Port Hudson so important?" she asked.

"In the Confederate blockade of the Mississippi, Port Hudson anchors the south, while Vicksburg anchors the north," Thomas explained. "If the Confederates can hold both, they'll keep east-west communication open via the Red River, which flows from Texas into the Mississippi between the two fortifications."

"I suppose that's why they moved the capital from Baton Rouge to Shreveport, since it's on the Red River," Rachel said.

"Exactly. The Red River is a lifeline, bringing grain and beef from Mexico through Texas into the Confederacy, as well as sugar, salt, and other supplies. It's also a backdoor for arms and goods from Europe, smuggled through the neutral Mexican port of Matamoros and then transported across Texas. If the Confederates lose Port Hudson and Vicksburg, the Union will control the entire Mississippi, cutting the Confederacy in two."

More concerned about their immediate situation, Rachel asked, "So how do we cross the river?"

Thomas scanned the horizon, assessing the path ahead. "There's a ferry just there," he said, pointing toward a distant spot on the riverbank.

Before they could take another step, a sharp voice cut through the stillness. "Halt! Who goes there?"

A Confederate sentry stepped into view, his bayonet fixed and glinting in the light. He was a lean man, perhaps in his thirties, with a bulging wad of tobacco distorting one cheek like a squirrel with a mouthful of nuts.

Thomas turned toward him, unfazed by the weapon leveled at them. "Evening, friend," he said with easy calm.

The sentry narrowed his eyes and took a few steps toward the wagon, spitting a thick brown stream of tobacco juice onto the ground as he approached. Rachel's stomach churned at the sight, the bitter stench of tobacco making her fight the urge to recoil in disgust.

"Let me see your pass," he barked.

Thomas reached into his pocket and pulled out his pass.

The sentry raised an eyebrow, his suspicion evident as he examined the pass. "This is signed by General Banks," he muttered, twisting his expression into a sneer. "That's only good for Union territory. Where exactly are you coming from, and what's your business here?"

Thomas remained calm, though the air between them was charged. "We're peddlers out of Baton Rouge," he said smoothly. "Union-held, yes, but we've got shoes to sell at Port Hudson."

The sentry's eyes narrowed as he spat another wad of tobacco onto the ground, the dark stain marking his growing mistrust. "Like I said before. Union pass don't mean a damn here, mister. You're crossin' into Confederate territory now. If you want to pass through, you'll have to clear it with me." His fingers tightened on his rifle as if to emphasize the threat.

Rachel felt her pulse quicken, and she struggled to remain calm.

The sentry's eyes lingered on Thomas, waiting for a response.

"This lady beside me here is my sister. Her husband died fighting for the Cause at Shiloh, and we're trying to join our relatives across the line. Everybody leaving Baton Rouge headed north has to have a pass from the Union."

The sentry handed back the pass. "Sorry 'bout your husband, ma'am," he said, tipping his visored kepi cap.

"Thank you, sir," she replied softly.

Turning to Thomas, the sentry said, "You don't sound like no peddler to me, mister. You sound like one of them college boys. You say you got shoes to sell?"

"Yes. A few dozen pairs and some boots. All used, but in good condition."

"Can't say we don't need shoes. We got men marchin' 'round barefoot."

"Can we cross?" Thomas asked.

"Follow me. I'll tell the waterman to take you over. It's just up the way a piece."

With the sentry leading the way, Thomas guided his wagon behind him. The road soon became marshier, and Nellie slowed to a snail's pace from the drag of the mud on the wagon's wheels.

"It ain't far now," the sentry called back.

Within minutes, the sentry reached the ferryman while Nellie struggled to catch up.

When Thomas pulled up to the ferryman, he asked, "How much do you charge to take a wagon across?"

"Ain't no charge. The rebels pay me."

"Thanks," Thomas said, stepping down from the wagon and guiding a hesitant Nellie toward the ferry. "Might take a minute. Looks like Nellie's not too fond of deep water."

"Must be her first time," the ferryman grinned. "An apple'll fix that in a jiffy."

"You happen to have one on you?"

"Always keep a few for the stubborn ones," the ferryman replied, fishing an apple from his jacket pocket and handing it over. "Have to use 'em on my team when they don't feel like pullin' the ferry back. I swear they've got me trained."

"Much appreciated," Thomas said, taking the apple and using it to coax Nellie forward.

Rachel, sitting in the wagon, watched the ferry with a mix of fascination and unease. Though she had seen ferries along the river at various plantations, often pulled by teams of horses, she could only recall being on one as a child with her father. Gripping the edge of the seat, she braced herself, her mind drifting to the unsettling fact that she had never learned to swim. Her fear stemmed from childhood memories of leeches along the riverbank: slick, silent creatures that clung to muddy shallows and tangled reeds. In her nightmares, they lurked just beneath the surface of dark water, waiting to attach to bare skin.

"Works like a charm," the ferryman called, noticing Nellie eagerly taking the apple from Thomas's hand. "Just keep her steady while I untie the raft and push us off," he said, grabbing his oar. "I'll yell at my buddy across the way to have his horses pull us t'other side."

Once the ferry was safely moored on the other side of the river, Nellie needed no coaxing to pull the wagon onto solid ground.

"That's a good girl," Thomas said, stroking Nellie's face. He glanced up at Rachel and called, "You all right, Sis?"

"Yes," she replied, relieved that the wagon had finally reached dry ground, yet unsettled by the way he called her sister when she was beginning to feel something for him that was anything but sisterly.

A young sentry, barely in his teens, sat astride a well-groomed chestnut stallion on the riverbank. "You folks can follow me," he called to Thomas, his voice still reedy, not yet deepened by manhood. "Ain't nobody I know of gonnah pass by here soon." The sentinel pointed toward the distant woods. "It's a little marshy here, but the trail ahead leads to higher ground, lined with pine trees and a few palmettos on either side. Beyond that, the ground's even higher and dryer, with nothin' but tall pines and thick briar underbrush."

"Thanks," Thomas said, climbing up to his seat in the wagon.

"That soldier seems friendly enough," Rachel said. "Such a young man."

"Wait until he tells his buddies what we have stashed in the back. We'll be a sight for sore eyes when we reach the camp."

Rachel smiled pleasantly. "I should think so. The soldier across the way said some men are walking around barefoot."

"I don't know if you noticed that boy's shoes. The wood pegs are coming loose, and the soles are starting to fall off. He'll be mighty glad when he sees our hand-stitched ones."

Thomas followed the youthful sentry up the dirt road as it climbed to higher ground and wound through a pine forest, his eyes drawn to the deep ravines flanking the path. Any troops that veered off the trail would find themselves trapped in these trench-like formations, thick with vines and thorny undergrowth. He observed that a group of soldiers, including several conscripted slaves, was chopping down small trees and brush to fill the ravines, further fortifying the natural barriers. This left only the main trail, which could easily be blockaded and defended by a phalanx of soldiers, their formation ensuring a clear, unobstructed shot at the enemy.

Further along, a field cleared of pine trees was visible, where countless rows of dust-brown canvas army tents of various types lined the road, stretching far into the distance. Some soldiers milled about, while others sat on barrels and crates, cleaning their weapons.

The sentry guiding Thomas and Rachel slowed his horse to ride alongside their wagon. "You folks can take a couple of the officers' tents we ain't using yet. We're expectin' more troops from Camp Moore and Texas any day now. Mess is around six. It ain't fancy, but y'all are welcome to grab a plate."

"Thanks," Thomas said.

"One more thing," the sentry added.

"What's that?"

"What you got to sell in that wagon?"

"Mostly shoes, but we got a lot of other stuff," Thomas returned.

"How much you want for a pair 'o them shoes?"

"A dollar."

"They the good ones?"

"The best you'll find. The shoes are all hand-stitched and are almost like new. And the boots are saddle-stitched to stand up to marching."

"A buck ain't bad for the shoes. Last time I bought myself a pair, they set me back five. Could you let me know before you start sellin' 'em so I can buy a pair? Don't mean to sound selfish or nothin', but your wagon ain't able to hold 'nough shoes for everbody who needs 'em."

Thomas's expression softened, a flicker of quiet amusement touching his features as he took in the sergeant's roundabout plea. The young man clearly wanted a pair of shoes but hesitated to ask outright.

"What's your name, soldier?"

"Ernest Johnson, sir."

"Thomas," he replied, extending a hand. "And this is my sister, Rachel. We're up from Baton Rouge way. I'll let you know before we set up shop."

The sergeant leaned in slightly, lowering his voice in a confidential tone. "I wouldn't mention the shoes right now, if I was you. Best wait 'til morning. If word gets out you've got good shoes and boots, you might start a barefoot stampede."

Thomas grinned. "Sounds like good advice."

"You ain't related to the Simpsons in Baton Rouge, are you?"

Thomas tilted his head, thinking. "Seems my grandmother mentioned some Simpsons somewhere along the way."

A warm smile spread across Ernest's face. "Then I reckon we're cousins."

"Could be, Ernest. Think you might show me around once we're settled? I hear you've got some heavy artillery up on the bluff."

Pride lit the young man's eyes. "That ain't the only place we've got the big guns. Plenty of lunettes are scattered around. I'll find you a horse to ride with me while yours gets a rest—looks like that old hag's earned one. Not much else for me to do once I get y'all to your tents and settle your horse in for the night." He paused, then added with an affable shrug, "Least I can do for kin."

41

To Catch a Spy

As the sun dipped low behind the pine trees, the sky above the Port Hudson camp transformed into a brilliant canvas of twinkling stars, growing sharper and brighter against the darkening background.

Soldiers huddled around the last flickering embers of the campfire, lit stubby cigars, shared stories of Shiloh, and spoke nostalgically of home. The mournful notes of a lone harmonica floated through the gentle evening breeze, blending with the sharp, rhythmic calls of tree frogs.

Sitting beside Thomas, Rachel responded to the attention of several soldiers with a gentle smile, her eyes modestly cast down as she engaged in light conversation. The men, respectful with their "Yes, ma'am" and "No, ma'am," lingered by the campfire, clearly enjoying the rare company of a single woman traveling with her brother. They eventually headed off to their tents one by one, casting glances back as though hoping for an excuse to linger longer.

"Goodnight, Miss Rachel," the last soldier said, tipping his hat.

"Goodnight, sir," she replied softly.

Once the last soldier retired, Rachel and Thomas sat alone by the glowing embers of the campfire.

"How was your tour of Port Hudson today?" Rachel asked.

"I was impressed with what they've accomplished in such a short period," Thomas said, poking at the embers with a stick. Tiny flames sprang to life, dancing for a moment before fading back into the coals.

"Such a nice young man to show you around," Rachel remarked, though she sounded disinterested.

"Yes, he was. When we returned, I let him pick out a pair of shoes for his trouble."

"That was kind of you," Rachel said, stifling a yawn as she stretched. "I'm sorry, Thomas, I'm exhausted. I spent the afternoon entertaining the troops. Several officers asked me if I would accompany them to a ball at Linwood Plantation next Saturday. Seems they don't get many lady visitors here when they're on leave."

"The Morgans have been staying with relatives at Linwood since Baton Rouge was occupied. The family has gone out of their way to entertain the officers at their plantation while fortifying Port Hudson."

"You know the Morgans?"

"Very well. I worked in Judge Morgan's practice before he passed. His daughter Sarah often visited the office. She idolized her father."

"I think Levi mentioned a Judge Morgan once," Rachel said, her voice trailing. "But I never met the family." She stretched and yawned again. "I really must get to bed. I'm exhausted."

"I'll see you early tomorrow," Thomas said as she prepared to leave. "We've got a long day ahead."

Rachel stood and smoothed her skirt, the firelight flickering against the gentle contours of her face. "Goodnight, then."

"Goodnight, Sis."

She walked off into the darkness, the soft swish of her skirts fading with her footsteps.

Thomas stayed by the fire, the quiet surrounding him. He watched where she had gone, still and thoughtful. There was a rare strength and gentle charm about her. It was something he had come to depend on without fully realizing it. She carried herself with quiet dignity, unlike the superficiality of coquettes who smirked through plantation parlors in peaceful times.

He had called her "Sis," as he must. But as the embers released their last whispers of heat, Thomas felt something stirring inside him beyond admiration, and wondered how long he could keep pretending to be her brother.

Inside his tent, Thomas pulled out the envelope Lytle had given him. Sitting on his cot, he carefully sliced through the twine with his pocketknife and sorted the contents. Mixed in with the portraits of Confederate soldiers were photographs of Union military formations, encampments, and artillery stationed in Baton Rouge. *Just as I thought,* he told himself, setting aside the portraits of Confederate soldiers for later distribution, before standing with the Union photos in hand to exit his tent.

Outside, Thomas glanced around to ensure he was alone before returning to the campfire. The crackle of embers mingled with the fading calls of the tree frogs, giving way to the softer, steady chirping of crickets in the stillness. With deliberate care, he tossed several Union photographs onto the embers, where they burst into flames and curled like burning autumn leaves. With a final flick of his wrist, he threw the last of them onto the fire.

Destroying what could have been a crucial advantage for the Confederacy brought him a slight sense of victory. But the real prize lay in the valuable intelligence he had gathered during the young sentry's tour of the stronghold earlier today. The boy had eagerly revealed every detail of the fortifications, proud of his knowledge, never suspecting he was giving away far more than he should.

The crackling of burning photographic paper and chemical odor was soon joined by the soft sound of footsteps approaching from behind. Thomas turned, his eyes narrowing as a guard stepped into the firelight.

"What are you burning?" the guard demanded.

"Just some papers," Thomas replied, trying to keep his tone casual, even as he realized he had made a serious mistake by destroying the photographs out in the open.

The guard stepped closer and spotted the last photographs smoldering among the embers. Using his bayonet, he pinned one of them out of the fire and stomped on it to extinguish the flames. "These look like Union military formations," he muttered before calling out sharply, "Sergeant Davis. Over here, on the double!"

The sergeant quickly approached. "Yes, Lieutenant. What seems to be the problem?"

"I caught this man burning photographs of Union military operations. Baton Rouge, most likely, since he told a sentry that's where he came from. He claims he's a peddler, but I suspect he's a spy. Take him to his tent and get somebody to help tie him up. We'll deal with him in the morning."

"Yes, sir," the sergeant responded with a crisp salute.

"I'm not a spy," Thomas protested, his voice steady but tense.

"Sir," the sergeant said, "I overheard this man asking Sergeant Johnson for a tour of the fortifications earlier today."

"Not a spy, you say?" the lieutenant snapped, his expression hardening. "We'll see what Sergeant Johnson says in the morning."

Sergeant Davis held his bayonet against Thomas's back. "Best you come quietly, mister. You can explain yourself at your court-martial first thing in the morning."

Hearing a scuffle from Thomas's tent, Rachel stood from her cot and cautiously peeked through the small opening in her tent flap to see a guard standing outside with his back turned. Quietly, she opened the flap wider, her eyes drawn to the flickering shadows on Thomas's tent wall. She stared in disbelief at what appeared to be two men struggling with a third figure who had to be Thomas.

She knew better than to get involved. As a woman, she could do little to help him, and getting caught could make things worse. But what had Thomas done to deserve such treatment?

Moments later, she heard Thomas shout, "I'm telling you, I'm not a spy!" A muffled sound followed his defiant cry, then silence as the men exited his tent.

"A spy?" she whispered in disbelief, her heart racing. Pressing her ear against the flap, she strained to catch the conversation between the two men outside.

"I caught him in the act, burning photographs of Union formations in Baton Rouge," the first man said. "And he spent the day with Sergeant Johnson, getting a tour of our defenses."

"Do you think the woman with him is a spy, too?" the second man asked.

"Who knows? Tomorrow, the Colonel will get to the bottom of it."

When the two men walked away, Rachel peeked out her tent flap and saw the armed guard still stationed in front of Thomas's tent. What could she do? Was it true that Thomas was a spy? And what if they decided she was a spy as well?

Without thinking, Rachel touched Levi's watch, which was still hanging around her neck. Its familiar weight grounded her. *What would he have done?* she wondered. Her heart pounded. *Was this war to claim yet another life she cared about?*

She pressed her lips together. *There must be another way. There has to be. But what?*

She turned to the back of the tent, dropped to her knees, and tugged at the canvas. It was secured tightly; the stakes hammered deep into the earth. She gritted her teeth and yanked at one, finally creating a small gap between canvas and soil. "Think, Rachel," she murmured. "You won't have another chance."

After several attempts, she wriggled through the opening, breathing heavily as she emerged outside. Brushing dirt from her dress, she stood and glanced toward Thomas's tent, her heart still pounding. Quietly, she approached and crouched down, pulling several stakes loose to lift a corner of the canvas. Slipping under, she gasped at the sight of Thomas, trussed like a hog and gagged on the ground.

His eyes widened when he saw her, and he tried to speak, but she quickly pressed a finger to her lips and then gently removed the gag.

"I left a pocketknife on the cot," Thomas whispered. "See if it's still there."

Rachel spotted the glint of steel, partially concealed beneath a fold of the sheet. She grabbed the knife and began cutting through the ropes.

Once he was freed, Rachel slipped back under the canvas, and he followed closely behind.

Outside, Thomas stole a glance around the corner. A lone guard leaned against a post, a cigar glowing at his lips, oblivious to their escape. Together, they cautiously navigated the maze of tents, their soft footsteps blending with the chorus of snores, occasional murmurs from soldiers lost in dreams, and the haunting screams of those ensnared in nightmares.

When they reached the camp road, Nellie was still tied to a tree, standing patiently beside a scatter of hay and a battered tin basin half-filled with water.

Thomas helped Rachel onto the wagon seat, then stepped around to the rear.

She watched as he crouched low, pried the lid off a tin of bear grease, and dipped a rag-wrapped stick into the pungent salve. He quickly worked the grease into each wheel hub.

When he finished, Thomas wiped his hands on a clean rag, untied Nellie's lead, and climbed up to his seat. He flicked the reins without a word, and the wagon moved forward silently into the night.

Once they were safely out of earshot, Thomas stopped the wagon and jumped down from his seat to steady Nellie. "It's all right, girl," he whispered, stroking her jowl reassuringly. "I just need to get a few things out of the back."

Rachel watched Thomas unload the wagon, hurriedly tossing shoes and boots onto the road. Curious, she climbed down to help.

"Why are you throwing all the boots and shoes out?" she asked.

"If there's one thing that'll slow them down, it's just that," he said, a determined glint in his eyes.

After he had finished, Rachel asked, "What now?"

"Let me help you back onto the wagon so you can watch," Thomas said. He guided Rachel into her seat, climbed beside her, and took hold of the reins. With a soft click of his tongue, he urged Nellie forward over the marshy ground. "Come on, old girl, you've got this."

Minutes later, they reached the ferry. It was moored for the night with no ferryman, sentry, or horses in sight. Thomas halted the wagon and jumped down, rushing to the ferry. He severed the mooring ropes with several quick slashes of his pocketknife, and the current swiftly swept the ferry downriver.

Returning to the wagon, Thomas moved it forward about ten yards and stopped. He grabbed a broom from the back and returned to where he had unloaded the shoes, carefully sweeping away the wagon tracks and his footprints as he walked backward to the wagon.

"The rebs will think we took the ferry downstream. Now, we follow the road along the river until daybreak," Thomas said as he climbed back into the driver's seat. "We'll stop at the first plantation with a ferry since we need to reach the other side to get to Baton Rouge. Someone will take two peddlers across, either out of Southern hospitality or for a good fare." He pulled a money pouch from under the seat and handed it to her. "Good thing they didn't search the wagon back at the camp."

Rachel sat quietly, holding the money pouch, her thoughts racing. She turned around in her seat, marveling at how Thomas had thrown the footwear on the road to slow their pursuers, cut the ferry loose to mislead them, and brushed away their tracks.

From how Thomas had taken control of their escape, it was evident he was far more than just a lawyer. *Who is this man?* she wondered. Though she had been the one to release him, his calm precision and strategic planning had now led them to safety. Their roles in the escape complemented each other perfectly.

A rare stillness settled over her as she watched the stars shimmer like diamonds across the river's gentle ripples. Silver-bellied mullet leaped from the water, their sleek bodies catching the moonlight before vanishing into the current below with a splash. The beauty of the peaceful scene was untouched by the weight of war or worry.

She glanced at Thomas, silhouetted against the night, his posture relaxed, though she sensed his mind still turning over the next steps ahead. There was a quiet strength in him that made her feel secure.

Rachel looked away quickly, her heart unexpectedly full. She had vowed never to feel this way again after losing Levi. But the truth pressed gently against her resolve: she was beginning to care for Thomas in a way that both frightened and consoled. It was not only his protection she cherished, but the way he listened to her and trusted her.

Beneath the moonlight, she realized that her feelings for him were no longer something she could ignore.

The sharp crack of a shot echoed along the riverbanks, shattering the silence. Rachel swayed in her seat, on the verge of tumbling from the wagon.

"Whoa, Nellie!" Thomas called, bringing the wagon to a sudden halt. He jumped from his seat and dashed to the other side, catching Rachel in time to soften her fall. As he steadied her, his eyes caught a blood stain on the sleeve of her dress. A bullet had wounded her right arm.

"It's only a graze, Rachel. You'll be all right," he reassured her, though her wide-eyed expression showed she was in shock.

Crouching behind the wagon with Rachel safely on the ground, Thomas peered around its edge. In the moonlight, a horseman in civilian clothing approached. Recognizing him as a sharpshooter armed with a rifle, Thomas quietly returned to his side of the wagon and retrieved his revolver from under the seat. Keeping low, he glanced around Nellie and saw that the man had stopped just a few yards ahead.

With a single shot, Thomas hit the man square in the chest, causing him to fall off his horse and hit the ground. Thomas quickly ran over to the man, confirming that he was dead. He rifled through the man's belongings, pulling off a leather ammunition bag before dragging the body to the side of the road. After slapping the sniper's horse on the rump to send it running, Thomas glanced down and noticed a Whitworth rifle beside him, a prized British weapon smuggled to the Confederates by blockade runners.

He reflected that, despite England's official declaration of neutrality, the government seemed to turn a blind eye to manufacturers supplying arms to the Confederacy. These transactions were cleverly disguised in shipping manifests, falsely listing the destination as China.

Returning to the wagon with the sniper's rifle and ammunition bag, Thomas stowed them securely under the tarp covering the wagon bed. He then quickly lifted the tarp's edge and reached inside to grab a clean rag. Kneeling beside Rachel, he saw the blood oozing from the gash in her arm.

"I need to tend to your wound," he said gently, before ripping the blood-stained sleeve of her dress.

After securing a makeshift dressing with a tight knot, he gently lifted Rachel onto the wagon. He then retrieved a blanket, draped it over her, and climbed aboard, pulling her close into his arms.

"Does it hurt badly?" he asked when he saw that she was alert again.

"No," she said faintly, her lip trembling. "But I'm frightened, Thomas. Is the man who shot me gone?" she asked, her gaze clouded with pain and fear as she searched his face.

Thomas hesitated, then nodded, gently stroking her hair, recalling her father's comforting touch during childhood mishaps. "Don't be afraid, Rachel. He's gone."

At that moment, the sharpness of the wound dulled as Rachel felt herself wrapped in the comfort of his embrace. For the first time in her life, she gasped for air, but it was not from pain or fear. *Why does my heart tremble so?* she wondered.

"Are you all right?" Thomas asked, his eyes widening.

Rachel exhaled slowly as she met Thomas's gaze. The tenderness in his eyes stirred something deep within, and words failed her. Surrendering completely to the overwhelming rush of emotions flooding her heart, she realized that she had fallen deeply, irreversibly in love.

42

EMANCIPATION PLANTATION

Sunday morning broke softly with the first rays of sunlight filtering through a canopy of tender, emerald-green spring leaves that arched over the road. Yet the canopy was open enough that, high above, beneath a cloudless turquoise sky, migrating pelicans could be seen gliding in elegant formations, their broad wings slicing effortlessly through the air. Below them, swallows darted and swooped with playful agility, their sleek bodies and forked tails tracing intricate patterns in the soft morning light.

"Look up there," Thomas said to a weary Rachel. "A flock of pelicans. It's a good omen."

Rachel returned a silent nod, feeling the pain in her arm worsening as her gaze traced the flight of the birds gliding effortlessly across the sky. She knew the pelican was incorporated into Louisiana's state seal, an ancient symbol of resilience and selfless love. Mother pelicans were said to rip open their breasts to feed their chicks their flesh when food was scarce. Their presence brought her a small yet welcome sense of comfort.

Around a bend in the river, a manned ferry appeared in the distance, with a ferryman, a passenger, and a buggy. Across the river, beyond a stand of oak trees, lay a sugarcane field, signaling the proximity of a plantation.

"Now that it's daylight, we have a decent shot at crossing here," Thomas said. "The ferryman seems to know what he's doing, bringing that man and his buggy across. Besides, the river forks here, so it's not as wide. We can manage the second part of the fork later."

"Aren't you worried the ferry might get washed downriver?" Rachel asked, an edge of tension in her voice. "They're no horses with ropes drawing it across to this side."

"Take a closer look," Thomas said, nodding toward the water. "There's a rope stretched across the current to guide the ferry."

Rachel exhaled a sigh of relief. "I suppose it's safe. Maybe the plantation's owner will take us in," she said hopefully.

"Once they see you're wounded, I'm sure they'll give us food and shelter. It's the Southern code…unless you've switched sides and become a Yankee after that rebel shot you."

Rachel forced a smile. "Yes, it is the Southern code," she replied, ignoring his remark. The truth was too complicated, and she wasn't ready to open that door yet.

"It will be some time before we can reach Baton Rouge to have a doctor examine that arm. Best we see if we can get some honey and sugar at the plantation to stop any infection."

Thomas pulled the wagon to a halt beside the landing, waiting for the ferryman to reach them.

The Negro ferryman, his arms as thick as most men's thighs, skillfully navigated the river with a large pole, pausing occasionally to grasp the lifeline and rest from battling the current.

Moments later, the ferryman tossed a rope ashore. Thomas caught it and tugged until the ferry beached.

"Thank you, suh," the ferryman called, tossing his pole on shore and mooring the ferry securely to a post. Once the ferry was secure, he motioned to his passenger to disembark with his wagon.

When the wagon left, the ferryman shouted, "Y'all Yankees or Rebels?"

"We have a pass from General Banks," Thomas called back.

"Reckon that means y'all be Yankees. You got that wagon loaded down? Don't want it to sink my ferry."

"No. It's almost empty," Thomas assured him.

"Go 'head and pull it on. Then git down off yo' wagon to steady yo' hoss. We might git to rockin' and I don't want to lose nobody," the ferryman warned. "'Specially no good hoss."

Thomas smiled at the man's wry humor, stepping back from the riverbank to guide Nellie, now an experienced passenger, onto the ferry. Once the wagon was secure, he held Nellie's reins and whispered, "Good girl. Nice and steady."

The ferryman untied the ferry, took his pole, and pushed it away from the riverbank. Eyeing Thomas, he asked, "Where you folks be headed?"

"Baton Rouge."

"What yo' names?

"My name is Thomas. My sister here is Rachel."

"Mine's Lijah. Looks like yo' sister has a hurt arm. She git shot by one'uh them rebel guerrillas?"

"Yes, she did," Thomas said. "We'll need to change that dressing."

The ferryman grimaced, struggling with the pole. "You need tuh see Mama Mary. She's thuh ole conjur woman on thuh plantation 'cross the ribber. She can fix that arm up in a jiffy."

"Which plantation is this, Lijah?" Thomas asked.

"We'se call it 'Mansipashun Plantation,'" the ferryman announced proudly, managing to speak while straining to fight the current. "Cause now we nigguhs own it. 'Leastways 'til somebody come and tells us different. Mighty fine place, sitiated where thuh ribber splits in two, so we gots ribber in thuh front and ribber in thuh back."

"So, what happened to the plantation's owners?" Thomas asked.

"Massah took his Misses and no 'count younguns and skedaddled when the Yanks come. Yanks took most everythin' from the Big House. We even hepped 'em pack it all up, 'cause us slaves ain't used to that fancy White folk stuff nohow."

"After we see Mama Mary, do you think we could stay a few days until my sister gets better, Lijah?"

"Shore 'nough, Mr. Thomas. We gots lots of food if you don't mind sweet taters and chicken with the massah's whisky to wash it down your gullet. Even gots a little bacon now the massah and all his no count younguns gone and left all thuh hogs behind." Lijah grinned from ear to ear. "First time most 'o us et high on thuh hog. We use'ta just git thuh feet, thuh ears, thuh tail, thuh snout, and thuh ears." He chuckled, "Sometimes they even thro'd us thuh squeal on Sundays."

"We appreciate the hospitality, Lijah," Thomas returned with a broad smile. "I can pay for our food and lodging."

"Keep yo' money," Lijah said with a grin. "Massah had us dig a deep hole under the big oak out back and bury his trunk o' gold. Tole us not to let the Yanks find it. Took four strong men to get it in the ground. Took fewer to dig it back up after he left." His grin widened. "Don't recall massah sayin' nothin' 'bout us not usin' it for what we need."

Once ashore, Lijah mounted his horse, and Thomas followed in his wagon along the oak-lined riverbank, then turned to follow a narrow path through a sugarcane field leading to Emancipation Plantation.

The estate was modest by plantation standards, with a whitewashed, two-story Big House nestled among the cane fields. In the distance, rows of abandoned slave cottages dotted the landscape, silent reminders of a past left behind by their former residents, who had moved on to enjoy the luxury of their former owner's mansion.

Pulling up to the entrance of the Big House, Thomas asked, "Is that the crack of a horsewhip I hear?"

Lijah grinned broadly. "Yassah. That be thuh sound of thuh chastisement o' Big John."

"Big John?" Thomas asked, eyebrows raised.

"Yassah, Big John. He be thuh 'ole massah's fo'man," Lijah said with a dramatic wave of his hand. "Ain't nothin' worse than a nigguh man who think he be White. When Big John look in thuh glass ever mornin' and lather up to shave, he see a White man. Then he spend thuh whole day, from can't see to can't see, puttin' down his own people fo' thuh massah. Then he go home to a nice place with a fancy karsene lamp and feed his big fat belly with all thuh hog meat thuh massah give 'im, while thuh rest o' us eat molassus and stone cold corn pone in thuh dark. Only thing can straight'n Big John out's a good whippin' to 'mind him he still be a nigguh like all thuh rest of us is. And when we's done whippin' him, we gonnah tie 'im up and toss 'im on thuh ferry up at Pote Hudsun, where thuh Rebs can put 'im to work diggin' ditches all day in thuh hot sun."

Thomas nodded but held his tongue, letting Lijah's scornful litany pass without interruption. It was plain enough that Big John—a fellow Negro who drove his own people mercilessly from "can't see to can't see," the bitter phrase slaves used for the grinding toil from first light to nightfall—was loathed not just for his cruelty, but for the way he had taken up the habits and airs of the White overseers, as if brutality could buy him a place among them.

"If y'all step down from thuh wagon and hitch yo' horse to thuh post at thuh house," Lijah said, "y'all can set up on thuh front porch and rock in thuh shade while I fetch Mama Mary to look at yo' sistah's arm."

"Thank you," Thomas replied, stepping down from the wagon to help Rachel. "You mind if I get water from that pump over yonder?"

"Hep yo'self," Lijah said, heading down the dirt path alongside the cane field. "It be used so much, it don't need no primin'."

"Thanks," Thomas said as he helped Rachel up the porch steps. After settling her into a rocking chair, he walked over to the pump near the edge of the porch. Working the handle until clear cold water gushed from the spout, he filled a bucket halfway and carried it back to Rachel.

"Here," he said, handing her the enameled dipper.

Rachel accepted the dipper with her good arm and sighed gratefully. "Thank you, Thomas. My throat's parched."

"So's mine," Thomas said, taking the dipper after she had finished.

Setting the bucket on the porch, they sat in companionable silence, watching as a gentle breeze rustled through the leaves of the nearby trees. A tabby tomcat wandered into the yard, only to be chased off by dive-bombing bluejays, leaving the yowling cat scurrying away with a few tufts of fur missing. The ensuing tranquil scene was punctuated by the occasional sharp crack of the whip coming from around the house, a reminder of Big John's ongoing chastisement.

Thomas glanced down the path and spotted Lijah returning, accompanied by a stout elderly black woman wearing a white turban. Dressed in a simple smock and apron, she carried a wooden crate with a handle. As they drew closer, Thomas noticed the crate contained glass bottles of various colors separated by neatly folded white rags.

"I got mo' work to do," Lijah said, tipping his hat as he left. "Mama Mary will fix yo' sistuh up."

"Thank you, Lijah," Thomas called after him.

Mama Mary stepped onto the porch with a warm, knowing smile. "Hear yo' sistah got shot by them infernal reb guerrillas," she said. "They got them fancy guns from England. Some of 'em come 'round here shootin' cans off thuh fence rails so far off I could hardly see 'em."

"Yes, ma'am," Thomas replied. "My name is Thomas, and this is my sister, Rachel."

"Folks 'round here call me thuh conjur woman. You can call me Mama Mary. My mama learned me how to heal folks with what thuh good Lord made to grow in thuh woods."

"Do you think you could treat my sister's arm?" Thomas asked.

Mama Mary leaned forward, carefully unwrapping the bandage around Rachel's wound. "Hmm," she murmured. "Ain't so bad. Nothin' I can't fix with a coneflower plaster."

She sat on the porch step and began selecting items from her crate: a bottle of honey, a jar of dried coneflower petals, and coneflower roots from the echinacea plant. Using a mortar and pestle, she ground the herbs with the honey into a paste. Satisfied with the consistency, she added a few drops of witch-hazel, blending it into the mixture.

"Here we is," Mama Mary said proudly, applying the poultice to Rachel's wound with a small wooden spoon. "This'll sting a bit, baby, but it'll feel better soon."

Rachel winced but didn't cry out.

"You all right, chile?" Mama Mary asked gently.

Rachel managed to coax a faint smile. "I'm fine. It's just cold."

Mama Mary wrapped the wound with a clean white rag, tying it securely.

Rachel looked up at her. "It's already starting to feel better."

"Told ya, honey. Mama Mary know what best."

"Thank you," Thomas said, reaching into his pocket. "How much do I owe you?"

Mama Mary let out a raspy laugh that rippled from head to toe. "You don't owe me nothin', young fellah. Thuh conjur woman work fo' thuh Lord. He pay me in heaven."

"Thank you so much," Rachel added sincerely.

"How long before we can remove the bandage?" Thomas asked.

"Don't let her lift nothin'. Best she stay rockin' out here on thuh front po'ch awhile. Later on, keep her in bed. Call me in thuh mornin' when she's rested, and I'll come check on her."

"We'll stay until she's well enough to travel if that's all right," Thomas offered.

"Course you can," Mama Mary said, as though leaving now was unthinkable. She reached into her crate and pulled out a small brown glass bottle. "Take a spoonful o' this willow bark tea 'fo bedtime, baby, and agin in thuh mornin'. It'll fight thuh fever."

"Thanks again," Thomas said.

"See y'all later," Mama Mary said, gathering her crate. "Lijah wants me to put a poltice on Big John's back. He want that mean nigger healed real good 'fo they send 'im upriver to Pote Hudsun. Rebs don't want no damaged goods."

After she left, Rachel turned to Thomas with a wry smile. "Seems the whole plantation can't wait to get rid of Big John."

Thomas grinned. "Yeah, but not before the chastisement's done."

43

THE SUGAR HOUSE

Early Tuesday morning, Mama Mary carefully unwrapped the dressing around Rachel's arm. "Lookin' purty good," she declared. "Once I cleans it up a bit and makes another poultice, wrap it proper, y'all be ready to go 'bout y'alls business."

Rachel smiled warmly. "It feels so much better, Mama Mary. You've been wonderful. But you didn't have to wash and iron my dress." She paused, brushing her fingers over the sleeve. "When I put it on, I noticed the tear where Thomas had to rip the fabric was mended. And this lace you added to cover the mend with a matching piece on the other sleeve is beautiful. The dress is even lovelier now than it was before."

"Pshaw! It ain't nothin'," Mama Mary replied, brushing off the compliment with a wave of her hand, though her face lit up with an unmistakable pride.

"Everyone here has been so kind," Rachel added. "This is only the third time I've stayed overnight on a plantation."

"What other plantations you been to?" Mama Mary asked, curious.

"My brother and I stayed at Buttonwillow, near Port Hudson," Rachel explained.

Mama Mary nodded knowingly. "I knows that lady. She treat her slaves real good. Tried to set 'em free, but the gov'ment stopped her."

"Yes, that's true," Rachel agreed. "And she was a lovely hostess."

"What was the other plantation you stayed at?"

Rachel paused, her memories drifting back. "Well, when I was a child, my father took me on a day's buggy ride to Judah Benjamin's Bellechasse Plantation, about twenty miles south of New Orleans. It was near the river like this. I remember it was a beautiful fall day, and he took my sister and me to the sugar house to make pull candy." She laughed softly. "Even though he had me butter my hands, the candy was so hot it burned."

Mama Mary smiled tenderly, a distant look in her eyes. "I 'member fall use'ta be the best time o' year for my two little boys. They use'ta beg me to take 'em out back so they could pull some candy." Her expression darkened. "That was 'fo the massah sold 'em downriver. Ain't never seen 'em since."

Mama Mary's words hit Rachel hard; the reality felt like a heavy stone on her chest. She tried to fathom the unbearable pain of a mother losing her children, torn from her arms and sold like property, all because of the color of her skin.

Her thoughts turned to her young nephew, Noah. The very idea of someone taking him from her sister, never to be seen again, was a nightmare beyond comprehension. Rachel shuddered as she pictured her sister's heart breaking as if Noah were nothing more than a piece of livestock to be bought and sold on the auction block. She couldn't imagine her baby sister surviving the loss.

Rachel swallowed hard, her throat tightening with emotion as she reached out and placed a comforting hand on Mama Mary's. "I hope that one day you find your boys. I know they still love you," she whispered, her voice thick with sincerity.

"Thank you, chile," Mama Mary replied softly, a tear welling in her eye.

Rachel reflected that it was the first time she had held a negress' hand. The sensation, warm though unfamiliar, felt deeply human, bridging a silent divide. In that moment, Rachel understood more than ever the horror and cruelty that had kept people of different races from experiencing such sacred and straightforward connections.

Mama Mary wiped her tears with a handkerchief, then, like a lever pulled to shift the course of a train, her face brightened, and her eyes sparkled once more. "How 'bout we walk down the lane to the sugar house, Miss Rachel?"

Rachel, caught off guard, blinked. "I thought sugar houses were closed in the summer."

"Yes'm," Mama Mary said with a gentle smile, "but I reckon you might like to see it anyways. Might bring back some good memories."

Rachel returned a warm smile. "I'd love to, Mama Mary."

Mama Mary pulled open the massive barn doors of the sugar house, their heavy hinges groaning in protest, and Rachel followed her inside.

"Ain't nobody here now," Mama Mary said, glancing around the cavernous space. "But come fall, when they haul in all that cane, this place get real hot with the men workin' them boilin' kettles over yonder."

Rachel surveyed the expansive interior. High rafters arched overhead, sunlight filtering through the gaps above the row of sunken copper kettles, all embedded in a long brick furnace. They were empty and polished, shining like rose gold, prepared for the next harvest.

Mama Mary gestured toward the furnace. "Thuh men outside the sugarhouse stoke the fire with wood to heat the juice. The men inside here keep movin' it from one kettle to the next 'til it thickens. That last one is where it turns to dark molasses."

Rachel watched as Mama Mary mimed a worker using a long wooden ladle to scoop molasses into a narrow trough. "It flows from this here trough to a bigger trough on that far wall, where it cools down."

"This brings back memories," Rachel said, standing beside the final kettle. "But everything looks so different from the sugar house at Mr. Benjamin's plantation. I don't remember seeing all these beautiful kettles."

"That's 'cause most big plantations got a bettah way to make sugah," Mama Mary explained. "What we gots here with these kettles is what they call a 'Jamaica Train.' A while back, a freedman down in New Orleans named Norbert Rillieux, made a big machine that done away with them kettles and made it safer and quicker to make sugah. I don't know how it work, but folks say his contrapshun made the massuhs more money and kept the slaves from gettin' burnt all the time."

"I think I've heard of him," Rachel said, nodding thoughtfully.

"His daddy was a rich white massuh who had him by a Creole woman on his plantation in New Or-leens. He sent Norbert to Paris to get edicated 'cause he was real smart. The Rillieux family heard 'bout Norbert teachin' college over there and comin' up with a better way to make sugah. They axed him to come back home and show everbody what he could do. He did, but his family had a fallin' out 'fo he could, fightin' over who could claim Norbert's machine. Then Norbert made it on his own time with his own money. Then other people come to see it and copied it without ever a please or thank yah."

"That's fascinating," Rachel said."

Mama Mary's expression turned pensive."There wuz 'nother free man of color who had a big hand in gettin' the whole sugah bizness started."

"Who was that?" Rachel asked.

"His name was Antoine Morin," Mama Mary said. "He come from Saint-Domingue. Folks nowadays call it Haiti, but he was edicated in France like Norbert. A White planter, Étienne de Boré, heard 'bout him and brought him to New Or-leens to learn how he wuz makin' sugah from cane. 'Fo that, folks were growin' tobacco and indigo, 'cause they didn't know how to get the sugah outta the cane and make much money," Mama Mary explained.

"How long ago was that?" Rachel inquired.

"Some time 'fo 1800," Mama Mary replied.

"That's before I was born," Rachel said, surprised. "I suppose that's why I've never heard of him."

"That's 'cause Étienne de Boré, the White man who hired him, claimed all the credit for what he done," Mama Mary continued. "You ask any planter up and down this ribber they'll all tell you how that Boré fellah made 'em rich."

Rachel fell silent, pondering the irony that two men of color, Morin and Rillieux, had laid the foundation for Louisiana's prosperity built on the backs of slaves. Without their ingenuity, the state might never have prospered as it did. And yet history, written by those in power, failed to recognize the people who had shaped it.

Later that afternoon, Rachel and Thomas waved goodbye to Lijah, who stood on the ferry, fading from sight as they continued toward their destination. The final stretch felt safer since Lijah had assured them that there were no bushwhackers along the stretch from Emancipation Plantation to Baton Rouge.

"I enjoyed our stay back there," Rachel said softly. "Mama Mary is better at what she does than most surgeons I've known who've had two full years of training."

"She certainly is," Thomas agreed. He paused, his expression shifting. "I thought I'd lost you back there. When the sniper's bullet hit your arm, and you tumbled from the wagon... I've never been so scared in my life."

Rachel glanced down at her bandaged arm. "It all happened so fast. One moment, I was sitting there, and the next...I was...in your arms."

Thomas's voice was low as he looked her in the eyes. "I thought you were gone. If you hadn't come back to me...." His voice trailed off.

Rachel gave him a teasing smile. "Well, you can't get rid of me that easily."

Thomas returned a fleeting smile, but the look in his eyes remained serious. "I never want to feel that way again, Rachel."

Rachel's heart swelled at the quiet sincerity in his voice. "You won't," she whispered.

The unspoken emotions between them grew, and after a pause, Rachel added, "I don't really feel like you're my brother, Thomas."

Thomas's brow lifted in surprise. "Oh? Then, who do you feel like I am?"

Rachel hesitated, her voice faltering. "It's not a woman's place to say." Regret flickered as she realized she had opened a door she wasn't ready to walk through.

"Unless the man says he loves her first," Thomas finished softly. "That's what you meant, isn't it?"

"Whoa, Nellie," Thomas called, pulling her reins. After Nellie came to a stop, he turned to look into Rachel's eyes. "Rachel, I think I love you."

Rachel cocked an eyebrow with a grin. "You *think* you love me? That's the best you've got, sir?"

Thomas's tone softened. "Rachel, I love you."

Her playful smile slipped away as she caught her breath, startled by the intensity of his gaze. "You're serious, aren't you?" she whispered, her voice barely audible. Suddenly, it seemed like there was not enough air for her to breathe.

"I couldn't be more serious," Thomas said. "You're the strongest, smartest, and most beautiful woman I've ever known. No one else could've saved me like you did at Port Hudson. If not for you, I'd have been shot as a spy come sunrise."

Rachel's practical side surfaced. "Well, I couldn't let that happen, spy or not," she said lightly. "It didn't take me long to decide that."

Thomas leaned in without another word, his arms drawing her close. Their lips met softly at first, then deepened with an intensity that matched their emotions.

When their kiss ended, their foreheads rested gently against each other. Thomas leaned back to gaze into her eyes. "I could spend the rest of my life with you, Rachel," he whispered.

Rachel's heart raced, and with a soft smile, she said, "And I with you, Thomas."

44

RETURN TO BATON ROUGE

Rachel took Thomas's hand to step down from their wagon at the levee in Baton Rouge. She marveled at the lively scene. Troops hurried past, freedmen unloaded cannons from Union ships, and the air was thick with the clamor and urgency of war.

"If it weren't for the war, this would be a perfect spring day," she said, taking in the fresh air and basking in the warmth of the sunshine.

As they stood together, she gazed at Thomas with the certainty of a new purpose unfolding within her, a promise of a future she hadn't dared to imagine before.

Thomas squeezed her hand gently as if divining her thoughts. "You and I will make it through this war, Rachel."

The quiet conviction in his voice felt like a lifeline, steadying her resolve. "Yes," she said softly. "Together."

Thomas glanced at the levee, alive with the movement of troops unloading weapons. "I don't think I've ever seen so many Parrott rifles in one place."

"Where?" Rachel asked, puzzled. "I don't see any rifles. And surely, they weren't designed for shooting parrots!"

Thomas chuckled. "No, my dear, they're not for shooting parrots," he explained, adjusting the strap on his satchel. "They're named after their inventor, Captain Robert Parker Parrott. Unlike the bird, his name is spelled with two t's. He cast the first of those beauties at the West Point Foundry. The metal band at the base makes them safer to fire by reinforcing the barrel, reducing the risk of explosion. They're called rifles instead of cannons because the barrels are rifled, which gives them far better accuracy than smoothbores."

"Do they still make the smoothbore kind?"

"Yes," he explained, "they each have their purpose. The rifled cannon typically fires explosive shells or solid shots and is more effective at longer distances. In contrast, the smoothbore offers more versatility at short ranges, as it is more easily loaded and can fire various projectiles, including cannonballs, canister, and grapeshot. The rebels can use them to return hot shot from the bluffs at Port Hudson."

"What's hot shot?" Rachel asked.

"Cannonballs heated red-hot before firing," Thomas explained. "The men call them 'great balls of fire.' They use them to set ships on fire."

Rachel smoothed her skirt and glanced at the cannons with a skeptical look. "They sound quite deadly. But they still don't look like rifles."

Thomas chuckled. "No, I suppose they don't."

"No offense to Mr. Parrott," Rachel sighed, "but I'd have called them 'rifled cannons' to avoid confusion." A flicker of weariness crossed her face. "Maybe Milton was right when he wrote that those 'devilish engines' must have been invented in hell to wage war against heaven."

Thomas remained quiet, having learned that sometimes the surest wisdom lies in silence, especially when a woman speaks her heart.

Rachel shielded her eyes and glanced down the road. "When do you think we'll find a place to stay?" she asked, making her impatience evident. "I'm dying for a hot bath and a quiet night in bed curled up with a good book." She noticed the grin spreading across Thomas's face and knew exactly what he was thinking, but let it go.

"We can probably get a couple of rooms at the same place we stayed before heading to Port Hudson," Thomas offered as if reeling his thoughts back just enough to play it safe.

"I recall a stable nearby," Rachel added thoughtfully. "Nellie will appreciate that."

Thomas gave her a curious glance. "I never asked you. Did you find your accommodations acceptable the last time we passed through?"

"They were fine," Rachel said, her tone softening at the memory. "And the biscuits at breakfast were incredibly light and fluffy," she added, eager to reexperience the simple pleasure.

"I rather fancied the fig preserves they served with them," Thomas said. "Then it's settled. Giddy up, Nellie."

As they headed to the boarding house, Thomas spotted a stationery shop on the next corner. "Would you mind terribly if I stopped for a moment to pick up a few supplies?" he asked.

"Not at all," Rachel replied. "After that, I could use a stop myself if we come across an apothecary."

"There's one on the next block, as I recall, assuming it's still in business," Thomas said, slowing the wagon to a halt in front of the stationery shop.

"Will you be a while?" Rachel asked as he stepped down from the wagon.

"I won't be long at all," Thomas assured her. "I know exactly what I want."

"In that case, I'll wait here," she said, reflecting on how she envied how swiftly men made their purchases without agonizing over options. Unlike women, who often combed through everything to find what they wanted at the best price, men seemed to know exactly what they needed and wasted no time getting it.

Thomas was met with familiar, comforting scents inside the stationer's shop: the earthy aroma of freshly sharpened pencils mingled with the metallic tang of graphite. At the same time, the drawing paper carried a faint mustiness from the lingering humidity.

As the ancient oak floorboards moaned wearily beneath his steps, Thomas let his gaze drift along the shelves. His eyes settled on an assortment of sepia pencils from A.W. Faber, a German firm renowned for producing some of the finest pencils in the trade. After carefully selecting a range of colors, he added a pad of laid sketching paper and a small pouch of gum arabic to his purchase, then made his way to the counter.

"Find everything you need?" the young shopkeeper asked as he began wrapping the items.

"Do you happen to have matches?."

"I've a few Lucifers left."

"Lucifers will do fine."

"Good choice. Although the sulfur odor can irritate the nose, they're easy to light and burn longer."

Thomas returned a playful grin. "I'll be sure to crack a window before I strike them."

Tallying up the order, the salesman said, "You're lucky we still have those sepia pencils. We can't get any more from Europe these days."

Thomas nodded. "Yes. Like everyone else, I can't wait for the war to be over."

"That comes to two dollars and fifty cents," the salesman said apologetically. "But rest assured, you're getting the very best."

Thomas retrieved three tiny one-dollar gold coins from his pocket, each bearing the distinctive "O" mark of the New Orleans Mint. With a soft metallic clink, he laid them neatly on the glass display counter.

"Thanks," the boy said, sliding them into the till and handing over the packages and ten silver half-dimes in change. "Don't see many of these one-dollar gold coins anymore."

Thomas nodded with a faint smile. "That's the last of mine. They're easy to lose, and they're not being minted any longer."

"Stop by if you need anything else, mister," the boy offered cheerfully.

"Thanks. I will," Thomas replied, tucking the wrapped supplies under his arm as he stepped out into the sunlight.

Outside, Thomas spotted two stray bricks lying abandoned on the sidewalk, silent casualties of the ongoing war. He bent down, carefully picked them up, and secured them in the back of the wagon with the supplies he had purchased from the shop.

Circling the wagon, he loosened Nellie's reins from the hitching post, giving her a gentle pat before climbing onto the driver's seat. Turning to Rachel, he asked, "Did you enjoy your people-watching?"

"I didn't have much time," Rachel remarked, shifting her gaze from the street to him. "Not many townspeople left, anyway. Most of them are soldiers or workmen."

"That's true," Thomas said. "Next stop, the apothecary."

Rachel leaned back as the wagon lurched forward, her gaze drifting over the battered storefronts in various stages of repair. Contrabands shuffled past with buckets of paint and rolls of canvas, restoring new life to the damaged facades. Nearby, shopkeepers huddled in small groups, exchanging cautious hopes that normalcy might soon return, allowing them to earn a living and support their families again.

"I've always loved watching people on the street," Rachel said as they traveled along the row of shops. "In the fall, my father and I often sat on our balcony for hours, watching the world drift by. It fascinated me to see all sorts of people, young and old, short and tall, skinny and stout, dressed in their best or worst. The parade never ended. Sometimes, it was more entertaining than a traveling minstrel show."

"I believe it," he said, a grin tugging at the corner of his mouth as he pulled on the reins. "You never know what kind of characters you'll meet. The whole world's a stage, after all, isn't it?"

Rachel's gaze followed a child skipping along the sidewalk, trailing behind her mother, carrying a breadbasket. "Yes, but the stage looks different now," she murmured, her voice softening. "Yet the show goes on just the same with the war assigning everyone new roles."

Thomas glanced at her, his expression reflecting a quiet understanding. "And some of us are cast in roles we never auditioned for," he added, flicking the reins lightly to keep the weary Nellie moving.

Thomas returned to his quarters after sharing a hearty, family-style supper around the boarding house table and seeing Rachel to her room. He carefully set the two salvaged bricks on the floor, arranged his supplies on the small table at the foot of the bed, and, utterly drained, collapsed in a weary sprawl across the mattress.

Planning only to rest his eyes for a few minutes, he drifted into a deep slumber.

When he awoke, twilight cast a soft glow over the room. Feeling unexpectedly refreshed from the unplanned nap, he swung his legs off the bed and walked to the table. He retrieved a Lucifer, struck one on the heel of his boot, and lit the whale oil lamp, fanning away the sulfur fumes that filled the air. The lamp's flame sputtered and flickered, then steadied, casting a warm glow over the room.

"Miss my kerosene lamp," he muttered, disappointed with the dimmer whale oil light.

Bending down, he picked up the bricks and positioned them in front of the table's back legs. Then, he lifted the legs onto the makeshift risers. Next, he adjusted the slant until it felt right and stepped back with an approving nod. "That's better," he muttered, the table reminding him of his tilted drawing board back home.

He unwrapped his sepia pencils and carefully tore a clean sheet from his sketch pad, setting it aside. He then positioned the paper on the table with gum arabic.

With the soft glow of the lamp illuminating the blank page, Thomas settled into his chair to begin sketching Port Hudson's fortifications for his upcoming meeting with Brigadier General Cuvier Grover.

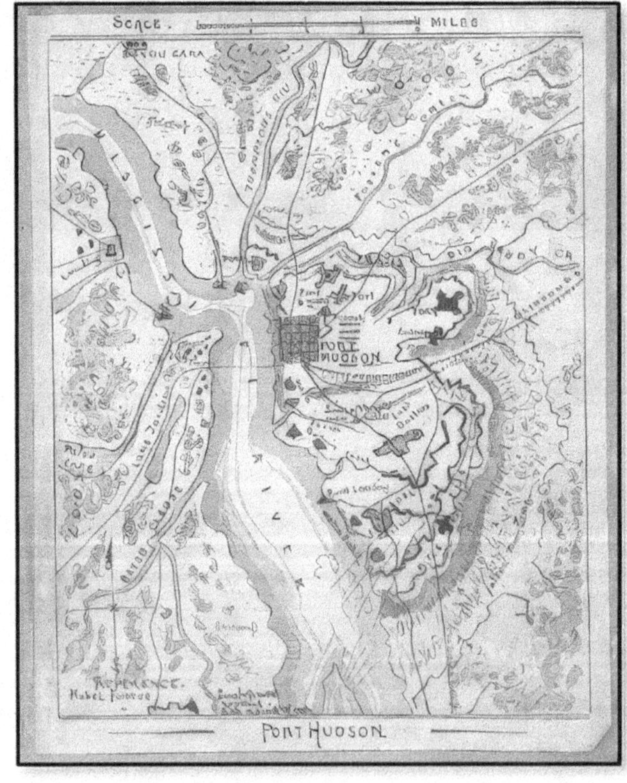
SCALE. MILES
BAYOU SARA
MISSISSIPPI
PORT HUDSON
RIVER
REFERENCE.
Rebel Forces
PORT HUDSON

45

DEBRIEFING THE GENERAL

Thomas secured Nellie's reins to the hitching post in front of the two-story Pentagon Building, just a few blocks from the boarding house where Rachel was still asleep. He took a deep breath of the cool early morning air, grabbed his leather satchel, and approached the door on the ground floor bearing General Cuvier Grover's name.

His light knock was met with a sharp, "Come." Stepping inside, he was greeted by a dimly lit room thick with the scents of aged wood, well-worn leather, and lingering cigar smoke.

Crisp military charts bearing fresh notations hung beside meticulously framed maps of Napoleon's European campaigns. The contrast caught Thomas's eye. It wasn't just the rarity of the Napoleonic maps that impressed him, but the deliberate pairing: present strategy informed by lessons from the past.

As Thomas took in the scene, he was struck by Grover's commanding presence. The general, a man in his mid-thirties with a weathered complexion, stood up from his work, revealing a medium build, around six feet tall, with a solid physique typical of a career military man. Dressed in his dark blue officer's uniform, with gold epaulets, polished brass buttons, and rank insignia, Grover's sharp, piercing blue eyes added to his authoritative demeanor. His neatly trimmed brown hair, beard, mustache, strong jawline, and prominent brow gave him a stern, determined expression.

"General Banks sends his greetings, Thomas," Grover said, stepping forward to extend a handshake. "He expressed his disappointment at being unable to meet with you personally to hear your report from Port Hudson, but pressing matters have kept him in the field."

Thomas returned the handshake with a slight smile. "I understand, General. On my way here, I took the opportunity to observe some drills and couldn't resist getting a closer look at a few of the Parrott rifles."

Grover's eyes gleamed with pride. "The Parrotts aren't just powerful. They're remarkably accurate at long range because of their rifling and banding. With them, we can fire from well beyond the range of the Confederate guns, and our eight and ten-inch siege mortars will deliver heavy shells to soften up their fortifications." He paused, clearly relishing the details. "Farragut's Dahlgrens, though, are the real beasts. Smoothbore, but they can fire explosive shells and solid shot at a shorter range. The versatility of those cannons will give our Navy control of the river while our land forces close in."

The general's profound understanding of every weapon available, whether by land or river, impressed Thomas.

Please, have a seat," Grover said, gesturing toward a straight-back chair at his cluttered worktable. The worn oak floorboards creaked as he moved to his oak swivel chair on the other side, the sound echoing softly in the otherwise quiet room.

"Thank you," Thomas replied, settling in.

"May I offer you a drink?" the general asked. "A cup of coffee? A shot of brandy? Perhaps a good cigar?"

"No, thank you," Thomas replied, shaking his head politely.

The general chuckled. "Ah, that's right, Thomas. You were one of Pinkerton's men before he left government service. I hear he frowns on indulging in life's finer pleasures."

Thomas offered a quick grin at the general's playful jibe as he collected his thoughts. "I suppose it's best to start by describing the various land approaches to Port Hudson."

A smile softened the general's otherwise stern features, fleeting but genuine. "I respect a man who skips the pleasantries and gets straight to the point," he said.

"Thank you," Thomas said, leaning forward, his hands resting on the table's edge. "Approaching Port Hudson from the north, through Bayou Sara, the terrain is primarily swamp, as you and General Banks already know from your maneuvers there. Your men must cross a small offshoot of the Mississippi that winds through the bayou, followed by Thompson's River, before reaching the first Confederate fortifications. The area is hazardous, teeming with cottonmouths and alligators."

"Beyond that," Thomas continued, "there's Big Sandy Creek to cross before reaching the primary fortified zone, which the rebels call 'Fort Desperate.' As the name suggests, it's their defense of last resort. Positioned on high ground, it gives them a commanding view of any Union forces approaching from the north. The area is heavily fortified with ravines, earthworks, trenches, and artillery positions. The Confederates have cut down scrub and small trees, piling them into the gullies. Now it's almost impossible to traverse."

"And if we can breach it?" the general asked.

"If Fort Desperate falls, I estimate that the entire garrison will collapse soon after," Thomas replied. He paused, watching the general's eyes narrow, clearly visualizing the difficult terrain and weighing the risks. He wasn't used to having his opinions considered so deeply by high-ranking officers.

General Grover scribbled notes on the pad beside him. "And what about the approach from the south?"

Thomas shook his head firmly. "I wouldn't recommend it, sir. The southern approach is the most heavily fortified. The defenses extend onto a well-guarded bluff at a sharp bend in the river. Any attack from that direction would be suicide. We can explore an eastern approach instead once I show you the layout of the fortifications."

Thomas unrolled his sketch across the table, carefully anchoring the corners with a paperweight and a book on the general's desk. The map revealed a meticulously detailed rendering of Port Hudson's defenses, with terrain features, artillery placements, and troop positions rendered in precise strokes of colored pencil.

"What kind of artillery do they have?" the general asked.

"They have howitzers and heavy cannons, including twenty-four- and thirty-two-pounders. Some are positioned on the river but can be adjusted to face inland. They also have smaller field guns dispersed along their lines."

The general gave a measured nod, absorbing the details.

"Note that I've outlined the Confederate fortifications," he said.

Grover leaned in, clearly impressed by the level of detail. "I heard you were taken prisoner and escaped under the cover of darkness. How in tarnation did you manage to escape with this?"

Thomas met his gaze calmly, unaware that news of his escape had reached Baton Rouge. "I didn't. I drew it from memory last night after arriving in Baton Rouge."

The general stared at him incredulously. "From memory...last night?" he echoed.

Thomas gave a modest smile and nodded.

"Young man, you have an extraordinary gift," the general said, leaning back in his chair in admiration. "This map is as detailed as any sketch we'd get from an artist aboard one of our spy balloons, but we've never flown one over that area. Believe me, I've asked. I saw their effectiveness during the Peninsula Campaign, but General Banks insists on what he refers to as more discreet means of gathering intelligence."

Thomas kept his quiet demeanor, letting the word *discreet* pass without comment. The irony was not lost on him. Banks disliked balloons because they were not discreet, yet Thomas's work at Port Hudson, supported by Banks, had proved anything but discreet.

"I've always had a knack for recalling details," he said. "It served me well in this case, and I hope it will assist in your planning."

The general pored over the map again, his eyes carefully tracing every line and notation. "It certainly will," he said, the weight of the new intelligence appearing to give him a new sense of confidence. "I'm certain General Banks will be more than pleased."

Thomas, content with the general's praise, hesitated. "I was wondering, General, would the paymaster happen to be quartered here in Baton Rouge?"

The general chuckled. "Son, I don't trouble the paymaster for work that needs to stay off the books. Besides, General Banks told me to spare no expense with you. Now I see why."

Opening his desk drawer with a key from his pocket, he pulled out a metal box and placed it on his desk. He opened it to reveal the gleam of gold coins.

"Tell me, how much does Uncle Sam owe you, son?"

46

HOMECOMING

As sunset gilded the New Orleans sky, lamplighters moved with practiced efficiency through the fading light, their long poles reaching up to coax life into the city's gas lamps. One by one, the lanterns flared, casting golden pools along the cobblestone streets and softly illuminating the faces of couples strolling arm in arm, their laughter breaking the hush of evening.

Thomas hopped out of the cab and extended his hand to Rachel, steadying her descent onto the pavement in front of her house. He placed her carpet bag neatly on the stoop and quickly brushed his trousers.

"A lot easier traveling without our trunks," he remarked with a wry smile. "I'll bet the boys up at Port Hudson had a fine time rifling through our things."

Rachel smirked. "I hope they enjoy doing my laundry."

Thomas chuckled. "It couldn't possibly be worse than mine."

Rachel glanced up, her playful expression softening as her gaze settled on the sky, now painted with brilliant streaks of gold and crimson.

"Look at that sky," she whispered, her voice catching with awe. "Have you ever seen anything more beautiful?"

Thomas glanced upward, watching the last rays of sunlight dissolve into deep indigos along the horizon. But his gaze drifted back to Rachel, captivated by how the fading light brushed the soft lines of her face with a golden glow. "I have, indeed," he said softly.

Rachel caught the look in his eyes and laughed, tapping his arm. "Oh, Thomas!" she teased, but her smile faded quickly. "I'm so glad to be home after our journey," she said, "but I miss Nellie terribly."

"I'm sure she's enjoying her rest after all we put her through." He paused, a thoughtful look on his face. "I don't think I ever told you her story."

"No," Rachel said. "You didn't."

"I got to talking with one of the men aboard the *Natchez* on the first leg of our trip, and he told me she was being sold to a stable in Baton Rouge since she was getting too old for heavy work, but could still manage a jog-trot. So, I tracked down the stable and hired her for our journey."

"I'm glad," she said, impressed by his effort. "The poor girl did seem to struggle with our wagon at times."

"I made sure that she has a good home now. Nothing but lighter work for her these days." He paused. "Do you think you might want to have a horse again?"

Rachel's eyes sparkled. "If I have someone to ride with," she said, her tone warm and inviting.

Thomas grinned with the charm of a man who enjoyed a lady's company, but let the sentiment pass without comment.

Rachel turned her attention to the window of her parlor. "That's odd," she murmured, her brow furrowing as her eyes lingered on the darkened window. "There's usually a lamp lit in the parlor by now. Sarah likes to read there before she takes her book to bed."

Her words trailed off as the house's stillness pressed down around her.

"Wait here, driver," Thomas called back at the cab. "I'll see the lady to the door, then I'll need a ride to my place."

Rachel's face lit up with excitement at the thought of being reunited with her family. "Sarah and Jacob are going to be so surprised! And I can't wait to hug Noah and cover his chubby little cheeks with kisses first thing tomorrow morning." She reached to the chatelaine at her waist and removed her brass door key. "Do you think I should knock or use the doorbell since Sarah's not expecting me?"

Thomas tilted his head thoughtfully. "It might be a good idea. Showing up unannounced could be a bit of a shock."

Rachel reached to knock on the door, but Thomas gently stopped her, a flicker of concern in his eyes. "Actually," he said softly, "maybe I should head out now. It might be overwhelming for Sarah to see you coming home with a stranger. She already has much to attend to."

Rachel's expression softened. "You're right."

Thomas leaned in and kissed her lightly on the cheek. "See you in the morning."

"I can't wait." Her smile was warm and reassuring. "Tomorrow, I'll tell them all about you and our journey. Then, I'll catch you up on everything."

Thomas gave her one last lingering glance before climbing back into the cab. "I'll leave once you're inside," he called.

"Goodnight!" Rachel called back, throwing him a kiss as she twisted the knob on the doorbell. When no one answered, she frowned and rang it again, now feeling uneasy. Still nothing.

With a quiet sigh, she slipped her key into the lock, turned it, and pushed open the creaking door, making a mental note to grease the hinges. Picking up her carpet bag, she stepped inside and quietly shut the door behind her, waving goodbye to Thomas.

The hallway lay in darkness. Turning to the parlor, its familiar outlines were dim, with only the light of the streetlamps filtering through the sheer curtains. She set her bag beside the sofa table, reached up to remove the lamp's glass shade, struck a match, and touched it to the wick. The flame flared, and she adjusted it until the warm light bathed the room in a soft glow.

As the lamplight spread across the space, something unexpected emerged from the darkness: a large wooden rocking horse standing in the center of the room.

"Noah," she whispered, her heart swelling with recognition. Stroking the rocking horse's carved mane, she marveled at the craftsmanship and beauty of the wood grain. "Such a lovely creature you are. You must belong to him."

Rachel admired the detailed craftsmanship of the wooden horse. With just the slightest touch, it gently rocked, awaiting its rider. She smiled gently as she imagined Noah perched atop the saddle. His little hands would hold on tight with the determination only a child could muster. She could almost hear his laughter and feel the weight of his tiny body leaning into hers as she steadied him.

She left the parlor with a wistful sigh, relieved to be safely home. As she ascended the stairs, her footsteps fell softly on the carpet runner, each step carrying her closer to the reunion she had dreamed of for so long. At the top, she paused to light the gas sconce outside the master's bedroom, watching as the flame flickered to life and cast its soft light along the walls.

Noticing no light from beneath the bedroom door, Rachel slowly opened it. In the soft glow of the hallway light streaming in, she saw Sarah and Jacob lying sound asleep under the covers, their breathing steady and peaceful. Nearby, Noah slumbered in his crib, his tiny form snug in the soft flannel nightshirt she had bought for him before she left on her travels.

"Such an angel," Rachel whispered with a tender smile, resisting the urge to scoop him up in her arms.

She carefully closed the door and crossed the hall to the smaller bedroom. Hesitating, she gently tapped on the door, wondering if Jacob's caretaker might still occupy the room. When no response came, she turned the knob and peeked inside.

By hallway light, she could see that the bed was neatly made, but the room lacked personal belongings, which confirmed that the caretaker no longer stayed overnight. Rachel felt relieved; things had changed, and the family was adjusting. Perhaps Jacob was well enough to return to work. At that moment, she felt a sense of accomplishment: she had fulfilled her duty to hearth and home as resolutely as any soldier on the battlefield.

She entered the bedroom, closed the door behind her, unbuttoned her shoes, and sank into the deep feather bed with a contented sigh.

"This is heaven," she whispered as the soft feather mattress swallowed her weary body. The crisp scent of fresh, sun-dried linens enveloped her, soothing her tired muscles. Her eyelids grew heavy as the room around her slowly dissolved at the edges. The soft creaking of the house in the cool evening air faded as she surrendered to the twilight of sleep, slipping effortlessly into the world of dreams.

The morning sunlight filtered softly through the bedroom curtains, and the comforting aromas of coffee and sizzling bacon gently aroused Rachel. Faint and joyful, a child's laughter echoed from downstairs, adding to the moment's warmth. She slowly regained her sense of place and sat up to enjoy the familiar sounds. The savory aroma of bacon—such a rare luxury these days—was unmistakable proof that Sarah had received the funds Dr. Zacharie had promised.

Slipping into her dressing gown and slippers, Rachel eagerly descended the stairs, anticipating a lively morning with her family.

"Good morning!" she greeted cheerfully as she entered the kitchen, her heart filled with pride at the bountiful table.

"Rachel!" Sarah gasped, dropping her spatula as she flipped the bacon. It clattered loudly against the floor, spinning to a halt as she stood frozen, stunned by the sight of her sister.

The sisters rushed into each other's arms while Noah waved his spoon wildly from his highchair, squealing excitedly.

"Look, Sarah," Rachel beamed. "Noah remembers me."

"How long have you been here, sister?" Sarah asked, appearing confused by Rachel's appearance in a dressing gown.

"I arrived last night, but you were all sound asleep, so I stayed in the guest room," Rachel explained. "I found one of my gowns in the dresser drawer."

Sarah looked irritated as she picked up the spatula and washed it. "I'm glad I made up the room for you after Jacob's caretaker left."

Rachel leaned down to carefully hug a beaming Jacob. "You look well!" she said warmly.

"I've been doing much better," Jacob replied. "I've been following the doctor's advice and can now stand from a chair by myself."

Rachel offered a gentle smile, choosing her words with care. "That's wonderful," she said, mindful of his struggles. She leaned over to use a napkin to wipe the grits off Noah's face and kiss him on the cheek. "Look how big you've grown, young man!"

"Try picking him up," Sarah teased as she flipped the buttered toast on a cast-iron griddle and fried eggs in a skillet.

Rachel removed Noah from his highchair with a laugh. "Goodness, big boy, you've been eating well!" she exclaimed, kissing him again before placing him back in his highchair.

Sarah rescued the toast just as it began to burn around the edges. "You must be hungry after being on the road for so long. Take a seat so I can serve up breakfast."

After they all gathered around the table, Jacob recited a brief prayer in Hebrew and then translated the words into English. Together, they began their meal.

Over coffee, Sarah mused, "Maybe one day they'll put a window in a coffee pot so we can see it percolate until it's just the right color. I don't know how many pots of coffee I've thrown out because I brewed it too long when Noah needed attention."

"Who knows?" Rachel laughed. "We do live in an age of invention."

Jacob nodded eagerly. "Speaking of the latest inventions, I love reading about new developments in steam engines and the creative ideas for traveling through the air with hydrogen balloons. The whole idea is fantastic. Imagine floating above the world with the birds flying by! *Scientific American* is worth every penny."

"It's mostly men reading about those new thingamajigs, isn't it, dear?" Sarah asked, amused.

"Probably," Rachel agreed before Jacob could respond, while they all savored the warmth of gathering around a bountiful breakfast table as a family once more.

After breakfast, Sarah and Rachel tidied up the kitchen, washing and drying the dishes while Jacob captivated Noah with his animated version of "Hänsel and Gretel."

"Noah just loves the part about the witch and her gingerbread house," Sarah observed, her eyes twinkling with amusement. "Jacob has told him the story so many times that he knows it by heart."

"Look how wide Noah's eyes are!" Rachel exclaimed. "Jacob has reached the part where the children shove the witch into the oven."

"I can't help but cringe at that," Sarah admitted, wrinkling her nose.

Rachel chuckled. "It's all magic to him."

"Perhaps," Sarah conceded with a smile. "Children do inhabit a world of their own, don't they?"

"Remember how Father convinced us Cinderella was real?" Rachel said, her voice tinged with nostalgia.

"Such a captivating story," Sarah reflected, "and with a strong moral too: overcoming adversity to find true happiness."

As Rachel placed the last dish on the drying rack, Cinderella's story and her own seemed to share more than a few parallels. She, too, had faced her share of hardship, shouldering burdens to support her family through difficult times. Perhaps happiness with Prince Charming wasn't just a fairy tale; it might be waiting at the end of her struggles, just as it had for Cinderella.

Rachel wiped her hands on a dishcloth, saving the thought for later. "Why don't we continue our chat in the parlor while Jacob entertains Noah?"

"Of course," Sarah replied, hanging her apron on a wall hook by the stove.

On their way to the parlor, Rachel pondered how to approach the topic of the impending deadline for locals to swear the Oath of Allegiance at the Customs House. Thomas had mentioned that General Banks was tightening regulations, reverting to Butler's policy of property confiscation and the threat of deportation to the Confederacy. This move was necessitated by Lincoln's determination to eliminate any resistance to his plan for Louisiana to become the first state to reunite with the Union.

The sisters sat across from each other in the dimly lit parlor, the gentle murmur of Jacob's voice drifting in from the kitchen as he entertained Noah. Rachel's hands were clasped in her lap; her eyes locked onto Sarah's.

"Sarah," Rachel began softly, "I wanted to ask if you plan to sign the Oath of Allegiance so you can stay here in New Orleans."

"Never!" Sarah said firmly.

Rachel reached for her sister's hand. "You have a roof over your head here, Sarah, a safe place for your family. Yes, New Orleans is occupied, but there's peace under Union control. Crime is practically unheard of now that martial law and curfew are in effect. Going deeper into the Confederacy is dangerous. Who knows what awaits you there?"

"Peace? This is hardly peace!" Sarah retorted, withdrawing her hand. Her tone was edged with bitterness. "How can you call it peace when all that I've known has been stripped away? The Union has robbed me of everything I hold dear, everything I grew up with. For Heaven's sake, they've taken Jacob's arms, depriving him of the ability to provide for his family. He can't even hug Noah." She paused, choking on her words. "Or me."

Rachel leaned forward. "What about Jacob and Noah? How can you take them into that uncertainty? You know as well as I do that parts of the Confederacy are crumbling. The Union advances every day, and tensions are growing. You'd be walking straight into the thick of it."

Sarah's expression hardened, and her voice grew angry. "This is no place to raise our son. At least there, we'll be among friends and won't be under the thumb of men who have no respect for our way of life. Every day, I see it all slipping away: our traditions, our standing, even…even our dignity. My servant was taken from me. What will happen to us once the colored men are freed en masse? Mayhem could break out any day with all the slaves pouring in from the plantations; it's a powder keg waiting for a match."

"Ginny left, yes," Rachel said, "as did my Rebecca, but they wanted their freedom. Can you genuinely begrudge them that? Look around you, sister. Try, just for a moment, to put yourself in their place. For the first time, slaves like Ginny and Rebecca have a chance to build their own lives. It may feel strange, but perhaps we must learn to live without them."

Sarah leaned back, folding her arms defiantly. "Easy for you to say, Rachel. You never relied on Rebecca the way I did my Ginny."

"You're not thinking clearly," Rachel replied, her voice dropping to a pleading whisper. "Jacob needs stability, especially now. How do you think he'll fare away from the city, away from the resources he needs?"

"You can't imagine what Jacob is enduring, Rachel. His nightmares are a battlefield of their own. He wakes in the dead of night, screaming, his clothes and sheets soaked with sweat and urine. I have to strip the bed, wipe him down, and ease him into something clean before he can rest again. When I try to comfort him, he tells me he sees himself lying wounded on the cold ground of a moonlit graveyard, a winged Angel of Death looming overhead. He says it feels like the very breath of life is being drawn out of his body. When I think the nightmare has finally released him, he whispers that in his dreams, he still has his arms, but then wakes up to the haunting stench of seared flesh and the brutal truth..

That's horrible," Rachel murmured, her voice trembling as she fought back tears. She suddenly recalled that Passover, a celebration of deliverance and protection, was just weeks away. But how could Jacob find solace in it now, after all he'd endured? She wondered if, in those agonizing nightmares, he felt forsaken, left at the mercy of the Angel of Death by the very God who had once commanded His people to mark their doors with the blood of the lamb for protection and deliverance.

"That's why I want to take him away from here, where he won't have to see all those Union soldiers everywhere he looks," Sarah said, her voice resolute. "We'll stay with Eugenia and Philip. They've written that they've sufficient room and are willing to help us. Jacob will be among friends, and he'll be able to recover and find work again. Eugenia has already said she would find an amanuensis who can assist him in joining Philip's practice. She and Philip agree that he can work from their home, so he doesn't have to meet clients."

Rachel's hands tightened in her lap, her shoulders slumping as she made a last attempt to reach her sister's heart. "And what about me, Sarah? You're all I have left. If you leave…" Her voice caught, and she looked away to hide the tears in her eyes. "Who knows when I'll see you again?"

Sarah's expression softened, a hint of sorrow breaking through her steely resolve. "Maybe you can live with the occupation, but I can't. I want to be somewhere I can hold onto some shred of our former life, where Noah can grow up without Union rule over his head, and Jacob can eventually recover."

Rachel's gaze dropped to the floor, her voice barely a whisper. "I can never convince you, can I, Sarah?"

Sarah shook her head, her voice steady. "No, you can't."

They sat in silence for a long moment. At last, Sarah gently took Rachel's hands, cradling them in a warm, steady clasp. "I want you to know how much I appreciate everything you've done for us," she said. "I honestly don't know what Jacob and I would have done to feed ourselves and Noah without the income you provided. Every week, a mysterious middle-aged man would knock on the door and drop off the money he said you sent us."

Rachel smiled with pride. "That was Dr. Zacharie, a friend of Rabbi Gutheim."

Rachel hesitated before speaking again, a blush creeping onto her cheeks. "I wanted to tell you I met a young man I fancy."

Sarah's brows rose, her voice softening. "What's his name?"

"Thomas. Thomas Manget."

"What is his profession?"

"He's an attorney from Baton Rouge. He once owned a plantation but sold it to concentrate on his profession."

Sarah's eyes sparkled with a touch of curiosity. "I'll have to ask Jacob if he knows this gentleman. Will he stay in New Orleans or leave for the Confederacy?"

"He plans on staying," Rachel replied, glancing down, her hands clasped in her lap.

"Do you think you might marry him?" Sarah asked, meeting her sister's gaze directly.

Rachel nodded, looking down as she murmured, "Yes."

A thoughtful silence passed before Sarah spoke again. "Passover's coming soon. Would you like to invite him to join us for our Seder?"

Rachel's thoughts raced. How could she bring someone like Thomas, practically an abolitionist, to meet her family? She quickly found a response. "I think he'll be out of town with some relatives."

"I see," Sarah replied, disappointed.

At last, she rose, pausing in the doorway with a look of bittersweet determination. "One day you'll understand, sister," she murmured, her voice barely above a whisper. Then, without another word, she turned and left the room.

Rachel sat alone on the parlor sofa, gazing through the window at the street. Her heart sank under the weight of the realization that her family, along with the remnants of their shared past, was vanishing into the waning shadows of the Confederacy.

47

PASSOVER

Golden light filled the room with the setting sun, highlighting the linen-covered dining table where Sarah, Rachel, and Jacob sat together preparing to celebrate Passover. Noah nestled contentedly in his mother's lap, his tiny fingers curled against her arm. Sarah and Rachel wore elegantly draped white lace tichels over their hair while Jacob sat quietly, a black silk yarmulke resting on the crown of his head.

Rachel stood to light the Sabbath candles, stepping into Sarah's role as the family matriarch to allow her to care for Jacob. Her voice recited the ancient blessing reverently, echoing through the millennia. The candle flames flickered to life, their soft glow ushering in not only Sabbath but the festival of deliverance. As the flames flickered, they bridged centuries of tradition, reaching back through generations of women who had kindled these same lights with the same words on their lips.

Rachel "ברוך אתה אדוני אלהינו מלך העולם, אשר קדשנו במצותיו וצונו להדליק נר של יום טוב," recited reverently, then repeated the blessing in English: "Blessed are You, Adonai our God, Ruler of the Universe, who sanctified us with the commandment of kindling the light of the festival."

Sarah cradled Noah, who was accustomed to lighting the candles every Friday evening for Sabbath. Yet, as always, his eyes widened with wonder, enchanted by the gentle dance of the flickering flames.

Jacob, his face glowing with pride, leaned in to kiss Noah on the cheek. "One day, Noah, it'll be your turn to ask the Four Questions during Passover. But tonight, Daddy will ask them for you."

Noah giggled up at his father, clapping his hands with delight.

"Look, everyone!" Jacob exclaimed with a grin. "I think he already understands what Daddy's telling him!"

"I do think you're right, Jacob," Rachel said. As she watched Jacob's tenderness toward Noah, a quiet joy filled her heart. Yet beneath that warmth, a faint ache tugged at her; she had hoped they might attend schul and celebrate the Seder with their congregation this year. Once more, her dress would remain tucked away in her armoire, its fabric preserved by the cedar wood lining and infused with cherished memories of life before the occupation. It waited, patient and untouched, for another Passover in another year. Over time, it had transformed into a quiet symbol of the community and fellowship she yearned for, the joy of sharing the holiday with others in freedom.

"I love how you've arranged our mother's Seder plate, Sarah," Rachel said wistfully. "It brings back so many fond memories."

"Yes," her sister replied warmly, running her finger gently along the edge of the family heirloom. "Even the tiny little chips along the edge are filled with memories of when you and I washed it with all the other dishes. How careless we were in our youth! We had no idea how we would grow to treasure it."

"And with the blockade of British goods, it's become truly irreplaceable," Rachel added, her thoughts drifting to the rifle used by the sniper who had nearly ended her life. *How ironic, she mused, that instruments of war were readily available while symbols of peace and solidarity had all but disappeared.*

Sarah's expression softened with sadness. "If you're set on staying in New Orleans, you should keep it here. But when you're ready to join us in LaGrange, remember to bring it with you." Beneath her gentle tone was a quiet urgency, as if she hoped Rachel wouldn't wait too long to join her family.

Sensing the subtle nudge, Rachel rested a hand lightly on Sarah's arm. "Let's not dwell on that now, sister. We'll revisit it another time. For now, let's savor the joy of Passover and the blessing of being together as a family. This year, we mark the Hebrew year 5623."

"And may we continue for generations to come," Jacob said, smiling warmly at Noah.

"Amen," Rachel said, her heart aching as she put aside the thought that Jacob could not reach out to tousle Noah's hair as she could, a tender gesture now forever lost to him.

"The best I could find for the bitter herb was chicory root," Sarah said almost apologetically.

"That works perfectly well," Rachel replied, noting the chicory in the center of the Seder plate. "And I see you found some matzoh." She paused. "It does look a bit different, though."

"Now that the federals are reopening trade routes, leavened bread is everywhere, but finding anything unleavened is a real challenge," Sarah said. "So, I decided to bake it myself, but it seemed hopeless without a pricking wheel to punch all those tiny holes to keep it flat and crisp. I had to resort to stabbing it a thousand times with a fork."

Rachel was amused at the image of Sarah furiously attacking the dough. "We should count ourselves lucky you didn't give up entirely. It's a fine piece of matzoh, sister."

"Thank you," Sarah said through a proud smile.

"At least our streets aren't swarming with women rioting for bread like they were in Richmond yesterday," Rachel said. "I heard they had to call in the troops and threaten to fire into the crowd to stop the mob from smashing windows and looting stores. Can you believe that Jefferson Davis himself rode through the streets, tossing his pocket change into the crowd of women?"

Sarah's eyes widened. "How dreadful! Poor President Davis must have been desperate to solve the problem. But how could you possibly know about this, Rachel, since it happened only yesterday? It's far too soon for it to be in the papers."

Rachel immediately realized she had spoken too freely, knowing her sister's undying loyalty to the Confederacy. Thomas had mentioned the Richmond bread riots just before leaving on his mission the night before, likely from catching up on telegraph reports. Quickly considering a plausible explanation, she added, "I overheard some soldiers talking about it below our balcony when you were in the kitchen preparing breakfast."

"I'm sure we'll see it in the papers then," Sarah replied. "Those poor women. They *had* to have been desperate to feed their children. I hope there isn't a food shortage in LaGrange when we arrive."

Rachel nodded thoughtfully. "We really should be grateful for the food we have here, where we can enjoy it in peace," she said, subtly weaving in her suggestion that Sarah might be better off staying in New Orleans. Wanting to shift the conversation away from her earlier misstep with the news from Richmond, she quickly added, "So, Sis, how did your shopping for the rest of the Seder plate go?"

"Except for the lamb shank, the rest was easy enough: the egg, parsley, and *charoset*. I used Mother's recipe for the *charoset*: fresh fruit, walnuts, wine, sugar, and cinnamon. Of course, I had to make it from memory since she never wrote anything down."

"I have to admit, I was never any good at roasting the egg," Rachel said, chuckling.

"Oh, how could I forget! You always burned it," Sarah teased, wrinkling her nose. "The kitchen smelled like burning sulfur for hours." Her laugh softened, a wistful look glimmering in her eyes. "I pitied dear Daddy. Do you remember what he used to say?"

"'Smells like Hell itself!'" Rachel replied, mimicking their father's voice with playful exaggeration.

The sisters dissolved into gleeful laughter, the sound carrying the warmth of a shared holiday memory.

"Well, you've outdone yourself, Sis," Rachel said, catching her breath. "The egg's roasted to perfection. Daddy would be proud."

"Sarah's always been a great cook," Jacob said, smiling. "That's why I married her."

Sarah playfully swatted his leg. "Jacob! You told me you married me because I was the most beautiful woman you'd ever laid eyes on."

"Well, that's true too, darling," he said.

Rachel chuckled, shaking her head. "You two are adorable," she said, amused by her brother-in-law's smooth, diplomatic charm and pleased to see him enjoy a moment of levity.

As she watched her sister and brother-in-law exchange playful banter, Rachel lamented that Thomas could not join them for the Seder. His absence weighed on her, though perhaps it was for the best. She feared that Thomas's presence, with his abolitionist convictions and Union sympathies, however inadvertently revealed, might have fractured the fragile peace she longed to preserve for this sacred evening.

Rachel rose to mix a little wine with water for Noah. "Where did you come across this wine, Sarah? It has an unusually delicate bouquet and a deep, rich color."

Sarah's face lit up with pride. "*I didn't* buy it. I fermented it myself from raisins since fresh grapes are so expensive."

"Oh. Elijah's Draft," Rachel said, genuinely impressed. "I had forgotten about the Jewish custom of making wine from raisins when commercial wine wasn't available. Maybe you should consider cornering the market on raisins in New Orleans and starting a winery. I could work the sisterhood for investors."

Sarah laughed, shaking her head. "Me? Starting a winery? Perish the thought! I had no idea what I was doing. Mr. Schmuelson at shul shared some of his brewing secrets with me. He even lent me a wine vat and showed me how to use a hydrometer to monitor fermentation. The whole process is surprisingly scientific."

"That was so generous of him," Rachel remarked. "Jacob, will you say the *kiddush* over this wonderful wine your wife made?"

"ברוך אתה אדוני, אלהינו מלך העולם, בורא פרי הגפן," Jacob chanted. "Blessed are You, Lord our God, King of the universe, who creates the fruit of the vine."

Sarah gently lifted Jacob's wine cup to his lips.

Rachel's heart sank as she watched her brother-in-law sip his drink, as helpless as a child, his empty sleeves dangling limply beside his body. Losing his arms not only meant losing his independence but also a part of his manhood, as his sense of identity was tied to providing for his wife and child. *How awful he must feel!* she mused. *Once, he could have done this himself without a second thought.*

Still, she reminded herself to be grateful that Jacob had come home alive, and she prayed that, in time, he might find his way back from the shadows of his sorrow and reclaim his place as both father and husband.

"Now for your wine, sir," Sarah said to Noah, helping him lift his cup to his lips. Jacob and Rachel beamed as the toddler eagerly sipped, a stream escaping the corner of his mouth and trickling down his cheek. Sarah gently wiped it away with her napkin.

"Shall we proceed with the handwashing?" Rachel asked, reaching for the tray with moistened napkins, which were prepared for the ritual cleansing. She froze as she extended it toward Jacob, realizing that his missing hands would make the gesture impossible.

Without hesitation, Sarah leaned over to take the napkin from Rachel, cleansed her own hands, and then gently wiped Jacob's cheeks with the same care she might offer a child.

Rachel's breath caught. She blinked hard against the welling tears. Steadying herself, she began the prayer of purification, remembering the rabbi's admonition that intent and participation to one's best ability matter most.

"רִיבּוֹנוֹ שֶׁל עוֹלָם, כַּאֲשֶׁר רָחַצְתִּי אֶת יָדַי, כָּךְ נַפְשִׁי וְרוּחִי יִהְיוּ טְהוֹרוֹת. טַהֵר אֶת לִבִּי וְהַשְׁרֶה שָׁלוֹם בְּתוֹכִי, כְּדֵי שֶׁאֶזְכֶּה לִכְבוֹת אֶת הַחֵירוּת וְהַגְּאוּלָה בְּלֵב שָׂמֵחַ וּבְנֶפֶשׁ שְׁלֵמָה. אָמֵן." Then, she repeated the words in English: "Master of the Universe, as I have washed my hands, so may my soul and spirit be made pure. Cleanse my heart and grant me inner peace so that I may fully experience the freedom and redemption of this night with joy and tranquility. Amen."

"Amen," Sarah and Jacob echoed together.

Sarah then reached for the parsley from the Seder plate, dipped it into salt water, and offered it to Jacob. "בָּרוּךְ אַתָּה אֲדוֹנָי, אֱלֹהֵינוּ מֶלֶךְ הָעוֹלָם, בּוֹרֵא פְּרִי הָאֲדָמָה," she recited reverently. She glanced tenderly at Jacob before translating, "Blessed are You, Lord our God, King of the universe, who creates the fruit of the earth."

Looking down at Noah, who sat wide-eyed beside her, Sarah added gently, "Noah, the salt water reflects the bitter tears shed by the slaves and the hope for renewal."

As the words of the Seder filled the room, Rachel found herself troubled. How could she sit with her family to celebrate deliverance from slavery with gratitude, knowing that children like Mama Mary's on the Emancipation Plantation were being torn from their mother's arms and sold into lives of misery? The thought gnawed at her. Were Jews truly so special? Yes, they were the Chosen People, but chosen for what? Didn't that honor come with a duty to all human beings, regardless of the color of their skin?

Breaking the silence, Sarah picked up the matzoh from the center of the Seder plate and broke it into four pieces. She recited the blessing over the bread: "בָּרוּךְ אַתָּה אֲדוֹנָי, אֱלֹהֵינוּ מֶלֶךְ הָעוֹלָם, הַמּוֹצִיא לֶחֶם מִן הָאָרֶץ." "Blessed are You, Lord our God, King of the universe, who brings forth bread from the earth."

Then she continued with the blessing specific to the Passover Seder: "בָּרוּךְ אַתָּה אֲדוֹנָי,

אלהינו מלך העולם, אשר קדשנו במצותיו וצונו על אכילת מצה." "Blessed are You, Lord our God, King of the universe, who has sanctified us with His commandments and commanded us to eat matzoh."

She broke the matzoh, gave a small piece to Jacob, another to Noah, and handed a third to Rachel.

"This is Noah's first Passover," Sarah said warmly, brushing a lock of his hair from his forehead. "Who should read the Four Questions for him?"

Rachel turned to her brother-in-law with a smile. "Jacob, are you ready to read the Four Questions on Noah's behalf?"

"Yes," Jacob replied, his face softening. "In a few years, he'll be able to ask them himself, even before he learns to read."

Rachel held the *Haggadah* steady for Jacob, positioning it so he could see the words clearly. He leaned forward slightly, his voice resonant and warm as he began to read the Four Questions.

"Why is this night different from all other nights?" Jacob read, pausing to glance at Noah, who sat wide-eyed. "On all other nights, we eat bread or matzoh, but on this night, only matzoh."

Jacob's gaze shifted to Rachel and Sarah as he continued, his tone taking on a gentle, storytelling rhythm, as though weaving a memory for Noah to cherish and pass on to his children in the future. "On all other nights, we eat all kinds of vegetables, but on this night, we eat only bitter herbs. On all other nights, we do not dip our food even once, but on this night, we dip twice. And on all other nights, we eat either sitting or reclining, but on this night, we all recline."

Rachel turned the page, guiding Jacob through the *Haggadah*. He read aloud with steady conviction, recounting the Israelites' bondage in Egypt, their liberation through Moses, and the great miracles of the Exodus. His voice carried a quiet strength, filling the room with a sense of shared history and purpose.

As Jacob finished, he turned to Noah. "One day, you'll tell this story, too, son," he said. "And you'll understand how our past gives us hope for the future."

Rachel cleared her throat and glanced at the *Haggadah*. "Shall I continue reading?"

"Please do, Sis," Sarah said with a nod, her face aglow with pride at Jacob's interaction with Noah.

Rachel took a breath and read reverently. "Blessed are You, Oh Lord our God, King of the universe, who has chosen us from among all people, raised us above all tongues, and made us holy through His commandments. And You, Our God, have given us in love Shabbats for rest and festivals for happiness, feasts and festive seasons for rejoicing this

Shabbat day, and the day of this Feast of Matzoh, and this Festival of Holy Convocation, the Season of our Freedom in love, commemorating the departure from Egypt."

The room grew quiet as the Seder rituals unfolded, each prayer and action drawing the family deeper into their ancient ancestors' liberation story.

Yet, as Rachel participated, her unease only grew inside her. She cherished the traditions, the history, and the love of her family, but she couldn't silence the questions rising in her heart: What did freedom mean if others still lived in chains? How could she celebrate the deliverance of her people while others were left in bondage simply because of the color of their skin? Weren't we all children of God? How long could she remain silent about her newfound convictions?

Rachel's gaze lingered on Noah as he eagerly reached for another piece of matzoh, his innocence a reminder of future generations and the hope they embodied for a better world where freedom and dignity belong to all people, not just a chosen few.

48

MAY DAY

Rachel and Thomas rode into City Park at a gentle canter as the May Day festivities began. Nearby, students from Madison Girls' School stepped down from the streetcar that had taken them from downtown across St. John's Bayou Bridge. Their colorful silk skirts swirled with each step as they made their way toward the oak grove at the park's edge, their joyful laughter floating on the breeze like notes from a flute.

Seated astride a golden chestnut mare Thomas had hired for her, Rachel wore a tan riding habit. Her polished boots gleamed in the sunlight. Leather gloves covered her hands, and a smart top hat perched on her head as she guided her horse forward.

Thomas, astride Midnight, his sleek, jet-black Morgan stallion, reached into his saddlebag and withdrew a gift box elegantly wrapped in fine paper and tied with a crimson ribbon. He extended it to Rachel with a warm smile. "Happy birthday, Rachel."

Her eyes widened with delight as she accepted the box. "Oh my! Should I open it now?"

"Of course," he replied, his grin widening as he watched her anticipation.

Rachel carefully loosened the ribbon and peeled back the wrapping, setting the paper and bow neatly aside. As she opened the box, she gasped softly. Inside lay a pair of supple, exquisitely crafted brown kid leather riding gloves and a matching leatherbound edition of *Sonnets from the Portuguese* by Elizabeth Barrett Browning, its pages' gilded edges catching the light.

She removed a riding glove to trace her finger over the smooth leather cover of the book. "Truly, I could not have asked for more thoughtful birthday gifts," she said with heartfelt appreciation.

Lifting the volume, she opened it with reverence. The crisp scent of fresh pages drifted up, stirring fond memories of her father's library. As she carefully leafed through the book, her fingers paused on her favorite sonnet: "How do I love thee? Let me count the ways."

Her smile softened, and she looked up at Thomas, her gratitude shining in her eyes. "Thank you, Thomas. Truly."

Thomas's expression softened as she read silently. "When was the last time you celebrated your birthday?"

Rachel hesitated, her eyes drifting as she searched for an answer. "I can't recall. April has always been unkind to me. Both of my parents died in April. The war began when Fort Sumter was fired upon in April. My husband died at Shiloh in April. New Orleans was occupied in April. It's as if my birthday rides on the coattails of all those sorrows."

Thomas reached for her hand, his grip warm and steady. "You know, I could list just as many unfortunate events around my birthday in December."

Rachel tilted her head inquisitively. "Such as?"

"Well, the Trent Affair in December '61 nearly landed us in another war with England. And just last December, there was Grant's General Order No. 11 expelling Jews from his military district and unleashing a wave of antisemitism. I'm certain I could come up with a long list, given enough time to think about it."

Rachel squeezed his hand. "I take your meaning. But somehow, the losses tied to my birthday feel more personal."

Thomas met her sad gaze. "Then maybe we'll make it a tradition to share something good every year on your birthday."

"Yes, my love. We must." Suddenly, her attention was caught by the swirling flurry of the young girls' colorful dresses in the oak grove. "Aren't they lovely?" she murmured, a soft smile across her face. "Like a flock of butterflies."

"Lovely, indeed," Thomas agreed. "The bloom of youth is still fresh on their cheeks— such a fleeting, innocent age. Just look at them soaring through the air on those rope swings the sailors are hanging from the tree branches. I see Captain Walters, the commander of the gunboat *Kineo*, supervising his men."

Rachel nodded, a trace of wistfulness in her voice as her father's words on growing older echoed in her mind. "Yes, *Tempus fugit*. If only youth could linger a little longer."

"Would you really want to go back to be that age again?

"I'm not certain I ever truly was that age, Thomas. I was the older sister, always looking after Sarah."

Thomas nodded and reached out to take her hand. "That's true. They say the older child is the responsible one. You never had an older brother to watch over you."

"I didn't need one, thank you," Rachel replied, pulling her hand away with a playful smile.

"Fair enough," Thomas said, chuckling. "You've always been more than capable of taking care of yourself."

Rachel smiled inwardly, pleased that independence was a trait Thomas found attractive in a woman.

"Shall we tether our horses over yonder in that clearing under the oaks, so we have a good view of the festivities?"

"Let's," Rachel said, following Thomas's lead to a spot with a clear view of where the girls were gathering.

After bringing his horse to a stop, Thomas helped Rachel dismount, then unbuckled the leather strap that secured their picnic basket to his saddle.

"I've been thinking about your suggestion of meeting your family," Thomas said, his voice sincere. "You're a courageous woman, Rachel. It takes strength to challenge the values you were raised with, especially when the world feels so divided."

Rachel looked down, her fingers gently brushing the edge of the tablecloth. "It hasn't been easy. But after everything we've been through and seen, it's hard *not* to question some things."

Thomas poured the wine and handed her a glass. "You won't have to face it alone."

She met his eyes, the promise behind his words comforting her. "I know," she whispered. Her expression grew sad. "I've been thinking about Sarah and Jacob leaving with Noah."

"Yes," Thomas replied. "I know that's been weighing on you."

"I tried to convince Sarah to stay here in New Orleans, but she wouldn't hear of it."

"What reason did she give you for leaving?"

"She said she was tired of living under occupation."

"But the occupation keeps us safe, and it will be over at war's end."

"And I told her as much. But she said it's not just about the Union soldiers in the streets, but the way forces beyond her control shape everything: the traditions, the old ways."

"Where she plans to go is far more dangerous," Thomas said, his brow tightening with concern. "Once Port Hudson and Vicksburg fall—and they will—Grant and Sherman will push hard toward Atlanta and beyond. My money's on 'Unconditional Surrender' Grant and 'Uncle Billy' Sherman wreaking havoc all the way to the sea."

"And that leaves my family below Atlanta directly in their path," Rachel said, her voice tightening. "I have no idea how the Union will approach the remainder of the war, but, inevitably, their new home in LaGrange with Eugenia and Philip will eventually be caught up in the fighting."

"I've learned that when I've done everything I possibly can, sometimes I just have to let go. It's one of the hardest things in life to accept."

"Letting go, you say?" Rachel echoed softly, thinking about Thomas's dire prediction of the war's course.

He nodded. "Yes."

Rachel managed a faint smile. "You're such a practical man," she said. "I wish it were that easy for me."

Her smile faded as her thoughts drifted inward, becoming quiet as she sipped the wine, savored its bouquet, and unwrapped the Roquefort cheese. She placed the cheese on the small oak cutting board, slicing it carefully while appreciating its fragrance, and then divided the portions between two plates.

"Would you like a larger piece?" she asked, hoping to lighten the mood.

"No, this is perfect," Thomas replied, reaching for a strawberry to pair with his cheese.

Rachel's eyes softened. "I haven't told you about Noah yet."

"I've been looking forward to hearing about the little tyke."

"I wish you could have seen him on his rocking horse," Rachel said fondly.

"He's old enough for a rocking horse?" Thomas asked, surprised.

"With a little help from his mother. He's still working on his balance."

"The rocking horse will help with that. Can he walk yet?"

"Only if he's holding onto something or when someone's holding his little hand."

Thomas's expression softened, his eyes warm. "You must've had such a grand time with him. He's still young enough to play 'This Little Piggy' with his toes."

Rachel threw her head back, laughing. "You should have seen him when I did just that. I barely get out, 'This little piggy went to market' before he breaks into the most delightful giggles you've ever heard. He's such a happy child."

"Noah sounds adorable. And how is Jacob faring?" Thomas asked.

"He's improving...at least physically. He has shown significant progress in standing and walking independently. They no longer need anyone to live in the house to help them. Sarah says that he exercises his legs every morning and practices his balance on his own." She hesitated. "But he still resists being seen in public. Sarah says it's a struggle to get him outside occasionally to get a little sunshine." She frowned. "Of course, the stares and whispers behind his back don't help."

"It'll take time," Thomas said gently. "Maimed soldiers bring the horrors of the battlefield home with them to face an uncertain future. They all bear scars, whether their wounds are visible or buried deep inside."

Rachel nodded, his words sinking in as she recalled visiting the St. Louis Hotel hospital with Loreta and finding Jacob without his arms. The memories of that day stirred something in her, and she thought of the painful sights of soldiers' faces that still appeared in her nightmares.

"May I offer you a strawberry?" Thomas asked, extending the basket toward her with a soft smile.

"Thank you," she said, picking out a bright red one. "It's so difficult to find fresh strawberries in the market. And when you do, you must finish them soon, or they get soft."

"Did you tell Jacob and your sister about me?" Thomas asked, raising an eyebrow.

"Yes, I did."

"And would you mind sharing what you told them?"

"Well," she began with a teasing smile, "I mentioned how tall, dark, and handsome you are."

Thomas grinned.

"And," she continued with a playful glint in her eyes, "I told them you were a Union spy."

Thomas's grin vanished, giving way to wide-eyed surprise. "No! You didn't."

Rachel burst into laughter. "Of course not, Thomas. They'd despise you if I had told them about our little adventure at Port Hudson."

He wiped his brow in exaggerated relief. "Whew!"

"When I get home tonight, I'd like to tell them I invited you to our house for supper later in the week, but I need to discuss that with you first."

"That sounds delightful," Thomas replied, grinning. "And how exactly do you plan to introduce me?"

She hesitated for a moment, then gave him a playful smile. "As a friend. A gentleman friend." Her eyes sparkled mischievously. "I am allowed, you know," she added teasingly.

Thomas chuckled. "Yes, I suppose you're old enough to have a 'gentleman friend.' That will do for now."

Rachel joined in his laughter and reached for his hand. "Should I tell them you'll visit?"

He paused. "I'm not sure I'll be free before your family leaves New Orleans, depending on my obligations."

"Perhaps you can join me in seeing them off, then."

"I will try," Thomas assured her. He nodded toward the lively scene unfolding a few yards away, saying, "Just look at those girls dancing. Their feet are barely touching the ground."

"And listen to that music!" Rachel exclaimed, her eyes brightening as she tapped her foot to the lively rhythm of the polka playing in the air. "I've never seen an all-girl band."

"I haven't heard a polka in some time," Thomas remarked, his thoughts turning back to the polka composed for Mrs. Lincoln when she held the grand reception celebrating the refurbishing of the East Room.

The lively dance unfolded to the polka's unmistakable "oom-pah" cadence: the accordion's bright, playful chords on the upbeat, perfectly paired with the tuba's deep, resonant notes anchoring the downbeat.

"Are you going to ask me to dance, sir?" Rachel asked playfully, finishing a strawberry. "Or must I ask you?"

Thomas settled his wine glass on the tablecloth and stood to offer his hand. *"Madame, puis-je avoir cette danse?"*

"Mais oui, Monsieur," she replied with a smile, taking his hand.

The couple stepped into the lively rhythm of the music, twirling and laughing as they danced across the grass, the polka light and carefree, Rachel's riding habit sweeping gracefully with each turn. Thomas led with spirited confidence, both caught up in the moment's joy. As the tempo quickened, they danced faster, their feet barely touching the ground, until they were out of breath as the music reached its crescendo and faded away. Exhausted, they stopped, still holding hands, their laughter mingling with the cheerful sounds of the celebration.

Suddenly, Thomas drew her into a tender embrace, his lips engaging hers in a soft, lingering kiss.

"Thomas, not here! The girls might see us," she said, pushing him away, her protest lacking conviction.

Thomas's grin was playful, his eyes glinting with mischief. "How clumsy of me, my love. Next time, I'll be more discreet when I steal a kiss."

Rachel shifted the conversation as the two settled back onto the ground. "It's such a joy to see these young girls having fun," she said, her gaze following the lively scene. "I'm glad their school arranged this celebration. I can't wait to watch them wrap the Maypole and crown their Queen."

Thomas sat beside her, his gaze softening. "You know, many of those girls have fathers who marched off to war for the Confederacy. And yet here they are, dancing alongside their friends whose fathers came from points north into New Orleans to replace the merchants who fled the occupation."

Rachel nodded thoughtfully. "Yes, wouldn't it be grand if everyone on both sides could get along as easily as they do? They seem so carefree, dancing and laughing as if nothing could ever come between them."

"Tabula rasa," Thomas remarked, a knowing edge to his tone. "The only hope for mankind."

Rachel nodded, her expression serious. "Yes, from Cicero to Locke, the philosophers understood. Only by writing a new story on the blank slate of the next generation can we hope to achieve lasting peace and harmony." Her voice softened as she trailed off, her gaze growing distant. She took a slow sip of wine, meditating on the young girls dancing gracefully in the distance while they circled the Maypole.

"Thomas," she ventured, her tone earnest, "when do you think this war will end?"

"I'm no prophet," Thomas said solemnly, pausing to gather his thoughts. "I wish I could tell you how it's all going to unfold, but it's impossible to see past the chaos right now."

"But truly," Rachel persisted, "Which side do you believe has the greatest chance of prevailing?"

Thomas exhaled slowly, holding her gaze. "I'm not a betting man, but if I were, I'd put my money on the Union. They have superior resources, and their leaders possess the resolve and the larger population to wage a war of attrition if necessary."

Rachel nodded, unperturbed by his answer. She had long suspected as much. The agrarian South, reliant on enslaved labor, could not compete with the industrial might of the North. Furthermore, with the Emancipation Proclamation in effect, enslaved people were escaping to Union camps, not only freeing soldiers from menial tasks but, in some instances, taking up arms and bolstering the ranks of the Union army to fight for their liberation.

The certainty of Union victory brought Rachel no solace. A far greater trial lay before her: envisioning a future where freedom meant more than emancipation or the mending of the Union. True liberty demanded reckoning with past wrongs and reshaping the very pillars of society.

49

Exodus of the Registered Enemies

Rachel stood next to Sarah at the bustling uptown terminus of the Pontchartrain Railroad station on Elysian Fields Street near the French Market. The rhythmic clatter of iron-rimmed wheels on the cast-iron tracks echoed throughout the station, punctuated by the long, shrill screech of the train's brakes. As if exhausted from its journey, the locomotive emitted a final deep wheezing chug, releasing clouds of hissing steam into the morning mist that stubbornly lingered against the warmth of the rising sun.

Sarah cradled Noah tightly in her arms while Thomas gently pushed Jacob's wheeled chair toward the door to a passenger car, where a station porter stepped forward to assist.

Rachel leaned over to kiss Noah's cheek, her voice trembling. "Auntie Rachel will see you soon, my love," she whispered, her eyes brimming with unshed tears.

Sarah, her own emotions raw, met Rachel's gaze. "Remember what you always told me about promises, big sister."

Rachel's eyes sparkled. "Yes. One must always keep one's promises."

"All aboard," the conductor's voice rang out, piercing the stillness of the station. "Only registered enemies departing New Orleans may board. This is the last run. No friends or family members are allowed."

Sarah called out, "But sir, can't my family ride to the steamer just to see us off?"

"I'm sorry, ma'am," the conductor replied, his tone firm. "Like I just said, this is the final trip, and there's not even standing room for family on the train."

Sarah sighed softly, her eyes meeting Rachel's. "Oh, dear, I was hoping you and Thomas could see us off at the steamer."

Rachel gave a bittersweet smile. "It seems we must say our goodbyes here, sister."

Thomas reached into his pocket, pulled out two Double Eagles, and offered them to Sarah. "Noah will need a new rocking horse," he said with a smile. "Rachel mentioned how much he loved riding his Chester."

"Thank you," Sarah replied, smiling as she took the gold coins. "Noah adored his Chester. I'll ask Eugenia to order another, just like the one she bought for him. She'll understand we couldn't bring it with us." She paused. "I'm sorry that we won't have a chance to get to know you better, Thomas."

"Let's plan for a reunion when the war is finally over," he said.

Rachel, working to keep her emotions in check, said, "Please give my love to Eugenia and Philip. I hope I'll be able to visit come Chanukkah. Perhaps, just perhaps, the conflict will be behind us by then."

Rachel knelt beside Jacob, brushing a lock of hair from his forehead before placing a tender kiss. "I love you, Jacob."

"I love you too, Sis," Jacob murmured, a tear sliding down his cheek. "You must come visit. Maybe even stay."

Rachel's smile quivered, but she nodded. "Yes, I will."

Thomas stood in front of Jacob, apparently resisting the urge to extend his hand. "It was good meeting you, Jacob. I wish you and your family all the best."

"Thank you, Thomas," Jacob replied, his voice thick with emotion. "And I wish you and Rachel happiness."

"Jacob, do you want us to lift you in the chair, or would you rather walk?" Thomas asked, his hand already moving to help.

"I'd prefer to walk," Jacob said with quiet determination.

Thomas watched as Jacob stood from his chair, then followed him up the stairs to the train to make sure he kept his balance. "I'll get your chair," he said, turning to head back down as Jacob entered the train.

Rachel embraced Sarah and Noah once more, holding them as if the warmth of the hug could delay their departure. When she finally let go, her hand instinctively gripped the stair rail, her knuckles turning white. The rail was her anchor, the only thing holding her upright as she fought to maintain her composure. She blinked back tears, trying to appear strong, even though her heart ached with fear that this might be the last time she would see them for a long time, or perhaps ever again, given that they were traveling deeper into the Confederacy, where the uncertainty of war loomed over them.

"You might suggest to Thomas that he avoid the sun," Sarah whispered. "He's nearly as dark as an octoroon. Keep him inside for a while, and he'll lighten up."

Rachel froze. The words struck her like a slap, their cruelty hidden beneath a genteel murmur. A sharp retort rose to her lips, but she swallowed it, not wanting to disrupt the family farewell. "Safe travels, Sarah," she said evenly, her smile tight, her heart pounding.

Once Thomas and the conductor lifted the invalid chair onto the train, the other passengers boarded, and soon Sarah and Jacob disappeared inside.

Rachel turned to leave the station with Thomas, but hesitated, glancing back. Through the mist-fogged window, she glimpsed Sarah seated with Noah in her lap, their faces barely visible behind the glass. Sarah raised a finger to trace the shape of a heart onto the window.

"I love you, too," Rachel called, waving with a strained smile as she blew a kiss. Her mind flashed back to her childhood when she and Sarah would trace hearts on fogged-up windowpanes to say goodbye to their father as he and his horse disappeared into the mist on winter mornings.

The locomotive announced its arrival with a loud whistle as it steamed into Port Hickok on the southern shore of Lake Pontchartrain, finishing its fifteen-mile journey around noon.

The morning fog had lifted, and the day was bright and beautiful at Port Hickok, frequently visited by New Orleans residents for picnics, swimming, and horseback riding. Today, however, the train was full of the last of over one thousand New Orleans residents, primarily women, who had refused to take the Oath of Allegiance to the Union.

The conductor and a gentleman on the train carefully lowered Jacob's wheeled chair down the steps of the passenger car and onto the station platform. Sarah cradled Noah in her arms while another passenger kindly helped steady Jacob as he descended the steep steps.

"Much obliged," Sarah said with a smile to the conductor and the two gentlemen who had helped her family.

The two men tipped their hats in unison, each offering a polite "ma'am" with a flicker of pity in their eyes.

She forced a smile, choosing to ignore it. Pity, at least, was easier to stomach than the whispered remarks she'd overheard, suggesting that it might have been kinder if he hadn't come back at all, leaving her free to marry a man who could provide.

The conductor, already stepping back onto the train, said, "Y'all have a safe trip, ma'am. God bless."

"Thank you," Sarah replied, placing Noah on Jacob's lap and securing him with a wide sash wrapped around his father.

Gripping the handles of Jacob's wheeled chair, her eyes lifted to the towering white Lake House, standing majestically at the end of the famed Shell Road. Paved with crushed oyster shells from New Orleans, the road was a testament to the culinary tastes of its residents.

A long, slow-moving line of people had already formed, waiting to enter the Lake House. Sarah had read in the papers that passengers were now being thoroughly searched for contraband. It seems that, on the last trip, enemies fleeing into Secessia had smuggled bottles of quinine and other supplies needed by Confederate troops concealed within their undergarments and babies' strollers.

Sarah was relieved to read that, after the outrage caused by women being inspected by soldiers on the first trip, General Banks recruited a group of female Union loyalists to take on this delicate task.

Most ladies seeking to leave were dressed in their colorful Sunday best, holding parasols as if the day were a joyous occasion. Friends lined the paths of their departing loved ones, offering tearful farewells, kisses, and lingering embraces. Their emotions were a poignant blend of joy and sorrow, much like the bittersweet goodbyes at a funeral when the departed are sent off with hopes that they will leave behind their burdens and walk on streets paved with gold in Paradise.

Sarah reflected that the women leaving were, like herself, probably close to penniless and without significant property holdings. In contrast, many planters, bankers, and wealthy merchants who had fled the occupied city early on had deeded everything to their wives. These women had taken the Oath of Allegiance, staying behind with no real intention of remaining loyal to the Union once Confederate troops returned.

After what felt like an eternity waiting in line, Sarah pushed Jacob's wheeled chair into the vast hall of the Lake House, now repurposed with partitions to accommodate Union inspection teams. The hall was tense as women and men were herded into separate sections.

"I'll take the child," a plainly dressed, middle-aged woman said, unfastening Noah from Jacob's lap. "We need to inspect his clothing as well as yours," she added, grabbing Sarah's travel bag.

"I'm going with you," Sarah insisted, her voice edged with alarm as the stranger carried Noah away.

"As you wish," the woman replied, leading Sarah to the women's section. Her attire was practical and straightforward, in contrast with Sarah's voluminous dress.

"What about my husband?" Sarah asked, hurrying to keep up with the woman.

"He'll be searched by one of the soldiers. You'll see him again past the inspection stations," the woman answered, her tone suggesting she was weary of answering the same question countless times.

Inside the women's inspection station, tables stacked with garments lined the walls, and women stood in various stages of *déshabillé*. A few, entirely nude, crossed one hand over their chests and the other over their lower bodies, their postures mirroring Botticelli's *The Birth of Venus* in a vain attempt to shield themselves from the humiliating exposure. Nearby, inspectors moved methodically, their hands deftly rifling through seams, hems, and linings of shed garments with the precision of those well-versed in uncovering hidden contraband.

Sarah stared in shock. "Must I strip naked?"

"That's the idea, ma'am," a second, taller, and younger inspector responded, looming over her without a hint of sympathy. "You Southern Belles have a talent for hiding quinine and other items in your clothing and on your person. We have our methods to ensure nothing gets through the lines to aid the enemy."

The enemy, Sarah reflected bitterly. Was she branded an enemy for trying to protect her family, including her infant boy and crippled husband? Reluctantly, she began undressing while watching the other inspector undress Noah, meticulously checking the hems of his little coat and even inspecting his baby linen. Was a child of his age also to be branded an enemy?

Once Sarah stood exposed entirely, the inspector gave her a curt nod. "Lift your breasts."

Sarah complied, lifting each breast until the woman was satisfied that nothing was concealed beneath them.

"Now, bend over," the inspector barked.

"Bend over?" Sarah echoed in disbelief.

"Yes, you heard me. Bend over. Touch your fingers to the floor."

Furious, Sarah followed the instructions, her face burning with humiliation. She had never experienced such an invasion of privacy, and the indignity of it all was nearly unbearable.

"You're clear back there; now lean back against the table and spread your legs," the inspector ordered, her tone devoid of compassion.

Sarah was aghast. *The nerve of this woman!* But she complied, enduring the cursory inspection of her most private areas.

"You may put your clothes back on," the inspector finally said, her task complete.

Sarah dressed quickly, feeling a profound sense of shame at the violation of her person. The older inspector quickly checked Noah and redressed him, satisfied there was no contraband. As she adjusted her dress, Sarah's mind raced, trying to reconcile the indignity she had just endured with the resolve she needed to maintain for Jacob, Noah, and the uncertain road ahead.

"Now for your luggage," the inspector said, turning to Sarah's bag on the table. "Are your papers inside?"

"Yes," Sarah replied. "I'll get them for you."

"I'll find them," the inspector said coldly. "I have to inspect everything myself."

The inspector methodically removed each item from the bag, laying them out on the table one by one: toiletries, baby linens, makeup, a baby bottle, and various pieces of clothing, all subjected to her thorough scrutiny. Then she pulled out a straight razor. "This is contraband," she declared, tossing the razor into a large bin on the floor beside the table.

Poor Jacob, Sarah thought with a pang, declining to give her tormentor the satisfaction of an objection. *He'll miss me shaving him in the morning. It's one of the few simple pleasures he has left.*

When the inspector came across a book in Sarah's bag, she held it by the spine and shook it, ensuring nothing was hidden within its pages. Satisfied that it was free of contraband, she opened the cover and said with a smirk, "You Southern Belles never cease to amaze."

Sarah blushed, feeling yet another intrusion into her privacy.

The inspector then picked up a small bottle of clear liquid. "What's this?" she asked.

"It's my husband's medicine," Sarah said.

The inspector uncorked the bottle, dipped her fingertip into the liquid, and brought it to her lips for a taste. Wrinkling her nose, she declared, "It's laudanum," before setting it aside in a metal tray with other confiscated medicinals.

"But he needs it to fall asleep," Sarah protested, her voice tinged with desperation.

"He'll be fine on the steamer," the woman replied dismissively. "It'll rock him to sleep like a baby."

"Nothing on the little boy," the older woman said, returning a confused but fully clothed Noah to his mother.

Once Sarah's belongings were summarily returned to her bag and Noah was safely back in her arms, the taller woman led her out of the inspection area. Jacob was waiting in his wheeled chair just outside.

The inspector gestured toward a path filled with their fellow registered enemies, all making their way toward the *J.D. Brown*. The massive sidewheeler, billowing clouds of black smoke, waited to carry them across Lake Pontchartrain to the pier at Madisonville, where they would board a train bound for deeper Confederate territory.

As they approached the steamer, Sarah felt the weight of the journey pressing down on her. The *J.D. Brown* was not just a means of escape but a lifeline, pulling her family away from the world they had known and into the fragile promise of a better future. Yet, amid the uncertainty, Sarah clung to the hope that this path would eventually lead to freedom and a new beginning for her family, especially once Rachel joined them.

She reminded herself that the Confederates were still holding firm against the Union attacks on Richmond in the east and the assaults on Vicksburg and Port Hudson in the west. With the aid of divine Providence and reinforcements and supplies along the Red River from Texas, there remained a glimmer of hope that they might one day return to their home in New Orleans and rebuild their lives together in the world they once knew.

As the last rays of sunset filtered through the parlor, Rachel sat alone on the sofa, struggling to breathe under the weight of her grief. Slowly, the crushing tightness in her chest began to loosen, though the exhaustion from lack of sleep was relentless. The initial shock had passed, but the sorrow remained heavy and unyielding. She sank onto the sofa, her head resting on a pillow, eyes fixed blankly on the ceiling. The numbness gradually gave way to a profound ache as the reality of her loss settled in.

Sarah, Jacob, and Noah were gone, banishing themselves from New Orleans as sworn enemies of the Union. The thought of moving forward without them filled her with despair. She knew she would have to carry their memory with her, learning to live in a world that felt emptier without them until she could be reunited after the war.

As night fell, Rachel stared at the warm, glowing orb of the kerosene lamp, her thoughts drifting to Thomas, who had brought a flicker of light into her darkest days. She recalled the terror she had felt at Port Hudson, believing she might lose him forever. She couldn't let that happen. Summoning every ounce of courage, she had risked her life to free him, knowing her fate hung in the balance. Later, when a sniper's bullet nearly took her life, it was Thomas who saved her, stopping the bleeding and staying by her side until he could get her to safety and comfort her through her healing.

Thomas had become more than her anchor; he was her lifeline, her hope for a future filled with love and renewal after the darkness of conflict and loss. She imagined the life they could build together—a marriage, children, and the joyful sound of laughter filling their home—and the reunion she longed for with her sister and the rest of her family.

She had a vision of them together, the bonds of love stronger than ever, sitting around the supper table saying the *Berachah* over the wine and bread, lighting the Sabbath candles, sharing stories, and finding comfort in each other's presence.

The boundary between wakefulness and sleep slowly dissolved. In the twilight of her dreams, the promise of love and family offered hope and healing, comforting her as she faced the trials ahead.

50

JUBILEE

Rachel stepped onto her balcony to enjoy the soft sunlight and gentle breeze of late afternoon. Her heart quickened as shouts, cheers, and bursts of singing stirred vivid memories of Mardi Gras parades and revelry.

She leaned over the wrought-iron railing to gaze at the lively scene below. Dozens of newly freed men and women, barefoot and draped in tattered garments, danced wildly with an unrestrained joy that echoed their newfound freedom. Their faces glowed with exhilaration, their voices rising in jubilant song as they swayed to the deep, resonant pulse of the drums.

The powerful sound surged through Rachel's chest, synchronizing with the rhythm of her heartbeat. The sound was so commanding that it seemed even the deaf might feel it reverberating through the marrow of their bones.

Little ragamuffins darted among the adults, blissfully unaware of their place in the world. They collided randomly with legs and arms as they clapped their hands and twirled to the rhythm. Their innocent laughter, unbothered by the jostling of their ecstatic elders, was as infectious as the beat that echoed through the streets.

"Jubilee! Jubilee!" echoed beneath her balcony. The celebration might have been unsettling, even threatening, for planters accustomed to demanding restraint from their slaves, but to her, it felt like an expression of heartfelt joy.

She rested her bare arm on the balcony railing. The cold wrought iron felt unyielding, reminding her that the old world, shaped by centuries of tradition, would not be easily undone. Yet, beneath its deceptive permanence, the steady drumbeats echoed through the streets, a relentless rhythm carrying the promise of freedom.

The sudden sound of the doorbell jolted Rachel out of her reverie. She hesitated, glanced at the loud celebration, and then turned away to go downstairs.

Rushing to the front door, she cautiously cracked it open and saw Thomas. She breathed a sigh of relief and stepped aside for him to enter.

"Come in," Rachel said. "I was beginning to worry about you. Are you all right?"

"I'm fine," he reassured her, pulling her into a gentle embrace before following her into the parlor.

There was something in his tone that she couldn't quite place, which made her even more nervous. She sank into the softness of the sofa, trying to steady herself. "I know it's the Fourth, Thomas," she began, her voice faltering slightly, "But I've never seen Negroes celebrate it like this. It's rather odd, don't you think?"

"What to the slave is the Fourth of July?" Thomas asked. "Those were the words Frederick Douglass asked in his speech a decade ago, denouncing the hypocrisy of a nation that proclaims liberty while keeping millions enslaved."

He paused, his gaze searching hers as he settled in beside her. "I suppose that's because the poor souls never truly had anything to celebrate on the Fourth until now."

Confusion flickered across Rachel's face, and Thomas's expression softened with understanding. "Yesterday, the Confederate army was defeated in Pennsylvania at Gettysburg. Today, they surrendered Vicksburg, and Port Hudson seems to be soon to follow."

"How do you know all this?" Rachel asked, her voice tinged with amazement at how swiftly the news had traveled.

"The telegraph lines are buzzing with it," Thomas replied." And where they're down, messengers rushed to the nearest station to pass it along."

As Rachel absorbed Thomas's words, the joy on the streets below began to take on meaning. With the Union now on the verge of taking control of the Mississippi River and its plantations all the way to Missouri and Illinois, it marked a momentous occasion reminiscent of the biblical tradition in *Leviticus*, where every fiftieth year brought the forgiveness of debts, the return of land, and the liberation of slaves. This day fulfilled that ancient promise for these newly liberated souls, heralding a profound shift in the world she had known.

As the realization settled in, a swirl of emotions churned within her. The old world was crumbling, but perhaps something better would rise from its ashes.

Thomas reached into his vest pocket, pulled out a *carte de visite*, and handed it to Rachel. On it was the image of a slave with his back to the camera, his skin crisscrossed with raised welts from countless lashings.

"Oh!" Rachel exclaimed, recoiling as if the card had scorched her fingers, quickly thrusting it back to him. "Where on earth did you get that? It's dreadful!"

"I understand that it is set to appear in today's issue of *Harper's Weekly*, along with the backstory," Thomas said, slipping the card back into his pocket. "It's already causing quite a stir among the abolitionists."

"As well it should. It utterly disproves the planters' paternalistic claims of treating their slaves humanely." She recalled that it was for this reason that Thomas had sold the plantation he had inherited.

"Indeed, it does," Thomas agreed. "I'm sorry it disturbed you so deeply, but I felt it illustrated what I was trying to convey about the joyous celebration on the streets."

"Do you know this man's name?" Rachel asked, still unsettled by the image.

"His name is Gordon. He and three fellow slaves fled their plantation and managed to evade capture by rubbing themselves with onions and running through swamps to throw the hounds off their scent."

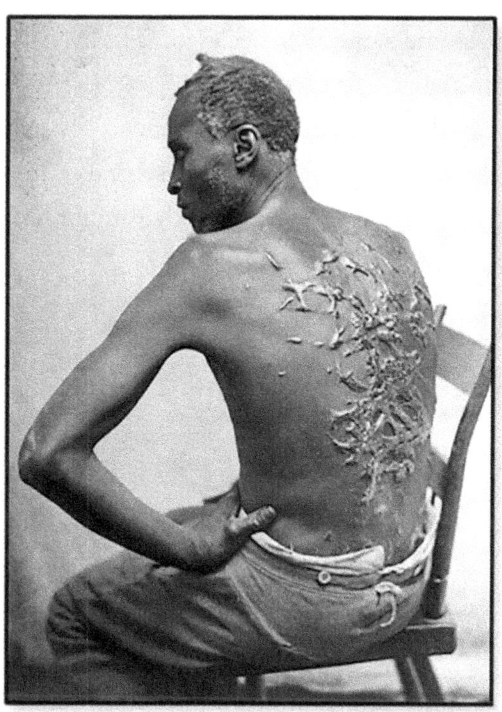

"That was certainly clever."

"Three of them, including Gordon, survived the escape and made it to the Union camps in Baton Rouge. There, Gordon was treated for his wounds and later joined Banks's *Corps d'Afrique*, where they gave him a rifle and taught him how to fire it."

"Where was that horrifying photograph taken?" Rachel asked.

"It was taken in Baton Rouge by McPherson and Oliver."

"What does it say on the back of the card?" Rachel asked, her initial shock at the cruelty giving way to a deeper appreciation of the truth Thomas was revealing. She could sense that it had affected him deeply as well.

Thomas retrieved the *carte de visite* again and read the inscription. "Contraband that marched forty miles to get to our lines."

"I'd love to learn more about Gordon's story," Rachel said, her curiosity piqued.

Thomas replied, "I should have a copy of today's edition of *Harper's Weekly* in a few days, depending on General Banks's courier. I'll bring it over as soon as I get it."

"What is happening here in Louisiana will profoundly impact people up North and even people of conscience in the South. It reminds me of the overwhelming response to Harriet Beecher Stowe's *Uncle Tom's Cabin*."

"Yes," Thomas agreed. "As I recall, President Lincoln greeted Mrs. Stowe last year by saying, 'So you are the little woman who wrote the book that started this great war.'"

Rachel nodded thoughtfully. "I believe it was Richelieu, the lead character in Edward Bulwer-Lytton's play of the same name, who declared, 'The pen is mightier than the sword. Take away the sword; states can be saved without it.'"

"Would to God the South had heeded that sentiment," Thomas lamented.

As Thomas's words, spoken with the reverence of a prayer, lingered in the air, Rachel, too, wished the South had chosen a different path that might have spared Levi. Yet now, she couldn't imagine a future without Thomas.

IMPERIAL

51

UNVEXED TO THE SEA

THURSDAY, JULY 16

The *Imperial*'s steam whistle sounded a deep note that slowly ascended an octave, its ghostly resonance lingering along the levee until its echo returned, weaving a haunting harmony that stretched across the river and through the streets of downtown New Orleans.

Union soldiers lined the railings on the lower deck, their elation palpable after recent victories at Vicksburg and Port Hudson. These triumphs opened the waters of the mighty Mississippi, rekindling hope and fueling patriotic fervor just days after the Fourth of July.

The sharp blast of the whistle pierced the afternoon air. Cheers rang out, hats flew skyward, and handkerchiefs fluttered wildly.

"Ste-e-e-eamboat a'comin'!" bellowed one man, his voice booming over the din as if the colossal three-decker required a herald to trumpet its arrival.

The crowd pressed forward, eyes straining for their first glimpse of the floating giant that churned toward them, its paddlewheel slicing the water with powerful thrusts. Steam hissed, the lowering gangplank creaked and groaned under its weight, and for a moment, the riverfront seemed to hold its breath, suspended between the echoes of war that once raged upon the river and the promise of peace and prosperity now glimmering along its banks.

"Hear that mooin' and squealin'?" a man in a blacksmith apron asked, tilting his head toward his friend with a knowing grin. "That's the sound of them cattle and hogs they're bringin' in from Texas. Ain't had me no bacon in a month a' Sundays."

"Well, you might not plan on fixin' yoreself none now, neither," his friend advised.

"Just wait'll you see how much they want for a slab a' bacon. You gotta shoe a lotta horses to eat that good."

Standing beside Thomas at the levee, Rachel reminisced about the days when steamboats laden with goods from ports as far north as St. Paul, Minnesota, were a regular sight. But now, the arrival of a grand steamship traveling from the North, with its towering smokestacks and bustling decks, felt almost surreal against the backdrop of a city still bearing the scars of conflict.

"So, it flows again, unvexed to the sea," Thomas reflected, echoing President Lincoln's words.

"Yes," Rachel said, her voice heavy with sorrow. "And it's borne upon a river of countless tears shed by fallen soldiers on both sides, flowing slowly to the sea." A shiver crawled down her spine. "I feel as though their ghosts, drifting in the mist at the water's edge, have found passage aboard the ship."

"Do you believe the country will ever again become so divided?" Thomas asked, putting his arm around her waist.

"I pray not," Rachel whispered, enjoying the comfort of his embrace. Her gaze remained fixed on the mighty *Imperial* as it moved downriver to moor, the weight of the past heavy on her heart. "When it's all over, let's hope this conflict has taught us something."

Thomas gently steered Rachel away from the crowd, guiding her behind a stack of wooden crates, where the din of cheers faded. With a soft, loving smile, he reached into his coat pocket and, with a slow, deliberate motion, sank to one knee. Opening his hand, he produced a small silk-covered box tied with a delicate pink ribbon.

Rachel's hand trembled as she untied the ribbon and lifted the lid, revealing a ring of Russian gold with its warm, rosy hue, crowned with a breathtaking step-cut emerald. The gemstone shimmered in the soft light, its vibrant green depths flickering with the promise of eternal love. On either side, two brilliant rose-cut diamonds flanked the center stone, catching the light with their icy fire and enhancing the emerald's verdant glow, giving the ring an air of quiet elegance.

"Thomas!" she gasped, pressing her hand to her mouth in disbelief. "Emeralds are my favorite gem. And diamonds are my birthstone."

Thomas looked up at her, still kneeling. "Rachel, my love, will you marry me?"

Her heart surged, and her breath momentarily caught in her throat. "Yes! Oh yes, Thomas! I will marry you."

With a look of quiet joy, Thomas rose to his feet, gently lifting the ring from the box and sliding it onto her finger with care as if sealing a promise. "I had it made at Tiffany's," he murmured.

Rachel stared at the perfect fit, astonished. "How did you know my size?"

Thomas grinned. "Remember when we first returned to New Orleans, and I tied that string around your ring finger to teach you how to make a Jacob's ladder? When I slipped it off, I kept the string and sent it to Tiffany's to size the ring."

Her eyes widened in amazement. "Thomas! You didn't!"

He laughed softly, brushing a tear from her cheek.

Rachel turned her finger slowly, mesmerized by the deep shades of green swirling inside the gem. "It's incredible, Thomas. I've never seen anything quite like it."

Thomas wrapped her in his arms, drawing her close. As she surrendered to his warm embrace, the world around her seemed to dissolve. His kiss was tender, slow, and unhurried. When their lips finally parted, she gasped, breathless and dizzy, as if the earth had moved beneath her.

"Mercy me," she whispered, her voice quivering.

Before she could gather herself, an elderly man peeked around the corner with an eager grin. Suddenly, a jubilant crowd swarmed around them, clapping and cheering.

Hand in hand, they slipped through the crowd, making their way toward their streetcar. Antoine's awaited, promising a meal that would mark a new beginning.

After returning home from a romantic dinner at Antoine's, Rachel carried a pot of hot water upstairs and indulged in the comfort of a warm bath enhanced with bathing salts and dried rose petals. She lingered in the water until it cooled, reluctant to leave the peace it offered. When she finally rinsed and stepped out, she toweled off and slipped into her favorite summer nightgown.

Sighing, she stepped into her bedroom, lit the lamp, smoothed the bed linens, and climbed into bed, sinking into the familiar embrace of the feather mattress. The window was slightly open, and the night air whispered through the sheer curtains, carrying the sweet, intoxicating scent of jasmine from the courtyard.

Though her body felt relaxed, her mind buzzed with thoughts flickering from one to the next like fireflies on a summer night: Thomas's tender gaze, the warmth of his hand enveloping hers, his romantic proposal of marriage, and the lingering sweetness of wine on her lips after a candlelit meal at Antoine's.

She allowed herself to drift into the afterglow, hoping that sleep might finally come somewhere amid these tender reflections. But it did not.

Her thoughts drifted to her library, and she considered reading to help her drift off to sleep. Her father had filled the library with the classics, but she had read most of them, some more than once. As she lay there, flipping through a mental catalog of familiar titles, a vivid memory surfaced: Sarah, curled beneath the quilt, lost in a book clutched tightly in her hand as if guarding some precious secret. Rachel had often watched her sister with quiet admiration, wondering what hidden worlds she had tucked away in her bedside drawer.

Intrigued by the memory, she slipped out of bed, stepping barefoot across the cool wooden floor to her sister's dresser. Pulling open the top drawer, she found a small stack of books, their covers concealed beneath plain brown wrapping.

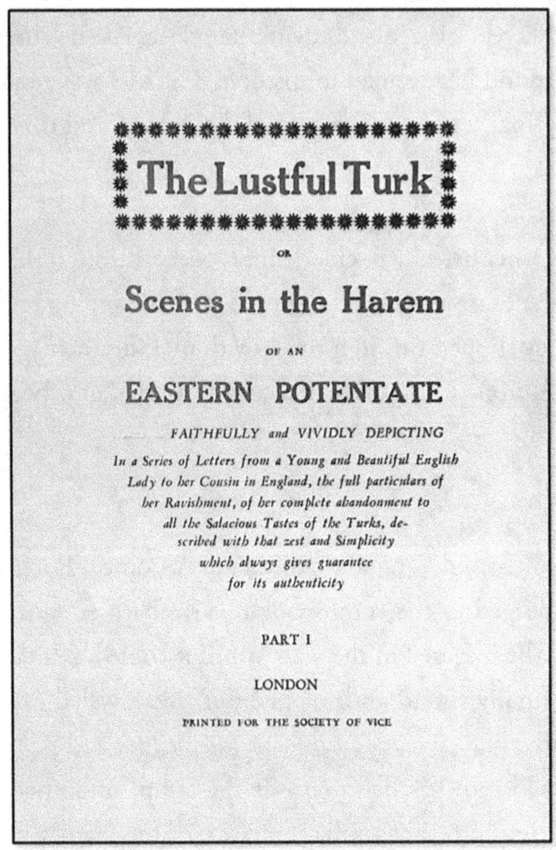

She plucked one from the pile, curious about her sister's bedtime reading. Returning to bed, she nestled beneath the covers and opened the book to its title page. "Oh, my!" she whispered. "*The Lustful Turk, or Lascivious Scenes from a Harem.*" Her eyes widened, half in disbelief, half in fascination. The title alone felt scandalous, as well as its assertion that it was printed by the "Society of Vice." Its extended title promised a glimpse into an erotic world far removed from the most private conversations among women.

Intrigued, Rachel flipped through the pages to find that the story consisted of a series of letters, confessions, really, penned by a young Englishwoman named Emily Barlow and posted to her friend Sylvia Carey. The early correspondence recounted how Emily had been captured by Mediterranean pirates and sold into the harem of the Dey of Algiers, a powerful Turkish ruler known for his wealth and the beauty of his concubines, whom he adorned with jewels and gold.

Rachel's heart quickened as she read, drawn unwillingly yet irresistibly into the tale of Emily's descent from fear and defiance to a reluctant yielding. What startled her most was the confessions of a woman discovering a kind of pleasure within her surrender, as though some hidden part of herself had been awakened.

"Heavens," Rachel breathed, her voice barely audible. Her cheeks grew warm as she lingered on a letter in which Emily described, in startling detail, the climax of her experience. Intrigued, she read on for a few more pages, then closed the book with a soft sigh, setting it on the nightstand as a bemused smile played at her lips. *There is more to Sarah than I ever knew,* she thought.

Her gaze drifted upward, her thoughts slipping from the fictional Emily to her own life with Thomas. A gentle contentment settled over her as she lifted her hand into the lamplight, mesmerized by the flame dancing inside the emerald of her engagement ring, as if the stone held a secret fire of its own.

Then, a curious thought stirred beneath her reverie. What was this thing called love—one of the so-called passions of the soul? Was her love for Thomas pure and chaste, the kind the philosophers praised? Or was it touched, even kindled, by the type of desire she had just read about: raw, physical, unspoken? Could it be both? Perhaps the scholars were wrong to separate the heart from the body so clearly. Maybe love, to be complete, must burn with both passion and purity.

But as her gaze lingered on the ring, her thoughts suddenly shifted to Levi. A shadow fell over her heart as she remembered the young man lost on the battlefield at Shiloh that she had buried and mourned. A whisper escaped her lips before she realized she had spoken: "Memory jar."

The words hung in the quiet room like the faintest echo of something from the distant past. She blinked, recalling how Emma, at Emancipation Plantation, had mentioned creating a memory jar for someone she loved.

"I should make one for Levi," Rachel murmured. The thought took root in her heart, growing with each passing second until it felt impossible to ignore.

Determined, she slipped out of bed again, returned Sarah's book of illicit pleasures to her dresser drawer, and padded down the dark staircase to the parlor. On the mantel, beneath the soft glow of moonlight filtering through the windows, lay the mourning brooch containing Levi's hair. She picked up the brooch from the mantel and removed his watch from around her neck.

Stepping into the kitchen, she set Levi's watch and the mourning brooch on the counter, then reached into the cabinet for a pristine Mason jar. A faint, clean scent of untouched glass drifted out as she unscrewed the metal lid. Tilting the jar, she gently slid the mementos inside. The watch landed with a soft thud, followed by the faint metallic tap of the brooch against it, as though the weight of Levi's memories had finally found their resting place.

She tightened the lid with care as if she was sealing not just the jar but a part of her past. Tomorrow, she would paint a small red heart on the glass with Levi's name inside, and set it on the parlor mantel above the gentle warmth of the fireplace to honor his memory.

52

THE GHOST AND MRS. DURAND

Rachel finished sewing the last seed pearl onto her white lace-over-satin wedding gown, a carefully crafted labor of love. Holding the gown before her, she stepped over to her tall dressing mirror in the corner. "Perfect, she whispered, posing to admire the intricate lace cascades and tiny, gleaming pearls.

She had meticulously planned every detail of her upcoming nuptials: the engraved invitations, the rabbi, and the chuppah for the synagogue. A vendor from the French Market would arrive soon so that she could choose the flowers.

She had curated every aspect of the ceremony, right down to the choice of Mendelssohn's Wedding March, a composition initially written for a performance of Shakespeare's enchanting tale, "A Midsummer Night's Dream." This play held a special place in her heart, especially for its portrayal of the Amazon Queen bride, Hippolyta, whose name meant "She who unleashes the horses."

She had left no stone unturned to ensure a splendid wedding, and Thomas was generous with her budget.

As for the food, she had engaged Antoine's, the restaurant where she and her betrothed had first dined before their journey to Port Hudson, to furnish the finest fare for the occasion. From the elegant dishes and carefully chosen wines for the wedding supper to the abundant Champagne that would set the night aglow, every detail would reflect Antoine's celebrated refinement and ensure the festivities lingered long into the evening.

The food had to be kosher because Rabbi Illowy was conducting the ceremony. He agreed to oversee the culinary arrangements and secured separate areas for restaurant kitchen preparation.

Carefully returning the gown to the cutting table, Rachel perused the guest list. It would be an intimate affair, with Thomas requesting invitations for only a handful of his friends from Baton Rouge, one of whom would serve as his best man. Her synagogue acquaintances had RSVP'd, but the absence of her family still weighed heavily upon her.

As pre-wedding jitters crept in, Rachel briefly considered canceling the ceremony and running away to marry in secret. But she quickly dismissed the thought with a resigned sigh, realizing how a wedding with friends attending would be a cherished memory.

The honeymoon, on the other hand, offered a glimmer of excitement. She had entrusted Thomas with the planning and eagerly anticipated being surprised.

Taking a seat at her vanity, Rachel gazed into the looking glass, picturing herself as Mrs. Thomas Manget. She imagined mingling with guests at the reception. "Mrs. Manget," they would say. "How lovely you are in that magnificent wedding dress. I do love the seed pearls." The thought filled her with a flutter of excitement, effervescent and light, like Champagne bubbles rising to the surface of a crystal glass.

Suddenly, the sound of the doorbell shattered her reverie. She glanced toward the library, where the mantel clock had just struck ten. *The florist*, she thought, eager to answer the door.

She hurried downstairs in anticipation. But as she cracked open the door, she gasped. Levi stood on the stoop, wearing a black frock coat, his expression distant and solemn.

The world tilted beneath her, her mind reeling from the impossible sight of Levi standing before her as if summoned from the grave. Was it truly him? Had she buried the wrong man?

A chill swept through her. Her legs buckled, and she crumpled onto the floor. She stared up in stunned disbelief, yet was now certain she was looking into the face of the man she believed she had lost forever.

"Levi?" Rachel asked incredulously as she recovered to find herself cradled in his arms.

"Yes, darling, it's me," he said, kissing her forehead as tears streamed down his cheeks. "I was released from the Union prison camp at Fort Delaware just weeks ago."

"Prison?"

"Yes," he said, standing to extend a hand. "Here. Let me help you up."

"But I buried you," Rachel sobbed, her face streaked with tears as she stood and took a seat on the sofa. "I grieved for a year until I had to shed my mourning clothes to work and support the family."

"Work?" he asked incredulously, sitting beside her and taking her hand. "When I heard New Orleans had fallen, I wrote, telling you I held preferred stock in Colt's Manufacturing Company in Connecticut for legal work I did for the owners. I kept it in our safety deposit box in New York. You could have sold the stock to support yourself. It has to be worth over $10,000 now, thanks to the war. That's over four years of the salary I earned before I left. How did you come to believe I was dead?"

Rachel was stunned at the irony of it all. Her fate would have been different if she had known about the stock. There would have been no House of the Rising Sun, no peddling into the Confederacy, and no Thomas. The room seemed to spin as she struggled to grasp the reality before her.

Managing to answer Levi, she said, "First, I never received any letters. Then, after Shiloh, I received what they claimed were your remains. The body was so disfigured that the undertaker insisted on a closed-casket funeral."

"You never received any of my letters?"

"Not a single one."

"That explains why you thought something had happened to me. But how did they identify the body of the man you buried?"

Rachel stood abruptly, her heart skipping a beat as she realized she was still wearing the engagement ring Thomas had given her. With guilt tightening her chest, she turned to the fireplace and carefully slid the ring off her finger, discreetly tucking it beneath the mantel cloth. She then reached for Levi's pocket watch from the memory jar. Taking a moment to compose herself, she returned to the sofa and handed it to him. "Here," she said softly. "They said they found it in your pocket."

Levi's eyes widened with sudden realization as he looked at the watch. "Now I understand. The man you buried was a thief, Rachel. He stole my watch while I was asleep."

Rachel cried, wringing her hands as she sat down beside him. "Oh, Fate, how can you be so cruel?"

Levi's expression saddened, and he slipped the watch into his pocket. "Aren't you happy to see me, darling?"

Rachel struggled for words, grappling with the flood of conflicting emotions. Beside her was the husband she had mourned deeply, even though she was forced to cut her grieving short to support her family.

But now, she had moved on and found love with another, and so many things had changed over time. Yet, here he was, her husband: the one who had gone off to war to defend her, the one she had vowed to love "until death do us part." Hadn't she honored her promise? Hadn't she loved him until she believed that death had taken him from her?

What should she do now? How could she possibly explain her wedding preparations to him? And how could she disclose Levi's unexpected return to Thomas?

More pressing still, how could she rekindle the fading embers of her love for Levi if she chose to remain his wife? And how could she extinguish the flame that now burned so brightly in her heart for Thomas?

The two men represented starkly different paths, and she was at a crossroads. She felt like a house divided against itself, once whole and filled with love, joy, and certainty, now torn apart. Faced with this impossible choice, she realized she could not hold on to her past with Levi while embracing the future with Thomas.

Regaining her composure, she said, "It's good that you're alive." She caught herself, feeling that her words lacked any genuine emotion.

Levi's face fell, disappointment evident in his eyes.

Rachel could see that he had hoped for a declaration of love and a rush of tears after such a long absence, but she could not bring herself to say the words he longed to hear.

"It must have been terrible in that prison," Rachel said, trying to summon words of comfort for the man she had once loved.

"It was," he said, lowering his head. "I try not to dwell on the filthy, crowded conditions: the rats, the spoiled rations, and all of the sick and dying around me."

"How horrible!" Rachel exclaimed.

"All I could think about was the day I would finally get out. I found an old, rusted nail and scratched a line on the wall for each day I endured. As the days passed, and I began running out of space on the small patch of plastered wall where I kept my tally, a guard escorted me to the warden's office. I was told I would be released if I signed the Oath of Allegiance and swore never to take up arms against the Union again. Even though signing that oath felt like a death sentence, worse than any bullet through the heart, I did it to be with you."

"I can't imagine how difficult that must have been," Rachel said. "How did you manage to get home?"

"I made my way into Confederate territory on foot, and by the occasional good graces of travelers who let me hitch rides on their wagons. Once in Richmond, I found a cousin, and he helped me buy some decent clothes and loaned me sufficient money until I could return home and sell some stock to pay him back."

"That took much courage," Rachel said, meaning it, yet she could not speak with the loving voice she once found so natural when she talked to him.

"I know this has been quite a shock, darling," Levi said gently. "You need time alone to adjust." He stood to leave. "I'll find a place to lodge tonight and tomorrow night. That will give you time to think. Perhaps we can have supper at Antoine's on Wednesday evening around eight? I could come by with a cab at seven-thirty."

"Yes," Rachel replied with a pained smile at the irony of his suggestion of Antoine's as he leaned over to kiss her. The thought of a quiet romantic supper at Antoine's with Levi, a place that once held the promise of their shared dreams as it had later with Thomas, now felt like an impending confrontation with a past that no longer aligned with her present.

As the door closed behind him, Rachel's facade of calm crumbled, and she sobbed uncontrollably. She moved to the window, watching her husband disappear down the street as he had done when he marched off to war. Tears blurred her vision as the enormity of her situation settled over her.

After Levi left, Rachel was plagued by voices in her head. Some chided her, while others attempted to console her, insisting she had done nothing to deserve such a terrible fate. *If only I had received his letters!*

The sunlight streaming through her parlor windows slowly retreated across the floor, fading as evening approached, yet she could find no peace. Desperate to escape her thoughts, she decided to go to bed early.

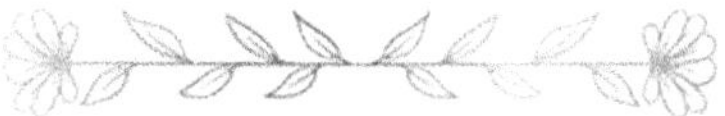

After changing into her nightgown, Rachel lay awake, sleep eluding her as her mind raced with thoughts. "Curse this war!" she exclaimed, striking the bed in frustration. "And curse that Beauregard, that so-called saint of the South, for igniting the conflict."

As she stood at the window, what weighed most heavily on her heart was the aftermath of a war waged primarily over economic disputes, leaving a trail of human misery in its wake. Countless lives had been lost, families were torn asunder, and neither side had a clear plan for reunification or for integrating Louisiana's more than three hundred thousand freed slaves into society.

Her husband and her brother-in-law had marched off to war with valor, believing they were defending their homes against an encroaching enemy bent on destroying their way of life. At the time, she and Sarah had been filled with pride, oblivious to the more profound truths Butler had voiced in his departing speech. His words still echoed in her mind, maintaining that the war was a "struggle for power, where the few seek to maintain control over the many."

She concluded that Jacob and Levi had been mere pawns on a vast chessboard. Jacob had returned home to his wife and newborn son, robbed of both his arms and his inner peace, confined to an invalid chair, while Levi had endured imprisonment for over a year, only to return to a marriage that had been interred with his memory.

Rachel knew she wasn't the woman her husband had left behind. Sooner or later, Levi would realize that as well. Would he accept the new version of her, even if she found the strength to try to love him again?

She remembered that Eugenia had handed her the remnants of Loreta's laudanum concoction before she left for Georgia. Perhaps the comfort she sought, the solace of Morpheus's embrace, waited for her at the bottom of that bottle.

53

THE SAZERAC COFFEE HOUSE

At nine o'clock in the evening, Levi entered the Sazerac Coffee House. Located at 13 Exchange Alley in the French Quarter, the establishment offered a more genteel atmosphere than most other coffeehouses.

The Sazerac was renowned for its namesake cocktail that began ceremoniously with two chilled glasses, each essential, like a bride and groom waiting to be joined in perfect union. The bartender swirled Absinthe carefully in the first glass, leaving its seductive aroma and bitter complexity behind. Then he blended cognac or rye whiskey with Peychaud's Bitters and sugar in the second glass, stirring the ingredients over small ice cubes until they harmonized into a uniquely smooth, flavorful mixture.

Finally, the two glasses came together, melding two distinct flavors into one inseparable union. The result was a drink greater than the sum of its parts, as if the flavors, like two hearts in marriage, had been destined to form the perfect union.

The bartenders at the Sazerac Coffee House, where the cocktail originated and gave its name to the drink, were much like officiants at an altar, perfecting the ritual with practiced hands. To connoisseurs, the Sazerac was more than a drink; it was a celebration of tradition, artistry, and magic.

To Levi's surprise, the bar was crowded, unlike Monday nights before the occupation. Among the patrons were Union soldiers and visitors from local plantations, who conducted business between bouts of pleasure.

Though the men exchanged jokes and clinked glasses, the presence of blue uniforms unsettled him. As a returning Confederate soldier, he could not ignore the quiet insult of drinking alongside the very men who had once been his enemy, now casually at ease in the heart of a city they had conquered. It was an unsettling and leveling scene, and Levi felt like a stranger in a strange land.

Several women in elegant, colorful dresses evocative of French cabaret dancers sat at one end of the bar. However, their fulsome powdered bottoms were provocatively exposed in a competition for the gentlemen's approval. This practice, originating in Parisian cabarets, had slipped into the French Quarter like a whispered secret and then to bars across Canal Street, where upper-class gentlemen staunchly denied its existence when in polite society.

On the bar top in front of each bare-bottomed contestant was a place card with a number. Dapperly dressed gentlemen approached the women to leer, note the number identifying their choice for the best derrière, and hand their selections to the bartender, who placed the votes in a jar for later tabulation. Each participant in the contest received free drinks for the evening. At the last call, the winner was awarded brass tokens for a week's worth of complimentary beverages until the next competition.

The contest served a dual purpose: it provided affluent customers for the establishment and introduced the entrants, who distributed their *cartes de visite*, bearing their professional names and the address of The House of the Rising Sun, conveniently located just down the street in the French Quarter.

Waiting for a place at the bar, Levi scanned the room. He noted that much remained the same as when he had marched off to battle, except for the Union soldiers sitting with female companions at tables.

He recognized some of the planter class as former clients. These men, owning twenty or more slaves, had, along with their sons, been exempt from military service and were now allowed to keep their slaves under certain conditions if they were in federally occupied territory. For them, little had changed except for a temporary decline in trade caused by the war. With control of the Mississippi River returning to Union forces, business was gradually returning to normal, and their sons had been spared from combat.

Levi's thoughts turned to Rachel and all that had shifted between them. So much had changed, yet the ache he felt at her cool reception cut deeper than he expected. He had marched off to war believing he was doing his duty by defending his property, his honor, and his family. He had stared down death without flinching and suffered the indignities of imprisonment. And now, after all he had endured, he was met not with joy or relief, but with a polite distance that left him feeling hollow.

Still, he could not fault her entirely. She had believed him dead. The weight of that falsehood, carried for so long, must have plowed deep furrows in her heart. He mourned the pain she must have endured and the burdens she had borne alone. It wounded him to learn of her financial hardship, and of the ruin that Union occupation had wrought.

When he left her, he could not have foreseen the fall of New Orleans or the collapse of their Confederate currency. He had believed she would be safe, provided for, untouched by the worst of the war.

But now, with his return after serving with honor in the war, he was determined to set things right. He would patiently repair what had been broken between them. He would court her again, as he had when they first met, with her favorite French chocolates and roses from the flower vendor in the French Market.

And if he returned to his law practice and sold his shares in Colt, they might begin again entirely. They could build a grand home in the country, or maybe even live his dream of acquiring a small plantation. Then they could raise a large family and put the war behind them. That was the vision he clung to now: not the smoke and blood of battle, or the confines of prison, but the quiet promise of domestic peace, the life they were meant to share before everything went to ruin.

The clinking of glasses and a burst of laughter snapped him back to the present. The tavern was crowded, noisy, and thick with the scent of tobacco. Levi spotted a young gentleman at the bar finishing a conversation with another man, and, wasting no time, he wove through the crowd to claim the newly vacated seat.

"Evenin'," the gentleman said as Levi settled in at the bar.

"Evenin'," Levi replied, pleased that he had found a seat. He noted the fine tailoring of the man's suit, reminding him of his planter clients.

"What'll it be, sir?" asked the bartender, a short, stout man with a handlebar mustache.

"Something strong."

"Double Sazerac?"

"Sounds good," Levi said, watching as the bartender situated two glasses on the bar to begin the Sazerac ritual.

"You lost your gal?" the young man beside him asked with a knowing grin.

"Why'd you ask that?" Levi responded, irritated by the stranger's presumption. He had hoped to sit and reflect on his thoughts without interruption.

"You look like a man who's lost his gal," he said.

"No. I'm a married man," Levi said, hoping to end the conversation.

"That explains it," the man chuckled, leaning back with a shake of his head. "A wife will wear a man down quicker than whiskey or war. You look like you've had a fair share of both."

"Here you go, one double Sazerac," the bartender announced, placing the drink in front of him.

"Thanks," Levi said, taking a big gulp.

"Better slow down," the bartender advised. "That'll hit you faster than you think."

"Name's Robert," the gentleman seated next to him said, extending his hand.

"Levi," he replied, shaking it and noting the soft, callous-free hand of a man who had never engaged in a single day of manual labor.

"You get a good look at them gals at the end?" he asked, nodding toward the women competing in the bare bottom contest.

"Yeah," Levi returned nonchalantly.

"Which one did you choose?"

"I didn't."

"You must have one hell of a wife," Robert said with a chuckle. "I'm not married, but I know how you feel. I still can't get my mind off a young filly I met at the Sun recently. Madame says she left the same day I saw her. Says she went off with some rich doctor old enough to be her father."

Levi remained silent, finishing his drink. "I'll have another, bartender."

"Yes, sir," he responded, setting up two more glasses to mix the signature drink.

"Don't I know you from somewhere?" Robert asked, examining Levi's face.

"It's possible. I was an attorney here in town before the war."

"That's where I remember you," Robert said. "You handled the sale of some of my family's slaves. The place was becoming littered with little Sambos."

"What plantation was that?" Livi asked, becoming increasingly irritated by the man.

"Weeping Willow."

"Yes, I recall that transaction vaguely. It was just before I left."

"I thought so."

Levi leaned into his drink as the young man beside him droned on, hardly pausing for breath.

"Anyway, let me tell you about Clarissa, my current fling. She's been unbearable lately," the young man drawled, his voice dripping with vanity and boredom. "I mean, she's beautiful, of course, or I wouldn't waste my time with her. No one can deny that. But she's so... ordinary. All she talks about is her next society ball and who will come with whom. It's tiresome."

Levi raised an eyebrow, his lack of interest apparent, but the young man continued.

"Clarissa was fun for a while, but she's just so predictable. You know what I mean?" He flashed a perfect smile, apparently expecting agreement from a fellow male.

Levi nodded politely, trying to hide his disdain for the young man's superficiality and idle complaints of someone who had been spared the horrors of war due to his station in life.

"And the way she fawns over her jewelry," the young man continued with a dismissive wave. "As if a few diamonds are supposed to impress me," he bragged, holding up his hand to display a diamond the size of the nail on his little finger.

Levi sighed. This was a person who had been handed everything and yet found satisfaction in nothing.

"I'll have to let her down gently," the young man mused, more to himself than Levi. "Can't have people saying I'm heartless, can I?"

As he prattled on, Levi became increasingly irritated.

"Didn't you get married just before you left New Orleans?"

"Yes," Levi returned.

"I remember your wife now. A real beauty."

"Yes, she is."

"She looked a lot like…"

Levi, tiring of the conversation, set his drink down on the bar and asked, "Like who?"

"Your wife looked like that girl I saw at a certain house in the French Quarter a few months ago. Hard to forget a red-headed beauty like that."

"You are mistaken, sir," Levi snapped. "My wife would never work at an establishment of that nature."

"Is her name Rachel?"

"Yes," Levi said, taken aback that the man knew her name.

"I spoke briefly with her, and we exchanged names. And she had bright red hair like your wife." His smile turned into a sneer. "Damn shame I didn't get a chance to see what she could do with those juicy lips of hers."

Levi felt the blood rise to his face. "Now see here, mister, I'm telling you you're mistaken."

"Didn't you join the army shortly after you got married?"

"Yes, I fought at Shiloh. But you are mistaken about my wife."

"'Fraid not, brother. Many women took to the profession when their husbands left them to make ends meet. Can't blame 'em." Robert winked. "If I were you, I'd have her checked out for the clap, though."

Levi downed his drink in one gulp, turned, and slugged the man full force in the jaw.

"Damn!" Robert yelled, reeling from the blow and grabbing the bar to regain his balance.

Amid animated conversations about the recent draft riots in New York, the bar fell silent, and patrons turned to watch. The tension was palpable.

"You, sir, have sullied my wife's honor," Levi declared, his voice cold and controlled.

Robert steadied himself, a mix of anger and shock on his face that now bore the red imprint of Levi's fist. "I meant no offense, sir, but I will not retract my words as I spoke the truth. Name your terms if you wish to defend your wife's honor."

Levi's eyes narrowed. "Very well. A duel. Name your weapon, your second, and the place."

Robert straightened his jacket, his expression hardening. "Dueling Oaks tomorrow at dawn. My second will be Mr. Hawthorne. I will borrow Dr. Lindsay's dueling pistols. He's a family friend. You may choose whichever weapon you prefer and load it yourself."

Levi nodded curtly. "So be it. I will introduce my second at the dueling field. We shall settle this matter then."

"Agreed. If you have no objection, I'll ask Dr. Lindsay to serve as the physician, as required under the Code Duello. He is also familiar with the operation of his pistols and can provide instruction if needed."

"Agreed," Levi answered firmly, still furious. He turned on his heels and strode toward the door. His adversary tossed down the last of his drink and followed closely behind.

A murmur spread through the crowd like the ripple of a stone tossed into still water, and the atmosphere grew taut with anticipation.

"Hey, Joe," one patron called, leaning over the bar. "What just happened between them two?"

The bartender shrugged, wiping down a glass without looking up. "Can't say for certain, Sam. I heard something about a woman. But with all I got goin' on back here and everybody havin' fun, I can't really tell you what they said."

Patrons leaned toward one another, whispering predictions about the outcome, each man weighing the odds of the duelists.

A frenzied exchange of bills began. "Robert, he's dueled before," someone muttered, sliding a greenback across the bar. "But the other guy's been a soldier, far as I can tell. He won't miss," another man declared, raising the stakes with a crisp Union States two-dollar bill.

Wagers multiplied like wildfire, spreading from the bar to the tables, as men speculated on whose nerve would hold, who would fire first, and which poor soul would be left bleeding out on the ground.

The bartender, wiping the counter with a slow, practiced hand, watched the frenzy with quiet amusement.

Duels had been outlawed and made a criminal offense, but the thrill of betting on two men settling their pride the old way still had a hold on these folk. For them, it was merely another evening in New Orleans, where destinies could shift with the turn of a card or the discharge of a firearm.

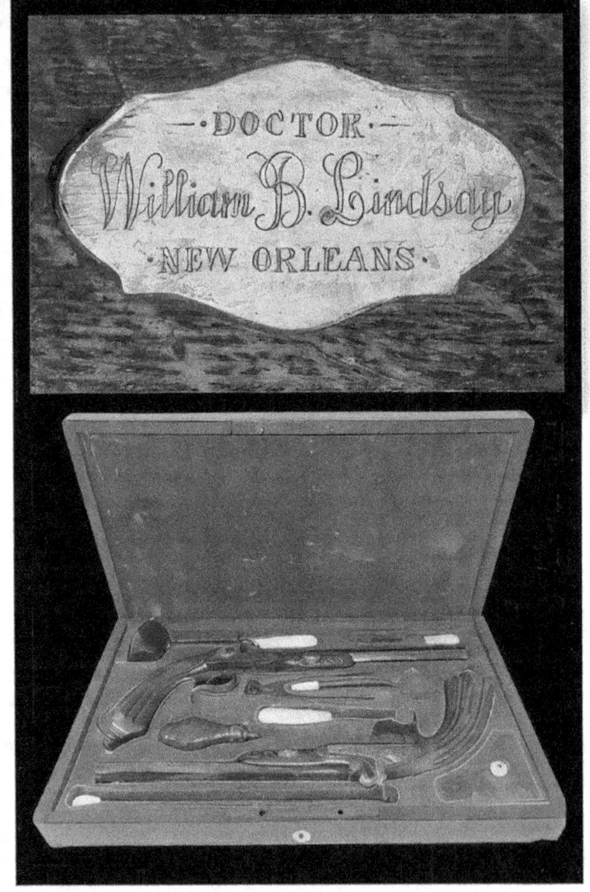
·DOCTOR·
William B. Lindsay
·NEW ORLEANS·

54

DUELING OAKS

At dawn's first light, the thunder of hooves shattered the silence of the oak grove, heralding the approach of a stately black calash drawn by four sleek stallions. They moved with a terrible grace, their cadence echoing the march of Revelation's dread riders: Pestilence upon his White Horse, War astride his blood-soaked Red, Famine atop the Black, and Death trailing in their wake on his Pale steed.

The grove was known to the English as Dueling Oaks and to the French as Chênes d'Allard, named after Jean Louis Allard, the Frenchman who once owned the plantation where the great oaks stood. Though dueling within the city limits was strictly illegal, it was located beyond them at the far northern end of Esplanade Avenue.

The ancient oaks stood like solemn sentinels, their gnarled branches cloaked in veils of Spanish moss that stirred in the breath of dawn, whispering secrets of the storm that loomed just beyond the horizon. A silvery mist coiled low around their roots like a mourner's shawl, cloaking the blood-soaked earth in a ghostly pall. It was a stage set for sorrow, and the grim tragedy soon to play out seemed ordained by the land itself.

The elegant calash, its black leather hood neatly folded down, glided to a halt under the steady hand of a Negro coachman, his silver hair neatly cut and pomaded. Dressed in immaculate livery with matching black gloves, he remained motionless at the reins, upright and dignified.

"Be ready to steady the horses," Robert instructed, his voice sharp and indifferent, as cold as the sheathed steel sword he wore at his side. "I don't want these beauties spooked at the sound of gunfire."

The coachman touched the brim of his hat as if saluting the Grim Reaper. Those who knew him well understood the nature of the gesture; after all, he had sat behind these reins through many duels, watching men fall like so many leaves in autumn. He bore silent witness to each fatal shot, never speaking a word, not because he had none to say but because his tongue had been taken after a stray remark, leaving him mute to the violence and cruelty of his young master.

"May I assist you, Dr. Lindsay?" Robert asked, addressing a slender, bearded man in his sixties, who slowly emerged from the carriage leaning heavily on a walking stick crowned with a silver cobra with ruby eyes that glowed in the light as he moved.

"Thank you, no, Robert," the doctor replied grimly, revealing his pain. "I can manage. Just takes me a while."

Robert stepped aside, patiently waiting as the elderly man descended. Once the doctor was clear, Robert slipped off his baldric and scabbard, carefully placing the sword on the floorboard. Then, with the same deliberate care, he reached for the polished monogrammed wood case containing the dueling pistols.

Robert's second, John Hawthorne, descended next. Impeccably dressed, with jet-black hair and deep-set brown eyes that gleamed with perpetual cynicism, he paused to close the carriage door behind him.

"You're actually going through with this, Robert?" John asked, his words laced with an air of arrogant amusement, underscored by the faint hint of a British accent. "You know the bloke doesn't stand a prayer."

Robert's grin sharpened, a flicker of cruelty dancing in his eyes. "I know. I'll be merciful and aim for his shooting arm to give him a flesh wound. Men of his class need a lesson in humility. He had his chance to back down."

Dr. Lindsay gave Robert a disapproving glance but kept his voice even. "At least let me show your challenger how to handle his weapon. It's the only honorable thing to do."

Robert shrugged, handing the doctor the pistol case. "Fine by me. I suppose it's only fair. I could load one of those beauties and hit a tin can at twenty paces blindfolded."

The three set off toward the oak grove, where two young men were engaged in spirited mock combat with practice foils beneath a sprawling, moss-draped oak. Nearby, their middle-aged *maître d'armes* was unpacking masks and gloves from a wooden crate for the morning's *assaut*.

Robert approached and said, "You might want to find another place to practice your fencing, gentlemen. There will be a duel of honor here shortly."

"A duel of honor?" the taller youngster echoed, wide-eyed. "Swords or pistols?"

"Pistols."

"Mind if we watch?"

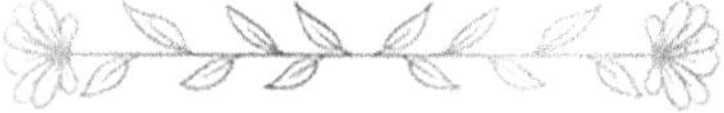

"Be my guest," Robert said. "Just keep aside, out of the line of fire."

"God be with you, son," the driver said, tipping his hat as Levi paid the fare and stepped out of the cab at Dueling Oaks.

"Thank you, sir," Levi said, waiting for his friend, Abe, to exit.

"Is that your opponent standing over yonder with those men?" Abe asked.

Levi turned to see Robert and two others, the older of them holding a physician's satchel. "Yes, that's him, his second, and the doctor friend he mentioned."

"If I'm not mistaken, that's Dr. Lindsay," Abe said. "Some folks call him 'Dr. Death,' since he has such a passion for duels. He even has his own custom-made set of pistols."

"Interesting," Levi said. "Robert told me that the pistols he chose belonged to Dr. Lindsay. I had no idea that the good doctor was into dueling. I only knew of him from his reputation for treating cholera victims."

"Levi," Abe said, a sober look on his face, "When I saw you standing at the door late last night, it was as if Lazarus himself had risen from the dead."

"I can only imagine the shock," Levi replied. "I'm sorry to have distressed you."

"No need to apologize, Levi, my dear friend. When I realized it was you, I was overjoyed to hear your voice and know you were safe and well."

Levi lowered his head without saying anything, thinking about how his friend's reaction to seeing him alive was so different from his wife's.

"Listen, we talked all night about the good times. I tried to avoid the topic of this duel, hoping you'd have a chance to cool down and reconsider after the liquor wore off. Now, I'm begging you to reconcile with your opponent. If you permit me, I'll negotiate a gentleman's agreement with his second, according to the Code Duello. Rachel needs you, Levi." He paused. "Does she know about this?"

"No," Levi said gravely. "She does not. She's been through enough already."

"For God's sake, Levi, what if you don't survive?" Abe asked, his eyes welling up with tears. "What torture will she go through then? She's already buried you once."

"I don't plan to die, my friend. But if I do, would you promise to go to our home this evening at half past seven? That's when I had planned to meet her to take her to Antoine's."

"Of course," Abe said.

"And give her my pocket watch."

Abe nodded silently.

Levi placed a hand on his friend's shoulder. "Thank you, Abe. I must defend her honor, no matter what the outcome. It's the only thing we have left after the occupation."

After a brief exchange of formalities, Dr. Lindsay approached Levi with his case of dueling pistols. "Have you ever dueled before, young man?"

"No, sir."

"Then let me show you how to handle these," the doctor said, his tone professional. "Robert told me you were in the military, but these pistols aren't like anything you've ever fired."

Dr. Lindsay eased open the wooden case bearing his name engraved on a silver plate, revealing the polished pistols nestled inside. Selecting one with a palsied hand, he held it almost reverently. With the precision of long practice, he demonstrated the process of loading: pouring the powder, seating the bullet, and tamping it down with the ramrod.

Levi watched intently, noting the faint, earthy scent of bear grease, a favorite for lubricating firearms. Once the lesson was complete, he practiced loading and firing several single shots, each echoing through the grove. The flintlock pistol felt awkward and foreign in his hands, so different from the familiar grip of his army-issued Colt. Yet, with every pull of the trigger, his confidence grew. He began to understand the weapon's rhythm: the careful load, the deliberate aim, and the moment of trust in the flint's strike. By the last shot, the pistol no longer felt like a relic but like an instrument he could command.

When the time came to begin the duel, Abe and John loaded the powder for the men. Levi was asked about his choice of distance, and he chose ten paces.

Dr. Lindsay, holding a white handkerchief, stood between the duelists, several paces out of the line of fire. "Gentlemen, take your positions," he commanded.

Levi and Robert turned their backs to each other, pistols raised.

"Step off," came the command.

The opponents began the pace. The seconds stretched on, heavy with the gravity of the moment. At the tenth pace, they turned to face each other, pistols still raised.

Dr. Lindsay dropped the handkerchief.

"Bang!" The sound of the twin pistols firing struck the grove as one sharp, cracking report. A moment later, Levi dropped backward onto the grass, limp and motionless, while Robert clutched his chest and fell to his knees, his face contorted in pain and disbelief.

Abe rushed to Levi and looked down to see a hole in the middle of his forehead. "We won't be needing you, Doctor," he called over his shoulder. Looking down at his friend, he said, "I'll get word to Rachel, Levi. I love you. Go in peace."

With those words, Abe removed Levi's pocket watch from his body and held it in his hand, looking at the engraving on the case. "Forever," he whispered, a tear rolling down his cheek.

Meanwhile, Dr. Lindsay hobbled toward Robert, who had slowly leaned forward from his knees and toppled face-first onto the bloodied earth. Once the doctor turned him over to reveal a crimson stain spread across his chest, his practiced eye confirmed the shallow rise and fall of the ribcage and the labored breath. All were signs of a collapsed lung and death closing in with every ragged breath.

John rushed over to the doctor's side and saw blood trickling from his friend's mouth. "Is it as bad as it looks, Doc?"

Dr. Lindsay nodded affirmatively. "Bend down here and help me press that wound in his chest. He's got a wounded lung, and we need to slow the bleeding."

John pulled a handkerchief from his pocket and pressed it over the wound with both hands. Robert's breath came in shallow, labored gasps, each more strained than the last. His neck veins bulged, and his lips turned a bluish-purple.

Wide, frightened eyes looked up into the doctor's, silently pleading with him to pull him back from the brink. His blood-slicked lips moved, struggling to form words, but only a faint, wet gurgle escaped.

The doctor grimaced, hearing the familiar hissing sound from his chest that made his stomach sink.

Looking up at John, the doctor gave a grave shake of his head, then carefully removed a container of morphine powder from his worn leather bag. Mixing a dose, he administered it to ease the young man's suffering as the metallic scent of blood clung heavily to the morning air.

He gripped Robert's hand with quiet resolve, knowing that all he could offer now was companionship and a silent prayer. "Easy now, my boy," the doctor whispered, his voice steady and low as if he were delivering Robert—not into this world, as he had done at his birth, but into the next.

The doctor remained still by his young friend's side, offering what little comfort he could. Moments later, Robert's final breath slipped from his lips, soft and fleeting, as the wind whispered through the ancient oaks, rustling the leaves overhead as if delivering his soul to a distant shore.

John stood over his friend, tears in his eyes. "He never lost a duel in his life."

"No, John. Until now," the doctor agreed sadly.

Honor and pride had demanded their offering, and the earth, like an insatiable ancient god, drank deeply of the duelists' blood, an unspoken oblation beneath the sprawling branches of the hallowed oaks.

The muffled creak of wheels came from the edge of the grove, and soon, a black hearse rolled into view, pulled by a pair of dark horses. It seemed someone had anticipated this outcome and summoned the carriage in advance. The driver and two other men, dressed in somber black, climbed down to claim the victims.

The doctor used his cane to rise slowly to his feet, his old knees protesting, and stood beside John over Robert's body for a final moment, reluctant to leave the boy he had once brought into the world.

Together, the men from the hearse began the grim task of lifting the duelists' bodies.

As the doctor laid Robert's arm gently across his chest, he murmured one last prayer under his breath, swearing that this would be the last duel he would ever attend.

The hearse doors shut with a hollow thud, sealing the duelists inside: two mortal enemies, now lying peacefully, side by side in death.

The driver climbed to his place, gave a sharp flick of the reins, and the hearse rolled away.

Beneath the oaks, the grove grew still again.

"I'm ready to go now, John," Dr. Lindsay said.

John nodded and opened the carriage door for him, then circled to enter the other side.

The tongueless coachman flicked the reins, and the horses sprang to life. He lifted his eyes briefly to the sky, a trace of something like a silent prayer of thanks softening the lines of his face, before turning his attention back to the road and leaving vengeance to Providence.

The carriage wheels creaked into motion, leaving the ancient killing field behind, the blood of grudges and bitter rivalries sinking into the earth beneath the ancient oaks.

55

A HEART DIVIDED

Rachel sat distraught in Rabbi Illowy's office, clutching a tear-soaked handkerchief. With quiet compassion, the rabbi rose from his chair, moved around his desk, and sat beside her.

"Rachel," he began gently, "I don't mean to diminish your pain, but you are not alone in your struggle. History is filled with stories of countless wives who endured the long, agonizing wait as their husbands vanished into the horrors of war. Yet, just as these wives began to rebuild their lives and move on, their husbands returned, standing on the doorstep like ghosts."

Tears welled up in Rachel's eyes. "What did those women do, rabbi?"

"There are numerous stories with various endings. But in your case, you had every reason to believe Levi was deceased. I know because I was there when Rabbi Gutheim conducted the funeral service."

Rachel remained silent, drying tears from her eyes.

"If you no longer wish to remain married to Levi, you will need to obtain a *get*, a proper Jewish writ of divorce. The civil courts, too, must be addressed, but the *get* must come first. This would allow you to marry your new love if that is your chosen path. Regardless of your decision, you must speak with both men, Rachel. They deserve to hear the truth from your own lips."

"That is the torment I carry in my heart, Rabbi. I love Thomas more, but I feel honor-bound to Levi, and I don't know if time will ever change that."

"Rachel, when you fell in love with Thomas, you were, in every way that mattered, a widow who had already grieved your loss. My dear child, the Almighty does not hold you to blame."

"I know, Rabbi, but I still feel guilty, as if I'm betraying Levi."

"Matters of the heart are more complicated than just your own feelings, Rachel. You have to think about Levi and Thomas, too. If you tell Levi you've fallen in love with someone else, he might decide to leave and start over." The rabbi paused, then added, "On the other hand, when Thomas finds out Levi is alive, he may choose to step away, believing it wrong to remain between you and your husband. Considering how you described him as an honorable man, that seems likely."

"Are you telling me I could lose both of them?" Rachel asked tearfully.

The rabbi nodded sadly. "Yes, Rachel. As I just explained, the choice is not yours to make alone. It rests also in their hearts."

Rachel wrung her hands. "I don't know how I could ask Levi for a divorce."

"I understand how difficult this is, my dear," the rabbi said softly, a note of compassion in his voice.

"Oh, Rabbi," she pleaded, "How do I end this torment?"

"Once you have spoken with both Levi and Thomas and told them your feelings, the matter will resolve itself, one way or another."

Rachel nodded slowly, acknowledging the wisdom of his words.

"Is Levi staying with you?"

"No. He said he would find lodging and take me to supper on Wednesday evening at Antoine's."

"When you have supper, let him open his heart and speak his pain. Most importantly, avoid discussing your feelings about him. Instead, tell him you want him to come with you to meet me in my office. Also, ask Thomas. All should be laid bare before God and one another."

Rachel shuddered but braced herself, accepting the rabbi's advice. "What time can you receive us here, Rabbi?"

"Thursday morning, say around ten."

"I'll speak with Thomas after I leave here and ask him to join our meeting on Thursday," she declared. "When I have supper with Levi on Wednesday evening, I'll also let him know."

The rabbi leaned forward and gently touched Rachel's hand. "May Heaven grant you the strength to walk the path set before you. I will keep you in my prayers."

"Thank you, Rabbi," she said with a gentle smile. "Right now, peace seems beyond my reach. I can only hope for divine guidance."

Rachel,
my love forever,
Levi

56

THE FINAL FAREWELL

Answering the doorbell, Rachel opened her front door to find Thomas standing on the stoop, a somber expression on his face, the kind worn after a friend's funeral. The late afternoon sun stretched his shadow across the threshold like a dark omen.

"May I come in?" Thomas asked, his voice unusually formal.

"Please," Rachel replied nervously, stepping back to let him enter. The tone of his voice and the look in his eyes told her that whatever bothered him was serious.

"I think it's best we sit in the parlor," he suggested.

Rachel led him into the parlor, torn between the urgency to hear what he had to say and the dread of the ill tidings he might bear. Once seated on the sofa, she broke the silence, her voice hesitant, betraying the tension that mounted in her neck and shoulders. "Before you say anything, Thomas, I must tell you something."

Thomas met her gaze, his eyes searching hers, silently pleading for answers.

"Yesterday, I had just finished sewing seed pearls on my wedding gown when there was a knock at the door. I thought it was the flower vendor arriving for our appointment, but when I answered, I was shocked to see who it was."

"It was Levi," Thomas interrupted, his voice cutting through the air like a blade.

Rachel's eyes widened. "How could you possibly know?" she asked, her voice barely above a whisper.

"I just need to know one thing, Rachel. Do you still want to marry me?" Thomas's voice was steady but tinged with vulnerability.

"Oh, yes," Rachel cried, tears welling up. "That's why I asked Rabbi Illowy to meet with the three of us to express my feelings to you and Levi."

"Do you still love him?" Thomas asked, his voice soft but intense, as if bracing himself for the answer.

Rachel pulled back, meeting his eyes with a newfound resolve. "Thomas, I had no idea Levi was alive," she said, her voice trembling as she struggled to hold back a flood of emotions. "Yes, I loved him…once. But I buried him over a year ago. I stood by his grave and mourned his death as if my heart had been ripped from my chest. I grieved for him, for our life together, and for the future we would never have. To have him suddenly reappear, alive and standing before me, felt like seeing a ghost. I thought I had laid him to rest, along with all our shattered dreams."

"But do you still love him?" Thomas persisted.

Rachel hesitated, caught off guard by the flicker of distress in his expression, a look she had never seen on his face before. Searching for the right words to express her turmoil, she spoke from the depths of her soul. "At some level, I suppose I still care for him, Thomas. But after crying through the night, I realized that what I'm feeling now is more guilt and a sense of duty. I mistook those feelings for love. But now I see they are rooted in the past, tied to memories and responsibilities that no longer define who I am. Levi marched off to fight, protecting his family and upholding a world I no longer recognize as just. I can honor his courage and still reject the cause he defended. I need to step out of the shadow of the past and grow into the woman I want to be, not the girl I was raised to be. And I want to do it with you."

Thomas pulled her into a gentle embrace and kissed her forehead. "You don't know how much it means to me to hear you say those words," he whispered, his relief palpable. The room fell into a heavy silence.

Thomas's expression grew solemn. "I had to hear that first. Now, there's something I must tell you."

Rachel's heart skipped a beat, her eyes wide with anticipation.

"Levi perished earlier this morning in a duel," Thomas said quietly.

"No!" Rachel gasped. "Where?"

"Dueling Oaks."

"But he was just here yesterday! How could this have happened?"

"Last night, Levi went to the Sazerac Coffee House. With all the noise in the bar, no one caught every word, but most agreed that he and another man were arguing over a woman after both had had a few drinks. The other man had a reputation as both a philanderer and a hothead. I reckon he said something that wounded Levi's pride."

Rachel's thoughts whirled, struggling to grasp the meaning of his words. "Why didn't he tell me? I could have stopped him."

"A gentleman rarely seeks permission from a lady to defend her honor," Thomas replied gently.

"But it's so senseless," she protested.

"Yes. And, in the end, both Levi and his opponent perished in the duel."

A numbness crept over Rachel, rousing uncertain fears. Was the man at the coffee-house the brash young man who had approached her at the House of the Rising Sun from that desperate time when the need to survive eclipsed shame? If so, should she confide in Thomas and hope he understood, or let the man's knowledge die with him, buried in silence?

"I can't imagine how difficult this must be for you," Thomas said, his voice filled with compassion. "I finally found where they took Levi's remains. After explaining that we're engaged, the undertaker gave me this."

Thomas handed Rachel Levi's watch.

Rachel held it in her hand, staring at it in disbelief. She had returned it to Levi just the day before. Here it was again, inexplicably back in her possession, as if she had stepped across the threshold into one of those dim and terrifying chambers Poe described, where the ordinary became grotesque. In the stillness, the watch no longer marked time—it ticked malevolently, like a mechanical echo of Levi's heart, still beating somewhere just out of reach in defiance of death.

She had already mourned Levi. Could she summon the strength to mourn him again? The confusion and grief were overwhelming. Her heart ached for the loss, the shock of his return, and now for this final farewell.

"If you'll allow me," Thomas said softly, taking her hand, "I think it best that I make the arrangements for Levi's funeral."

"What about the man already buried in his grave?" Rachel asked, her voice trembling as she struggled to process the surreal situation. "The man who stole Levi's watch and caused all this pain?"

"There will be legal matters to resolve," Thomas explained. "We'll need to have him exhumed. Since there's no way of identifying him, I'll arrange for him to be buried in the paupers' cemetery. Even a thief deserves to be laid to rest with some measure of dignity."

Rachel nodded silently, acknowledging what Thomas said. Yet inside, she seethed with anger toward the stranger who had caused her so much sorrow.

"Do you want me to get the date of death changed on Levi's headstone?"

"No," Rachel said, tears welling up again. "Please leave it the same. For me, that's the day he died. All the rest of this..."

"All the rest of this is a living nightmare," Thomas said, finishing her sentence as her voice trailed off.

Rachel toweled off after her bedtime bath, dusted herself with cornstarch, and slipped into her nightdress before settling into Levi's side of the bed that had been Sarah's while he and Jacob were away.

When she noticed his pocket watch resting on the bedside table, tears welled up in her eyes. She reached over to her side of the bed for her handkerchief. Picking up the watch, she read the inscription, thinking how the events in her life had caused her to grow wiser. "Yes, Levi," she whispered, "we were younger then, and believed our love would last forever."

With these thoughts, Rachel cradled Levi's watch, stood, and went to the parlor. She reached for the memory jar she had meticulously crafted for him and unscrewed the lid carefully, then tilted it, allowing the watch to slip inside beside the mourning brooch Eugenia had gifted her. As the metal met the glass with a clink, she screwed on the lid for the second and final time.

She stood silently, her fingertips resting on the cool glass of the memory jar as if to leave one last blessing, then placed it back on the mantel. Lifting the edge of the mantel cloth, she reached underneath and took out her engagement ring, sliding it onto her finger as she sealed the past and embraced the future.

57

JUDAH BENJAMIN

As rosy-fingered dawn blossomed over Richmond, a sleek black carriage drew to a halt at the corner of Twelfth and East Clay Streets, just beyond the wrought-iron fence enclosing the Confederate White House grounds.

Perched atop Shockoe Hill, the mansion's stately columns and portico crowned the summit as if marking the temple of a god, casting long shadows over the city still stirring from slumber. From this commanding height, the winding thread of Shockoe Creek shimmered in the valley below, and the rooftops of distant homes looked no larger than scattered toys left behind by some careless child.

Like the estate it approached, the carriage was managed by enslaved hands. A teenage liveryman stood beside a neatly uniformed, gray-haired butler whose erect bearing exhibited a dignity not granted but earned from endurance.

With movements as smooth as the carriage's wheels, the driver stepped down, handing the reins to the liveryman. Then, the butler stepped forward to open the carriage door, his hand extending to assist his passenger.

"Watch your step, Dr. Zacharie," he cautioned.

"Thank you," he replied, leaning heavily on his silver-handled cane, a necessary support since he injured his knee just before sailing from New Orleans to Mobile, where he boarded the train. He appreciated the butler's concern for his safety since the arduous three-day journey to Richmond, with no sleeping cars and no means to bathe on the train, had only compounded his misery, leaving him physically and mentally drained. Yet, after success-fully establishing a network of peddler spies in New Orleans to report back to General

Banks, he was now committed to negotiating a peace treaty with the Confederacy, despite not being officially authorized to do so.

"What's your name, young man?" Zacharie inquired, his gaze turning to the attentive butler.

"Isaiah, sir," the butler responded with a trace of a smile. "I'll have your trunk brought up to your room. Is there anything else you require for your stay?"

"A warm bath would be most welcome," Zacharie said, already anticipating the relief of changing his travel-worn clothes and soaking his injured knee.

"I'll see to it that you have a bath drawn, sir, as soon as you've settled in your room."

"Thank you," Zacharie said, catching the surprise in the servant's eyes as if the simple courtesy of asking his name was something he seldom heard. "What's behind that wall with the large iron gates just ahead of us?"

"That's the stables, sir," Isaiah said proudly. "President Jefferson owns the best stables in Virginia."

"I'm certain he does," Zacharie said, his gaze shifting to take in the substantial grayish-white stucco mansion, its neoclassical design emphasized by towering Doric columns. He noted the attentive service provided by Davis's slaves, no doubt brought with him from the elegant surroundings of Brierfield, his cotton plantation along the Mississippi River, just south of Vicksburg.

It was a bitter irony that the plantation, once emblematic of Davis's wealth and privilege, now lay in Union hands, while the grand house he occupied in Richmond was nothing more than a rented refuge. Homeless and without a country, he now desperately fought to forge his own nation in the crucible of war.

Following Isaiah through the iron gate, flanked on either side by two stern-faced Confederate soldiers in crisp uniforms, Zacharie's eyes were drawn to the imposing structure before him. The size of the three-story building was daunting, and he couldn't help but contemplate the considerable number of slaves required to maintain such a vast estate. Beyond the upkeep of the grand house itself, there was the endless labor necessary to attend to the personal needs of Davis and his staff, including general cleaning, lawn and garden maintenance, laundering, cooking, transportation, stabling, and the myriad other tasks demanded by a household of this scale.

Then, a fleeting thought crossed his mind. Could the Confederate President ever relinquish his slaves in favor of paid laborers, given his deep-rooted belief in a rigid social hierarchy and attachment to the life of elegance and privilege that it afforded? To dismantle the institution of slavery would mean overturning the very foundations upon which his beliefs were built, reminiscent of Alexander H. Stephens' infamous "Cornerstone Speech" of 1861, where he declared that slavery was the cornerstone of the Confederacy and the natural and proper place for Africans in society.

Turning his attention to the grounds, Zacharie noticed the mansion's front lawn was beautifully trimmed. It was bordered by low, autumn-blooming shrubs and shaded by tall maple trees. A few maple leaves had already turned and fallen, some onto the ground and others onto the shrubs, decorating them with the bright fall hues.

Zacharie gripped the iron railing of the front steps, ascending the stone stairs with careful deliberation until he reached the porch.

Isaiah followed, stepping ahead to open the massive front door, which revealed a spacious, elliptical entry hall adorned with golden faux marbling on the walls. Two alcoves flanked an open double door straight ahead. In the alcoves stood life-size statues of two Greek muses: Thalia, the goddess of comedy, and Melpomene, the goddess of tragedy, both daughters of Zeus. Thalia, crowned with an ivy wreath, held a shepherd's staff in one hand and a mask of comedy in the other. Opposite her, Melpomene, also crowned with ivy, gripped a sword and a mask of tragedy.

Although the statues appeared to be made of bronze, Zacharie noticed a small chip in the finish at the base of Melpomene, revealing the alabaster beneath. He allowed himself a crooked grin, recalling the adage about gods with feet of clay, brought low by hidden flaws.

The irony, of course, was that Davis and the Confederacy, like false idols, had built their Cause on a fragile foundation. They embodied the illusion of strength, grandeur, and righteousness, yet beneath that veneer lay the cracks of pride, stubbornness, and dependence on an unsustainable system rooted in human misery.

The foyer's floor was covered with an oilcloth displaying a vibrant geometric pattern, mimicking the elegance of imported tiles and naturally drawing the eye toward the open double doors leading to a spacious central parlor, which was carpeted with a French Savonnerie rug that featured a delicate floral motif. Inside, an Italian Neoclassical sofa with rosewood trim and twin oval-backed side chairs, upholstered in raised-pattern silk brocatelle, showcased an elegant floral motif that was coordinated with the Savonnerie rug. The expansive window was adorned with lace sheers and complemented by velvet drapes in a harmonizing hue.

Zacharie surmised that a prominent Richmond citizen had likely designed this palatial Greek Revival-style mansion years earlier. Perhaps he was a patron of the arts with a theatrical flair: the golden faux marbling on the foyer's walls, the bronze-finished plaster statues in the alcoves, and the painted oil cloth flooring struck Zacharie as an elaborate stage. It now seemed populated by actors striving to project a nobility they did not possess.

Isaiah led the doctor through the entry hall and past an archway to the right.

As Zacharie approached the stairwell ahead, his gaze swept upward and downward along the broad, spiraling staircase connecting the basement below to the floors above. Its curves were evocative of the intricate design inside a chambered nautilus. He carefully ascended the winding staircase, passing two more bronzed plaster statues: Hera, Zeus's regal wife, and Athena, the goddess of wisdom, warfare, and strategy, said to have sprung miraculously fully armored from her father's head.

To Zacharie, these plaster goddesses were as inauthentic as the mortals who played at nobility within these walls. Both were part of the same elaborate charade, figures in a meticulously crafted production designed to project power and legitimacy.

"This is your room, Dr. Zacharie," Isaiah announced, opening the door to a bedroom at one end of the hall on the second floor. "I trust you will find everything to your satisfaction."

"Thank you," Zacharie replied, catching his breath from the climb as he stepped into the expansive room, which he estimated to be over twenty feet long and nearly as wide. A blazing oak fire crackled in the fireplace at the far end, anchoring the space, while two large windows offered a view of the front lawn and a quiet cul-de-sac beyond the portico.

"Your trunk will be sent up shortly," Isaiah assured him, "and I'll have the housekeeper bring more firewood."

"Thank you very much," Zacharie said, unaccustomed to such attentive service.

Isaiah paused as he was about to close the door. "I nearly forgot, Dr. Zacharie. Secretary Benjamin is expecting you for breakfast in the dining room downstairs. When you're ready, pull on the bell cord at the head of the bed, and I'll escort you downstairs."

"Please let Secretary Benjamin know I'll be delighted to join him," Zacharie said, his stomach already rumbling at the thought of a warm breakfast.

Isaiah nodded and departed with a courteous bow.

The doctor closed the door behind the dutiful servant, pausing momentarily as he leaned against it to take in the room. He stepped over to the window, drawing the curtains halfway to soften the bright morning sunlight, then moved toward the fireplace to warm himself. Turning around, he surveyed the furnishings: a feather bed, a washstand, and a small dresser topped with a bowl of apples and oranges. Unlike the upscale hotels he was accustomed to, there was no bathroom, only an enameled chamber pot placed discreetly beside the bed. On either side of the bed stood nightstands, each bearing an ornate oil lamp featuring a milk glass shade and a box of matches. A Bible lay on the nightstand nearest the door.

Zacharie stepped over to the washbasin, carefully pouring water from the porcelain pitcher. Its surface was decorated with colorful floral patterns that reminded him of the fine British china his wife purchased after they were married. He dipped the rag hanging on the nightstand into the cool water and wiped his face, savoring the refreshing relief it offered after his journey. Yet, he still longed for the warm bath Isaiah had promised.

As he toweled his face dry, he moved to the bed. He sat down, gathering his thoughts and mentally preparing for his upcoming meeting with Judah Benjamin, his fellow Israelite and a man often referred to as the "brains of the Confederacy."

This would be a meeting with an uncertain outcome, as both secessionists and abolitionists were equally convinced that God was on their side, leaving hundreds of thousands of enslaved people caught in the crossfire. All the while, the fate of the Union hung precariously in the balance.

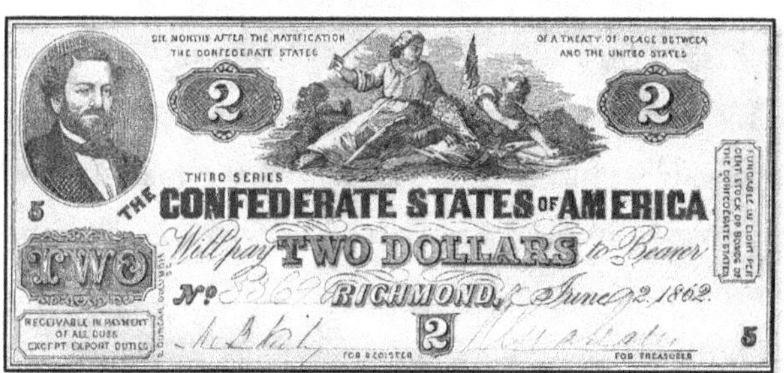

Refreshed after Isaiah arranged a room with a tub full of warm water for him to bathe and change into a clean suit from his trunk, Dr. Zacharie followed him down the spiral staircase to the foyer. They continued through a short hallway and turned right to enter a room with a large table in the center.

Zacharie stood admiring the grandeur of the principal dining chamber. It was crowned by an ornate bracketed cornice and dominated by a massive, gilded plaster ceiling medallion, from which hung a magnificent brass gasolier. A wall-to-wall Brussels carpet with an elaborate floral design anchored the floor, while green and gold brocatelle draperies and white lace sheers framed the windows, matching the upholstery of several small sofas lining the walls.

Horsehair-upholstered chairs surrounded an expansive rosewood dining table, while a green lambrequin in matching brocatelle draped over the marble mantel. Above the mantel, a gilded Rococo Revival mirror reflected the room's lavish furnishings worthy of European royalty.

A portrait of George Washington hung prominently above a heavily carved, marble-topped mahogany sideboard. Zacharie thought it was an apt inspiration for Davis, who saw himself as the standard-bearer of a new nation. The painting embodied the ideals of independence and resistance against tyranny, much like the struggle Southerners had come to view as their own "Second American Revolution."

A bronze bust of the recently fallen Stonewall Jackson presided over the sideboard like a god of war, his stern gaze and chiseled features evoking the stoic tenacity and populist fervor of the Confederacy's emerging pantheon.

Judah Benjamin sat at the head of the massive oval dining table, leisurely savoring a cup of coffee.

The Secretary of State of the Confederacy was robust, apparently of average height, with a full head of curly black hair and a neatly trimmed beard that accentuated his face's smooth, youthful contours. His fair complexion and bright, lively eyes enhanced his warm, jovial demeanor.

"Good morning, Dr. Zacharie," Benjamin said with a boyish smile, standing to give his guest a handshake. "I trust your passage was a safe one."

"Good morning, Secretary Benjamin," the doctor replied, appreciating the exquisite tailoring of Benjamin's black silk suit and matching tie. "Yes, thank you," he added, instantly captivated by the pleasant, melodious tone of the man's voice. It wasn't the voice alone that had earned Benjamin his reputation as an orator, but it enhanced everything he said, like a fine instrument in the hands of a practiced musician. However, the lingering handshake surprised him, a detail no one had mentioned. It felt unusually soft and warm, reminiscent of a woman's touch, with a delicate sensibility.

"Please, have a seat," Benjamin offered, gesturing to the chair opposite him across the massive dining table.

"Thank you," Zacharie replied, taking in the nutty aroma of Benjamin's coffee. "The coffee smells sublime."

"Sarah," Benjamin called, summoning a young Negro woman into the room from her chores just outside the door. "Some coffee for Dr. Zacharie."

"Yes, Mr. Benjamin," she said, moving to the sideboard under the portrait of George Washington to retrieve a pot of coffee and pour a cup for the doctor.

Noticing the nearly empty sugar dish and the running-low cream pitcher, Sarah asked, "Would you like more sugar and cream with your coffee, sir?"

"No, thank you. I take mine black."

"Would you care for some scones?" Benjamin asked with a smile in his voice. "I understand you're British by birth."

"Well, yes, I would," Zacharie said. Though scones weren't his preference, he accepted them with a gracious smile.

"Sarah, bring Dr. Zacharie a plate of scones with fresh fruit, clotted cream, and strawberry jam," Benjamin instructed smoothly. "And for me, buttered toast with jam and two poached eggs with cheese grits."

Zacharie chuckled, catching the British touch in Judah's order for his food. "I am of British descent but not of British inclination," he quipped, though he doubted from the servant's expression that a scone could be found in the kitchen.

Benjamin smirked, the tease evident as he asked, "Would you prefer biscuits and redeye gravy, then?"

"Just the biscuits, thank you," Zacharie replied. "Also, some butter and honey, with two poached eggs, would be grand."

Benjamin gave a slight nod of approval, making it clear that the order would proceed only through his word. "Sarah, bring Dr. Zacharie two poached eggs and serve his biscuits with butter and honey."

"Yes, sir," the maid replied deferentially, stepping out of the room.

"The coffee is delicious," Zacharie remarked, now familiar with the man's humor.

"Yes. I have it imported from St. Croix."

"That's where you were born, isn't it?"

"Yes. My ancestors were Sephardic Jews who fled Spain around the time of Columbus and settled on the island. But I was quite young when my parents later moved to the States, so I have no memories. I suppose I became accustomed to the coffee when my family enjoyed it in Charleston, where they raised me."

"No doubt that's also where you developed a taste for cheese grits," Zacharie returned with a smile.

Benjamin laughed, rubbing his stomach. "I do have a weakness for Southern cooking. I even brought Sarah along from my plantation in New Orleans. She makes a superb gumbo."

The doctor smiled to himself, knowing Benjamin's plantation, like Davis's, had been confiscated.

Eager to move past the usual Southern pleasantries and discuss his mission, Zacharie reached into his vest pocket, withdrew his billfold, and pulled out a Confederate two-dollar bill bearing the likeness of Benjamin. "I received this as the change from a twenty-dollar Gold Eagle on my way here," Zacharie remarked, holding up the bill with a knowing look. "A fair likeness of you, wouldn't you say?"

Zacharie chose not to mention the inferior quality of the wood-pulp paper and printing in flat black ink, a clear reminder of the Confederacy's struggle to match the craftsmanship of Union currency printed with oil-based ink on high-quality rag paper containing silk threads.

Benjamin glanced at the bill and shrugged indifferently. "I suppose. As you can imagine, our options for engravers and printers are currently quite limited. The engraving was done by Keatinge and Ball's printing here in Richmond."

Zacharie narrowed his eyes as he examined the fine print on the bill. "There's an interesting clause here," he said, reading aloud with measured emphasis. "'The Confederate States of America will pay two dollars to the bearer six months after the ratification of a treaty of peace between the Confederate States and the United States.'" He looked up, one brow slightly raised. "That sounds like the kind of language you might have drafted."

"I did," Benjamin replied. "I wanted the disclaimer to clarify that the bill is a promissory note. It holds no redeemable value until the ratification of a peace treaty."

Zacharie nodded, pleased to have steered the conversation back on course. "If I understand correctly, you are saying this currency cannot be redeemed for silver or gold until a peace treaty with the Union is negotiated. Is that accurate?"

"Yes," Benjamin confirmed.

Zacharie continued, "So, it would proceed logically that this two-dollar bill, like all Confederate paper currency, represents an unsecured debt and is essentially worthless to the bearer unless a peace treaty is secured?"

"Correct," Benjamin replied, a trace of irritation in his voice.

"And should you successfully negotiate such a treaty, you'll then be obligated to pay the bearers of this currency its face value in gold or silver upon demand?"

"Indeed," Benjamin said. "And we intend to honor that obligation."

Zacharie observed a flicker of chagrin in Benjamin's expression, signaling that his point had resonated with a man well-versed in legal nuance. He tucked the bill back into his wallet and slipped it into his vest pocket. "Rest easy, my friend," he said. "After you negotiate a peace treaty with the United States, you'll owe two dollars less since I intend to keep this one as a souvenir."

"Enter," came a voice through the heavy door after Secretary Benjamin tapped lightly. The tone betrayed nothing of the weighty decisions being made by the man behind the door, who aspired to be the leader of a new nation.

Benjamin carefully entered the study, stepping into the dimly lit room with a quiet sense of reverence. The scent of fine, hand-selected Virginia tobacco lingered in the air, mingling with the rich aroma of antiquarian leather-bound volumes that filled the bookcases along the walls.

Sitting in a tailored gray suit at his impeccably oiled and polished rosewood desk, cluttered with a stack of orders, maps, and correspondence, was President Jefferson Finis Davis, the youngest of ten children. It was rumored that he was given the middle name "Finis" by his mother, who reportedly prayed he would be her last.

Davis's brown hair, streaked with gray, piercing blue eyes behind wire-rimmed spectacles that seemed to miss nothing. His neatly trimmed chinstrap beard, threaded with silver, lent him an air of composed authority. Yet, the burden of his responsibilities lay heavy upon him, carved in lines upon his face.

A solitary beam of mid-morning sunlight filtered through the half-drawn curtains, casting a golden band across the desk. Tiny dust particles danced in the sunbeams. Their slow movement was barely perceptible as the President meticulously reviewed the documents before him with a furrowed brow.

Davis gestured toward the high-backed leather armchair across from his desk without lifting his eyes from the papers. "Have a seat, Judah."

"Thank you, sir," Benjamin replied with due respect to his liege as he settled into the chair.

For a moment, the tense silence in the room was broken only by the crackling and popping of oak logs in the fireplace, the rustle of papers, and the deliberate scrape of Davis's modest iron-tipped pen as he executed his signature in a single, bold stroke.

Davis finally leaned back, his piercing blue eyes shifting from the documents to meet Judah's patient gaze. "Have you spoken with Dr. Zacharie?" he asked, his tone devoid of curiosity or concern, the dispassionate inquiry of a man accustomed to calculating the cold facts of strategy, much like tallying the casualties from the latest skirmish.

"Yes, Mr. President," Benjamin confirmed. "Dr. Zacharie is intelligent and fueled by ambition. He began his presentation with force, but as the sound and fury subsided, it dissolved into triviality. From what I can gather, he's convinced he will be remembered as the Benjamin Franklin of diplomacy."

"Ambitious, indeed," Davis agreed, a sardonic smile curling at the edge of his lips upon the invocation of Franklin's name. "And what did he have to say?"

"Nothing that we haven't already learned from our agents in New Orleans. The crux of his proposal is that his superiors believe we would agree to free our slaves in exchange for a token payment, as well as payment for our debts tied to the currency we've printed, and the offer of their support in a war with Mexico against France's Austrian proxy Maximillian. They seem to believe that we would be attracted to the idea of establishing a Confederate empire stretching from Mexico through South America and Cuba."

"Someone should tell the good doctor that we abandoned the feverish dream of a Golden Circle long ago. I believe it was sometime after the Mexican War and countless failed attempts to acquire Cuba, including your own Senator Solé's ill-fated Ostend Manifesto."

"A rather noble but ill-conceived effort," Benjamin said. "Cuba should have been ours long ago."

"As for France installing that Austrian, Maximilian, as their proxy Emperor of Mexico," Davis continued, "it is clearly a violation of the Monroe Doctrine, which forbids any European power from interfering in the affairs of independent nations in the Western Hemisphere. Neither Lincoln nor I can enforce it alone, and we won't be acting together."

Benjamin nodded, acknowledging the truth in Davis's words.

"The war is well upon us, Judah, and now the question is not how we got into it but how we are to get out of it," Davis continued, his tone shifting to one of grim determination. "But I will see the lining on the inside of my coffin before I will give up our independence and bend a knee before the Union. Besides, we don't need Lincoln to send us to war with Mexico. We would be better invested in allying with Maximillian, not becoming his enemy."

"I agree, sir. The timing of Dr. Zacharie's arrival is calculated. It comes after our setback at Gettysburg, which halted our northern incursion, and Vicksburg, which split the Confederacy in two. It underscores Lincoln's confidence. He now believes he can negotiate from a position of strength."

Davis raised his hand, signaling he wasn't finished, though a flicker of pain briefly broke through his otherwise stoic expression at the mention of the recent defeats in both the Eastern and Western theatres. "When you first suggested meeting with this man, I was against it for precisely that reason. The timing isn't ideal for us, and Lincoln knows it. But given what you've shared, I'm glad we proceeded. Now, he has laid all his cards on the table."

Benjamin felt vindicated in his decision to meet with the doctor. "He has indeed. And we've revealed nothing of our intentions."

Davis gave a wry smile. "It amuses me that the Grand Usurper still clings to the notion that we are engaged in this conflict simply over the issue of slavery, as if he alone has the right to define it. Yes, slavery is our God-given right, but our true purpose is the pursuit of freedom: from oppressive tariffs, from lack of representation, from a distant government that presumes to dictate our fate."

"What Lincoln cannot fathom," Davis continued, his tone sharpening with resolve, "is that I would, if necessary, raise the stakes on his Emancipation Proclamation by leasing the slaves from their owners, enlisting them into our ranks. Planters would receive compensation at the war's end, and the slaves would receive freedom in exchange for their loyalty to our Cause. I would even go as far as granting them, in some measure, the dignity of personhood. That's a recognition they have never been afforded. For the preservation of our independence, I would go that far."

Secretary Benjamin nodded gravely, recognizing the enormity of the task ahead.

"Now, I'm counting on you to work your charm," Davis said with a smile. "Flatter the man. Get to know him. Tell him his ideas have merit, but you require time for careful consideration. Have our servants cater to his every need and treat him as an honored guest. Then, send him off cordially with my regards, leaving him with high expectations for his meeting next Sunday with my Secretaries of War and the Navy at City Point, as we had initially agreed. And advise my Secretaries ahead of his arrival that I said to extend him every courtesy when he arrives, but reveal nothing."

Benjamin immediately grasped the subtlety of the President's strategy. "I understand, sir."

Davis offered a slight nod, a subtle gesture of approval. "By all accounts, Old Abe seems to have some regard for this strange little man, though, from what you've told me, he's inexperienced in diplomacy. The first thing he'll do after leaving City Point is go rushing to Lincoln, proclaiming he has secured terms for a peace treaty." Davis's voice remained calm, almost detached, as he continued. "At the very least, entertaining him buys us the time we need to strengthen our Secret Service operations in Canada, which might tip the balance of power in our favor."

Benjamin's silent nod conveyed his understanding. He recognized that in the theatre of war, Davis's strategy of deception and delay was as vital a weapon as any sword, rifle, or cannon on the battlefield.

For a moment, silence reigned, broken only by the soft ticking of the French Empire mantel clock. Cast in gilt bronze, it depicted Poseidon surging into battle, trident aloft, astride a chambered nautilus drawn by rearing sea beasts. Its artistry was exquisite, its symbolism unmistakable.

Like the Confederate White House itself, the clock was a vision of power forged in fantasy: grand, defiant, yet doomed.

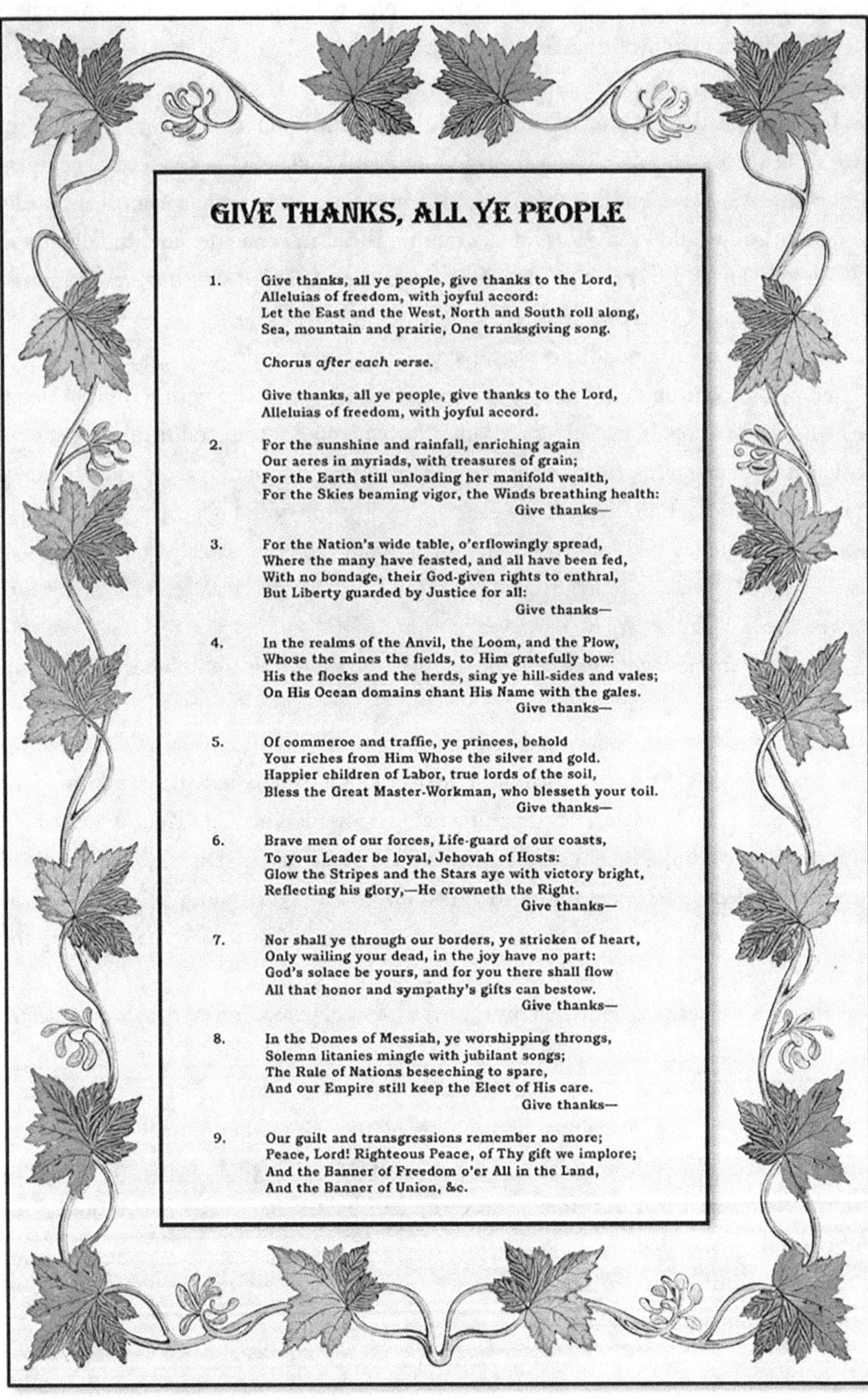

GIVE THANKS, ALL YE PEOPLE

1. Give thanks, all ye people, give thanks to the Lord,
Alleluias of freedom, with joyful accord:
Let the East and the West, North and South roll along,
Sea, mountain and prairie, One tranksgiving song.

Chorus after each verse.

Give thanks, all ye people, give thanks to the Lord,
Alleluias of freedom, with joyful accord.

2. For the sunshine and rainfall, enriching again
Our acres in myriads, with treasures of grain;
For the Earth still unloading her manifold wealth,
For the Skies beaming vigor, the Winds breathing health:
    Give thanks—

3. For the Nation's wide table, o'erflowingly spread,
Where the many have feasted, and all have been fed,
With no bondage, their God-given rights to enthral,
But Liberty guarded by Justice for all:
    Give thanks—

4. In the realms of the Anvil, the Loom, and the Plow,
Whose the mines the fields, to Him gratefully bow:
His the flocks and the herds, sing ye hill-sides and vales;
On His Ocean domains chant His Name with the gales.
    Give thanks—

5. Of commerce and traffic, ye princes, behold
Your riches from Him Whose the silver and gold.
Happier children of Labor, true lords of the soil,
Bless the Great Master-Workman, who blesseth your toil.
    Give thanks—

6. Brave men of our forces, Life-guard of our coasts,
To your Leader be loyal, Jehovah of Hosts:
Glow the Stripes and the Stars aye with victory bright,
Reflecting his glory,—He crowneth the Right.
    Give thanks—

7. Nor shall ye through our borders, ye stricken of heart,
Only wailing your dead, in the joy have no part:
God's solace be yours, and for you there shall flow
All that honor and sympathy's gifts can bestow.
    Give thanks—

8. In the Domes of Messiah, ye worshipping throngs,
Solemn litanies mingle with jubilant songs;
The Rule of Nations beseeching to spare,
And our Empire still keep the Elect of His care.
    Give thanks—

9. Our guilt and transgressions remember no more;
Peace, Lord! Righteous Peace, of Thy gift we implore;
And the Banner of Freedom o'er All in the Land,
And the Banner of Union, &c.

58

THE PRESIDENT'S HYMN

Rachel and Thomas strolled arm in arm along Canal Street, savoring the crisp fall breeze as they perused shop windows, stopping occasionally to admire the merchandise.

"Such a delightful time of year," Rachel said with a contented sigh.

"Yes," Thomas agreed. "A fine day to be out and about." He caught sight of something in a nearby window. "Look there," he said, guiding her toward the window of A. E. Blackmar's music shop. "There's a copy of 'The President's Hymn,' written for the national Thanksgiving holiday Lincoln just declared."

"That's strange. Blackmar is known for publishing Confederate songs. Sarah obtained her copies of 'The Bonnie Blue Flag' and 'God Save the South' from him last year."

"I thought Blackmar fled when the occupation began," Thomas said.

Rachel nodded. "He moved to Augusta. Odd that his sign is still up."

"Shall we take a look inside?" Thomas asked.

"Let's."

As they pushed the door open, a bell tinkled overhead. An older man greeted them warmly, "Come in, folks! Take your time and browse at your leisure."

"Thank you," Thomas said. "May we look at the 'President's Hymn' you have displayed in the window?"

"Certainly!" said the shopkeeper as he shuffled over to a nearby wall display. "I keep copies right here." He selected two sheets from a tidy stack and then handed them to

Thomas. "Please, take a seat," he added, gesturing toward a table and chairs in the center of the room.

"Thank you, sir," Thomas said, handing Rachel a copy of the sheet music as they sat at the table. He studied the cover of his copy while running a finger along the printed text. "Written by Reverend William Augustus Muhlenberg, set to music by J. W. Turner, and published by A. D. F. Randolph in New York."

"That's right," the shopkeeper affirmed, stepping closer. "These copies are fresh in from New York. I have a press in the back, but I can't print them here without permission."

"Are you the new owner?" Thomas asked.

"No, sir. I'm Mr. Blackmar's typesetter. Before he left for Augusta, he asked me to mind the shop until the war ends. It's good to step away from the presses now and then and speak with folks."

"Does Mr. Blackmar still own the shop?" Rachel inquired.

"Yes, ma'am. At least, his wife does. She signed the Oath of Allegiance and paid the property taxes before they left town."

Thomas shot Rachel a knowing glance, a silent reminder of how wives, legally forbidden to own property without their husbands' permission, became invaluable during the occupation.

Thomas opened the sheet music, admiring a printed insert of a set of lyrics beautifully framed by delicate fall leaves. On the back of the insert was an advertisement for Blackmar's shop.

"When you buy a copy, that card is compliments of the house," the shopkeeper said proudly.

"You printed this?" Thomas asked.

"Yes, sir. But I can't sell it since I don't have the rights. I came up with the idea of giving it as an advertisement. I've already put a stack in the lobby of the St. Charles Hotel." He gave a sly smile. "Can't play the hymn without the music, can you?"

"That's clever," Thomas remarked, seeing Rachel enjoying reading the music inside her copy. "I'd like to buy two copies."

The old man scratched his head. "Hate to tell you, but that'll be a dime a copy. If I could print it here, I'd only charge a nickel."

Thomas pulled out two Seated Liberty silver dimes and handed them over.

"Would you like them wrapped?" the shopkeeper asked, apparently pleased with the sale.

"No need," Thomas replied. "Mind if we sit awhile to look at the music."

"Y'all take your time. Can I offer a cup of coffee or a cup of tea? I just brewed both."

"Would you like something to drink?" Thomas asked Rachel.

"A cup of tea would be lovely," she replied.

"And for you, sir?"

"Coffee, black, please."

"I'll have it out in two shakes of a lamb's tail," the shopkeeper promised, disappearing through the back door. Moments later, he returned with a tray bearing two steaming cups, which he set down with a clatter.

After he disappeared again, Thomas asked Rachel, "Did you notice that all of the Confederate sheet music is no longer on the shelves?"

"Yes, I did. I suppose all of it was confiscated."

"And burned," Thomas added. "What do you think of the hymn?"

Rachel took a sip of her tea. "First, thank you for buying me my copy. As to the hymn, I appreciate the mention of hope for freedom, given that so many people live in bondage. But it's hard to imagine that happening without ending this war."

"Speaking of which," Thomas said, "today is election day. General Banks ordered an election of local officials as part of the President's reconstruction plan."

"Who gets to vote?" Rachel asked.

Thomas blushed. "Only white men who've sworn loyalty to the Union."

Rachel shook her head. "That doesn't sound much like freedom from bondage to me."

"No," Thomas admitted. "But it's the first step on a very long journey."

As Rachel folded her sheet music, she felt the fragile hope woven into its verses flicker inside her. Far to the north, she could only wonder if President Lincoln, in whose honor the hymn was written, carried a similar hope in his heart.

PORD'S NEW THEATRE.
Tenth Street, near E.

JOHN T. FORD · · · · · Proprietor and Manager.
(Also of Holliday street Theatre, Baltimore.)

MONDAY EVENING, NOVEMBER 9, 1863.
Last Week of
MR. J. WILKES BOOTH,
And Messrs. CHAS. WHEATLEIGH,
HARRY PEARSON,
G. F. DE VERE,
AND THE GRAND COMBINATION COMPANY.

THE MARBLE HEART.

Phidias..
Dochalot } ·················· Mr. J. Wilkes Booth.
Diogenes
Volage } ·················· Mr. Chas. Wheatleigh.
Georgias
Chateau Margaux } ·········· Mr. Harry Pearson.

ON TUESDAY—HAMLET.

ADMISSION:

Dress Circle........50 cents | Orchestra Chairs....75 cents
Family Circle........25 cents | Private Boxes....$10 and $6

☞ Box Sheet now open, where seats can be secured
without extra charge.   oct 4—

59

Booth's Marble Heart

Shortly after seven o'clock in the evening, the orchestra began playing "Hail to the Chief" in the newly renovated Ford's Theatre in Washington, D.C.

Backstage, President Lincoln waited with the First Lady and her friend Sallie Clay, daughter of U.S. Minister to Russia, Cassius Clay. Behind him stood his private secretaries, John Hay, and John Nicolay.

Dressed in formal attire, the Presidential party entered the onstage box by the staircase from a private corridor, prompting the audience to rise in a wave of acknowledgment and respect. The orchestra swelled, filling the hall with the triumphant notes of "Hail to the Chief." The President's carefully choreographed entrance heightened the drama of the evening, drawing every eye to the stage.

When the Presidential party reached their seats, they settled into plush, velvet-upholstered opera chairs in a specially designed Presidential box installed after the 1862 fire. Positioned stage left, the box provided a clear view of the performance while offering the audience easy sightlines of the President and First Lady.

This intentional stagecraft created a sense of closeness between the President and the audience, enhancing the shared experience of the event. Many attendees, especially women, eagerly looked forward to catching a glance of Mrs. Lincoln's evening gown, adding extra flair to the scene.

As the applause faded and the audience returned to their seats, the orchestra shifted effortlessly into a lively medley of familiar tunes. The music welcomed a distinguished gathering of judges, congressmen, and Washington dignitaries, further elevating the event's grandeur.

The evening's play was *The Marble Heart*, or *The Sculptor's Dream*, Charles Selby's English adaptation of *Les Filles de Marbre* by Thiboust. After debuting in London in 1854, Selby's melodrama crossed the Atlantic, premiering at San Francisco's American Metropolitan Theatre.

Its success on the East Coast followed, where Edwin Booth portrayed the dual roles of Phidias, a sculptor in a dream sequence set in ancient Rome during Act I, and, in subsequent acts, Raphael, a tragic artist in contemporary Rome.

Tonight, however, the spotlight was on Edwin's younger brother, John Wilkes Booth. Having performed the play in Baltimore in March 1862 and at Chicago's McVicker's Theatre the following August, John Wilkes was well-versed in his role and ready to captivate his audience.

Lincoln's attendance was no coincidence. He had recently seen John Wilkes Booth perform *The Apostate* at Grover's Theatre, not far from Ford's. Booth's portrayal of Hemeya, a Moorish nobleman grappling with being forced to convert to Christianity, resonated deeply with the President, a man of profound personal convictions who believed in the separation of Church and State. After a demanding week filled with military briefings and preparation for his upcoming address at Gettysburg, Lincoln welcomed the distraction of theatre, especially a production featuring an actor he had admired for his intensity and passion.

While Lincoln quietly scanned the playbill, his secretaries, John Nicolay and John Hay, sat just behind him, discreetly taking notes as they observed the audience. Meanwhile, the First Lady leaned toward her friend, Sallie Clay, as their animated conversation flowed easily.

"What a beautiful theatre," Mary Todd remarked, her eyes glimmering with satisfaction. "The renovation makes it far more elegant than the original."

Sallie nodded, surveying the opulent surroundings.

"The red velvet seats and matching carpet are especially exquisite," Mary Todd continued. And those gold curtains draped over the balcony boxes, along with all the flag bunting, are simply stunning. I still can't believe Mr. Ford managed this on a modest $20,000 insurance claim."

Sallie smiled playfully. "Try to enjoy the evening without critiquing the décor, dear." With a wink, she added, "Don't look now, but every woman in this audience is turning green with envy over your gown."

Mary Todd leaned closer, assuming a conspiratorial voice. "You're starting to sound like Abe when he's in one of his grouchy moods about my penchant for decorating. I thought he'd never forgive me for the expense of the East Room carpet. He didn't even give me a chance to explain that it was a bargain!"

Suppressing a laugh, Sallie whispered back, "Well, you did go a bit over budget."

"What's a little over budget compared to the praise of Washington's elite? Even the French ambassador's wife remarked that our ballroom rivals theirs."

Sallie grinned. "High praise, indeed, from the land of Louis XIV."

"Yes, though she said it in French to a companion. I suppose she assumed I wouldn't understand her."

Hearing bits of the lively conversation, Lincoln leaned in with a knowing smile. "It sounds like the two of you are having more fun than the playbill promised, and the performance hasn't even begun."

Mary Todd shot him a playful look. "It's nothing you'd find important, dear. Just frivolous matters unworthy of the attention of a man with the nation's weight on his shoulders."

Lincoln raised a brow, feigning offense. "If it's about my alleged grouchiness, I just *might* be interested."

The women chuckled, and Mary Todd gently disarmed him with a quick kiss. The gesture prompted scattered applause from the audience.

Lincoln grinned, nodding toward the balcony. "We might consider reserving one of those private booths next time. Wouldn't want to steal the show."

Mary Todd blushed.

Behind them, Nicolay and Hay exchanged amused glances.

Sallie shifted the topic smoothly. "I met John Wilkes Booth backstage a few years ago."

Mary Todd perked up with interest. "Oh? Do tell."

"He's in his twenties, a bit taller than average, and athletic, with that gorgeous wavy jet-black hair and mustache. And his smile! It lights up the whole room. He has a way of charming everyone—especially the ladies."

Mary Todd's blush intensified as she noticed the grin tugging at her husband's lips.

Before the conversation could continue, the gasolier overhead dimmed, and the sconces around the auditorium followed. Meanwhile, the gas footlights at the stage's edge flared, signaling the audience to take their seats.

"This new lighting design creates such an atmosphere," Mary Todd whispered. "I just hope they don't bore us with some long-winded speech for the prologue."

Lincoln raised a brow, his tone reflective. "I've thought the same. The Bard had it right when he said that brevity is the soul of wit." He paused thoughtfully. "I've been working on my remarks for Gettysburg, you know. They must be brief but carry the weight of what's been lost. Those fallen men deserve no less."

Sallie smiled affectionately at the couple's interplay. "You two never stop working, do you?"

Mary Todd nudged her friend. "Look, Sallie! It's Mr. Ford."

A distinguished man of medium build, Ford's neatly groomed mustache and beard lent him an air of authority. His black tailcoat, perfectly tailored and complemented by a merlot-colored tie, gave him a polished, professional appearance. Reaching center stage, he paused, offering a respectful bow toward the President before beginning his introduction with the flair of an actor.

"Ladies and gentlemen, welcome to Ford's New Theatre. For those unfamiliar with me, I am John Thompson Ford, founder and manager of this establishment." Turning to the President with an outstretched hand, he said, "It is a great honor, Mr. President, to have you with us this evening in our magnificent, newly renovated theatre, nestled in the heart of Washington's vibrant cultural scene. Would you do us the honor of rising to greet the audience?"

Lincoln rose, his towering frame unfolding, and retrieved his top hat to wave it in a broad gesture to the cheering crowd.

After a lengthy standing ovation, Ford continued his address once Lincoln had retaken his seat.

"We are especially pleased to present tonight's production, *The Marble Heart*, or *The Sculptor's Dream*, a tale that transcends the ages from Pygmalion in ancient Greece to the present, revealing the anguish of men who seek perfection in art, yet find themselves caught up by the passions and vicissitudes of unrequited love."

"Tonight," he continued, "we are privileged to present a dear friend of mine, the exceptionally gifted John Wilkes Booth of the illustrious Booth family, in the dual roles of Phidias and Raphael. *The Marble Heart* has mesmerized audiences worldwide, beginning in London and continuing across our great nation, from the bustling streets of San Francisco to the grand stages of New York. It is our honor to experience this remarkable performance in the heart of the capital tonight."

He paused for a round of applause.

"Now, ladies and gentlemen, without further ado, please sit back and enjoy the performance. Thank you for supporting the arts at Ford's grand new theatre."

As the plush, red velvet curtain rose, the heavy fabric slowly gathered at the bottom, curling upward in gentle arcs, creating a sense of anticipation. The curtain continued to rise until it nestled in bunches at the top, revealing the cluttered setting of a sculptor's studio. A centerstage gasolier gradually illuminated the scene, complementing the warm glow of the footlights. Blocks of white *papier-mâché*, fashioned to simulate marble partially chiseled into form, stood among scattered tools, creating an atmosphere of creative chaos.

Upstage, near the very back, a vibrant green curtain draped a large wood frame set before the black backdrop, defining the area. It seemed to conceal something yet to be unveiled by the artist, intensifying the audience's anticipation of the masterpiece it concealed.

Booth, portraying Phidias, the sculptor of the Parthenon, dressed in a slate-colored shirt adorned with a white Grecian border, a Phrygian cap, tan pants, and high shoes, stepped onto the stage to the strains of violins playing a melancholy tune. His movements were heavy and labored, shoulders slumped, head slightly bowed, as though the weight of the world bore down upon him. His pale face, lined with worry, reflected his inner torment. He slowly approached the mysterious green curtain, stood momentarily, and pulled it open to reveal statues of three beautiful women so perfect they appeared alive.

The somber music of the melodrama, paired with his downtrodden demeanor, perfectly displayed Booth's mastery of his craft, moving the audience to feel his character's anguish as if it were their own.

Phidias's torment stemmed from falling in love with his models and being heartbroken that their statues could not be his because they belonged to his wealthy patron.

When the patron arrived to claim the sculptures, Phidias's friend, Diogenes, proposed an unusual solution: Phidias and his patron should present their cases to the statues and let them decide their fate. When they followed his advice, to everyone's astonishment, the statues, living actresses covered in white grease paint and draped in togas, opened their eyes, smiled, and reached out to the wealthy nobleman, rejecting the love of the poor sculptor, Phidias, in favor of a more elegant abode.

The scene concluded with workmen entering to cart the statues away, leaving Phidias in despair, crying out, "Ah, monsters of ingratitude! They forsake me!"

Phidias was left heartbroken, his face buried in his hands, while his friend Diogenes delivered the story's moral to the low accompaniment of weeping violins: "O, marble hearts, marble hearts! False ones of the past, false ones of the future. Woe to the man who loves you, for your gold-bought smiles have always been, and always will be, the ministers of ruin, misery, and death."

The mournful cry of the violins swelled from the orchestra, each long-drawn note dripping with sorrow, underscoring the anguish onstage.

Diogenes exited, leaving Phidias frozen in his grief as the curtain fell on Act I.

At the close of the dream sequence, stagehands rearranged the props and removed the large wooden frame and green curtain containing the three "statues" that had come to life. The stage was then set for an artist's retreat in the forest of present-day Fontainebleau.

While the crew buzzed about the dimly lit set like worker bees in a hive, Booth stood in the wings behind the heavy velvet curtain, just moments away from taking the stage. His index finger, trembling with anticipation, traced the familiar lines of his script, marked with his marginalia. A lamp flickered behind him, casting a menacing shadow that loomed over the narrow backstage walls.

Then, his gaze drifted through a gap at the curtain's edge.

There he was. President Lincoln sat in his onstage box behind a railing, tall and unassuming. His posture was relaxed as he conversed quietly with his companions.

Booth's jaw tightened, and his grip on the script hardened. He had known in advance that his sworn adversary would be attending tonight's performance, but the actual sight of him was another matter.

His anger crept upon him, insidious and relentless, like the constricting grip of an anaconda. Each moment tightened its coils, squeezing his ability to think clearly and rationally. The pressure mounted steadily, every word Lincoln spoke to those around him and every casual gesture serving as another twist of the serpent's powerful body.

Booth lowered his eyes to the script to regain his focus. He reviewed the changes he had penciled in earlier that day for Acts IV and V, murmuring the lines softly to himself, his voice low and intense.

The adjustment in Act IV felt especially fitting, as the script touched on abolition, a subject that only stoked the embers of his fury. But his final change in Act V held his focus the longest. The slight change would go unnoticed by anyone in the audience, yet in Booth's mind, it was monumental, ensuring that the play's closing line became more than just dialogue: it would transform into a dagger, a final, lasting impression aimed squarely at his enemy.

The original line, "I will have your heart! It is marble! It is marble!" was meant to be spoken in the delirium of a lover's passion. But Booth had altered the line with four words that resonated deeply with his convictions about Southern sovereignty, a belief reinforced by his friendship with President Jefferson Davis and his three-month stay in the Confederate capital earlier in the year.

"You are a traitor," he whispered, the appellation dripping with venom as it slid from his lips. It wasn't just a line delivered in a play; it was a damning verdict aimed squarely at the man in the presidential box.

The stage dissolved around him at that moment, and the performance became a vessel for something far darker. He didn't know how or when, but the day would come when he would make the tyrant pay for every drop of precious blood he had caused to be spilled on the sacred soil of the South.

Satisfied with his changes, Booth placed the script on a small prop table.

The stage manager called his cue. Booth rolled his shoulders back, squared his stance, and took a deep breath, waiting for the curtain to rise. This was his moment.

"Wasn't it amazing how those actresses portrayed the statues?" Mary Todd asked, turning to her friend during the entr'acte. "Can you imagine having to remain perfectly still, covered in that white grease paint on your face and arms? The very thought unsettles me. I would surely suffocate."

Sallie gave her a playful nudge. "Look at Abe. A moment ago, he was praising Booth's performance. Now, I do believe he's nodded off."

Mary Todd smiled knowingly. "My husband has a remarkable talent for sleeping bolt upright. But, mark my words, as soon as the curtain rises, his eyes will pop open, and if you ask him, he'll swear he never closed them."

"That must be how he manages to handle so much with so little sleep," Sallie said softly.

Mary Todd nodded. "If you only knew. I need my sleep mask to block out the light of his lamp until he finally comes to bed and extinguishes it. Sometimes, I wonder if he ever makes it to bed or if the oil just ran out."

"Oh, I think they are about to begin," Sallie said, taking note of the dimming house lights.

On cue, the violins led the orchestra, their bows caressing their strings to create a warm, resonant tone that swelled and ebbed as softly as the rise and fall of a lover's sigh.

The curtain rose slowly, revealing an idyllic wooded retreat for artists in the Forest of Fontainebleau. In the foreground, Marco, a stunning yet cold-hearted coquette driven by a pursuit of wealth and status, moved effortlessly among a circle of noblemen. All of them took turns mocking her about her fortune-hunting ways, singing, "Tis the chink of gold you love."

Rather than take offense, Marco embraced her reputation. She set her sights on Raphael, an artist renowned for his considerable savings from a life of frugality and his penchant for beauty. With calculated ease, she identified him as her next conquest.

Just as she had expected, the unsuspecting Raphael walked in, his attention immediately drawn to Marco's charm. Yet his attention drifted just as quickly to another beauty, Clementine, whose gentle charms stirred something unexpected in him. Seizing the moment, Raphael gallantly offered Clementine a carriage ride, only for Marco to intervene, shifting the attention back to her.

Caught between the two beauties, Raphael hesitated but ultimately chose Marco. As they exited arm in arm, Marco cast a triumphant smirk over her shoulder at Clementine, leaving her competitor humiliated in the wake of their departure.

As the curtain fell on Act II, Sallie exclaimed, "The nerve of that, Marco!"

"And Raphael's no better," Mary Todd added with a disdainful shake of her head. "The man's a complete muttonhead."

"There has to be a peripeteia coming later, my dear," Sallie replied.

"Let's hope so. Without a twist in the plot, the play falls flat."

"Oh, the house lights are coming up. It must be intermission," Sallie said, glancing around.

"That's what the playbill says," Abe remarked dryly, pointing to the order of performance.

Mary Todd turned to Sallie. "Shall we head to the retiring room? I'm dying to see how they've decorated it."

"An excellent idea, my friend. Besides, I need to freshen up a bit."

After the intermission, the audience fell silent as Booth, playing Raphael, strode onto the stage to begin Act III.

Raphael stood before his latest creation, which, although unfinished, seemed to embody the essence of a Greek goddess. Her delicate features were frozen in a serene expression, and her eyes were cast downward as if contemplating her existence. Flowing robes clung to her form, their intricate folds hinting at movement as though she were not merely a statue but a goddess on the verge of stepping free into the world of mortals.

While Raphael stood consumed by his sculpting, his mother implored him to find a wife. She told him he needed someone to love him and bear his children. Though he indulged her concerns, he admitted that he endlessly chased perfection in his art but had never found it in any living woman.

In a rapid-fire chain of events, Raphael became increasingly infatuated with Marco, who skillfully deceived him into believing she returned his love. At the same time, she reveled in the luxuries he showered upon her. But once his fortune was spent, Marco distanced herself from him, and he returned to his home. There, he was unable to work and fell into depression. Then, on the dare of her noblemen friends, Marco sent for him, claiming she had a change of heart. He revived and rushed out of his studio to visit her.

As the curtain fell on Act III, accompanied by gay music reflecting Raphael's renewed hopes of capturing Marco's heart, Mary Todd and Sallie resumed their commentary on the play as the house lights brightened.

"So much like a man," Sallie said. "So easily deceived by a temptress."

"Yes," Mary Todd agreed, nudging her husband. "Except for my faithful Abe."

"What do you think of the young Booth's performance?" Abe asked, redirecting the conversation.

"I think he's marvelous," Mary Todd said. "He can create a convincing character and pull you into his world."

"Precisely," Sallie agreed. "I saw him as Richard III. It allowed him to bring his energy and charm to the stage while portraying a menacing character, unlike himself."

"I know Abe enjoyed seeing him, didn't you, dear?"

"It was a delightful evening. I found myself drawn to his performance. More so than any other actor I've seen."

While the audience chatted and commented on the play, Booth paced restlessly backstage, his shoes striking the floor in sharp, deliberate steps as the tension knotted in his chest. Act IV was fast approaching, and with it, the moment he had rehearsed obsessively. His heart pounded relentlessly against his ribs as he clenched and unclenched his fists, repeatedly running the lines through his mind.

It was his chance to channel the contempt that had been simmering in him for months. He would hurl his line like a dagger, each word a disguised indictment of the tyrant he loathed.

"Death and dishonor! I can endure no more!" he mouthed, barely above a whisper, his lips curling into a sneer. He raised his fist to the air, feeling the raw energy build within him as he imagined himself onstage, facing not just an audience but the very man he blamed for the destruction of the South and the desecration of his ideals.

In the upcoming act, his character, Raphael, would be accused by Monsieur Veaudore, a pompous aristocrat, of admiring *Uncle Tom's Cabin* and sympathizing with abolitionists. Booth could not have dreamed of a more fitting provocation. The accusation mirrored everything he despised: the abolitionist agenda, the war, and what he believed was the tyranny of Lincoln's administration. What better moment to reflect his outrage than now, when the words carried the dual edge of theatre and reality?

Booth rehearsed the scene again in the dim backstage shadows, his body tense. First, he would stride toward Veaudore as written in the script. Then, with a sudden pivot, he would turn sharply, not toward the actor as directed in the script, but toward Lincoln. His eyes would lock onto the President's, and he would let his fury explode in that single, piercing line: "Death and dishonor!"

Satisfied that he had mastered every word, every inflection, and every glance meant for Lincoln, Booth allowed himself to relish what was to come.

In Act V, the final act, Raphael would descend fully into madness, hallucinating that his unfaithful lover, Marco, was taunting him from the darkness. Booth's pulse quickened as he imagined Lincoln oblivious to the rage he would unleash since each word was cloaked in the guise of performance.

On his knees, Booth rehearsed the moment Raphael crumbled, his voice cracking under the weight of desperation. Mouthing a frenzied shout directed toward the imagined specter of Marco, his entire body stirred with rage. "I cannot work; I cannot breathe while you are there! Your breath is pestilence; the glare of your eyes scorches my soul!" His hands shook as he paused, gasping, the fury burning fiercely inside him.

Then the pivotal moment, where Raphael's breakdown would mirror Booth's own. With a sudden, explosive energy, Booth sprang to his feet, his eyes wide and wild. His breath came in short bursts as he thrust out his hand, trembling with rage, and mouthed, "What? You laugh at my misery? Tyrant! You are a tyrant! I will have your heart! It is marble! It is marble!"

Each word would fall with the weight of conviction, his delivery measured and relentless, like hammer strokes against an anvil, forging raw steel into the keen edge of a blade. With each rising cadence, the blade would be sharpened further, honed to a lethal edge, poised for the moment he would strike.

The audience would see only a lovesick artist ensnared in a web of delusion. But Booth knew the truth. This would be no mere performance.

Just before the curtain call, he murmured with quiet finality, "Tonight is the dress rehearsal for what may be the grandest act of my life."

The rising curtain of Act IV revealed an elegant residence in a villa in the Boie de Boulogne. Marco mixed and mingled with the noblemen who teased that Raphael would steal her from them. Marco responded, "Psha! How can you be so absurd!" signaling her intent to toy with Raphael.

Making good on her promise, Marco greeted Raphael coldly when he arrived, and a friend gratuitously entered to point out that she had fleeced him of his life savings and made a fool out of him. To turn the knife in his wound, a haughty nobleman, Monsieur Veaudore addressed Raphael.

"By the way," Veaudore said, "hadn't I the pleasure of seeing you in a box at the theatre about two months ago, with Mademoiselle Marco, weeping at the sorrows of Uncle Tom?"

Raphael objected, "Sir...I..."

Veaudore pulled out his pince-nez and examined Raphael's face. "Yes, I am right, though I did not quite recognize you then. I presume from the ardor with which you applauded the liberal speeches that you are for the emancipation of Blacks?" Finishing the insult, Veaudore casually retrieved a case and pulled out a cigar.

Raphael spun angrily toward Lincoln in response, his gaze blazing with unspoken fury, his fist raised. "Death and dishonor! I can endure no more!" He then whirled back toward Veaudore, who treated the confrontation as a jest. As Raphael prepared to strike, Marco's entrance, accompanied by the familiar lilting tune that had become her dramatic signature, instantly dispelled the tension in the room.

Marco used the occasion to tell Raphael that she did not love him, whereupon he languished in despair and left. Marco's friends then laughed at her, taunting that Raphael was manipulating her to break up so he could return home to the arms of Marie, a simple, orphaned country maiden who loved him. Believing the noblemen, Marco was furious and vowed to coax him back to her, not out of love but to prove her prowess.

Raphael returned, and Marco made her move, but he told her that he had been standing outside and had heard everything. He spurned her advances and exited again, leaving her with her friends, who claimed they had won the bet. Enraged, she vowed to win him back again. "I'll double the wager: forty, fifty, a hundred Louis. I'll win him back again."

The curtain fell, accompanied by a melody of hope and aspiration, with strings elevating the theme through soaring harmonies. Meanwhile, the flute's bright, airy tone glided effortlessly above the ensemble, evoking the sound of swallows in flight. The music built to a crescendo of promise and possibility, leaving the audience with an enduring sense of hope as the final romantic chords faded into the atmosphere.

"Poor Raphael. He's such a romantic," Sallie said.

Mary Todd nodded. "He should have followed his mother's advice and married the poor orphan girl. What was her name?"

"I believe it was Marie. She was such a simple girl that I'd also almost forgotten about her. Yet, I do recall that she seemed to care about him."

"Yes, she did," Mary Todd agreed.

Hearing the women share their views on Raphael's affairs, the President said, "It appears we are in store for the final act. Do you have any guesses as to what happens?"

"He could just marry Marie," Sallie suggested.

"Oh, no. That's far too simple," Mary Todd said. "These melodramas never end that way. The resolution must be much more dramatic, even tragic."

"Perhaps he becomes a hermit," Abe suggested, "rejecting all the women in his life."

Mary Todd elbowed him. "Spoken like a man."

Sallie chuckled at the couple's interchange.

"The house lights are dimming," Mary Todd said. "Now for the final act.

Act V opened in Raphael's studio once more, where he discovered that his mother had died out of despair over his refusal to accept Marie, the orphan, as his true love. Raphael vowed to honor his mother's wishes to protect the young girl and treat her as his sister. Marie was devastated, as she was fond of him and had hoped to be his wife.

Left alone, Raphael rambled on about his responsibilities and how he still loved Marco until he spiraled into madness as the stage plunged into darkness, with a single gaslight casting eerie shadows across his tormented face. Violins played in *sul ponticello* style, their harsh, dissonant tones weaving a foreboding melody, a chilling premonition of the tragedy to come.

In the throes of delusion, Raphael imagined his faithless lover taunting him from the shadows. Overwhelmed with fury, he collapsed to his knees directly in front of the President, his voice cracking as he shouted in a frenzied tone, "I cannot work. I cannot breathe while you are there! Your breath is pestilence. The glare of your eyes scorches my soul!" He paused, trembling with rage. "What? You laugh at my misery? Tyrant!"

With a sudden surge of manic energy, Raphael—transfigured through Booth—leapt to his feet, his wild eyes locked onto a startled Lincoln. His hand thrust forward in a threatening arc, and he howled, "You are a tyrant! I will have your heart! It is marble! It is marble!" The accusation echoed like a curse, reverberating through the hushed theatre.

On cue, Volage rushed in to console his tormented friend. But Raphael, now fully consumed by despair, crumbled under the weight of his torment. Moments later, he collapsed into Volage's arms with a final, shuddering breath.

As the curtain fell on the tragic tableau, the mournful strains of the violins swelled, mirroring the heartbreak onstage. The music lingered, a lament that held the audience captive even as they stirred from their spellbound stillness.

"I think he meant his last dying line for you," Sallie whispered to the President.

"I rather think so myself," he replied, appearing unshaken.

Beside him, Mary Todd's face tightened with concern, her hands clasping together in her lap.

The President leaned over to her, his voice scarcely above a whisper. "I cannot let this rest," he said solemnly. "I must invite him to the Executive Mansion to extend my hand as our guest."

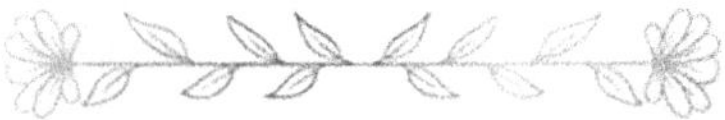

Backstage, as actors wiped away their makeup and returned their costumes to the wardrobe, a stagehand approached Booth, who sat at his dressing table. The mirror reflected the streaks of grease paint still clinging to his face.

"President Lincoln asked me to deliver this to you, Mr. Booth," the stagehand said, handing over a neatly folded note.

"Thank you, John," Booth replied, pausing momentarily to rub cold cream across his face. Unfolding the paper, his eyes scanned the message. It was a congratulatory note from Lincoln, commending his performance and concluding with an invitation to dine at the Executive Mansion.

Booth's expression twisted, his jaw tightening as rage flickered beneath the surface. With a sneer, he crumpled the note into his fist and tossed it onto the floor. "Tyrant!" he hissed through clenched teeth. "This is from the President who opens his doors to abolitionists and welcomes freedmen like Douglass to dine with him. I'd sooner rot in my grave than shake hands with a man who thinks such company is equal to mine."

60

THE OLIVE BRANCH
AND THE SWORD

Rachel stepped onto her front stoop, where the crisp December air nipped at her cheeks and carried the scent of chimney smoke from neighboring fireplaces, rich as a hearthside memory. The freshly delivered December 5th issue of *Frank Leslie's Illustrated Newspaper* lay at her feet, still stiff and cool from the outdoors. She picked it up carefully, picturing the spark that would brighten Thomas's eyes when he saw the latest engravings.

"It's such a beautiful, brisk morning, with barely a cloud in sight," she said cheerfully, stepping into the parlor to sit on the sofa beside Thomas. "Can you believe tonight is Christmas Eve?"

Thomas smiled contentedly, enjoying the soft light filtering through the curtains. "Everyone out on the streets is wishing each other peace and goodwill."

Rachel tilted her head thoughtfully. "One can only hope."

Thomas unfolded the newspaper. "Let's see if they've printed Lincoln's speech at Gettysburg." He scanned the pages until an illustration of the event caught his eye in the centerfold. "Ah, here it is."

Rachel leaned closer, her gaze following his finger to an illustration of Lincoln standing on a raised platform speaking to the masses. "Looks like a decent crowd."

"Yes," Thomas replied. "I'm surprised the President wasn't worried about his safety."

"Heaven forbid!" Rachel exclaimed, pressing a hand to her heart.

Thomas turned the pages and angled the paper so they could read it together. "Here's the speech on page eleven."

Rachel's brow furrowed as her eyes skimmed the brief text. "Is that all of it? Just three paragraphs on a single page?"

"With room to spare," Thomas noted with a wry smile. "I've never known a politician to be so frugal with their words."

"I find it refreshing," Rachel said. "They usually drone on for hours."

"Shall I read it aloud?" Thomas asked.

"Please do."

Clearing his throat, Thomas began, his voice steady and deliberate as though channeling Lincoln's cadence: "Four score and seven years ago, our fathers brought forth on this continent a new nation, conceived in Liberty and dedicated to the proposition that all men are created equal...."

When he finished, Rachel sat quietly, her thoughts swirling. "It's incredible. Not a word of bitterness after so much war and suffering. The whole thing sounds noble, as if he's reaching for something higher in all of us."

Thomas nodded, his expression contemplative. "Or, as he would say, 'Our better angels.' It's a call to unity. I admire his vision for the future and his fortitude in completing the Capitol Dome during wartime, insisting on hoisting the Statue of Freedom to the top just weeks ago. Many criticized him for that, but he refused to turn the Capitol into a mausoleum."

Rachel's gaze drifted momentarily as she thought of her family in LaGrange. "People in the market are saying General Grant is headed East now that the Mississippi flows freely again."

"Grant has become a national hero," Thomas said. "I've heard that Congress passed a resolution to have a gold medal struck in his honor."

"They don't call him 'Unconditional Surrender Grant' for nothing," Rachel said, though she kept her worries about her family to herself.

"Indeed," Thomas replied. "There are even whispers of him as a future president."

Rachel raised an eyebrow. "Isn't that a bit premature?"

"Perhaps," Thomas conceded, "but the message is clear: while Lincoln extends the olive branch, Grant wields the sword." He paused, the firelight catching a flicker of hesitation in his eyes. Then, with a measured breath, he turned to her. "Speaking of the future... I was wondering if we might revisit our wedding plans."

Rachel lowered her eyes, her voice soft but steady. "There may be gossip, given that Levi perished in a duel this year, but I've given it thought. No matter how much I wish I could, I can't change the past."

"So we have a date?" Thomas asked gently.

Rachel met his gaze, her eyes brimming with unshed tears of joy. "We do."

"And that would be?" he prompted, taking her hand.

"Sunday, January 3rd."

Thomas leaned back, surprised. "That's just over a week away!"

"So much has changed," Rachel murmured. "Since my family left New Orleans, they won't be attending the wedding. Rabbi Gutheim departed about the same time, having helped his congregants secure safe passage. Dr. Zacharie also left, aiming to collaborate with Judah Benjamin to negotiate peace."

"Yes, Thomas said. "All of that has changed. "And now I'm working here in New Orleans with General Banks to keep an eye on the secessionists. At least I won't be traveling anymore."

"Do you have anyone you want to invite?" Rachel asked.

"No."

"Then it's just you and me," Rachel said softly, thinking of how most of Thomas's friends had gone off to war.

"So, where does all of that leave your plans for the wedding?" Thomas asked.

"Well, the lack of guests means there will be no wedding supper and no need for all the other arrangements required for a large ceremony. Rabbi Illowy leans much more toward orthodoxy than Rabbi Gutheim, so I asked if he could adjust his usual ceremony to incorporate more English. He kindly agreed to make an exception but insisted on saying the usual blessings in Hebrew and drafting a traditional *Ketubah* for our marriage contract."

Thomas grinned, his tone playful. "Well, it *has* been a long time since *my* bar mitzvah, and my Hebrew has gotten rusty. I'd really like to understand what I'm agreeing to."

Rachel continued, disregarding his humor. "I'll wear my wedding gown, and the *chuppah* I designed will remain, but it'll just be you, me, the rabbi, and whoever else he deems essential to make it official. Nothing else matters. Let the tongues wag away!"

Thomas's smile warmed. "An intimate wedding suits me just fine. And tell me, Mrs. Manget-to-be, what plans do you have once we're married?"

Rachel's eyes sparkled with mischief. "If I tell you, you'll think I've lost my senses."

"Never."

"I want to be a teacher," she declared.

"Teacher? Where? What? Who?"

"At one of the new schools for freed children here in town."

"Teaching the ABCs and counting to ten?" he asked incredulously.

"Exactly," Rachel replied, her enthusiasm overflowing. "It would be a joy to help them grow."

Thomas gave her hand an encouraging squeeze. "It's a noble challenge, darling. When do you plan to start?"

"The day after our wedding."

"No honeymoon? I thought you wanted me to surprise you."

"Not yet. This way, we'll have an excuse to take one every year."

Thomas considered this with a smile. "How about we sneak away for a horseback ride in City Park before the wedding? We could have a picnic."

Rachel laughed, her face lighting up. "As Shakespeare said, 'My kingdom for a horse,' but alas, I have neither."

Thomas squeezed her hand reassuringly. "Leave that to me, darling. I'll take care of everything."

"Do you think you could hire one like Nellie?" she asked wistfully.

"I'll do my best," he said with a mischievous glint in his eye.

1864

THE RISE OF
RECONSTRUCTION

61

DORÉ

By mid-morning, sunlight filtered through the moss-laced branches of the live oaks in City Park, casting dappled patterns on the ground below. Thomas reined in his wagon just before an arched stone bridge that crossed a gently murmuring creek. A few yards ahead, a middle-aged man stood beneath a low-hanging branch, where two horses were loosely tethered. Weathered and sunburned, he wore a broad-brimmed straw hat, and a long, grizzled graying beard spilled down his chest as he slowly chewed a stem of straw, his gaze fixed somewhere in the distance.

Stepping down to approach the man, Thomas greeted him with a nod. "Much obliged, Fred, for fetching the horses."

Fred gave a subtle nod. "My pleasure, Mr. Manget. I understand you and your lady friend plan to ride along the lake this morning. I'll wait here 'til you're ready and take the horses back to the stable." He reached into the pouch of his saddle and pulled out an envelope. "Mr. Johnson sent your receipt for the mare. He said to fill out the breeding papers with her name so he can record it."

"Much appreciated," Thomas said, taking the papers and shooting the liveryman a warning glance, his eyes flicking briefly toward Rachel to ensure she had not overheard the exchange.

"Sorry," the man said, looking embarrassed. "Didn't know."

"We won't be more than a few hours," Thomas said, his tone betraying a slight impatience to shift the conversation elsewhere.

Fred gave an easy smile. "Picked yourself a mighty fine day for a ride. Warm for this time of year." Settling into the shade, he pulled out a soft, worn pouch and thumbed free a thick coil of Southern Twist, tearing off a chaw with practiced ease before tucking it in his cheek.

Thomas secured the papers and stepped back to the wagon, offering Rachel his hand. "Let me help you down, my love."

"Thank you, my dear," Rachel said primly, stepping from the wagon with a wicker picnic basket. Her gaze lingered on the horses. "I see you brought Midnight. I didn't know they hired out such beautiful horses as this one you brought for me."

Thomas beamed with pride. "I thought you'd take a fancy to your new mare."

Rachel placed the basket on the ground and ran a hand along the mare's face, her touch gentle. "She's gorgeous," she murmured, admiring the animal's golden coat. Then she paused, catching the meaning in Thomas's words. "Wait. What did you say?"

Thomas's grin widened. "She's your wedding gift."

Rachel gasped. "Thomas! You're wonderful!" Throwing her arms around him warmly, she asked, "Does she have a name?"

"That's for you to decide," he replied with a broad grin.

Rachel tilted her head, bemused. "She's never had a name?"

"No," Thomas answered, shaking his head. "The stable just gives their stock a number and a foal date for the breeding record. The breeding record leaves a blank space for the new owner to name her."

Rachel melted as she gazed into the horse's gentle brown eyes. "Doré," she murmured, her voice soft and warm. Her hand glided affectionately along the mare's sleek golden mane, a tear of joy slipping down her cheek. Wiping it away, she nodded with quiet certainty. "Doré," she said again, savoring the name. "It suits her perfectly. She's golden."

Doré let out a soft whinny and nodded as if in agreement.

"Thomas, look!" Rachel called out. "She likes her name!"

Thomas chuckled, his eyes twinkling. "Either that or she smells the food in the picnic basket."

Rachel gave him a playful slap on the arm. "Either way, I think she loves me just as much as I love her."

"What do you think of her saddle?"

Rachel ran her fingers along the smooth, supple saddle. The seat was wide and padded for comfort, and the stirrups were perfectly adjusted to her legs. The softly oiled finish gave the leather of the saddle and stirrups a smooth, rich texture, preventing chafing. She noticed how the lower pommel and cantle would make mounting and dismounting easier, and the deeper seat provided an extra sense of security.

"It's wonderful," she said, her fingers brushing over it with sincere admiration. She inhaled deeply, her eyes brightening. "Nothing quite like the smell of fresh leather."

Rachel placed her foot in the stirrup and quickly swung into the saddle. She settled comfortably, immediately aware of how well the saddle balanced her weight across Dore's back. The mare stood still, ears flicking as she gave a soft snort as if approving of the thoughtful design.

"This feels like my favorite chair at home," she said delightedly. "How did you know how to have it made so perfectly?"

Thomas's chest swelled with pride. "Do you remember when you went with me to my saddler when I was shopping for a new saddle?"

"Yes," she said.

"I told him what I was planning for you, and he observed your posture and noted the styles you admired. I then returned with Doré for him to fit her. That's how he was able to craft everything for you." He grabbed the picnic basket and secured it to his horse. "Shall we go on our ride?"

"Before we do, would you mind fetching the box I asked you to pack in the back of the wagon?" Rachel asked, dismounting her horse.

"Of course," Thomas replied. He turned, retrieved a large parcel wrapped in brown paper and bound with twine, and set it before her at the back of the wagon.

"Would you open it?" she urged.

He raised an eyebrow. "Now?"

"Yes," she said with a smile that left no room for refusal.

Thomas drew his pocketknife, sliced the twine, and peeled away the paper. Beneath was a walnut case, with an inset silver plate monogrammed with his initials. He unlatched it and eased open the lid. Inside, velvet lining cradled a gleaming set of instruments: compasses, dividers, and ruling pens, fashioned of brass and ivory. Nestled alongside were a clutch of slender colored pencils, neatly bound sticks of pastel chalk, and a small case of graphite leads. A bone-handled penknife, meant for sharpening nibs and points, lay in its own slot.

For a long moment, he was silent, running a fingertip along the smooth arc of a compass. At last, he looked up, his eyes shining. "Rachel," he murmured, "you could not have chosen better. I will cherish these always."

Rachel threw her arms around him, and for a moment they held each other, lost in the tenderness of the exchange.

"How did you know I liked to draw?" he asked, still holding her close.

"Do you remember the colorist's shop in Baton Rouge?"

"I do."

"Well, while you were out the next day, I returned and spoke with the shopkeeper. He told me what you had purchased. From there, the rest was easy. We still have a stationer in New Orleans who imports from New York."

Thomas smiled. "You're amazing. Let me secure this in the wagon so we can go for our ride."

"By all means," Rachel said.

Thomas secured his gift and gestured toward the stone bridge ahead. "What do you say we cross the bridge and find a spot under those oaks just beyond it?"

"That sounds lovely," Rachel agreed.

Fred, sitting in the shade, grinned as he watched the two mount their horses. "Ain't young love a sight to see," he muttered, popping a fresh piece of chaw.

Rachel and Thomas crossed the bridge, its stone arch reflected in the shimmering creek below. On the other side, they saw a quiet clearing ahead, shaded by gigantic oaks, their sprawling limbs draped with long strands of Spanish moss swaying gently in the breeze.

Thomas slowed Midnight as they reached the clearing. Sunlight filtered through the moss-draped branches, casting a lacework of shadows on the ground. He glanced over at Rachel. "What do you think? Should we stop here?"

Rachel met his gaze, lingering more on him than on the clearing he had chosen. "Perfect," she murmured.

Rachel dismounted Doré, and Thomas followed, stepping down with the picnic basket. He placed it on the ground and carefully unfolded the embroidered linen tablecloth covering the food. The intricate, colorful floral patterns in x-shaped stitches of roses, violets, and ivy leaves curled gracefully along its borders.

"Let me help," Rachel offered, taking hold of a corner.

Together, they spread the tablecloth across the grass, the vibrant colors catching the afternoon light. Thomas admired the intricate work. "Such a beautiful piece," he remarked. "Who did the needlework?"

"I did," Rachel said. "I spent countless hours stitching each blossom and leaf of my favorite flowers. It marked the days when Sarah and I were lonely, and I found comfort in the work."

Thomas nodded thoughtfully, offering no further words as they sat across from each other.

"I brought a baguette, some cheese, and corned beef," Rachel said. "Nothing that might spoil easily."

"Perfect," Thomas replied, arranging the food, plates, and silverware.

Rachel looked back into the basket and pulled out two bright red apples, holding them up with a puzzled expression. "I don't remember packing these," she said. "How curious."

Thomas chuckled with a mischievous grin. "I slipped them in while you were busy naming Doré. I thought she might enjoy sharing our picnic. And we can't leave out Midnight."

Rachel's face lit up with delight. "What a thoughtful daddy you make," she teased, standing to offer one of the apples to Doré, who eagerly accepted it, crunching with enthusiasm.

"Look, Thomas!" Rachel exclaimed, her voice filled with excitement. "She loves it!"

"I had a feeling she would."

Now turning to Thomas's stallion, she said, "Now one for you, Midnight," and offered him the second apple.

Pleased to see that the horses enjoyed their treats, she returned to her seat, her eyes sparkling. "Shall we slice the bread for our sandwiches?"

"Ready when you are," Thomas said, reaching for the loaf. "I'll slice."

"I'm famished," Rachel admitted, her hands busy organizing the other ingredients.

After Thomas carefully sliced the baguette and spread butter on each piece, Rachel took the bread and layered relishes, mustard, and thin slices of corned beef, wiping away the excess salt before gently placing the top slice of bread.

Thomas grinned as Rachel handed him his sandwich, a towering stack of ingredients that looked more ambitious than practical. "This might require some strategy," he quipped, eyeing the stacked layers. "The last time I encountered an impossible sandwich like this was in New York, just before the war. I'd gone to Niblo's Garden to see *Blue Beard* and stopped by one of the German eating houses afterward."

Rachel's eyes sparkled with amusement. "What a lovely compliment. Let me know if it's missing anything you want," she said, her tone playfully inviting.

Thomas leaned in, taking a careful bite from the edge. "Mmm," he murmured, nodding as he swallowed. "Exactly the way I like it."

The couple fell into a comfortable silence, savoring their sandwiches with unhurried delight. Each bite seemed to draw them closer, their eyes consuming the warmth and tenderness reflected in the other's expression. Their gazes met often, lingering in a wordless communion that spoke louder than any conversation.

After a long pause, Thomas's face took on a serious look. "Rachel, before our wedding, I must tell you something."

Sensing the sincerity in his tone, Rachel tried to lighten the moment. "You're not already married, are you?" she teased.

Thomas chuckled, although there was an unmistakable sadness beneath it. "No, definitely not. However, I do need to tell you about my past."

Rachel leaned in, her eyes filled with concern and curiosity. "I'm here, Thomas. Tell me."

He took a steady breath. "My father told me that my mother died giving birth to what would have been my younger sister, so he raised me alone since no other family was living in the area. I don't remember my mother, and he never took me to visit her grave, no matter how often I asked."

Rachel reached for his hand. "I'm sorry, Thomas. He must have been grief-stricken and unable to accept her passing."

"He was a good father in many ways," Thomas continued, "but looking back, I realize he spoiled me. Being his only child, he doted on me. But as I grew older, I realized that he had a darker side."

Rachel squeezed his hand, bracing herself for what he might say.

"He was cruel to his slaves."

"That must have been difficult for you, darling."

"It was," he admitted. "I threw myself into school and sports—anything to stay away from the plantation. I hated seeing the way he whipped them for things he called slacking. I had to believe that if I had a mother, she would have restrained him."

Rachel's eyes glistened with unshed tears. "That's heartbreaking."

Thomas leaned over and kissed her gently on the cheek, then took a deep breath. "There's more. When I learned Louisiana was planning to secede, I traveled to Washington and offered my services to President Lincoln's security team, led by Allan Pinkerton."

Rachel's eyes widened. "So, they were right about you at Port Hudson? You are a spy!"

"Yes, but not with Pinkerton now, since he's resigned from the government. I'm working with General Banks to track the movement of secessionists here in New Orleans and gather intelligence," Thomas said, his gaze steady and unwavering. "I couldn't stand with the South when they fought to preserve slavery, even though it was in my best financial interests as the sole heir of a plantation. If I were going to fight, it had to be for something better."

He looked into her eyes and saw the tears in them. His tone softened as he continued, "You need to understand, Rachel. Until this war ends, I'll often be away on assignments. And I'll have to set up a separate residence as discreet quarters to shield my identity. But when it's over, I'll return to being an attorney and come home every night." He held her gaze, his voice low and earnest. "Knowing all this, do you still want to marry me?"

Rachel's voice trembled with emotion as she replied, "Oh, yes, Thomas! More than ever."

As they embraced, her mind drifted to the past year's trials, the moments of desperation when she had been willing to sacrifice her dignity to keep her family afloat. Those memories weighed heavily on her now that Thomas had disclosed his past, pressing her to unburden her soul, to speak truths she had long kept locked away.

"I have some secrets to share with you as well, Thomas," Rachel began, her voice hesitant.

Thomas met her gaze, his face softening as he listened.

She paused, weighing her words, then continued, "There was a time when I was so desperate to support my family that I went to the House of the Rising Sun."

Thomas's gaze didn't waver. "Go on," he urged gently.

Rachel swallowed hard. "I was ready to sell myself," she confessed, her voice trembling. "Thank heaven, Dr. Zacharie saved me that first day before anything could happen."

Thomas reached for her hand, holding it firmly. "Whether something happened or not, it changes nothing. I love you, Rachel. You did what you could to survive and support your family. That's all that matters."

Rachel hesitated, uncertainty gnawing at her. A confession lingered on her lips, and she knew she had to say it. "There's one more thing." She took a breath, then pressed on. "I think that man at the bar with Levi that night had met me, just briefly, at the House of the Rising Sun. I do remember a young man asking my name. If that was him... if Levi knew that, then I'm responsible for his death."

Thomas shook his head. "No, Rachel. Levi didn't have to defend your honor. Duels were meant for self-appointed aristocrats; a relic of men obsessed with pride and status. Levi wasn't even part of that social class. That planter's son could've declined the challenge and spared both of their lives."

The couple sat silently, their hands entwined. Their confessions had fallen like rain, cleansing their souls and leaving the air around them fresh and alive with the promise of a better tomorrow.

62

A NEW FOREVER

Rachel and Thomas stood beneath a *chuppah* covered with pink roses woven into a garland of greenery near the *bema* in the Dispersed of Judah synagogue. Rabbi Illowy stepped before them with his walking cane to begin the ceremony.

The rabbi was in his fifties, hailing from Bohemia. He was known for his piercing gray eyes, which he would fix intently on any congregant who dared to nod off during his services, a silent signal that never failed to prompt an embarrassed nudge from their companion. He wore a neatly trimmed beard, a dark suit with a matching cravat, and a black, brimless cap prevalent among Central European Jewish communities.

The synagogue was empty except for Rachel, Thomas, Rabbi Illowy, and two male witnesses required by state law and Jewish tradition, just as Rachel had wished. Convincing the rabbi to omit the traditional *minyan* of ten males for the wedding to be halachically valid had been quite a task.

This moment belonged to them alone. It was a sacred space free from spectacle, where their wedding vows would intertwine underneath the floral canopy of the *chupah*, the symbol of their first home together. Here, they would embark on their journey toward a new forever.

They waited for the rabbi to station his walking cane, find his place in the prayer book, and arrange the instruments of the marriage ceremony: the wine bottle, the goblets, the wedding glass wrapped in a silk scarf for the groom to break, and a pen for signing the *Ketubah*, the sacred marriage contract. They exchanged stolen glances, trying not to smile.

Thomas looked lovingly at his radiant bride, her gown of white lace and satin flowing like a soft breeze, the seed pearls glimmering in the candlelight. The delicate strands of *essence d'orient* pearls cascaded down her back like a shimmering waterfall, each bead catching the light with a quiet brilliance.

Rachel, in turn, beamed with pride at her groom in his impeccably tailored black silk suit. He stood as the embodiment of refined strength and quiet resolve, her perfect mate for the path they would now walk together.

Before them stood Rabbi Illowy, his white prayer *tallit* with blue stripes draped over his shoulders. He was bathed in the soft glow of twilight, which was filtering through the windows, marking the traditional beginning of a new day in Judaism. The last rays of sunlight merged with the flickering candlelight, casting an ethereal glow over the room.

"Today," Rabbi Illowy began, his voice carrying softly under the *chupah*, "we bear witness to a covenant between two souls. Not only a promise for this day but a vow for all days to come, through joy and trials yet unseen. Rachel and Thomas, may your love be both a shelter and a guiding light."

Rachel stepped closer to Thomas, her breath easing into a natural rhythm as the warmth of his arm brushed against hers. Thomas gently took her hand, his thumb tracing a small, comforting circle — a symbol of eternity — against her palm. In that simple touch lay a quiet promise, an unspoken vow that resonated with the rabbi's blessing.

Rabbi Illowy recited the traditional blessing over the wine, the rhythmic sound of his voice carrying the ancient Hebrew chant across the ages, binding hundreds of generations together in an unbroken chain from the past to the present.

As the blessing concluded, he offered the ancient prayer that sanctifies a marriage. "Blessed are You, Lord our God, King of the universe, who created the groom and the bride."

Rachel's heart fluttered as Thomas turned to her, holding the small gold band destined for her slender finger. His hands were steady as he met her eyes and spoke softly, "With this ring, I bind my heart to yours." He slipped the ring onto her finger, the cool metal warming instantly against her skin and finding its place beside her engagement ring. She followed suit, placing a wider gold band on his finger and repeating the same vow, her voice a steady counterpoint to her racing heart.

At the end of the vows, the rabbi held up the *Ketubah*, a contract of devotion, its text carefully prepared in advance according to two thousand years of Jewish tradition. With great care, he read aloud the covenant within, affirming the groom's promise to love and support his wife, cherish her as his equal, and build a home filled with trust and compassion. The *Ketubah* acknowledged the matrilineal nature of Judaism, detailing provisions for Rachel and any future children in the event of their marriage dissolution or if Thomas were to pass away before her.

When he finished, the rabbi handed Thomas a pen. "I took the liberty of dating it," he said with a gentle smile. "Today is the twentieth day of the month of Tevet, in the Hebrew year 5623."

Thomas signed first, his pen stroke bold and assured.

The rabbi nodded to two men seated silently in the front pew, inviting them forward to witness the document. Each took the pen in turn, their signatures binding the contract in the eyes of tradition, faith, and law.

The *Ketubah* was complete, now bearing the seal of their shared commitment and the signatures of two impartial witnesses. It would soon be framed and hung with honor in their home, a testament to love and devotion, protected behind glass, that would endure as the years passed.

As the witnesses stepped away, Rabbi Illowy lifted a silver goblet, its surface adorned with delicate engravings of grapevines and clusters of grapes that gleamed in the warm light. Offering a blessing that wove ancient promises into the present, he handed the cup to Rachel and Thomas to share, sanctifying the moment that joined them in spirit and tradition.

With hands intertwined, the couple sipped from the cup, tasting the richness of the wine, a symbol of their shared life ahead. At that moment, they acknowledged both the sweetness and the bitterness that might lie along their path, the intricate vines on the cup echoing the twists and turns of a future they would navigate together.

Rabbi Illowy wrapped a thin silk cloth around a delicate crystal glass for the final ritual and set it near Thomas's foot. "The breaking of this glass," he intoned, "reminds us that even in our greatest joy, we acknowledge the sacredness and fragility of life, just as the Temple in Jerusalem was destroyed in antiquity."

Thomas looked at Rachel one last time, a tender smile passing between them before he lifted his heel. The glass shattered beneath his foot with a sharp crack, followed by a resounding "*Mazel Tov!*" from the rabbi and the witnesses.

Thomas pulled her into his arms, and they shared their first kiss as man and wife beneath the sweetness of the *chuppah.*

Antoine's held a special enchantment that evening. The candlelit room, reserved for the newlyweds, glowed with intimate charm. A bottle of *Veuve Clicquot* Champagne chilled in a bucket beside their table, while at its center rested a delicate arrangement of white rosebuds entwined with rosemary sprigs, their fragrance softly perfuming the air. Flickering candlelight cast a warm, golden hue over the *Ketubah,* laid out carefully on the pristine linen before Rachel.

After studying it carefully, she sighed and said, "It all looks so formal, like a mortgage."

Thomas chuckled, a knowing glint in his eye. "Why do you think so many of our people become attorneys? We are rooted in thousands of years of accountability, shaped by the Torah's laws that make us natural custodians of legal tradition."

Rachel smiled admiringly, leaning into his easy confidence. "Spoken like a true attorney. No objections here, counselor."

"As you know, I'm more Jewish by heritage than by observance, but one tradition I value, besides the emphasis on education, is the respect Judaism accords to women." He nodded toward the marriage contract. "You can see that respect embedded in the *Ketubah*, with its clear outline of a husband's obligations."

"Speaking of obligations," she said, "I haven't yet decided what to do with the Smith & Wesson stock Levi left me. Selling it and investing in something more stable, perhaps gold, might be wise. Levi had predicted the stock would drop after the war and had no plans to hold onto it."

"I think he was right. That stock is unpredictable and tied too closely to firearms demand," he replied thoughtfully. "I've been considering investing in the Pennsylvania Rock Oil Company. Kerosene production is advancing, and it's a cheaper alternative to whale oil for lamps and heating. It could hold promise."

"That makes sense," Rachel nodded. "Oil might shape the future in ways we can't imagine now. Maybe that would be the best investment."

"Just not all of it," he advised with a grin. "Perhaps a variety of investments for broader security would be more prudent. It could include a little oil stock and something more traditional, like railroads."

A glint of anticipation sparkled in her eyes. "Maybe it's time for our first business meeting as a couple. It's never too early to start planning for our family's future."

"Nothing would make me happier," he replied, reaching for her hand.

Thomas's gaze softened, resting on a large leather-bound volume on the table. "The rabbi was thoughtful to give us that book of remembrance as a wedding gift," he said.

Rachel traced the raised golden Hebrew letters on the leather-embossed cover, absorbing their meaning through touch alone. *Generations*, she mused, lingering on the gold letters of the title as if the power of family and legacy were embedded in the surface itself: a tactile connection to something larger than herself.

"Once I've filled in my side of the family tree, we'll add yours," she murmured, enjoying a quiet sense of continuity as she imagined the future they would build together.

Thomas grinned. "Let's hope our branches don't cross somewhere back in France, say in Évian-les-Bains, which some associate with the Garden of Eden due to its idyllic setting."

Rachel's eyes sparkled with joy. "I suppose they might."

"We can always add some new names to the mix," he teased.

"Oh, I already have a list prepared," she replied, a playful glint in her eye.

"A list?" he asked, caught off guard.

Rachel returned a wry smile, squeezing his hand. "I've only chosen a dozen, but I left room for the ones we'll dream up together."

Thomas reached for the *Veuve Clicquot* without missing a beat and poured two glasses. "Here's to us and our future generations. *L'Chaim!*"

"*L'Chaim* — to life!" Rachel replied, raising her glass. The cheerful sound of glasses clinking echoed the love they shared.

As she took a quiet sip, Rachel's gaze lingered on the sparkling golden liquid, its tiny bubbles rising to the surface in delicate streams.

Thomas's selection of *Veuve Clicquot,* or "Widow Clicquot," stirred something in her; it wasn't simply a fine Champagne, but one famously crafted by Barbe-Nicole Clicquot, a woman who, after her husband's death, transformed the modest family winery into an international empire.

Rachel marveled at the unspoken tribute in Thomas's choice. In a single gesture, he honored her as an equal partner.

63

THE COLORS OF FREEDOM

Rachel watched her hired hackney depart in the hush of early morning light at Congo Square. Drawing her cloak tightly around her, she turned toward the entrance of the address she'd been given for the Freedman's School. It was an unassuming two-story brick structure just a few doors from where she had met Loreta two years ago.

So much had changed. She felt almost as if everything had become a strange dream, the kind one might recount only to question its reality. Once, she had been so desperate to support her family that she turned to prostitution. Yet, from that low point, she had unwittingly found herself swept into a spy mission to Port Hudson, risking her life to save the man with whom she traveled from execution as a Union spy. She returned home to lose her sister and regain her husband, only to lose him again in a duel. Then she married the man she knew to be a spy. And now, against all odds and the conventions of her time, she had chosen to become a teacher at a school for freed slaves, a decision as audacious as it was transformative.

Rachel reflected that her life bore an uncanny resemblance to Gerty's in Maria Cummins' *The Lamplighter*. Like the story's heroine, her journey through hardship had been shaped by improbable twists of fate and the kindness of unlikely allies, leading her toward a renewal she scarcely imagined possible.

If she could have traveled back in time to reveal the decisions she would make to her former self and the twists and turns that would follow, she would have thought her future self utterly mad. But now, standing at the threshold of her new life in front of the school building, she felt ready to embrace whatever future lay beyond the door.

Despite the lack of a sign on the building identifying it as a school, she knocked on the door, which had no doorbell. She waited, the seconds stretching into minutes, with no response. Just as she raised her hand to knock again, the door swung open, revealing a tall, sharply dressed freedman in his early sixties.

"Please come in, Mrs. Durand," he invited in Jamaican Patois, his baritone voice as smooth and warm as the rich aroma of freshly brewed Jamaican coffee that wafted out the door to greet her. "We've been expecting you. My name is Mr. Chinn."

"It's a pleasure to meet you, Mr. Chinn," Rachel replied, captivated by the charm of his island accent. "I haven't had the chance to inform you that I was recently married. My married name is Manget."

"Congratulations to the groom, Mrs. Manget," Mr. Chinn offered pleasantly.

Rachel's gaze then caught the initials, V. R. M., boldly seared into his forehead, raising scars. Recognizing them as a slave brand, she quickly looked away, determined not to let the brutal mark of ownership fix her attention.

"It's a pleasure to meet you, Mr. Chinn," Rachel said, extending her hand. As she did, she caught the subtle, earthy scent of sandalwood cologne.

Following Mr. Chinn's welcome, she was greeted in the foyer by a younger freedman, a middle-aged freedwoman with a neatly tied tignon and a tea towel in hand, and five school-aged children—two boys and three girls—standing in a reception line. What immediately struck her was that only one of the boys appeared to be Black, while the other boy and three girls looked White.

"Everyone, I'd like to introduce you to our new teacher, Mrs. Manget," Mr. Chinn announced.

"Good morning, Mrs. Manget," the group chorused in unison.

"Good morning, everyone," Rachel replied, her gaze lingering on the children as she adjusted to the sound of her married name. She turned to Mr. Chinn and asked, "Are these my students?"

"You have these five right now," he said. "We are expecting one more later this afternoon. They range in age from seven to eleven. Let me introduce you. First, we have Master Charles Taylor, then Mistress Rebecca Huger. Next, we have Mistress Rosa Downs, then Mistress Augusta Broujey, and Master Isaac White." He paused. "What do we say, children?"

"Pleased to meet you, Mrs. Manget!" the children exclaimed in chorus, the boys offering polite bows while the girls performed practiced curtsies.

"A pleasure to meet you all," she said, offering her first curtsy since childhood, caught off guard by the children's charm.

"And these are our staff, Miss Mary Johnson and Reverend Robert Whitehead," Mr. Chinn said. "Miss Johnson prepares our noon meal, and Reverend Whitehead is our minister and my assistant."

"A pleasure to meet you, Mrs. Manget," Miss Johnson greeted with a curtsy.

"A pleasure to meet you," the Reverend Whitehead added with a slight bow.

"I'm delighted to meet you all. I look forward to working together," Rachel replied warmly.

"Children, let's show your new teacher her classroom," Mr. Chinn suggested, motioning to a door in the vestibule. "Please," he said, nodding to Rachel, "After you."

The spacious classroom, which had once been a sunroom, now radiated an air of purpose and charm as a place for learning. Sunlight poured in through expansive windows, illuminating six neatly arranged school desks, each equipped with pencils and slates, as well as well-worn reading primers acquired from the local schools. The students' desks faced the teacher's desk, a modest yet commanding piece positioned against the far wall.

Behind it, two large black chalkboards dominated the space, framed by a proudly displayed U.S. flag mounted between them. The chalkboards were meticulously prepared with a well-worn eraser, a pointer, and neatly aligned chalk sticks occupying the troughs below. Above the chalkboard, someone had carefully hand-lettered the alphabet in elegant French cursive.

On one chalkboard, a welcoming message was written in bold, flowing cursive: Welcome, Miss Durand.

Mr. Chinn quietly slipped past the children, took the eraser, and carefully removed Rachel's old surname from the board, replacing it with her new one. "There," he said, with a firm voice that suggested years spent guiding students and correcting their work.

"How lovely," Rachel said, her smile widening at the greeting written on the chalkboard. Her gaze shifted to a wicker basket on the desk, brimming with vibrant oranges and kumquats, their stems still bearing fresh green leaves.

"The children thought you might enjoy taking home some fresh fruit," Mr. Chinn said with a smile.

Rachel lit up at the kind gesture. "What a lovely gift! It appears to have been picked fresh from the orchard. Thank you so much, children. Or should I say, students?"

"You're welcome, Mrs. Manget," the children responded in unison, their young voices reminiscent of a practiced chorus in a school play.

Leaning close, Mr. Chinn whispered to Rachel, "You ought to have seen the younglings at the French Market. Took them the better part of an hour to choose the ripest fruits and reckon out their dearly earned pennies."

Suddenly, Rachel felt a deep sense of belonging, almost like having family again. It was a place where she was loved, valued, and, perhaps, needed once more.

MAISON
DES ESCARGOTS

64

Maison des Escargots

Rachel followed Thomas into a modest restaurant and said, "I've never heard of this restaurant." A large sign at the entrance read *Maison des Escargots* and featured a big snail, its beautifully painted shell reflecting the soft, silvery light of the moon, which hung low in the starry sky.

"Most people haven't," Thomas replied with a grin. "That's one of the reasons I like it. It's never crowded. It's only open for supper, with fresh escargot that's authentically French and gumbo that's truly Creole."

"Escargot and gumbo are my favorite, of course," Rachel said, her eyes lighting up. "Especially with warm, crisp French bread and butter."

"Then you won't be disappointed," he assured her.

She glanced around the room, noting the empty tables. "I don't see a host."

"There's no host here."

"How unusual," Rachel murmured, following Thomas to a table.

The décor was minimal: clean yet worn, with white linen-covered tables, each featuring a single unlit candle set in an empty wine bottle as its centerpiece. The surrounding walls were painted a pale green, and the gas wall sconces were more functional than decorative.

After seating Rachel, Thomas took his place across from her.

A young waiter soon appeared, sporting a peach-fuzz mustache and dressed in a crisp white shirt, sharply creased black trousers, and a white apron. "May I take your order, Monsieur?" he asked without offering a menu.

"Yes, please," Thomas replied. "We'll each have a salad with a dressing of olive oil and wine vinegar, a bowl of gumbo, escargot with two loaves of French bread—extra butter, please—and a chilled bottle of your white table wine."

"Certainly, Monsieur," the waiter nodded before departing.

Rachel was surprised that Thomas had not asked her what she wanted before ordering.

When the waiter was out of earshot, he leaned in, grinning, and whispered, "That's all they serve."

Rachel smiled. "As long as what they serve is good, who needs a large menu or a more refined ambiance?"

Thomas's eyes sparkled. "Sitting here with my beautiful wife is all the ambiance I could ever ask for." Reaching into his pocket, he pulled out a vesta case and struck a light, bringing it to the candle stuck in the wine bottle at the center of the table. "There we go. Now I can see your lovely face better."

"You're so sweet," Rachel said, glancing down to admire her emerald and diamond engagement ring. As she moved her hand, the gem caught the light of the newly lit candle, its various shades of green flickering like fire. She looked up at Thomas, noting how the soft, warm candlelight highlighted his handsome appearance.

"A penny for your thoughts," Thomas said, catching her gaze.

"I was sitting here thinking how handsome you are…and how much I love you."

"What a coincidence," Thomas replied, smiling. "I was sitting here thinking how beautiful you are…and how much I love *you*." He reached for Rachel's hand, and they sat quietly, hands clasped, lost in each other's gaze.

When the waiter returned, he expertly balanced a large serving tray on one hand to place it on a nearby side table. He set the dishes before them with the efficiency of a seasoned professional. "Your gumbo," he said, placing a large pot of gumbo with a ladle between them. "Your utensils," he added, setting silverware wrapped in a plain napkin beside their plates. "Your wine," he continued, smoothly uncorking the bottle and setting it in front of Thomas with two glasses. "And your warm bread, fresh from the oven," he concluded, placing a basket before them, each loaf wrapped in a napkin and accompanied by a dish filled with scoops of butter shaped with a spoon.

"Thank you," Thomas said, offering a polite smile.

"May I bring you anything else?"

"No, thank you," Thomas replied.

The waiter departed with the empty tray, leaving Rachel smiling. "I wonder why he even bothered to ask if he could bring anything else?" she teased. "What more could we have ordered in a place without a menu?"

"Nothing, except dessert and coffee later," Thomas replied with a playful grin. "And, just like the main course, the dessert selection is extensive: pecan pie…or pecan pie. No hurry. Let me know when you've finally made up your mind."

"Ah, just as I suspected," Rachel said, playing along. "It's a difficult decision, and it may take me some time to weigh my options."

Settling the coarse cotton muslin napkins on their laps, they began savoring the escargot, dipping pieces of warm French bread into the pools of garlic butter nestled in each shell. Their eyes met in a silent exchange of shared pleasure in the delicate flavors.

Thomas poured a glass of white wine for himself and one for her. Looking at the label, he said, "I see they still have white Scuppernong wine from Dahlonega, Georgia," he remarked. "None of that is getting across the line anymore."

"That name sounds familiar. Isn't that a small mining town in north Georgia, where there was an early gold rush?

"Yes, indeed. It all began in 1828, two decades before the California Gold Rush, when early settlers stumbled upon nuggets on the streets. Dahlonega's gold boom grew so large that a U.S. Mint was established in the town, producing coins until the outbreak of the war. Bearing the distinctive 'D' mintmark, some coins are still circulated today." He laughed, "My dollar gold ones are all gone now, either spent or lost because they were smaller than a dime. The smallest coin ever minted by the United States."

"You sound like a true numismatist," Rachel said.

"Maybe one day I'll start a collection. The Dahlonega gold dollars are scarcer than those minted elsewhere."

Rachel reached for her glass, and Thomas raised his for a toast.

"Here's to sharing the best escargot in New Orleans with the world's best wife," he said warmly.

"To the best husband a woman could ever want," Rachel replied, clinking her glass against his. "My, this wine is sweet," she said.

"Yes," Thomas replied. "Scuppernong wine tends to be quite sweet. It's usually considered more of a dessert wine, but it's the only one they serve."

"It's different from the *Chablis* served at Antoine's, but I like it."

Thomas set his glass down and turned his attention to her. "I haven't had the chance to hear about your first day at school. I came home late last night and left early this morning, so we had no time to talk."

"I hardly know where to begin," Rachel replied, taking a bite of her salad.

Thomas teased, "It's usually best to start at the beginning, proceed to the middle, and go to the end."

Rachel grinned at Thomas's reference to Aristotle's *Poetics*, where he wrote that every well-crafted narrative has a beginning, a middle, and an end. "You can be so silly sometimes, my love. I suppose I should start with when I knocked on the school door, and a well-dressed freedman gentleman opened it. He introduced himself as Mr. Chinn. At first, his name struck me as Chinese, but I recalled that it could just as well be English, considering he was from Jamaica."

"Yes, Chinn is British, though not a surname one encounters often," Thomas agreed, leaning in as he ladled gumbo and carefully buttered a slice of bread for Rachel.

She took a bite, relishing the crusty bread. "What I saw afterward surprised me even more," she continued.

"Oh?" Thomas encouraged, raising his brows as he ate.

"First, I discovered it was one of the Freedmen's schools, overseen by a Mr. Bacon, with Mr. Chinn in charge." She paused, then added, "I must compliment this bread. It is truly my weakness."

"Mine as well," Thomas murmured, dabbing his mustache with a napkin.

Rachel chuckled softly as he wrestled with the smear of butter, determined to tame it amidst the bristles of his beard. "Mr. Chinn also introduced me to a younger freedman, Reverend Whitehead, their minister, and Mr. Chinn's assistant. They seem quite prepared to grow their school."

"It's good that they're ready to expand," Thomas noted.

"They even have a cook, Mary Johnson, who fled from a plantation. She had scars on her arm. During lunch, I asked her how she had come by them."

Thomas paused, looking up from his meal. "What did she say?"

"She told me she had been half an hour late serving her master's coffee because her mistress expanded her chores, and he lashed her three times on the arm. The very next day, Union soldiers passed through, and she fled straight to them."

"And they took her in?"

Rachel nodded. "Yes, they did. They escorted her to New Orleans, where she was hired as the school's cook. And Thomas, let me tell you, the cornbread and black-eyed peas she served were nothing short of extraordinary."

Thomas said, "Sounds like you won't need to pack a lunch for school."

"That is indeed convenient. The school now has only six pupils. The sixth, a young girl, came in at the end of class, so I only met her briefly."

"A small class must be a delight for you. It allows you to devote more attention to each student."

"Yes, but it was not the class size that caught me off guard. It was that four out of the six students appeared to be White. The youngest girl looks like a little porcelain doll. I could have just scooped her up in a hug."

"She sounds charming, dear."

"She was. But what shocked me was that Mr. Chinn had the branded initials of his former owner on his forehead."

"That must have been quite unsettling for you."

"To say the least. Outlawing branding should be straightforward now that slavery is in the process of being abolished."

"That should certainly be among the priorities on the new legislative agenda once Banks manages to hold elections. President Lincoln has been pushing hard on the issues of Reconstruction and the return of Louisiana to statehood. He wants it to be the first. Along with his speech to Congress last December, the President proclaimed that whenever the voters of a seceding state re-establish a loyal state government, it should be accepted back into the Union."

"Would that mean the government would establish separate schools for Whites and Coloreds? I cannot imagine how they could manage it when telling the races apart is difficult, if not impossible, for many."

"General Banks expressed similar frustration," Thomas remarked. "In New Orleans, the lines between White and Colored were often blurred, especially when it came to free men of mixed ancestry enlisting in the *Corps d'Afrique* or the regular army. It made his task all the more complicated."

It reminds me of last year when White people complained about Negroes boarding the streetcars downtown," Rachel added. "Butler's soldiers taunted them, saying they had no problem sharing a bed with their slaves, so why balk at sitting beside them?"

"There's more than a little truth to that," Thomas remarked, raising an eyebrow as he sipped his wine.

"How on earth will society adapt to all this?" Rachel wondered aloud. "For generations, the government has used skin color to separate the races. Now, skin color is no longer a reliable indicator. Will the new government force everyone to carry identification and document their racial heritage?"

"God help us, I hope not," Thomas replied. "Though I wouldn't put it past some hardliners to start digging through old records to prove ancestry."

Rachel shuddered yet remained silent, recoiling at the thought.

"I suppose," Thomas continued thoughtfully, "the issue will only fade when people recognize that skin color is merely a physical trait, nothing more, and has no bearing on a person's character."

She sighed. "I doubt we'll live to see that day, Thomas."

"Perhaps not, my dear. But one day, far into the future, after much struggle, bloodshed, and hardship, I believe it will come to pass."

"Setting skin color aside," she continued, "if I had closed my eyes today in the classroom, I would have found all the students equally intelligent."

"Does that surprise you?"

"Society didn't teach me to see slaves as people with minds or feelings, Thomas," she said. "You have shown me a different world, where respect is earned and given freely, not due to wealth or birthright, but because of character."

"I chose you," he said gently, taking her hand, "because you have a good heart and a brilliant mind. Most importantly, you are unafraid to grow. That's what makes you remarkable."

"Dessert, anyone?" The waiter's voice broke in unexpectedly, his sudden appearance pulling them back to the present.

"I believe the lady is still weighing her options," Thomas replied with a perfectly straight face.

Rachel's smile widened as she struggled to keep from laughing—both at Thomas's dry humor and the earnest expression on the waiter's face, given that there was only one dessert choice.

65

THE GRAND REUNION

The St. Charles Hotel bustled with anticipation as it became the epicenter of a grand assembly, orchestrated by the well-connected Mrs. Benjamin Rush Plumly and sponsored by her husband, Major Benjamin Rush Plumly. The hotel's expansive parlors, segregated for the evening—one for ladies and the other for gentlemen—stretched an entire block. Draped with national banners and floral arrangements, the grand venue exuded an air of patriotic elegance.

Dozens of prominent wives attended the ladies' parlor, their identities overshadowed by their husbands' names. This reflected the customary British common law doctrine of coverture, which dictated that a woman's identity and property were subsumed under her husband's control. Among the *femmes covert* were Mrs. Nathaniel P. Banks, Mrs. Stone, Mrs. Beckwith, Mrs. Holabird, Mrs. Waldron, Mrs. Major Howe, Mrs. Colonel Bostwick, and Mrs. Wright.

In the gentlemen's parlor, newly commissioned portraits of Major General Nathaniel P. Banks and Vice Admiral David Farragut, created by the renowned maritime artist Mauritz Frederik De Haas, stood prominently draped in Army and Navy flags, paying tribute to their steadfast leadership.

The event attracted over five hundred guests, including the distinguished Major General Banks and Rear Admiral Farragut, as guests of honor. By Banks's side stood Brigadier General James Bowen, recently appointed Provost Marshal of the Department of the Gulf, who managed civil matters.

The harmonious strains of a ten-piece band wove through the air, complementing the lively conversations and the clinking of Champagne glasses. The room teemed with palpable energy, charged by the patriotic fervor of Union leaders committed to preserving the Union and shaping Louisiana's future.

Notably, representatives of New Orleans' long-established elite, previously hesitant to attend Union gatherings, were present, signaling a significant shift in the city's social dynamics. The presence of these influential civilians at Union events indicated a growing acceptance of the new order and a desire to align with the prevailing power structure to influence the city's future.

At the front of the room, between the looming freshly painted portraits of Banks and Farragut, Major Plumly tapped his Champagne glass with a silver spoon. "Gentlemen, may I have your attention, please?" The room quieted. "I am honored here tonight by your presence. We have assembled a group of Union officers and statesmen, all to honor your roles in achieving our recent local victories and steel ourselves against the monumental task ahead of us to reunite our nation. Turning to the portraits behind him, he said, "On this wall hang the portraits of Major General Banks and Rear Admiral Farragut, two of our nation's heroes who played major roles in reopening the passage along the mighty Mississippi. As our President said, 'The Father of Waters again goes unvexed to the sea.'"

The crowd applauded, a wave of appreciation and support rolling through the room.

"And soon, Major General Banks will turn his efforts to opening the Red River from Shreveport to Texas."

A thunderous applause rose again, the excitement building.

"And Rear Admiral Farragut will bring his formidable fleet to bear upon Mobile."

The applause swelled, voices lifting in cheers.

"So tonight, let us strengthen our resolve, gird ourselves for the challenges ahead, and, in the words of the late Daniel Webster, celebrate 'Liberty and Union, now and forever, one and inseparable.'"

The room erupted once more, applause and the rhythm of stomping feet resounding like the steady drumbeat of an advancing army.

As Thomas mingled among the distinguished guests dedicated to assuring a Union victory while poised to shape the future of Reconstruction, he recognized George W. Miller, a prominent New Orleans resident who operated a boarding house on Felicity Street between Baronne and Dryades Streets. The establishment had gained a reputation as a gathering place for itinerant actors and other visitors, some of whom were suspected of harboring Confederate sympathies.

General Butler had once marked Miller for banishment to Ship Island. However, when General Banks arrived, he opted to monitor Miller's activities instead and tasked Thomas with infiltrating his operations. Of particular interest was Miller's association with the famous actor John Wilkes Booth, who was rumored to be planning a performance in the city between late March and early April.

Booth had already drawn the attention of Union agents due to his increasingly overt Confederate sympathies and remarks overheard backstage as well as directed at the President during a performance of *The Marble Heart* in Washington last November.

Thomas recognized the seriousness of his mission. He suspected that Miller's boarding house was more than just a home and a meeting place for Confederate sympathizers; it might also be a center for covert activities. Booth's upcoming visit increased the urgency, as his presence could rally local Confederate supporters.

Thomas's task was straightforward: infiltrate Miller's circle, gather intelligence on Booth's plans, and report any threats to Banks.

"Mr. Miller," Thomas said, extending his hand. "My name is Thomas Manget. My father was a planter up near Baton Rouge."

"Ah, yes, Master Manget," Miller said, returning the handshake. "I know your father's reputation as a strict taskmaster. He often stayed in my boarding house on his trips to New Orleans."

"I seem to recall him speaking of you as well," Thomas said. "I wanted to speak with you because word has it that Mr. Booth may be rooming at your boarding house soon."

"Yes, he has written to me asking for accommodations."

"Would it be an imposition for me to meet Mr. Booth when he arrives?"

"Seeing that you are our people, I can arrange that. Do you have an address where I might dispatch a message when he arrives?"

"Certainly," Thomas said, retrieving his *carte de visite*, which bore the address of "General Delivery, New Orleans Post Office."

To my dearest love,
Rachel

66

VALENTINE'S DAY

Just before noon, Rachel glanced out the parlor window and saw Thomas in front of the house, tying his horse's reins to the hitching post and retrieving something from the bench seat of his phaeton. At the sight of him, her heart gave a quiet flutter. She had missed that feeling—the warmth that settled low in her chest, like embers stirred to life at the whisper of his name.

She turned from the window and quickly walked into the foyer. "Thomas!" she greeted, opening the door wide. "I was beginning to worry about you. I knew you had to be out of town on business, but I had expected you back sooner."

"Sorry to be late, darling," he replied, stepping to the doorway to kiss her cheek. "Happy Valentine's Day." His arms were laden with a dozen soft pink roses, a box of chocolates, and an intricately decorated Valentine's card. He gave her a playful grin. "I'd give you a proper hug, but as you can see, I'm a bit encumbered."

"Oh, Thomas!" she exclaimed, her eyes bright with delight as she took the roses. "Let's sit in the parlor before the fire so I can admire these properly while you get warm."

In the parlor, Thomas removed his overcoat and draped it over the end of the sofa. He then took the roses from her and offered her a Valentine before settling beside her with the roses on his lap.

Rachel's eyes widened with delight as she noticed the loving inscription, "To my dearest love, Rachel." She looked up, visibly moved. "The design reminds me of the roses on my *chuppah*," she murmured. "Who created this?"

"There's an elderly woman in Baton Rouge who makes these cards each year for

Valentine's Day," Thomas explained. "She crafts the roses and leaves from tissue paper, then arranges them on lace with a heart appliqué. She even mentioned that the paper backing is made from linen."

"How beautiful," Rachel whispered, running her fingers gently over the intricate flowers and lace.

Thomas's smile spread across his face.

Rachel's gaze returned to the card, savoring every detail. She felt a warmth in her heart, grateful for the care her husband had taken to make the day so special.

Thomas leaned in and gently pressed his lips to hers. The kiss was soft and unhurried, a tender moment that lingered.

"Should I find a vase for the roses, so they stay fresh?" he asked.

"Yes, please. They will wilt soon without water, and I want to enjoy them as long as I can," she replied, still feeling the afterglow of the kiss. "You can find a vase in the kitchen pantry on the top shelf."

Thomas disappeared into the kitchen with the roses, leaving Rachel alone with her valentine. She continued admiring the card, savoring the beauty of each handmade detail.

Thomas soon returned with a serving tray, a large flower vase filled with water, and two cups of tea. He placed the tray on the table before the sofa, arranged the roses in the vase, and set them on the mantel. "I thought you might like to share a warm cup of tea by the fire and enjoy some chocolates," he said.

Rachel opened the heart-shaped box of chocolates, carefully unwrapping a piece. "Mmm," she murmured, savoring the taste. "These are delightful. Here, have one."

Thomas accepted a chocolate with a smile. "These are delicious," he said, relishing the rich flavor.

"The fire is wonderful, isn't it?" Rachel asked, gazing into the fireplace. "And I love where you placed the roses so I can enjoy them." She leaned forward to take a sip of her tea. "Shall we toast?"

"*Mais certainment, Madame,*" Thomas said, raising his cup.

"*L'chaim,*" she said. "To life — with each other."

"*L'chaim,*" he returned.

I never did ask you about the reunion you attended at St. Charles last week. I read about it in the *Daily True Delta*, but I'd like to hear what it was like being there."

"It was rather grand," Thomas said. "All the top brass and just about every local official you can name. They dedicated portraits of Banks and Farragut and spoke of reconstruction."

"Reconstruction?" Rachel inquired. "Isn't it premature to discuss rebuilding while the war continues?"

"President Lincoln insists that Louisiana be the first state readmitted to the Union," Thomas began. "He believes that moving as soon as possible toward reuniting the secessionist states shows strength. To that end, General Banks is organizing elections and other initiatives based on the Ten Percent Plan."

"The plan that ten percent of a state's voters have to swear an oath of allegiance to the Union?"

"The very same. Towards that end, General Banks has appointed Brigadier General James Bowen as Provost Marshal to oversee civil affairs while he leads the Red River Campaign."

"I see," Rachel said thoughtfully.

"They also discussed establishing public schools," Thomas continued.

Rachel's curiosity was piqued. "Oh?"

"Yes," Thomas said. "There was hesitation about integrating schools, but some insisted that all races should attend together."

"I can understand the difficulty," Rachel said sadly. "Some White people are still resisting mixing with freedmen."

Thomas finished telling the story of the reunion, leaving out what was most important to him: his chance encounter with George Millier, and his plan to meet John Wilkes Booth and others suspected of conspiring to aid the Confederacy.

As their conversation naturally waned, an unspoken understanding passed between them. They reached for each other's hands; the touch was charged with the excitement of young love.

Without breaking their gaze, they rose together, moving silently up the staircase toward the sanctuary of their bedroom.

67

THE INAUGURATION OF GOVERNOR HAHN

By mid-morning, golden sunlight drenched Lafayette Square, illuminating the busy junction of St. Charles and Poydras Streets. It filtered through the canopy of fresh spring leaves, casting a delicate chiaroscuro across the ground as shifting patterns of shadow and light played beneath the trees.

The square's strategic location in the heart of French Town, with the iconic City Hall and St. Charles Hotel visible nearby, made it an ideal site for the inauguration of the first elected governor of Union-occupied Louisiana.

A wooden platform, erected for the occasion, stood in the heart of the square, draped in red, white, and blue bunting that rippled in the gentle spring breeze. Union flags and banners reflected federal authority and the hope for a restored nation.

A throng of citizens gathered throughout the morning, bringing their pastries, fresh fruit, and jugs of coffee, water, or hard cider as suited their tastes. Many ladies brought colorful parasols to shade their fair complexions from the sun.

On the platform stood Michael Hahn, his figure sharp against the backdrop of the blue morning sky. He was a man of medium build, his features framed by neatly trimmed dark hair and a beard in the style of a cavalier. His black frock coat was immaculate, and in his hand, he held a letter from President Lincoln on Executive Mansion stationery. He stood proudly, soon to be inaugurated as Louisiana's first occupation governor, after his successful election on February 22, less than two weeks earlier.

The air hummed with the low murmur of conversation, punctuated by the distant clang of a blacksmith's hammer from Chartres Street and the faint, rhythmic beat of a military drum corps approaching from the east.

Banks stood to Hahn's right, his hands clasped behind his back, his posture as stiff as his neatly pressed blue uniform. His presence underscored the military authority still dominating New Orleans. Union officers, local dignitaries, and prominent citizens filled the seats on the platform, their faces a spectrum of hope, skepticism, and solemn pride.

A notable feature of the event was the musical accompaniment provided by the renowned band leader Patrick S. Gilmore. He assembled all available military musicians in New Orleans, supplemented by civilian talent, creating a combined force of over five hundred performers. This grand assembly, dubbed by him a "monster concert," was the first of its kind in the nation.

The notes of "The Star-Spangled Banner," "Battle Hymn of the Republic," and "My Country 'Tis of Thee" enhanced the celebratory atmosphere, reinforcing the Unionist sentiments of the gathering. The swelling music echoed off the facades of nearby buildings, blending with the crowd's energy.

A hush settled over the square as Hahn stepped forward, his shoes thudding lightly on the wooden platform. The crowd's murmur faded into expectant silence. He unfolded the letter he held with care, his fingers steady despite the moment's weight. Hahn's gaze swept the crowd, and for a moment, his eyes lingered on the rows of freedmen standing toward the front: men, women, and children whose lives had been irrevocably changed since the beginning of the occupation.

"Fellow citizens of Louisiana," he began, his voice clear and strong. "I have in my hand a letter from President Abraham Lincoln. I will read it now, for its message belongs to you as much as it belongs to me."

The crowd stilled, drawn in by the gravity of his tone. Hahn's eyes returned to the page, and he read aloud:

Executive Mansion, Washington, February 27, 1864.

To Michael Hahn, Governor-elect of Louisiana:

I congratulate you on having fixed your name in history as the first free-state governor of Louisiana. Now, you are about to have a Convention, which, among other things, will probably define the elective franchise. I barely suggest for your private consideration whether some of the colored people may not be let in—as, for instance, the very intelligent, and especially those who have fought gallantly in our ranks. They would probably help, in some trying time to come, to keep the jewel of liberty within the family of freedom. But this is only a suggestion, not to the public, but to you alone.

Yours truly, A. Lincoln

The crowd's reaction was a swell of emotions after hearing the President's urging to "let in" the "very intelligent" of the colored people to the legislature. The newly freed slaves clasped their hands together, their faces a blend of awe and resolve. Soldiers nodded solemnly, and one man shouted "Amen!" across the square. Women dabbed their eyes with handkerchiefs, overcome by the moment's gravity.

Hahn folded the letter slowly and slipped it into his coat pocket. He lifted his eyes to meet the crowd once more. "This is not merely an inauguration," he continued, his voice rising in stentorian tones. "This is a commitment to justice, progress, and the preservation of the Union. President Lincoln's vision is not one of vengeance but of unity. My solemn duty is to ensure that Louisiana leads the South not into the darkness of rebellion but into the light of a free and prosperous future."

Cheers broke from the crowd, beginning in scattered bursts but growing in strength like a rising tide.

Hahn raised his hand, calling for quiet. "Today, I take an oath not merely as a man but as a servant of the people. The task before us will not be easy. It will demand every ounce of our will and every spark of our compassion. But with God's grace, we shall prevail."

Reverend Thomas Conway stepped forward to offer a benediction. He lifted his hands toward the sky, his palms open as if gathering the people's prayers. "Almighty God," he intoned, his deep voice resonating with power. "Bless this man, this people, and this land. May we walk with righteousness and mercy, and may the wounds of war give way to the healing of peace."

"Amen," came the crowd's thunderous reply, their voices blending.

As Hahn lifted his right hand to take the oath of office, the sun's light caught the polished brass of a Union soldier's belt buckle in the crowd as he sat in a wheeled chair. General Banks raised his hand in a silent salute to the soldier as Hahn's voice rang out: "I, Michael Hahn, do solemnly swear..."

Rachel and Thomas stood at the back of the crowd, taking in the moment.

"Do you think the other states will come along?" Rachel asked.

"In time," Thomas said solemnly. "This was Lincoln's special project, and it has yet to be finished."

"A journey of a thousand miles begins with a single step," she murmured, almost to herself, recalling one of her father's favorite sayings.

"That's the idea," Thomas replied softly. "That's the whole idea."

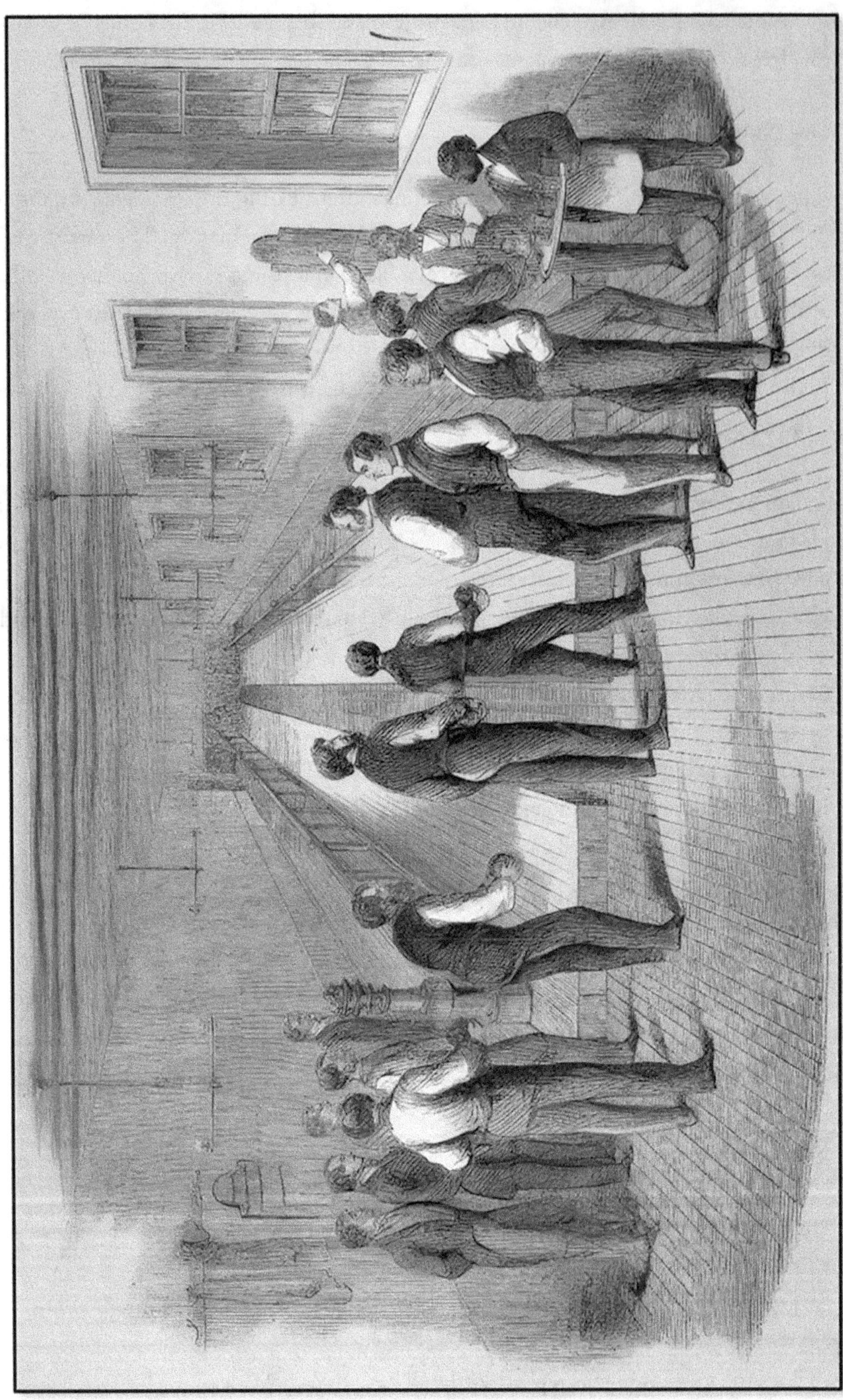

68

BOOTH PLAYS NEW ORLEANS

Draped in a silk night robe, John Wilkes Booth sat comfortably in a leather-upholstered armchair, his gaze drifting around his familiar room in New Orleans. He found comfort in this retreat and enjoyed the company of the owner, George Miller, a fellow Confederate known for his hospitality.

Booth also appreciated the refined elegance of the lodging and its prime location in the upper section of the city, where affluence and British heritage intertwined to afford him a comforting sense of belonging. The only Negroes in sight were gardeners, servants, or liverymen essential to upholding the genteel comforts of the household and tending to the needs of its discerning guests. More importantly to him, they knew their place.

A glass of bourbon rested in Booth's hand as he browsed through the theatrical notices and reviews of local newspapers, his eyes scanning the columns intently. In a departure from routine, he had purposely refrained from reading the theatrical reviews until the conclusion of his engagement in town, dedicating his days to rigorous rehearsals and his nights to spirited revelry with friends at the local taverns.

Now, with his three-week run drawing packed audiences and eliciting enthusiastic applause and repeated curtain calls, he anticipated glowing reviews from the critics. He reassured himself that their positive critiques would compensate for the negative feedback to his previous engagement in Nashville, where one critic observed that he looked "tired."

Eagerly anticipating his debut performance as Shakespeare's malevolent, humpbacked monarch, Richard III, at the St. Charles Theatre on Monday, March 14, newspapers in New Orleans had dispatched reporters to pen their reviews. Several seasoned critics had already witnessed two earlier renditions of the same play at the same theatre: first by Booth's late father, the British Shakespearean actor Junius Brutus, and later by his elder brother, Edwin. Consequently, expectations were high for the younger Booth's performance, and critics arrived anxious to delve into their troves of superlatives.

Struggling to focus his blurred, double vision, Booth squinted at the *Times-Picayune* review of *Richard III* by the light of the kerosene lamp on the bedside table. Drunkenly slurring, he read, "Great expectations of Mr. Booth's ability as a tragedian had been formed... mainly because he is the son of one who, as Gloster, had no equal, and the brother of one who, as a tragedian, already occupies a proud position. We think these expectations have not been fully satisfied...his performance disappointed us."

What more, he asked himself, could he have done to deliver a better performance? Determined to captivate New Orleans' notoriously jaded audience, he had selected Colley Cibber's condensed version of *Richard III* from Samuel French, carefully adjusted with more violent action than Shakespeare had portrayed. He had thoroughly reviewed every scene, crafted precise stage directions, and even sent his prompt book weeks ahead through Union lines so the local cast could rehearse. He had practiced his part a thousand times, perfecting his timing and delivery. Aside from an inconvenient bout of laryngitis, he was as prepared as anyone could be, even more so than his father or brothers had ever been.

Tearing the review to shreds, he angrily flung the paper strips on the floor beside his chair. Reaching for *The Daily True Delta* next, he read, "His acting last Sunday night gave assurance that he will, when time and experience have settled on his brow, be fully equal to his sire."

He could have basked in the reflected glory of his father's legacy in the review, dismissing the tempered praise. However, it was more than he could tolerate when coupled with the *Times-Picayune* acclaim for Edwin's performance as Richard III. "May the devil take my father! And damn my brother, as well!" he hissed, tearing *The Daily True Delta*'s review to shreds. His intended shout was reduced to a raspy oath, stifled by persistent laryngitis that had plagued him for days.

Damn his family, indeed. Soon, he would have the chance to prove himself against his older brothers, Edwin and Junius, in his upcoming performance of *Julius Caesar* as a prestigious fundraiser in New York for the dedication of a statue of William Shakespeare in Central Park. He vowed that his Mark Antony would outshine Edwin's Brutus and Junius' Cassius, leaving no doubt who was the best of the Booths.

Racing through several more papers, he found that the reviews were no better for the fourteen performances he had given over the last three weeks. These ranged from Shakespeare's high tragedy, *Hamlet,* to the English version of Théodore Barrière's Pygmalion-esque play, *The Marble Heart,* to Bulwer-Lytton's convoluted but popular melodrama, *The Lady of Lyons*. He had performed his entire bathetic repertoire to ensure there was something for everyone, hoping to attract large audiences since he was now low on funds and needed cash.

Reaching for the last newspaper in the stack, *The Times-Democrat*, he read, "Seldom have we seen a man whose age and talent so well evinces that dramatic talent is intuitive, and not to be cultivated with years…Mr. Booth seeks not to play a part, but to be intrinsically of it."

"Finally," he smirked, carefully folding the paper and setting it aside on the nightstand, savoring his solitary laurel.

A growing sadness overcame him as he stared at the shredded newspaper pile beside his chair. His three-week engagement in New Orleans, initially planned for five weeks, had been cut short by his unexplained loss of energy, laryngitis, and a growing lack of interest in the things that once gave him pleasure.

Even when he left the theatre for an evening of tenpins, he had to feign enjoyment while drinking with his friends. For some reason, he felt distant and detached, unable to experience the joy that once came with camaraderie and freely flowing spirits.

He had also noticed a growing inability to restrain himself from expressing hatred for the Yankees and the occupation. Before New Orleans, he had played in the Union-occupied city of Nashville and had managed to maintain his composure.

But New Orleans was different. Here, his hatred of all things Northern grew stronger. He even broke into a public performance of "The Bonnie Blue Flag," a song outlawed in the city since Butler's original occupation. He had laughed when his drinking buddies abandoned him, dispersing just before Union officers arrived. Fortunately, he managed to charm an officer who had enjoyed one of his performances, claiming he had heard the song somewhere, was visiting the city, and had no idea it was banned.

He suspected that the deep-seated anger smoldering beneath his melancholy had begun when he witnessed the city's social structure crumble under occupation. The St. Charles Theatre, once the pinnacle of New Orleans high society, now welcomed free Negroes and Union soldiers, transforming what had been a bastion of the city's social elite into a space that locals viewed as tarnished by the changes of the war-torn era.

Then there was his performance as the central character in *The Marble Heart*. It brought back memories of Washington last November when he played the same role at Ford's Theatre, with Lincoln in attendance. Seeing the man he deemed a heartless autocrat seated in a specially designed box on stage had instantly ignited a burst of anger. He remembered directing his most venomous lines toward the President while he sat with his wife and their friends, doing everything he could to resist the urge to leap over the railing and strangle him.

He also recalled his indignation at receiving Lincoln's note backstage after the play, inviting him to the Executive Mansion.

While staring at the empty whiskey bottle on the lamp table, there was a knock at the door.

"Who's there?" he asked, barely able to understand his own slurred words.

"It's me, George," came the reply. "Did I wake you, John?"

Booth wrestled with getting to his feet, not bothering to close his nightrobe to cover his nakedness. Cracking the door open, he saw his friend, George Miller, the boarding house proprietor.

"Oh!" Miller exclaimed upon seeing Booth in déshabillé. Deliberately shifting his gaze, he looked past him at the shredded newspapers, dirty socks scattered across the floor, and an empty whiskey bottle on the bedside table. "Beg your pardon, John. I see you're indisposed."

Unfazed by his nakedness, Booth casually tied his robe. "How may I help you?" he asked, trying to maintain a dignified demeanor while suppressing a hiccup.

Backing up a step because of the offensive odor of stale whiskey and unwashed socks, Miller asked, "Since you're leaving tomorrow, John, would you join me downstairs for a special breakfast to see you off?"

Booth yawned. "It will be my pleasure."

"Good. I'll see you in the morning around ten," Miller said, smiling at his inebriated friend. "Enjoy the remainder of your evening."

69

THE SECRET ROOM

At precisely ten o'clock the next morning, Booth came down the stairs dressed in his travel attire and polished brown shoes, carrying a matching leather valise. He appeared alert and cheerful as he entered the dining room.

The room was spacious, featuring a bank of windows that filled the area with natural light and a wall of walnut bookshelves. The central dining table, set beneath a sparkling crystal gasolier, was elegantly draped with a white lace tablecloth and a gold linen runner. A sterling silver epergne adorned the center of the table. From its polished base rose four slender, hand-blown crystal vases, surrounding a larger central vase. Each vase was shaped like a flower blossom, with a deep throat on a delicate silver stem, and held a single pristine red rosebud.

At the head of the table sat Booth's host, George W. Miller, a well-dressed man of medium height in his late thirties with a neatly groomed beard. To Booth's surprise, he noticed Hiram Martin, his ten-pin bowling companion from the previous evening, sitting beside Miller. Martin was a young man of about his age and build, but not as handsome.

"Good morning, John," Miller greeted, standing to shake his friend's hand. "Ready for the road again, I take it."

"Good morning, George," Booth replied, flashing his signature smile. "I didn't expect to see you here after last night, Hiram. Especially after I won the last few rounds of tenpins and emptied your purse."

Martin laughed, standing to shake Booth's hand. "Wouldn't miss the chance to see a fellow Southron off, old friend. I didn't expect to see you up this early after our evening of libations. I don't know if you remember, but I took care of your tab and gave you a ride home in the cab so you wouldn't end up in the calaboose."

"I am in your debt, sir," Booth returned with a stage bow.

After the men took their seats and exchanged pleasantries about their camaraderie over the past three weeks, a Negro woman entered the room with a cart. She served a large loaf of freshly baked Sally Lunn bread wrapped in a linen napkin and placed in a wicker basket. She also served butter and orange marmalade in matching Blue Willow serving pieces. She then set a chilled bottle of Champagne in an ice bucket on a stand nearby.

"Thank you, Fanny," Miller said. "The bread smells delicious. I'll let you know if we require anything else."

"Yassuh," Fanny returned, leaving the room.

"That old darky makes the best Sally Lunn bread this side of England," Miller said, opening the napkin to break off a piece of the warm delicacy and place it on his bread plate. "Here, have some," he added, passing the basket to Booth. "You'll find it's buttery, but not too sweet."

"It does smell delightful," Booth agreed, appreciating the crisp crust as he broke off a piece. "Reminds me of the Sally Lunn bread my brother Edwin and I enjoyed when we traveled to Bath back in '54 during our London tour."

"I couldn't help but notice that you finally read the reviews, John," Miller ventured, changing the subject.

Booth glowered. "Damn the critics," he growled. "I hope they all rot in hell."

"Damn them to hell!" Martin agreed, pounding his fist on the table.

"I say pay no heed to the literary Philistines," Miller advised with a knowing smile. "Critics are like shadows at sunset, John, long and dark but fleeting, while your admirers, like the light of dawn, are steady and enduring, illuminating the path ahead."

Booth smiled at his friend's support. "Thank you for the kind words, George."

"The folks in this town have gone thirsty a long while, John," Martin said. "They've had nothing but Christie's Minstrels to quench them. You were an oasis in the desert."

"Speaking of being dry," Miller said, standing to reach for the Champagne. "It's the last bottle I managed to hide from the Yanks. Why don't we have some refreshment for ourselves?"

"Hear, hear!" Martin cheered. "Now that's the spirit."

Miller popped the cork and filled three crystal glasses. Lifting his glass, he said, "A toast."

"Yes," Martin echoed, raising his own. "A toast to our esteemed guest… the rascal!"

Miller added, "To John Wilkes Booth, our friend and world-renowned actor."

"Hear, hear!" Martin cried as their glasses clinked together in a sharp, celebratory sound.

After downing their drinks, Miller passed the warm loaf of bread around the table. "I can't get enough of this," he commented, savoring his buttered bread. "And don't forget to taste the marmalade. Fannie made it fresh from oranges in my garden."

Martin's features sobered. "George, you're the historian among us. How in tarnation did we get ourselves into this war?"

Miller arched an eyebrow, a glint of mischief in his eye. "Are you inviting me to give one of my lectures?"

Martin chuckled. "I suppose so if it would help me understand how we got ourselves into this mess in the first place."

Miller leaned back in his chair. "To understand how we arrived at this bitter moment in our nation's history, we must start at the beginning and explain a series of decisions—compromises, they were called—that have led us to this war."

He took a sip of Champagne. "First, let's consider the Three-Fifths Clause, written into the Constitution in 1787. At the time, the Founding Fathers grappled with how enslaved people would be counted in the census. The Southern states, whose economies were deeply rooted in slavery, insisted that slaves be fully counted to increase their representation in Congress while simultaneously arguing they should not be counted for determining their share of federal taxes. The Northern states strongly opposed this contradiction. The compromise? Each enslaved person would be counted as three-fifths of a human being, allowing the South greater representation in Congress and the Electoral College, as well as lowering the apportioned taxation of the Southern States."

"That much I know," Martin said. "The Constitution grants us the right to own slaves, as President Davis has maintained."

"So much for the first compromise. Then came the Missouri Compromise of 1820. By this time, the tensions over slavery were growing as our nation expanded west. Missouri wanted to enter the Union as a slave state, but that would upset the balance between free and slave states. To placate both sides, Congress admitted Missouri as a slave state and Maine as a free state. More importantly, it drew a line at the 36°30′ parallel across the Louisiana Territory. North of that line, slavery was to be prohibited—except in Missouri, of course. Many in the South argued that Congress had no right to restrict slavery in any state without amending the Constitution. However, the South ultimately gave in because the compromise brought peace for a time but later became a symbol of division and political tension."

Miller paused, his gaze shifting out the window to the horizon as if he could see the specter of conflict rising from the ground. "Then the Mexican War provided us with vast new territories, and the question loomed: Would Congress allow slavery? Once again, politicians sought to strike a balance, this time in the Compromise of 1850, without amending the Constitution. California entered the Union as a free state, but the South got its due with a stricter Fugitive Slave Act, which compelled even the free states to return escaped slaves to their rightful owners. The act enraged abolitionists and fueled the Underground Railroad, causing further tensions. Meanwhile, the territories of Utah and New Mexico were left to decide the matter of slavery for themselves through popular sovereignty. This notion was destined to come back and haunt us in regional conflicts."

The men's faces were grim. Miller took a breath to continue.

"And then, in 1854, came the Kansas-Nebraska Act. Senator Stephen Douglas, seeking Southern support for a transcontinental railroad, introduced legislation that created the territories of Kansas and Nebraska, allowing their settlers to decide whether to permit slavery through popular sovereignty. In doing so, the legislation nullified the Missouri Compromise line, opening new lands for owning slaves. The result was bloodshed. 'Bleeding Kansas,' they called it, as pro-slavery and anti-slavery settlers clashed in violence and murder. It tore apart political parties, led to the rise of the Republican Party, and brought us one step closer to the brink of war."

Miller glanced around the room, his gaze steady and deliberate. "You see, my friends, these four compromises—made in 1787, 1820, 1850, and 1854—were like coal torpedoes thrown into the furnace of the nation's conflicts, each one destined to ignite and explode in its own time."

"I don't think I've ever heard anyone explain it so clearly, George," Martin said. "Thank you."

"My pleasure."

"I never did ask you, George," Booth said, appearing restless. "Speaking of slaves, how did you manage to keep that servant of yours? You didn't sign the Oath of Allegiance, did you?"

"I give her a room and a small salary, and she says she's happy staying here. She told me she has nowhere else to go since her last owner sold her children years ago. Little has changed in our relationship, except that she is no longer my property." He leaned back in his chair. "In a strange way, I don't mind. It relieves me of the responsibility of providing for her in her old age."

"As long as you can use her to cook and clean, I suppose that's good."

"I find the relationship satisfactory," Miller agreed, his attention drifting. "I never asked you, John. How do you feel about joining our resistance?"

"Resistance?" Booth asked, trying not to speak with his mouth full.

"When we've finished our breakfast, I want to show you something you might find interesting," Miller replied, pulling out his pocket watch. "Enjoy your coffee. I expect a new friend to be joining us soon."

After the trio finished breakfast, Miller led his guests to his bookcase. "I'm proud of my library," he said, gesturing to shelves of gold-embossed leather-bound classics.

"Yes," Booth agreed, his eyes alighting on a thick volume of Shakespeare's works beside a slimmer collection of Sophocles' seven surviving plays. "Quite an extensive collection."

"Seems someone's at the front door," Miller said, hearing the faint ring of the doorbell.

He stood and stepped briskly to the door and opened it, revealing Thomas Manget, dressed in a dark blue suit.

"Come on in, Thomas," Miller greeted warmly. "You're just in time to meet John and his friend, Hiram Martin. We are just finishing breakfast."

Manget stepped inside, removing his hat with a polite nod. Miller led him back to the dining room. "Gentlemen, this is Thomas Manget. Thomas, John Booth, and his tenpin companion, Hiram Martin. Thomas grew up on a plantation just upriver near Baton Rouge. I knew his father some years ago when he stayed at my boarding house on his trips to New Orleans."

Booth extended his hand with a theatrical flourish, although it was apparent he was uncomfortable being upstaged by another handsome man, and especially one taller than him. "A pleasure to meet you, sir. Any friend of George is a friend of mine."

Manget nodded and gave a reserved smile as he shook his hand. "Likewise. Your fame certainly precedes you."

Booth returned a self-satisfied smile.

Martin leaned in and offered his hand. "Good to meet you, Thomas."

"Good to make your acquaintance, Hiram," Manget said, shaking his hand.

After a few moments of conversation, Miller stepped toward the bookcase flanking the windowed wall, his fingers grazing the spines as if searching for something more than a title until he triggered a hidden lever. The bookcase groaned softly, then swung outward on concealed hinges to reveal a narrow, shadowed stairwell.

Miller reached for a lantern mounted on the wall at the head of the stairs and lit it. "This way," he said, leading the way downstairs.

At the bottom, a door opened into a dimly lit room illuminated by a single gasolier. The space was sparse but functional, dominated by a round table. Shelves lined the walls, holding documents, maps, and a small collection of Revolutionary-era weapons.

Miller stepped to the table and poured glasses of whiskey for his guests. He raised his own in a toast. "To the Confederacy," he said, resolutely. "May it long endure."

Martin followed, but Thomas hesitated, declining the offer of a drink with a slight shake of his head.

Booth caught the gesture and turned to him. "You'll forgive my candor, Mr. Manget, but as the Moor once said, 'Men should be what they seem.' Tell me, sir, are you one of Pinkerton's men?"

Thomas's lips twitched into a faint smile. "I'm my own man, Mr. Booth. But I'm curious where you came up with that notion."

Booth leaned against the table, his dark, recessed eyes glinting. "I take pride in being a good judge of people. It comes from years of peeling back masks, onstage and off. It teaches a man to read what lies beneath the surface. And you, sir, seem the very picture of temperance."

Thomas's gaze held steady. "A useful quality, don't you think, Mr. Booth, in these times when one must be on their guard?"

"Indeed, Mr. Manget," Booth said, raising his glass. "Especially when traitors bear a smile."

"That Pinkerton fellow is on his own now, John," Martin said. "He's here in New Orleans investigating fraud for the Feds, cleaning up after the Beast and his cronies."

Miller nervously cleared his throat, gesturing to the chairs around the table. "Shall we get to business, gentlemen?" He placed his lantern on the table and took a seat. "John," he said, pointing to the wall in front of him, "could you turn the gasolier up? The valve's over there on that wall."

Booth stepped to the valve and turned the gas up.

"There," Miller said, apparently pleased with the level of light in the room.

After each man extinguished his lamp, Booth noticed a wall of portraits now visible in the light. "I like your Gallery of Heroes, George."

"Thank you," Miller replied. "I call it 'Our President and All His Men.' It's my tribute to the greatness of the President of our emerging nation and the leaders shaping its destiny."

"All those men served in the Mexican War," Manget observed.

"Yes, they did," Miller said. "And every one of them joined our fight for Southern independence."

"It's a shame old General Twiggs is no longer with us," Martin said. "He gave his all, poor soul,"

Miller said, "Yes. Being well advanced in years, he only lasted about a year after falling off his horse here in New Orleans in '61."

Booth remarked, "The horse probably didn't mourn the portly gentleman's departure."

Martin, clearly uncomfortable with his friend's remark, shifted the focus. "I notice our national flag to the left of President Davis," he said. "But what is that symbol to his right?"

Miller leaned back in his chair, steepling his fingers as he spoke. "I'm glad you asked.

Gentlemen, what I've shared is only a part of the larger plan. The Confederate Secret Service isn't working alone. Have any of you heard of the Knights of the Golden Circle?"

Martin nodded slowly while Booth and Thomas remained silent. "I've heard whispers of a secret society devoted to expanding Southern influence into Mexico, the Caribbean, and beyond. I know they were quite active in Texas before the war. Are they still around?"

"Yes," Miller replied, his voice low and serious. "The Knights have been instrumental in our cause since before the war began. Many members of President Buchanan's Cabinet, including Secretary of War John Floyd and Treasury Secretary Howell Cobb, were part of the order. They facilitated the transfer of federal arms and supplies to Southern states, ensuring we were well-prepared for war even before we seceded."

Booth's eyes narrowed. "Secret societies," he muttered impatiently. "Shadowy figures pulling strings and working the levers from behind the curtain. Why haven't they ensured our independence if they're so powerful?"

Miller's expression became serious. "Because they know timing is everything, my friend. The Knights are patient, methodical, and well-organized. They're working to destabilize the Union on multiple fronts: economically, politically, and militarily. Their agents are already in place, waiting for the right moment. Lincoln's capture is just one piece of the puzzle."

Booth stood abruptly, pacing the room. "You speak of plans and patience while Lincoln tightens his grip on this nation: martial law, suspension of habeas corpus, shutting down newspapers. The man's a tyrant, plain and simple! If the Knights are so bold, let them *act* boldly. Kidnapping him isn't enough. The man must be removed, permanently."

Miller shifted uncomfortably in his chair. "John, the Knights aren't about chaos. They're about methodically achieving their goals. The Knights agree that the key to victory is leverage, not martyrdom. Kidnapping Lincoln would paralyze the Union leadership and force them to negotiate. An assassination, however, would ignite the fury of the North and doom our cause forever."

"So where are these Knights? Where is their headquarters?" Booth asked.

"The Knights have integrated into the Confederate Secret Service. Right now, most of them are safely located across the Niagara in Canada, beyond the reach of the Union."

Booth stopped pacing and turned to face the others. "I hear your words, but my conviction remains unchanged. I'll visit Canada, meet these so-called masterminds, and see their grand plans firsthand. I'll also determine what role I might play."

"Then it's settled," Miller replied firmly. "You'll contact our allies in Canada, and they'll keep us informed of your efforts through couriers."

The men settled into their chairs, the gravity of their purpose palpable as the meeting began in earnest. Miller moved to a side table, retrieving a large, rolled map to spread across the surface before them. "Gentlemen," he said, his tone measured, "all this talk of eliminating Lincoln, one way or the other, is premature. What lies ahead is far greater. We're laying the groundwork for an assault on Washington come summer."

"Washington?" Martin gasped as he saw the map spread out before him.

"Yes, Washington. General Lee knows the Union is planning another drive on Richmond this spring, but he plans to counterpunch this time. The Second Corps— Jackson's old command—will come up through the Shenandoah and cross the Potomac for the capital. This will create panic in Washington, force redistribution of Union troops, and may even create an opportunity to nab Lincoln himself."

Thomas leaned in, taking mental notes of Miller's map.

THE REBEL ATTACK ON WASHINGTON. D.C.
By Genl. JUBAL A. EARLY. Confederate Army.
PLAN OF THE REBEL ATTACK ON WASHINGTON. D.C. JULY 11th and 12th 1864.
Maj Genl. H.G. Wright. Union Forces 20,000 — Rebel Force 12,000 under Genl Early & Breckinridge
POTOMAC
RIVER
GEORGETOWN
WASHINGTON
FORT STEVENS
FORT SLOCUM
FORT RENO
FORT KEARNY
FORT MANSFIELD
FORT GAINES
BATTERY KEMBLE
BATTERY CAMERON
TENNALLYTOWN
ROCK CREEK
RESERVOIR
REBEL LINE
EARLY 11th JULY
GEN EARLY
19th CORPS
Copy of Official Plan made in the Office of Col. Alexander. U.S.A. Chief
Engineer of The Defences of
Washington
by R.K. Sneden. Topg Engr. U.S.A.
Sept 1864.

State of Louisiana

An Ordinance

To abolish Slavery and Involuntary Servitude

We The people of the State of Louisiana, in Convention assembled, do hereby declare and ordain as follows:

Section First: Slavery and Involuntary Servitude except as a punishment for Crime whereof the party Shall have been duly Convicted are hereby for ever abolished and prohibited throughout the State.

Section Second: The Legislature Shall make no law, recognizing the right of property in Man.

Adopted in Convention at New Orleans on this Eleventh day of May, in the year of our Lord, One thousand eight hundred and Sixty four, and Eighty Eighth of the Independence of the United States of America.

E H Durell
President
of the Constitutional Convention of the
State of Louisiana.

A true Copy
John E. Neilis
Secretary

32988

70

Louisiana Adopts
New Ordinance

Rachel leaned back against the upholstered arm of the couch in the library with her stockinged feet tucked beneath her. Lost in thought, her fingers wandered along the seam of the cushion. Outside, a steady rain tapped softly against the panes of the French doors, its gentle cadence breaking the hush of early evening.

Thomas sat beside her, his legs stretched out on the ottoman, one ankle crossed over the other. His cravat was loosened; his coat draped carelessly over the arm of a nearby chair. A single kerosene lamp on the side table cast a pool of golden light across the room, catching the faintest glimmer of silver in his hair. He turned a page in his law journal, brow furrowed, eyes keen with focus.

"Thomas," Rachel said quietly, not looking at him.

"Hmm?" He asked, his eyes continuing to scan the text before him.

She shifted, resting her elbow on the back of the sofa, her gaze now fixed on him. What is the difference between the ordinance that abolished slavery and the new Louisiana Constitution that did the same? What's the need for having them both?"

His eyes lifted slowly, pulling his focus away from the legal text. He blinked, glanced toward the rain-streaked French doors as if gathering his thoughts, then set the journal aside. "Think of it this way. The Ordinance Abolishing Slavery, which they passed today, was like a law. The moment they voted on it, slavery was no longer legal in Louisiana. But an ordinance can be easily changed with the ebb and flow of politics. It can be repealed with a vote."

Rachel gave a slight nod of acknowledgment. "But not so with the Constitution?"

"Exactly," he said, his eyes meeting hers with the patience of a man guiding a client along a complicated legal path. "The Louisiana Constitution isn't just a law. It's the very foundation of the state's authority. It takes a convention, a whole new agreement from the people, to amend. And it takes time."

Rachel considered his explanation, her fingers tapping lightly against the edge of the sofa cushion. "So, the ordinance was passed to make sure it ended quickly. Then the Constitution will assure it is fixed."

"Precisely," he said. "The ordinance is Louisiana's way of showing Lincoln and Congress that it is serious about rejoining the Union. They didn't want to wait to amend the Constitution, so they passed the ordinance immediately. It was a token of sincerity."

Her eyes flicked up to him. "A gesture of good faith or a plea to be let back in?"

Thomas raised an eyebrow. "Maybe both. Louisiana sought to prove that it could be the first Reconstruction state that Lincoln had envisioned. The ordinance was the legislature's opening argument for the abolition of slavery. The Constitution will be their closing argument, solidifying their case."

She kissed him on the cheek. "Remind me to invite you to speak to my class sometime."

Absorbed in his thoughts, he leaned back, his hands resting on his thighs. "Lincoln needs a test case. A Southern state that can show the rest of them how it can be done: peacefully, and with dignity. He needs to prove his Ten Percent Plan can work. And that's what Louisiana was trying to do. They thought if they abolished slavery and drafted a constitution that banned it for good, then they'd be accepted back into the fold."

Her eyes grew distant as her gaze drifted toward the rain-soaked French doors. "But they didn't give freedmen the right to vote," she said quietly. "Not in the ordinance. Not in the Constitution."

"No," Thomas said sadly. "No, they didn't."

She turned her eyes on him, sharp now, her jaw set. "What good is freedom then?"

He shifted uncomfortably. "I'm afraid it isn't as simple as that."

"It never is," she muttered, leaning back against the sofa, her arms folded, thinking of how the slaves were now freed only to be without a voice. Her gaze settled on the French doors, tracking the rain as it slid down the rippled glass in thin, glistening lines. "Do you think they'll change it one day? Establish the right of freed slaves to vote in the nation's Constitution, I mean."

Thomas sighed. "The world's turning, Rachel. But it's turning slowly."

Her mouth curved into a wry smile as she nudged Thomas with a playful shove. "Maybe the world just needs a little push."

"That's my wife," Thomas said with a proud grin, drawing her close.

The rain fell harder, drumming against the roof in a steady, rhythmic cadence. Its echoes reverberated through the eaves like the low murmur of a distant crowd, each raindrop a voice contributing to the swelling chorus. From there, it spilled into the gutters with the rush of hurried whispers before splashing onto the street in silent puddles.

The patter of the falling rain reminded Rachel of the voices of martyrs. Once defiant, they soared on high, only to falter and sink into silence.

71

Congo Square Celebrates Emancipation in Louisiana

Saturday, June 11

On a humid Saturday morning nearing noon, the air around Congo Square stirred with growing anticipation. The celebration was unprecedented, its significance resonating deeply in the hearts of all who gathered. The shouts of street vendors offering butter-roasted pecans and warm pralines blended with the laughter of children as they darted through the throng, creating a symphony of joy that filled the square.

Beneath the ancient oaks of the Square, once a place of worship and lamentations for slaves, thousands of freed men, women, and children now gathered to celebrate Louisiana's abolition of slavery, turning the sacred ground into a place of joy and deliverance.

The square itself pulsed with color, movement, and sound. Women in bright calico dresses swayed to the melodies of spirituals. Their colorful headscarves, tied in intricate patterns in a tradition passed down through generations, told silent stories of survival, endurance, and ancestral memory.

Men stood tall, some in their Sunday best, while others proudly wore the blue uniforms of Union soldiers. Their faces were a mosaic of joy, disbelief, and quiet pride. Even those who had spent their entire lives in bondage walked with newfound dignity, holding their heads high as if they were finally unburdened by centuries of oppression.

At the heart of the square, a rough wooden platform stood adorned with banners that fluttered in the sticky breeze. A line of speakers awaited their turn, their expressions a mixture of solemnity and exhilaration. Each was prepared to voice the hope and pain that had defined generations.

Shortly after noon, a preacher stepped forward, raising a hand to quiet the crowd. "Today," he proclaimed, "we do not stand as property but as people. As God's children who have carved freedom out of fire and fury, we will carry this torch for generations yet unborn."

The crowd erupted in cheers so loud and fervent that the ground seemed to quake. Women raised their arms to the heavens, tears streaming down their cheeks. Children clung to their parents, their wide eyes reflecting the weight of a moment they could not fully understand.

Then, from the edge of the square, the drums began. The rhythm was slow at first, like the steady pulse of a heartbeat, but it gradually intensified, resonating through the air with an ancient, elemental rhythm. The sound called forth dancers from the crowd, their feet striking the earth with a force that seemed to echo across time. Each movement spoke of pain and defiance, of survival and ultimate liberation.

"Glory, hallelujah!" an elderly man cried, clutching a tattered Bible in one hand and his grandson's small hand in the other. His voice, trembling with age and emotion, was a testament to endurance. "Thank the Lawd! We are free at last!"

Men lit torches as the sun dipped, flames flickering against the encroaching darkness. The glow illuminated faces etched with hope and determination. Groups gathered in clusters—some dancing jubilantly, others exchanging stories of escape, resistance, and dreams of reuniting with loved ones. An elderly woman, her back stooped from decades of toil in the cane fields, raised her wavering but proud voice in song, her words carrying the weight of a lifetime. "Swing low, sweet chariot," she began with a steadiness that belied her age.

The crowd joined in, their voices blending into a powerful chorus that reverberated through the square and beyond. "Coming for to carry me home…"

Amidst it all, a young mother stood silently, her baby balanced on her hip. Her gaze was fixed on the horizon, her eyes shimmering with tears. She whispered to the child, "All this is for you."

As the celebration swelled, the drums suddenly fell silent. All eyes turned to the stage, where a mother knelt beside her young son. She gently touched his shoulder and whispered, "Go now, Lizah. Make Mama proud. Speak the words of Jesus when He gave that sermon high up on the mountaintop."

With a deep breath, Lizah stepped onto the stage, a single candle flickering in his hand.

The humid breeze threatened to extinguish its flame, but the boy shielded it carefully. His voice, thin but steady, rang out over the crowd.

"Ye are the light of the world," he began. "A city that is set on a hill cannot be hidden. Neither do men light a candle and put it under a bushel, but on a candlestick, which gives light to all in the house. Let your light so shine before men, that they may see your good works, and glorify your Father which is in heaven."

He paused, glancing back at his mother for approval. She beamed at him with pride. Turning to face the sea of faces, she added, "This is our light now, and one day it will grow into a glorious flame."

The crowd erupted once more, their cheers blending with the primordial beat of drums in the torchlit night.

72

HORACE GREELEY'S NIAGARA FALLS PEACE EPISODE

THURSDAY, JULY 21

While the freedmen of Louisiana rejoiced in their newfound liberty beneath a sweltering sky, the question of lasting peace still hung precariously over the nation. Far to the north, where the cooling mist of Niagara mitigated the summer heat, three Confederate envoys gathered at the stately Clifton House on the Canadian side, clinging to the frail hope that a modest overture to Horace Greeley—editor, abolitionist, and self-appointed emissary—might somehow pry open the gates of reconciliation.

Across the churning river, on the American side, John Hay stood at the railing beyond the International Hotel's wide veranda, his eyes fixed on the silhouette of the Clifton House rising through the mist. Between them, Horseshoe Falls thundered with elemental force, its roar a relentless echo of the fury and division that continued to convulse the country.

So near, and yet so very far, Hay reflected. The river that divided the United States from British Canada measured barely a mile across, yet it seemed to separate two worlds. On the far bank, peace lingered like a sigh. On this side, a wounded nation bled out its conscience, struggling to preserve its body and soul.

Lincoln had sent him north from Washington to accompany Greeley, not to negotiate, but to deliver a letter and observe the response once it passed into Confederate hands.

"To whom it may concern," Hay murmured. It was hardly a stirring overture. The message that followed was stark, uncompromising, and left no room for negotiation. It offered safe conduct to Washington, but only on the condition of a full return to the Union, something Jefferson Davis had already declared unthinkable.

Hay understood why they had been sent. Lincoln had no illusions that peace would be achieved, nor did he expect the Southern commissioners to accept terms that required surrender. This was Greeley's errand, not his own. In truth, Lincoln had consented to the scheme not out of optimism but out of necessity, telling him that his efforts, "might save us from a Northern insurrection."

Hay understood that Lincoln's concerns were far from imagined. With the presidential election drawing near and Copperhead agitation stirring unrest among the Peace Democrats, the contest for public sentiment had become as critical as any fought with cannon or saber. Through his command of the *New York Tribune*, Greeley held considerable influence over the Northern conscience. However slim, there remained a chance that his carefully crafted editorials might reach further into the hearts of wavering readers than the incendiary rhetoric of *The Liberator*, still resounding with the fierce, unyielding voice of William Lloyd Garrison.

As Hay scanned the patio, he noticed a steward offering wine cards to guests at nearby tables. He beckoned the man, who stepped over with a polite bow and presented a list of offerings.

Château Lafite Claret, five dollars. Sparkling Catawba, three dollars and fifty cents. All prices are payable in greenbacks. Premium allowed on gold.

Hay studied the card. Considering that a skilled laborer earned little more than a dollar or two a day, he concluded that the guests assembled here were not factory workers.

"Oh, John, there you are," called a sharp voice behind him.

He turned to see Horace Greeley.

Now in his fifties, the bespectacled editor bore the restless energy of a man forever at odds with the world. Once wiry, he had grown heavier, though the unkempt mane of white hair still clung defiantly to his head, its disorder matched only by the theatrical beard beneath his chin. His familiar frock coat hung about him like an old obligation, ill-fitted to the summer heat and testimony to a life unconcerned with fashion or ease. Everything about him spoke of unrelenting principles and a profound impatience with dissent.

"Come, let us sit," Greeley said, gesturing toward a table, his tone more a directive than an invitation.

With a sigh, Hay eased into a chair and leaned forward on his elbows.

"John," he began, his voice settling into the rhythm of habitual debate, "I want to thank you for accompanying me while I've been attempting to parley with the Confederates across the river."

"It's also been quite the flurry of dispatches between you and Holcombe, Thompson, and Clay," Hay replied.

"Steward," Greeley called abruptly. "Do you have any grape juice?"

"Grape juice, sir?"

"Yes, grape juice," Greeley repeated, his tone as indignant as a temperance speaker in a taproom.

"What kind would you prefer?"

"Concord grape."

"I'm afraid Concord grapes are not yet in season, sir, but we have freshly pressed Niagara grape juice. The grapes arrived this morning, and our chef reserved a small amount before fermenting the rest for table wine."

"Very well," Greeley said with a vague wave of his hand.

"And for you, sir?" the steward asked Hay.

"Saratoga Springs water, without ice."

"Would you like lemon?"

"Yes, thank you."

Greeley tapped his fingers against the tabletop. "The President's letter you handed me on arrival did nothing to help matters."

Hay chose his response carefully. Any reply risked igniting a long, unwinnable argument. "You mean the salutation?"

"Exactly. That cold, impersonal 'To whom it may concern' has caused no end of trouble. Clay and Holcombe responded this morning. They refuse to accept any negotiation that requires submitting to national authority and insist that they lack the power to agree to terms that leave no room for an honest peace."

Just then, the steward returned. "Your grape juice, sir, compliments of the chef. And here is your Saratoga Springs, with lemon." He placed the carafe and glass on the table. "Will there be anything else, gentlemen?"

"No," Greeley replied curtly.

"I'll leave the ticket," the steward said, placing a tray on the table.

"I'll get it," Greeley muttered, laying a few coins on the tray. "Keep the change."

"Much obliged, sir," the man said.

Greeley ignored the water and sipped his grape juice, then pulled his gold pocket watch from his vest. He flipped open the lid, checked the time, and shut it again with a soft snap. "My efforts have come to naught, John," he said quietly. "There will be no negotiation."

The words were not delivered with his usual fire. Instead, resignation settled over him like the mist rolling off the falls.

Hay leaned back and exhaled slowly. Despite his frequent frustration with Greeley's bombast, he felt a flicker of sympathy. "It does seem," he said softly, "that all hope has fallen."

Without another word, Greeley stood up and walked away, his broad back slightly stooped in defeat, leaving Hay alone beneath the distant rumble of the falls.

73

FARRAGUT CAPTURES MOBILE BAY

General Nathaniel Banks sat behind his desk in the St. Charles, reviewing the dispatch detailing Farragut's triumph at Mobile Bay. Across from him, Thomas Manget sat quietly, waiting for the general to speak.

Banks laid the report down, his fingers drumming thoughtfully on the desk. "Mobile Bay is ours, Thomas. No small feat for Farragut, considering the Confederate ironclads, the torpedoes, and Buchanan's tenacity. What's your read on it?"

"Admiral Buchanan's training at the Naval Academy equipped him to be a formidable opponent," Thomas said.

"Yes, and the CSS Tennessee he commanded was a powerful warship with ramming capabilities."

"Pity he gave up his position in the U.S. Navy to join the Confederacy. He could have been a great asset for the Union."

"Yes," Banks agreed. "And now, after sending his sword to Rear Admiral Farragut as a sign of surrender, he's a Union prisoner recovering from his wounds. That's hard to accept for a man of his standing, well into his sixties."

Banks handed Thomas the report.

Thomas read that disaster had struck shortly before eight o'clock in the morning when the *USS Tecumseh*, leading the charge, struck a torpedo and sank almost instantly. The ship vanished beneath the waves, taking nearly all her crew to a watery grave.

As Thomas continued reading the dispatch, the words gave way to powerful images. He saw the fleet hesitate, commanders faltering as torpedoes stationed beneath the waterline exploded, claiming hulls and lives with every blast.

In his mind's eye, Farragut rose like a vision, high in the rigging of the *Hartford*, clinging to the shrouds as though born to the mast, his voice cutting through the smoke and din: *"Damn the torpedoes! Full speed ahead!"*

The *Hartford* surged forward, her bow knifing through the bay, Farragut's stentorian cry galvanizing the entire fleet. One by one, the Union ships followed, braving the withering fire from Fort Morgan and the hidden terror below. Torpedoes bobbed like sleeping beasts beneath the surface, yet miraculously, most failed to detonate.

By eight o'clock, the *Hartford* had passed the forts, battered but alive. From the port quarter, Confederate gunboats—*Selma*, *Morgan*, and *Gaines*—raked her decks with fire. Thomas watched, still in the theater of his mind, as Farragut ordered the *Metacomet* to cast off and pursue. She gave chase, swift and unrelenting, until the *Selma*, overwhelmed, struck her colors.

And still the battle roared on. He saw the shadow of the ironclad *Tennessee*, massive and implacable, bearing down under the command of Admiral Franklin Buchanan. By half past eight, the Union fleet had wheeled about to meet this final menace. The *Monongahela* struck first, ramming the ironclad's flanks, followed by the *Lackawanna*. Then came the *Hartford*, her guns firing at near point-blank range, her broadside crashing into iron with thunderous resolve.

Smoke poured from the *Tennessee*, choking the crew. Shells tore through her gunports like claws. Inside, Buchanan refused to yield, even though he was gravely wounded. Only after her rudder was gone, her engines failed, and her decks lay in ruin, did the ironclad finally drift into stillness. At ten o'clock, the Confederate flag came down, and silence settled over the bay like a shroud.

Thomas held the vision of Farragut aloft, clinging to the tarred ropes of his flagship as he surveyed the battle's end. At last, the admiral descended to the deck: blood-streaked, soot-covered, but triumphant.

"A bold victory, sir," Thomas said, his thoughts returning to the room. "Farragut's decision to press forward, torpedoes be damned, secured the bay. But the implications of this are what interest me most. The Confederacy's Gulf trade is effectively sealed off now. We've severed their last lifeline to the outside world between New Orleans and Mobile."

Banks allowed himself a rare smile. "Indeed, Thomas. Mobile and New Orleans are no longer at odds, giving us control of the Gulf. With the bay secure, we can move troops, supplies, and goods between the two ports more easily. That strengthens our control of the entire Gulf region."

"That, and an open Mississippi, will encourage trade and facilitate post-war reconstruction efforts."

Banks stepped over to the window, gazing out over the bustling streets of New Orleans. "All of this is encouraging for my mission here."

Thomas rose and moved to stand beside him. "Exactly, sir. "The consolidation of these ports, the steady flow of cotton and sugar, and the reopening of secure trade routes will restore Southern commerce in critical areas."

Banks turned to face him with a resolute gaze. "It's ironic, isn't it, Thomas? Farragut, New Orleans' native son, has delivered the decisive blow to Mobile."

Thomas offered a knowing nod. "First New Orleans, then Mobile. The man has cemented his legacy. Not to mention his support in the victories at Port Hudson, Baton Rouge, and Vicksburg."

"Those victories didn't just win territories; they freed up trade routes." Banks said. "Cotton harvesting has just begun near New Orleans. All of Louisiana will follow in a few weeks, and the Mississippi is now open for transporting the crop to market."

"Yes," Thomas said. "Production plummeted from millions of bales a year before the war to a fraction of that. It can only go up from there."

Banks clasped his hands behind his back, his voice carrying the weight of responsibility. "And now, with Louisiana ratifying its new Constitution, we must continue our work. It's up to us to ensure that this hard-won advantage doesn't slip through our fingers."

"Speaking of which, General," Thomas said, "I have some troubling developments to share regarding the Confederate Secret Service."

Banks leaned back in his chair; one eyebrow arched. "You mean beyond the plan to attack Washington that you reported earlier?"

"Yes, sir," Thomas replied, his expression somber. "I didn't mention it during that briefing because I needed to verify the details first."

"And what have you uncovered?"

"It seems there's a second plan underway," Thomas said gravely. "This one involves kidnapping the President—or murdering him in cold blood."

74

ATLANTA BURNS

News of Atlanta's fall broke over New Orleans like a tidal wave, crashing over the levee and flooding the city with dread. The heart of the Confederacy lay crushed and smoldering in Sherman's wake. Within an hour, word of it had swept from the telegraph office to every corner of the city.

Rachel's heart clenched at the cries rising from below her balcony while she sewed by lamplight in the study. Abandoning her work, she threw open the French doors and stepped outside. The crisp early fall air swept against her face as she leaned over the iron railing to witness the commotion below.

People gathered in small clusters along the darkening streets, clutching one another as their voices wavered between disbelief and grief. Some wept openly, while others murmured bitter recriminations about the Union forces and the devastation Sherman had left in his wake. Lamentations rose like a dirge, threading through the city.

Yet Rachel did not see the people below. Her gaze drifted to the horizon, where the present dissolved into the past in her mind, playing like a magic lantern's grim show. A chariot of swirling fire appeared, red and vengeful, blazing with unrelenting fury. Flames surged upward, twisting and churning like Ezekiel's wheel within a wheel, an insatiable force that stretched its fiery arms toward the heavens, casting its wrathful fire over the city.

It was the sights and sounds of the occupation in the harbor all over again, echoing through her mind. Black smoke unfurled, curling like spilled ink in water, dark and suffocating. Wooden ships filled with bales of cotton turned to pyres, their masts collapsing, consumed by ravenous flames. The voices of Confederate captains commanding their vessels to be soaked in kerosene and set ablaze rather than surrender them to Federal hands.

She saw Rebecca, her slave, standing near the hearth, her wide eyes frozen, resembling an ebony statue with ivory eyes. She hadn't asked Rebecca what thoughts gripped her; the answer was written all over her face: she was witnessing the death of one world and the birth of another.

Rachel returned her gaze to the horizon, her chest tightening—not from the memory of the fires or the haunting look on Rebecca's face, but from the knowing.

Like Cassandra, burdened with the curse of foreseeing the inevitable yet powerless to change it, Rebecca intuitively grasped the truth with chilling clarity. This was how it ended: not with banners lowered in orderly surrender, but with flames indifferent to the countless lives they consumed.

"Rachel?"

The sound of her name cut through the specters of her mind. Her head automatically turned toward the voice, her fingers loosening from the balcony railing. She blinked, and the terrifying images of the magic lantern in her mind faded.

"Are you all right?" Thomas asked gently, stepping toward her. "For a moment there, you seemed a thousand miles away."

Her eyes flicked toward him, narrowing. "Hold me, Thomas. Just hold me, please."

He pulled her close, glancing over her shoulder at the levee. A flicker of understanding crossed his expression. "You're thinking about Atlanta, aren't you, darling? How it recalls the harbor here during the occupation."

Rachel exhaled slowly and pulled away, her eyes settling on the pale gray line where the sky met the earth. "Yes," she murmured. "But it's different. During the occupation, the ships in the harbor were already dead when the flames consumed them: hollowed out, stripped bare, just waiting to sink to a watery grave." Her fingers traced the cold iron rail that anchored her in the present. "But Atlanta was alive, a city crying and struggling for breath as the flames consumed her. Now, her people are scattered, without food, shelter, or anyone to bind their wounds. They don't even have their horses to bear them away from the devastation."

Her tear-filled eyes darted to meet his. "Sarah and her family are still in LaGrange, just south of Atlanta. Do you think she's safe with Jacob and little Noah?"

He said nothing, only staring down at the street below as if weighing her words like a man calculating the bridge's strength before crossing. His gaze lingered on a woman in the street with a child clinging to her skirt. His eyes grew distant and thoughtful. When he finally spoke, his voice was resolute.

"Sherman didn't start the fire in Atlanta. He only targeted military infrastructure for destruction. It was General Hood of the Confederacy who ordered the detonation of train cars loaded with ammunition, sparking much of the blaze. And LaGrange is a good seventy miles southwest of Atlanta," Thomas said, tightening his arm around her. "If Sherman's headed anywhere next, it will be east, straight for Savannah."

She turned away from him, her eyes locked on the distant horizon. The sky darkened, but still, she imagined the faint glow of flames. Her throat tightened as she thought of Sarah standing in the doorway of her house with Noah on her hip. Would she run, hoping that Jacob could keep up? Or would she stand still, frozen in fear, just as Rebecca had done during the occupation of New Orleans?

"Do you think Jefferson Davis will surrender now?" Rachel asked.

"No," Thomas replied without hesitation. "From what I know of him, he will never surrender. Word has it he's touring cities around Atlanta, holding rallies in support of the war, and encouraging every able-bodied man, regardless of age, to join his cause. I even hear he's offering pardons to soldiers who abandoned the battlefield if they return. His next stop is Macon."

A comforting silence eventually fell between them as they held hands. The only sound was the clamor on the streets below and the distant clang of a ship's bell downriver.

"If Sarah needs you," Thomas assured her quietly, cradling her again in his arms, "we'll find a way to get you to her."

75

JEFFERSON DAVIS
RALLIES MACON

The proud city of Macon, home to eight thousand souls, buzzed with uneasy anticipation as crowds gathered and milled about the town square. The late September sun warmed the damp soil, which was still drying from recent rainfall. Farmers in worn homespun clothing stood behind businessmen and elected officials dressed in tailored suits, bow ties, and hats. Gold watch chains gleamed as they draped gracefully across the vests of the more affluent.

Toward the back of the crowd, women with tired eyes clutched small children at their sides, still grieving the loss of their older sons who had eagerly marched off to war. Everyone anticipated the arrival of Jefferson Davis, the man they spoke of reverently as their President.

Several reporters from the *Macon Telegraph* stood with pencils and journals in hand, prepared to record Davis's speech for the press. One remarked wistfully that no device yet existed to capture the President's voice for posterity. Another answered that no politician would allow their words to be set down by a machine.

When their President finally ascended the platform after his short carriage ride from the train station, his slight frame seemed dwarfed by the weight of the occasion. His face, etched with the strain of leading a beleaguered Confederacy and the recent loss of its Gate City of Atlanta, a half-day journey north of Macon by rail, was framed by neatly combed graying hair. He surveyed the sea of faces before him, embracing the mingled hope and despair that mirrored his private struggles.

"Ladies and gentlemen, friends and fellow citizens," he began. "It would have gladdened my heart to have met you in prosperity instead of adversity. But friends are drawn together in adversity. The son of a Georgian who fought through the first Revolution, I would be untrue to myself if I should forget the State in her day of peril."

"Though misfortune has befallen our arms from Decatur to Jonesboro, our cause is not lost. Sherman cannot maintain his long line of communication and retreat sooner or later, and he must. And when that day comes, the fate that befell the army of the French Empire in its retreat from Moscow will be re-enacted. Our cavalry and our people will harass and destroy his army as did the Cossacks that of Napoleon, and the Yankee General, like him, will escape with only a bodyguard."

Applause and cheers erupted from the crowd.

"How can this be most speedily effected?" he continued as the crowd fell silent. "By the absentees of Hood's army returning to their posts. And will they not? Can they see the banished exiles? Can they hear the wail of their suffering countrywomen and children and not come? By what influences they are made to stay away, it is not necessary to speak. If there is one who will stay away at this hour, he is unworthy of the name of a Georgian. To the women, no appeal is necessary. They are like the Spartan mothers of old. I know of one who had lost all her sons except one of eight years. She wrote me that she wanted me to reserve a place for him in the ranks. The venerable General Polk, to whom I read the letter, knew that woman well and said that it was characteristic of her. But I will not weary you by turning aside to relate the various incidents of giving up the last son to the cause of our country known to me. Wherever we go we find the hearts and hands of our noble women enlisted. They are seen wherever the eye may fall or step turn. They have one duty to perform, and that is to buoy up the hearts of our people."

"I know the deep disgrace felt by Georgia at our army falling back from Dalton to the interior of the State, but I was not of those who considered Atlanta lost when our army crossed the Chattahoochee. I resolved that it should not, and I then put a man in command who I knew would strike an honest and manly blow for the city, and many a Yankee's blood was made to nourish the soil before the prize was won."

"It does not become us to revert to disaster. Let the dead bury the dead. Let us, with one arm and one effort, endeavor to crush Sherman. I am going to the army to confer with our generals. The end must be the defeat of our enemy. It has been said that I abandoned Georgia to her fate. Shame upon such a falsehood. Where could the author have been when Walker, Polk, and General Stephen D. Lee were sent to her assistance? Miserable man. The man who uttered this was a scoundrel. He was not a man to save our country."

The crowd applauded and cheered.

"If I knew that a general did not possess the right qualities to command, would I not be wrong if he was not removed? Why, when our army was falling back from northern Georgia, I even heard that I had sent General Bragg with pontoons to cross into Cuba. But we must be charitable."

A ripple of subdued laughter passed through the somber crowd, a brief and fragile moment of relief sparked by Davis's wry dismissal of the outlandish rumor.

"The man who can speculate ought to be made to take up his musket. When the war is over, and our independence is won, who will be our aristocracy? I hope the limping soldier. To the young ladies, I would say when choosing between an empty sleeve and the man who had remained at home and grown rich, always take the empty sleeve. Let the old men remain at home and make bread. But should they know of any young men keeping away from the service who cannot be made to go any other way, let them write to the Executive. I read all letters sent me from the people but have not the time to reply to them."

"You have not many men between eighteen and forty-five left. The boys—God bless the boys—are as rapidly as they become old enough going to the field. The city of Macon is filled with stores, sick and wounded. It must not be abandoned when threatened, but when the enemy comes, instead of calling upon Hood's army for defense, the old men must fight, and when the enemy is driven beyond Chattanooga, they too can join in the general rejoicing."

"I'm ready to fight!" an elderly man cried out, thrusting his fist high into the air as he steadied himself with his other hand firmly gripping his cane. The gesture ignited a wave of cheers and raised fists from the crowd, their voices echoing "Fight, fight," and swelling with renewed fervor.

"Your prisoners are kept as a sort of Yankee capital. I have heard that one of their generals said that their exchange would defeat Sherman. I have tried every means and conceded everything to effect an exchange to no purpose. Butler the Beast, with whom no Commissioner of Exchange would hold intercourse, has published in the newspapers that if we would consent to the exchange of Negroes, all difficulties might be removed. This is reported as an effort of his to get himself whitewashed by holding intercourse with gentlemen. If an exchange can be effected, I don't know, but I might be induced to recognize Butler. In the future, every effort will be given as far as possible to effect the end. We want our soldiers in the field, and we want the sick and wounded to return home."

"It is not proper for me to speak of the number of men in the field. But this I will say, two-thirds of our men are absent. Some are sick, some are wounded, but most of them are absent without leave. The man who repents and returns to his commander voluntarily appeals strongly to executive clemency. But suppose he stays away until the war is over, and his comrades return home when every man's history is told; where will he shield himself? I rely upon these reflections to make men return to their duty, but after conferring with our generals at headquarters, if there be any other remedy, it shall be applied."

"I love my friends, and I forgive my enemies. I have been asked to send reinforcements from Virginia to Georgia. In Virginia, the disparity in numbers is just as great as it is in Georgia. Then I have been asked why the army sent to the Shenandoah Valley was not sent here. It was because an army of the enemy had penetrated that Valley to the very gates of Lynchburg, and General Early was sent to drive them back. This he not only successfully did, but, crossing the Potomac, came well-nigh capturing Washington itself, and forced Grant to send two corps of his army to protect it. This, the enemy, denominated a raid. If so, Sherman's march into Georgia is a raid. What would prevent them now if Early was withdrawn from penetrating down the Valley and putting a complete cordon of men around Richmond? I counseled that great and grave soldier, General Lee, upon all these points. My mind roamed over the whole field."

"With this, we can succeed. If one-half of the men now absent without leave will return to duty, we can defeat the enemy. With that hope, I am going to the front. I may not realize this hope, but I know there are men there who have looked death in the face too often to despond now. Let no one despond. Let no one distrust, and remember that if genius is the beau ideal, hope is the reality."

As his speech ended, Davis's voice faltered briefly, a flicker of exhaustion betraying the weight he bore. But he stood straight, his final words resonating like a benediction. "Hold fast, my friends. As long as we stand united, our cause is not lost. May God defend the right."

The crowd surged forward, their cheers drowning out the distant church bells, floating over the rooftops and the square like a prayer carried by the wind.

As Davis descended from the platform, he shook hands with those who pressed close, offering gratitude and encouragement. Behind him, the makeshift podium stood empty, a silent witness to the hope and resolve he had kindled in a weary people.

Watching Davis disappear into the crowd, two women stood arm in arm, their tear-stained faces etched with the weariness of sacrifice.

"I sent five sons to fight," the first woman murmured, her voice wavering between sorrow and quiet defiance. "I believed in the cause. I believed it was righteous. But now, my husband and all my boys lie silent in their graves, save my little Robert, who just turned eighteen. He plans to enlist next week. I cannot help but wonder…was their sacrifice too high a price to pay for honor?"

Looking around nervously, her companion pressed her hand gently. "Softly, my dear, I pray. To speak of such loss marks us as traitors," she urged in a hushed voice. "May God have mercy on us mothers, for who else will?"

76

RED RIVER REGRETS

Nathaniel Banks leaned against his desk, gazing through the tall windows of his office in the St. Charles Hotel. Midday sunlight poured in, warming the room. Outside on the levee, a steamer's whistle pierced the air, its sharp tone mingling with the shouts of merchants, the clang of streetcars, and the steady clatter of carriages. It was an unending cacophony of a resilient city determined to endure in the wake of upheaval and occupation, as it had throughout its history.

His thoughts wandered, carrying with them the bitter sting of irony. He had replaced Butler—a man notorious for his heavy-handed rule and opportunistic profiteering—only to find himself on the verge of being replaced after the humiliating failure of the Red River Campaign. Two generals, two legacies, both defined by failure.

Failure. The word clung to him like a stubborn stain, seeping into his memories of the long march through the swamps of Louisiana. It was his version of Lady Macbeth's damned spot, impossible to wash away, no matter how hard he tried.

He believed in his plan and thought it would be his defining achievement, but instead, it became his undoing. Poor timing, treacherous swamps teaming with alligators, unreliable subordinates, inadequate supplies and troops, and a relentless enemy conspired against him. Unfortunately, his name was now tied not to triumph but to retreat from a campaign that had drained resources and morale with little to show for it.

His jaw tightened as he turned to the neat pile of papers on his desk. Lincoln's words rang in his memory, spoken with quiet resolve when he first took command: "Restore the

Union, General. Do so with honesty and fairness. Heal the wounds of this city and bring its people back under the flag, not through force alone, but with trust."

He had done his best to carry out those orders. Where Butler had wielded power like a cudgel, he had sought to govern with transparency and fairness. He had worked to improve the city's infrastructure, restore its economy, and ensure the fair treatment of its people, regardless of their social status. And while his military record now bore the blemish of the Red River Campaign, he took solace in knowing he had acted with integrity.

But that solace did little to quiet the gnawing guilt that accompanied thoughts of his wife and the ignominy she was left to bear. He ran a hand across his brow, closing his eyes momentarily. She was over a thousand miles away, in the social whirl of Washington, where the news of his failures had no doubt spread like wildfire. He could picture her now, her graceful composure masking the hurt and embarrassment she must feel. How many cruel whispers behind her back had she endured at soirées and dinners, even in her own home?

Banks shook his head, a bitter smirk on his face. "So much for Nathaniel Banks, the self-made man," he muttered. His voice sounded hollow in the quiet room. "You've made her a gossip topic, a woman who must explain away your failure while holding her head high. She deserves better."

He rose from his chair and crossed to the window, but the view of the bustling levee offered no solace. With hands clasped behind his back, he spoke aloud to his reflection in the glass.

"You did what you could. You brought order to chaos. You gave this city stability, fairness, and a reason to believe in the Union again. But Washington won't see that. They'll forget that you ended starvation, opened schools for children born in bondage, replaced slave labor with wages, helped rekindle commerce along the course of the Mississippi, and rooted out corruption. All they'll remember is Red River."

The reflection stared back: silent, worn, but unflinching. "You made your share of mistakes," it answered, voice steady in his mind. "But you led with honesty. And if that honesty costs you your command, so be it. Better to leave with honor than rule with shame."

The clang of a ship's bell echoed faintly from the river, pulling him back to the present. He stood there for a long moment, watching the water flow south, its destination sure, even as his path seemed lost in the swirling currents of failure and regret.

"In some ways, I pity the President," Banks said, speaking to the thin air. "I can only imagine the embarrassment of learning of Butler's corruption, followed by my military failures."

Turning from the window, he focused on the maps pinned to the wall. Once tools of strategy and ambition, they now served as stark reminders of his missteps, leaving images of battlefields in his nightmares.

Without hesitation, he seized one by the edge and yanked it free with a sharp rip that tore through the room's stillness. He watched as the paper drifted to the floor, then moved to the next map and the next, pulling them down until the wall stood bare.

"No more pins on a map. No more boots wading through bayous," he murmured, staring at the grim reminders of failed campaigns scattered across the floor.

A sharp knock at the door cut through his self-recrimination. Drawing a steady breath, he called, "Enter."

The door opened, and Thomas Manget stepped inside, his gaze sweeping over the fallen maps scattered like battle casualties.

"A clean slate, is it?" Manget asked, his tone wry.

"In a manner of speaking," Banks replied, his smile grim and his eyes resolute. He gestured to the chair opposite him, his tone warmer than usual. "Come in, Thomas. I've been expecting you. Before I depart, there's much to discuss. My mission here is done, but yours is far from over."

77

A Sister's Ultimatum

As Rachel stepped cautiously across the planks at the levee, the cool evening fog enveloped her, obscuring all but the dim red glow of a cigar in the distance, piercing the mist like a watchful, demonic eye.

She paused, holding her breath, unable to discern the shape shrouded in the vapor. Slipping quietly behind a stack of shipping crates, she waited and watched, hoping the figure would move on.

"Hey, John," a voice called through the dampness. "Want to join me? I just brewed a pot of coffee at my post. Ain't nobody out here but you, me, and them damn river rats."

"Sure, Jack," came the reply, followed by the faint hiss of his cigar falling on the wet planks.

Their footsteps soon faded into the distance.

Rachel leaned out cautiously from her hiding spot, listening for other voices or movements. Hearing none, she emerged, advancing slowly toward where the men had stood. As she drew closer, her heart raced as the faint outline of someone emerged from the thick fog. It was a woman shrouded in a cloak, her hood casting deep shadows over her partially obscured face. The mysterious figure advanced step by step until she passed into the dim glow of a solitary gas streetlamp, illuminating her face.

"Loreta?" she gasped.

Rachel quickened toward the woman who had once been a soldier and a spy, then a nurse who had kindly led her to Jacob. Her mind raced with questions. Why had Sarah sent her a telegram that day, delivered by courier, asking for a clandestine meeting at such an hour? Was it news of Grant or Sherman, perhaps an update on their movements as they advanced deeper into Georgia?

"Rachel, it's good to see you," Loreta said, extending her hands.

Rachel clasped her hands, still anxious to understand the reason behind this secret meeting. "It's been a while," she said. "So much has happened."

"Yes," Loreta agreed. "I have news for you, but I must deliver it in haste. It concerns your family."

"My family?" Rachel's heart quickened. "Pray tell me they're all right."

"Yes, they are safe," Loreta assured her. "Sherman's forces have marched on from Atlanta, and LaGrange's women's militia, the Nancy Harts, are prepared to defend the town should Union soldiers arrive."

"The Nancy Harts?" Rachel asked.

"They're a militia named after the Revolutionary War heroine Nancy Hart. These women have trained since the early days of the conflict, determined to protect their homes. They drill regularly, but, like most women, they know when to reason their way out of a fight."

Rachel nodded, a faint sense of reassurance flickering within her. It seemed unthinkable that any Union general would choose to be remembered for leaving the bodies of dead women in the streets rather than accepting an offer for a peaceful resolution. "Thank you for the news," she said quietly. "It's a relief to know my family is safe."

Loreta's expression turned serious. "There's something else I need to tell you. It's about Thomas."

"Thomas?" Rachel felt her stomach knot. "What about him?"

"He's a Union spy," Loreta said with an edge in her voice.

Rachel stiffened but maintained her composure, determined not to betray anything. "I don't understand."

"He was one of Pinkerton's men before working with General Banks. I thought you should know."

Rachel's voice tightened. "You do realize he's my husband?"

"I do," Loreta said, her tone softening. "And because of that, I feel compelled to inform you about his blood."

"What do you mean?"

Loreta paused, casting a glance around to confirm they were still alone. "Thomas's father was Jewish, but his mother, Josephine, is a quinteroon and Catholic. Their story began with a single encounter when his father visited the Poydras plantation and was captivated by the young Josephine. From what I understand, the attraction was mutual."

Rachel froze, the revelation striking her like a thunderclap. "Thomas never told me."

"To be fair, Thomas may not know," Loreta said. "His father insisted on raising him alone, allowing Josephine to visit him occasionally as a child. No doubt he was concerned about anyone knowing of Thomas's lineage. But you need to understand the practical implications that will affect your life. Under Louisiana law, since he is a hexadecaroon, your marriage isn't recognized, and any children you have will be considered colored. Their futures here will be severely limited unless you move North."

Rachel's thoughts turned in anguished circles, not because of Thomas's ancestry but because of his lack of awareness. Would she now bear the responsibility of informing him about his lineage so he would have the opportunity to reunite with his mother?

"Thank you for telling me, Loreta," Rachel said after a long pause. "I'll think about what you've said."

Loreta reached out, placing a hand on Rachel's arm. "There's also another message. It's from your sister."

"Oh?" Rachel's voice wavered.

"First, she wants you to know that she, Jacob, and Noah are faring well. She also wants you to know that your heart was in the right place when you worked with me to get the contents of Eugenia's trunk shipped to LaGrange. However, she wants you to know that if you stay with Thomas, she will no longer consider you her kin. But if you leave him and join your family in LaGrange, she will accept you with open arms."

The words cut through Rachel like a dagger. She drew a measured breath, steadying herself, her voice unwavering despite the ache that tightened in her chest. "Please tell her that I love her. And let her know that if she ever replaces hate with love in her heart, we can reunite when this war ends."

Rachel watched as Loreta turned without replying and retreated into the mist, her silhouette vanishing as quickly as it had appeared.

A moment later, a river rat the size of a small cat scurried across the damp planks, its claws tapping faintly in the silence she left behind. It paused near Rachel, nose twitching, as if scenting something, then slipped through a gap between the boards and vanished into the shadows below.

Rachel watched its passage without alarm. The creature seemed fitting, a grim little messenger trailing the bitterness of Sarah's words. Its presence was low and furtive, its teeth no less sharp than the ultimatum her sister had sent.

It was then that Rachel began to understand the full weight of her reply to her sister's demand. Her words were spoken before thought could catch them, drawn up from some place deep within her soul.

Yet even though the conviction in her answer bypassed any conscious consideration, she could not shake a gnawing sense of failure. She had spent years being a big sister to

Sarah, yet somewhere along the way, she had failed to instill in her the ability to love others unconditionally. Now, she was left with the trauma of being separated from her family forever—unless she could find a way to reach her conscience.

"One step at a time," she told herself softly, "That will be a challenge for another day."

As Rachel cautiously navigated the familiar streets to avoid Union patrols, her thoughts turned to the dilemma that consumed her. How could she disclose the truth about Thomas's heritage to him? And how would he react to the revelation of his mixed-race lineage in a South deeply entrenched in taboos about miscegenation?

78

ALONE

Rachel sat motionless on the edge of her bed, her hands trembling. Her thoughts turned to Thomas, the one person whose strength she depended on. Yet the truth of his heritage, still hidden from him, cast a long shadow over everything.

He would be returning home tonight and deserved to know the truth about the mixed-race blood that coursed through his veins in a world that sought to shame and punish such truths. Yet, she had considered keeping it from him, telling herself it was for his protection, just as his father and mother had. Was it something he truly needed to know?

Then again, how could she shield Thomas from the truth that Josephine was his mother? And what if their children bore features that betrayed their father's lineage? More importantly, how would they chart a path forward in a place where his heritage would invite scorn and condemnation?

Rachel's chest tightened as she rose from the bed. The light from the kerosene lamp on the bedside table cast flickering shadows across the room as she moved to the window and drew back the heavy curtain. The streets below were hushed, the occasional sound of hooves on cobblestones breaking the stillness of the dimly lit street. She pressed her palm to the cool glass, willing clarity to come.

"Alone." The word escaped her lips, an unguarded whisper she hadn't meant to voice, not even in the privacy of her thoughts. The war had stolen so much: her family, her certainty about the world, and the secure place she once believed she held within it.

And now, she would have to turn Thomas's world upside down.

She fell back onto the bed, the mattress yielding softly beneath her weight as her body sank into its embrace. Yet it offered no comfort to her troubled mind. Her eyes drifted to the ceiling, its blank expanse stretching above her like a *tabula rasa*. She waited for the future to be written, just as the wall once bore the ominous handwriting in the Book of Daniel, foretelling King Belshazzar's fall.

She squeezed her eyes shut, willing the ceiling to remain blank, to hold its secrets. Yet, even in its emptiness, it seemed to mock her, a reminder that the answers she sought might come in ways she wasn't prepared to face.

Thomas entered the bedroom to find Rachel fully dressed and fast asleep atop the bedcovers, illuminated by the soft glow of her table lamp. He paused, his gaze lingering lovingly on her for a moment. Then, he moved to his side of the bed and began to undress.

"Thomas?" Rachel asked, rubbing her eyes.

"I didn't mean to wake you," Thomas said.

"What time is it?"

"It's almost midnight, darling."

"I'm so glad you're home," she said, sitting up to stretch.

Thomas finished pulling off his shoes and circled the bed, leaning over to kiss her. "I'm glad to be home, as well." He paused. "Why are you still dressed?"

"I must have fallen asleep waiting for you," she said, yawning. "How was your trip?"

"It went well, thank you. Much is afoot among the Confederate sympathizers."

"Anything here in New Orleans?"

"Yes," he said.

"Then we're safe," she said with a smile. "You're here." She sat up in bed and moved over. "Come sit by me, Thomas. There's something I need to tell you. Something important."

He circled the bed to sit beside her. "Go on."

Rachel drew a steadying breath. "It's about Josephine."

"Josephine?"

"Yes. From Buttonwillow. She's not just a family friend, Thomas. She's... she's your mother."

Thomas blinked. "My mother?" he echoed incredulously. "How...how could that be? My mother died in childbirth."

"That's what your father told you," Rachel interrupted gently. "But Josephine gave birth to you. She was young, just a girl, and your father loved her, but their love was forbidden."

Thomas leaned back, his brows furrowing as the pieces began to fall into place. "Josephine is...a quinteroon," he said slowly. "That means I'm a hexadecaroon."

"Yes," Rachel confirmed. "From what I can tell, your great-great-great-grandfather was a Negro. Your father kept it hidden, perhaps to protect you from the harshness of our world."

For a moment, Thomas said nothing. Then he exhaled, shaking his head with a faint, incredulous smile. "Rachel, I…I don't even know what to say. It's so unexpected. I can't believe Josephine is my mother."

Relief flooded Rachel's face, and she reached for his hand. "I feared you'd be upset, but I should have known better. Thomas, you've always been a man of great heart." She paused, then added softly, "I love you as you are. This changes nothing for me. It makes me admire you even more that you embrace your heritage."

His fingers tightened around hers, and he kissed her on the forehead. "You're incredible, Rachel." His eyes softened.

"There's something else," Rachel said. "Josephine is Catholic, not Jewish."

Thomas appeared stunned. "That means I'm not Jewish by birth."

Rachel's heart ached to hear the sudden vulnerability in his voice. She gently cupped his cheek, guiding his gaze back to hers. "Thomas, neither of us follows orthodoxy, and you've adopted Deism. What defines us isn't our lineage or heritage. What matters is how we shape ourselves, create our life together, and share our love."

"You're right, dear," he said, embracing her.

"And I love you," she whispered, holding him tightly. "There is one other thing," she said, pulling away.

"Yes?" Thomas asked.

"I feel so guilty," Rachel admitted.

"About what?" he pressed.

"Eugenia's trunk," she said hesitantly. "I never told you about it. I agreed to help her send it to LaGrange with Loreta's assistance. Loreta later told me that Sarah thanked me for helping get the contents to her and said I did the right thing, whatever that meant."

Thomas returned a mischievous grin. "You have no idea what was in that trunk, do you?"

Rachel's curiosity sparked. "No," she replied. "Do you?"

"Maps," he said, a glint of pride in his eyes. "Maps of strategic Union troop locations. But Eugenia and Loreta didn't know that those maps weren't from their agents in New Orleans. I drew them. I altered the numbers and locations to make our strongest fortifications look weak and our weakest look strong, then placed them in the hands of double agents."

Rachel's brows furrowed in confusion. "So, does that mean…"

"Exactly," Thomas interrupted, his smile widening. "They attacked our strongholds, thinking them vulnerable, and avoided our weak points, believing them impenetrable. That's one of the reasons they're losing so badly."

"Did you come up with this plan on your own?" Rachel asked, her tone a mix of surprise and admiration.

Thomas's smile turned proud as he nodded.

Rachel silently leaned into his embrace, her earlier guilt melting into a quiet admiration for his ingenuity. "I was thinking," she said, pulling away from him. "Life is much more interesting now that I'm married to a hexadecagonic fellow. There are so many more sides of you than I realized."

Thomas burst into laughter, remembering his Euclidean geometry and the sixteen-sided figure Rachel was comparing to his one-in-sixteen-part African blood.

FOR SALE
AT
AUCTION

79

THANKSGIVING

Rachel and Thomas strolled hand in hand along the uneven cobblestones of Faubourg Tremé, the lively district just north of Rampart Street that marked the edge of the French Quarter. They delighted in the crunch of the autumn leaves beneath their feet and the nostalgic scent of distant bonfires.

The fall air at the outdoor market was rich and intoxicating, carrying the mingling aromas of freshly baked bread of various varieties, savory gumbo bubbling in cast-iron pots suspended from tripods over crackling wood fires, chicken fricassée, and the sugary warmth of pralines cooling in rows spread out on waxed paper.

The faint, briny scent of oysters being expertly shucked by Negro women around a table with glinting oyster knives wove itself into the air. The shimmering oysters, set out on thin wooden planks with various spicy sauces made from Scotch bonnet peppers and other Caribbean chilies, beckoned to eager oyster enthusiasts.

The streets pulsed with a living symphony of color and motion, where French, Spanish, and Caribbean accents intertwined like instruments in concert, rising and falling with the rhythm of the crowd. Vendors leaned over makeshift wooden stalls and carts, their voices bright and animated, hawking their offerings with a cadence as lively as the city itself.

A Creole woman with a brightly patterned tignon tied high on her head stood at the heart of the bustle, gracefully ladling thick, fragrant shrimp étouffée into waiting bowls of rice, the aroma filling the air with its promise of warmth and satisfaction. The colorful tignon, once mandated for women of African descent by the Spanish to distinguish them from White women, had, a century later, become embraced as a stylish accessory and a way to celebrate their heritage.

Nearby, a young Negro boy strained against the handle of a wooden press, squeezing juice from sliced ripe oranges that glistened like miniature suns under the slant of late afternoon light. Each squeeze released an essence of citrus into the air, a vibrant contrast to the deep, savory aromas of the simmering dishes.

Together, the sights, sounds, and smells of the market enveloped Rachel and Thomas, a feast for the senses that captured the neighborhood's vibrant culture.

"Do you think any of the vendors will take us to court for stealing the smell of their baked goods?" Rachel teased, her tone light as she recalled the old Arabic tale of a poor man hauled before a judge for simply savoring the baker's aromas without paying.

"If they do," Thomas replied with a grin, "I'll pull out a gold coin, and the judge will rule that the vendor's delight at the sight of the gold is payment enough."

Rachel laughed, her eyes wandering to a tray of sliced apples covered with honey and arranged in an enticing display. She exchanged a glance with Thomas, who obligingly reached for several pennies and placed them in the vendor's hand. The vendor, an older man with a weathered face and a cheerful air, handed Rachel a piece of honied fruit wrapped in parchment paper, then another to Thomas, who savored its sweetness.

The sounds of a fiddle, drums, and a tambourine rose above the din from beneath a giant Live Oak tree where a small group of street musicians had gathered. Their melodies were a lively blend of French, Spanish, and African influences. The rhythm was infectious, and Rachel found her step unconsciously quickening to the beat.

Children darted between the adults, laughing as they chased each other with carefree abandon. Occasionally, they bumped into unsuspecting adults, eliciting startled looks or indulgent chuckles from those too charmed to scold.

Thomas pointed toward a woman balancing a huge tray of beignets on her head, the powdered sugar forming a pale, sweet-smelling cloud as she navigated the crowd. Nearby, a boy with smudged cheeks sold *calas*, warm rice fritters piled high in a basket. Rachel bought two, their golden crust yielding a soft, sweet interior that melted on her tongue. She offered one to Thomas, who eagerly accepted the treat.

"Honest Abe did it again," Thomas said, bending down to pick up a trampled political broadside of the McClellan-Lincoln presidential election from earlier in the month.

Rachel smiled proudly. "Yes, indeed. His victory secured the promise of reunifying the nation and freeing the slaves."

"He also assured you of a career in teaching children. I was struck by how this broadside placed McClellan's and Lincoln's platforms in stark contrast."

"I haven't seen that one," Rachel said. "So many circulated before the election. They seemed to be raining from the sky like cats and dogs."

"It says here that this one is by Siebert, a printer based in New York City." He handed the broadside to her. "As you can see, it's divided into two scenes. The one on the left is entitled 'Union and Liberty,' showing Lincoln shaking hands with a common workman holding a handsaw, with a background of mixed-race children running out of a schoolhouse. The one on the right is entitled 'Union and Slavery,' depicting McClellan in military uniform shaking hands with Confederate President Jefferson Davis. Notice the slave auction taking place behind them."

"That *is* a stark contrast," Rachel said, examining the sheet. "It's visually striking, but do you think it accurately depicts their respective platforms?"

"In a very simplistic manner of speaking, yes," Thomas said, taking the broadside back to toss in a trash bin along the way. "Lincoln, running as a Republican under the National Union Party banner, was for continuing the war until the Confederacy was defeated, abolishing slavery, and carrying out Reconstruction to reintegrate Southern states and heal the nation. McClellan, a Democrat, ran with a party divided between the Peace Democrats, or Copperheads, who favored an immediate and unconditional settlement with the Confederacy without discussing slavery, and the War Democrats, who supported the war effort but were critical of what they considered Lincoln's high-handed manner."

"So, if I understand correctly," Rachel said, "Lincoln was for abolishing slavery and preserving the Union, while McClellan had to deal with a divided party that wanted peace at any price without giving a fig about slavery."

"Close enough," Thomas said with a grin. "You summed it all up rather nicely."

"Thank you," Rachel said, apparently pleased with her grasp of the two factions' differences. "Didn't you once tell me that you saw Mrs. McClellan dressed in secessionist colors to display her Confederate sympathies?"

"Yes, I believe I recall mentioning it in passing."

"One is left to wonder if her husband shared some of the same leanings."

"I suppose we will never know," Thomas said. "But he certainly was no stalwart abolitionist."

Rachel suddenly became solemn. "Thomas, do you think the war's end will unite us as a nation?"

"No," he replied without hesitation. "Peace after a storm is a comforting thought, but the storm doesn't always end when the rain clouds pass. The flood that often follows in the aftermath wreaks destruction long after the skies have cleared."

80

CHRISTMAS EVE

The early sunbeams danced through the French Market, painting the bustling vendors and holiday shoppers in soft, burnished tones as if Mother Nature had set up her easel in the square.

Rachel and Thomas huddled close in their heavy wool coats on Christmas Eve morning, sharing warm beignets and cradling cups of hot coffee in their hands.

"What a beautiful, crisp morning," Rachel said, inhaling deeply. "I love the smell of fresh coffee and bread just pulled from the oven."

Thomas sprinkled more powdered sugar over his beignet before taking a bite and washing it down with a sip of coffee. "There's a certain magic about this time of year," he mused. "How could anyone, Christian or not, argue with a holiday celebrating 'Peace on Earth and Goodwill toward Men?'"

Rachel's expression dimmed, the warmth in her smile fading. "If only mankind could live by those words."

Thomas breathed a reflective sigh. "Territory, nationalism, and the thirst for wealth and power, all wrapped in ethnicity and religion," he said, the weight of history clear in his tone. "Those forces have driven war since the beginning of civilization. They're woven into the fabric of every society."

Rachel nodded thoughtfully. "Religion has undoubtedly shaped history in ways that are less than holy. It's why our forefathers fled the religious wars in Europe and emphasized the importance of separating church and state."

"As you know, that's why I've always leaned toward Deism as most of our forefathers did," Thomas admitted.

Rachel leaned back, pondering. "I can understand Deism. In some ways, I've always felt that religions were man-made. There are so many of them, after all." She hesitated, then asked, "Thomas, would you want to raise our children to be Jewish?"

Thomas's response was immediate. "Of course. It's how I was raised. Besides, since you're Jewish by birth, as their mother, they will be Jewish. When they're old enough, they can decide for themselves what to believe."

A playful glint flickered in Rachel's eyes. "Let's return to the Peace on Earth part, shall we? I think I've had my fill of talk about war and religion."

Thomas sidled up to her, and the two sat savoring their coffee, beignets, and strolling carolers' songs.

"I'm looking forward to your students joining us for Christmas tonight," Thomas said, breaking the silence.

"Lily and Sam were thrilled when I invited them," Rachel said warmly. "The other children have places to go, but those two… they've always gravitated toward me. They're such affectionate, clever little souls."

"And the tree looks perfect," Thomas added.

"That's only because you found the fullest one at the market and somehow managed to haul it up the stairs to the library."

"It would still be bare without your decorations."

"And it would still be bare if you hadn't helped string the garlands and fasten the candles," Rachel teased, recalling Thomas's insistence on setting buckets of water by the tree. It had been non-negotiable, a part of his careful, methodical nature that required every precaution before he agreed to join her in the festive task.

Thomas leaned back, hands wrapped around his still-warm coffee cup. "Looks like it took both of us, then."

Their hands touched briefly, a gentle warmth spreading through Rachel, catching her off guard. "I'd kiss you, but…" She cast a playful glance around the bustling market, her smile teasing. "We're in public."

Thomas's cheeks flushed, though a mischievous grin curled at his lips. "I've yet to see any order forbidding public affection."

Rachel's laughter lingered in the crisp air. "No," she said, her eyes softening, "but my father, God rest his soul, certainly did. It was a strict rule for both of his girls."

Thomas chuckled, leaning in to whisper in her ear. "Your father's not here now to enforce that rule."

Rachel's smile deepened, the playful glint in her eye edged with a hint of nostalgia. "Even if he were, I'd petition for an exception."

Before Thomas could respond, the sound of strolling carolers drifted toward them, their harmonies weaving through the market air. The group, bundled against the chill, sang cheerfully about joy and peace, their voices rising above the bustle of vendors and shoppers.

Thomas tilted his head, savoring the music. "Christmas wouldn't be Christmas without carolers, would it?"

Rachel's eyes softened, the melody stirring something warm within her. "No, they're inseparable. Although my family never celebrated Christmas, we would gather around the piano and sing while Sarah played a few carols. 'Silent Night' was my favorite."

"Comment ça va?" croaked a raspy voice. Rachel turned to see a man adjusting the position of his hoop, atop which perched a brilliant parrot, its feathers a riot of green, red, and gold. The bird bobbed its head and offered another spirited *"Comment ça va?"* to every passerby, its cheerful French greeting startlingly clear, as if a Parisian street vendor had taught it.

"How delightful!" she exclaimed.

"Yes, but I wouldn't want that one in the parlor," Thomas said with a smile.

"Neither would I," Rachel agreed.

Thomas let the moment linger before continuing the conversation. "Have you found a present for Lily yet?"

"Done," Rachel replied. "What about Sam's gift?"

"Done."

Rachel gave a little shiver and shifted closer to Thomas. "The day is still young, darling. Let's have another cup of coffee, eat beignets until we can't manage another bite, and watch the world drift past."

The two sat nestled together in contented silence, enjoying coffee and smiling as they watched an elderly gentleman in a tall silk hat and ivory-handled cane bow graciously toward a middle-aged street vendor. With a theatrical flourish, she pinned a nosegay of fragrant Parma violets to his lapel, her eyes dancing with coquettish delight.

Sitting on the parlor sofa after returning from the French Market, Rachel's eyes sparkled with excitement as she carefully removed the paper wrapping from a large rag doll and placed it beside her, smoothing its lace-fringed dress with affection. "I'm so excited, I can scarcely contain myself!"

Thomas leaned in. "Look at that!" he exclaimed, lifting the doll with a broad smile. "A colored rag doll. The only time I've seen one like this was when a little slave girl had one on our plantation, playing with it in front of her cottage."

Rachel beamed. "I can't believe I managed to get one made for Lily. Last week, a Black lady at the French market was selling rag dolls for Christmas. All of them had either blonde or red hair. I asked her if she could make one with features that reflected her heritage. She was initially surprised, but then she gave me the sweetest smile and agreed to make one. I was embarrassed at how little she wanted to charge."

Thomas examined the doll's hair. "Look at that hair," he marveled, his fingers brushing the textured strands. "It's perfect."

"When I picked it up, she explained that she crafted it using the same method she had learned on the plantation. First, she twists thin rag strips into cords, then dyes them with the boiled walnut hulls and madder roots to achieve that deep, rich, reddish-brown hue. I couldn't have been more pleased with how it turned out, so I gave her a little extra."

"Lily's going to treasure her," Thomas said warmly, handing the doll back to Rachel. His eyes twinkled as he opened the package he had brought. "And look what I have for Sam."

Rachel's eyes sparkled. "Socks! The school cook mentioned that's all Sam wanted for Christmas. That boy!"

Thomas confessed, "I might've taken a little detour to the dormitory today to deliver something to match."

"You did?" Rachel asked.

"I thought they'd enjoy new clothes for the party tonight, so I dropped off a few items."

Rachel wrapped her arms around him, squeezing tightly. "You always remind me why I love you," she whispered, kissing him softly. Pulling away, her gaze was inquisitive. "But how did you figure out their sizes?"

With a sly grin, Thomas replied, "The school seamstress helped. She said she always keeps the students' measurements on hand since she never knows when she might need to whip something up."

Their conversation was interrupted by the sound of the doorbell.

"I'll get it," Thomas said, springing up from the sofa. "That should be the children."

When he opened the door, a freedman driver from the school stood on the stoop, straightening his coat.

"May I help you?" Thomas asked.

The driver gave a polite nod. "I've got two children from the school to deliver to this address. Is this the Manget residence?"

"Yes, it is," Thomas confirmed.

The driver turned and offered a hand to help Lily and Sam down from the cab. The moment their feet touched the ground, their faces lit with joy at the sight of Thomas. With giggles of delight, they ran toward him, and he knelt, arms wide, to embrace them both.

"Thank you, driver," Thomas called as the man returned to his seat. "I'll have them back to the dormitory by bedtime."

"Thank you, sir. They told me they need to be in by nine," the driver reminded, adjusting the reins.

Thomas gave a reassuring nod. "You have my word."

The driver doffed his hat and flicked the reins. The carriage rolled smoothly down the street, the rhythmic clatter of hooves fading into the quiet of the evening.

Thomas turned back to the children with a warm smile. "I see you two got the clothes I left for you at the school."

"Yes!" they chimed in unison.

Thomas chuckled. "Sam, you look very handsome. And Lily, you look beautiful."

"Thank you!" they said as Thomas ushered them inside.

The children followed Thomas up the stairs. As they reached the hallway, they stopped and gazed into the library. Their faces lit up with wonder as they beheld the Christmas tree and the presents.

"Come on in, Lily, Sam," Rachel called, offering two candy canes.

"Mrs. Manget!" Lily exclaimed as she and Sam took the candy canes and embraced her.

"Thank you," Sam said. "What kind of candy is this?"

"It's called a candy cane. It's all white, but it tastes a little like pull candy."

"I love pull candy," Sam said, licking the white cane.

"I do, too," Lily said, tasting hers.

"Have you children had supper already?"

"Oh, yes," Lily said. "We had a great big ham, yams, and biscuits."

"It was the biggest ham I've ever seen," Sam said. "Our master never even had one that big."

"Please, children," Rachel said, "sit on the sofa before we open gifts. I'll bring some hot cider with cinnamon sticks from the kitchen."

Lily and Sam sat on the sofa, and Thomas took the chair facing them.

"Did your parents work in the master's house?" Thomas asked.

"Our mama did," Sam said. "Our daddy was the master."

"What was your mother's work at the plantation."

"She was the cook. Leastways she was 'til the master sold her."

"He say she was bad," Lily volunteered, a tear coming to her eye. "He say she ate some of his food while she was cookin' it. She say she just tastin' it see if it needed salt."

"We heard her yellin' all the way outside where we were playin' with the other kids,"

Sam said. "We run inside, and the master was kickin' her while she was on the floor, all curled up with her hands over her face. He yelled at her, 'Now I gottah keep you from eatin' me outtah house and home.'"

"What happened then?" Thomas asked quietly.

"He looked at us real mean and said, 'That's what happens when you steal my food.'" Sam paused. "Then he just walked out like it was nothin'."

Lily's voice quivered as she spoke. "Mama didn't come to bed that night. The next mornin', when we went to the kitchen for our cornbread and milk, we found her." She paused, choking back tears before forcing herself to continue. "She had... this awful thing on her face."

"On her face?" Thomas repeated, frowning."Yes, sir," Sam answered. "It was like somethin' you'd put on a dog to stop it from bitin' you. There was a round piece of metal with holes over her mouth and a collar 'round her neck. A rod run over her head from front to back, holdin' it tight so she couldn't take it off. It had a lock, too, and only the master had the key. He left it on for two whole days 'fo he took it off to let her have a bite to eat."

Sam's voice softened as he spoke. "We had to tilt Mama's head back just to pour water through those tiny holes so she could drink."

Thomas's expression melded sadness with palpable anger; his jaw clenched tight as he listened.

Just then, Rachel's cheerful voice broke through the somber mood. "Here's the cider," she announced as she entered the library, a tray laden with refreshments in hand. "And some fruitcake, too. It's chock-full of pecans, cherries, raisins, and currants."

Thomas carefully took the tray and set it on the table in front of the sofa.

"Only one piece for each of you," she added, "We wouldn't want you to have a bad case of the collywobbles." She leaned over to whisper to Thomas, "I've got a special piece aged in essence of rum for you later, darling."

Thomas grinned.

Noticing tears on the children's cheeks, Rachel paused, her smile fading into concern.

Thomas gave her a knowing look, silently communicating that she should leave the matter be. "Enjoy your fruitcake, kids," he encouraged warmly.

The room filled with lighter chatter as Rachel served the cider, and the children shared tales from school.

Soon, Thomas stood, his voice brightening. "Who wants to open their presents?"

The children's faces lit up, and they clapped excitedly.

"Here's one for you, Sam," Thomas said, handing over a small bundle wrapped in paper and twine.

"And there's one for you under the tree, Lily," Rachel said, retrieving the rag doll she had hidden at the back.

Lily gasped at the sight of it. "She's beautiful! I've never seen nothin' like her, not even in the Big House." She hugged Rachel tightly, her small arms trembling with joy. "Thank you, Mrs. Manget."

"You're welcome, dear," Rachel replied gently as Lily sat down and cradled the doll like a baby.

Sam tore open his bundle and let out a cheer. "Socks!" he cried. "My old ones got holes in 'em. These'll keep my feet from freezin'!" He darted forward and hugged them both with all his might.

Thomas chuckled. "Glad to hear it, Sam. Looks like you're all set."

Then Lily looked shyly at Rachel, holding something behind her back. "I made you this," she whispered, revealing a small corn husk angel tied with bits of ribbon.

Rachel knelt to accept it, her eyes stinging. "She's lovely, Lily. I'll keep her always." She held the angel up to Thomas. "Would you place Lily's angel on top of the tree?"

"Certainly," he said, taking the angel and settling it into the top of the tree.

"How beautiful," Rachel said, a tear rolling down her cheek.

Sam, suddenly bashful, leaned forward to hand Thomas a folded piece of paper. "I drew a picture," he mumbled. "It's you and Ms. Manget. I didn't have no colors, but I tried real hard."

Thomas unfolded the paper carefully, holding it for Rachel to share. "It's perfect, Sam. I think you caught my best side."

Rachel's heart swelled with quiet joy. "These are the best gifts we could've hoped for."

Lily smiled as she held her doll close.

Sam said, "Nobody's ever been as good to us as y'all have. I'm glad there's White people like y'all."

After Thomas delivered the children back to their school, he and Rachel settled on the library sofa, enjoying the warmth of the fire and the soft glow of the candles on the tree, now flickering at the end of their wicks.

"I don't think I've ever seen a Christmas tree in a Jewish home," Thomas mused.

"Neither have I," Rachel admitted with a soft smile. "It does feel out of place, doesn't it?"

"I could get used to it, though," he said, pulling her closer.

"It's not like it belongs only to Christmas," Rachel added, glancing at the flickering candles among the branches.

Thomas tilted his head thoughtfully. "I know. Before Christianity, people celebrated winter by bringing evergreens and holly indoors as symbols of life enduring through the dead of winter."

"Exactly," Rachel nodded. "Father used to say that the early Christians borrowed those customs to mark the birth of Jesus, which they decided to celebrate near the winter solstice since no one had any idea when he was born. And that's how Holly's red berries and green leaves became part of Christmas."

Resting her head on Thomas's shoulder, Rachel sighed. "Honestly, to me, this tree isn't about religion. It's about embracing winter's stillness, kindling the fire of hope against the cold, and trusting that spring will return, bringing new life to the world."

Thomas pressed a kiss on her forehead. "Hoping for new life. Now *that's* a tradition I can get behind."

1865

A MAN FOR ALL AGES

81

NEWS FROM THE EAST

Rachel and Thomas sat on a folded quilt before the library fireplace, the warm glow of the flames casting a golden hue on their faces.

Rachel leaned forward and dipped her fingers into the cool water of her prized Bennington bowl, where the chestnuts had soaked overnight. She gathered a handful and set them on a linen towel. One by one, she scored an X into each softened end with a paring knife, then placed them carefully into a cast-iron pan.

"I was delighted to find marrons this year," she said proudly.

"They're my favorite," Thomas replied. "Once they're cooked, the flesh of these giant beauties is almost like a perfectly roasted sweet potato."

Rachel's expression softened with nostalgia. "I remember when my grandmother visited us from Paris when I was a child. She brought a box of the most exquisite *marrons glacés* for Chanukah. Such a special candied treat."

Thomas nodded. "I always preferred them over the local pralines. In my opinion, the thick caramel in pralines tends to overpower the flavor of the pecans."

"I couldn't agree more," Rachel said. She then fell into a pensive mood. "Thomas."

"Yes, dear?"

"Do you think this year will bring the peace everyone's praying for?" she asked, her voice tinged with hope.

Thomas nodded thoughtfully. "The tide does appear to be turning with Sherman's march to the sea, Lincoln's resolve, and soldiers deserting in droves from the Confederacy.

At this pace, the war can't last much longer." Thomas paused. "Then there's the upcoming Hampton Roads peace conference."

"Peace conference?"

"Yes. The first official peace conference of the war. The elder Francis Blair, editor of the *Washington Globe* and personal advisor to the President, played a crucial role in laying the groundwork for the meeting. The President himself will be there."

"Let us pray that he is successful," she said. Then she fell silent for a moment, gazing deep into the fire. "When I think of peace, I can't help but think of my family and how I desperately hope they are doing well."

"Yes," Thomas said. "I do as well. I can see little Noah on his rocking horse now."

Rachel kissed his cheek. "It was kind of you to give Sarah the money to replace his Chester," she said, though the gesture struck her with bitter irony, recalling her sister's vow to cut ties if she remained with Thomas because of his race.

Thomas returned her smile, savoring the warmth of her words. The room fell into a comfortable silence, punctuated by the crackling of the fire. After a moment, he broke the silence. "Jack came to mind today." He placed the chestnuts in a long-handled roaster and held them over the embers, stirring them gently with a broad wooden spoon.

"Jack?" Rachel glanced up, recognizing the name. "Wasn't he your childhood friend?"

"Yes," Thomas replied. "I visited him at the St. Louis Hotel hospital this morning. He's back from Sherman's march."

"How is he?" she asked, remembering her visit to the hospital where she found Jacob.

"Alive," Thomas said, though there was sadness in his voice. "But not without scars. He's…well, he's changed. He shared a story that stuck with me."

Rachel paused. "What was it?" she asked softly.

Thomas's gaze fixed on the crackling flames. "Sherman presented Savannah to Lincoln as a Christmas gift. But Jack… he doesn't talk about the battles, the skirmishes, or the victories, Rachel. He talks about the people left behind. Those who had to flee, risking their lives to gain their freedom."

"Sitting here together, safe and warm by this fire, it's easy for us to forget the human toll of it all."

Thomas nodded sadly, stirring the chestnuts as their shells began to blacken and split. "He said something else, too, about the slaves. He's seen ghosts. Not the kind we think of in stories around the campfire, but the phantoms of nightmares that linger in the darkness until twilight."

Rachel reached for the chilled white wine and poured two glasses, the pale golden liquid catching the firelight. She handed one to Thomas, her fingers brushing his. "To the ones who carry those ghosts," she said quietly, raising her glass.

Thomas met her gaze, his eyes filled with gratitude for her warm companionship. "And to those who fight to survive." They clinked their glasses gently, a note of fragile harmony in the quiet room.

"Whoa! I almost burned them!" Thomas exclaimed, taking the long wooden handle of the chestnut roaster and carefully transferring them to a waiting cast-iron *rechaud*. The chestnuts' aroma mingled with the faint fruitiness of the wine as they peeled them, revealing the tender flesh inside.

"They're not burned. They're perfect," Rachel remarked after a taste, her voice lighter as they allowed the moment to shift to the feast before them. They nibbled on the chestnuts, pairing their earthy, nutty flavors with the savory depth of rich, creamy Brie slices.

There was a sense of solace in their quiet library, with the warmth of the fire, the food, the wine, and each other's company. Their conversation ebbed and flowed as the evening deepened, touching everything from the day they first met to memories of their wedding day to idle dreams for their future together.

As the fire died to glowing embers, Thomas threw on another log and began recounting his visit to the hospital to see his friend, Jack.

The air in the St. Louis Hotel hospital reeked with the biting sting of antiseptics mingling with the sickly sweetness of ether, a noxious blend that floated above a chorus of groans. Pale morning light seeped through the high windows, wavering uncertainly as though it feared intruding upon a dark space saturated with suffering.

Jack, a young planter's son who recently returned from Savannah after fighting for the Union, sat upright in bed, propped on a pillow, his gaunt face hollowed by weeks of fever. His right arm lay cradled in a sling, his fingers curling aimlessly as if uncertain of their rightful owner.

Thomas sat in a chair beside him, hands clasped between his knees, his gaze steady on Jack's face. He said nothing, waiting patiently for his friend's words to come. "It was early December," Jack began, his voice distant as if slipping into a dream. "We were pulling out just as a storm set in. Had orders to rejoin the main column. Used a pontoon bridge to cross Ebenezer Creek. Seemed more like a river where we crossed it. Cold as hell, it was. No time to think, just haul and hammer, lay the planks and pontoons, then march." He paused, eyes fixed on something Thomas couldn't see. "But they came. Lord Almighty, they came."

"Who?" Thomas asked.

Jack blinked slowly. "The slaves," he said quietly. "Like a flood busting loose from a broken levee behind us. Men, women, children. They run like the devil hisself was nippin' at their heels." He scrubbed his face with his good hand, his eyes red from too many sleepless nights. "Never seen anything like it."

He glanced up pitifully at Thomas. "They knew, Thomas. You could see it in their eyes. They knew that bridge we were taking down behind us was their only road to freedom."

Thomas leaned forward, fingers laced tight. "Did many of them make it?"

"Some did. The ones that made it onto the bridge before we started taking it down. A few others reached the bridge on a log raft our men helped 'em hitch up to it." Jack's breath drew in slowly and deeply as if the world's weight sat on his chest. "But not all. Like I said, we were pulling the bridge apart behind us. General said we'd need it up the line. You ever try to tell a woman holding her baby up over her head in the ice-cold water you ain't got time to save it when she's drownin'?"

Jack didn't wait for Thomas to answer. "Halfway 'cross the river, that mama was sinking up to her neck, holding her baby up to me like she's offerin' it to God." Jack's voice cracked, his good hand curling into a fist on his knee. "I'll never forget her face, Thomas. Never. When I grabbed that baby and watched its mama go under, that was the moment I thanked God I left Baton Rouge to fight for the Union."

He rubbed his eyes hard, grinding the heel of his palm into the socket like he could scrub the images clean from his mind. "Some of them reached the bridge. Feet slipping on the wet planks, eyes wild, like animals backed into a corner. But we were pulling it apart, plank by plank. One second, they're clinging to something steady; next second, they're grabbing at nothin' but air."

Thomas's throat tightened, a hard ache settling in his gut.

"Don't think I didn't try like hell, Thomas," Jack's voice fell quieter, like a confession. "After I sent the baby on with another woman on the bridge, I hauled up a boy, couldn't have been more than ten. His hands were cold as ice, fingers clamped onto my sleeve like a crab that won't let go. I pulled him up, shoved him toward the line, and he run like hell. Didn't even look back. But I couldn't get 'em all. The water was too cold…." He shivered, immersed in the moment.

Jack's eyes squeezed shut as tears traced silent paths down his cheeks. "I still hear them crying out, Thomas, 'Don't leave us, Yanks! Please, Lord, don't leave us!'" He fell silent for a moment. "Voices full of pain, like fingernails scrapin' on a chalkboard inside my skull. Then the rebels reached the creek. Stood there and fired on the slaves. Didn't even have to aim. Picked 'em off one at a time like they was fish in the water."

Jack's eyes narrowed, his face hardening like stone. "Once we reached shore, there were land torpedoes," he muttered. "Eight-inch shells buried just deep enough in the road to blow a man's legs clean off if he stepped wrong. Damn rebel trick. I've seen it happen. Boy 'side me couldn't have been older than nineteen. One second, he's laughin' and runnin' like hell; the next, he's lyin' on the ground screamin' with no legs to run on. Blood everywhere." He glanced at his bound arm. "That's how I got this. Doc says he may have to cut it off."

Thomas's eyes met Jack's with quiet understanding.

"After that boy died, Sherman made them Reb prisoners who planted them torpedoes walk the ground first," Jack added. "Said if they're gonna lay the road to Hell, they're gonna be the first to walk it."

They sat in silence, the groan of a soldier down the hall drifting toward them.

Thomas's eyes shifted to Jack's face, watching as his friend's breath slowed, eyes half-lidded with pain and exhaustion.

"Do you think most of them made it?" Thomas asked.

Jack's gaze drifted to the window, his eyes narrowing as if he were tracking figures only he could see beyond the glass. "Some did," he reflected, his voice as reverent as a eulogy. His brow furrowed, and his eyelids drooped; his words were muttered like a man speaking in his sleep. "Some always do, don't they, Thomas?"

Thomas watched Jack until his breathing slowed, then rose slowly to reach and pull up the threadbare sheet to cover his chest. "Sleep well, my friend," he whispered, resting a hand gently on his feverish forehead. "And may God grant you peace."

Rachel leaned into Thomas, resting her head on his shoulder. Her eyes closed as her breath synchronized with the slow, soothing rhythm of his chest's rise and fall. The warmth of his presence, the soft glow of the fire, and the lingering flavors of sweet wine and roasted chestnuts wrapped around her like a comforting blessing.

"I can't believe we've been married for a year this month," Rachel said.

"It seems like yesterday," Thomas agreed.

They sat in stillness, holding each other. The fire's gentle crackle underscored the quiet peace of the room, while the distant whistle of the wind beyond the French doors reminded them of the cold world outside.

82

THE HAMPTON ROADS
PEACE CONFERENCE

The *River Queen*, a privately owned Union-contracted sidewheel steamboat, lay anchored at Hampton Roads, a vast natural harbor in southeastern Virginia at the confluence of the James, Elizabeth, and Nansemond Rivers.

The still waters and sunlit shorelines belied a past marked by fire and fury. In March 1862, the ironclads *USS Monitor* and *CSS Virginia* collided here in a battle that shattered the age of wooden warships and heralded a new era of naval warfare. Their brutal stalemate became a living embodiment of the ancient "irresistible force paradox," where an unstoppable force meets an immovable object, each incapable of prevailing.

The paradox extended beyond the battlefield, reflecting the very nature of the war itself. Like the unstoppable force, the Union surged forward with industrial might, boundless manpower, abolitionist fervor, and the conviction that the nation must remain whole. Its factories relentlessly churned out weapons, ships, and rail lines at an unprecedented pace, driven by a belief in progress and an unyielding will to preserve the Union.

On the other side stood the Confederacy, immovable in its resolve to protect a way of life rooted in agriculture, slave labor, hierarchy, and the doctrine of states' rights. It clung to the idea that sovereignty lay with the states, not a distant federal government. With generals steeped in tradition and soldiers fighting on familiar soil, the Confederacy's strength lay in its defensive posture and unrelenting resolve. Like the immovable object, it did not need to advance. It simply had to endure.

The *River Queen's* saloon, the chosen meeting place for this official peace negotiation between the Union and the Confederacy, exuded an air of opulence and sophistication. The polished mahogany table gleamed under the muted light of brass fixtures, positioned amidst fine naval furnishings. Rich, olive-drab velvet drapes framed the rectangular windows, evoking the atmosphere of an aristocratic drawing room rather than the stark strength and functionality of a naval vessel's round portholes.

President Lincoln sat slightly stooped over on one side of the table. His inimitable expression bore a blend of solemnity and cordial warmth that reflected the moment's gravity while preserving his approachable demeanor. Beside him, Secretary of State William H. Seward maintained the poise of a seasoned diplomat and negotiator, his sharp gaze studying the Confederate envoys facing him across the table.

Opposite them, a diminutive Vice President, Alexander H. Stephens of the Confederacy, appeared frail from his bout with tuberculosis. John A. Campbell, the Confederate Assistant Secretary of War, carried himself with a grave, unyielding dignity befitting his station. R. M. T. Hunter, Confederate senator and former Secretary of State, sat stiffly, his wearied face betraying the strain of the conflict.

Just outside the room stood two of Lincoln's bodyguards and two Confederate agents.

President Lincoln, a hint of a smile on his face, opened the meeting shortly after arriving at ten o'clock in the evening. "Gentlemen, I appreciate your making the journey, and I trust that you have been made comfortable and provided with a meal to your liking. I have always found this ship and its crew to be most accommodating and have chosen it many times for my travel."

Stephens nodded. "We appreciate the hospitality of your crew, sir, and hope that our meeting will yield fruitful results and foster mutual respect between our respective nations."

"This war has brought much suffering to both our peoples," Lincoln said. "I hope we might find common ground to bring it to a swift and just end."

Adopting a firm stance, Stephens said, "Mr. Lincoln, we share that hope. But common ground seems elusive when the demands upon us are tantamount to unconditional surrender. Your terms appear as non-negotiable as they have been since the exchange of letters between our representatives and your Mr. Greeley at Niagara Falls."

Lincoln leaned back. "Mr. Stephens, I would rather not discuss surrender or the past. Reconciliation is the goal. After so much bloodshed, let neither side claim a hollow, vainglorious victory. Let your people return to the Union not as vanquished foes but as brothers coming home to their families."

"And what, sir," Hunter interjected, "awaits our people upon returning? Homes lay waste, an economy is in ruins, and a social fabric is torn asunder. The sudden emancipation of a vast, uneducated, and potentially violent slave population unprepared for the responsibilities of citizenship poses challenges that cannot be ignored. How does the Union propose addressing these profound upheavals in our society?"

"We are all familiar with the work of the great Adam Smith, the British economist who maintains that slavery is more expensive than using paid labor," Lincoln continued. "He also argues that slaves have little incentive to maximize output because, regardless of their effort, they can only acquire the bare minimum they need to survive, which leads to their unrest."

Stephens narrowed his eyes. "Even if we accepted his argument, sir, you cannot expect us to change the foundation of our economy overnight."

"By rejoining the Union, Mr. Stephens," Lincoln said, "your representatives would gain the opportunity to delay the ratification of the Thirteenth Amendment, which has already passed Congress and seeks to abolish slavery. This will happen shortly if you do not return. If you do return, you would have enough states to delay the amendment's ratification long enough to change your society's economic basis. General Banks has successfully demonstrated a transition from slavery to salaried labor in Louisiana. I would gladly arrange for you to review the accounting ledgers of the plantations he examined to assure you of the financial advantage of shifting from slave to compensated labor."

Seward spoke next, his calm, deliberate tone cutting through the tension. "Mr. Hunter, I must remind you that this conflict did not begin with the question of slavery, at least from the Union's side. The Union's initial purpose was to preserve the Constitution and prevent disunion. Slavery, as you well know, is guaranteed within the framework of that Constitution, and we did not seek to disturb it where it already existed."

Hunter's demeanor hardened as Seward continued.

"But the course of this war has changed the landscape entirely. When your Confederacy chose to sever its ties with the Union, it abandoned the protections afforded by the Constitution. As a result, it is no longer shielded under its provisions. Therefore, it has become a central issue in our divide, not by our choosing but by your secession."

Seward paused as if to gauge the reception his forceful words received from the Southern delegation.

Hunter's face reddened, but he responded with restraint. "You speak of protections under the Constitution as if they were a kindness bestowed upon us by your benevolence, but I tell you, sir, those protections were never yours to grant. The Constitution is no sword for you to wield as you please. It was a compact agreed to by sovereign states, each with an equal claim to its protection. It was you, the North, that first breached the compact, trampling on the rights of our people and denying us the liberty to govern our affairs. You are mistaken if you believe we have abandoned those protections by secession. Nay, we have reclaimed them. For if sovereignty means anything, it means the right to withdraw from tyranny when it comes calling in the guise of union."

"We do not speak of this lightly, Mr. Hunter," Seward said, "nor without understanding the profound changes it brings. The Union does not seek to impose further hardship upon you or infringe upon your legitimate rights. Instead, we extend our hand in partnership to rebuild a nation where every citizen, free and equal, can thrive. It will not be easy or swift, but it is the only way to ensure that the sacrifices made on both sides were not in vain."

Stephens's eyes narrowed beneath a furrowed brow. The man who once proclaimed slavery the "cornerstone" of Southern society now sat face-to-face with the agents of its irrevocable end. "Mr. Seward, will the Union guarantee the safety of our citizens and leaders if we choose to lay down arms?"

Lincoln joined in; his voice was soft and earnest. "Mr. Stephens, I have no desire for vengeance. I aim to heal this nation and provide financial aid for reconstruction."

"Mr. Lincoln," Stephens began, his tone sharp but controlled, "abolition would do more than disrupt our economy. It would strip the South of its political power. Without the Three-Fifths Clause, we would lose a sizable portion of our representation in Congress."

Lincoln leaned forward, his expression calm and reassuring. "Mr. Stephens, I understand your concern, but let me assure you, the latest census indicates a potential gain if you are willing to treat all men as full citizens. This increase in representation would ensure that your region's voice becomes even stronger."

Stephens hesitated, his gaze narrowing. "You present a persuasive case, Mr. Lincoln, but you failed to mention that the numbers still favor the North by an overwhelming margin. That same census you reference counts your population at 22.3 million, including slaves in the North. Compare that to the mere 1.4 million votes we might gain by granting freedom and enfranchisement to ours. And even then, the economic devastation of losing our labor force far outweighs any minor gains in representation."

Before Lincoln could respond, Campbell interjected, his tone sharp, "And what of our other property, Mr. Lincoln? Will the government confiscate what little remains to us as contraband of war, the way it has our slaves?"

Stephens shot Campbell a pointed look, a silent signal to temper his tone, before turning to hear Lincoln's response.

The President's expression steeled, though his voice remained steady. "Beyond your slaves, who will no longer be regarded as property, you have my word that this government does not seek to become a tyrant."

Hunter leaned forward, his eyes narrowing. "What about those who have sacrificed everything for the Confederacy? Will they now be branded as traitors?"

"No, Senator," Lincoln replied, his words deliberate and measured. "They will be remembered as Americans, as will the fallen of the Union whose sacrifice I honored at Gettysburg. There will be no trials, no executions. I assure you of that, so long as I am President."

"Mr. Lincoln," Stephens said, "with the understanding that we are not authorized to enter into any binding agreements, we *are* empowered to negotiate peace terms and present them to President Davis and his Cabinet."

"I understand," Lincoln said.

"Then let us proceed to negotiate, even if we continue until sunrise."

HARPER'S WEEKLY.

A JOURNAL OF CIVILIZATION.

Vol. IX.—No. 425.]   NEW YORK, SATURDAY, FEBRUARY 18, 1865.   [SINGLE COPIES TEN CENTS.
$4.00 PER YEAR IN ADVANCE.

Entered according to Act of Congress, in the Year 1865, by Harper & Brothers, in the Clerk's Office of the District Court for the Southern District of New York.

SCENE IN THE HOUSE ON THE PASSAGE OF THE PROPOSITION TO AMEND THE CONSTITUTION, January 31, 1865.

83

THE THIRTEENTH AMENDMENT

Shortly after the ink dried on their notes and the *River Queen* slipped back into the tide, the currents of change had already begun to course through the capital. In Washington's coffeehouses, where the air swirled with the mingling aromas of tobacco and damp wool from the pouring rain, young men entrusted with the care of the nation's conscience sat hunched over steaming cups, pondering what lay ahead.

The air inside Klemm's, the coffee house next to Ford's Theatre, was thick with the warm aroma of roasted Jamaican coffee beans and Havana cigars, accompanied by the clink of porcelain cups and the low murmur of conversation among Washington's elite. Sleet tapped gently against the warm windowpanes, melting into rivulets that meandered down the leaded glass caming, blurring the wintry world beyond.

John George Nicolay stirred his coffee absentmindedly, perusing *Harper's Weekly*. Across from him, his co-worker, John Milton Hay, sat back in his chair, his arms folded across his chest, studying his colleague's face.

"You've been quiet all evening, Nicolay," Hay said, tilting his chair onto its back legs. "Did you want to talk about tonight's play?"

"*The Toodles?* Not particularly," he replied, casually setting his spoon on the saucer. "By my count, the house employed at least a dozen claqueurs to prime the audience's enthusiasm for the comedic drivel. Mercifully, it had only two acts. Mrs. Lincoln praised it solely because John Wilkes Booth's brother-in-law, Clarke, played the lead. She seems to have taken quite a fancy to him."

"You must admit, though, that Clarke brought a certain charm to Timothy Toodle with his affable manner. But what would you prefer to discuss if you found the play so tiresome?"

Nicolay tapped his fingers lightly against the rim of his coffee cup, holding up the front page of *Harper's Weekly*. "I was thinking," he said thoughtfully, "about today's piece on the amendment. The Thirteenth."

Hay arched an eyebrow and glanced across the table at the front-page illustration of the U. S. House of Representatives passing the Thirteenth Amendment. "It's fair to say that half of Washington is talking about it as well," he reflected. "The other half is trying to ignore it, fearful of its consequences." He leaned forward. "What part of it is gnawing at you?"

Nicolay sat back, placing the newspaper on the table and rubbing a hand over his face. "It's not the amendment itself, Hay. It's Mr. Lincoln. I often think about what he told me years ago before we came to Washington. When I left my editorial position at the *Pike County Press* and began collaborating with him on his campaign in Springfield, he told me about the time he took a flatboat down to New Orleans as a young man. He said it was the first time he had seen a slave auction."

Hay leaned into the conversation, his interest piqued. "What did he say?"

"He said he saw whole families herded onto an auction block like livestock under the giant rotunda of the St. Louis Hotel. He watched a mother try to hold on to her baby, but the auctioneers ripped the child from her arms. She screamed, John! Screamed so loud that he swore he could still hear it long after he'd left the market."

Hay grimaced. He glanced down at his coffee, stirring it slowly with his spoon. "Well," he muttered, "that'll stay with you."

"It *did* stay with him," Nicolay said, tapping his temple. "Right up here. He told me he couldn't stop thinking about that mother's scream anytime he traveled on the Mississippi." Nicolay's eyes sharpened as he leaned forward. "That was the moment, Hay. That's where it started. He didn't say it outright, but I knew it then. That's where his aversion to slavery was born."

Hay took a long sip of his coffee, letting the warmth soothe the winter chill. "An aversion isn't the same as action," he said.

"True," Nicolay conceded, his eyes narrowing in thought. "But think about it, John. Consider how he framed his arguments when he ran for office. He didn't say he'd abolish slavery. He said he was in favor of controlling its expansion. He was cautious."

"Cautious because he had to be," Hay shot back. "Look at the Constitution, Nicolay. Slavery is baked into it with the Three-Fifths Clause. Then there is the Fugitive Slave Act and the Supreme Court's ruling in the Dred Scott decision that further reinforced the institution. Every attempt to pull it out was like trying to extract poison from a wound that had already spread to the heart. If he'd declared he'd end it from the start, he'd have been politically dead before he could hang his hat in the Executive Mansion."

Nicolay nodded, conceding the point, but something more was behind his eyes. "I agree," he said, his tone grim. "But you know as well as I that Lincoln didn't set out to free the slaves. He didn't believe he had the power to do it. He was determined to stop slavery from spreading west. But emancipation?" He let out a short, sharp breath. "Not until the war afforded him the opportunity."

"The Proclamation," Hay said with a slow, knowing nod.

"Exactly," Nicolay replied. "With a stroke of his pen, he stripped the South of its workforce and turned the slaves into soldiers and laborers for our side, all in the name of military necessity. He wasn't freeing them because he believed he had the legal right to do so under the Constitution. He freed them because it weakened the Confederacy and gave the Union a better chance to survive."

"And yet," Hay countered, a sly grin forming on his face, "his freeing the slaves is what will be remembered a hundred years from now. He'll be lionized as the Great Emancipator."

"Maybe," Nicolay said, his eyes flicking toward the rain-streaked window. "But you and I will remember it differently. We'll remember the Cabinet debates: Stanton pounding his fist on the table, Chase rattling off constitutional arguments, Seward insisting on waiting for a victory so it wouldn't seem desperate. Lincoln persevered through it all, John."

"And in the end," Hay said with a smile, "they all got in line."

"Only after Lincoln persisted," Nicolay added, his eyes meeting Hay's with quiet intensity. "He said it himself. 'The promise must be kept.'"

Hay tilted his head, his eyes sharp with curiosity. "And you think he was talking about the war?"

Nicolay shook his head slowly. "No," he said quietly. "I believe he was referring to that woman on the auction block down in New Orleans. The one whose baby was ripped from her arms." He paused, his fingers tracing the rim of his coffee cup counterclockwise as if he were trying to turn back the hands on a pocket watch.

For a moment, Hay remained silent. When he finally spoke, his voice was thoughtful. "That would make her the second woman to play a major role in the chain of events leading to the Emancipation Proclamation and ultimately to the Thirteenth Amendment."

Nicolay's eyes lifted, his brows drawing together in question.

"The first was Harriet Beecher Stowe," Hay continued, leaning forward as if the thought had just crystallized. "When Lincoln met her, he told her she'd written 'the book that started this Great War.'"

Nicolay's eyes brightened. "She was certainly the catalyst."

"Precisely," Hay agreed, his voice gaining momentum. "It's like something my college chemistry professor once described: an explosive reaction. It begins with two unstable elements. In this case, it was the South, with its volatile and reactive foundation of slavery, and the North, with its pent-up energy of abolitionist fervor. Along comes Stowe's *Uncle Tom's Cabin*, exposing the moral depravity of slavery and the fierce power of a mother's love as she risks everything to save her child. As you said, that was the catalyst, Nicolay. It sparked the violent reaction that led to the Civil War."

"Then along came the President," Nicolay added, his voice contemplative. "Initially, he acted as a catalyst inhibitor, trying to control the reaction, slow it down, and prevent it from burning too hot. But when that approach failed, he introduced a new ingredient to the reaction: emancipation."

"I'm convinced his inspiration for that was the slave woman in New Orleans," Hay said. "The war allowed him to act on his moral principles while strengthening the Union's position through increased manpower."

"That's right," Nicolay concluded, his gaze distant, as if he were watching the past unfold before him. "However, if we follow this analogy, there is one more piece to consider. Every reaction requires a solvent, a medium where it takes place."

"American society," Hay said. "A mixture of hope, fear, greed, ambition, and moral reckoning. It was everywhere, surrounding every interaction between North and South, seeping into every town square, parlor, legislature, and pulpit."

"Exactly," Nicolay replied. "It's the medium that allows every reaction to happen in the first place. Without it, the elements might remain separate, never colliding at all. But in that shared space, they came into contact. The solvent didn't *cause* the reaction but enabled it to occur. It was the necessary but not sufficient agent."

"Which is why it's still unsettled," Nicolay said with a glance toward the window. "The solvent doesn't simply return to its original state once the reaction ends. It holds traces of everything it's touched."

"The analogy isn't perfect," Hay said, "but it captures the essence of what happened. Two volatile elements, mined from the depths of sectionalism, acting in a social medium, met a catalyst. After that, no catalyst inhibitor could stop the spark of Secession from igniting an explosion so fierce that it forever changed the course of history."

The two colleagues fell into a thoughtful silence, kindred souls savoring the comforting afterglow of their shared intellectual insights.

The heavy sleet outside softened to a gentle rain, and the hum of voices around them grew louder as the evening progressed.

"Do you remember what the President said about Jefferson's view of slavery?" Hay asked.

Nicolay nodded. "Yes, I do. He said, 'We have the wolf by the ears, and we can neither hold it nor safely let it go. Justice is on one scale, and self-preservation in the other.'"

Hay turned toward the leaded glass window, his eyes tracking the slow trickle of water as it wove its way down the narrow channels of the lead caming. "Looks like the President's letting the wolf go now, doesn't it?"

"Not yet," Nicolay said softly, lowering his eyes. "Not until the Fourteenth passes and is ratified." He glanced up to meet his friend's eyes. "Citizenship, due process, and equal protection are the only ways to let it go for good."

"Poor wolf," Hay said. "In some respects, I feel sorry for the creature."

"How so?"

"Jefferson's wolf may gain its freedom," Hay responded, his gaze drifting as if peering into the distant future. "Yet, the unfortunate creature will soon confront hunters with traps and snares set with relentless purpose to reclaim what they believe belongs to them."

Nicolay commented, "That does seem inevitable. The old slave patrols will be transformed into a police force bolstered by the South's Black Codes."

Hay nodded gravely.

After that, they sat solemnly in shared silence, two young men with wisdom beyond their years, sipping coffee and considering a world in transformation.

Beyond the warm confines of the coffeehouse, tomorrow would see carpenters setting to work at first light, hammering boards into place for the inaugural platform rising beneath the unfinished ribs of the Capitol dome. There would be newsboys wading through puddles, their voices sharp in the chill air as they cried out headlines announcing Lincoln's upcoming address. Although the headlines themselves would reveal little, the articles beneath them would brim with speculation about whether the President would speak of peace, reconstruction, or the promise of liberty now enshrined in the heart of the Thirteenth Amendment.

84

LINCOLN'S SECOND INAUGURATION

Morning in the nation's capital dawned beneath a somber, overcast sky, its gray expanse reflecting the uncertainty of a country on the brink of peace, yet still shadowed by war. A steady drizzle fell, the cold, penetrating rain soaking through clothing and settling into bone as if nature herself shared the nation's weariness.

Despite the dismal weather, thousands gathered on the east front of the U.S. Capitol, their faces upturned toward the grand portico where Abraham Lincoln would soon stand. The rich organic scent of damp earth and musty wool overcoats filled the air, and the low hum of voices mixed with the soft patter of raindrops falling on fields of canvas umbrellas.

People came from all social classes: Union soldiers in weather-beaten blue uniforms, freedmen and women, curious onlookers, and government officials in formal attire. Many held newspapers or parasols to shield their heads; others braved the rain bareheaded. A sea of faces stretched as far as the eye could see, standing in the mud puddles of Capitol Hill, their feet cold and wet, straining to catch sight of the man who had become the nation's moral compass.

The Capitol's newly completed dome loomed above them. Former slaves stood gazing up at their handiwork with pride. The grand iron structure, painted white to harmonize with the marble façade of the building's new extensions, stood as a bold testament to Lincoln's unwavering vision of unity persisting through the trials of war.

Below it, most of the scaffolding had been cleared, except for what was needed to construct the platform on which Lincoln would deliver his second inaugural address. The plank-faced platform was simple yet sturdy, befitting the occasion's dignity. Soldiers stood at its perimeter, rifles in hand, eyes scanning the crowd with quiet vigilance.

A military drumroll echoed, sharp and commanding, as the crowd's murmurs faded into expectant silence. Heads turned as dignitaries emerged from the Capitol's central door. Cabinet members, generals, and Supreme Court justices took their places, each man's movements marked with deliberate gravity.

Lincoln's Vice President, Andrew Johnson, had already taken his oath of office. Still, his appearance was presaged by the uneasy whispers of those who had seen him earlier: sick, drunk, or something worse, some said. His words were slurred in a way that left many exchanging concerned glances.

All eyes, however, were fixed on the tall, gaunt figure that stepped forward next. Abraham Lincoln's familiar face was a map of weariness, his sunken eyes framed by deep creases that time and the war had prematurely etched into his leathery skin. He took off his stovepipe hat, revealing a head of unruly hair that had turned gray since his first inauguration four years earlier.

As Lincoln appeared, the rain ceased as if the heavens held their breath for this moment. The crowd's hush deepened, reverence filling the air. Many in the throng still recalled the stirring words of his celebrated address at Gettysburg, spoken just eighteen months ago to a nation battered by war.

Lincoln approached the table slowly, his gaze sweeping the mass of onlookers. His black coat hung loose on his frame; the fabric darkened from the damp. Sharp and searching, his eyes lingered on the soldiers, freedmen, and widows in mourning veils as if he were asking their silent permission to proceed.

His hand rested on Chief Justice Salmon P. Chase's personal Bible held before him; its edges were worn from years of use. He had appointed Chase last year to succeed the late Chief Justice Taney, author of the infamous Dred Scott decision.

"Raise your right hand," intoned Chase.

Lincoln's hand rose slowly, his long fingers straight, palm outward, his body still as stone. He gazed forward, his eyes fixed on some distant point. Chase's voice carried clearly in the rain-cooled air as he recited the words of the oath. Lincoln repeated them in a soft but firm voice, each word measured, each syllable spoken with the care of a man who understood their gravity.

"I, Abraham Lincoln, do solemnly swear that I will faithfully execute the Office of President of the United States and will, to the best of my ability, preserve, protect, and defend the Constitution of the United States."

His sharp, penetrating voice carried over the crowd, the familiar timbre causing men to remove their hats and women to clutch their children a little tighter. When he lowered his hand, a cheer rose from the crowd, growing until it became a roar. Flags waved, caps hurled through the air, and the rain-soaked assembly surged with the unspoken relief of those who had feared this day might never come.

Lincoln's eyes shifted downward to glance at Chase's tattered Bible before he turned to face the crowd. He took a breath, hands gripping the sides of the table before him, his fingers curling around its edges as if bracing himself. The rain had begun again, softly at first, but none of the crowd moved to leave.

"Fellow countrymen," he began, his voice resonant and calm. "At this second appearing to take the oath of the Presidential office, there is less occasion for an extended address than at the first. Then, a detailed statement of a course to be pursued seemed fitting and proper. Now, at the expiration of four years, during which public declarations have been constantly called forth on every point and phase of the great contest which still absorbs the attention and engrosses the energies of the nation, little new could be presented."

His words echoed over the crowd like a solemn hymn, each sentence a note in a larger, unspoken melody. The crowd, drenched but unmoving, hung on every word. It was not a call to arms nor a declaration of triumph. It was something else entirely: a meditation on sorrow, the shared burden of a divided people, and a prayer for the elusive yet sweet hope of reconciliation.

"With malice toward none, with charity for all, with firmness in the right as God gives us to see the right, let us strive on to finish the work we are in, to bind up the nation's wounds, to care for him who shall have borne the battle and for his widow and his orphan, to do all which may achieve and cherish a just and lasting peace among ourselves and with all nations."

The rain thickened as he spoke, yet no one chose to leave what felt like a profound spiritual experience, a ritual purification that washed away their tears and replaced sorrow with awe and respect.

The crowd's roar had quieted to a reverent silence. Many wept, and not just the widows. Hardened soldiers, some on crutches, blinked back tears as they thought of their lost comrades.

The President's gaze lingered once more on the crowd below him. His lips bore not a smile but an expression of resolve. He tipped his head in acknowledgment and turned, his steps slow as he retreated through the great doors of the Capitol.

The rain fell harder now, soaking into hats, coats, and cloaks. Yet the crowd remained, even as the man himself vanished, lingering as if unwilling to let the moment slip away, reluctant to return to the world as it had been before those hallowed words were spoken.

85

SARAH MORGAN

The afternoon sun beamed down Canal Street, its bright light glinting off shop windows with the gentle warmth of March. New Orleans breathed in the moist breeze from the nearby riverfront, intertwined with the faint sweetness of jasmine and honeysuckle from the nearby uptown neighborhoods, mingling with the rich aroma of brewed coffee and the toasty scent of roasted chicory drifting from cafés downtown. The rumble and sharp clang of streetcars pulsed steadily through the city's arteries, echoing along the bustling thoroughfare.

Sarah Morgan, a petite young woman, paused along the sidewalk. Her porcelain complexion was framed by long brown hair that spilled in soft waves from beneath her feathered hat. Her tresses brushed her shoulders, grazing the delicate white lace collar that lay softly atop her dark blue dress. A fashionable double pendant necklace featuring a single draping feather complemented her hat and completed her ensemble.

Sarah's intelligent brown eyes fixed intently on the shop window at Madame Olympe Boisse's boutique, the most prestigious millinery in New Orleans. Her gloved hands rested just under her chin, and the slight tilt of her head suggested she was weighing which creation might best suit her fancy.

Walking with Rachel, Thomas caught sight of Sarah, recalling the girl he had once known when he clerked at her father's law firm. She had matured into a striking young woman.

"Sarah!" he called, his voice rising above the street's bustle.

She turned, her eyes scanning the crowd until her face lit with recognition. "Mr. Manget," she said, her voice bright with surprise.

Thomas weaved through the crowd, waving a hand in greeting. Rachel quickened her pace to match his strides.

"It's been too long, Sarah," he said warmly. "I hardly recognized you. You've grown into such a proper young lady."

"You're kind to say so, Mr. Manget," Sarah replied gracefully, offering her hand. "It's a wonder to see you after all this time."

He took her hand briefly but then waved it off with a grin. "None of this 'Mr. Manget.' You're making me feel like an old man. Call me Thomas, please." He glanced to his side. "Allow me to introduce my wife, Rachel."

Rachel's face brightened with a friendly smile. "Thomas has spoken fondly of you and your father, Sarah. It's a pleasure to meet you."

"The pleasure is mine, Mrs. Manget," Sarah said with a hint of a curtsy.

"Thank you, but you must call me Rachel. There's no room for formalities among friends." She glanced into the shop window. "I see you're looking at hats today."

Sarah's eyes lit up. "I always stop here when I'm downtown. The ever-changing creations of the display artists never fail to captivate me."

"Why don't we find a place where we can sit and have the chance to talk properly?" Rachel suggested. "You and Thomas haven't seen each other for a month of Sundays."

Sarah's smile widened. "What a fantastic idea!"

They soon found a charming tearoom between a dry goods store and a jewelry shop. Thomas held the door open for the ladies before following them inside.

The air was filled with the warm, comforting aromas of brewing tea leaves and fresh beignets. Lace curtains softened the sunlight into gentle beams, casting a cozy glow across the room.

Thomas guided Rachel and Sarah past a cluster of customers to a table by the window. He pulled out their chairs before taking a seat next to Rachel.

"Shall we have tea?" he asked, glancing between them.

"Yes, please," Sarah replied with a nod.

"I'd like some beignets as well," Rachel said, her gaze shifting toward the faint sound of batter meeting hot oil from the kitchen.

A youthful waiter with wavy black hair approached. "Would you like to place your order?" he asked cheerfully, retrieving a pencil from behind his ear.

"Hot tea and beignets for everyone," Thomas said.

"Congou or Bohea?" the waiter asked, his eyes shifting to each of them.

Thomas looked at Rachel and Sarah. "Any preference?"

"Either would be fine," Rachel replied. "What about you, Sarah?"

"Congou, if it's all the same."

"Three Congou then," Thomas told the waiter. "With sugar, cream, and lemon, if you would."

The waiter returned a crisp, "Yes, sir." He scribbled on his notebook, tucked his pencil behind his ear, and strode toward the window that opened into the kitchen.

As the gentle clatter of porcelain and the low hum of conversation filled the room, Thomas leaned forward. "What brought you to New Orleans, Sarah? Last I heard, you stayed with family at Linwood Plantation after Baton Rouge was occupied."

Sarah's face grew wistful. "We settled at Linwood as long as possible, hosting officers from the entrenchments at Port Hudson on weekends to lift their spirits. It was comforting to be surrounded by loved ones, safe from the distant roar of shells exploding. I cherished the stillness and used it to catch up on my reading." She paused, drawing a breath that exhaled in a sigh.

"When the Yankees moved upriver, my mother and I fled to the relative safety of the town of Port Hudson, keeping away from the fortifications on the river. We stayed there briefly, managing with meager accommodation. Then, we boarded a train from Port Hudson to Clinton, Mississippi, where our journey grew more arduous. By wagon, we pressed on over rough terrain that shifted from deep, clinging mud to jarring, rocky inclines. At last, we reached Amite, where we boarded the Northern Line, disembarking north of Lake Pontchartrain before finally arriving here."

"It was a long and grueling journey," she continued, "especially so after a terrible accident in our barouche before I left home. My back has never been the same. I can still feel the sharp prodding of those surgeons with their instruments of torture. Honestly, I'm unsure which was worse, the injury or the cure."

"That must have been dreadful," Rachel said, her voice filled with sympathy.

The waiter returned, balancing a tray on one hand above his head. He set down the platter of beignets, the porcelain teapot, cups, and small dishes for cream, sugar, and lemon. A faint puff of finely powdered sugar rose from the warm beignets, carrying the pleasant sweetness of heated sugar laced with vanilla.

"Will that be all?" he asked, his gaze shifting politely between them as he placed silverware wrapped in linen napkins on the table and adjusted the teapot's handle to face Thomas.

"Yes, thank you," Thomas replied, nodding as he reached for the teapot and tilted it carefully to pour a steady stream of steaming tea into each cup. He then went for the platter of beignets, offering them to Rachel and then to Sarah before helping himself.

Sarah sipped her tea, pausing as though weighing her words. "The soldiers ransacked our house, you know. They took anything they could carry and shattered the rest. Books were strewn like refuse across the library floor. Precious heirlooms were destroyed. Such Philistines! No appreciation for anything of beauty or worth."

"That's terrible," Rachel said, her voice soft.

"What's worse, I had to let Jimmy go when we fled," she said.

"Jimmy?" Rachel asked.

"Yes, my beloved pet bird. I named him after my younger brother. He was precious to me. I did get my Jimmy back after a while when a Negro man climbed a tree in our neighborhood to capture him for me after he saw my distress. I still believe dear Jimmy flew back to our street because he missed me."

"That was kind of the man," Rachel said.

"And then the Capitol," Sarah added as if, in her prolonged lament, she had heard nothing of what Rachel said. "They burned it. Baton Rouge will never be the same without our Castle on the Hill."

Thomas shook his head, his gaze distant. "I understand it was an accident. Still, a pity."

"Yes," Sarah agreed, "but the aftermath of accidents is just as cruel as the aftermath of intentions when you're left behind to live with it." She glanced up, her face still sad. "Now we're staying with my older brother, Philip. He's a judge here now. Mother and I rarely speak with him since he sided with the Union. It's a cramped house with none of the comforts of our home in Baton Rouge, but it's better than having no roof over our heads and living in constant fear of being shelled."

"Are you and your mother both well now, though?" Rachel asked, leaning forward with concern. "That's all that truly matters."

"It's been a hard few years," Sarah said. "My father's asthma finally took him in '61, just before the war, and then my brother Henry…" Her voice faltered. "He died in a duel defending our family's honor the same year. Then, my brothers, Gibbes and George, succumbed to illness in the camps. Mother has never recovered from the loss." Her eyes lowered to her teacup.

Thomas glanced at Rachel's face, noting her painful expression at Sarah's mention of a duel taking her brother.

"So much loss," Rachel said. "I'm so sorry for your family."

Sarah's shoulders lifted slightly and then fell as she let out a resigned sigh. "It's the way of things, isn't it?" She looked up with a sad smile. "And you, Thomas? What's become of you since you left clerking for my father?" A flicker of amusement crossed her face. "You've earned a few silver hairs since you left."

"I'm practicing law here in New Orleans now," he replied casually, glancing at Rachel with a silent look acknowledging a necessary social lie. "It's kept me busy."

Sarah's gaze shifted to Rachel. "And what of you, Rachel?"

Rachel's smile widened. "Trying to keep up with my husband, mostly," she said lightly, not mentioning her teaching children for the new Freedman's Bureau. "We've been through more than our share of adventures, but I'm glad to have him by my side."

Thomas reached beneath the table to squeeze Rachel's hand.

As the conversation shifted from one topic to another, Rachel praised the fresh produce at the French market, resulting from the lifted blockade, before transitioning to this year's fashion.

Sarah wrinkled her nose at the mention of the latest Parisian haute couture. "Too many fancy bows and frills and not enough style for my taste."

Rachel smiled self-consciously, her hand instinctively brushing the bow on the back of her dress as she avoided meeting Sarah's eyes.

"My mother is a very practical woman," Sarah said with a grin. "She always told me to stuff all my old dresses into a big barrel. Then, flip it over and open it from the bottom when it's full. Behold! The latest fashion sensation!"

Rachel and Thomas laughed, charmed by Sarah's playful take on how yesterday's styles often return to the height of fashion.

"The war's changing everything," Sarah said after a pause. Her voice grew thoughtful. "Only time will tell if it's for the best. I've considered that one day in the far future, with the knowledge we will have, we will look back at what will then be the dead past and see that all has been for the best for us in the end. Then we will wonder how we could ever have been foolish enough to await each hour in such breathless anxiety."

Rachel nodded slowly at the wisdom of her words. "One can only hope."

"I must be going," Sarah announced suddenly, gathering her gloves. "I've already bored you two lovely people with my prattling. I rarely get a chance to chat with fellow Southerners these days. But Mother always frets if I leave her alone for over an hour or two. She had such an ordeal with taking the Oath of Allegiance demanded of us to pass the line. After losing so much because of the war, it nearly killed her to swear allegiance to the enemy. The officer had to threaten her with prison to cause her to relent. Afterward, she cried incessantly for the rest of our journey and prayed the rosary constantly."

"Such a pity you must leave so soon," Rachel said. "I was enjoying our conversation."

"It's been a pleasure meeting you, Rachel. And it's good to see you again, Thomas. We should all get together soon."

"Yes, we should. Perhaps at our house for tea," Rachel suggested.

"That would be delightful."

"Take care of yourself," Thomas said, rising from his chair.

Rachel bid a "God be with you," watching Sarah leave the shop.

Thomas sat back down, his gaze following her. "She's grown up."

"Such a tragedy, losing her father and three brothers, her family home, and her health all within a short space of time. She's endured more than most young women ever will, yet she bears it gracefully and manages to stay in good humor."

Thomas nodded. "Yes. And she demonstrates a wisdom beyond her years."

Rachel's eyes twinkled with quiet amusement. "I'm glad she never caught a glimpse of the back of my dress. She'd be mortified after what she said about French fashions."

Thomas looked up from his tea. "Pray tell. What would she have seen?"

"Don't you remember where you bought it for me last week when we went shopping? How I objected because it was outrageously expensive, but you insisted on buying it because you liked how it looked on me?"

"Yes, but I don't recall the shop."

"It came from New Orleans's boutique that imports the latest fashions from Paris. And it has a big pink bow on the back to prove it!"

NEW ORLEANS
NEW ORLEANS

86

JUBILEE ON CANAL STREET

Revelers crowded Canal Street, their cheers swelling as Union soldiers marched in triumph down the broad thoroughfare, moving with solemn pride beneath a sky fluttering with the Stars and Stripes. The parade rivaled the grandest spectacles of Mardi Gras past, though the occasion bore a weight far beyond mere revelry.

The polished boots of soldiers struck the cobblestones in rhythmic unison, the sound echoing off the façades of buildings festooned with bunting. Freedmen danced at the margins, women waved handkerchiefs from balconies, and children darted about, wide-eyed at the spectacle.

Above them, people crowded onto balconies, leaning eagerly over the wrought-iron railings, waving handkerchiefs and scarves as they called out their joyous "Hurrahs!" to the soldiers below. One little boy, spotting his father among the ranks, scrambled over the railing. His mother gasped and caught him by his suspenders, pulling him back to safety with a firm grip to the cheers of the women surrounding her.

On the street below, men in tired uniforms marched with their shoulders squared, their eyes fixed forward, a gleam of victory in their gaze. Interspersed among them, the *Corps d'Afrique* strode with heads held high, their dark faces resolute and proud, bearing the Stars and Stripes with a dignity hard-won on fields where they had bled and sacrificed for the freedom that now filled the air.

Union flags waved from hands and balconies, a bright red, white, and blue ripple against the sky. The soldiers' voices rang out as they broke into verses of "Hail Columbia:"

> Hail, ye heroes, heaven-born band!
> Who fought and bled in freedom's cause,
> And when the storm of war was gone,
> Enjoyed the peace your valor won…

Their singing mingled with the crowd's cheers as if each note carried the weight of every battle and hardship endured along the way. Some soldiers glanced up, smiling at the faces above them, nodding to the cheers of people who had long awaited this day.

As they turned a corner, the troops' voices swelled again in unison, rolling out with renewed vigor:

> Firm, united let us be,
> Rallying round our liberty,
> As a band of brothers joined,
> Peace and safety we shall find.

The chorus rang out with a force that united the hearts of soldiers and citizens of all races in that moment of relief and joy, a collective acknowledgment that the long, dark shadow of war was finally lifting with the fall of Richmond earlier in the month.

Thomas stood with Rachel near the Customs House, where Union officers busily processed Confederate prisoners, soon to be sent back to their homes.

"Look up there," Thomas said, nodding toward the tall windows of the Customs House where several men in Confederate gray leaned out, waving their arms and cheering.

Rachel tilted her head, squinting up at the prisoners. "Strange, isn't it, that they're cheering for a parade of Union soldiers?"

"Usually, yes," Thomas replied. "But for now, most have put aside their differences. I'd wager they're just eager to see their families again."

Rachel grew quiet, her gaze thoughtful. "Strange how things change so dramatically," she murmured. Her thoughts drifted to her sister and other Southerners who had fiercely clung to the "Cause" and the "peculiar institution" upon which it was founded. How passionately they had fought to preserve a fragile, illusory world now crumbling before their eyes.

Thomas glanced at her. "You know, it isn't entirely settled yet. Though Lee surrendered to Grant, I've heard that General Johnston's rebel forces are still engaged with Sherman in North Carolina. And General Taylor is still holding out with rebel forces in Alabama, Mississippi, and Eastern Louisiana, not far from us."

Rachel's expression grew distant, her brow furrowing. "And as long as Jefferson Davis is on the run…"

"Precisely," Thomas said, nodding. No one knows what he might be planning. Rumors are he is organizing a band of guerrillas in the Appalachians, where they would be difficult to root out. Other people think he might yet attempt something more desperate."

"At least we're safe here," Rachel said quietly.

"Yes, and with Major General Canby in Mobile and Brigadier General Grierson having left here to join him, the two will press through the remaining pockets of rebel resistance. General Taylor is a practical man. Soon, no corner of the South will be controlled by the Rebels."

Rachel said nothing, absorbing Thomas's words. The South she had known was in its death throes, and all that remained was to lay to rest the old traditions and brace for an uncertain future. In her heart, she hoped that Sarah and her family were safe, and looked forward to reconciling with her.

The jubilant music from the parade receded into the distance as the soldiers marched onward, clearing the street. The crowd gradually dispersed, a quiet hum of conversation replacing the cheers.

Rachel's mind drifted to more profound questions. She gazed at Thomas with pleading eyes. "Will this war ever end?"

Thomas's chest rose and fell with a deep, deliberate sigh. "Civil wars never end," he declared.

Rachel's brow furrowed in confusion. "But Richmond has fallen, and the Confederacy is left in shambles," she said, leaning forward as though her nearness could cause his answer to be different.

Thomas shook his head sadly. "The gunfire will end, and the battles will fade into history. The armies will march home, and the cannons, finally silent, will be melted down and recast into church bells, tolling an uneasy peace. But the deep division carved into men's hearts will endure for decades, if not longer."

Rachel's lips parted, yet she hesitated to speak. Her eyes, wide with disbelief, searched his face for any sign that he did not truly mean what he had just said. "So, you're saying there's no hope?" she inquired, her voice barely above a whisper.

"There is hope," Thomas said, his demeanor softening. "But only when love replaces hate in people's hearts. That is when it will truly end."

A storm of questions raged through Rachel's mind. Could former enemies reunite, binding their wounds and setting aside years of hatred and bloodshed? Would families, like her own, torn apart by loyalty to one side or the other, ever find peace across their divides?

Rachel turned to her husband. "With emancipation now in motion, do you think this country, in its rebirth, can truly become a place where all races may one day walk side by side?"

"Perhaps," Thomas replied, his voice tinged with uncertainty.

"I don't mean as strangers, but as fellow citizens, united by strength of character and a shared commitment to the words of our Declaration of Independence: that all men are created equal and endowed by their Creator with certain unalienable rights."

"A noble goal, my love," he replied, placing his arm around her shoulders.

As the sun dipped toward the western horizon, the last echoes of the parade faded into memory like a tide pulling back from the shore. In the streets where flags had waved, and voices had soared in song, quiet now settled over the city, leaving behind scattered rose petals and rice.

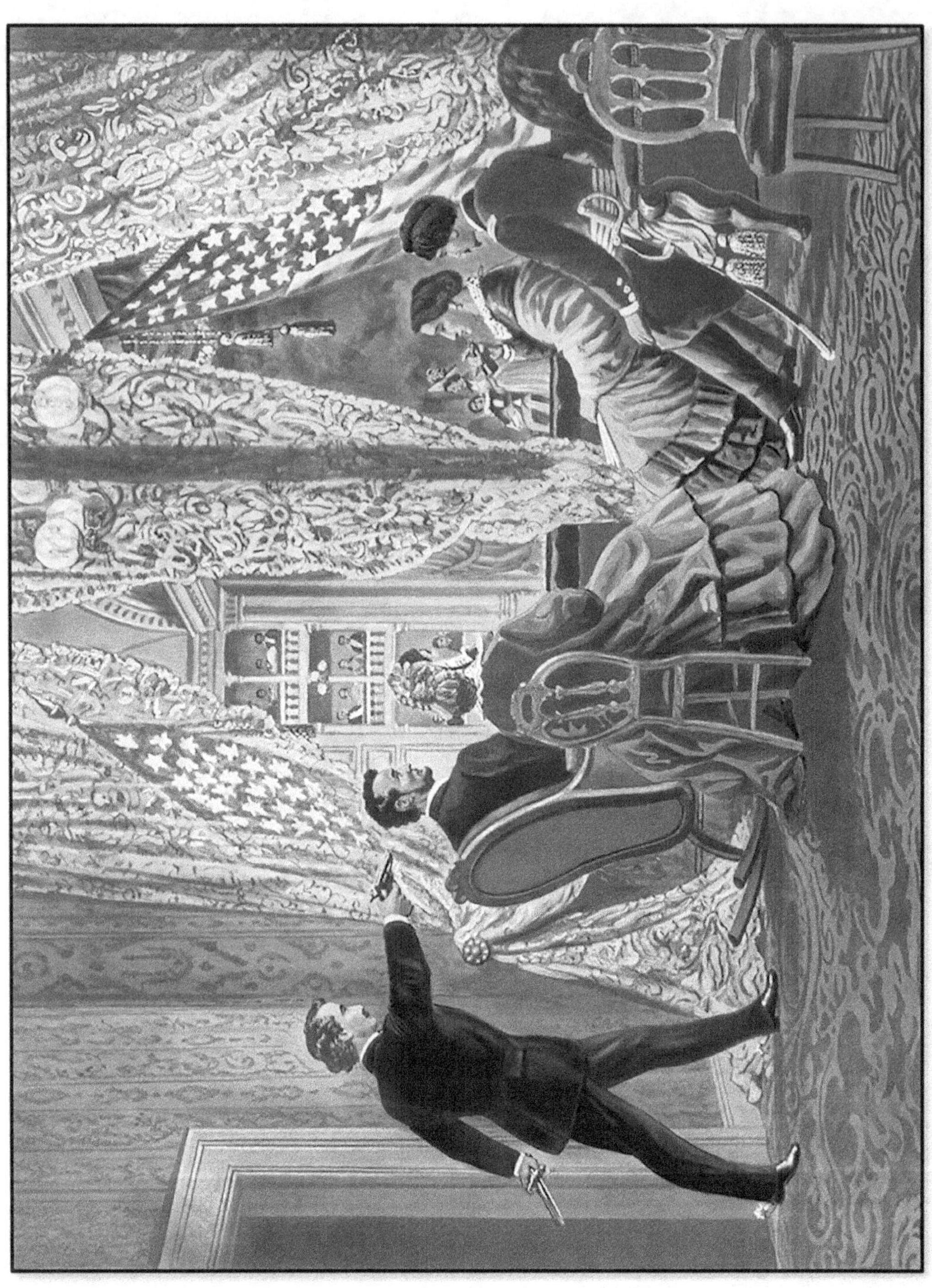

87

OUR AMERICAN COUSIN

Far to the north, in the nation's capital, the same April twilight that marked the end of Jubilee in New Orleans unfolded with deceptive calm. The bells of Christ Church Episcopal tolled nine, their chimes echoing through the pleasant spring air along the Potomac.

John Wilkes Booth emerged from the National Hotel, his figure sharply outlined against the evening light. Dressed impeccably in formal attire, he cut a striking figure with a gleaming top hat perched atop his dark curls. Walking with confidence, his mind churned with dark thoughts. The memory of last month's foiled plot with John Surratt to kidnap President Lincoln and trade him for Confederate prisoners still gnawed at him. Yet even in his brooding, Booth clung to a grim solace: while abduction had failed, assassination remained within his grasp.

He would finally execute his plan tonight, culminating in weeks of careful plotting and meetings with Confederate Secret Service agents in Canada following his theatrical engagement in New Orleans the previous year.

George Sanders, a fervent advocate for the assassination of heads of state, including French Emperor Napoleon III, had particularly influenced him. Both shared the conviction that eliminating tyrants was the sole path to securing the freedom of nations, both at home and abroad.

The night was calm and clear, the stars faintly twinkling against the gaslit haze that lingered above the bustling streets. The city, still reveling in the hard-won peace after a long and bloody civil war, was alive with celebration. Passersby exchanged cheerful greetings and sang, and laughter emerged from the crowded taverns, creating a tableau of joy that clashed with Booth's brooding thoughts.

He frowned, his jaw tightening as he passed the revelers. Their merriment felt like a cruel mockery, a gloating celebration of the South's inglorious defeat. Born and raised on the modest Tudor Hall plantation near Baltimore, Booth carried his family's values and traditions with a steadfast sense of pride. Now, that pride was seared with bitterness.

When the war erupted, Booth saw President Lincoln as a tyrant who had initiated a campaign of devastation under the guise of unity. To Booth, Lincoln bore sole responsibility for the hundreds of thousands of lives lost in a war he viewed as Northern aggression.

Booth's steps quickened as he envisioned his role in the history books of future generations. This was no ordinary night and no ordinary play. It would become his stage tonight, and he would assume the lead in a drama that would immortalize him.

The gas streetlamps illuminated his path as he strode toward Ford's Theatre, where Lincoln and his party would be enjoying *Our American Cousin*. Booth's mind churned with the details of the plan. He thought of his co-conspirators: George Atzerodt, assigned to kill Vice President Andrew Johnson; Lewis Powell, tasked with assassinating Secretary of State William Seward; and David Herold, his steadfast companion, who would help Powell to escape. Their coordinated efforts would plunge the North into chaos and, perhaps, just perhaps, give the South a chance to rise from the ashes.

As Booth approached Ford's Theatre, the lively sounds of the city began to fade. The streets grew quieter as revelers filtered into taverns along the way. The warm glow of the theatre illuminated the sidewalk ahead, its inviting light spilling onto the cobblestones like a beacon summoning its star performer.

Weeks of preparation centered around Mary Surratt's tavern in Surrattsville, Maryland, a remote haven just 13 miles southeast of Washington. The tavern was a hub for Confederate sympathizers and a reliable meeting spot.

As he walked, Booth envisioned his escape route again, reviewing the sequence like cues in a play. David Herold, his companion and trusted guide, would join him after the deed was done. Herold's role tonight as a trained pharmacist was not only to accompany him and treat any injuries he might sustain during his mission, but also to assist Powell in the grim task of murdering Secretary of State Seward. After completing their missions, Booth and Herold would rendezvous at Soper's Hill, a prearranged meeting point beyond the Navy Yard Bridge. From there, they would ride south to Surratt's Tavern, where weapons and supplies for the next leg of their escape route awaited them.

Every detail was a carefully rehearsed note in Booth's grand opus, each step bringing him closer to his stage to play the lead role. This was his moment: the culmination of months of meticulous plotting with his co-conspirators.

The streets grew quieter as Booth approached Ford's Theatre, with the festive crowds retreating into nearby establishments. Ahead, the warm glow of the theatre beckoned like limelight awaiting its lead actor.

His musings were interrupted by the lively strains of music and laughter coming from Taltavul's Star Saloon, nestled next door to the theatre. The sound tugged at him, and he paused for a drink or two to steady his nerves before completing his mission.

"John!" called a sharply dressed man behind the bar wearing a barkeep's apron, his neat mustache twitching with a smile as his face brightened at the sight of his famous patron.

"Peter!" Booth returned, his tone jovial as he perched on a barstool and reached over to shake the proprietor's hand. "My usual."

"One stiff shot of whisky and water coming up," Peter replied, deftly decanting the drink.

Booth took the glass of whiskey and glanced around the crowded tavern. A group of stagehands huddled at a corner table, grabbing quick drinks before the next set change. Their conversation was lively, punctuated by laughter, as they prepared to scurry through the private passageway connecting the saloon to the theatre. This convenient route allowed food and drink to flow freely to the actors and stagehands bustling behind the scenes.

Peter leaned casually against the bar, watching Booth. "You have any plans for this evening?" he asked.

Booth took a measured sip of his drink before answering. "Oh, I just thought I'd hang around and catch a couple of scenes."

"I hear Lincoln's there tonight," Peter said, lowering his voice slightly.

"Oh?" Booth replied, raising an eyebrow, though his tone remained nonchalant.

"Yeah. He insisted on sitting in the private balcony box. He didn't like the box Edman built for him onstage."

"Ed did a fine job on that box," Booth remarked, swirling the whiskey in his glass before draining it smoothly. "Shame to have to take it down."

"Rumor has it Lincoln wanted his privacy," Peter said with a shrug. "Can't imagine what he considers privacy, being President and all."

"Privacy," Booth replied with a sardonic smile, his tone laced with irony at the thought of the man lying in his coffin six feet under the ground.

Peter turned to serve another customer, and Booth rehearsed the play's flow in his mind. The timing was everything. He would wait for the line that never failed to elicit uproarious laughter from the audience. Tonight, the line would be delivered in falsetto by Harry Hawk, cross-dressed as the brash American, Asa Trenchard, who confronts the pompous British aristocrat, Mrs. Mountchessington: "Don't know the manners of good society, eh? Well, I guess I know enough to turn you inside out, old gal. You sockdologizing old mantrap!"

A wicked smile crossed Booth's face, envisioning how the audience's laughter would swell, drowning out the sharp crack of his derringer's single shot, a sound no louder than the pop of a Champagne cork. Enchanted by the comedy onstage, the audience would remain blissfully unaware of the tragedy unfolding in the balcony until the horror finally took center stage when he leaped down into the spotlight.

Booth set his empty glass on the bar and adjusted his top hat. "I think I'll slip over to Ford's."

Peter nodded, giving him a knowing smile. "Come on back after you've had a gander. I'll set you up with another round."

Booth returned the smile with a slight nod. "I just might," he replied, tipping his hat before slipping into the private passageway from the bar to the theatre's rear entrance. Upon emerging into the dimly lit alley, he moved stealthily toward Ford's private stable, where the bay mare he had hired earlier from Pumphrey's livery awaited him.

The mare stirred as he approached, her ears flicking at the sound of his footsteps. Despite having only one good eye, she recognized him instantly since he had chosen her before, appreciating her speed and reliability. She had auditioned well for her crucial supporting role in tonight's daring escape.

Booth ran a hand down her sleek neck. "Easy now, girl," he said, his voice low and steady. He checked the saddle, ensuring the girth was snug but not too tight, then gave the cinch a final tug to ensure it was secured correctly. Satisfied, he gathered the reins and led the mare toward the backstage door of Ford's.

After tethering his mare in the shadows beside the wall, he rapped lightly on the door. The knock rang out, sharp and hollow in the stillness of the alley.

"John!" a voice called from within. "Come on in."

The door swung open, revealing Edman Spangler, a sturdily built man of average height with deep-set eyes and a constant air of fatigue. Booth stepped inside and greeted him with a handshake.

"I'd recognize that knock anywhere," Spangler said with a smile.

"How's the play?" Booth asked casually, although his mind was focused on his role.

"The play's been a resounding success," Spangler grinned. "Standing ovations and sold-out crowds at every performance."

Booth smiled. "I'm glad to hear that. I returned tonight because the President invited me to the Executive Mansion almost two years ago after my performance here in *The Marble Heart*." He chuckled softly. "Had to send my regrets at the time because of other obligations, but when I heard he'd be here tonight, I thought the least I could do was stop by and pay my respects."

Spangler laughed. "I remember that performance. Fall of '63, wasn't it? The President and Mrs. Lincoln were sitting in that special onstage box Mr. Ford had me build for them. You played Raphael, and if I recall, you delivered some harsh lines his way. He really wasn't expecting that."

Booth laughed with him, the memory briefly piercing his grim concentration. "No, he wasn't. I hope to catch him by surprise tonight as well."

"You always were a prankster," Spangler said.

"Are you assisting with the production?" Booth asked, glancing around the bustling backstage area.

"They've got me touching everybody up between acts," Spangler replied with a shrug. "Fancy that. A carpenter doing makeup."

Booth smirked. "You're a man of many talents, Ed."

The two men shared a laugh, but Booth's thoughts soon drifted back to his plan. "Ed, I wonder if I might ask a favor."

"Anything, John," Spangler replied without hesitation.

"Would you mind looking after my mare? I hitched her outside, hoping to catch a few minutes of the play."

"I'd be glad to," Spangler said. "Better hurry, though. They're beginning Act III shortly."

As Spangler headed into the alley to attend to the mare, Booth moved purposefully to the stage wing. The familiar scent of sawdust and old varnish filled his senses, mingling with the faint laughter of the audience beyond. He paused in the shadows, his gaze lifting toward the draped double balcony box reserved for the President and his party.

The gaslights illuminated the stage where *Our American Cousin* unfolded, a comedy often veering into farce. Booth's sharp eyes scanned the presidential box, its bunting framing Lincoln's unmistakable profile. The President reclined in his chair, his posture relaxed, his face serene. The sight quickened Booth's pulse, adrenaline and resentment rising in his chest. He swallowed hard, willing himself to look away. *Not yet*, he thought.

Booth adjusted his coat and slipped into the corridor. He passed through the lobby, stepped through a side door, and emerged into the cool night air, where he walked briskly back to Taltavul's Star Saloon.

The murmur of patrons enveloped him inside the saloon, but he felt distant from the room's warmth, as if separated by an invisible barrier. He reached the bar and slid onto a stool, catching Taltavul's attention.

"Scotch," he said tersely, then added, "Make it a strong one."

Taltavul glanced at him, his brow furrowing slightly. "John? Is everything all right?"

"Fine as cream gravy, Peter." Booth forced a tight smile. "I get a little nervous watching someone else perform. I don't know why. Something about not having control, I suppose. So many things I would have done differently."

Taltavul nodded knowingly as he poured the drink. "Here," he said, sliding it toward Booth. "This should help."

Booth lifted the glass and took a long sip. The whiskey burned as it slid down, yet the fire did little to ease his nerves. His mind raced with vivid images of what lay ahead: the gunshot, the leap from the balcony onto the stage, the midnight ride into history. He signaled for another whiskey, the tremor in his hand betraying his inner turmoil.

The second drink softened the sharp edges of his thoughts. The panic receded slightly, giving way to a sense of detached determination. When he finally stood, he smoothed his jacket and ran a hand over his mustache, offering a polite smile to a young woman who gave him a coy wink as she passed by with her beau.

Stepping back into the alley, the crisp air struck his face, sharpening his focus. Booth moved as if trapped in a dream, each step toward Ford's Theatre steeped in an eerie sense of unreality unfolding according to a script he couldn't change. His resolve strengthened as he reached the familiar glow beneath the backstage door.

Re-entering the theatre, he slipped silently through the wings, his steps measured as he descended the short flight of stairs from the stage. The faint sound of the audience beyond the heavy curtain was a steady murmur, occasionally punctuated by laughter. His destination lay ahead: the dress circle, where Charles Forbes, Lincoln's trusted valet and attendant, stood at the door leading to the presidential box in the balcony overlooking the stage.

Booth approached casually with the confidence of a familiar face and said, "I'm John Wilkes Booth."

Forbes, a sturdy, freckled Irishman with an unassuming demeanor, nodded in recognition. The famous actor needed no further introduction. Stepping aside, Forbes said, "I'm certain the President will be happy to see you, Mr. Booth. He often speaks of you."

Booth offered a forced smile, tipping his hat slightly. "Mind if I ask who his guests are tonight?"

"There's Mrs. Lincoln, of course," Forbes began. "Major Henry Rathbone and his fiancée, Miss Clara Harris, are seated with them. General Grant was expected to attend but sent his regrets at the last minute."

The mention of Grant's absence struck Booth like a slap in the face. His sources had informed him that the general had planned to be present, and he had mentally set aside a single bullet from his derringer for the President and a thrust of his hunting knife for the man many in the South feared as Lincoln's likely successor. His plan to undermine the Union's leadership would have worked better with Grant included, but he quickly pushed his frustration aside to concentrate on his primary target.

"Thank you for letting me know," Booth replied, removing his hat. "Mind if I remain here to enjoy a bit of the play before I head upstairs to wait for the President?"

"Please do," Forbes said politely, stepping aside to allow Booth a moment of quiet observation. "I'll be glad to keep your hat while you visit."

"Thank you," Booth said, handing him his hat.

Booth lingered just outside the door, his gaze drifting toward the stage, where the play unfolded. The audience's laughter grew louder, rising like waves, and Booth's pulse quickened. The moment was drawing near.

He leaned against the wall, his gaze fixed intently on the Presidential Box where Lincoln sat, immersed in the play and laughing at its humor. The scene before him seemed almost surreal, the warm glow of the gaslights illuminating Lincoln's relaxed profile. Booth's eyes drifted to the balcony rail, mentally confirming the details of his escape route. He estimated the drop to the stage below was a manageable nine-foot leap, and the heavy curtains framing the box would provide a convenient aid in his descent.

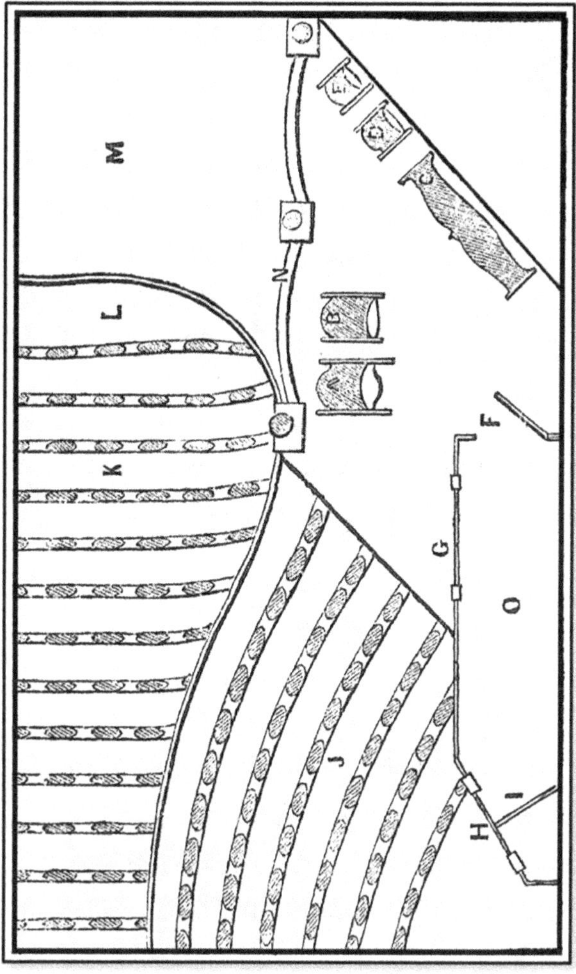

F. The Stage
G. Closed door
H. Entrance to the corridor.
I. The bar used by Booth to prevent entrance
J. Dress circle (Mezzanine)
K. The parquette (Orchestra Level)
L. The foot-lights
M. The stage
N. Place where Booth vaulted over to the stage below Lincoln's box
O. Dark corridor leading from the dress circle to Lincoln's box

Booth glanced toward the stage, taking note of the actors' movements. The play had reached the second scene of the third act. Now was the moment. He nodded to Lincoln's valet, who unlocked the door to the stairwell.

"Thanks," he said, flashing a polished stage smile as the valet secured the door behind him. A few steps ahead, he opened the door to reveal the stairway leading to the hallway that opened onto the Presidential Box, his heart pounding. As he slipped inside and softly closed the door behind him, the audience's noise dulled to a faint murmur. His hand brushed against the derringer hidden beneath his coat, its cool weight grounding him. He took a steady breath, feeling the gravity of the moment. Everything had led to this. There was no turning back.

Booth's mind flickered briefly to his earlier preparations. He had positioned Lincoln's customary rocking chair to the left of the Presidential box earlier that day, ensuring a clear and direct shot from the moment he entered. His meticulous planning left nothing to chance: only a single shot separated success from failure.

At the top of the stairs, there was a third door, leading to the dark corridor that led to Lincoln's box. Stepping inside, he paused to retrieve a wooden board he had concealed that day. Carefully, he propped it up against the door to block it, ensuring no one could follow him or interfere.

The corridor felt suffocatingly narrow, its dim light casting long shadows. Booth approached the double doors to the Presidential box. He crouched slightly, locating the small peephole he had drilled earlier using a gimlet, and widened it with his pocketknife. Peering through, he saw Lincoln sitting precisely as he had planned, his tall frame relaxed in the rocking chair positioned just six feet inside the door. His wife, Mary Todd, sat beside him, leaning in to speak, her hand resting lightly on her husband's arm.

Listening to the actors deliver their lines in a play he had practically memorized, Booth held his breath, his nerves taut. Then came the line he had waited for, cutting through the quiet tension like a knife.

Booth silently mouthed Asa Trenchard's words as the brash American character scolded the pretentious Mrs. Mountchessington for mocking her lack of refinement: "Don't know the manners of good society, eh? Well, I guess I know enough to turn you inside out, old gal. You sockdologizing old mantrap!"

The audience erupted in laughter, the sound swelling and spilling over the theatre. Darting through the right-hand door of the Presidential box, he drew his pistol and fired a single shot at close range. The roaring laughter from the audience drowned the crack of the derringer.

The bullet struck President Lincoln behind the left ear, piercing his brain. Lincoln slumped forward in his chair, unconscious. Mrs. Lincoln turned in shock, her husband's blood spattering her gown. Her scream, piercing and raw, shattered the ambiance of the theatre, drawing the attention of the audience, who sat bewildered and frozen, unsure whether this horrifying moment was part of the performance or a tragic reality.

Sitting next to the President, Major Henry Rathbone immediately jumped to his feet, seizing Booth's arm in a desperate effort to apprehend him. Booth, undeterred, dropped the pistol to the floor and pulled out his hunting knife. With a savage slash, he cut into Rathbone's arm, the blade slicing deep, leaving the major reeling backward, clutching a wound that gushed a stream of blood with every heartbeat.

Freed from Rathbone's grasp and knife still in hand, Booth moved swiftly to the edge of the box. Gripping the balcony railing with his left hand, he paused, his voice cutting through the stunned and screaming crowd: "*Sic semper tyrannis!*" The phrase, immortalized by Brutus in *Julius Caesar*, echoed through history and Booth's past when he had performed the assassin's role at New York City's Winter Garden Theatre.

Vaulting over the edge of the balcony, the spur of Booth's boot snagged on the bunting, tearing the fabric as he plummeted to the stage. He landed heavily, dropping to one knee, a jolt of searing pain shooting through his leg. Gritting his teeth, he pushed himself up, ignoring the increasing agony.

Booth brandished his knife with a theatrical flair before the stunned audience, his voice cutting through the chaos: "The South shall be free!" His eyes briefly met Harry Hawk's, who, as Asa Trenchard, had just unwittingly delivered Booth's cue. The actor stood frozen on the stage's apron, his face a mask of terror. The tilt of his slipping blonde wig, exposing the short, dark brown hair beneath, added an absurd flourish to the macabre tableau.

Booth advanced toward Hawk, his limp barely slowing him down. The actor, eyes wide, fled in panic, darting toward a staircase leading into the wings. Booth followed, but the actor vanished through a concealed tormentor door into the dimly lit backstage area, while Booth headed for the exit to the alley.

Suddenly, Edman Spangler emerged from the shadows, pale and shaken. Silently, he opened the back door for Booth and locked it after him. "May God have mercy on your soul, my friend," Spangler whispered, bowing his head.

Emerging into the cool night air, Booth's thoughts raced. The defiant words of Satan in Milton's *Paradise Lost* flashed through his mind: "Unconquerable will, and study of revenge, immortal hate, and courage never to submit or yield."

"Mr. Booth!" a thin, nervous voice called out. He turned to see a young stable hand standing by his one-eyed mare. "Mr. Spangler told me to watch One-Eyed Nellie for you. He said he had work to do inside."

Booth nodded curtly. "Thank you," he said, taking hold of Nellie's reins and pulling himself into the saddle. Pain shot through his injured leg, but he stifled a groan and managed to steady himself to mount his horse, his determination unshaken.

Booth urged the mare into a relentless gallop, her hooves pounding against the cobblestones. Above, the moon cast a pale light on the deserted road as he raced away from the city to rendezvous with David Herold, his riding companion waiting at Soper's Hill.

Driven by determination, he rode into the darkness, poised to swallow both man and beast into the depths of hell.

88

THE EMANCIPATION OF LINCOLN

The dimly lit East Room of the Executive Mansion was crowded with guests, their numbers spilling into the adjacent Green Room. Once the setting of Mrs. Lincoln's regal reception, the space had been transformed into a chamber of mourning, its former splendor eclipsed by the shadow of war, and in its place, a darkness made visible.

The once-colorfully adorned windows were now draped in black, befitting the solemn occasion. The magnificent crystal gasoliers hung like fireflies ensnared in black netting; the brilliance of their prisms faded but not extinguished. In the center of the room, a giant catafalque hung with black curtains formed a tent over Lincoln's coffin on a high platform edged with matching bunting.

Grief-stricken and inconsolable, the First Lady remained in her bedroom, refusing to attend the funeral services, her curtains drawn against the world. A litany of earlier tragedies deepened her anguish: the devastating loss of two young sons to disease and the deaths of three brothers, a half-brother, and a brother-in-law, all of whom perished fighting for the Confederacy.

Now, she had lost the husband who had stood steadfastly by her, shielding her from cruel whispers and false allegations of Confederate sympathies that had only added to her sorrows.

General Grant, a battle-hardened leader familiar with the sight of countless soldiers perishing under his command, sat alone at the head of the catafalque in full uniform. He exuded the image of a hero on a pedestal, yet his face shone with silent tears as he looked down with a clenched jaw at the coffin of his beloved Commander-in-Chief.

Vice President Andrew Johnson stood solemnly with the Cabinet. His presence served as a quiet yet powerful assertion of Constitutional Order amid the chaos of war, a visible reminder that, even in the face of violent upheaval, the principles of governance and the peaceful transition of power could endure.

Reverend Charles Hall, an Episcopal clergyman in ecclesiastical vestments, opened the service with a traditional prayer from 1 Corinthians 15:20. "But now is Christ risen from the dead," he intoned, a declaration affirming the power of faith to assure eternal life.

After Reverend Hall's opening prayer, Reverend Phineas D. Gurley, a stern-looking man with long sideburns framing his resolute face, stepped to a podium to address the mourners. He spoke not only as a minister but also as Lincoln's pastor from the New York Avenue Presbyterian Church and as a confidant of the President.

"As we stand here today," he began solemnly in a commanding baritone, "mourners around this coffin and the earthly remains of our beloved Chief Magistrate, we recognize and adore the sovereignty of God."

The Reverend called on the nation to bow before God's infinite majesty, emphasizing that divine providence guides all events while human understanding is limited. "His way is in the sea, and His path in the great waters, and His footsteps are not known," Gurley declared, encouraging the mourners to place their faith in God's plan.

The reverend reflected on the nature of Lincoln's assassination, noting, without immortalizing the name of Booth, "It was a cruel, cruel hand, that dark hand of the assassin, which smote our honored, wise, and noble President, and filled the land with sorrow."

Yet, he urged the mourners to look beyond the assassin's hand to "the chastening hand of a wise and faithful Father," reminding them that God's purposes, though inscrutable, are always just. He called on the people to drink from the bitter cup given to them, just as Lincoln had borne the burdens of war with grace and perseverance.

Gurley's eulogy turned to Lincoln's character, praising him as "simple and sincere, plain and honest, truthful and just, benevolent and kind." Regarding his integrity, Gurley said he was "thorough, all-pervading, all-controlling, and incorruptible." It was this steadfast morality, he maintained, that made Lincoln a fitting leader during a time of national peril, and his calm reliance on God's providence had inspired confidence in others. Gurley recalled Lincoln's words to a gathering of clergymen, "Gentlemen, my hope of success in this great and terrible struggle rests on that immutable foundation, the justice and goodness of God."

Closing his eulogy, Gurley urged the nation to "have faith in God." He declared, "Though our beloved President is slain, our beloved country is saved. Liberty itself is immortal."

His parting message was one of hope, rooted in faith, as he declared that a "brighter, happier day" for the nation would surely come from this trial.

When the service ended, mourners filed out in orderly lines, emerging through the north door to stand on the driveway and await the procession to the Capitol.

A sea of grievers pressed together beyond the Executive Mansion gates with grief etched into every face. Men stood with hats in hand, their eyes red-rimmed and downcast, while women clutched handkerchiefs to their faces. Wide-eyed children clung to their mothers' skirts.

At precisely two o'clock, the great doors of the Executive Mansion opened, and silence rippled through the parting crowd like a tide pulling away from the shore. From the shadowed entrance, an honor guard emerged into the sunlight, their movements precise. Six stalwart soldiers bore the President's coffin on their shoulders, their faces stoic. The coffin, draped in the Stars and Stripes, seemed to glow faintly in the soft afternoon light.

The honor guard moved as one, the men's boots striking the ground in unison as they approached the waiting funeral wagon. Draped in heavy black crepe, it resembled a rolling catafalque fit for a fallen king. Six regal white horses, their manes braided with black crepe ribbons, stood like silent sentinels before the gathered crowd.

With precision, the honor guard eased the President's coffin onto the wagon's platform. Church bells across the city began to toll. The cortège emerged from the Executive Mansion gates, escorted by a cavalry regiment. Behind them rolled two artillery batteries, the cannons painted jet black for the occasion.

A battalion of marines led the funeral march with precision, their rifles glinting in the light. Two infantry regiments followed; their steps synchronized to the mournful beat of muffled drums. At their head rode the commander of the escort, his staff trailing behind, their somber expressions reflecting the profound loss etched across the faces of the crowd.

A dirge floated through the air, explicitly composed for this day. The slow and deliberate rhythm of the drums marked the passage of time as the procession moved forward. The deep, resonant beats seemed to echo within the souls of those gathered, stirring profound emotions that bound the crowd in shared mourning.

Mounted Marine, Navy, and Army officers followed the hearse, with dismounted officers behind them. These men had known Lincoln as their President, commander-in-chief, and a beacon of hope and unity.

The crowd along the avenue stood in hushed reverence. Women clutched handkerchiefs to their faces, their tear-filled eyes fixed on the pageantry before them. Veterans of the war stood solemnly. As the hearse passed, a little boy standing by his father's side raised a crisp military salute.

When the procession neared the Capitol, a profound silence enveloped the scene. The marble steps, swathed in black, loomed like a solemn altar, poised to receive its sacred burden.

Minute guns thundered in the distance, reverberating reports punctuating the somber quiet.

Beneath the great dome he had ordered built during the winds of war, Lincoln's coffin was carried into the rotunda.

The ceremony went beyond mourning: it was a nation offering its grief and gratitude to the man who had become both the heart of its suffering and the hope for its rebirth.

89

GENERAL BANKS RETURNS
TO NEW ORLEANS

Nathaniel Banks stood watching the heavy April showers lash against the windowpanes of his old office in the St. Charles Hotel. The sheets of rain blurred his view of the streets below, where puddles collected in the uneven cobblestones and rivulets of water streamed through the gutters. Though the city bustled beyond the windowpane, it felt distant, as if veiled by the grief that had settled in his chest.

Along the levee, horses hauled wagons loaded with crates under sagging tarps, their hooves splashing through the muck, while a steamer let out a shrill whistle that seemed to slice through the thick, drumming rain. The sound mingled with the cries of merchants hawking their wares from beneath dripping awnings, the shuffle of freedmen moving cautiously through the chaos, and the clatter of carriages whose wheels splashed water onto the sidewalks.

Banks's thoughts wandered, bringing with them the biting irony of his situation. He had assumed command after Butler toward the end of 1862, replacing a man notorious for his heavy-handed rule and personal gain, only to be succeeded by General Hurlbut in July 1864 following the disastrous Red River Campaign.

After Hurlbut's tenure ended in April of this year, bogged down in the same quagmire of allegations of corruption that plagued Butler, he found himself back in this office with his old desk, chair, and weighty responsibilities. This time, however, the focus had shifted. It was 1865; the war was over, the President had been assassinated, and his Vice President was in office. The challenge now was Reconstruction.

Banks turned away from the rain-streaked window, his hands clasped tightly behind his back and let out a slow breath. "Reconstruction," he muttered to himself. "It's a grand term. But what exactly are we rebuilding?"

His eyes drifted back to the window, where he watched the rain pounding against the glass. "How do you govern a city that defies every rule and expectation? Freedmen stepping into a world that resents their freedom. Former masters who still wield their wealth and influence like weapons, Black Codes creeping in like rot beneath the surface, undoing the victories we bled for. And yet, the work must go on. It's not about me or my failures. It's about those people trying to carve out lives for themselves from the ruins. If we falter now, we condemn them to a new kind of bondage."

Banks rubbed his temple, feeling the weight of every decision he had made and those yet to come. "Reconstruction isn't just about mending roads and rewriting codes. It's about rebuilding trust, if that's even possible. It involves tearing down the old scaffolding of hate and ignorance, piece by piece, and praying there's enough strength to hold up the structure when the storm rolls in." He turned to his desk and picked up a report on vigilante groups in the countryside. "The war ended slavery, but the fight for equality is just beginning. And God help me. I'm not sure we're ready for that battle."

A knock at the door pulled him from his reverie. Banks straightened his coat with a deep breath, the weight of his musings disguised behind his practiced military demeanor. "Come in," he called, his tone steady though the storm inside him raged on.

"General Banks," Thomas greeted, stepping inside and closing the door quietly behind him. "Welcome back to New Orleans."

"Thomas," Banks said warmly, extending his hand for a firm shake as Thomas placed his umbrella on the stand beside the door. "I'm glad you could come. Please take off your McIntosh and have a seat. May I offer you anything?"

"No, thank you," Thomas replied, draping his raincoat across an empty chair, then took a seat across from Banks.

"Much has happened since we last spoke," Banks said cordially.

"Yes, it has," Thomas agreed. He paused briefly before adding, "You know I've returned to my law practice."

"I'm sure Rachel is pleased."

A smile crossed Thomas's face. "She certainly is. We can finally have more time together."

"A shame about the President," Banks said after a moment's silence.

"Yes, it certainly is," Thomas said gravely. "I don't know how things will proceed without him."

"You mean Reconstruction?" Banks asked.

"Exactly. President Johnson is far more sympathetic to the South than Lincoln ever was."

Banks frowned, his jaw tightening. "That's what troubles me. He's too comfortable with the former slaveholders as well. My sources inform me that he opposes granting civil rights to freedmen."

Thomas nodded slowly. "That doesn't bode well for the future."

Banks paced the room as he spoke. "First, I was tasked with that infernal offensive up the Red River. Now, I'm expected to handle Reconstruction under a President who seems determined to undermine it. What am I? The King of Lost Causes?"

Thomas remained composed, though Banks's uncharacteristic display of frustration struck him. "Congress is still on your side, sir," he offered. "The Black Codes here and elsewhere are already stirring alarm. I don't think there's much sympathy up North for handing the South everything it wants after all these years of sacrifice."

Banks paused, exhaling slowly before returning to his chair. "That's true," he conceded. "There is gathering resistance."

Thomas asked, "Is there anything I can do to help?"

Banks met his gaze. "Yes, Thomas, there is something." He paused, allowing the gravity of the admission to settle, then continued with a lighter tone. "Would you be willing to take on a new assignment? It comes with good pay, low risk, and little travel."

Thomas raised an eyebrow, intrigued. "And what service would I be expected to render?"

"Practical and insightful advice," Banks replied, a faint smile breaking the seriousness of his expression. "You're good at reading situations, Thomas. And people. That's what I need now. Someone I can trust to tell me what they *really* see, not what they *think* I want to hear."

Thomas tilted his head thoughtfully. "I'd consider it."

Banks's expression shifted, a determined edge creeping into his tone. "Then let's talk Black Codes and how the Confederates are plotting to undermine Reconstruction."

A knock at the door interrupted the conversation.

"Come," Banks called.

Allan Pinkerton stepped inside, rainwater dripping from his umbrella, hat, and rumpled suit. His presence filled the room. He was a man with an air of authority, and the weight of unfinished business was etched into his features.

Pinkerton was in his early forties. A stout and ruggedly built man of average height, his physical presence reflected years of hard work and travel. His thick, graying beard framed a face marked with deep lines, a testament to the stresses of his profession. His sharp, penetrating eyes conveyed an intensity that seemed to cut through pretense.

"Allan. Good to see you," Banks said, surprised to see him.

The detective chief set his umbrella down and removed his hat, revealing a thinning hairline. He nodded to both men. "I've come on a personal matter, Nathaniel," he said, with a trace of a melodic Scottish accent. He paused to take note of Thomas. "Thomas, good to see you."

"Good to see you as well, sir. Should I leave to afford you privacy?" he asked, standing to shake his hand.

"No. Sit. Make yourself comfortable."

Thomas engaged in a half-smile, returning to his seat and recalling his former employer's abrupt manner.

Banks gestured to a chair. "Have a seat, Allan."

Pinkerton sat facing Banks, his expression grim. "I should never have left Lincoln's side. The damn fool had no real protection. Nobody could convince him that Booth wasn't his friend. That scoundrel walked in and out of Ford's Theatre as if it were his own home. If I'd been there…" He trailed off, his hands tightening into fists.

"No one can change what happened," Banks assured him.

Pinkerton looked at Thomas, his eyes almost pleading. "We saved him once."

Thomas nodded sadly, "Yes, sir, we did."

"Back in '61, it was," Pinkerton reminisced. "You were with me then. Do you remember that little widow, Kate Warren?

"Very much so," Thomas said fondly.

"Best female detective I've ever had. She's the one who infiltrated the Confederate spy ring with her feminine charms. I swear, that woman could convince you she was the Queen of England if that's what it took to complete her mission."

Thomas laughed. "She could also play quite the Southern Belle."

"That's why she's working with me here in New Orleans," Pinkerton said. "My job is to investigate and root out abuses in federal contracts. The President, God rest his soul, told me it was too much to burden you with, Nathaniel, especially since he wanted you to focus on Reconstruction without being weighed down by all the details. Butler and Hurlbut left a mess, and I've been assigned to help you put things in order. However, it all ties back to the Reconstruction issue. We need to know who we're dealing with when awarding federal contracts. If we don't get it right, we're just building a house on sand."

Banks's gaze flicked to Thomas. "You hear that, Thomas? One of you deals with graft and corruption, and the other deals with Black Codes and paramilitary groups, reporting your findings to me."

Thomas met the men's eyes, his voice calm but resolute. "Agreed. We'll need a coordinated effort."

Pinkerton sat back in his chair, appearing resolute. "Then we'd best get to work."

90

THE RESURRECTION
OF CODE NOIR

The dancing firelight of Antoine's chandelier in the main dining room refracted through cascading faceted crystals. Each flicker of the gas flames danced from prism to prism, filling the room with magic.

The low murmur of refined conversation flowed through the room, mingling with the gentle clink of silverware on porcelain plates. Slender waiters, dressed in *tenue de serveur*, moved briskly between the linen-draped tables, their white aprons crisp and immaculate.

Rachel and Thomas sat across from one another at a small table near the elegantly draped window. The rich aromas of sauces, buttered oysters, gumbo, and fresh French bread filled the air, but neither seemed to be engaged in their dining as the rising bubbles in their Champagne glasses marked the passage of time.

"Is there a problem with the cuisine, Monsieur?" a garçon asked incredulously as he stopped on his way to another table.

"No," Thomas replied. "We're just enjoying each other's company."

"*Bien,*" he returned smiling, continuing to serve other guests.

"Thomas," Rachel began, "I heard troubling reports from Opelousas today at school. The local authorities have passed a Black Code. From what I understand, it's reminiscent of the old *Code Noir*, aiming to suppress the freedoms of the newly emancipated slaves."

Thomas sighed. "The local politicians with secessionist sympathies perceive the Freedmen's Bureau's reforms as threats to their way of life. The Black Codes are their effort to maintain a racial hierarchy and reestablish a labor force that mirrors slavery as closely as possible under the guise of 'law and order.'"

Rachel clasped her hands in her lap. "Who's law and who's order? They act like emancipation never happened."

"That's the idea," Thomas replied, his gaze steady on hers. "They couldn't call it slavery anymore because of the Thirteenth Amendment. But it's slavery, plain and simple, only now it hides behind the guise of law and order. The chains are written in ink instead of seared into flesh."

Rachel's brows knitted tighter. "What's in it, this Black Code?"

"First of all, if a freedman's found without work," Thomas began, "he's charged with vagrancy. And once charged, he's fined. If he can't pay the fine, he's leased out to work it off without any pay on the same plantation he thought he'd escaped."

Rachel's fingers curled around the stem of her Champagne glass. "Leased? You mean hired out like a mule or a wagon?"

"That's right," Thomas said, his voice dropping a note lower. He leaned forward in his chair, his eyes scanning the other patrons as if he expected to be overheard. "Sent back to work off a debt they'll never get ahead of. It's just another chain. If they're not 'vagrants,' then they're 'workers.' And that's a distinction with no honor. It's 'freedom,' but only on paper."

Rachel's voice was sharp with disbelief. "It doesn't take an attorney to know that no one is free if they're not free to leave their employer."

"Exactly," Thomas said, his lips pressing into a grim line. "It's even worse for their children. If the parents are seen as 'unfit' — and guess who is the sole arbiter of that? — then the children can be 'apprenticed' to their former masters. The apprenticeship lasts till they're twenty-one and is transferable to another planter on another plantation, effectively restoring the slave trade."

Rachel lifted a hand to her mouth, her eyes distant, as if she were seeing something far away. "They're stealing the children again, Thomas. Separating them from their mothers."

Thomas's gaze hardened. "Yes, they are."

Rachel's voice was quiet and controlled, but her words reflected her anger. "They're afraid of them, Thomas. Afraid of them being educated, afraid of them gathering. Afraid of what'll happen when the freedmen no longer live in fear."

"That's right," Thomas said, leaning in closer, his eyes sharp with intensity. "And the courts won't help, either. The inequities persist until Congress enacts a Fourteenth Amendment, as Stevens and Sumner advocate, guaranteeing equal protection under the law and fundamental civil rights. As it is now, black folks can't serve on juries, can't afford an attorney, and can't testify against a White man. They're left defenseless in a system designed to keep them oppressed."

"In other words, they're free from slavery, but they have no civil rights. And who's going to change this in the meantime, Thomas?"

Her husband's jaw tightened, his gaze meeting hers. "Until Congress acts, freedmen are not likely to gain more rights under the law. But there's still hope, Rachel. They can organize and fight. Some long-term freedmen business owners in town are already holding private meetings to organize an underground movement."

"An armed resistance?" Rachel asked incredulously. "Haven't we had enough bloodshed?"

"Perhaps, at some point," Thomas said, "people will find it in their hearts to appeal to their better angels. President Lincoln's words from his speech at Gettysburg came to mind when I first heard about the Black Codes passing. I've memorized most of them by heart. He said, 'We here highly resolve that these dead shall not have died in vain. That this nation, under God, shall have a new birth of freedom, and that government of the people, by the people, for the people, shall not perish from the earth.'"

Thomas saw tears welling up in Rachel's eyes.

"What oft was thought, but ne'er so well expressed," she replied, recalling Alexander Pope's praise of Shakespeare.

He reached across the table to gently squeeze her hand. "Shall we enjoy our food while it's still warm and our Champagne while it's still cold?"

Rachel dabbed her eyes with her handkerchief, then lifted her Champagne glass, her smile steady.

Thomas raised his glass in a toast, invoking the cry of the French Revolution. "*Liberté, Égalité, Fraternité!*"

Their crystal Champagne flutes touched with a soft, resonant chime, echoing freedom's call through the ages.

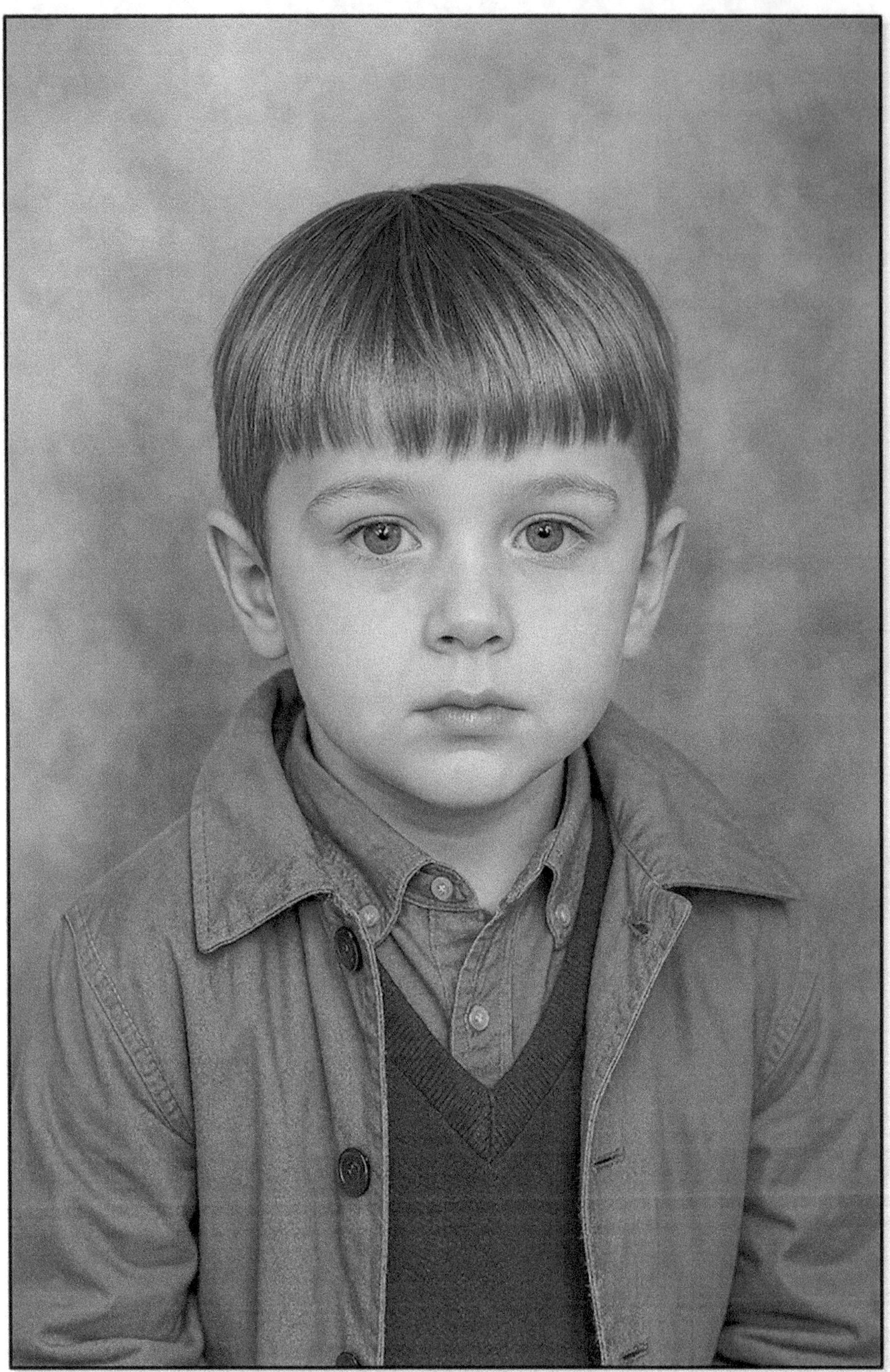

91

A Voice from the Past

Rachel brewed a fresh pot of coffee in the kitchen and then went upstairs to check on Thomas, who usually awoke to the enticing aroma. Peeking into the bedroom, she saw he was still asleep at nearly nine in the morning. Gently closing the door, she decided not to wake him, as he had been working on legal documents into the early hours.

As she descended the staircase to open the front door, she heard the familiar rhythmic clippity-clop of horses' hooves on the street.

"Mornin', Mrs. Manget," the postman said, tipping his cap as he approached her. "Lovely day."

"Good mornin', Henry," Rachel replied. "Do we have anything today?"

"Yes'm. Only one letter. It's for you from someone in LaGrange, Georgia."

"LaGrange?" Rachel asked, immediately thinking of her sister.

"Yes'm. They just resumed mail service from LaGrange. I heard that the Nancy Harts negotiated a peaceful surrender with the Yankees after the Rebs fled the town. Smart group of women, them Nancies."

"And brave, too," Rachel said, taking the letter.

"Yes'm. You have yourself a good day, Mrs. Manget."

"Thank you, Henry," she said, waving. "You as well."

Rachel was surprised that the letter was from Eugenia Phillips. Why would Eugenia write now? She hadn't heard from her since Butler released her from Ship Island and banished her from New Orleans almost two years ago.

Returning to the parlor, Rachel sat on the sofa and eagerly opened the envelope. A small photograph fluttered to the floor as she unfolded the letter. She bent over to pick it up and saw that it was Noah. He was beautiful, with big, bright eyes and a face as soft and round as a ripe peach. Picking up the photograph, she longed to hold him, hug him close, and kiss his sweet face.

As her attention turned to the letter, her hand began to tremble with the growing fear that it might contain bad news about her family.

LaGrange, Georgia   April 20, 1865

My Dearest Rachel,

I trust this letter finds you and Thomas in good health. My prayers are with you both, always. Mr. P. told me that he has heard that Thomas is thriving in his practice and that you are devoting your talents to teaching. Please accept my sincerest wishes for your happiness.

Thanks to the courage of the brave Nancy Harts, our homes and property have been spared. Only military assets were destroyed. I must even commend our town's namesake, a Union colonel, for his integrity in forbidding his men from looting the homes of LaGrange. It is a small mercy amidst so much loss.

It pains me deeply to share the sorrowful news that Sarah and Jacob have succumbed to typhoid fever. Local health officials insisted on an immediate burial and quarantined us in our house. Thank God that little Noah and the rest of our family were spared.

My dearest Rachel, I am so sorry that this news must reach you this way.

Young Noah grows swiftly, like a tender sapling after spring rain, and he has become a handsome little fellow. He has his father's eyes. Yet his nights are restless, filled with tears and cries for his mother and father. I have told him they have gone on a long journey, but his questions grow harder to answer each day.

Rachel, I wonder if you and Thomas might meet Philip and me, perhaps in Mobile, now under Union control, so that Noah might come to live with you in New Orleans. He needs the stability and love that only you can provide. If this is agreeable, please telegraph me at your earliest convenience so that we can arrange everything without delay.

Though the war has officially ended, I fear the conflict is far from over. The scars left by this great upheaval will not heal easily. This nation remains bitterly divided, and I tremble at what lies ahead. For now, I take solace in my Christian friend's wisdom: "Sufficient unto the day is the evil thereof."

When I read of President Lincoln's death proclaimed across the papers last week, a strange and solemn tide of emotions overtook me. I had prayed for an end to this bitter strife for four long years. Yet, this was not the end I had prayed for. His death, I fear, will only deepen the nation's wounds. Once seen in the South as a tyrant and in the North as a savior, he has transcended these divisions. His legacy will shape us all, for better or worse. As Secretary Stanton so eloquently declared, "He belongs to the ages."

Please write soon, my dear Rachel, and know that my heart is ever with you and Thomas.

With My Deepest Sympathies,

Eugenia

Rachel's hand shook as she placed the letter in her lap.

Sarah and Jacob were gone.

The news struck her like an arrow through the heart, leaving an ache that radiated through every limb. Sarah, with her gentle ways, and Jacob, with his quiet presence and warm smile. Both are gone, leaving Noah without a father or a mother.

The room felt suddenly oppressive; the walls seemed too close, and the air was too thick. She rose abruptly and crossed to the window. The sounds of the street outside— children shouting, a vendor calling out his wares—seemed surreal.

Her gaze drifted out the window, where the sun cast shadows over the rooftops. Somewhere, Noah was crying for his parents, his young heart too innocent to grasp the permanence of their absence. A lump rose in her throat, and she clutched the window's edge, her knuckles turning white.

A wave of guilt followed swiftly on the heels of her grief. While Sarah lay dying, she had been here with Thomas, focused on her survival and future. She had promised to protect her family, yet she had failed them when it mattered most. Now, she was left to step into the void and provide Noah with the stability he desperately needed.

Rachel drew a deep breath, steadying herself. She could do this. She *would* do this. Whatever else she had lost, she still had the strength to love and care for Noah.

Returning to the sofa, Rachel sat down heavily. She picked up the letter again, her eyes lingering on the words about President Lincoln's death. Eugenia's reflection on his legacy struck a chord. "He belongs to the ages." Rachel let the phrase roll over her, the weight of its finality sinking in. So much had been lost. Not just lives but a way of life, a certainty about the world that would never return. Rightly or wrongly, it was gone.

A tear slipped down her cheek, and she let it fall. "Sarah, dear sweet Sarah," she whispered, her sister's name breaking on her lips.

She carefully folded the letter and tucked it back into the envelope. Then she rose again and walked to the mantel, holding the letter and Noah's picture in her hand. There was her memory jar, the one she had crafted for Levi. Inside it was his watch and the mourning brooch that Eugenia had given her.

Rachel placed the envelope and Noah's picture gently on the mantel, then picked up the jar, its cool surface smooth against her palm. Opening the lid, she slid the envelope inside, settling it among the relics of her past. This, too, was a part of her story now. It was a memory of all that remained of her kin, except for Noah, whose picture she carefully propped up against a photo of her and Thomas.

Clutching the jar to her chest, she felt its coolness slowly yield to the warmth of her body as if drawing life from her embrace. One day, when Noah was old enough to understand his heritage, this jar would belong to him. For now, it was hers to guard, a fragile repository of love, grief, and hope for the future.

"Is that coffee I smell?" Thomas asked, entering the parlor.

"Good morning, dear," Rachel said, carefully returning the memory jar to the mantel. "Are you ready for breakfast?"

"Am I ever," he said, hugging her and giving her a peck on the cheek. Drawing back, he said, "You've been crying. What's the matter, darling?"

"It's about my family in LaGrange. There's something we must speak about."

LITTLE
ANGELS
Canal

92

LITTLE ANGELS

Rachel and Thomas, dressed to the nines for the matinee performance of *The Wicklow Wedding* at the Varieties Theatre, strolled arm in arm along Canal Street, enjoying the warmth of the afternoon sun and the sweet aroma of pastries wafting from the bakery storefronts.

"I suddenly feel an urge for a fresh, warm brioche with fig preserves. What about you, darling?" Thomas asked.

"Sounds delightful," Rachel said, smiling brightly. "I'm famished."

Thomas pulled out his Waltham half-hunter pocket watch, its polished gold case gleaming in the light. He glanced through the small glass inset on the cover at the blued steel hands sweeping across the white enameled dial. "It's only a quarter past one," he said. "We still have an hour or so before curtain time."

As they entered the bakery, rows of glass cases greeted them, displaying shelves of enticing golden brioche and delicate madeleines. Plates of *pain perdu* and sugar-dusted beignets rested alongside an abundant display of confections, their appearance as inviting as their promise of sweetness.

"May I help you?" the matronly Irish woman asked from behind the counter.

"What would you have, my dear?" Thomas asked Rachel as he removed his hat.

"Goodness. What *wouldn't* I have," she replied.

"You *are* hungry," Thomas said with a chuckle.

"Let's see..." Rachel's eyes drifted slowly along the case, her gaze lingering on each confection as if tasting them in her mind. "I'll start with two of the madeleines, of course," she said. "Oh, and the beignets look delightful. I'll have two of those as well."

The stack of baked goods on the counter grew as Thomas watched in disbelief.

"There," Rachel declared with satisfaction. "Do you have ice cream?" she asked the shopkeeper.

"No, my lady," the woman replied incredulously, shaking her head. "That would be Jackson's ice cream parlor, just a few doors down to the left as you leave."

"Pity," Rachel sighed, though her disappointment was short-lived.

Looking bemused by Rachel's ravenous appetite, Thomas stepped to the register.

"That will be one dollar," the shopkeeper said with a smile. "My best sale of the week."

After paying for the treats, Thomas turned to Rachel. "Shall we sit and enjoy some of these before we continue shopping? Fingers can get sticky."

Rachel took the lead, sitting at a small round wrought-iron table with a glass top. Thomas joined her, placing the tray of sweets on the table.

"Looks like we'll need more room," he remarked, setting the shopping bag and his hat on an adjacent table. "Since we're the only ones in the shop, I don't think anyone will mind."

"I know exactly where I'll start," Rachel said, reaching for a madeleine. "Oh, I'm sorry, darling. I forgot to ask for coffee. Cream and sugar, of course."

"Right away," he said, rising from his chair. He returned to the counter, purchased two cups of coffee, and brought them back on a tray with cream and sugar to see that Rachel had already finished her madeleine.

"These are divine," she said, wiping her fingertips with a napkin.

"I'm glad you're enjoying them," Thomas replied, placing the coffee and cream on the table. He set the empty tray on the next table, beside their shopping bag and his hat, and sat beside her.

"Shall we share a beignet?" he asked.

"We have two," she reminded him with a grin. "I'll take one, please."

Thomas handed her a beignet, his eyes narrowing with curiosity as he watched her. She had always been a delicate eater, and he was surprised to see her consume so many pastries in one sitting.

Rachel added cream and sugar to her coffee, stirring it slowly before breaking off a piece of the beignet. She dipped it into the steaming coffee, letting it soak for a moment before taking a bite. Then she glanced around suddenly. "Good thing there are no British here. They consider the French terribly rude for their dunking habits," she said with a playful grin.

Thomas's eyes crinkled with amusement. "I doubt that the British are coming, my dear. Feel free to dunk your pastries to your heart's content."

Rachel broke off another piece of beignet. "Then I shall," she declared, dipping it again with a flourish.

After savoring the last bite of her treat, she delicately dabbed her mouth with a napkin. "What's the name of the play we're seeing tonight?"

"*The Wicklow Wedding.*"

"Have you read any reviews?" she asked.

"No," Thomas replied. "I believe it's about a peasant girl set in 1709 during the Irish Rebellion. She secretly marries a messenger who gets arrested for spying, and she orchestrates his daring escape."

Rachel gave Thomas a knowing smile. "Does anything about the plot strike you as familiar?"

Thomas chuckled, rolling his eyes. "Vaguely," he said.

The couple finished their pastries and left the bakery to resume their window shopping, intrigued by an array of newly imported European goods: silks, silver trinkets, and bonnets brimming with colorful feathers and roses, reminiscent of paintings of fashionable French ladies strolling along the Champs-Élysées.

Rachel paused to admire a millinery shop and asked, "Which hat would suit me best?"

"Perhaps I'll buy you one of those feathered creations," he teased, gesturing toward a flamboyant hat with brilliant plumage. "You'd look like a beautiful exotic bird."

Rachel laughed playfully. "And I suppose you'd claim me as your rare specimen?"

"Caught and caged, my dear. But you're so clever, I doubt I could keep you caged for long."

"You're terrible!" she retorted, giving him a playful swat.

As they continued their stroll, Rachel's gaze grew wistful. "Now that the war is over and we're assured safe passage, it will be such a joy to bring Noah home to be part of our family."

"Yes," Thomas agreed. "I've booked one of those new Pullman coach accommodations for our travel. The berths are versatile, with beds that fold down to provide comfortable, padded seating. I'm also told that the dining is superb."

"That sounds perfect," Rachel said with a soft smile. "I can't wait to hold him."

"It will be quite the experience for Noah," Thomas added. "I was a teenager when I took my first train ride, but it was nothing like the luxurious Pullman cars of today."

"Perhaps Noah will have a little brother or sister one day," Rachel said, watching his face.

Thomas's eyes sparkled. "That would be grand. Maybe one of each."

They stopped before a shop with gilded letters on the window that read "Little Angels." An unreadable smile with a touch of mischief crossed her face as her gaze lingered on the display of baby clothes.

"Did I mention I visited Dr. Zimmerman's office this morning?" she asked, her tone light.

Thomas's brow furrowed. "Is Doré unwell?"

Rachel let out a laugh. "Doré is as healthy as ever."

"Then why visit our veterinarian?" he asked.

She tilted her head, her eyes sparkling. "Didn't you know that Dr. Zimmerman is also a physician? And quite experienced with foaling?"

Thomas's gaze flicked to the tiny garments in the window, then slowly back to hers. "You mean…"

Rachel nodded, her heart racing as she watched the wonder grow in his eyes.

Without a word, he swept her into his arms, lifting her off her feet in a breathless embrace. Her heart soared as he held her close, his arms strong and assuring.

At that moment, the world vanished, and the two of them were suspended in a silence more eloquent than words.

When he finally released her, she asked softly, "Are you happy?"

Thomas exhaled a shaky breath, his smile radiant. "Happy? I've drawn up Noah's adoption papers, and we're having a baby now. Sweetheart. I'm not just happy. I'm the luckiest man alive."

1920

EPILOGUE

BATON ROUGE

Rachel and Thomas sat hand in hand on a rocking settee on their front porch in Baton Rouge, enjoying the gentle spring breeze as they watched their great-grandson, David, roll a hoop along the sidewalk with a stick.

The boy's laughter rang out each time he kept it upright, his delight infectious as the hoop spun smoothly over the pavement.

Rachel smiled warmly, a distant look in her eyes. "Watching David play takes me back. I wanted to play hoops with the neighborhood boys when I was a little girl. Jack, a skinny child with asthma, was the only one who'd play with me. The others teased him and called him a sissy for playing with a girl. Eventually, they bullied him so much that he stopped. After that, I played alone, spinning the hoop around my waist, losing myself in the rhythm, until Mama ran outside and told me to stop because it wasn't ladylike."

She chuckled softly. "Later, Daddy pulled me aside, wrapped me in a warm hug, and said, 'You're my little tomboy.'"

Thomas squeezed her hand. "Jack sounds like a kind soul. And your daddy was a good man. I wish I could have met him."

Rachel nodded wistfully. "Jack became a judge and married a lovely girl from our neighborhood."

Thomas chuckled. "And the other boys?"

"Billy, the worst of the bullies, ended up in jail for disturbing the peace."

They fell into a companionable silence, watching David play.

After a moment, Rachel spoke again. "Thomas, I've been thinking. You've recently discussed purchasing a new car. What if we keep the Model T instead of trading it in so David can have it when he's old enough to drive?"

Thomas laughed. "If that car sits unused until David can drive, the only thing holding it together will be baling wire."

"I know I'll never drive it again," Rachel admitted. "I nearly broke my arm the last time I tried to crank it. I much prefer riding Daisy to the general store when you're at work."

"I thought all of the hitching posts downtown had been removed."

"A few remain," Rachel said. "But sometimes cars are parked in front of them. People can be so inconsiderate."

Thomas hesitated before replying. "It might not be safe to ride Daisy into town much longer, darling. There are too many cars on the road now."

Rachel sighed. "You're right. She does get a bit nervous around cars, especially when they backfire. I suppose I'll take her riding in the country instead. I'll ride into town with you in your car when I need to go."

A thin, middle-aged, colored woman appeared at the screen door, her apron snug around her waist, a hairnet holding back her graying curls. "I'm done with the cleanin', done with the dishes, and done with makin' up the beds, Mr. Thomas," she declared. "It's Friday, and I need to pick up a sack of groceries on my way home to fix supper."

Thomas reached for his wallet with the familiarity of a well-practiced ritual. He counted out five one-dollar bills and added a few coins. "Here you go, Annie," he said, pressing the money into her hand. "A little extra since you scrubbed the porch yesterday."

"Ain't no trouble, Mr. Thomas. I try to keep y'all's place like I keep my own."

"We appreciate you, Annie," Rachel said warmly.

"And I 'preciate y'all," Annie said, slipping the money into her apron pocket. "I best get on before the store closes."

"Can I give you a ride, Annie?" Thomas asked. "It's warm for May."

"No, sir. Ain't but half a mile down the lane to the quarters. These old bones need to keep movin'."

"Have a good weekend, Annie," Rachel said.

"Y'all too," Annie said, stepping off the porch with careful deliberation.

"Bye, Aunt Annie!" David called, pausing his hoop to wave.

"Bye, precious. See y'all next week."

As their maid walked away, Rachel watched her thoughtfully. "It feels like just yesterday that Annie would have been a slave. Now, even though she's in a servile position to White people, she's free to make her own choices and works to support herself and her son since her husband passed away. She told me Amos has straight A's and is heading to vet school in Kansas next year, since they still won't let Colored people into colleges in Louisiana. Unfortunately, we have a long way to go before there's equal opportunity for Coloreds."

"Amos is a smart kid," Thomas said, gently steering the conversation toward a more positive note. "He will be the first in Annie's family to have a college degree. Always has his nose in a book when he's not rescuing injured birds."

Rachel chuckled. "Yes, and he names them all. Even buries the ones that don't survive in his backyard, putting up crosses and praying for each of them."

Thomas smirked. "Didn't Annie say his cat, Kitty, keeps digging them up?"

"Yes. Kitty isn't the best guest to invite to a bird's funeral."

Thomas adopted a mock-serious tone. "Kitty came not to bury them but to feast upon them."

Rachel grinned, rising to her feet with a dramatic arm sweep. In her best stage voice, she intoned, "Friends, birds, and backyard companions, lend me your ears! Kitty has come not to bury these poor creatures but to feast upon them. The mischief cats do live after them; the good is oft interred with the sparrows. So let it be with these birds!"

Thomas laughed. "Well played, my dear. Though I think Kitty would prefer another sparrow to a eulogy."

Their laughter intertwined as they savored the moment.

Rachel sat down again and leaned against Thomas, resting her head on his shoulder. "It feels like we've been together our whole lives."

He kissed her hair. "Fifty-six years, to be exact."

"Working on fifty-seven. We were so young back then. Everyone believed the war between the states was so horrific that we'd never fight another one."

"Especially not a war in Europe," Thomas said. "At least this time, soldiers from the North and South are fighting on the same side."

"And in the air." Rachel shook her head in wonder. "Who would have thought men would ever fly? Back in the day, aeronauts' balloons were tethered to the ground."

Thomas nodded. "I never imagined movies in the theaters replacing live actors, or electricity in our home, either."

"Or electric light bulbs," Rachel added. "So much easier to read or sew at night now."

Thomas chuckled. "You know, in 1843, the Commissioner of Patents claimed human improvement was advancing so fast that progress would soon come to an end."

Rachel laughed. "Sounds like he was talking himself out of a job."

"Or just lacked imagination. Last night, I read in *Popular Science* that they're developing a device called a radio. It receives electromagnetic signals broadcast through the air and converts them into sound."

"Amazing," Rachel said. "It's like something out of Jules Verne. But I don't want voices coming into my home uninvited. And can you imagine what politicians would do with a contraption like that?"

Thomas chuckled. "Perish the thought."

They sat quietly for a while.

Rachel sighed. "So much is changing, Thomas. Sometimes, I feel like an ancient relic behind the glass in a museum exhibit."

Thomas kissed her forehead, stroking her silver hair. "You're not a relic, my love. You're my beautiful wife. And you're right here with me in the perfect place and time."

A giggle from the sidewalk broke their reverie. David pointed at the porch and called out to passersby with childish glee, "Looky, y'all! Grandma and Grandpa are smoochin' again!"

ACKNOWLEDGMENTS

This journey began in a classroom at Dalton College in Dalton, Georgia, where Professor Thomas Luke Manget brought U. S. history to life with passion. Each lecture was more than a lesson; it was an invitation to witness the unfolding story of a nation. I was captivated, caught up in his enthusiasm. From those moments, the seeds of this novel were planted. One of its central characters bears his name, though the resemblance ends with his good looks and strength of character. The figure who moves through these pages is wholly fictional and should not be confused with the real Professor Manget.

The following year, my journey took me to New Orleans, where I immersed myself in original Civil War documents housed in the archives of Tulane University, the Historic New Orleans Collection, the Jewish Museum, the Mardi Gras Museum, and Confederate Memorial Hall. The exhibit at Vue Orleans was an immersive experience, providing an observation deck with a sweeping view of the city. The dedicated staff at each of these institutions generously shared their time and expertise, making my prolonged research process a true joy.

I would be remiss if I didn't mention the incredible cuisine of The Court of the Two Sisters, Tujaque's, Antoine's, Brennan's, Galatoire's, and The Gumbo Pot. Each evening was a memorable dining experience, and I enjoyed meals at each of them on multiple occasions.

From there, I traveled north to Baton Rouge, where the old Capitol building, the Louisiana State Library, and the Louisiana State Museum revealed a treasure trove of history. Among the exhibits at the State Museum was an experimental Confederate submarine and a bracelet made from General Beauregard's uniform buttons. The museum's displays were full of insight. The nearby Sugar Museum proved to be another hidden gem, offering a deep look into the history of Louisiana's sugar plantations and the legacy of enslaved people who contributed their expertise to the industry.

One of the most memorable stops along the Mississippi River was the Whitney Plantation. It was refreshing to see a plantation where history was preserved rather than whitewashed or turned into a wedding venue. A guided tour of the grounds, along with an exhibit honoring the enslaved children who once lived there, provided a profoundly moving experience.

I also came across the town of New Roads, where I met Brian Costello, a gracious historian and author, a native Louisianan with a keen interest in Julian Poydras, the founding father of Louisiana, and a love of his state's history. His books add depth to the land and its people, and he is one of the few remaining speakers of Louisiana Creole French.

Exploring New Roads, where Brian works as the town historian from his office in the library, I was fascinated by the tranquil lake that was once a part of the mighty Mississippi River as it changed course over the centuries, forming what's now known as "False River."

At Port Hudson, just north of New Roads, the park rangers were generous with their time and knowledge, sharing many materials and primary sources about one of the last Confederate strongholds on the Mississippi River. They spoke passionately about an upcoming re-enactment of the siege.

In Vicksburg, I visited the Vicksburg Civil War Museum, the first such museum founded by an African American. The owner, Charles Pendleton, was a gracious host and eager to answer questions. A particularly moving exhibit was a "breeding cage," where enslaved women were confined as breeding stock.

While in Vicksburg, I stayed in a historic mansion that had been spared from Admiral Farragut's shelling only because the owners had offered it as a hospital.

The Vicksburg National Military Park was vast and profoundly moving, featuring the salvaged and reconstructed *U.S.S. Cairo* gunboat as a somber reminder of the war.

Along the river, I observed the enduring strength of the levee system, which still protects the banks of the Mississippi River. Yet, I was saddened to see the once-fertile farmland now dominated by oil fields and refineries.

When I returned home, I dedicated myself to reading for four years, including works by Nicolay and Hay, as well as Abraham Lincoln's letters. I also read every available journal by those who endured the war, while sharing their heartaches and joys.

I wish to acknowledge Steven Smith, military historian, and Dan Hanks, copy editor, whose thoughtful guidance and revision suggestions proved invaluable, for even the most diligent writer is ill-served when acting alone as his editor.

Finally, my artists contributed significantly to illustrating this volume. Alper Yumerov restored and colorized all archival images for the color print edition of this work, while K. Henriott-Jauw and Mirshad Aakif created pen-and-ink illustrations that were digitally post-processed by Alper Yumerov or the author.

Throughout this journey, my wife has been my greatest supporter and source of inspiration.

ILLUSTRATIONS

Disclaimer: Many historical images in this text exist in multiple collections, making it challenging to cite a photograph as "original" when a negative can produce numerous prints. The term becomes even more complex when studios produced many prints bearing backmarks that collectors consider original.

All period images have been enhanced for better resolution, restored, and colorized for the full-color print and e-book editions by digital artist Alper Yumerov.

AI-generated images are created in ChatGPT by C. Arthur Ellis, Jr.

The author holds copyrights from commissioned artists.

Book Cover: C. Arthur Ellis, Jr., using AI, with lettering modified by Alper Yumerov. Author portrait on back cover by April Curtain with after-processing by Alper Yumerov.

Frontispiece Title Page: The primary image on this page is by Julius Bien, lithographer, and is known as *Scott's Great Snake* [Elliott's Map of the United States], map (Cincinnati: J. B. Elliott, 1861), Library of Congress Geography and Map Division, https://www.loc.gov/item/2003627080/

Prologue: Wood engraving, Mrs. Lincoln's East Room reception, February 5, 1862, attributed to "our social artist," possibly Henry Lovie. *Frank Leslie's Illustrated Newspaper*, February 22, 1862.

Chapter Illustrations:

Chapter 1
1. Portrait of Rachel Manger was drawn by Mirshad Aakif and enhanced by Alper Yumerov.

Chapter 2
1. (Center) portion of a painting by Julian Oliver Davidson, sometime before 1892, portraying New Orleans Harbor on April 25, by Farragut's ship, the *Hartford*, and fires from the burning of cotton and ships by Confederates. (Left) St. Louis Cathedral photograph by C. Arthur Ellis, Jr. (Right) Christ Church by an unknown artist.

Chapter 3

1. View from Rachel's balcony, AI-generated by C. Arthur Ellis, Jr.

Chapter 4

1. Illustration of Mumford and the flag by Alfred R. Waud, *Harper's Weekly*, May 17, 1862.

Chapter 5

1. Photograph of Eugenia Phillips by an unidentified photographer, probably the Brady studio, is stored in Box 22, referenced at this Library of Congress site. https://findingaids.loc.gov/db/search/xq/searchMferDsc04.xq?_id=loc.mss.eadmss. ms011144&_faSection=contentsList&_faSubsection=series&_dmdid=d296095e24&_ start=1&_lines=125

Chapter 6

1. Cover image from *Report of the Sanitary Commission of New Orleans on the Epidemic Yellow Fever of 1853*, retyped in Microsoft Word by C. Arthur Ellis, Jr., then integrated with a facsimile of the background of the original cover using AI. The original image is available at: https://archive.org/details/reportofsanitary00newo

Chapter 7

1. The original of this black and white drawing of Mumford's hanging is displayed in an exhibit at Confederate Memorial Hall in New Orleans, and was captured by C. Arthur Ellis, Jr. using an iPhone. Artist unknown. The display also included related artifacts, such as a piece of rope allegedly used to hang Mumford. Colorized by Alper Yumerov.
2. Photograph of William Bruce Mumford by Theodore Lilienthal. See entry, "William Bruce Mumford," *Alchetron: The Free Social Encyclopedia*. Colorized by Alper Yumerov.

Chapter 8

1. Original engraving of the French Market by Jason E. Taylor. *Frank Leslie's Illustrated Newspaper*, September 14, 1867, p. 409. Colorized by Alper Yumerov.

Chapter 9

1. Lieutenant DeKay's sword. Image from a family posting on Find a Grave: https://www.findagrave.com/memorial/112048541/george-coleman-dekay.

Chapter 10

1. General Benjamin Franklin Butler, photographed by Matthew Brady in his studio, 1861. National Portrait Gallery. Colorized by Alper Yumerov.

Chapter 11

1. Madame Larue, engraving from *Butler's Book,* p. 511. Butler does not individually credit illustrations in his work, but the imprint page lists Colonel John B. Bachelder, E. A. Schoelch, Frank Hendry, and "others" as contributing artists. Colorized by Alper Yumerov.

Chapter 12

1. (Left) Photograph of Phillip Phillips by an unknown photographer, probably Brady studio, and colorized by Alper Yumerov. It is in Box 22 in the Library of Congress collection referenced here: https://findingaids.loc.gov/db/search/xq/searchMferDsc04.xq?_id=loc.mss.eadmss. ms011144&_faSection=contentsList&_faSubsection=series&_dmdid=d296095e24&_ start=1&_lines=125

(Right) Photograph of Reverdy Johnson by Matthew Brady, archived in Mathew Brady Photographs of Civil War-Era Personalities and Scenes, compiled 1921–1940, documenting the period 1860–1865 (National Archives Identifier: 524418). Colorized by Alper Yumerov.

Chapter 13

1. Eugenia Phillips. This is the same photograph as in Chapter 6 with the exception that the jewelry has been digitally altered; it now features an amber pendant with an embedded ant. Digital art by Alper Yumerov.

Chapter 14

1. Acrostic sampler created in MS Word by C. Arthur Ellis, Jr., based on an acrostic cited by Doyle, page 217. The footnote reads: "Quoted in Parton, *Butler in New Orleans,* 340; New Orleans Civil War Papers, Folder M 32, Tulane University Archives, New Orleans." However, aside from Doyle's reference to the original Tulane materials, no such acrostic appears in an electronic search of James Parton's, *General Butler in New Orleans: History of the Administration of the Department of the Gulf in the Year 1862: By an Account of the Capture of New Orleans, and a Sketch of the Previous Career of the General, Civil and Military,* 11th Edition. New York: Mason Brothers, 5 & 7 Mercer Street, 1864. Available at: General Butler in New Orleans : Parton, James, 1822-1891 : Free Download, Borrow, and Streaming : Internet Archive

Chapter 15

1. Drawing of Loreta Velazquez, signed "REA," circa 1876, from *The Woman in Battle* by Loreta Janeta Velazquez. Published by subscription, Hartford, T. Belknap, 1876. REA was John Rea Neill, known for illustrating the *Land of Oz* series and *Little Black Sambo.* The image has been digitally altered by C. Arthur Ellis, Jr., using AI to replace the original white background with a brown background.
2. Image of Shiloh battlefield AI-generated by C. Arthur Ellis, Jr.

Chapter 16

1. Image of the St. Louis Hotel Lobby converted to a hospital is based on an original sketch by K. Henriott-Jauw that was digitally modified using AI by C. Arthur Ellis, Jr.
2. Alper Yumerov created this image of Jacob in the hospital based on photographs of double amputees archived in the Surgeon General's Office, Army Medical Museum, War Department, Washington, D.C. Photographs of this type were used to gain support for awarding pensions to disabled veterans.

Chapter 17

1. Kaleidoscope image AI-generated by C. Arthur Ellis, Jr.
2. Portrait of Abraham Lincoln by George P. A. Healy, 1887. National Portrait Gallery in Washington, DC.
2. This photograph of Issachar Zachary in later years is archived in the American Jewish Historical Society. The American Jewish Historical Society is located in the Center for Jewish History on West 16th Street in downtown Manhattan.

Chapter 18

1. 1861 Fort Monroe etching by Edward Sachse, published by E. Sache & Co. Smithsonian Museum, Harry T. Peters "America on Stone" Lithography Collection. ID Number DL.60.3788. Catalog Number 60.3788. Link to original record:
   http://n2t.net/ark:/65665/ng49ca746b4-e836-704b-e053-15f76fa0b4fa

Chapter 19

1. Francis Bicknell Carpenter, *First Reading of the Emancipation Proclamation of President Lincoln*, 1864, oil on canvas, House Collection, H-216 Lincoln Room, U.S. Capitol, Washington, D.C. The painting depicts President Lincoln presenting the draft of the Emancipation Proclamation to his Cabinet. Left to right: Secretary of War Edwin Stanton; Secretary of the Treasury Salmon P. Chase; President Lincoln; Secretary of the Navy Gideon Welles; Secretary of the Interior Caleb Smith; Secretary of State William H. Seward; Postmaster General Montgomery Blair; and Attorney General Edward Bates. The painting was later engraved for printing by Alexander Hay Ritchie.

Chapter 20

1. Engraving of General Benjamin Butler by Charles Stanley Reinhart for *Harper's Weekly*, ca. 1896. Original in Library of Congress Prints and Photographs Division, Swann Collection of Caricature and Cartoon (788). Call Number: SWANN-no. 1316.
   https://www.loc.gov/pictures/item/2009617225/

Chapter 21

1. St. Charles Theatre illustration by G. Tolti. Library of Congress Control Number 2004669145. Date unknown.
2. Pile of burning dummies sketched by K. Henriott-Jauw, colorized by Alper Yumerov.

Chapter 22

1. Image of the Hyde and Goodrich store was AI-generated by C. Arthur Ellis, Jr., based on the original pen and ink by K. Henriott-Jauw.

Chapter 23

1. St. Charles lobby image was AI-generated by C. Arthur Ellis, Jr., based on the original pen and ink by K. Henriott-Jauw.
2. Photograph of General Banks, backmarked "Published by F. & H.T. Anthony, 501 Broadway, New York from Photographic Negative in Brady's National Portrait Gallery." Retrieved from:
   https://uncledaveys.com/all-items/photographs/cdv-photographs-union-generals/nathaniel-banks-cdv-photograph/
3. Image of Zouave soldiers AI-generated by C. Arthur Ellis, Jr.

Chapter 24

1. Cartography reproduced by written permission of artist Dick Gilbreath. The exact details of the original are preserved in this color and resolution-enhanced version by Alper Yumerov.
2. The 1861 White House China, imported from France, featured a central image sketched by Mrs. Mary Todd Lincoln and hand-painted by E. V. Haughwout and Company, New York. This piece is part of the Raleigh DeGeer Amy Collection, "Official White House China."
3. The image of Tujague's stand-up bar was digitally created and colorized by Alper Yumerov, using multiple historical photographs.

Chapter 26

1. Dispersed of Judah synagogue by Myers, W. E., *The Israelites of Louisiana: Their Religious, Civic, Charitable and Patriotic Life, N. O., LA, n.d. (about 1904)*; available at New Orleans Public Library, Louisiana Division (R296 M99), and in the Louisiana Research Collection, Tulane University.

2. Photograph of Rabbi Gutheim by an unknown photographer, archived in Temple Sinai, New Orleans.

Chapter 27

1. House of the Rising Sun image AI-generated by C. Arthur Ellis, Jr.

Chapter 28

1. Engraving by Theodore R. Davis. "Battle of the Handkerchiefs," *Harper's Weekly*, May 16, 1863. Vol. 7, No. 333.

Chapter 29

1. Original pen-and-ink image by Mirshad Aakif, with digital enhancement by Alper Yumerov.

Chapter 30

1. Image of Charles Perrault's *Histoires ou Contes du Tems Passé Avec des Moralités* retrieved from: https://www.nocloo.com/charles-perrault-biography/

Chapter 31

1. "Plantations of the Mississippi River from Natchez to New Orleans, 1858," by Adrien Persac. 1931 reprint archived at TSLA Map Collection, 42389, Tennessee State Library & Archives, Tennessee Virtual Archive
https://teva.contentdm.oclc.org/digital/collection/p15138coll23/id/8929

2. "General Banks Addressing the Louisiana Planters in the Parlor of the St. Charles Hotel, New Orleans," by Francis H. Schell, *Frank Leslie's Illustrated Newspaper*, March 28, 1863.

Chapter 32

1. Image of Antoine's Restaurant, AI-generated by C. Arthur Ellis, Jr.

Chapter 33

1. Steamboat *Natchez*, Thomas Nast etching, *Harper's Weekly*, December 5, 1863.

Chapter 34

1. Photograph of old State Capital Building ascribed to McPherson & Oliver, Baton Rouge, circa 1863. Suydam (G.H.) Collection, Mss. 1394, LSU Libraries, Special Collections.

Chapter 35

1. Photograph by Andrew David Lytle after the fire of January 1863. Numbered 113 in the LSU Libraries Special Collections, Andrew D. Lytle's Baton Rouge Photograph Collection. https://louisianadigitallibrary.org/islandora/object/lsu-sc-p15140coll12%3A286

Chapter 36

1. Image of Rachel and Thomas traveling along the Mississippi, AI-generated by C. Arthur Ellis, Jr.

Chapter 37

1. Button Willow Plantation is fictional. This illustration is by artist Marie Adrien Persac as an embellishment on *Norman's Chart of the Lower Mississippi River from Natchez to New Orleans*, by Benjamin Moore Norman, publisher, 1858. Lithographed by Pikes Peak Lithographing Co., Colorado.

2. Slave cottages at Laurel Hill Plantation in Jefferson County, Mississippi, near Rodney, Mississippi, created by C. Arthur Ellis, Jr. using AI.

Chapter 38

1. Image of dining room in fictional Button Willow Plantation AI-generated by C. Arthur Ellis, Jr.

Chapter 39

1. Emma's cabin was digitally created by Alper Yumerov, incorporating a photograph of Lincoln over the fireplace by Alexander Hesler, 6/3/1860, published by Herbert George Studio, Springfield, Illinois.

2. *A Plantation Burial*, by John Antrobus, 1860. Archived in the L. Kemper and Leila Moore Williams Founders Collection at The Historic New Orleans Collection.

3. Thomas, as a tinkerer, was digitally created by Alper Yumerov.

Chapter 40

1. Illustration appears on page 500 by J. R. Hamilton, *Harper's Weekly*, August 8, 1863. This image is entitled "Port Hudson from the Opposite Bank of the River."

2. *"View of Indiana artillery, Port Hudson, LA,"* albumen print, 1863. The photograph depicts Union soldiers with a cannon behind breastworks, likely belonging to the 1st Indiana Heavy Artillery, during the Siege of Port Hudson. Library of Congress Prints and Photographs Division, digital ID cph.3b15279. The photographer is unknown, but McPherson & Oliver, operating out of New Orleans, were at Port Hudson and photographing during this time. Colorized by Alper Yumerov.

Chapter 41

1. First Wisconsin Light Artillery at Baton Rouge, credited to A. D. Lytle, from *The Photographic History of the Civil War*. Francis Trevelyan Miller, editor-in-chief; Robert S. Lanier, managing editor. New York: Review of Reviews Co., 1911. Vol. 8, p. 248. This was taken in 1864, not 1863.

Chapter 42

1. Cropped image from a diptych by Millard R. Judd Sr. (1911–1983), now in the author's private collection. Judd was an American artist celebrated for his realistic depictions of Florida's rural landscapes, particularly those in the state's northern and central regions. This scene takes place within the story's timeline, depicting a ferryman navigating the Suwannee River at Suwannee Springs, just north of the author's home in Live Oak, Florida, in the days before a bridge spanned the river. Image colorized by Alper Yumerov.

Chapter 43

1. The illustration shows sugar processing using copper kettles through the Jamaica Train method, which was used by many plantations in Louisiana before the development of the more

efficient vacuum method. The painting is by William Clark as part of a series published as *Ten Views in the Island of Antigua, in Which Are Represented the Process of Sugar Making, and the Employment of the Negroes in the Field, Boiling-House, and Distillery* (1823). William Clark was a U.S. citizen who lived in the West Indies for three years and drew scenes of the sugar production process imported into Louisiana. The publication is reproduced here: https://collections.britishart.yale.edu/catalog/orbis: 4515711

Chapter 44

1. *The Banks Expedition—Scene on the Levee, Baton Rouge—Contrabands Coming into Camp,* by Alfred R. Waud. *Harper's Weekly*, March 14, 1863,

Chapter 45

2. General Cuvier Grover, image in the U.S. National Archives with the local identifier 111-B-2525, from Brady's Photographs of Civil War-Era Personalities and Scenes.

3. The original of this map of the Battle of Port Hudson is by Robert Knox Sneden, provided by the Virginia Museum of History & Culture, Virginia Historical Society. The map has been digitally altered to show only the Confederate positions since this is what Thomas would have seen while he was there.

Chapter 46

1. This illustration is a composite of Victorian rocking horses manufactured in England. It was AI-generated by C. Arthur Ellis, Jr.

2. Jacob's dream illustration was AI-generated by C. Arthur Ellis, Jr.

Chapter 47

1. This is one in a series of Seder plates manufactured by Ridgway, a well-known Staffordshire pottery company founded in the 18th century. This piece was registered in 1923 but closely resembles designs from the mid-1800s. The plate is still widely available online.
https://jewishmuseum.org.uk/exhibitions/museum-on-the-move-bradford-pesach-2024/

Chapter 48

1. May Day Illustration, by J. R. Hamilton, *Harper's Weekly*, June 6, 1863, page 357. Colorized by Alper Yumerov.

Chapter 49

1. Registered enemies arriving at Port Hickok by an unnamed "special artist," *Harper's Weekly*, May 7, 1863, page 156. Colorized by Alper Yumerov.

Chapter 50

1. Image of Rachel on her balcony observing the jubilee was AI generated by C. Arthur Ellis, Jr.

2. Photograph of Gordon, by William D. McPherson and J. Oliver, 1863. Identified as "Scourged Back," Reproduction Number: LC-USZC4-793. Colorized by Alper Yumerov.

Chapter 51

1. Arrival of the steamboat *Imperial* at New Orleans from St. Louis, July 16, 1863. From a sketch by Mr. J. R. Hamilton, *Harper's Weekly*, August 8, 1863, p. 501. Colorized by Alper Yumerov.

2. Title page of *The Lustful Turk*. This work is currently in publication and is widely available through online bookstores.

Chapter 52

1.   The image of Levi at the door was AI-generated by C. Arthur Ellis, Jr.

Chapter 53

1.   Image of the Sazerac Coffee House bar was AI-generated by C. Arthur Ellis, Jr.

Chapter 54

1.   Image of Dueling Oaks colorized from a drawing by Harry Fenn based on an old photograph and print, retrieved from "Dueling in Old Creole Days," by Louis J. Meader, in *Century Magazine,* Vol. 74, #2, June 1907.

2.   Image of Dr. Brashear's dueling pistols and case obtained from the website of Guns International.com, where they were listed for auction in 2025.

Chapter 55

1.   Image of Rachel's hands AI-generated by C. Arthur Ellis, Jr., and enhanced by Alper Yumerov.

Chapter 56

1.   Image of Levi's pocket watch with engraving digitally created by Alper Yumerov.

Chapter 57

1.   Image of the Confederate White House exterior from an early 20th-century postcard made by Tichnor Brothers, a producer of souvenir postcards. The family name is alternately spelled Ticknor or Teichner.

2.   Image of the entry hall in the Confederate White House, AI-altered by C. Arthur Ellis, Jr., from a photograph archived in the American Civil War Museum in Richmond, Virginia, to remove contemporary electric lamps on statues of goddesses and replace them with their original attributes before renovation.

3.   The 1853 oil-on-canvas portrait of Judah Philip Benjamin, painted by Adolph D. Rinck, is preserved in the Historic New Orleans Collection, located on Royal Street in New Orleans. It bears accession number 1959.82 HNOC.

4.   Image of Judah Benjamin on $2 bill, Texas State Library and Archives Commission.

Chapter 58

1.   This embellished image of "The President's Hymn," was created by C. Arthur Ellis, Jr., using AI. The actual sheet music is archived in the Alfred Whital Stern Collection of Lincolniana. Also cataloged by the Library of Congress.

https://www.loc.gov/resource/lprbscsm.scsm0185/?st=gallery

Chapter 59

1.   Photograph of John Wilkes Book on his *carte-de-visite.* The backmark reads, "Haines & Wickes, Photographers, 478 Broadway, Albany, N.Y." Copies are archived in multiple locations, including the Gilder Lehrman Collection at The Gilder Lehrman Institute of American History, 49 W. 45th Street, New York, NY 10036. Catalogue ID: GLCO5136.23.

2.   *Ford's Theatre Playbill for The Marble Heart,* starring John Wilkes Booth, November 9, 1863. A copy is archived in the Brooklyn Academy of Music. Facsimile of John Wilkes Booth's signature added by C. Arthur Ellis, Jr.

Chapter 60

1. This is a cropped image of a photograph of Lincoln delivering his address at Gettysburg, printed from the original glass plate negative, which was unidentified until 1952, when Josephine Cobb, working at the National Archives, recognized Lincoln in the image. Source: NARA, Rare Photo of Lincoln at Gettysburg:

    http://blogs.archives.gov/prologue/?=2564

    David Bachrach, a 20-year-old photographer at the time, is credited with the photo. The image is archived in the Library of Congress's Prints and Photographs division under the digital ID ds.03106:

    http://hdl.loc.gov/loc.pnp/ds.03106

2. Image of Grant Congressional Commemorative Coin retrieved from:

    https://www.nps.gov/subjects/ulyssesgrantexhibit/military-career.htm

    The coin is exhibited at the Smithsonian National Museum of American History, NMAH AF.93729.

Chapter 62

1. Image of Rachel and Thomas under the Chuppah AI-generated by C. Arthur Ellis, Jr.

2. (Left) Image of Thomas signing Ketubah. (Right) Image of Rachel and Thomas holding a wine goblet. Both images were AI-generated by C. Arthur Ellis, Jr.

Chapter 63

1. The engraving, titled "Emancipated Slaves, White and Colored," is based on a photograph taken by Charles Paxson and Myron Kimball, and was published in *Harper's Weekly* on January 30, 1864, page 69.

Chapter 64

1. Image of the fictitious Maison des Escargots Restaurant created by Alper Yumerov.

Chapter 65

1. Image of the Grand Reunion at the St. Charles created by C. Arthur Ellis, Jr., using AI.

Chapter 66

1. Image of Valentine, AI-generated by C. Arthur Ellis, Jr.

Chapter 67

1. Image of Governor Hahn's Inauguration by special artist C.E.H. Bonwill, *Frank Leslie's Illustrated Newspaper,* April 2, 1864, p. 24.

2. Portrait of Governor Michael Hahn by John Genin, archived in the Louisiana State Museum.

Chapter 68

1. *The Prince of Wales and Suite Playing at Ten Pins, at Zimmerman House, Niagara.* Engraving appears in *Illustrated News of the World*, November 3, 1860. Artist unknown.

Chapter 69

1. Bookcase with hidden door AI-generated by C. Arthur Ellis, Jr.

2. Image of Confederate generals is a composite from multiple sources on the internet, AI generated by C. Arthur Ellis, Jr.

3. Plan of the Rebel attack on Washington, D.C., July 11th and 12th, 1864. Robert Knox Sneden, 1832-1918. Virginia Historical Society, P.O. Box 7311, Richmond, VA 23221-0311 USA. http://hdl.loc.gov/loc.ndlpcoop/gvhs01.vhs00256

Chapter 70

1. Ordinance abolishing slavery, signed by E. H. Durell. Archived in Abraham Lincoln papers: Series 1. General Correspondence. 1833-1916: Louisiana Constitutional Convention, Wednesday, May 11, 1864.

Chapter 71

1. Image of celebration in Congo Square, AI-generated by C. Arthur Ellis, Jr..

Chapter 72

1. Image of John Hay looking across the Niagara River at the Clifton House, AI-generated by C. Arthur Ellis, Jr.

Chapter 73

1. Original painting of Farragut on the *Hartford* at the invasion of Mobile Bay by William Heysham Overend, commissioned by the Fine Art Society, by galleries in London and Glasgow. The Fine Art Society produced and distributed prints of Overend's work, beginning to sell them in November 1883. The original painting is now in the Wadsworth Atheneum Museum of Art in Hartford, Connecticut.

Chapter 74

1. Image of Atlanta burning, AI-generated by C. Arthur Ellis, Jr.

Chapter 75

1. Image of Jefferson Davis delivering his speech to the townspeople of Macon, AI-generated by C. Arthur Ellis, Jr.

Chapter 76

1. Image of General Banks in his office in the St. Charles AI-generated by C. Arthur Ellis, Jr..

2. Thomas Nast's wood engraving, "Battle of Pleasant Hill, Louisiana," appeared in the May 7, 1864, edition of *Harper's Weekly*.

Chapter 77

1. Image of Loreta in night mist AI-generated by C. Arthur Ellis, Jr.

Chapter 78

1. Image of Rachel's bedroom AI-generated by C. Arthur Ellis, Jr.

Chapter 79

1. Political broadside by Martin W. Siebert, 1864. Printer, 28 Centre Street, Corner Reade, New York City. No artist is credited. Archived at the Library of Congress: http://hdl.loc.gov/loc.pnp/cph.3a04824

Chapter 80

1. Illustration of Rachel and Thomas at the French Market, AI-generated by Arthur Ellis, Jr.

2. Image of a slave woman with a metal gag digitally created by Alper Yumerov.

3. Image of Lily and Sam with their presents by the Christmas tree AI-generated by C. Arthur Ellis, Jr.

Chapter 81

1. Image of chestnuts on hearth AI-generated by C. Arthur Ellis, Jr.
2. Image of slaves trying to escape to the Union pontoon bridge, AI-generated by C. Arthur Ellis, Jr.
3. Image of a slave woman handing her baby to a Union soldier to save it from drowning, AI-generated by C. Arthur Ellis, Jr.

Chapter 82

1. *River Queen* docked at Hampton Roads, wet plate collodion photo by Alexander Gardner. Archived in the National Archives and Records Administration, Washington, D.C. Digital colorization by Alpi Yumerov.
2. Image of Hampton Roads meeting AI-generated by C Arthur Ellis, Jr.

Chapter 83

1. Cover of *Harper's Weekly*, February 18, 1865.
2. The image of Lincoln on a flatboat travelling to New Orleans was AI-generated by C. Arthur Ellis, Jr. The inset image of the woman having her baby torn from her arms at a slave auction was inset by Alper Yumerov.

Chapter 84

1. Photographer Alexander Gardner. Library of Congress Prints and Photographs Division Washington, D.C. 20540 USA.
   http://hdl.loc.gov/loc.pnp/pp.print. Library of Congress Control Number 2009633604. Photo digitally colorized and Lincoln's head inserted for better resolution by Alper Yumerov.

Chapter 85

1. Portrait of Sarah Morgan by an unknown photographer, possibly David Lytle. Archived at Wilson Special Collections Library, University of North Carolina, Chapel Hill. Colorized and enhanced by Alper Yumerov.

Chapter 86

1. Image of Jubilee on Canal Street, AI-generated by C. Arthur Ellis, Jr.

Chapter 87

1. *The Assassination of President Lincoln at Ford's Theatre, Washington D.C., April 14th, 1865.* Hand-colored lithograph by Currier & Ives, 1865. Archived in the Metropolitan Museum of Art.
2. Floor plan of Ford's Theatre, *Harper's Weekly*, Saturday, April 29, 1865, Vol IX, No. 435, pages 257-258.
3. Illustration of Booth fleeing D.C. AI-generated by C. Arthur Ellis, Jr.

Chapter 88

1. Engraving of Lincoln lying in state in the East Room by C. E. H. Bonwill, *Frank Leslie's Illustrated Newspaper*, May 6, 1865, pp. 100-101. Colorized by Alper Yumerov.
2. "Lincoln's Funeral Procession in Washington, *D.C.*" Engraving by Alfred R. Waud. Engraver unknown. Published in *Harper's Weekly*, May 13, 1865. Colorized by Alper Yumerov.

Chapter 89

1. Illustration of street scene along levee AI-generated by C. Arthur Ellis, Jr.
2. Alan Pinkerton albumen silver photograph by Matthew Brady, circa 1861, Library of Congress, LOT 4192 (Brady-Handy Collection). LOC Control No: 2004665380.

Chapter 90
1. Illustration of Antoine's AI-generated by C. Arthur Ellis, Jr.
2. Illustration of meeting of freedmen AI-generated by C. Arthur Ellis, Jr.

Chapter 91
1. Illustration of Noah generated by C. Arthur Ellis, Jr.

Chapter 92
1. Illustration of Rachel and Thomas standing outside Little Angels AI-generated by C. Arthur Ellis, Jr.

Epilogue: Illustration of Rachel and Thomas on front porch AI-generated by C. Arthur Ellis, Jr.

CHAPTER NOTES

Prologue: Chandeliers and Silk Gowns in the Shadow of War

1. In the 1800s, the White House was referred to as the Executive Mansion, while the Confederate equivalent in Richmond was called the Confederate White House.
2. "Mary Todd Lincoln Polka," accessed April 25, 2025. https://soundcloud.com/vishneskiaudio/mary-todd-lincoln-polka
3. The description in this chapter follows the account in "The Grand Presidential Party at the White House," *Frank Leslie's Illustrated Newspaper*, February 22, 1862, 216.
4. The Lehrman Institute site is an excellent resource on the occasion and has references. "East Room: redecoration and Willie's Death" Accessed April 29, 2025.
5. A good source for the history of the East Room from construction through various refurbishments is "East Room." Wikipedia.
6. Marion Southwood reports on the event in *Beauty and Booty*, pp. 98-102.

Chapter 1: Where Is Apollo Now?

1. Taylor, "The Civil War Experiences of a New Orleans Undertaker." Casanave (275–76), an African American undertaker, founded his business with an inheritance from Jewish businessman and philanthropist Judah Touro, who had employed him as a clerk.
2. Casanave placed an ad in the March 15, 1865, *New Orleans Tribune* to notify customers that he was moving his establishment to Toulouse Street but appeared to keep stables at his old location. During the Civil War, New Orleans undertakers served both Union and Confederate soldiers, shipping bodies across states to families who could afford the service. While many of the dead from the Battle of Shiloh were transported by train to New Orleans, some were buried in mass graves at the battlefield. Some Confederate remains were shipped northward to higher ground in Baton Rouge, as the low-lying delta around New Orleans made in-ground burial difficult, and above-ground vaults were too expensive..
3. Tememe Derech Cemetery was established as a Jewish cemetery in New Orleans in 1858 and was later renamed Gates of Prayer Cemetery in 1939. Following Jewish tradition, all burials are in-ground and oriented eastward toward Jerusalem.

Chapter 2: The End of Days

1. This portrayal of Eugenia Phillips during the Union invasion of New Orleans is primarily based on her diary, "Journal of Mrs. Eugenia Phillips, 1861-1862." She notes April 14 as the approximate date of the fire in the harbor, Lovell's departure, and Farragut's arrival. On that day, Farragut's ships were positioned below Ft Jackson and Ft St. Philip and had not yet crossed

the passage to New Orleans, which they wouldn't do until April 24. Knowing the forts would soon be breached, Lovell evacuated his troops before April 25. The Phillips papers are archived in the Library of Congress. Her diary is in Box 1: https://findingaids.loc.gov/db/search/xq/searchMferDsc04.xq?_id=loc.mss.eadmss. ms011144&_faSection=contentsList&_faSubsection=series&_dmdid=d296095e24&_ start=1&_lines=125

2. Marion Southwood's diary, *Beauty and Booty*, p. 20, cites April 25 as the date of Farragut's arrival, which is consistent with most historical accounts.

3. Sarah Morgan's diary, *The Civil War Diary of a Southern Woman*, pp. 47 and 48, reports her account of the cotton burning and Farragut's arrival on April 26.

4. Chester G. Hearn's *The Capture of New Orleans*, 1862, gives detailed information on the capture of New Orleans.

5. The tolling of bells, burning of cotton, and departure of Lovell are placed on April 14 based on Eugenia Phillips' account in her diary.

6. According to the United States Navy Department, Farragut arrived on April 25 in Chapter 2. Official Records of the Union and Confederate Navies in the War of the Rebellion. Series I, Volume 18. Washington, D.C.: Government Printing Office, 1904.

7. "The Capture of New Orleans," by Charles J. Wexler is part of a series published by The Essential Civil War Curriculum, a Sesquicentennial project of the Virginia Center for Civil War Studies at Virginia Tech. It provides an excellent summary of the defenses of New Orleans and the strategy behind the invasion planned by Farragut, Porter, and Butler, who worked together as a team. He is one of the few authors to credit Butler with supplying the coal to fuel the invading fleet. Without this advantage, the Confederates would have had more time to strengthen their defenses by completing additional ships, which might have changed the outcome of the invasion.

8. Rachel references the article "The Defences of the Mississippi" in which the citizens of New Orleans were assured of their defenses below the city. The article appeared in the *New Orleans Daily Picayune* on April 5, 1862.

9. John S. D. Eisenhower explores Scott's Anaconda Plan in *Agent of Destiny: The Life and Times of General Winfield Scott*.

Chapter 3: The Nightmare

1. No references.

Chapter 4: Mumford and the Flag

1. Three articles describing the Mumford incident are:

    a. Robert P. Broadwater, "William B. Mumford became a Southern hero for defying Union sailors in New Orleans," *America's Civil War*, November 2005, Vol. 18, Issue 5, p. 20.

    b. Andres Haugen, "Patriotic Fervor, the Civil War Press and the Execution of William B. Mumford," Louisiana History: *The Journal of the Louisiana Historical Association*, Vol. 63, No. 2 (Spring 2022), pp 191-236.

    c. "Particulars of the Execution of William B. Mumford for Hauling Down the Union States Flag," *The New York Herald*, June 19, 1862, page 1.

2. Butler's account of the Mumford case is given on pages 439-446 of *Butler's Book*.

3. An exhibition case at the Confederate Memorial Hall, New Orleans,` contains the drawing of Mumford's execution along with a piece of the rope used to hang him.

4. The word "marines" was not capitalized in the 1800s since it was not yet a formal standing corps of the U. S. military.

5. "God Save the South, Confederate Civil War Song." The site contains lyrics to "God Save the South."

   https://www.youtube.com/watch?v=YysIg_ERg24

6. Vermont native Armand Edward Blackmar moved to the South in the 1850s to teach music at Centenary College of Louisiana in Shreveport. By 1860, he was in business with his brother Henry, selling "musical merchandise of every description" in New Orleans. Blackmar was one of the largest publishers of sheet music in the South, especially during the early years of the Civil War. He published a wide variety of music under his own name and various pseudonyms, including the first edition of "The Bonnie Blue Flag" in 1861. The following site of The Historic New Orleans Collection references Blackmar:

   https://vop.omeka.net/exhibits/show/goods-of-every-description/music/blackmar?

Chapter 5: Eugenia Visits Rachel and Sarah

1. The portrayal of Eugenia Phillips in this chapter is based on her *Journal of Mrs. Eugenia Levy Phillips, 1861–1862*, archived in Box 1 of the Phillips's papers in the Library of Congress:

   https://findingaids.loc.gov/db/search/xq/searchMferDsc04.xq?_id=loc.mss.eadmss.
   ms011144&_faSection=contentsList&_faSubsection=series&_dmdid=d296095e24&
   start=1&_lines=125

   The journal is also available in print: "Journal of Mrs. Eugenia Levy Phillips, 1861–1862." Marcus, Jacob R. Memoirs of American Jews, 1775–1865: 3. Philadelphia: Jewish Publication Society of America, 1956.

   Phillips's remarks concerning General Butler, the Union occupation of New Orleans, her imprisonment in Washington, D.C., and her association with Varina Davis, the wife of Confederate President Jefferson Davis, are drawn directly from entries written during that period. Her account of Butler's alleged profiteering, particularly his manipulation of Confederate currency, is also based on this diary. According to Phillips, Butler first rendered Confederate money worthless by issuing General Order No. 29 on May 27, 1862. He then purchased large amounts of the devalued currency. Soon after, a local newspaper influenced by Butler published a report claiming that the English government and the U.S. government were preparing to recognize the Confederacy. This fueled speculation, driving up the value of Confederate money, which Butler then sold at a profit.

2. Phillip Leigh, *Trading with the Enemy: The Covert Economy during the American Civil War,* offers detailed accounts of Butler's corruption and profiteering during the occupation, with a good summary of his net gains on pages 70 and 71.

3. Hearn, Chester G. *When the Devil Came Down to Dixie: Ben Butler in New Orleans,* pages 6 and 196, reports that Butler's brother, Andrew, is believed to have made $1-2 million from illegal cotton trading. He notes that Andrew's personal worth was about $150,000 when General Butler arrived in New Orleans. When Butler died in 1893, his estate was valued at

over $ 7 million, most of which was accumulated while he was in New Orleans. These figures roughly equate to at least ten times their amount in today's currency. Hearn also mentions the chamber pots with Butler's image on the bottom.

4. In *Butler's Book*, Butler recounts his use of sugar for ballast instead of sand, pages 384-385.

5. Clara Solomon, a 16-year-old, documents her response to General Order 28 on pages 367-370 of her journal, edited by Elliott Ashkenazi and published as *The Civil War Diary of Clara Solomon: Growing up in New Orleans, 1861-1862*.

6. For a more detailed examination of women's roles in occupied New Orleans and General Order 28, see Alecia P. Long's main article, "(Mis) Remembering General Order No. 28: Benjamin Butler, the Woman Order, and the Historical Meaning," in LeeAnn Whites and Alecia P. Long's edited volume, *Occupied Women: Gender, Military Occupation, and the American Civil War*.

7. The mention of a Negro minstrel banjo player appears on page 41 of *Beauty and Booty*.

8. Robert E. May's, *Slavery, Race and Conquest in the Tropics: Lincoln, Douglas, and the Future of Latin America*, is the definitive account of the Knights of the Golden Circle and their role in shaping the Civil War, including their efforts to help the Confederacy establish a "Golden Circle" of nations extending slavery through Mexico, Cuba, and parts of northern South America. May, an attorney by profession, spent years researching period newspapers, journals, books, letters, and other primary sources at the National Archives and Library of Congress, uncovering a compelling story often overlooked by scholars.

9. Gail Jarrow notes on page 50 that Beauregard used fake cannons made of logs, called "Quaker guns," as decoys to deceive Union aeronauts into overestimating his firepower.

10. Alexander Stephens, vice president of the Confederacy, delivered his "Cornerstone Speech" in Savannah, Georgia, on March 21, 1861. The full text was published in the local newspaper, the *Savannah Republican*, under the title "Vice President Stephens' Speech," on March 22, 1861.

11. One announcement of Christie's Minstrels' performance at the Camp Street Theatre appears in the *New Orleans Daily Picayune*, February 24, 1863, page 2, titled "Christie's Minstrels." Butler cancelled all public celebrations under martial law.

Chapter 6: First, Do No Harm

1. Sanitary Commission of New Orleans. Report of the Sanitary Commission of New Orleans on the Epidemic Yellow Fever of 1853. New Orleans: Printed at the *Picayune* Office, 1854. A reprint is available on Amazon: https://www.amazon.com/Report-Sanitary-Commission-Orleans-Epidemic/dp/1298986486

2. An unnamed doctor referred to on p. 399 in *Butler's Book* as giving a treatise to Butler. This chapter suggests that the doctor was Dr. Smith and that the treatise was Dr. John Leonard Riddell's *Memoir on the Nature of Miasm and Contagion,* published in 1836 by N. S. Johnson in Cincinnati, Ohio. This work was presented before the Cincinnati Medical Society on February 3, 1836, and is considered a significant early contribution to the germ theory of disease. In this publication, Riddell challenged the prevailing miasma theory, which attributed diseases to "bad air" or noxious vapors. He proposed instead that microscopic organisms, or "animalcules," were the true agents of contagion. This perspective was notably ahead of its time, predating the widespread acceptance of germ theory by several decades. Riddell also

later participated in the 1854 New Orleans Sanitary Commission report on the yellow fever outbreak.

3. Dr. Mercer's encounter with Butler to plead for Mumford's life is recounted in *Butler's Book*, pp. 442.443. It is also recounted in Beauty and Booty, p. 147.

4. Butler mentions the Confederate plot of yellow fever in *Butler's Book*, pp. 396-397.

5. *Butler's Book*, p. 396, mentions churches praying for pestilence to come as divine intervention.

Chapter 7: The Hanging of William B. Mumford

1. "Particulars of the Execution of William B. Mumford for Hauling Down the United States Flag," in the *New York Herald*, June 19, 1862, p. 2, column 1, describes the hanging, noting that the body hangs for thirty minutes until Dr. W. T. Black, Surgeon of General Shepley's staff, along with Dr. George A. Blake of the U.S. Sanitary Commission, ascertained that Mumford's heart had stopped beating.

2. Butler reports his encounter with Mrs. Mumford in *Butler's Book*, p. 441.

3. The Memorial Hall Confederate Civil War Museum has a display with the illustration of Mumford's hanging as well as a piece of the rope allegedly used to hang him.

4. Butler, in *Butler's Book*, p. 441, states that he chose the site of the U. S. Mint for the hanging based on the Spanish custom of exacting punishment at the crime scene.

5. A messenger from Farragut's ship was dispatched to demand, "The Confederate flag must be hauled down from the federal mint and replaced by the Stars and Stripes." Captain Henry W. Morris, hearing of Farragut's demand but under no order to do so, sent ashore marines from the USS Pocahontas to raise the U.S. flag over the mint at gunpoint before the city's surrender. Once ashore, Morris' marines warned the angry mob that his ship, the Pocahontas, would fire upon anyone attempting to remove the Union flag. An account of this is given in "Particulars of the Execution of William B. Mumford for Hauling Down the United States Flag," *New York Herald*, June 19, 1862.

6. Another account of hanging is posted at:
https://en.wikipedia.org/wiki/William_Bruce_Mumford

Chapter 8: The French Market

1. "Culture and Connections: The French Market's Enduring History" discusses the history of the French market:
https://frenchquarterly.com/history/culture-and-connections-french-markets-enduring-history

2. Catherine Cole's *The Story of the Old French Market, New Orleans*, written in 1916, is an account of the history of the French Market:
https://louisiana-anthology.org/texts/cole/cole--old_french_market.html

Chapter 9: The Funeral of Lieutenant DeKay

1. "The Hamlet General." *The New York Times*, October 14, 1862, reflects public frustration with McClellan's hesitation following the Battle of Antietam and uses the "Hamlet" metaphor to characterize his indecisiveness. This reputation followed him into his run for President against Lincoln.

2. The description of the funeral procession and service, as well as mention of Eugenia Phillips, are reported in "The Funeral of Lieut. Dekay Disgraceful Exhibitions by the Rebel Sympathizers

Resistance to Cotton-Burning-Shameful Outrages-Louisiana in a State of Anarchy." *The New York Times*, July 13, 1862, p. 1.

3. A photo of Lieutenant DeKay's sword is posted by his family on Find a Grave: https://www.findagrave.com/memorial/112048541/george-coleman-dekay.

Chapter 10: Eugenia's Arrest

1. *Butler's Book*, page 421 states, "The women, she-adders, more venomous than he-adders, were the insulting enemies of my army and my country, and were so treated."

2. Eugenia Levy Phillips, "Journal of Mrs. Eugenia Levy Phillips," 1861-1862. Eugenia Phillips' journal quotes the sign in Butler's office: "There is no difference between a He and a She adder in their venom." She was sentenced to Ship Island by General Order 150.

3. William J. Seymour's post-war memoir, *The Civil War Memoirs of Captain William J. Seymour: Reminiscences of a Louisiana Tiger*, recounts his ordeal with Butler.

Chapter 11: An Incident Involving Madame Larue

1. This account of Larue's actions is based on *Butler's Book*, pp 511-512, where the illustration used for this chapter appears as a black-and-white line drawing. The date of the incident is not mentioned in his book. Butler recounts that her husband appeared before him and was chastised for not controlling his wife, for which he was imprisoned, but he does not mention Madame Larue appearing before his court before he sentenced her to serve time on Ship Island. The account in this chapter is fictional, but it is likely that Butler summoned her to appear in his court as a formality before he rendered her sentence.

2. After she survived Butler, a March 22, 1874, *New-Orleans Times* "Card of Thanks" reports that Madame Larue was named the godmother of a fire engine and that she was awarded a prize for having the best-dressed animal.

3. Marion Southwood's Journal, *Beauty and Booty*, p. 266, reports an inventory of items from one of the ships that Butler sent home for himself. The inventory included diamonds, silver table service, gold jewelry, six stallions, and five poodles.

Chapter 12: Should Auld Acquaintance be Forgot?

1. Bernard C. Steiner's *Life of Reverdy Johnson*, p. 58, gives an account of Johnson's involvement in the Dred Scott case and his being dispatched to New Orleans, with footnotes to primary sources.

    His citation for the text of the Johnson report on New Orleans is 37th Cong. 3rd Sess., Exec. Doc. 16; vide Series I War of Rebellion Record, vol. 15, p. 474.

Chapter 13: Eugenia's Return

1. Eugenia Levy Phillips, "Journal of Mrs. Eugenia Levy Phillips," 1861-1862. Eugenia Phillips' diary quotes the sign in Butler's office: "There is no difference between a He and a She adder in their venom." She was sentenced to Ship Island by General Order 150.

Chapter 14: Eugenia's Diary

1. Parton references this acrostic in *General Butler in New Orleans*. His working papers for the book also contain references on page 340, and may be found in the New Orleans Civil War Papers, Folder M 32, Tulane University Archives, New Orleans. "Bill No. 2" refers to one of two New Orleans toughs known as "Red Bill No. 1 and No. 2."

2. Eugenia Phillips' diary was used to develop the narrative for this chapter.

Chapter 15: Rachel's Mission

1. See *Butler's Book* on boys taunting a soldier about yellow fever deaths, p 398

2. Loreta's story is based on *The Woman in Battle: A Narrative of the Exploits, Adventures, and Travels of Madame Loreta Janeta Velazquez*, by herself.

3. Account of gilded letters of store columns and taking down signs given by Marion Southwood, *Beauty and Booty*, p.63.

4. September 20, 1862, page 3, article in *The Daily Delta* reports on the play, *Servants by Legacy*, being performed aboard the *Pensacola* under the City Intelligence Section with the title, "Theatricals on the River." The play's date is given as Tuesday, September 16.

5. Loreta's story of Farragut and Vicksburg from "On to Vicksburg," chapter 7 in *Tomblin's Civil War on the Mississippi*.

6. The statement about New Orleans being safer than Timbuktu was cited by Julia LeGrand in *The Journal of Julia LeGrand*, New Orleans, 1862-1863, on page 82 of the 1911 edition.

Chapter 16: An Army of Shadows

1. See Hlemprière, "The Old St. Louis Hotel." Digital Humanities Studio, Loyola University New Orleans Department of History. December 18, 2015.

2. For a history of the St. Louis Hotel, see "St. Louis Hotel" in Wikipedia. Last modified April 25, 2025.

Chapter 17: President Lincoln Receives Dr. Zachary

1. During the Civil War, the White House was known as the Executive Mansion. There was also no Oval Office, just an office for the President off his bedroom.

2. Gail Jarrow. *Lincoln's Flying Spies: Thaddeus Lowe and the Civil War Balloon Corps* documents the Balloon Corps.

3. Ernest L. Abel's *Lincoln's Jewish Spy: The Life and Times of Issachar Zacharie* was used to construct the narrative and details of this chapter.

Chapter 18: Dr. Zachary's Follow-up Visit

1. For the history of Ft. Monroe, see Weinert and Arthur's *Defender of the Chesapeake: The Story of Fort Monroe*.

2. For a discussion of the Anaconda Plan, see Bill Wiemuth's *The Civil War Anaconda Plan: Explore the Drama of the Union Strategy That Won the War*.

Chapter 19: Lincoln's Cabinet Meeting

1. *Artemas Ward's book* was initially published in 1862 by George W. Carleton in New York. It is available as a reprint from Leopold Classic Library (January 26, 2016). Artemas Ward was the pseudonym used by Charles Farrar Browne. David Herbert Donald gives reference to Lincoln reading this passage to his Cabinet members in, *Lincoln*, page 514.

2. "Lincoln and the Cotton Trade," Chapter 26 in Thomas H. O'Connor's *Lords of the Loom*, gives insights into the complexities of the cotton trade during the Civil War.

3. Doris Goodwin's book, *Team of Rivals: The Political Genius of Abraham Lincoln*, gives detailed backgrounds and descriptions of Lincoln's Cabinet members.

4. *Trading with the Enemy: The Covert Economy During the American Civil War* by Philip Leigh is an exhaustive treatise on the complexities of the commerce between the North and the South during the Civil War.

5. Salmon Chase's notes made during this Cabinet Meeting may be found in Chase's diary, *Inside Lincoln's Cabinet: The Civil War Diaries of Salmon P. Chase,* pp. 149 ff.

Chapter 20: Butler's Farewell

1. Butler's speech is on pp 538-541 of *Butler's Book.* When he published his memoirs, he commented on how local attorneys respected his appointed judges in a footnote on page 540: "As proof of such, upon the retirement of Major Bell from the bench of the provost court, the local lawyers and others who had attended it presented to the major a valuable cane, accompanying the gift with expressions of esteem and gratitude, far more precious than any gift could be."

Chapter 21: Our Maryland

1. An announcement of *Our Maryland, or, the Battle of Antietam,* written by a local playwright, appears on page 3 of The *Sunday Delta,* December 28, 1862. No other information was found. After requesting additional information from Ms. Mary Lou Eichhorn, Senior Reference Associate at the Williams Research Center of The Historic New Orleans Collection in July 2025, she responded, "There is insufficient data to speculate about the author's identity, and I found no evidence indicating the production went on tour to other cities."

2. "Hail Columbia" was first written in 1798, with lyrics by Joseph Hopkinson and music adapted from "The President's March" (1793) by Philip Phile. Originally composed as a patriotic song during the Quasi-War with France, it remained popular throughout the nineteenth century. During the Civil War, it was frequently performed at Union rallies, parades, and theaters, often alongside "The Star-Spangled Banner" and "Yankee Doodle," serving as a public declaration of loyalty to the Union.

3. Butler's planned mannequin parade to celebrate the New Year's issuance of the Emancipation Proclamation is recounted by Julia LeGrand in her diary entry on January 1, 1863, p. 61.

4. "The Year of Jubilo," also known as "Jubilo," or "Kingdom Coming," was written by Henry C. Work, a Unionist white man, in 1862, just before the issuing of the Emancipation Proclamation. One mention of slaves singing the song along the banks of the Mississippi above New Orleans as Union gunboats passed is cited by Tomblin, p. 187. The lyrics incorporate various anecdotes that Work had heard from slaves. "Jubilo," derived from Spanish, is a song of intense jubilation that celebrates impending freedom for the slaves after one master flees his plantation. The song lyrics are written in plantation Creole, an obsolete dialect that preceded African American vernacular English. The lyrics are rarely sung now, although the original version is available by streaming through Amazon and YouTube: https://www.youtube.com/watch?v=kPpq4Lf-f7M
The melody has since been used in numerous Disney cartoons and other Western films, as well as in Ken Burns' Civil War documentary, where it is frequently associated with the appearance of General Grant.

Chapter 22: The Poison Pen

1. Marion Southwood, *Beauty and Booty*, p. 204, gives her account of the pen in the chandelier.

2. Unlike today, the practice of using multiple pens to sign important presidential documents did not exist in Lincoln's time, so there was only a single pen used in the signing. In the author's email correspondence with Daniel Hinchem of the Massachusetts Historical Society on July 21, 2023, he states, "To the best of my knowledge, once the pen passed from Lincoln to Livermore (by way of Sumner), the pen was not displayed in a way as laid out in Ms. Southwood's story, and our provenance is fairly clear based on the written record." It is left to the reader to decide whether Marion Southwood fabricated the story of the pen displayed in the chandelier, and, if so, to consider what motive she might have had. Alternatively, it is possible that General Banks used a duplicate pen to illustrate his point, and Ms. Southwood, believing it was authentic, recorded it as the original used to sign the Declaration of Independence. In that case, both Mr. Hinchem and Ms. Southwood would be correct in their respective accounts.

3. On p. 58 of her journal, Julia LeGrand reports on the fear of an uprising of negroes should Lincoln decide not to sign the Emancipation Proclamation and Banks returning firearms to the white population to protect themselves.

Chapter 23: The General and the Doctor

1. For a history of the St. Charles Hotel, see New Orleans (La.). *St. Charles Hotel. Souvenir of New Orleans,* "the City Care Forgot."

2. For a brief history of Otis Elevator, see the Otis Elevator site: https://www.otis.com/en/us/our-company/history

3. Jason Goodwin's *Otis: Giving Rise to the Modern City: A History of the Otis Elevator Company* explores the history of the Otis Elevator in detail.

4. In his *The First and the Bravest. Gettysburg, PA*, McAfee discusses the Louisiana Tigers in the Civil War and their origins in the Tiger Rifles of the Louisiana Volunteers.

5. For an account of General Banks, his life and career, see James G. Hollandsworth, *Pretense of Glory: The Life of General Nathaniel P. Banks.*

6. Abel, in *Lincoln's Jewish Spy: The Life and Times of Issachar Zacharie*, p. 94, discusses Zacharie learning of peddler spies from General Dix during his stay at Fort Monroe. He also writes of Banks's letters to Zacharie asking him to "spare no expense" in traveling to New Orleans to assist him with gathering intelligence. Abel references all correspondence between Zacharie and various parties in New Orleans, in preparation for his visit. Incidents in this chapter are covered on pages 63, 64, 65, 66, 73, 84, 85, 93, and 94. Abel also discusses Zacharie's business ventures in California, his brief chiropody practice in New Orleans, and his exploits elsewhere.

Chapter 24: Dr. Zachary Dines with General Banks

1. Margaret Brown Klapthor gives a history of White House china throughout various administrations in her book, *Official White House China.* She was a distinguished Smithsonian curator and a respected authority on White House history. She served as the longtime head of the First Ladies Collection and Division of Political History at the National Museum of American History.

2. Sarah's *When General Grant Expelled the Jews* gives a scholarly account of General Grant's Order 11.

3. Account of Beauregard's Bells given by Marion Southwood, *Beauty and Booty*, pages 73-77. She reports on the original request for bells by Beauregard to Butler's deployment of them as the ship's ballast, and then the auction in New York.

4. The map used in this chapter to illustrate Banks' explanation of his campaign to Zachary was created by cartographer Dick Gilbreath, who has given his permission for this publication. Alper Yumerov colorized his map.

5. For an account of Lincoln's purchase of the German newspaper and printing press, see Harold Holzer's. *Lincoln and the Power of the Press: The War for Public Opinion*, page XV.

Chapter 25: Tête-à-Tête at Tujague's

1. See Tejal Rao's, "A Legendary New Orleans Restaurant, 160 Years in the Making." *Eater*, September 2, 2016. The restaurant offered set fare meals with no menu.

Chapter 26: Dr. Zachary Goes to Shul

1. Scott Langston's "James Koppel Gutheim" in the *Southern Jewish History Journal* examines Rabbi Gutheim's life and impact in the American South.

2. The Dispersed of Judah synagogue was designed by W. A. Ferret Jr. and built by the firm of Little & Middlemiss in 1857. See Myers's, The Israelites of Louisiana: Their Religious, Civic, Charitable and Patriotic Life, N. O., LA, n.d. (about 1904); available at New Orleans Public Library, Louisiana Division (R296 M99), and in the Louisiana Research Collection, Tulane University. The location of the Dispersed of Judah Synagogue, named only as a "Synagogue," along with the name of its "Minister," J. K. Gutheim, is listed on page xxii, "Churches and Ministers," as being at "Carondelet a. [at] Julia," in Charles Gardner's New Orleans Directory for 1861.

3. The arrangement between Jesse R. Grant, General Grant's father, and the Mack brothers came to light when Jesse sued them in the Superior Court of Cincinnati. The *Cincinnati Enquirer* printed the petition in January 1864, later reprinted by the *American Jewish Archives Journal*. In it, Jesse alleged that the Macks promised him a quarter share of the profits if he could secure a permit through his son to buy cotton in Union-occupied territory and ship it to New York for sale.

4. "Fly in his tent" was used as an expression in this chapter because "fly on the wall" was not used at the time. The desire to be a fly to be present where one otherwise could not be reflects this idea, which goes back to Act 3, Scene 3 of Shakespeare's *Romeo and Juliet*. In that scene, Romeo laments that even carrion flies landing on Juliet's hand or lips are luckier than he is to be near her. Shakespeare was the first to introduce this idea.

5. William Kursheedt was a Union loyalist and one of the founders and president of the Dispersed of Judah congregation. He sent a list of names of potential peddler spies to Zachary on January 7, 1863. The letter is in the Banks Papers, Box 26. (Iss book p 216)

Chapter 27: The House of the Rising Sun

1. Reference to Sun King and prostitutes shipped from prison on p. 1, *Brothels, Depravity, and Abandoned Women: Illegal Sex in Antebellum New Orleans*, by Judith Kelleher Schafer.

2. The House of the Rising Sun in this chapter is fictitious, created from a blend of New Orleans houses of prostitution.

Chapter 28: Battle of the handkerchiefs

1. Dimitry, Adelaide Stuart. "The Battle of the Handkerchiefs," The Haskell Monroe Collection: *Life in the Confederacy*, accessed October 2024: https://library.missouri.edu/confederate/items/show/2319

2. Mary Ashley Townsend, also known as Xariffa, was born in New York in the early 1800s. She went on to become a renowned poet in New Orleans, and in 1870, her collected volume, *Xariffa's Poems*, was published by J. B. Lippincott in Philadelphia.

3. The March 21, 1863 issue of *Harper's Weekly* reports the prisoner exchange, p. 186, in the article, "Extraordinary Excitement in New Orleans."

Chapter 29: The Serendipitous Spy

1. No references.

Chapter 30: Rachel's Farewell

1. No references.

Chapter 31: High Noon at the St. Charles

1. This meeting was reported in *Frank Leslie's Illustrated Newspaper*, March 1863, p. 14.

2. Educating the slaves is discussed in "Education as a Vehicle of Racial Control: Major General N. P. Banks in Louisiana, 1863-64." Author(s): Keith Wilson, in The Journal of Negro Education, Vol. 50, No. 2 (Spring, 1981), pp. 156-170. Published by: Journal of Negro Education.
    https://www.jstor.org/stable/2294849l

3. Thomas is referring to Karl Marx and Friedrich Engels, *The German Ideology* (1845–46), in *The Marx-Engels Reader*, ed. Robert C. Tucker, 2nd ed. (New York: W. W. Norton, 1978), 172.

4. The paintings on the walls were most likely by Marie Adrien Persac, a French-born artist popular among planters of the period. Persac's life and works are described in *Marie Adrien Persac*, by Poesch and Vlach.

Chapter 32: Antoines

1. Roy Guste, Jr.'s *Antoine's Restaurant Since 1840: Cookbook and History* is authored by a fifth-generation member of Antoine's family and provides a historical overview and culinary tour of the famous French Quarter restaurant. It features anecdotes, family stories, photographs, and recipes that detail the restaurant's journey from its founding in 1840 to the present day.

Chapter 33: Steaming to Baton Rouge

1. Louis Hunter's *Steamboats on the Western Rivers: An Economic and Technological History*, offers a detailed examination of steamboat development, operations, and the dangers they encountered. He examines the impact of technological advancements and economic factors on steamboat travel, including detailed accounts of boiler explosions and their effects on river commerce. This book is essential for understanding the larger context of steamboat activities and accidents during that era.

Chapter 34: Baton Rouge

1. William Spedale's *The Battle of Baton Rouge, 1862*, offers a detailed account of that year's battle, enriched with period photographs, sketches, and maps. Spedale provides insights into the

city's devastation, including the destruction of buildings and the impact on local landmarks. The book also discusses the aftermath, such as the burning of parts of the city by Union forces to prevent Confederate reoccupation. It's particularly valuable for its visual documentation of Baton Rouge's wartime transformation.

2. Dennis Dufrene's *Civil War Baton Rouge, Port Hudson and Bayou Sara: Capturing the Mississippi*, provides a detailed account of the Civil War's impact on Baton Rouge, including the strategic significance of the Old State Capitol. It discusses the building's occupation by Union forces, its use as a garrison, and the devastating fire that gutted its interior in December 1862.

Chapter 35: Souvenir

1. Mark Martin's, *Andrew D. Lytle's Baton Rouge: Photographs, 1863–1910*, provides insight into the work of Andrew David Lytle (1834–1917), a prominent photographer based in Baton Rouge, Louisiana, during the Civil War era. Born in Ohio, Lytle began his photographic career as a daguerreotypist in Cincinnati. In 1858, he moved to Baton Rouge, establishing a studio on Main Street. His work encompassed both portraiture and field photography, capturing the city's daily life and significant events. During the Civil War, Lytle provided photographic services to Confederate and Union forces, documenting military encampments and naval vessels, including Admiral Farragut's fleet.

2. The Andrew D. Lytle Photograph Collection (Mss. 2600), housed at Louisiana State University's Hill Memorial Library, includes images from 1862 to 1903, featuring portraits, military encampments and drills, cityscapes, and scenes of daily life.

Chapter 36: Poydras & Port Hudson Road

1. No references

Chapter 37: Buttonwillow Plantation

1. Buttonwillow Plantation is fictional, as are Josephine and the plantation staff.

Chapter 38: Le Petit Dejeuner

1. "Julien de Lallande Poydras." Wikipedia. Last modified April 28, 2025. https://en.wikipedia. org/wiki/Julien_de_Lallande_Poydras

Chapter 39: Emma's Kitchen

1. An article on Hush Harbors with references for further reading is on Wikipedia: https://en.wikipedia.org/wiki/Hush_harbor

2. Memory jars have their roots in African memory jugs. An article with references may be found on Wikipedia: https://en.wikipedia.org/wiki/Memory_jug

Chapter 40: Port Hudson

1. Edward Cunningham discusses Port Hudson and the campaign in *The Port Hudson Campaign, 1862-1863*.

Chapter 41: To Catch a Spy

1. No references.

Chapter 42: Emancipation Plantation

1. The Emancipation Plantation and the geography of the Mississippi River portrayed here are fictional.

Chapter 43: The Sugar House

1. Antoine Morin, the father of sugar granulation and a free man of color, lived before photography, and no portrait has survived. However, the portrait of the plantation owner, Étienne de Boré, who took credit for his work, survives. See, "Sugar Granulation on the Boré Plantation," here:

   https://neworleanshistorical.org/items/show/1655

2. The Jamaica Train method described in this chapter was employed by many plantations in Louisiana before the invention of the more efficient vacuum method. William Clark describes this process with illustrations as part of a series, *Ten Views in the Island of Antigua, in Which Are Represented the Process of Sugar Making, and the Employment of the Negroes in the Field, Boiling-House, and Distillery (1823)*. William Clark was a U. S. citizen who resided in the West Indies for three years and drew scenes of the sugar production process that was imported into Louisiana.

3. Norbert Rillieum, a free man of color, invented the multiple-effect evaporator, which replaced the Jamaica Train process. It was much more efficient and safer for workers. See the booklet by Judah Ginsberg, *Norbert Rillieux and a Revolution in Sugar Processing* (Washington, DC: American Chemical Society, 2002), April 18, 2002:

   https://www.acs.org/education/whatischemistry/landmarks/rillieux.html

Chapter 44: Return to Baton Rouge

1. No references.

Chapter 45: Briefing the General

1. Ezra Warner gives an account of General Cuvier Grover in *Generals in Blue: Lives of the Union Commanders*. General Grover's brigade mounted a notable bayonet charge against Confederate forces in the Second Battle of Bull Run.

Chapter 46: Homecoming

1. No references.

Chapter 47: Passover

1. Staffordshire is a county located in the West Midlands region of England. It is renowned for its rich industrial heritage, particularly for its significant contributions to the ceramics and pottery industries. The area has been well-known for centuries for its pottery manufacturing and exquisite hand-painted designs, with famous brands such as Wedgwood, Spode, and Ridgway emerging from Staffordshire. The seder plate shown is a 1923 pattern by Ridgway, but it reflects styles produced in the 1850s.

2. The Haggadah—the text read during the Passover Seder—has ancient origins but reached its current recognizable form during the early medieval period. Its sources are layered, reflecting centuries of evolution from biblical commandment to rabbinic interpretation to liturgical poetry. The text has many variations, including abbreviated versions for shorter Seder ceremonies.

3. The bread riots in Richmond were reported in the *New York Times*, April 8, 1863. "Bread Riot in Richmond: Three Thousand Hungry Women Raging in the Streets, Government and Private Stores Broken Open."

Chapter 48: May Day

1. The celebration of May Day by the Madison Girls' School in City Park in New Orleans in 1863 was captured in an engraving entitled "Celebration of May-Day by the Madison Girls' School in the City Park, New Orleans—Crowning the May Queen," based on a sketch by J. R. Hamilton. An illustration of the celebration appears in *Harper's Weekly* on June 6, 1863. An article describing the event is on page 362, with credit given to an unnamed "Times correspondent."

2. A front-page article in the *New York Times* on May 18, 1863, also gives details of the May Day celebration, along with other events in New Orleans. Its rather lengthy title is "Our New Orleans Correspondence.; Wonderful Cavalry Exploit Grand Demonstrations at the St. Charles Hotel May Day Celebration Registered Enemies and Gen Banks' Proclamation The Rebel Prisoners at Algiers Highly Exciting News from Gen. Banks' Army." The article notes that two-thirds of the girls were daughters of Confederate soldiers. It also notes that Union officers assisted in the celebration, supplying canvases to cover the grass so the girls could sit, and then stringing up rope swings for their entertainment.

Chapter 49: Exodus of the Registered Enemies

1. March 7, 1863, article, "Affairs in New Orleans: Return of Registered Enemies to Dixie," by "Special Affairs Correspondent," Mr. J. R. Hamilton, *Harper's Weekly*, p. 157.

2. "The War in America: Arrival of a Federal Steamer with Flag of Truce at Madisonville, Lake Pontchartrain" in the *Illustrated London News*, April 11, 1863, p. 401, features an illustrated article about the arrival of a steamer at Madisonville, Lake Pontchartrain, carrying an earlier group of registered enemies.

3. "Registered Enemies," *Times-Picayune*, May 12, 1863, p. 2. The article lists what registered enemies may take with them: "…a sufficient quantity of food for ten days' subsistence, a reasonable amount of clothing, and the beds and bedding necessary for their own use."

Chapter 50: Jubilee

1. Gordon's scourged back was photographed by the team of William D. McPherson and J. Oliver, who were active in New Orleans and Baton Rouge in the 1860s. Abolitionists distributed the image widely in Northern newspapers, including *Harper's Weekly*, July 4, 1863, 429.

2. Frederick Douglass's "What to the Slave Is the Fourth of July?" was an address delivered in Rochester, New York, on July 5, 1852. It was printed by Lee, Mann & Co. in 1852. It was also included in an anthology, *The Frederick Douglass Papers: Series One—Speeches, Debates, and Interviews*. Volume 2: 1852–1859, edited by John W. Blassingame, 1–28. New Haven, CT: Yale University Press, 1982.

Chapter 51: Unvexed to the Sea

1. J. R. Hamilton's sketch of the event and an article on the arrival of the Imperial at New Orleans from St. Louis on July 16, 1863, are published in *Harper's Weekly*, August 8, 1863, p. 501, in an article entitled, "Opening of the Mississippi River."

Chapter 52: The Unexpected Visitor

1. No references.

Chapter 53: The Sazerac Coffee House

1. Around 1850, Sewell T. Taylor sold the Merchants Exchange Coffee House to focus on importing spirits, notably the French cognac Sazerac-de-Forge et Fils. The new proprietor, Aaron Bird, renamed the venue the Sazerac Coffee House. It was here that the Sazerac cocktail is believed to have been first served, blending Sazerac cognac with bitters crafted by local apothecary Antoine Amédée Peychaud. Today, the coffee house on Canal Street is a dual distillery and museum, housing items from its history. An article with references on the history of the Sezerac is posted at:

   https://en.wikipedia.org/wiki/Sazerac

2. The House of the Rising Sun is fictitious.

Chapter 54: Dueling Oaks

1. Jochum, Kimberly, "Dueling Oak," New Orleans Historical, accessed April 24, 2025. **https://neworleanshistorical.org/items/show/109.**

2. "Dueling in Old Creole Days," by Louis Meader in *Century Magazine*, Volume 74, Number 2, June 1907.

3. Hamilton Cochran's *Noted American Duels and Hostile Encounters* describes duels of historical interest in the United States. It also includes the text of the Code Duello.

Chapter 55: Caught Between Loyalty and Love

1. Rabbi Gutheim had left New Orleans by this time, but he appears here to preserve continuity. The rabbi that Rachel would have met with was Rabbi Illoway, who remained in New Orleans through the war.

   An article with references to Rabbi Illoway is posted at:

   https://en.wikipedia.org/wiki/Bernard_Illowy

Chapter 56: The Final Farewell

1. No references.

Chapter 57: Judah Benjamin

1. The meeting between Judah Benjamin and Issachar Zacharie took place on September 27, 1863, at City Point, Virginia, rather than Richmond, where Zacharie had stopped on September 22 during his journey to the event. The participants included Zacharie, Benjamin, Secretary of the Navy Stephen R. Mallory, Secretary of War James A. Seddon, and Richmond's Provost Marshal General John H. Winder. E. Lawrence Abel discusses this meeting, and the newspaper reports about it in *Lincoln's Jewish Spy: The Life and Times of Issachar Zacharie*, Chapter 19. General Banks, Issachar Zacharie, Judah Benjamin, Jefferson Davis, and President Lincoln all showed interest in this informal gathering but preferred it not to be an official negotiation in Richmond.

2. Collier et al.'s *White House of the Confederacy: An Illustrated History* chronicles the history and restoration of the Confederate White House. The authors meticulously explore the building's history, detailing its construction in 1818 as a private residence for Dr. John Brockenbrough and his wife, following his appointment as president of the Bank of Virginia. Dr. Brockenbrough sought a home that reflected his elevated social standing, resulting in a house with an elaborate design and carefully curated furnishings. The house underwent several ownership changes and was remodeled and redecorated multiple times before Richmond

purchased it in 1861 to lease to the Confederacy. The most significant renovation was the addition of a third floor. Though now a prominent feature, the impressive elliptical entry hall is not original to the house; it was added by one of its subsequent owners before 1861. The alcoves containing the two Greek Muses remain as they were since the house's construction, though the lamps held by each goddess were electrified. In traditional Greek iconography, Thalia, the Muse of comedy, is depicted with an ivy wreath, a mask of comedy, and a shepherd's staff. At the same time, Melpomene, the Muse of Tragedy, is shown with an ivy wreath, a mask of tragedy, and a sword. The illustration in this chapter aims to reconstruct the statues' original appearance, featuring their attribute before these elements were likely altered to accommodate first gas and later electric lighting fixtures. The tile floor currently in place is a modern attempt to replicate the original oilcloth pattern typical of entry floors from that era. Once adorned with faux marbled paint, the walls are now covered with marbled wallpaper. Much of the furniture consists of reproductions, but some pieces were acquired from owners whose relatives had purchased the original furniture from the house over the years. Floor plans of the Confederate White House are available from the Library of Congress at:

https://www.loc.gov/resource/hhh.va0517.sheet?st=gallery

3. Judah Benjamin's life is depicted in James Traub's *Judah Benjamin: The Brains of the Confederacy*. Benjamin was a brilliant and secretive man who destroyed all his private papers before his death. He was widely rumored to be fond of his gentlemen friends, and especially his brother-in-law. His wife tormented him with her many lovers and left him to live in Europe, taking their daughter with her.

4. Jews like Judah Benjamin, who desired to assimilate in the antebellum South and aspired to the Southern aristocracy, are discussed by Abraham J. Peck in "That Other 'Peculiar Institution' Jews and Judaism in the Nineteenth-Century South." Peck writes of these Jews, "They claimed to be descended from the noble and aristocratic Jews of Spain and Portugal, the Sephardim, when in fact, very few actually were." (P. 102).

5. Bonnie K. Goodman, in her online article, *The Mysterious Prince of the Confederacy: Judah P. Benjamin and the Jewish Goal of Whiteness in the South* (2019), Academia.edu, discusses the desire of Judah Benjamin to assimilate into Whiteness in the South.

6. The engraving of the Confederate bill was executed by Keatinge and Ball's printing in Richmond. See George B. Tremmel, *A Guide Book of Counterfeit Confederate Currency: History, Rarity, and Values*. Atlanta: Whitman Publishing, 2007.

7. Jefferson Davis would later express the sentiments stated here in his conversations with Judah Benjamin in his message to the Second Session of the Second Confederate Congress delivered in Richmond on November 7, 1864.

8. Jefferson's Poseidon-themed clock in this work is a fictitious device to create a metaphor. He did, however, keep a cherished white marble French mantel clock in his office, its soft ticking a steady companion as he labored over his papers. A photograph of Jefferson's clock and its history is in Collier's book on page 76.

Chapter 58: The President's Hymn

1. Paul Richard Powell's thesis, *A Study of A. E. Blackmar and Brother, Music Publishers, of New Orleans, Louisiana, and Augusta, Georgia: with a Check List of Imprints in Louisiana Collections*, gives a history of A. E. Blackmar's music publishing and music shop.

2. On October 3, President Lincoln proclaimed the first official national Thanksgiving Day to be observed on Thursday, November 26, and, "henceforth on the last Thursday of November of each year." Far from being an original idea, President George Washington had first proclaimed November 26 a day of national thanksgiving to give thanks for the new Constitution. From the pilgrims through Washington, though, none of these days of thanksgiving were ever declared a national holiday in perpetuity. In honor of this new national holiday, "The President's Hymn," also known as "Give Thanks, All Ye People," was written by Reverend William Augustus Muhlenberg, set to music by J. W. Turner, and published by A. D. F. Randolph in New York. It appears here:

    https://chroniclingillinois.org/items/show/19963?utm_source=chatgpt.com

Chapter 59: Booth's Marble Heart

1. *The Marble Heart*, also called *The Sculptor's Dream*, is Charles Selby's American version of Barrière and Thiboust's *Les Filles de Marbre*. Both are five-act plays. The literal translation of the French title is "The Girls of Marble," which was meant to imply the coldness of courtesans who drained lovers of their fortunes.

    The script, once distributed by Samuel French, is no longer available through that publisher. However, copies are still available from Skilled Books, an antiquarian publisher in India, through a U.S. online bookseller, Abe Books. While these editions have poor print quality, they provide a viable alternative for reading incomplete or difficult-to-read microfilm or online archives. After reading the play, I found many online synopses to be unreliable, often confusing characters. For example, Marco, Raphael's obsessive love interest, is sometimes mistakenly reported to be a man, which creates an interesting, though unintended, variation. Some descriptions also wrongly depict Raphael as a villain when, in fact, he is a victim of his obsessive love, which ultimately leads to his tragic end. This mistake probably comes from reports of John Wilkes Booth confronting Lincoln with threatening lines during the show—lines Booth ad-libbed since they aren't in the original script. In this chapter, artistic license is used to incorporate these threatening lines and gestures, placing them where the original script would naturally allow, without significantly altering the play.

    Creative license is also taken with the presence of Nicolay and Hay, who did not attend that evening's performance.

2. A thorough treatment of the music for the melodramatic theatre of the time may be found in Michael V. Pisani's *Music for the Melodramatic Theatre in Nineteenth-Century London and New York*.

3. Michael W. Kauffman, in *American Brutus: John Wilkes Booth and the Lincoln Conspiracies*, writes in detail about Booth's calculated presence and performance that night.

Chapter 60: Between the Olive Branch and the Sword

1. Lincoln's address was delivered on Thursday, November 19, 1862 to dedicate the Union cemetery for fallen soldiers who fought and died at Gettysburg, Pennsylvania. At the time, it was

not called the "Gettysburg Address." There was no formal response to the address from the Confederacy.

2. William R. Rathvon (December 31, 1854-March 2, 1939) witnessed Lincoln's speech as a 9-year-old and later recorded a 78-rpm record on February 12, 1938. It may be heard on the following link:

https://www.historyonthenet.com/authentichistory/1860-1865/2-sounds/2/19380212_Gettysburg_Eyewitness_William_V_Rathvon.html

Chapter 61: Doré

1. The stone bridge at City Park depicted in this illustration was constructed years later. The original was constructed of wood.

Chapter 62: A New Forever

1. A biographical sketch of Rabbi Bernard Illowy, born in Bohemia, is given at:

https://en.wikipedia.org/wiki/Bernard_Illowy

2. An article on the history of the Ketubah may be found at:

https://en.wikipedia.org/wiki/Ketubah

3. Barbe-Nicole Clicquot Ponsardin, known as the "Widow Clicquot," assumed control of her husband's Champagne house in 1805 and revolutionized the wine industry with innovations such as the riddling table. Her Champagne became popular across Europe, even amid Napoleonic wars and trade blockades. See Tilar J. Mazzeo, *The Widow Clicquot: The Story of a Champagne Empire and the Woman Who Ruled It.*

Chapter 63: The Colors of Freedom

1. The description of the school and its pupils and staff is adapted from "White and Colored Slaves," by C. C. Leigh, appearing on page 71 in the January 30, 1864, issue of *Harper's Weekly*. The illustration in the article depicts eight individuals who had been recently freed from slavery in Union-occupied New Orleans. Among them are five children—Charles Taylor, Rebecca Huger, Rosa Downs, Augusta Broujey, and Isaac White—and three adults—Wilson Chinn, Mary Johnson, and Robert Whitehead. Notably, several of the children appear to be White or nearly White, a deliberate choice meant to challenge Northern perceptions of slavery and evoke empathy from white audiences. The article mentions how this was one of many photographs circulated in the North by abolitionists.

2. An article on the impact of pictures like this in the North: "Disunion: The Young White Faces of Slavery." Mary Niall Mitchell. January 30, 2014. *The New York Times.*

3. Published in March 1854, Cummins's *The Lamplighter* was a sensational bestseller: it sold 20,000 copies in 20 days, 40,000 in eight weeks, and 65,000 within five months, trailing only *Uncle Tom's Cabin* in sales at the time. Perhaps the most famous derision from male authors came indirectly through Nathaniel Hawthorne, who, frustrated by the growing popularity of women writers, wrote in an 1855 letter to his publisher, William D. Ticknor,: "America is now wholly given over to a damned mob of scribbling women, and I should have no chance of success while the public taste is occupied with their trash." A full reference to Hawthorne's letter is given in the Bibliography.

Chapter 64: Maison Des Escargots

1. No references.

Chapter 65: The Grand Reunion

1. "Another Reunion," *Daily True Delta*, February 4, 1864, p. 2, describes this event.

2. Portraits of General Nathaniel P. Banks and Admiral David G. Farragut were commissioned to commemorate their significant roles in the Civil War. These portraits were created by the renowned artist Mauritz Frederik De Haas, known for his maritime scenes and depictions of naval engagements. De Haas's works often captured the valor and strategic prowess of naval officers, making him a fitting choice for portraying Admiral Farragut. The current location of these two paintings is not known, but some of this artist's work is part of the holdings at the Historic New Orleans Collection.

Chapter 66: Valentine's Day

1. No references.

Chapter 67: The Inauguration of Governor Hahn

1. Michael Hahn was the nineteenth governor of Louisiana. He served during the federal occupation of the state following the Civil War. Hahn's administration attempted to enfranchise black citizens and laid the foundation for a black school system. As governor, Hahn endeavored to implement progressive reforms, including advocating for African American suffrage and establishing a public education system for Black citizens. However, his administration faced significant challenges. Major General Stephen A. Hurlbut, who succeeded Banks, did not recognize Hahn's civil authority, leading to political friction. Consequently, Hahn resigned in March 1865 to accept an election to the U.S. Senate. However, the post-war Congress, dominated by Radical Republicans, refused to seat him, along with other Southern representatives, delaying Louisiana's full reintegration into the Union. See "The Restoration of the Union—Inauguration of Hon. Michael Hahn, Governor of Louisiana, on Lafayette Square, New Orleans, March 4." In *Frank Leslie's Illustrated Newspaper*, April 2, 1864, pp. 24-25.

2. In early 1864, bandleader Patrick S. Gilmore organized a "monster concert" in Union-occupied New Orleans, assembling hundreds of military and civilian musicians for a massive public performance. It is reportedly the first of its kind in the United States. Gilmore, who would later organize the National Peace Jubilee and World's Peace Jubilee in Boston, is widely regarded as a pioneer of large-scale American musical events. See Marwood Darlington, *Irish Orpheus: The Life of Patrick S. Gilmore, Bandmaster Extraordinary.*

Chapter 68: Booth Plays New Orleans

1. This chapter is based on "When Booth was Here," which appeared in the Sunday, March 9, 1902 issue of the New Orleans *Times-Democrat*. The article erroneously states that Booth stayed in New Orleans for three weeks for theatre engagements in 1863 when, in fact, this stay was in November 1864, which was much closer to the time when he assassinated President Lincoln only 5 months later on April 14, 1865. The article also erroneously states that General Butler was present in New Orleans when, in fact, he was replaced by General Banks in December 1862 and did not return until 1865.

2. Lucas, Alex Christian. 2020. "Assassin in the Cresent City: The Untold Story of John Wilkes Booth on his only visit to New Orleans in the Spring of 1864," The Macksey Journal: Vol. 1, Article 35. Available at:
https://www.mackseyjournal.org/publications/vol1/iss1/35

Chapter 69: The Secret Room

1. For a discussion of the Knights of the Golden Circle, see Robert E. May's, *Slavery, Race, and Conquest in the Tropics: Lincoln, Douglas, and the Future of Latin America*. Cambridge: Cambridge University Press, 2013.

2. David C. Keehn, in *Knights of the Golden Circle: Secret Empire, Southern Secession, Civil War*, discusses the role of the Knights in the Civil War.

3. For Booth's ties with the Confederate Secret Service, see Sandy Prindle, *Booth's Confederate Connections*.

4. Curtis, the younger half-brother of George Miller, owner of the boarding house where Booth stayed while in New Orleans, writes about the occasion in "When Booth was Here," March 8, 1902, *The Times-Democrat*.

Chapter 70: Louisiana Adopts New Ordinance

1. Refer to *Ordinances Adopted by the Constitutional Convention of the State of Louisiana*, May 11, 1864 (New Orleans: J. O. Nixon, State Printer, 1864), 4.

Chapter 71: Congo Square Celebrates Emancipation in Louisiana

1. Susannah J. Ural and Ann March Daly, in "Before Juneteenth: *What may be America's first Juneteenth.*" *The Atlantic*, June 17, 2024, documents a mass celebration on June 11, 1864, held in Congo Square, New Orleans, to commemorate emancipation in Louisiana. The gathering included soldiers, educators, schoolchildren, and civic groups, with speeches demanding "Freedom, Suffrage, Work, and Wages."

Chapter 72: Niagara Falls Peace Summit

1. Chapter 6 in "The Niagara Peace Episode," in Fahrney, Ralph Ray. *Horace Greeley and the Tribune in the Civil War* discusses the event.

2. Abraham Lincoln, "To Whom It May Concern," July 18, 1864, in Collected Works of Abraham Lincoln, ed. Roy P. Basler, vol. 7 (New Brunswick, NJ: Rutgers University Press, 1953), 457.

3. For a discussion of Lincoln's acute awareness of the power of the press, see Harold Holzer's *Lincoln and the Power of the Press*.

4. C. C. Clay and James P. Holcombe, "Letter to Horace Greeley," July 18, 1864, in Official Records of the Union and Confederate Navies in the War of the Rebellion, Series IV, vol. 3 (Washington, DC: Government Printing Office, 1900), 577–78.

5. Horace Greeley, "Letter to Abraham Lincoln," July 19, 1864, in Collected Works of Abraham Lincoln, ed. Roy P. Basler, vol. 7 (New Brunswick, NJ: Rutgers University Press, 1953), 460–62.

6. C. C. Clay, James P. Holcombe, and Jacob Thompson, "Letter to Horace Greeley," July 21, 1864, in Official Records of the Union and Confederate Navies in the War of the Rebellion, Series IV, vol. 3 (Washington, DC: Government Printing Office, 1900), 578–79.

7. Frank H. Severance, "The Peace Conference at Niagara Falls in 1864," *Publications of the Buffalo Historical Society* 18 (1914): 79–94.

Chapter 73: Farragut Captures Mobile Bay

1. See James P. Duffy, *Lincoln's Admiral: The Civil War Campaigns of David Farragut*.

Chapter 74: Atlanta Burns

1. Russell S. Bonds in *War Like the Thunderball: The Battle and Burning of Atlanta* describes Sherman's conquest of Atlanta and the burning of the city.

Chapter 75: Jefferson Davis Addresses Macon

1. Jefferson Davis's speech at Macon, Georgia, on September 23, 1864, may also be found in *The Papers of Jefferson Davis*, Volume 11, pp. 61-63, edited by Lynda Lasswell Crist et al.

2. The speech was originally published in the *Macon Telegraph*, Sept. 24, 1864.

Chapter 7: Red River Regrets

1. No references.

Chapter 77: A Sister's Ultimatum

1. No references.

Chapter 78: Alone

1. No references.

Chapter 79: Thanksgiving

1. No references.

Chapter 80: Christmas Eve

1. Susan Benjamin's *Sweet as Sin: The Unwrapped Story of How Candy Became America's Favorite Pleasure*, pp. 94-96, notes that 19th-century candy canes were all white and flavored, with stripes appearing in the early 20th century.

2. In his biography, *The Interesting Narrative of the Life of Olaudah Equiana, or Gustavus Vassa, the African*, on page 63, Olaudah Equiano, a slave, mentions the iron muzzle, writing, "… she had one particularly on her head, which locked her mouth so fast that she could scarcely speak; and could not eat or drink." Sir John Soane's Museum in London has one such device in its collection.

Chapter 81: News from the East

1. In early December 1864, Maj. Gen. Jefferson C. Davis's Union XIV Corps neared Ebenezer Creek, a swollen tributary of the Savannah River. With Confederate cavalry under Wheeler closing in, the army hastily constructed a pontoon bridge. As Union soldiers and wagons stampeded across, hundreds of newly freed Black families tried to cross. Once the last Union unit reached the far bank, Davis ordered the pontoons unlashed and floated downstream, leaving the refugees stranded. Panic ensued: some managed to wade or swim across, aided by desperate soldiers who felled trees or pushed makeshift rafts, but many drowned in the icy rush. Confederate cavalry arrived, some drowning souls were shot, and survivors were rounded up and returned to slavery.

2. Dennis Keating. "Jefferson C. Davis and the Ebenezer Creek Controversy." *Cleveland Civil War Roundtable*, June 7, 2020.

3. "The Ebenezer Creek Massacre, a prelude to '40 Acres and a Mule': https://spokesman-recorder.com/2021/02/01/the-ebenezer-creek-massacre-a-prelude-to-40-acres-and-a-mule/?utm

Chapter 82: The Hampton Roads Peace Conference

1. Since there was no agenda and no notes taken during this meeting, this is not an attempt to create an exact narrative of the discussion.

2. For a meeting summary, see pages 557-561 of Donald's, *Lincoln*, and refer to his chapter notes for more extensive primary sources.

Chapter 83: The 13th Amendment

1. An authoritative source on the 13th Amendment is Michael Vorenberg's *Final Freedom: The Civil War, the Abolition of Slavery, and the Thirteenth Amendment*. Cambridge

2. *The Toodles* was written by John Brougham, an Irish-born American playwright, actor, and comedian. It was often billed as "A Domestic Drama in Two Acts," and is a 19th-century farce with occasional slapstick centering on two dissimilar characters who both bear the name Timothy Toodles: the younger, leaner, "Toodles the Less," and his corpulent counterpart. The play was first performed in England as early as 1832 and reached American shores by the mid-19th century. The Full text of the play is on the web: https://archive.org/details/toodlesdomesticd00raym

Chapter 84: Lincoln's Second Inauguration

1. *Frank Leslie's Illustrated Newspaper*, March 4, 1865 contains an illustration and description of the event.

Chapter 85: Sarah Morgan

1. Sarah Morgan's character and conversations are drawn from her diary, *Sarah Morgan: The Civil War Diary of a Southern Woman*. Following her tragic accident and ensuing chronic pain, her writing becomes less energetic and expressive, although she remains stoic. Her often quoted musing about the future, beginning, "One day in the far future…" is on page 263 of her diary.

Chapter 86. Jubilee on Canal Street

1. There were many Union parades joined by slaves in 1864, and this is a fictional account that portrays a generic parade.

Chapter 87: Our American Cousin

1. This account is taken from "Abraham Lincoln was a John Wilkes Booth Fan," *Harper's Weekly*, Saturday, April 29, 1865, Vol IX, No. 435, pages 257-258.

2. Nicolay and Hay wrote extensively about Lincoln's assassination in their published works, especially *Abraham Lincoln: A History*, but neither was physically present at Ford's Theatre that night. Their accounts are secondhand but authoritative, drawn from their positions in Lincoln's inner circle and from careful historical inquiry.

3. Michael W. Kauffman gives a detailed account of the planning and assassination in *American Brutus: John Wilkes Booth and the Lincoln Conspiracies*.

Chapter 88: The Emancipation of Lincoln

1. The funeral sermon for President Lincoln, appears in the *New York Times*, April 20, 1865.

Chapter 89: Banks Returns to New Orleans

1. General Banks returned to New Orleans on April 21, 1865, and on April 22 formally resumed command of the Department of the Gulf, a position he held until June 3, 1865.

2. For a secondary account of Pinkerton and his time in New Orleans, see:

https://warfarehistorynetwork.com/article/allan-pinkerton/

3. For Pinkerton's own account of his service, see his autobiography, *The Spy of the Rebellion: Being a True History of the Spy System of the United States Army during the Late Rebellion*

Chapter 90: The Resurrection of Code Noir

1. Vernon Palmer's *Through the Codes Darkly: Slave Law and Civil Law in Louisiana* examines the unique origins of the Black Codes in Louisiana's history of slavery and their lasting impact.

Chapter 91: A Voice from the Past

1. Union forces occupied LaGrange, Georgia, on April 17, 1865, during the final days of the Civil War. The occupation was part of Wilson's Raid, a campaign led by Union General James H. Wilson aimed at destroying Confederate supply lines and infrastructure in Alabama and Georgia. Union Colonel Oscar H. LaGrange confronted the town, leading his troops into the area. Forrest Clark Johnson's *A History of LaGrange, Georgia, 1828–1900* describes this.

2. The occupation of LaGrange is notable for the involvement of the Nancy Harts, an all-female militia formed in 1861 by the women of LaGrange, Georgia. These women had trained and drilled throughout the war, preparing to defend their homes. When Union forces approached, the Nancy Harts met them and negotiated a peaceful surrender, ensuring the protection of civilian homes while Union troops destroyed strategic Confederate resources. See "Hart, Nancy Morgan." In *New Georgia Encyclopedia*, s.v. "Nancy Hart (c. 1735–1830)," updated ca. 2005.

Chapter 92: Little Angels

1. Paula June Thompson mentions the *Wicklow Wedding* performance in *A History Daybook of the English Language Theatre in New Orleans During the Civil War*.

Epilogue

1. Henry Ellsworth, the Commissioner of Patents in 1843, remarked in his report to Congress on page 6,, "The advancement in the arts, from year to year, taxes our credulity and seems to presage the arrival of that period when human improvement must end."

BIBLIOGRAPHY

Autobiographies, Diaries, Letters, and Journals

Butler, Benjamin F. *Butler's Book: A Review of His Legal, Political, and Military Career.* Boston: A. M. Thayer & Co., 1892.

Chase, Salmon P. *Inside Lincoln's Cabinet: The Civil War Diaries of Salmon P. Chase.* Edited by David Donald. New York: Longmans, Green and Co., 1954.

Chestnut, Mary. *Mary Chestnut's Civil War.* Edited by C. Vann Woodward. New Haven and London: Yale University Press, 1981.

Fahrney, Ralph Ray. *Horace Greeley and the Tribune in the Civil War.* Cedar Rapids, IA: The Torch Press, 1936.

Garcia, Céline Frémaux. *Celine: Remembering Louisiana, 1850–1871.* Edited by Patrick J. Geary. Athens and London: University of Georgia Press, n.d.

Hawthorne, Nathaniel. *The Letters of Nathaniel Hawthorne, 1853–1856.* Edited by Thomas Woodson, L. Neal Smith, and Norman Holmes Pearson. Vol. 17 of *The Centenary Edition of the Works of Nathaniel Hawthorne.* Columbus: Ohio State University Press, 1987.

LeGrand, Julia. *The Journal of Julia LeGrand, New Orleans 1862–1863.* Richmond: Everett Waddey Co., 1911.

Morgan, Sarah. *Sarah Morgan: The Civil War Diary of a Southern Woman.* Edited by Charles East. New York: Touchstone, 1992.

Paine, Halbert Eleazer. *A Wisconsin Yankee in Confederate Bayou Country: The Civil War Reminiscences of a Union General.* Edited by Samuel C. Hyde Jr. Baton Rouge: Louisiana State University Press, 2009.

Phillips, Eugenia L. "Journal of Mrs. Eugenia Levy Phillips, 1861–1862." Marcus, Jacob R. *Memoirs of American Jews, 1775–1865: 3.* Philadelphia: Jewish Publication Society of America, 1956. Copy at Manuscript. Library of Congress Manuscript Division, Washington, D.C. Cataloged in the P. Phillips Family Papers, 1832–1914.

Solomon, Clara. *The Civil War Diary of Clara Solomon: Growing Up in New Orleans, 1861–1862.* Edited by Elliott Ashkenazi. Baton Rouge and London: Louisiana State University Press, n.d.

Southwood, Marion. *Beauty and Booty: The Watchword of New Orleans.* New York: Published for the author by M. Doolady, 1867.

Velazquez, Loreta Janeta. *The Woman in Battle: A Narrative of the Exploits, Adventures, and Travels of Madame Loreta Janeta Velazquez.* New York: Firework Press, 1897.

Dissertations and Theses

Doyle, Elisabeth Joan. *Civilian Life in Occupied New Orleans,* 1862-1865. LSU Historical Dissertations and Theses, 228. Baton Rouge: Louisiana State University, 1955. https://digitalcommons.lsu.edu/gradschool_disstheses/228

Powell, Paul Richard. *A Study of A. E. Blackmar and Brother, Music Publishers, of New Orleans, Louisiana, and Augusta, Georgia: with a Check List of Imprints in Louisiana Collections.* M.L.S. thesis, Louisiana State University, 1978.

On-Line Publications

"Abraham Lincoln was a John Wilkes Booth Fan." Wikipedia. https://civilwarsaga.com/abraham-lincoln-was-a-fan-of-john-wilkes-booth/. Accessed April 27, 2025.

"Battle of the Head of Passes." Wikipedia. Last modified n.d. Accessed April 17, 2022. https://en.wikipedia.org/wiki/Battle_of_the_Head_of_Passes.

"Battle of New Orleans." https://newspaperarchive.com/free-newspaper-archives/war-history/civil-war/battle-of-new-orleans-p-2/. Accessed April 17, 2022.

"Benjamin Butler's Enlistment of Black Troops in New Orleans in 1862 on JSTOR." Last modified n.d. https://www.jstor.org/stable/4232388?seq=1. Accessed April 17, 2022.

"Bernard Illowy." Wikipedia. February 13, 2025. Accessed April 5, 2024. https://en.wikipedia.org/wiki/Bernard_Illowy

Chamberlain, Charles, and Lo Faber. "Spanish Colonial Louisiana - 64 Parishes." Last modified https://64parishes.org/entry/spanish-colonial-louisiana.

"The Civil War Months." Last modified n.d. Accessed April 17, 2022. https://civilwarmonths.com/about/.

"Civil War Music: God Save the South." Last modified n.d. Accessed April 17, 2022. http://www.civilwar.org/education/history/on-the-homefront/culture/music/god-save-the-south/god-save-the-south.html.

Coffee, Walter. "The Lord of Hosts Was with Us – The Civil War Months." Last modified April 24, 2022. Accessed April 24, 2022. https://civilwarmonths.com/2022/04/24/the-lord-of-hosts-was-with-us/.

"Compensated Emancipation." Accessed April 17, 2022. http://www.mrlincolnandfreedom.org/civil-war/congressional-action-inaction/compensated-emancipation/.

"The Corinth Campaign Finally Begins – The Civil War Months." Last modified n.d. Accessed May 3, 2022. Accessed August 15, 2025. https://civilwarmonths.com/2022/05/02/the-corinth-campaign-finally-begins/.

"Culture and Connections: The French Market's Enduring History." Accessed August 15, 2025. https://frenchquarterly.com/history/culture-and-connections-french-markets-enduring-history

Du Bois, W. E. B. *Isaac Brown: A Biography*. Philadelphia: George W. Jacobs & Company, 1909. Accessed August 16, 2025. https://books.google.com/books?id=SgoAAAAIAAJ&printsec=frontcover&source=gbs_ge_summary_r&cad=0#v=onepage&q&f=false.

"East Room." Wikipedia. Accessed August 25, 2025. https://en.wikipedia.org/wiki/East_Room.

"East Room: redecoration and Willie's Death." Accessed August 25, 2025. https://www.mrlincolnswhitehouse.org/the-white-house/downstairs-at-the-white-house/downstairs-white-house-east-room/east-room-redecoration-willies-death/index.html

Enslaved.org. "Journal of Slavery and Data Preservation." Last modified n.d. Accessed April 17, 2022. https://enslaved.org/search/all?name=Poydras&limit=20&offset=0&sort_field=label.sort&display=people.

"The Fall of Forts Jackson and St. Philip – The Civil War Months." Last modified n.d. Accessed April 26, 2022. https://civilwarmonths.com/2022/04/26/the-fall-of-forts-jackson-and-st-philip/.

"Fall of New Orleans and Federal Occupation." 64 Parishes. Last modified n.d. Accessed April 5, 2022. https://64parishes.org/entry/fall-of-new-orleans-and-federal-occupation.

"Farragut Career Academy." Accessed March 8, 2022.

https://www.farragutcareeracademy.org/about/farragut.jsp.

"Federals Bombard Forts Jackson and St. Philip – The Civil War Months." Last modified n.d. Accessed April 18, 2022. https://civilwarmonths.com/2022/04/18/federals-bombard-forts-jackson-and-st-philip/.

"Federals Target Forts Jackson and St. Philip – The Civil War Months." Last modified n.d. Accessed April 17, 2022. https://civilwarmonths.com/2022/04/17/federals-target-forts-jackson-and-st-philip/.

Frommer, Frederic J. "Abraham Lincoln Tried to Free the Enslaved Years before Emancipation." *The Washington Post.* April 16, 2022. Accessed August 1, 2025. https://www.washingtonpost.com/history/2022/04/16/lincoln-slavery-abolition-compensated-emancipation/.

Ginsberg, Judah. *Norbert Rillieux and a Revolution in Sugar Processing.* Washington, DC: American Chemical Society, 2002. Accessed April 18, 2002. https://www.acs.org/education/whatischemistry/landmarks/rillieux.html

"God Save the South, Confederate Civil War Song." Accessed July 5, 2025. https://americancivilwar.com/Civil War Music/song lyrics/God Save The South.html

Goodman, Bonnie K. *The Mysterious Prince of the Confederacy: Judah P. Benjamin and the Jewish Goal of Whiteness in the South.* 2019. Academia.edu. https://www.academia.edu/38410687/The Mysterious Prince of the Confederacy Judah P Benjamin and the Jewish Goal of Whiteness in the South.

"The Golden Circle Conspiracy | Ross Eric Gibson, Local History – Santa Cruz Sentinel." Last modified n.d. Accessed April 18, 2022. https://www.santacruzsentinel.com/2021/01/17/the-golden-circle conspiracy-ross-eric-gibson-local-history/

Hlemprière. "The Old St. Louis Hotel." *Digital Humanities Studio,* Loyola University New Orleans Department of History. December 18, 2015. Accessed August 1, 2025. https://docstudio.org/2015/12/18/st-louis-hotel-virtual-tour-of reconstruction-in-new-orleans/.

"Jewish Confederate Judah Benjamin's Contradictory Life – The Forward." Last modified n.d. Accessed April 17, 2022. https://forward.com/culture/476897/how-judah-benjamin-a-jewish-confederate-slave-owner-who-decried-slavery/.

Jochum, Kimberly. "Dueling Oak." New Orleans Historical. Accessed April 24, 2025. https://neworleanshistorical.org/items/show/109.

"John Surratt." Accessed July 5, 2025.
https://en.wikipedia.org/wiki/John_Surratt

"Julien Poydras (Poédras) | Louisiana Slave Conspiracies." Last modified n.d. Accessed April 17, 2022.
https://lsc.berkeley.edu/people/julien-poydras-po%C3%A9dras.

"Julien de Lallande Poydras." *Wikipedia*. Last modified April 28, 2025.
https://en.wikipedia.org/wiki/Julien_de_Lallande_Poydras.

"Ketubah." Wikipedia. Accessed April 17, 2022.
https://en.wikipedia.org/wiki/Ketubah.

Lehrman Institute. "Black Soldiers: Louisiana and Massachusetts." Last modified n.d. Accessed April 17, 2022.
http://www.mrlincolnandfreedom.org/civil-war/black-soldiers/louisiana-and-massachusetts/.

"Marie Therese Coincoin." 64 Parishes. Last modified n.d. Accessed February 9, 2022.
https://64parishes.org/entry/marie-therese-coincoin.

Modica, Michael Antonio. "The Civil War in Louisiana: General Banks' Failed Red River Campaign of 1864." University of Houston Clear Lake. Last modified n.d. Accessed April 17, 2022.
https://www.academia.edu/1180093/The_Civil_War_in_Louisiana_General_Banks_Failed_Red_River_Campaign_of_1864.

"Nathaniel P. Banks." Wikipedia. Accessed April 17, 2022.
https://en.wikipedia.org/wiki/Nathaniel_P._Banks.

"New Orleans in the Civil War | LSU Libraries." Last modified n.d. Accessed February 21, 2022.
https://www.lib.lsu.edu/special/research/manuscripts/guides/neworleans-in-the-civilwar.

Paxson, Charles. "Enslaved Children of New Orleans, 1863: A Spotlight on a Primary Source." *History Resources.* The Gilder Lehrman Institute of American History. Last modified n.d. Accessed April 17, 2022. https://www.gilderlehrman.org/history-resources/spotlight-primary-source/enslaved-children-new-orleans-1863.

Phillips, Eugenia "Journal of Mrs. Eugenia Levy Phillips, 1861-1862." Accessed June 28, 2025. http://www.jewish-history.com/civilwar/eugenia.html.

"Phillip Phillips (Lawyer)." Wikipedia. Accessed June 2, 2025.
https://en.wikipedia.org/wiki/Philip_Phillips_(lawyer)
"The President's Hymn."
See also:
https://chroniclingillinois.org/items/show/19963?utm_source=AI.com

Rathvon, William. Witnessed Lincoln's speech and later recorded a 78-rpm record on February 12, 1938. It may be heard on the following link, last accessed September 1, 2025: https://www.historyonthenet.com/authentichistory/1860-1865/2-sounds/2-historical/19380212_Gettysburg_Eyewitness_William_V_Rathvon.html

Rehder, Isaac B. "Sugar Plantation Settlements of Southern Louisiana, a Cultural Geography." Dept. of Geography, University of Tennessee, 1971. Last Accessed August 25. https://talltimbers.org/wp-content/uploads/2018/09/111-Rehder1979_op.pdf.

Rao, Tejal. "A Legendary New Orleans Restaurant, 160 Years in the Making." *Eater*, September 2, 2016. Last accessed July 8, 2025. https://www.eater.com/2016/9/2/12736732/tujagues-new-orleans.

Southern History Project. "Haiti and New Orleans: Revolution, Migration, and Legacy." Last modified n.d. Accessed April 17, 2022. https://tripodnola.org/wp-content/uploads/2019/05/Haiti-and-New-Orleans.Curriculum.pdf.

"St. Louis Hotel." Wikipedia. Last modified April 25, 2025. https://en.wikipedia.org/wiki/St._Louis_Hotel.

"Sugar Granulation on the Boré Plantation." https://neworleanshistorical.org/items/show/1655

"This Bushwhacking Must Cease – The Civil War Months." Last modified n.d. Accessed May 3, 2022. https://civilwarmonths.com/2022/05/03/this-bushwhacking-must-cease/.

"Unflinching Trust in God – The Civil War Months." Last modified n.d. Accessed April 23, 2022. https://civilwarmonths.com/2022/04/23/an-unflinching-trust-in-god/

Ural, Susannah J. & Daly, Ann Marsh. "Before Juneteenth: *What may be America's first Juneteenth,*" *The Atlantic*, June 17, 2024. Last accessed June 18, 2025. https://www.theatlantic.com/ideas/archive/2024/06/juneteenth-earliest-celebrations/678599/

"USS Albatross (1858)." Wikipedia. Accessed April 17, 2022. https://en.wikipedia.org/wiki/USS_Albatross_(1858).

Warner, Ezra J. *Generals in Blue: Lives of the Union Commanders*. Baton Rouge: Louisiana State University Press, 1964. Last accessed August 8, 2025. https://lsupress.org/9780807156162/generals-in-blue/

Wexler, Charles J. "The Capture of New Orleans." Accessed April 29, 2025. https://www.essentialcivilwarcurriculum.com/the-capture-of-new-orleans.html. Accessed April 27, 2025.

"William Bruce Mumford." Wikipedia. Accessed April 29, 2025.
https://en.wikipedia.org/wiki/William_Bruce_Mumford

Newspapers and Periodicals

"Another Reunion." *Daily True Delta*, February 4, 1864, p. 12.

"Bread Riot in Richmond: Three Thousand Hungry Women Raging in the Streets, Government and Private Stores Broken Open." *New York Times*, April 8, 1863.

"Christie's Minstrels." *New Orleans Daily Picayune*, February 24, 1863, p. 2.

"The Defences of the Mississippi." *New Orleans Daily Picayune*, April 5, 1862.

"Extraordinary Excitement in New Orleans." *Harper's Weekly*, March 21, 1863, p. 186.

"The Funeral of Lieut. Dekay Disgraceful Exhibitions by the Rebel Sympathizers Resistance to Cotton-Burning-Shameful Outrages-Louisiana in a State of Anarchy." *The New York Times*, July 13, 1862, p. 1.

"The Grant Family's Cotton Speculations. Official Record of the Grant–Mack Cotton Case in 1862." *Cincinnati Enquirer*, January 2, 1864. Reprinted in *American Jewish Archives Journal* 13, no. 2 (1961): 107–10. https://sites.americanjewisharchives.org/publications/journal/PDF/1961_13_02_00_doc_jewsUnion.pdf.

Frommer, Frederic J. "Abraham Lincoln Tried to Free the Enslaved Years Before Emancipation." *The Washington Post*, April 16, 2022.

"General Banks Addressing the Louisiana Planters in the Parlor of the St. Charles Hotel, New Orleans, LA." *Frank Leslie's Illustrated Newspaper*. March 28, 1863, p. 14.

"The Grand Presidential Party at the White House." *Frank Leslie's Illustrated News*, February 22, 1862, p. 216

Hamilton, J. R. "Affairs in New Orleans: Return of Registered to Dixie." *Harper's Weekly*, March 7, 1863, p. 157.

"The Hamlet General." *The New York Times*, October 14, 1862.

Keating, Dennis. "Jefferson C. Davis and the Ebenezer Creek Controversy." Cleveland Civil War Roundtable, June 7, 2020.

"The Grand Presidential Party at the White House." *Frank Leslie's Illustrated News*, February 22, 1862, p. 216

Leigh, C. C. "White and Colored Slaves." *Harper's Weekly*, January 30, 1864, p. 71.

"May Day." *Harper's Weekly*, June 6, 1863, p. 362.

"Opening of the Mississippi River." *Harper's Weekly*, August 8, 1863, 501.

"Our New Orleans Correspondence.; Wonderful Cavalry Exploit Grand Demonstrations at the St. Charles Hotel May Day Celebration Registered Enemies and Gen Banks'

Proclamation The Rebel Prisoners at Algiers Highly Exciting News from Gen. Banks' Army." *The New York Times*, May 18, 1863, p. 1.

"Particulars of the Execution of William B. Mumford for Hauling Down the United States Flag." *New York Herald*, June 19, 1862, p. 2.

"A Typical Negro." *Harper's Weekly*, July 4, 1863, p. 429.

"Registered Enemies," *Times-Picayune*, May 12, 1863, p. 2.

"Theatricals on the River." City Intelligence, *The Daily Delta*, September 20, 1862, p. 3.

"The Funeral of Lieut. Dekay Disgraceful Exhibitions by the Rebel Sympathizers Resistance to Cotton-Burning-Shameful Outrages-Louisiana in a State of Anarchy." *The New York Times*, July 13, 1862, p. 1.

"The Restoration of the Union—Inauguration of Hon. Michael Hahn, Governor of Louisiana, on Lafayette Square, New Orleans, March 4." *Frank Leslie's Illustrated Newspaper*, April 2, 1864, pp. 24-25.

"The War in America: Arrival of a Federal Steamer with Flag of Truce at Madisonville, Lake Pontchartrain," *Illustrated London News*, April 11, 1863, p. 401.

Plays

Selby, Charles. *The Marble Heart: A Romance of Real Life in Five Chapters*. India: Skilled Books.

Letters and Writings

Lincoln, Abraham, and David S. Reynolds. *Lincoln's Selected Writings: Authoritative Texts: Lincoln in His Era: Modern Views*. First edition. A Norton Critical Edition. New York: W. W. Norton & Company, 2015.

Books, Scholarly Journals, Encyclopedias, Congressional Reports and Papers

Abel, Ernest L. *Lincoln's Jewish Spy: The Life and Times of Issachar Zacharie*. Jefferson, NC: McFarland & Company, Inc., Publishers, 2020.

Benjamin, Susan. *Sweet as Sin: The Unwrapped Story of How Candy Became America's Favorite Pleasure*. Amherst, NY: Prometheus Books, 2016.

Bielski, Mark F. *A Mortal Blow to the Confederacy: The Fall of New Orleans, 1862*. El Dorado Hills, CA: Savas Beatie, 2021.

Blount, Russell W. *The Longest Siege: Port Hudson, Louisiana, 1863*. Jefferson, NC: McFarland & Company, Inc., Publishers, 2021.

Bonds, Russel S. *War Like the Thunderbolt: The Battle and Burning of Atlanta*.
Yardley, PA: Westholme Publishing, 2009.

Bowery, Charles R., Jr. *The U.S. Army Campaigns of the Civil War: The Civil War in the Western Theater 1862*. CMH Pub 75-7. Washington, DC: Center of Military History, United States Army, n.d.

Broadwater, Robert P. "William B. Mumford Became a Southern Hero for Defying Union Sailors in New Orleans." *America's Civil War* 18, no. 5 (November 2005): 20.

Butler, W. E. *Down among the Sugar Cane: The Story of Louisiana Sugar Plantations and Their Railroads*. Baton Rouge: Moran Publishing Corporation, 1980.

Clark, John Elwood. *Railroads in the Civil War: The Impact of Management on Victory and Defeat*. Conflicting Worlds: New Dimensions of the American Civil War. Baton Rouge: Louisiana State University Press, 2008.

Clark, William. *Ten Views in the Island of Antigua, in Which Are Represented the Process of Sugar Making, and the Employment of the Negroes in the Field, Boiling-House, and Distillery*. Published by Thomas Clay, Ludgate-Hill, London, 1823.

Cochran, Hamilton. *Noted American Duels and Hostile Encounters*. Philadelphia: Chilton Books, 1963.

Cole, Catherine. *The Story of the Old French Market, New Orleans*. New Orleans: The New Orleans Coffee Company. 1916.

Collier, Malinda W., John M. Coski, Richard C. Cote, Tucker H. Hill, and Guy R. Swanson. *White House of the Confederacy: An Illustrated History*. Richmond, VA: Cadmus Marketing, Inc., 1993.

Costello, Brian J. *The Life, Family, and Legacy of Julien Poydras*. New Roads, LA: John & Noelie Laurent Ewing, Printers, 2001. Note. This private publication is available only from the author, who resides in False River, Louisiana, and is the country historian at the city library.

Cummins, Light Townsend, Judith Kelleher Schafer, Edward F. Haas, Michael L. Kurtz, Bennett H. Wall, and Isaac C. Rodrigue. *Louisiana: A History*. 6th ed. Chichester, West Sussex: Wiley Blackwell, 2014.

Cummins, Maria Susanna. *The Lamplighter*. Boston: John P. Jewett and Company, 1854.

Cunningham, Edward. *The Port Hudson Campaign, 1862-1863*. Baton Rouge: Louisiana State University Press, 1963.

Darlington, Marwood. *Irish Orpheus: The Life of Patrick S. Gilmore, Bandmaster Extraordinary*. Philadelphia: Manley, Olivier & Klein, 1950.

Davis, Jefferson. *Speech at Macon, Georgia, September 23, 1864.* In *The Papers of Jefferson Davis,* edited by Lynda Lasswell Crist et al., vol. 10, 1864, 327–330. Baton Rouge: Louisiana State University Press, 1993.

Donald, David Herbert. *Lincoln.* New York: Simon & Schuster, 1996.

Douglass, Frederick. "What to the Slave Is the Fourth of July?" In *The Frederick Douglass Papers: Series One—Speeches, Debates, and Interviews. Volume 2: 1852–1859,* edited by John W. Blassingame, 1–28. New Haven, CT: Yale University Press, 1982.

Duffy, James P. *Lincoln's Admiral: The Civil War Campaigns of David Farragut.* Edison, NJ: Castle Books, 2006.

Dufrene, Dennis J. *Civil War Baton Rouge, Port Hudson, and Bayou Sara: Capturing the Mississippi.* Charleston, SC: The History Press, 2012.

Eisenhower, John S. D. *Agent of Destiny: The Life and Times of General Winfield Scott.* Norman, Oklahoma: University of Oklahoma Press, 1999.

Ellis, C. Arthur, Jr. *Of Mind and Man: The Historical Context of Rene Descartes' Contribution to Physiological Psychology.* Lutz, Florida: Gadfly Publishing, LLC, 2020.

Ellsworth, Henry L. *Report of the Commissioner of Patents Showing the Operations of the Patent Office During the Year 1843.* 28th Cong., 1st sess., H. Doc. 177. Washington, D.C.: Blair & Rives, 1844.

Equiano, Olaudah. *The Interesting Narrative of the Life of Olaudah Equiano, or Gustavus Vassa, the African,* Written by Himself. London: Printed for and sold by the author, 1789

Evans, Eli N. *Judah P. Benjamin: The Jewish Confederate.* New York: The Free Press, 1988.

Fahrney, Ralph Ray. *Horace Greeley and the Tribune in the Civil War.* New York: Columbia University Press, 1936.

Farragut, Loyall. *The Life of David Glasgow Farragut, First Admiral of the United States Navy, Embodying His Journal and Letters.* Reprint. New York: D. Appleton and Company, 1882. Scholar Select.

Flagel, Thomas R. *The History Buff's Guide to the Civil War.* Nashville, TN: Cumberland House, 2003.

Follett, Richard J. *The Sugar Masters: Planters and Slaves in Louisiana's Cane World, 1820–1860.* Louisiana Paperback ed. Baton Rouge: Louisiana State University Press, 2007.

Garrison, Webb B. *Civil War Curiosities: Strange Stories, Oddities, Events, and Coincidences.* Nashville, TN: Rutledge Hill Press, 1994.

Ginsberg, Judah. *Norbert Rillieux and a Revolution in Sugar Processing.* American Chemical Society, April 18, 2002.

Goodwin, Doris Kearns. *Team of Rivals: The Political Genius of Abraham Lincoln.* New York: Simon & Schuster, 2006.

Goodwin, Jason. *Otis: Giving Rise to the Modern City: A History of the Otis Elevator Company.* Chicago: Ivan R. Dee, 2001.

Gosnell, H. Allen. *Guns on the Western Waters: The Story of River Gunboats in the Civil War.* Louisiana Paperback ed. Baton Rouge: Louisiana State University Press, 1993.

Guste, Roy F. Jr. *Antoine's Restaurant Since 1840: Cookbook and History.* New Orleans: Carbery-Guste, 2015.

Hall, Gwendolyn Midlo. *Africans in Colonial Louisiana: The Development of Afro-Creole Culture in the Eighteenth Century.* Louisiana Paperback ed. Baton Rouge: Louisiana State University Press, 1995.

Harelson, Randy, Sexton, Richard, and Brian J. Costello. *New Roads and Old Rivers: Louisiana's Historic Pointe Coupee Parish.* Baton Rouge: Louisiana State University Press, 2012.

"Hart, Nancy Morgan." In *New Georgia Encyclopedia*, s.v. "Nancy Hart (c. 1735–1830)," updated ca. 2005.

Haugen, Andres. "Patriotic Fervor, the Civil War Press and the Execution of William B. Mumford," Louisiana History: The Journal of the Louisiana Historical Association, Vol. 63, No. 2 (Spring 2022), pp 191-236.

Hearn, Chester G. *The Capture of New Orleans,* 1862. Baton Rouge: Louisiana State University Press, 1996.

———*When the Devil Came Down to Dixie: Ben Butler in New Orleans.* Baton Rouge: Louisiana State University Press, 1997.

Hewitt, Lawrence L., and George C. Rable. *Port Hudson: The Most Significant Battlefield Photographs of the Civil War.* 1st ed. Knoxville: University of Tennessee Press, 2021.

Hollandsworth, James G. *Pretense of Glory: The Life of General Nathaniel P. Banks.* Baton Rouge: Louisiana State University Press, 2005.

Holzer, Harold. *Lincoln and the Power of the Press: The War for Public Opinion.* 1st Simon & Schuster hardcover ed. New York: Simon & Schuster, 2014.

Holzer, Harold, Edna Greene Medford, and Frank J. Williams. *The Emancipation Proclamation: Three Views (Social, Political, Iconographic).* Conflicting Worlds. Baton Rouge: Louisiana State University Press, 2006.

Hunter, Louis C. *Steamboats on the Western Rivers: An Economic and Technological History.* Cambridge, MA: Harvard University Press, 1949.

Isaac, Dix. "Communication from Major General Dix." New York: Comstock & Cassidy, Printers, 1864.

Jarrow, Gail. *Lincoln's Flying Spies: Thaddeus Lowe and the Civil War Balloon Corps.* 1st ed. Honesdale, PA: Calkins Creek, 2010.

Johnson, Forrest Clark. *A History of LaGrange, Georgia, 1828–1900; Genealogical and Historical Register of Troup County, Georgia*. 1st ed. 5 vols. Bound in 2 vols. Histories of LaGrange and Troup County. LaGrange, Georgia: Family Tree, 1987.

Jones, Terry L. *Louisiana in the Civil War: Essays for the Sesquicentennial*. Scotts Valley, CA: CreateSpace, 2015.

Kauffman, Michael W. *American Brutus: John Wilkes Booth and the Lincoln Conspiracies*. New York: Random House, 2004.

Keehn, David C. *Knights of the Golden Circle: Secret Empire, Southern Secession, Civil War*. Baton Rouge: Louisiana State University Press, 2013.

Klapthor, Margaret Brown. *Official White House China*. Washington, D.C.: White House Historical Association, 1999.

Langston, Scott. "James Koppel Gutheim." Southern Jewish History, vol. 5 (2002), pp. 71–102. Southern Jewish Historical Society.

Leigh, Philip. *Trading with the Enemy: The Covert Economy during the American Civil War*. Yardley, PA: Westholme, 2014.

Lincoln, Abraham, and Stephen Douglas. *The Lincoln-Douglas Debates*. Columbia, SC: Independently published, 2020.

Long, E. B., and Barbara Long. *The Civil War Day by Day: An Almanac, 1861–1865*. New York: Da Capo Press, Inc., 1971.

Lowenthal, Larry. *A Yankee Regiment in Confederate Louisiana: The 31st Massachusetts Volunteer Infantry in the Gulf South*. Baton Rouge: Louisiana State University Press, 2019.

Lucas, Alex Christian. "Assassin in the Crescent City: The Untold Story of John Wilkes Booth on His Only Visit to New Orleans in the Spring of 1864." *The Macksey Journal* 1 (2020): Article 35.

McAfee, Michael J. *Zouaves: The First and the Bravest*. Gettysburg, PA: Thomas Publications, 1991.

Marx, Karl, and Friedrich Engels. *The German Ideology*. 1845-46. In *The Marx-Engels Reader*, edited by Robert C. Tucker, 2nd ed., 172. New York: W.W. Norton, 1978.

McPherson, James M. *War on the Waters: The Union and Confederate Navies, 1861–1865*. Littlefield History of the Civil War Era. Chapel Hill: University of North Carolina Press, 2012.Marcus, Jacob R. "Journal of Mrs. Eugenia Levy Phillips, 1861–1862." *Memoirs of American Jews, 1775–1865*. Philadelphia: Jewish Publication Society of America, 1956.

Martin, Mark E. *Andrew D. Lytle's Baton Rouge: Photographs, 1863–1910*. Baton Rouge: Louisiana State University Press, 2008.

Marx, Karl, and Friedrich Engels. *The German Ideology*. Edited with an introduction by C. J. Arthur. New York: International Publishers, 1970.

May, Robert E. *Slavery, Race, and Conquest in the Tropics: Lincoln, Douglas, and the Future of Latin America*. Cambridge: Cambridge University Press, 2013.

Mazzeo, Tilar J. *The Widow Clicquot: The Story of a Champagne Empire and the Woman Who Ruled It*. New York: HarperCollins, 2008.

Meader, Louis. "Dueling in Old Creole Days." *Century Magazine* 74, no. 2 (June 1907

Mills, Gary B. *The Forgotten People: Cane River's Creoles of Color*. 8th printing. Baton Rouge: Louisiana State University Press, 1995.

Nevins, Allan. *The Emergence of Lincoln: Prologue to Civil War, 1859–1861*. Vols. 3–4 of 8 vols. New York: Charles Scribner's Sons, 1950.

New Orleans (La.). St. Charles Hotel. *Souvenir of New Orleans, "the City Care Forgot."* Hardcover. New Orleans: St. Charles Hotel, 2016.

Nicolay, John G., and John Hay. *Abraham Lincoln: A History*. 10 vols. New York: Century Co., 1890.

O'Connor, Thomas H. "Lincoln and the Cotton Trade." *Lords of the Loom: The Cotton Whigs and the Coming of the Civil War*. New York: Charles Scribner's Sons, 1968.

Palmer, Vernon V. *Through the Codes Darkly: Slave Law and Civil Law in Louisiana*. New Orleans: Quid Pro Books, 2012.

Parton, James. *General Butler in New Orleans: History of the Administration of the Department of the Gulf in the Year 1862: With an Account of the Capture of New Orleans, and a Sketch of the Previous Career of the General, Civil and Military*. New York: Mason Brothers, 1864.

Peck, Abraham J. "That Other 'Peculiar Institution': Jews and Judaism in the Nineteenth-Century South." Modern Judaism 7, no. 1 (February 1987): 99-114. Oxford University Press. http://www.jstor.org.stable.1396444.

Perrault, Charles. *The Complete Fairy Tales*. Translated by Christopher Betts: Oxford University Press, 2009.

Pinkerton, Allan. *The Spy of the Rebellion: Being a True History of the Spy System of the United States Army during the Late Rebellion*. New York: G.W. Carleton & Co., 1883.

Pisani, Michael V. *Music for the Melodramatic Theatre in Nineteenth-Century London and New York*. Iowa City, Iowa: University of Iowa Press.

Poesch, Jessie, and John Michael Vlach. *Marie Adrien Persac: Louisiana Artist*. Baton Rouge: Louisiana State University Press, 2000.

Porter, Horace. *Campaigning with Grant*. New York: Konecky & Konecky, 1992.

Prindle, Sandy. *Booth's Confederate Connections*. Gretna, Louisiana: Pelican Publishing Company. 2019.

Riddell, John L. *On the Nature of Miasm and Contagion. Cincinnati, Ohio:* N. S. Johnson. 1836.

Roland, Charles Pierce. *Louisiana Sugar Plantations during the Civil War.* Louisiana paperback ed. Baton Rouge: Louisiana State University Press, 1997.

Sanitary Commission of New Orleans. *Report of the Sanitary Commission of New Orleans on the Epidemic Yellow Fever of 1853.* New Orleans: Printed at the Picayune Office, 1854.

Sarna, Jonathan D. *When General Grant Expelled the Jews.* New York: Schocken Books, 2012.

Schafer, Judith Kelleher. *Becoming Free, Remaining Free: Manumission and Enslavement in New Orleans, 1846–1862.* Baton Rouge: Louisiana State University Press, 2003.

——— *Brothels, Depravity, and Abandoned Women: Illegal Sex in Antebellum New Orleans.* Baton Rouge: Louisiana State University Press, 2009.

Severance, Frank H. "The Peace Conference at Niagara Falls in 1864." *Publications of the Buffalo Historical Society* 18 (1914): 79–94.

Seymour, William J. *The Civil War Memoirs of Captain William J. Seymour: Reminiscences of a Louisiana Tiger.* Edited and introduced by Terry L. Jones. Baton Rouge: Louisiana State University Press, 1991.

Spedale, William A. *The Battle of Baton Rouge, 1862.* Baton Rouge, LA: Privately printed, 1976.

Stahr, Walter. *Seward: Lincoln's Indispensable Man.* 1st Simon & Schuster hardcover ed. New York: Simon & Schuster, 2012.

Steiner, Bernard C. 1914. *Life of Reverdy Johnson.* Baltimore: John Murphy Company.

Thompson, Paula June. Louisiana State University and Agricultural & Mechanical College. *A History Daybook of the English Language Theatre in New Orleans During the Civil War.* (Volumes I and II).

Tomblin, Barbara Brooks. *Civil War on the Mississippi: Union Sailors, Gunboat Captains, and the Campaign to Control the River.* Lexington: University Press of Kentucky, 2022.

Townsend, Mary Ashley (Van Voorhis), pen name Xariffa. *Xariffa's Poems.* Philadelphia: J. B. Lippincott & Co., 1870. Reprinted edition, Albuquerque. Hansebooks, n.d.

Traub, James. *Judah Benjamin: The Brains of the Confederacy.* Jewish Lives. New Haven: Yale University Press, 2021.

Tremmel, George B. *A Guide Book of Counterfeit Confederate Currency: History, Rarity, and Values.* Atlanta: Whitman Publishing, 2007.

United States, and Abraham Lincoln, eds. *The Emancipation Proclamation.* Bedford, MA: Applewood Books, 1998.

United States Navy Department. *Official Records of the Union and Confederate Navies in the War of the Rebellion.* Series I, Volume 18. Washington, D.C.: Government Printing Office, 1904.

Vorenberg, Michael. *Final Freedom: The Civil War, the Abolition of Slavery, and the Thirteenth Amendment.* Cambridge Historical Studies in American Law and Society. Cambridge: Cambridge University Press, 2001.

Waller, Adolph E. "The Vaulting Imagination of John L. Riddell." *Ohio History* 54, no. 4 (October–December 1946): 331–360.

Waller, Douglas C. *Lincoln's Spies.* 1st Simon & Schuster hardcover ed. New York: Simon & Schuster, 2019.

Ward, Artemus. *The Complete Works of Artemus Ward.* Scotts Valley, CA: CreateSpace Independent Publishing Platform, 2014.

Wiemuth, Bill. *The Civil War Anaconda Plan: Explore the Drama of the Union Strategy That Won the War.* History Highlights Series. Kindle ed. n.p.: History Highlights, 2022.

Weinart, Richard P., and Robert Arthur. *Defender of the Chesapeake: The Story of Fort Monroe.* 3rd rev. ed. Shippensburg, PA: White Mane Publishers, 1989.

Wilson, Keith. "Education as a Vehicle of Racial Control: Major General N. P. Banks in Louisiana, 1863–64." *The Journal of Negro Education* 50, no. 2 (Spring 1981): 156–70.

Winters, John D. *The Civil War in Louisiana.* Baton Rouge: Louisiana State University Press, 1991.

www.ingramcontent.com/pod-product-compliance
Lightning Source LLC
Chambersburg PA
CBHW082051090726
47909CB00010B/3004